# BACHELOR BRIDES COLLECTION

JENNY HAMBLY

Copyright © 2019 by Jenny Hambly

These books are sold subject to the condition that they shall not, by way of trade or otherwise, be lent, resold, hired out, or otherwise circulated without the publisher's prior consent in any form of binding or cover other than that in which it is published and without a similar condition including this condition being imposed on the subsequent publisher.

The moral right of Jenny Hambly has been asserted.

www.jennyhambly.com

# VOLUME ONE

ROSALIND

# ROSALIND
## A REGENCY ROMANCE

Jenny Hambly

**Bachelor Brides Book 1**

# CHAPTER 1

LONDON 1818

The Earl of Atherton had played quite recklessly tonight, not really caring whether he won or lost. Each throw of the dice had been accomplished with a negligent flick of his deceptively strong wrist. The vast quantities of wine he had been drinking just as recklessly, only showed in his slightly sprawled posture and the stormy look in his half-veiled grey eyes. His winnings had mounted steadily before him yet he seemed as disinterested in this as in everything and everyone else around him.

"I think," he drawled softly, "yes, I really think that I have had enough."

This drew various amazed glances from the other gentlemen who shared the table.

"I say G-George," stammered the long-suffering gentleman to his left, "that's the outside of enough, r-really it is, when you've been fleecing us all m-mercilessly all night."

The wintry gaze gentled as the earl's glance rested on his old friend Lord Preeve, whose slightly unfocussed, protuberant wide-blue eyes resembled nothing more than that of a startled rabbit. His glorious golden locks (quite his best feature) which had earlier been lovingly arranged by his fastidious valet, were now wildly disordered due to the frustrated tugs he had been giving them as the dice fell against him time after time.

A weary but fond smile curved the earl's lips as he rose gracefully and began slowly pocketing the pile of carelessly flung notes and golden coins before him.

"My heart would be quite, quite wrung if I didn't know you were rich as Croesus," he murmured. "Go home, John, Wrencham will be looking for a new position if he catches sight of the disaster you have made of your hair. Even if he had sent you out coup au vent, which I am fairly certain, dear chap, he did not, he would be shocked, quite shocked."

This gentle ribbing drew a grin from his companion on the right. There was no malice in it and they all knew there was no danger of this prophesied event occurring, it would be a brave valet indeed who would leave the employ of so rich and generally easy going an employer.

"W-well really, G-George, I suppose Townsend has barely anything to s-say to that mad riot of chestnut curls you sport, eh?" he protested.

"Nothing at all, my dear John, they are quite natural I assure you," he reassured his spluttering friend. "Quite the bane of my sisters' lives if they are to be believed." He turned to the quiet, neatly dressed man next to him, quirking one finely drawn dark brow. "Coming, Philip?"

Sir Philip Bray, ex-captain of the 15th Hussars,

had resigned his commission and reluctantly stepped into his late father's shoes on the occasion of his sad demise over a year ago. With rugged good looks, considerable charm and a natural aptitude for dancing, he was a firm favourite at every society function, yet despite countless lures having been thrown his way, had so far avoided the parson's mousetrap.

"With pleasure, my dear fellow, lead on," he smiled, pushing back his chair and getting only slightly unsteadily to his feet.

The steady drumming of some very white fingertips drew everyone's glance to the last occupant at the table. A large emerald glinted on one of the impatient digits. Everything about this gentleman was precise, no injudicious tugging had displaced a single hair of his close-cropped Caesar cut, his short sideburns framed his high, prominent cheekbones, and a thin patrician nose led the way to a pair of very thin lips whose natural expression seemed to be a sneer. A matching emerald tiepin nestled in the folds of his meticulously starched cravat, its glitter reflected in the cold green eyes that stared resentfully across at the earl.

"It wants three o'clock yet, Atherton," he drawled, not quite able to keep the bitterness from his voice. "I for one would like the chance to recoup some of my losses."

"Ah, Rutley," the earl sighed, "loath though I am to disappoint, I really have had enough you know."

A cynical smile twisted those thin lips. "Enough of winning?"

Hard grey clashed with agate green. "Enough of everything, my dear fellow, your revenge must wait for another occasion." The voice remained soft, but the implacable note was unmistakeable and offering only the briefest of bows, the earl turned and left the room.

It was this strange humour that had persuaded him to try the new discreet hell on King St. He wasn't in the mood to parry the usually pointless banter with which his cronies at Whites would have no doubt regaled him. His own unexpected succession to his late father's honours, had recently made him the butt of a wide range of singularly foolish marriage mart jests. Thank God his mourning status excused him from attending all the great squeezes of the season where he might be expected to do the pretty for the latest round of insipid debutantes.

Sir Philip accompanied his friend along Old Bond Street in companionable silence for a time, somewhat doubtful that Atherton was even aware of his presence so distracted did he seem. Only the odd hackney or the call of the night watchmen claiming a fine night and the advanced hour broke the silence.

"You've made an enemy of Rutley if I'm not much mistaken," he finally ventured.

Lord Atherton seemed to turn this thought over in his mind for a moment before shrugging somewhat fatalistically. "What, after all, can he do to me, Philip?"

Sir Philip's normally cheerful mien had temporarily deserted him, a slight frown lurked at the back of his usually smiling eyes. "Nothing, I should imagine," he conceded. "But I hear he's been playing deep and losing more often than not, there's talk that nothing but an heiress will keep his creditors from his door."

This depressing news seemed of little interest to Lord Atherton. "So he's likely to be the latest is he? I fail to see, however, what the devil that has to do with me."

A short laugh escaped his friend. "You're a damned cool fish tonight, George. It has, of course, nothing to do with you, but he had an ugly, almost desperate look about him and if looks were pistols, you'd have had a bullet through your brain tonight."

Atherton gave a rather harsh laugh. "At least that would save me from the prospective lists of suitable wives my well-meaning but annoyingly persistent sisters have already drawn up for me."

"I sympathise, dear chap, and whilst I acknowledge it to be tiresome to be seen as a fish to be caught on someone's none-too-subtle lure, I hardly think death preferable."

"I apologise, Philip. I am less than good company tonight. Have none of this season's beauties caught your eye yet?"

Sir Philip smiled. "Oh my eye, yes, but it is all so tame, so dull. None of them have any spirit. I'd rather have someone challenge me than smile charmingly and agree with everything I say." He suddenly laughed at himself. "You are making me as maudlin as you, dear fellow, it won't do."

At the point where Davies St met Grosvenor St, the friends parted. Lord Atherton carried on towards Grosvenor Square whilst Sir Philip proceeded towards Brook St. His friend's unusual mood preoccupied him so he didn't notice a dark figure, no more than a shadow, dart back into Brook Mews. However, this slight wraith had no interest other than to remain unseen and waited patiently until he had passed before continuing furtively towards the dark, winding Avery Row where a modest cart and horse awaited.

"Come on, miss, best away whilst this blindman's holiday lasts!"

The lithe figure climbed aboard and let out a low chuckle. "Stop fretting, Ned, all's well," she assured him.

A disapproving grunt was the only answer she received. Her reluctant escort showed an unerring knowledge of London as he led her down the less frequented alleys past Bloomsbury and into Holborn. It was not long before they pulled into the back entrance of Prowett's Coffee House on Red Lion Street, which any slightly impoverished gentleman could tell you served up an excellent ordinary but had no idea that a lady of undoubted quality was, at present, living upstairs.

Her room faced onto the street and a sudden shout of laughter drew her to her window. Drawing the curtain slightly to one side, she glanced outside. The street lamps threw just enough light for her to make out two entwined figures in the doorway opposite. A young man had his face buried in the ample bosom of his chosen companion for the evening. She saw the painted older lady draw back for an instant, her hand outstretched for payment before she allowed him to continue in his amorous pursuits. She sighed and let the curtain drop back into place. She only hoped that the poor unfortunate soul that was forced to tolerate the attentions of the young buck pawing her, was getting well paid for her services. It was a sight she had seen only too often since making her temporary home here to be shocked. It might have been expected that a lady of quality would have taken out her venom on the fallen woman but she had seen enough since her brief sojourn in town to realise that poverty was rife, and the women often didn't have a choice, whereas it seemed the young men had nothing to think of but their own pleasures. How she despised them. They were the privileged ones who were in a position of power and could, if they would, make some sort of difference to the world. But instead they used their wealth to further their own trivial pleasures, be it through gambling, drinking or whoring.

Reaching into her coat, she withdrew a slim case and dropped it onto the desk, before seating herself and pulling open one of the drawers. She retrieved a rather crumpled document and allowed a grim smile to curl her unfashionably full lips as she crossed out yet another name on her list. Lord Rutley would wake up tomorrow morning to find himself the latest victim of the Mayfair Thief. She regarded the closed case for a moment before opening it. The famous Rutley emeralds twinkled forgivingly in the light of the two candles that lit her small desk. Of course, the theft may have remained undiscovered for some time if she hadn't left her calling card. That would not have suited her purposes at all, especially if the latest rumours going around the coffee room downstairs that he was so badly dipped he was going to pay his addresses to the heiress of a prominent merchant in the city, young enough to be his daughter, were true. She was surprised he hadn't already sold them. That was after all, what her father had done with all but a few of her mother's treasures and those she had been forced to sell at a fraction of their worth to fund her present frugal existence. A tentative knocking on the door recalled her attention to the present.

"Come in, Lucy," she called softly, quickly adding the correct label to tonight's haul. It wouldn't do to get them mixed up, she did, after all, intend to return every item she had successfully stolen, eventually.

"Oh, look at you, Rosie," her old nurse scolded, grabbing the cloth that hung from the washstand. "Here, let me get that muck off you."

Rosalind submitted meekly to the rigorous scrubbing required to remove the soot from her face.

"Why can't you wear a loo mask instead? You'll be ruining that lovely complexion of yours if you're not careful. Where's all this going to end? That's what I want to know," Lucy grumbled. "You'll end up in Newgate and no mistake if you don't give up this lark soon."

Rosalind smiled fondly down at the plump, anxious face of her most faithful servant and friend, wondering which of the two hazards was bothering her old nurse more.

"Well, I don't happen to have a loo mask at present, but I admit it's not a bad idea," she conceded graciously, "but it will take more than a half-asleep watchman armed with a lantern and a stick or a couple of foxed gentlemen to catch me, Lucy, never fear."

Lucy took a step back and planted her small, capable hands on her wide hips. "Of course there's no danger at all, that's why you won't even take my Ned in with you."

Rosalind's smile faded. "He helps me enough as it is. I may not think the risk that great, but you know I won't put anyone else in danger. This is my game and I'll play it out."

Recognising the finality in her charge's clipped tones, Lucy sighed long and deep.

"Well, let's get you out of those clothes, my girl, they're positively indecent."

With no more ado she stripped the clinging breeches and dark, close-fitting coat from Rosalind's tall, willowy form, threw a nightgown over her head, cursorily dragged a brush through her raven locks and tucked her up in bed, her rough, disapproving attentions in no way concealing her very real affection.

Rosalind stretched limbs suddenly weary and offered a tired smile. "It's nearly over, only one left on my list."

Lucy paused in the act of packing away the items of clothing that had so offended her sensibilities. "Well, and what then, missy? What's to become of you when you won't even sell your haul? You may as well benefit from those as has stolen your inheritance from you."

"Go to bed, Lucy, you have to be up again in a couple of hours," Rosalind murmured even as sleep dragged her down into its clinging embrace.

Tonight the dreams came thick and fast. She was back at her childhood home, Roehaven Manor; her father had been drinking again and instead of showing his only child his usual careless affection he had locked her in her room. Confused and resentful, she had rebelled. Always a tomboy and excellent at climbing, she had thought nothing of opening her window and clambering onto the nearest branch of the tree outside, from where it was an easy descent to the garden.

Like a moth to a flame, she had been drawn to the lights in her father's study window. There she had found the reason for her incarceration. Around a small table by the fire sat her father and three gentlemen, none of whom she recognised not having benefited from a season in London. So engrossed were they in the turn of the cards she was in little danger of being seen. A hard anger had settled within her as she had studied her father's red, prematurely lined face, his thick brows drawn together in a fierce frown of concentration. She noticed his hand was slightly unsteady as he picked up the glass beside him and drained it.

He had taken to hard drinking and gambling after her mother's death five years previously, and she knew from the drastic reduction in staff at the manor that it was only a matter of time before they lost their home. As Willow, their long-suffering butler entered the room carrying another bottle of burgundy, she ducked beneath the stone lintel but not before she was sure he had seen her. A trusted friend, he did not give her away and she turned and ran in the moonlight through the increasingly wild gardens.

Her dream shifted and she was standing beside her father, gripping his hand tightly as she looked on her beautiful mother's pale, still face. Although she knew she was dead from the dreadful bout of influenza she had suffered, she still silently willed her to open those soft, gentle brown eyes.

Next, she was back in her bedroom, huddled under the covers, as they could no longer afford to have the fires going as a matter of course, when a loud shot shattered the night, causing her to shoot upright.

"Hush now, it's alright, my love. Lucy's here," came a soothing voice.

Rosalind forced heavy eyes open to find her shaking body clasped closely to her old nurse's bosom. Relaxing into the warm embrace, she allowed silent tears to fall. When this was all over, when all of the fine gentlemen who had bled her father dry had been punished in some small way, she hoped the dreams would stop.

# CHAPTER 2

Never at his best first thing in the morning when in town, Lord Atherton was not best pleased to be disturbed whilst still at breakfast. He raised surprised eyes to his butler Radcliffe, but that esteemed personage was quickly brushed past by the earl's impetuous sister, Lady Isabella Hayward. Intercepting a brief look of sympathy between them, Isabella laughed prettily.

"Yes, Radcliffe informed me you hadn't left the breakfast table yet, but it is already almost midday and I am really very busy this morning, so you will just have to make the best of it," she informed him, sitting down firmly.

"Another cup, my lady?" enquired Radcliffe impassively.

"Yes, if you please," she dimpled at him.

The earl sighed and laid his paper aside. Even dressed in a trim dress of black crape worn over black sarsenet, his sister still radiated a restless energy that failed to match her mourning colours. The necessary curtailment of her usual relentless whirl of social activities had resulted in an unwarranted interest in his own affairs that was as ill-judged as unwelcomed.

"I am of course honoured to think you can fit me into your busy schedule, Belle," he assured her, "but if you have come to inform me of the latest lady of excellent virtue and pleasing demeanour that has taken your fancy, don't. I find it a dead bore I assure you."

"Oh, you seem to find everything a dead bore at the moment," she pouted, but the grey eyes that almost exactly matched her brother's twinkled mischievously from beneath the softly upturned brim of her black poke bonnet. "Well, this might pique your interest; I happened to bump into my dear friend Miss Mowbray in Hatchards," she informed him, untying the lavender ribbons which, mourning or not, were knotted coquettishly beneath her right ear.

"Belle," Lord Atherton rapped out.

"Stop being such a crosspatch," the offended lady clucked. "She is not nearly beautiful enough for you so is, of course, not to be considered. You really don't deserve that I share the latest on-dit with you, you know."

"I believe I can stand the suspense," he drawled. The genuine hurt that momentarily darkened Lady Haywood's expressive eyes swiftly brought remorse. He reached for her hand and gently squeezed it. "Forgive me, love. I am not quite myself at present."

The little hand turned beneath his and returned the clasp. "You are feeling it dreadfully, I know," she murmured. "I never realised there was such a strong bond of feeling between you and Papa. It seemed to me you were always wrangling about something or other."

The grim, set look about his mouth silenced her but only for a moment. "Well, never mind. The thing is, Miss Mowbray's maid's brother works as a groom for Lord Rutley you know, and she had it from him that the Rutley emeralds are the latest heirlooms to be stolen."

She smiled as she realised she finally had his full attention.

"When was this?" he asked, surprised. "I have seen no notice in the papers."

"Well you wouldn't," she rushed on in hushed tones as if discussing state secrets. "It only happened last night."

Lord Atherton let out a low whistle. He didn't question the accuracy of the statement; the servants always knew everything before everyone else after all. Poor Rutley might have to follow Brummel across the Channel if he didn't snare his heiress soon. A slight twinge of guilt disturbed him as he recalled the quite large sum of money he had relieved him of the night before. The irony of it was he had no great love of gambling above the ordinary, it was only this persistent restlessness that seemed to have seized him recently that had sent him out at all.

The entrance of the butler with another cup and a fresh pot of tea might have been expected to have ceased his sister's penchant for gossip for a moment, but her brother was not at all surprised when it did not.

"Have you heard anything of the latest theft, Radcliffe?" she asked audaciously.

Although the allusion that he might take the smallest notice of gossip would have earned any of the lesser beings below stairs a sharp set down, he had always had a soft corner for Lady Hayward and so condescended to reply.

"I believe Lord Rutley is the latest gentleman to have been stripped of some of his most valuable assets," he replied with dignity. As Lady Hayward did not look quite satisfied he offered her another titbit. "Apparently a calling card bearing the inscription, 'For I will be merciful to their unrighteousness, and their sins and their iniquities will I remember no more,' was left behind." He paused a moment to let this sink in. "Hebrews, chapter eight, verse twelve, if I am not much mistaken."

Satisfied by the rapt expression on Lady Hayward's face and aware of the warning one on his harassed employer's, he judged it time to bow and withdraw.

Overcoming her momentary astonishment she blurted out, "Well really, George, I don't know how it could be called merciful to thieve from someone, although I am not at all shocked to discover Rutley is guilty of some iniquity. He always makes me shiver with those cold eyes of his; he reminds me of a deadly snake."

Lord Atherton looked unimpressed by this outburst. "My dear sister, you have discovered nothing but what some common thief has claimed, and I would ask you not to go about spreading any tales."

That fair lady pouted sulkily at such a suggestion and got impatiently to her dainty feet. "As you seem so set on being disagreeable I will take my leave of you," she declared with frigid dignity, but immediately spoiled the illusion by rushing on, "I think it vastly amusing that such a felon should scatter bible allusions behind him, and I doubt very much that it could be any *common* thief or that the victims are chosen at random. *And* I find it very hard to believe you are not as interested as the rest of society to discover the mystery behind it all."

"Believe it," he sighed. "I blame the lending libraries; you must all turn everything into a romance."

Lady Hayward didn't deign to reply, too busy in front of his handsome mirror, retying the ribbons on her dashing hat over her golden curls.

"Belle," he said rather more gently. "As you're not attending parties at the moment, I was going to suggest you post up to Atherton to bear Mother company. She should not be so much alone at such a time."

His sister's incredulous gaze spoke volumes as to her opinion of this suggestion. "Leave town now, when I have barely been back a fortnight? Really, George, I must not neglect poor Hayward so," she asserted firmly.

The earl's lips quirked at the image of staid, sensible Lord Hayward pining for his energetic, flighty bride. Although he undoubtedly doted on her, he would more likely be relieved not to have to drag her out of some scrape or other. Rising, he took her hand and kissed her cheek. "Lay your bristles, Belle, I would not wish to have Hayward's decline laid at my doorstep. I will probably go myself."

This revelation earned him a swift, warm hug. "I am so pleased, your visit will cheer poor Mama up more than mine ever could."

After handing his sister up into her barouche, Lord

Atherton climbed the steps to his noble mansion slowly. Loath though he was to own it, Belle had given him plenty of food for thought. Her suggestions about the nature of the thefts were disturbingly likely, but as he could think of no one he had particularly sinned against, which seemed to be the general gist of the calling cards, he was not unduly worried. Belle's assertion that his mother would be happier to see him concerned him more nearly; he was only too well aware that he had neglected her shamefully and was grateful that Belle had not thrown that accusation in his face, for he would have deserved it.

He did not venture out that evening but instead sat in his darkened study into the early hours with only a bottle of particularly fine Chambertin for company. The servants had long since gone to bed, and the quiet of the house contrasted sharply with the unquiet of his mind as his last argument with his father kept running relentlessly through his head. As was so often the case it had blown up over something quite trivial, in this case, a horse he had wanted to purchase. His father's gout had been particularly bad, and he had refused to countenance the idea. "You're nothing but an expensive wastrel," he had ranted. His undutiful son had been foolish enough to remind him of the rather large loan he had recently given to one of his old cronies who was far more of a wastrel than he could ever hope to be. The argument had escalated rapidly, harsh words being bandied on both sides. "Until you spend more time here learning about the estates you will one day inherit, you good for nothing gadabout, you'll get nothing more out of me. I've not had notice to quit yet and by gad I'll whip you into shape before I do!"

However, this hope had been destined to fail; his errant heir had made all haste back to town and within a week his irascible parent was dead. The suspicion that he had caused the fatal heart attack refused to leave him, but the guilt that accompanied it had not filled him with a desire to prove his father wrong, he had instead thrown himself into a life of the sort of dissipation his father had not completely unjustly accused him of.

A strange scraping sound coming from the window at the rear of the room that faced onto the small courtyard at the back of the house, recalled him from his unpleasant memories. "Well, I'll be damned," he muttered softly, at the same time gently opening one of the drawers of his desk and removing a small silver pistol. A sudden rush of cooler air into the room informed him that his visitor had gained entry and his eyes, already accustomed to the darkness, picked up a shadow darker than all the rest moving silently and stealthily towards the desk. He waited patiently until it was almost upon him before pushing himself out of his chair and grabbing the dark armful roughly around the middle, clamping the thief's arms to his sides in case he carried any weapon. He had braced himself to take a potentially heavy weight and was so unprepared for such a slim, slight form, he unintentionally lifted them right off their feet. Feet that were soon busily pummelling his shins as their owner wriggled like a desperate eel determined to make an escape. Realising he could hold the form encircled within one arm, he raised the hand with the pistol and pushed its cold, hard barrel against the side of their head.

"Be still, or I'll shoot," he snapped out.

Immediately the figure became statue-like in his arms, and as he lowered them to the floor, he made an interesting discovery. The hood of his assailant's long black cloak had fallen back in the struggle, and unless he was much mistaken, long tresses of silken hair were now covering the hand that still clamped the silent form to him. His nostrils twitched as he recognised the faint scent of jasmine. He turned them both and pushed his mute thief into the chair he had just vacated. "Don't move," he said curtly, moving swiftly to light the candle that had been left to light his way to bed. He then perched on the edge of his desk in stunned surprise as he took in the vision before him, starting with the long, long slim legs that were encased in close-fitting breeches; the rest of the slight figure was obscured by the cloak and a dark coat beneath. As he watched, the still silent intruder reached up to release the remainder of the hair that had already mostly escaped its knot. It fell in a glossy, wavy sheen almost to her waist and framed an almost preternaturally pale face. She now unhurriedly removed her loo mask and revealed eyes of the lightest amber, the enlarged black pupils the only sign of any nervousness. My God, she had the eyes of a tiger. Despite himself, Lord Atherton felt a flicker of amusement not untainted with admiration as he realised they were observing him just as closely with a cool, speculative interest.

A scuffling sound followed by a muffled grunt outside the window broke the silent spell that had held both occupants in the room momentarily immobile.

He quirked an enquiring eyebrow at his caged tigress. "A friend of yours?"

She gave a brief shake of her head.

"Damn," muttered Lord Atherton. "Get under the desk quickly. If you try to escape, I will not hesitate to stop you." Not pausing to see if his concise instructions were followed or to consider why he was protecting a thief who was clearly a menace to society, he strode swiftly to the window, thrusting it up far enough to enable him to lean out of it.

"Who goes there?" he snapped imperatively.

"Lord bless you, gov'ner, danged if someone ain't trying to slum your ken, er, what I mean is, if you ain't being robbed, sir," came an earnest voice as a thickset form in a thick frieze coat picked himself up from the cobbles beneath the window. "I seen him come up the mews and in past the stables with me own oglers. Then I spied a dark figure disappearin' through that very window, strike me down if I didn't. Best let me in, sir, I'll know how to deal with the thieving varmint."

"You are mistaken, my good man. Whilst I am reassured by the presence of a Bow Street Runner in the vicinity, in the light of recent alarming events, I am very much afraid to inform you, that whilst I approve of your diligence, you have in this case made a mistake."

As the earl started to withdraw back into the room, the startled runner rubbed his rather bulbous nose and protested vehemently, "But I saw something disappearin' through that window. It must be that pesky thief, I've been set on to watch out for him see."

Lord Atherton sighed with every appearance of boredom and sublime unconcern. "Yes I see, and although I hesitate to further blight your hopes, as I have not left this room tonight, it is quite impossible that I would be unaware if someone had entered it," he answered truthfully. "What you saw was possibly my cat, that disgraceful feline did indeed grace me with her presence not very many minutes since," he embellished, finding a store of hitherto unsuspected creativity.

A look of chagrin and doubt descended on the runner's face. "Are you sure you don't want me to cast me ogles over your ken, sir? I could 'ave swore I seen someone."

"No, it is quite unnecessary. Good night to you and good hunting." With that, he snapped the window shut, drew the rich velvet curtains and bent to retrieve a small object from the floor.

CHAPTER 3

Rosalind folded herself neatly into the cramped space underneath the desk and listened with bated breath to this conversation. She was well aware that the mention of the Bow Street Runners was both a warning and a threat. One part of her wanted to make a run for it, but a curiously fatalistic feeling had crept over her. It had been foolish to attempt the final theft so close to the last one. For weeks, the plotting of her limited revenge and the carrying out of her audacious plan had consumed her, had been the only thing that had given her life any direction at all. She had repeatedly ignored Lucy and Ned's warnings, too hard-headed and desperately needing to take some sort of action before she faced her bleak future. But she had been gripped by a seething madness. She had realised it finally, almost certainly too late.

When she had been struggling in those strong arms and then laid herself open to the amazed scrutiny of her captor, she had realised that the only person she had really succeeded in punishing was herself. Her father might have already brought their name into disrepute but she, she had put the crowning glory on it through her own actions. She went cold as all the ramifications of the Bow Street Runner caught up with her. To be dragged to a round-house, then a magistrate or court, for her identity to be revealed and her conduct judged under the meticulous, unforgiving microscope of the ton, would be unbearable. Even if they had condemned her father, his actions though shameful were hardly unusual, whilst for a female of gentle birth and upbringing to act as she had was unheard of, disgraceful and completely unforgivable.

"You can come out now." The voice was velvet laced with steel. It jerked her out of her reverie.

As she uncurled herself, the room was flooded with a soft light as the man she had so recently struggled with, lit a candelabra above the fireplace. Next to it were ranged two comfortable looking, wing-backed leather chairs. A brief nod directed her to one of them. She perched uncertainly on the edge of the one indicated and watched in bemused amazement as her 'host' poured a dark red liquid into two glasses. He handed her one before arranging himself comfortably in the other chair, leaning deep back into it and crossing his hessian-clad ankles.

He raised the glass and sipped unhurriedly as he considered her thoughtfully over the rim.

"I have undoubtedly been behaving in both a reckless and almost certainly foolish manner recently," he finally murmured softly, as if speaking to himself, "but this tops it all. I should, of course, have handed you over to the authorities, I may still do so." He took another thoughtful sip of his wine. "But I admit you have enlivened an otherwise tedious night, for that at least I am grateful."

Rosalind's eyes widened as she watched him put down his wine glass on the elegant rosewood table beside him and slowly begin to read a small rectangular card, her calling card. He read it aloud in a deep hard voice. "I came not to call the righteous, but sinners to repentance."

He let the words hang heavily between them for a moment. "I am, I admit, more than a little intrigued to discover what alleged sin I have committed against you, someone I am very sure I have never seen before this unexpectedly eventful evening."

As she continued to sit as if carved from stone, her alabaster face expressionless and her gaze fixed firmly on the floor, he added conversationally, "Who are you by the way?"

Rosalind slowly raised eyes that held a strange mix of regret and resolution. "Lady Rosalind Marlowe," she said in her low musical voice. "And you have committed no sin against me, sir, I..." she paused, taking an unladylike gulp of her wine, "I thought this the house of the Earl of Atherton."

She thought she saw a look of shocked surprise disturb the languid composure of the handsome face before her, but she may have been mistaken as a moment later his eyes were shuttered, and he offered only a brief nod in her direction.

"It is. I am Atherton."

It was her turn to look shocked. "But, but I thought he, you, would be a much older man."

Lord Atherton quirked one dark eyebrow. "My father died over two months ago. Is it possible that you knew him?"

Rosalind gulped. "No, not knew him, but of him." She felt as if a hard fist had clamped around her heart and suddenly found it hard to breathe. "I'm sorry, I didn't realise, I..." The room had started to spin, and she could say no more.

Lord Atherton moved with swift speed and grace to remove the wineglass from her nerveless fingers before it fell to the floor. He held it to her bloodless lips and encouraged her to take a sip then gently pushed her further back into the chair.

"If you think this show of female weakness will make me feel sorry for you, you are mistaken." His harsh voice flicked over her like a whip and brought her head back up with a snap. Her eyes flashed fire, and she felt the dizziness recede and a familiar anger fill her veins. He might be innocent of his father's sins, but she would be surprised indeed if he differed from him or any other gentleman of fashion in any great measure.

"I don't want you to feel sorry for me, I don't want anything from you, there is very little you or any of your kind can do to me anymore," she almost spat at him.

"That's better," Lord Atherton said, his tone again mild as if her loss of control had restored his. "Show your claws. However, your statement is both wild and inaccurate. There is the small matter of the Bow Street Runner who is, I'm quite sure, still lurking somewhere close by. You are quite notorious, my dear, and he would dearly love to be the one to receive the acclaim and the reward attached to the one who catches you."

His words snuffed out her anger as again the enormity of what she had done rushed in. "What do you want from me?" she asked, resentfully regarding him as he sat in a relaxed posture, one powerful thigh crossed over the other, his long fingers steepled before him. "Why didn't you hand me over?"

"I think an explanation is due to me, don't you?" he enquired more gently. "Or in your book, should the son suffer from the imagined sins of the father?"

Rosalind sighed as a deep weariness crept over her. "No, no, of course not." She curled herself into the corner of the chair and tucked her legs beneath her, allowing a waterfall of hair to cascade over her face. How she wanted all of it to be over, all of the pain, the humiliation, the anger, the bewilderment at the course her life had taken. She closed her eyes, and her mother's calm loving face swam before her. Her warm gaze held wisdom, sympathy and a gentle strength. Almost before she realised it, she had begun talking, her low voice almost expressionless as the whole sordid tale spilled from her. She left nothing out, explaining how she had found the list in the drawer of her father's study after he had shot himself. The list of all the people he owed money to and how much his reckless gambling had cost him, how she had made a copy of it before the lawyers came, not really knowing what she would do with it, only that she wanted to know everyone who had been even partially responsible for his downfall. How the estate had had to be sold and having no close relatives that she was aware of, how she had fled with only a few possessions to her old nurse, and how she had formed her mad plan to make those guilty for her circumstances suffer, if only a little bit.

Lord Atherton wasn't deceived by the controlled voice; he knew it masked a world of pain and heartache. His father's voice echoed at the back of his mind. 'How dare you dictate to me who is or isn't worthy of my help, you selfish whelp? When was the last time you helped, really helped anyone but yourself?'

Aware that a stilted silence had replaced the flow of words that had seemed to pour out of Lady Rosalind, he gathered his scattered thoughts.

"What do you intend to do with me now, my lord?" Those luminous, bewitching eyes regarded him warily, still with a hint of defiance.

"Do you really intend to return everything you have stolen?" he asked.

Now they flashed. "Every word I have spoken has been the truth."

"As you see it," he murmured cryptically.

His words had her on her feet. "What other way is there to see it? My father was miserable and desperate and a fool, but he was preyed upon by his so-called 'friends'." She paused, her breath coming short and fast. "And I, I have learned nothing, for I too have been miserable and desperate and a fool. If you are going to let me go, then for God's sake do it, Ned and Lucy will be worried."

Lord Atherton too was on his feet, blocking her way to the door. "Not quite so fast." His calm tone gave no indication of how tempted he was to smother those tempestuous words with a kiss. "Sit down." His own weakness made him harsh.

Rosalind sat. For a moment she had thought his eyes had burned like the embers of a smouldering fire, but now they regarded her indifferently again. She could not make head nor tail of this man. But then her experience of men was small, and what she had seen she did not admire.

"What did you plan to do once your reckless plan was complete?" he demanded.

Rosalind shrugged. "Find some respectable position, I suppose. Maybe apply for a post as a governess?"

The earl let out a crack of laughter. "My dear girl, have you looked in the glass recently? Who in their right minds would hire a governess attractive enough to turn the heads of any or all of the males in the household?"

Rosalind flushed. "Surely sir, you exaggerate, I'm sure…"

She got no further but was rudely dragged up by her shoulders and turned to face the mirror over the fireplace. She was uncomfortably aware of the heat of the man so close behind her but dutifully looked in the mirror trying to see what he saw. Her full lips were parted slightly, her face suffused with heat from the fire and his closeness, and her eyes were large, her pupils dilated. Her unbound hair added to her quite wanton appearance. Their eyes met and held. Time seemed suspended for an infinite moment, and then she stumbled as he suddenly released her, her knees unaccountably weak.

"Respectable you will be," he ground out harshly.

"It seems, Lady Rosalind Marlowe, that we are in each other's debt." He paced the room with a restless energy as he spoke. "You will never do as a governess, but I can see no difficulty in you acquiring a post as a companion to an older lady who will not worry if you outshine her in looks."

Rosalind bristled at his high-handed manner. "And no doubt, my lord, you know of just such a one, probably some purple-turbaned old dragon who will expect me to wait on her hand and foot for little or no thanks."

Despite himself, Atherton's lips twitched; both her spirit and her extreme youth were evident, in many ways she reminded him of Belle. "It is a little too late to be so fussy if we are to make you respectable again."

The undoubted truth of the statement made Rosalind bite back the unladylike temptation to tell him to go the devil. "Who is this Lady I am to be a companion to?"

"My mother."

Her lips parted in amazement. Wrong-footed, she was surly. "Your mother? Are you not afraid I will run off with the family silver?"

He leaned over and took her chin in a firm grip. "Enough. Swallow your spleen, you ungrateful chit. You're in the devil's own scrape, and I am trying to help you out of it."

"But why?" she said, pulling herself out of his grasp.

A wry smile twisted his lips. "Let's just say I don't choose that my family should be in any way responsible for your continuing decline in fortune. Is it a bargain?"

Bewildered, she simply nodded her agreement. She did not see that she really had much choice. From then on he was all business, covering her up with her cloak, retying her loo mask, pulling up her hood and insisting she wait whilst he flagged down a hackney cab and then bundling her inside following her closely.

Any alarm she may have felt at being alone with a strange man inside a small cab was soon overcome as he was all efficiency. He fired instructions at her for most of the way: she was to be ready to travel by midday tomorrow; she must be prepared to spend two nights on the road so she would need a female companion of some description for the journey to lend her respectability; she must arrange for the return of all the jewels she had stolen and so on. He helped her down from the cab in the lane behind the coffee house and dismissed it.

She was afraid for a moment that he meant to accompany her in and quailed at the thought of the scene that would inevitably ensue, however, he merely offered her a brief bow before disappearing back into the night. But of course, he didn't need to come in. He now knew everything and could count on her compliance as she had unwittingly placed Ned and Lucy in danger by revealing their whereabouts.

* * *

He walked swiftly, needing to put some distance between himself and Lady Rosalind, to try to put the crazy events of the night into some sort of perspective. Something he couldn't do with those large mesmerising eyes regarding him or the faint smell of jasmine making him want to bury his face in her neck and drink in the sweet scent of her. She seemed to fill him with desire and anger in equal measure. The anger was the harder of the two emotions to explain as it seemed to spring from more sources; anger that she could affect him like some callow youth rather than an experienced man who was always in control of himself around women, anger that one so lovely and innocent had been dealt the hand she had been given, and anger that she should have taken such foolish and dangerous risks.

So caught up was he in his internal monologue, he hardly noticed when someone fell into step beside him as he strolled through Mayfair.

"Ah, so glad to see you, my dear Atherton," drawled a cold, soft voice.

Quickly turning his head, it took a moment to register that Lord Rutley was now beside him, neat as wax as usual in his dark swallow-tailed coat, perfectly tied cravat, his white waistcoat with one gold fob hanging from it complementing the golden buckles on his black pumps.

"Rutley, I hope you have had a successful evening."

"Well, that still remains to be seen, Atherton. The night is not over yet. Might I suggest you accompany me home so I can take a touch at my revenge?" he asked with a smile that did not reach his eyes, the elegant walking stick tapping insistently against his black satin breeches belying his calm tone.

"It will have to wait, I'm afraid," he replied somewhat curtly. "I am going up to Atherton tomorrow on urgent business and must be away early."

The tapping came to an abrupt stop. "But this is very sudden. I hope nothing too serious?"

The earl felt his hackles rising at being delayed further. "Just some estate matters that need my attention," he clipped out.

Arched eyebrows winged upwards, and a smile more closely resembling a smirk twisted thin lips. "Business? Estate matters? I am all admiration, my dear fellow. It has never seemed to me that you took an interest in such, er, rustic pursuits."

That touched a spot already raw from rubbing. A feeling of intense dislike swept over him; this man was harder to be rid of than an irritating wasp. Tired of the verbal swordplay, he went for a home thrust. "Ah, but it is high time I did, it is our estates and our investments that enable us to enjoy the many and varied pleasures of town, after all, my dear fellow."

The barb hit home. It was well known that Lord Rutley viewed his only as a coffer to be dipped into and that the coffer was nearly empty.

Lord Atherton's eyes widened as he saw the scorching flame of green hatred blaze momentarily in the suddenly narrow eyes before him. So Philip had been right, another metaphorical bullet had just lodged itself deep in his brain, perhaps it was just as well he was disappearing for a while.

"Let's hope you are not the next victim of this damned thief whilst you are away," came the bitter reply.

Although he was sure there was nothing Rutley would like better, the irony washed over Lord Atherton in a wave of amusement, dousing his annoyance. "Why thank you for the reminder, most kind of you.

Perhaps I will take my mother's jewels down to her; they will be safer at Atherton. Goodnight."

On that parting shot, he turned towards Grosvenor Square but felt Rutley's resentful stare burning between his shoulder blades every step of the way.

CHAPTER 4

Rosalind had rather more explaining to do. When she did not make their rendezvous, poor Ned had bolted back home in a panic, only to have Lucy ring a peal over him for deserting her. They were both on the point of setting out in search of her when she returned. Lucy began to give her a severe scold but quickly perceived that most of it was going unheard as Rosalind sat in a state of bewilderment and numbed shock. Lucy then completed an abrupt volte-face, turning again on poor Ned who she apostrophised for a bumbling lobcock, ordering him to bring some wine to poor Miss Rosie before making himself scarce. The evening's events sounded even more unlikely in the re-telling, but apart from the odd gasp, Lucy remained silent until it was done. When Rosalind had finished, she simply nodded and responded on a note of grim satisfaction, "For I will restore health unto thee, and I will heal thee of thy wounds, saith the Lord; because they called thee an Outcast."

Rosalind smiled despite herself, "You should have been a vicar's wife, Lucy. I believe you know a bible quote for every occasion."

"Far too high and mighty for me, luvvie," dimpled Lucy. "Besides, most of 'em are more interested in lining their pockets than following the good Lord's teachings."

Rosalind frowned uncertainly. "But will it do? What, after all, do we know about Lord Atherton or his mother?"

"Well, you pitched yourself into a right bumble bath, missy, and no mistake, but handsome is as handsome does. If this here earl of yours was going to make trouble, he had plenty of opportunity to do so this very evening. And didn't he insist you travel with a companion to keep all respectable?" she pointed out as a clincher.

Rosalind's frown deepened. "Who shall I take? You are so busy here..."

Lucy was on her feet in an instant, her hands on her hips, bristling with disapproval and purpose. "Now you start listening to me, Rosalind Marlowe. Your sainted mother, bless her soul, begged me to look out for you as she lay there dying, not that starched up governess who always looked down her nose at me. You'll never know the heartache and worry I suffered when your father sent me away. As if I wouldn't have stayed for nothing. Heaven knows I've done my best. It went against the grain with me to let you have your head with that crazy plan of yours, but now you will do as I say. I'm coming with you tomorrow, and we'll see how the land lies. Ned will cope for a few days. I will arrange for his sister to come and help. Besides, who else will ensure you remember how to act and dress like a lady instead of the hoyden you've been allowed to be these last years?"

Rosalind's eyes lit with amusement. "Hoyden, Lucy?"

"Aye, hoyden. What else would you call it when you were allowed to run wild all over the estate after me and your governess left? And as for running all over town in breeches!"

Her outraged expression drew forth a low chuckle. As usual, Lucy had made everything seem better.

"It's no laughing matter, young lady, when I think of all those hours we worked our fingers to the bone altering your mother's gowns so you could look respectable," she chided, but Rosalind didn't miss the twinkle in her nut-brown eyes.

"What about the jewels? I have no time…"

"Now don't you go worrying your head about that, your part in that nonsense has finished."

"But who?" Rosalind stopped, an almost embarrassed flush had crept over Lucy's face.

"Never mind about who. Let's just say that my Ned knew some less than respectable people before I sorted him out, and he will know how it is to be done."

The not very agile Bow Street Runner suddenly sprang into Rosalind's mind, and a slow grin worked its way across her face. "They must be returned to Bow Street," she pronounced decidedly. "They need all the help they can get, and we'll need one more message, Lucy."

That much put-upon lady raised her eyes to heaven, but she did not disappoint. "For what shall it profit a man, if he shall gain the whole world, and lose his own soul?" She nodded once in a satisfied manner before bundling Rosalind upstairs to pack.

\* \* \*

Having breakfasted early, Lord Atherton was on the point of departure when he received a large package and a hastily scribbled note. Pulling out his quizzing glass, he scanned this missive impatiently.

*Dear George,*

*Please take down this parcel to Mama and give her my greatest love. Have a safe journey.*

*Your loving sister, Belle.*

*Oh, by the way, the latest is the heiress's father, though a cit, has turned down Rutley after all, his dislike of profligacy overcoming his desire to establish his daughter in the ton!*

He shook his head slowly, feeling a creeping disgust at the society he belonged to. Whatever one thought of Rutley, did a man really deserve to have his every mistake or embarrassment inspected and condemned by an indolent, hypocritical ton? These gossip weavers spun a web of half-truths and conjecture, poisoning reputations without compunction.

"Bad news, my lord?" enquired his concerned butler, hovering nearby, ready to hand him his hat and gloves.

"No," he responded shortly. "No news at all."

He arrived behind Prowett's Coffee House in his curricle, closely followed by his chaise to convey Lady Rosalind and her companion. He found both ladies ready to depart, their baggage at their feet. Quickly, he dismounted and strode towards them. He was a tall man, and his caped driving coat emphasized his size. He dwarfed Lucy as he bowed briefly before her.

"Mrs Prowett, I presume?" he asked with a small smile.

She offered him a curtsy in return and looked up at him from under her old fashioned bonnet, her nut-brown eyes offering him a sharp scrutiny. "Indeed sir, and if I might say so, you won't find a finer or kinder companion than Lady Rosalind if you advertised 'til the cows came home, my lord."

"Lucy," protested Lady Rosalind, flustered.

Lord Atherton transferred his attention to her. Her green pelisse and matching green bonnet were not of the latest fashion, but he saw nothing to despise in them. On the contrary, they brought out the warm tones of her eyes most effectively; eyes that looked far more shy and uncertain in the cold light of day. He bowed slightly more deeply and took her hand.

"Lady Rosalind, I look forward to seeing the truth of that statement as my mother deserves both kindness and respect."

The words were softly spoken, but Rosalind didn't miss the hard thread underlining them. Even as she felt herself bristle, they were being hustled towards the waiting chaise. He handed them up the steps himself and provided them both with a blanket as the postilion secured their luggage.

"My horses are rather fresh," he said, nodding towards a pair of restive, well-matched bays being walked by his groom. "So don't worry if I draw ahead of you for a short time; they need to stretch their legs." With a brief nod, he was gone, barely giving his groom time to jump up behind him before he swept out of sight.

As he weaved through the London traffic with calm skill, no one would have guessed at his inner turmoil. She had looked absurdly youthful. He would be surprised if she numbered more than eighteen years to her name. How did he explain her to his mother, who had steadfastly refused the benefit of even one of her relations as her companion? How did he explain to himself his actions? How did he feel about re-visiting the home that was his family seat but also the heart of the guilt and grief he felt for his father?

As he left the built-up environs of town and reached the edge of Finchley Common, he put his nagging worries aside and gave his horses their wish and let them go.

*** 

Lady Rosalind nibbled the end of one slender finger thoughtfully. "I think he's regretting it," she murmured, as the chaise made its more careful progress towards the edge of town.

"Well if he is, you will just have to show him he's wrong," smiled Lucy, patting her hand comfortingly. "Have you ever travelled in such comfort? It's his own carriage too," she sighed.

"How do you know?" Rosalind enquired. Lucy chuckled. "Where have your wits gone begging? Didn't you notice the crest on the panel? Two quite fierce-looking lions, a mangled snake at their feet."

She shook her head. "We were bundled in so quickly, I scarce had time to notice anything."

"Well, I hope you noticed how he paid us every observance, handing us into the carriage himself and giving us these lovely warm rugs. A true gentleman if you ask me."

Rosalind shrugged off-handedly. "They all appear gentlemanly, but I'll be surprised if he turns out differently from the rest of the greedy, shallow breed."

Lucy frowned worriedly at her charge. "Rosie, your experience has been bad, no one can deny it, but it is also limited. Living above an establishment where young bucks to and fro, isn't something you should have experienced but you must not judge too harshly. Young ladies aren't meant to see or hear foxed young gentlemen or overhear conversations not meant for ladies' ears. It's just part of growing up for them, my dear."

Rosalind sighed and leant back against the comfortable squabs, closing her eyes for a moment. "Listen, Lucy."

"Apart from the horses, I can't hear anything."

"Exactly," Rosalind concurred, smiling slightly. "The constant hum of London has gone."

Turning her head, she glanced out of the windows and saw that even the press of London traffic heading north had temporarily disappeared. As they rounded a bend, she saw the grassland sloped gently upwards towards a stand of trees swaying slightly in the brisk breeze. Then she spotted movement. It looked like two riders were cantering towards the road. How she wished she was one of them, riding had always been a joy for her. Thinking no more of it, she closed her eyes again and gave herself up to the gentle sway of the carriage.

The unmistakeable thud of hooves grew louder, and then a crack of gunshot brought her bolt upright, just as the chaise swayed alarmingly. She grabbed the nearest strap to stop herself plunging forwards, her other hand reaching into the pocket of her pelisse.

"Get down, Lucy," she whispered, her heart thumping uncomfortably fast. Opening the window, she saw the two riders were almost upon them, muffled up to the eyes. Not giving herself time to think, she pointed the small silver pistol she had retrieved, closed her eyes and fired it in the general direction of the nearest one. It was a lucky shot, he jerked awkwardly and clutched his shoulder. He shouted something in the direction of his companion, and they headed off again across the common.

Opening the door, Rosalind jumped down. The postilion was thankfully unhurt but busy calming the spooked horses. "Well done, miss," he said admiringly. "There's been no highwaymen that I ever heard of around these parts the last few years. Who'd o'thought it? And in broad daylight too!"

Rosalind, now pale and shaking a little, put up her chin. "They weren't very determined, were they?"

"Nor stupid, miss," he said, nodding up the road. Rosalind saw a cloud of dust and through it, a small group of horses galloping towards them. They all seemed to be wearing a uniform of some kind.

"Robin Redbreasts, ma'am."

She let out a slow sigh of relief. The irony wasn't lost on her; last night she had been lucky to escape the clutches of a Bow Street Runner and here she was offering up a prayer of thanks at her deliverance at their hands. As they came closer, she saw they were all dressed in dark blue coats and trousers, only the flash of their scarlet waistcoats and yellow buttons adding a splash of colour to their sober uniforms.

\* \* \*

Having galloped their fidgets out, Lord Atherton slowed his horses to a walk. He was on the point of turning the curricle, feeling that it was not quite the thing to leave the ladies alone when he spotted two familiar figures riding towards him. Pulling in, he waited for them.

"Atherton, you have missed such a farce as you have ever witnessed," called one of them.

"Good day, Philip, and to you, John. This is an unexpected pleasure."

"Y-you should have c-come with us, old boy," said Lord Preeve. "N-never laughed so much in my l-life!"

He quirked an enquiring brow. "Barnet races? Give me a moment to turn around before telling me all about it, will you? I'm accompanying my mother's companion to Atherton but fancied a gallop."

A noted whip, it took only moments for him to execute a neat turn. He listened with increasing amusement as between them, they regaled him with the result of the race between a grey mare and a bay gelding, both of whom had seen better days. The grey mare had become winded halfway round the course and had pulled up and started to munch the apples overhanging the rough track at that point. The race should now have been the gelding's of course, but the combined circumstances of the rider having imbibed too freely of his tipple of choice and his over-enthusiastic celebrations before the winning post had been reached, had been his undoing, resulting in him falling off as he broached the final bend.

They were still all laughing when they reached the brow of the hill and saw the situation below.

"George, isn't that your chaise surrounded by redbreasts?" murmured Sir Philip.

He had already sprung his horses and in a few moments came upon the scene, closely followed by his friends.

Sir Philip nodded at one of the patrol. "Hello Charlie, what's afoot?"

This individual might have been handsome if not for the deep scar that ran from his forehead to the corner of his mouth. He took the proffered hand and shook it warmly. "Hello, Captain Bray, sir. Would you believe these ladies were set upon by a couple of rascals, but owing to the young lady firing a shot at them and apparently winging one of 'em, they made off before we got here? Two of the lads have gone after them, but they had a start, so I'm not that hopeful."

Lord Atherton had visibly paled. Turning to the two ladies who stood beside the carriage, he bowed deeply. "Accept my apologies. I should never have left you. It won't happen again." He turned towards the postilion. "Any damage?" he said briskly.

"Not to speak of, sir, the horses were a bit spooked is all. It's miss we have to thank, let off her popper in a flash and dang me if she didn't hit one. That soon put paid to the blighters."

Atherton looked back to Lady Rosalind. Her white

face looked pinched with cold. He held out his hand. "Could I see it?"

Her eyes widened in alarm, but she reluctantly reached into her pocket and drew it forth. "I hope you don't mind that I, er, borrowed it," she said hesitantly.

His eyes shot back to hers as he took the pistol, his pistol, the very one he had threatened her with only the night before. She was looking at him anxiously as well she might the little minx.

"You are full of surprises, my dear," was all he said softly, fully aware of the interested gaze of those around them.

"By J-Jove that's a nice piece!" approved Lord Preeve, pressing closer, but his eyes were firmly fixed on the lady, a look of keen appreciation in them.

Lord Atherton was forced to introduce them but once bows and curtsies had been exchanged he hurriedly assisted the ladies back into the carriage before thanking and dismissing the patrol. He then led his friends a little way apart.

"Y-you damned d-dark horse," protested Lord Preeve. "W-where have you been hiding that d-dashed beauty?"

He had clearly not yet made the connection between Lady Rosalind and her father, but the fixed regard of Sir Philip told him he had. "I've not been hiding anyone, John, but she has been living a somewhat secluded existence due to, er, straitened circumstances. I'd rather you both forgot about both this incident and the lady herself, for now."

"I b-bet you would you d-devil, want to keep h-her all to yourself, eh?" responded his friend jovially.

As usual, Sir Philip said very little, but it was to the

point. "If such an unusual circumstance doesn't make the papers, I'd be surprised," he commented, blandly enough. "The mounted patrols have all but eradicated such incidents." He gave his friend a very direct look. "I'd say it would take someone very desperate to mount such an attack on this road in daylight."

"The world is full of desperate people," Atherton said. "I take it your friend Charlie was in the regiment?"

Sir Philip nodded.

"He is one of the lucky ones to find gainful employment; there are many others not so fortunate who may be forced to such desperate measures."

Sir Philip held his eyes steadily. "As you say. Don't worry, not a word will pass our lips, but if you don't return to town soon, expect a visit. Where do you stay tonight?"

"I'm hoping to make Fenny Stratford. I've a mind to pay the lock keeper a visit."

Lord Preeve had kept quiet during this exchange, feeling sure he was missing something, although what was beyond him. But this piece of casually dropped information was too much. "V-visit a lock keeper? N-not at all the thing, G-George. C-come to think of it, F-Fenny Stratford ain't all that either, m-much better accommodation to be f-found at Stony Stratford you know."

Sir Philip smiled knowingly at his friend. "The Grand Junction Canal? Finally taking an interest in your father's investments?"

"Just so," affirmed Lord Atherton before taking his farewell.

The small cavalcade made good time from there

on in, despite the somewhat hilly and often winding roads between Barnet and St Albans. But Rosalind would have preferred to continue to endure the frequent jolting that even His Lordship's well-sprung chaise could not prevent, rather than face him over tea in the private parlour of The George.

Due to the coming and going of servants bringing tea and seed cake, there was very little occasion for private discourse, but Rosalind took the bull by the horns in one such lull.

"I hope you will forgive me for borrowing your pistol," she ventured in a small voice. "It seemed prudent at the time."

As usual, Lucy sprang instantly to her defence. "Well, just as well you did as where was our fine lord in our moment of need? And to think of you acting as if you were used to firing on villains every other day."

Rosalind sent her stalwart supporter a look of entreaty, but Lord Atherton stepped neatly into the breach, accepting without a blink his fall from grace in this good lady's eyes.

"Please, don't apologise. I understand your reservations and am thankful you showed such forethought. Mrs Prowett is quite correct; I should not have left you in such a perilous position. If I had had any concerns as to your safety, you may be sure I would not have done it. The mounted patrols have, until now, effectively eradicated the nuisance of highwayman from the common."

A not very dignified snort from Lucy was his only reply. There did not seem to be anything left to say, so after finishing the repast provided for them, they made their way to Fenny Stratford, only stopping briefly at Dunstable to change horses.

The sun was setting as they broached the steep descent into the valley of the Ouse and glimpsed the roofs of their destination glimmering redly in the distance. Rosalind had long since shut her eyes in an effort to dim the thumping in her head which seemed to echo the rhythm of the pounding of the hooves against the hard-baked road but now looked around with vague interest. She had never seen a landscape quite like it; fertile pastures and wide cornfields spoke eloquently of the bucolic ideal on one side, yet as they crossed a hunchbacked bridge she saw a calm expanse of water giving a glimpse of the industrial efforts of the country. She was fascinated by the sight of a barge being towed by a huge horse in the distance and looked forward to taking a closer look.

They had soon pulled into the large and bustling yard of The Bull Inn and were shown to a large, commodious bedchamber that housed a very comfortable looking four-poster bed, a truckle bed for Lucy and a table set under the large window that gave views onto the canal.

Rosalind's suggestion that Lucy might share in her comfort in the larger bed was met with a firm rebuttal, as was the suggestion she joined her in the private parlour Lord Atherton had hired for dinner.

"You may forget what your correct station in life is, Rosie, I mean Lady Rosalind," she hastily corrected herself, "but I never have and never will. You are the daughter of an earl. Things may have got a bit too relaxed recently what with you living with me and all, but whilst in London I may be the proprietress of a respectable coffee house, here I am just your personal maid and don't you go forgetting it. Speaking of which, we better bustle about if you're to be ready any time soon; your dress is sadly crumpled, and your hair looks like you've been through a hedge backwards."

She dressed simply in a plain peach gown with a soft, well-worn shawl draped around her shoulders, her hair simply arranged in a top knot with curling fronds framing her face. Lord Atherton awaited her by the fire, his perfectly cut black tail-coat and close-fitting pantaloons emphasising an athletic figure that owed nothing to artifice. He bowed politely over her hand before pulling out one of the chairs at the table already set for dinner.

"You look charming, my dear. I'm not sure which I prefer, the waif in breeches or the young lady of refinement," he murmured provocatively as he seated himself opposite her.

Fortunately, she was spared the necessity of answering as a waiter appeared carrying various dishes. Their experiences were so wide apart it was not to be expected that an easy flow of chatter would enliven the table, so Rosalind, who had realised that she was quite famished, attacked the various dishes before her with the healthy appetite of the young. The soup was surprisingly good, she followed this with some roast chicken and asparagus and made good inroads into a delicious damson tart.

Lord Atherton covertly watched her with some amusement. More used to watching the ladies of his acquaintance pick at their food in a dainty manner, he found it refreshing that she employed none of the many maidenly arts to attract his attention or impress him with her femininity. But as the satisfying repast came to an end, she raised her eyes to his and gave him one of her direct looks.

"It has occurred to me that you will hardly have had time to let your mother know of my coming," she began somewhat hesitantly, "that there might be some awkwardness in my unexpected arrival."

Lord Atherton took a thoughtful sip of his wine before answering. "You are right," he affirmed. "And she may well resent it at first but trust me to smooth the way. She may not want a companion, but it is for the best. She is too much on her own, and I fear, must miss my father badly."

Lady Rosalind grimaced. "So I am neither expected nor wanted. What a delightful prospect for me."

"Have you a better one?" parried Lord Atherton. "As you have been living with your old nurse, I had presumed, perhaps wrongly, that you were friendless. But it occurs to me that as the daughter of an earl, you must have some relations?"

She shrugged. "Not that I know or want to know. My father's relations did not approve of his marriage to a squire's only daughter and one who had no wish to lead a fashionable life. The squire also did not approve of my mother's marriage. He felt my father was too unsteady, and it led to a rift between them. He died almost a stranger to me. My mother was a gentle, kind woman who enjoyed a quiet life in the country and made my father happy. He did not know how to go on without her, and I was too young to be of any use."

Lord Atherton heard the catch in her voice. "You

have been unfortunate with your relatives. My elder sister, Lady Harriet, married a squire, and although it was not the match my father had set his heart on, my parents put her happiness first. You must have been very lonely," he probed gently.

For a moment her eyes looked distant, but then she blinked and offered him a small smile. "I had my lessons at first, although I was a sad trial to my governess, always escaping to the stables and riding out across the estate. I was always happier outside than cooped up. It was a relief to us both when she was sent away."

"Yet you were thinking of becoming one," he reminded her. "Have you any accomplishments, apart from breaking and entering, of course?"

He saw the spark of resentment flash through her eyes and almost regretted his words, but he felt safer with the spirited Lady Rosalind rather than the pathetic orphan who tugged at his sympathy. He had not enjoyed the almost haunting melancholy that he had glimpsed when she talked of her parents. He noted the sudden mulish set of her jaw and watched with interest as she pushed back her chair and marched over to the writing desk in the corner. She returned in a moment armed with paper and then reached for her reticule, pulling out a short stub of pencil.

Lord Atherton felt slightly uncomfortable as he found himself on the receiving end of a piercing gaze that viewed him with objective interest as if he were a specimen under the microscope.

"Don't move," she hissed as he shifted in his chair.

She worked quickly, her hand making a series of

deft, quick strokes, pausing occasionally with her head tilted to one side before continuing in the same style.

It did not take many minutes before she had finished. Silently she handed it to him.

It was an excellent sketch. His likeness had been caught in those few deft strokes, and if he saw an arrogance which he did not recognise in the tilt of his chin and the challenge in his eyes, he was not one to cavil at such irrelevances. Lifting his eyes from the portrait in front of him, he looked admiringly at her.

"This is very good, and so quick too. Another surprise. I see I must be careful not to underestimate you."

She nodded briefly, accepting her due.

"But no more surprises tonight, if you please. I have to go out, there is someone I want to see, and I need you to promise you won't leave your room. This place has many visitors by road and canal, not all of them quality you understand."

As much as she resented his orders, she could see the sense in them. "I can see no reason for me to go out," she responded with dignity, rising to her feet. He rose too, picked up her sketch and accompanied her to the door of her chamber, whether from innate good manners, or to make sure she followed his orders, she was not quite sure.

Tired from the day's travels, she and Lucy retired to bed almost immediately. Lady Rosalind awoke some time later to find the moon shining through the window and slanting across her face. Unable to fall back to sleep, she slipped into her dressing gown, retrieved her pencil and searched through her rather battered portmanteau for her sketchbook.

Settling herself at the table by the window, she drank in the sight of the moon glinting on the still water, the lock keeper's cottage gleaming softly white in the distance. Quickly she became absorbed, trying to capture the still, almost otherworldly atmosphere of the scene. As she began to add the cottage to the sketch, she saw the door open and two figures shake hands. Although some distance away, she felt sure one was Lord Atherton and became certain when he began to walk back down the towpath; his long confident stride and something about the upright way he held himself giving him away.

Her attention shifted as she detected movement on one of the barges near the cottage. As Lord Atherton passed, two men stepped ashore. She could make out no more than two dark silhouettes but felt some alarm as she saw them come up behind Lord Atherton. One raised an arm and unconsciously she cried out, awakening Lucy. She saw Atherton slump. He was caught by one of the men and then dragged back towards the barge. Wasting no more time, she started stripping off her dressing gown.

"Lucy, do not ask me any questions; there is no time," she gasped out. "Lord Atherton is in trouble. Get my breeches out of the bottom of my portmanteau, quickly."

Lucy grumbled something about breeches and grown men being able to look after themselves but did as she was bid. In a matter of moments, she was dressed. Grabbing Lucy's cloak, she made for the back stairs. Hurrying across the humped bridge, she ran down the towpath towards the barge, diving swiftly behind a small clump of trees as she heard a creak as the small door of the barge opened, and the two dark figures emerged.

"His Lordship ain't gonna be none too happy if he hears we left 'im alone," said one of them.

"You worrit too much you young jabberknoll," laughed his companion. "That was a reet good knock you gave 'im on his bone box, and even if he do come round, he'd belong in a circus if he can get out o' them knots."

"I s'pose the odd flash of lightnin' won't do us no harm," his partner in crime conceded.

Lady Rosalind waited patiently for them to disappear before hurrying onto the barge. For a moment she thought she was too late. Lord Atherton lay awkwardly on his side as still as if he were dead. His feet were tied and his hands bound behind his back. She fumbled frantically with the fiendishly tight knots for some moments before finally acknowledging the futility of her attempts. Glancing somewhat wildly around, she noticed the stove and a small cupboard next to it. Yanking it open, she prayed for something sharp. Reaching for a wooden handle, she pulled out a huge carving knife.

"My boot," came a faint, familiar voice behind her.

"Thank God," she cried, turning back towards Lord Atherton. "Your boot?" she repeated, falling to her knees.

"Knife," he murmured, eyeing the fearsome one she wielded with some dismay. "Sharp and small."

The effort of talking seemed to have cost him much for he closed his eyes again on the words. She grabbed his leg just below the knee, firmly shutting her mind off from the feel of the strong steel-like muscles she felt there and slipped her small fingers into the top of his boot. It was the work of a few moments to retrieve the slim, deadly-looking blade. It sliced through his bonds with ease, and he was soon free if far from well. She helped him into a sitting position.

"Do you never do as you're told?" he muttered.

"Just as well for you I don't," she snapped back.

"I do not mean to be ungrateful, but what if they come back? How will you defend me then?" he challenged, his voice getting stronger by the moment.

"They won't. They have disappeared in the general direction of the Navigation Inn to partake in something called a flash of lightning," she said dryly. "I imagine they will be jug-bitten before too long."

Despite the seriousness of their situation and his aching head, a silent laugh shook those broad shoulders. "You have clearly enlarged your vocabulary since you have been in town, but pray, try to forget it before we reach Atherton."

With a sniff, she helped him to his feet.

"Thank you," he murmured, removing her hand from his arm, "but I will do now."

The short walk back to The Bull was uneventful until they approached the bridge, then they saw an alarmingly purposeful figure striding towards them. Even as Lady Rosalind shrank back, Lord Atherton surged forwards.

"Philip," he greeted his friend.

"Evening, George, you look sick as a horse, more adventures?" he enquired calmly.

"Indeed, but if you hoped to share in them, Galahad, you're too late. I have already been rescued."

Sir Philip's glance moved past Lord Atherton to the

silent figure behind him. His quick eyes widened as they took in the slender form, the cloak's hood failing to disguise the wide amber eyes that held his own, half defiantly.

"Lady Rosalind," he murmured softly.

"Let's get inside before the pleasantries," suggested Lord Atherton.

They had barely made the top of the back stairs before Lucy was upon them.

"The righteous is delivered out of trouble," she declared on a note of relief, casting an experienced eye over Lord Atherton. "You look likely to cast up your accounts and no mistake, my lord," she surmised. "Back to bed with you, my girl," she said, turning to Lady Rosalind. "I'll see His Lordship is made more comfortable."

"Lucy, you forget my station," she murmured, amusement lighting her eyes at the way Lucy spoke to all of them. Before that formidable matron could reply she turned to Lord Atherton. "One thing you probably should know. One of them referred to the fact that 'His Lordship' would not be pleased at them leaving you. It would seem you have an enemy, after all, my lord."

As soon as she had gone, Lucy turned her beagle eyes on Sir Philip. "Although I'm glad enough to see you, sir, you might think to take His Lordship's arm; it wouldn't take no more than a feather to send him over."

Neither gentleman was proof against Lucy's managing ways, so it was not until her prophesy had been proved correct and Lord Atherton's stomach had been relieved of its contents and his head bathed with vinegar, that they were left to themselves.

"I see you've still got your soldier's nose for trouble," smiled Lord Atherton.

"And all my faculties," he concurred, casting an eye about the room. "And as I have never found you to be untidy, I would suggest your room has been searched. Anything missing?"

Lord Atherton's gaze slowly took in the room, finally noticing that a drawer in the desk hung open and his greatcoat was in a huddle on the floor. His eyes came slowly back to the desk. "There was a package on the desk," he said finally.

"I assume that is what the hold-up was about? Might I ask if there was anyone who might have had reason to suppose you were carrying something of value, George?"

His head still thumping, it took Lord Atherton a few moments to piece together the events of the day, and then he started to laugh.

Sir Philip's brows shot up. "You think this a laughing matter? George, you could have been killed!"

"No, I am sure that was not the intention, and I am afraid I am somewhat to blame. I er, rather unwittingly baited the trap," he admitted.

He related his meeting with Lord Rutley the night before and saw comprehension dawn on his quick friend's brow.

"The cad! George, you should call him out for this!"

"Much as I sympathise with your feelings, Philip, I find I cannot kick a fellow when he's down. His humiliation is complete. His suit to the heiress has been turned down, which opens him wide to the gossip and ridicule of the ton but more to the point, his creditors will be calling on him in droves. He may be able to fob off his boot maker or his tailor by retiring to his crumbling estate and growing vegetables, but his debts of honour are another thing. He will be ostracised if he cannot raise the money."

Sir Philip regarded him seriously under frowning brows. "But what about your mother's jewels?"

Lord Atherton smiled wolfishly. "Now, my friend, we come to the cream of the jest. Imagine Rutley's anticipation when he holds that package in his hands, the eagerness with which he will shred the wrapping, only to find if I am not much mistaken, some material for my mother!"

Although a smile lurked in the back of his astute eyes, Sir Philip was still not quite satisfied. "I've a mind to waylay those rogues and beat the truth out of them. I believe I would enjoy it," he said slowly. "Rutley must have followed you. It would not be difficult to trace your route; your crest is quite memorable. He must have wasted no time in hiring those thugs to put you out of the way whilst another searched your room. My guess is he has gone on to Stony Stratford to await events. He would not risk staying here. I could quite easily track him down and teach him a lesson."

"Your feelings do you credit, and under other circumstances, I might approve," replied Lord Atherton. "But consider, as you pointed out the other evening, I seem to have already incurred his enmity and my rough treatment tonight was his means of teaching me a lesson. He will, in all likelihood, leave me alone now. However, if even a rumour of his possibly being related to today's events were to get out, his downfall would be complete, and he would not be able to show his face at any time in the near future. He would have real cause to hate me then, and it would be very tiresome to always be looking over my shoulder. As it stands, I cannot see that he has many choices; he must retire to his mouldering estate or flee the country in the hope that he can turn his fortunes around. I believe the latter event is more likely."

After giving it some thought, Sir Philip reluctantly accepted this line of reasoning.

"And Lady Rosalind?" he probed. "You made no mention of having made her acquaintance or of intending to accompany her to your mother, was it only two nights ago? An enterprising young lady, who has not only shot a supposed highwayman today but also flew to your rescue this evening, dressed shall we say, somewhat unconventionally?"

Lord Atherton considered his friend somewhat pensively before answering. "Unconventional, perhaps, and certainly impetuous, but still very much a lady, an innocent if you will and under my protection." He paused for a moment to let his words sink in. "And there, my dear Philip, we will leave the subject of Lady Rosalind."

CHAPTER 5

Perhaps not surprisingly, there was no sign of the barge in the morning. No doubt the unsuccessful felons had seen the wisdom of neither facing a potential confrontation with their escapee or their naturally disappointed employer. Sir Philip accompanied the small cavalcade, having apparently set himself up as watchdog, but they enjoyed an uneventful day's travel to Coventry, putting up at the King's Head. Any wish he might have harboured to further his acquaintance with Lady Rosalind was somewhat thwarted by the natural reticence of a young lady who had no wish to expand on either the events of her more distant or recent past. This rather pleased Lord Atherton, who had too often watched damsels succumb to the handsome face and undoubted address of his rather dashing friend.

Atherton Hall was situated some twelve miles from Shrewsbury, and although she felt a little anxious at meeting the dowager countess (her imaginings ranging from a stern-faced harridan in a turban to a frail, tear-stricken, inconsolable widow, who was never without her handkerchief), Rosalind looked about her with interest as they turned through a wide gateway with two imposing posts with two lions mounted upon their weathered pier caps. A long, neat avenue lined with mature elm trees led through a pleasant parkland, with a lake shimmering to the east in the late afternoon sunshine. Turning a bend, a home wood spread out to the west, and the first view of the house was attained. The large Palladian-style mansion seemed almost set alight with the sun heating its red brick and reflecting brightly off its many windows. Set towards the back of the imposing structure, two long lower wings spread out, their brick more mellow, softening the look of stern grandeur thrown out by the main house.

Their arrival may have been unexpected, but as they drew up on the gravelled forecourt in front of the elegant portico, they found a butler and two footmen already hovering under a series of classical columns, whose capitals were carved into the shape of acanthus leaves. Everything spoke of taste, symmetry and order. Lady Rosalind felt somewhat daunted; it was a far cry from the shabby, neglected house in which she had been reared.

Lord Atherton handed the reins to his groom and jumped down swiftly. "Sedgewick," he smiled at the white-haired butler, "I had no chance to inform you of my coming, or that I was bringing guests! Sir Philip will be staying for a few days, and I have brought Lady Rosalind Marlowe to visit my mother. Her maid, Mrs Prowett, will also be staying, though I am not sure for how long."

Sedgewick bowed graciously but permitted himself a small smile, the privilege of long-standing service allowing him the familiarity. "If I may say so, sir, your arrival will so please Lady Atherton that if you had brought a dozen persons with you, I do not think it would trouble her."

"Where is she?" he asked in a lowered tone. "I would like to announce our arrival myself."

"Of course, I shall make your guests comfortable whilst you go to her. I believe you will find her in the kitchen gardens, my lord."

The main gardens at Atherton were as neat and symmetrical as the house, but the kitchen gardens were his mother's domain. Here, she created a wonderful riot of nature where flowers, herbs, fruit and vegetable beds intermingled to create a beautiful and fragrant sanctuary. As he passed through the arch into the walled garden, a burst of colour greeted him. Bright yellow black-eyed susans and deep purple delphiniums vied for attention. As he passed further along the path, a plethora of scents assailed him, the more subtle, calming smells of rosemary and thyme being overridden by the delicate sweet peas. It was by one of the neat rows of asparagus that he saw his mother kneeling, apparently totally absorbed in her task of removing weeds.

She looked absurdly youthful for a widow with three grown offspring. A few blonde tresses still untouched by grey had escaped her bonnet, but her pretty face, still only home to a few fine lines, held a suggestion of melancholy and distraction.

"Mother," he said softly.

Her head shot up, shock and joy swiftly chasing themselves across her face.

"George, what a lovely surprise," she smiled, rising swiftly to her feet and stripping off her soiled gloves, before hugging him warmly.

He held her close for a moment, before putting her gently from him and wiping a smudge of dirt from her brow.

"I believe we have gardeners enough for this task, Mother," he frowned. "You look a little tired, my dear."

"How unchivalrous of you to say so," she laughed. "Jackson, our head gardener, would agree wholeheartedly with you, of course. He cannot get used to me insisting on doing this little chore myself, but I enjoy it vastly, I assure you. The gardeners are welcome to the rest of the gardens; I prefer to put my own touch on this one."

She tucked one small hand in his arm and began walking slowly back to the house with him.

"Out with it, what is it you want to say to me?"

He looked down into her twinkling grey eyes ruefully. "There is still no getting anything past you is there?"

"Well, my love, let's just call it mother's intuition, but something tells me that this unexpected visit might have a reason behind it?" She suddenly looked a little alarmed. "Belle hasn't got into a scrape, has she? She did faithfully promise me that she would try to behave, but I can't say I placed any great reliance on her being able to keep it. If only Hayward would be firmer with her."

"It strikes me as slightly unjust to expect Hayward

to succeed where all the rest of us have fallen lamentably short. But no, Belle is not in any trouble that I know of," he reassured her.

She looked at him shrewdly for a moment before directing him down a side path to a bench placed in front of a sidewall covered with green apricots and gooseberries.

"What scrape have you fallen into, George?"

"I have found you a companion," he plunged in, rushing his fences.

Lady Atherton's finely shaped brows shot up and her eyes glittered diamond hard. "Am I to believe that you have gone against my wishes in this matter, George?" she asked softly.

Lord Atherton felt himself almost reduced to schoolboy status. It was no meek spirit which had held together the Atherton household for the last thirty years. Though a loving spouse and parent, it was not through doting fondness that she had bound together such a diverse set of characters.

"If you will let me explain," he began.

"Yes, George, I really think you must, and for your sake, I hope your explanation is very, very, good."

It was not an easy interview. After several false starts, he could think of no better way of engendering his mother's sympathy than by telling her the truth.

Lady Atherton had not been prepared for such an amazing tale but had enough common sense not to interrupt with pointless questions. When he had finished, she held her own counsel for several moments.

"Well, my dear, that certainly was very enlightening," she murmured. "And you were quite right to share it with me. How can I resent this poor child when she has already been instrumental in rescuing you from that, that cowardly, good-for-nothing scoundrel?"

"Yes, Mother, but I am not at all sure you should mention it to her. It might embarrass her to think you know all."

The dowager countess gave her son a very straight look. "If and when, I find myself in need of your advice on managing recalcitrant children, George, I will ask for it!"

Lady Rosalind and Sir Philip were shown into a cheerful, primrose morning room whilst Sedgewick took Mrs Prowett to Mrs Simmons, the housekeeper. She showed no signs of the annoyance she felt that Sedgewick should be the first to know of the new arrivals but calmly sent a maid with suitable refreshments, whilst she welcomed Mrs Prowett and arranged for bed chambers to be made ready.

Lady Rosalind stood awkwardly in the middle of the room, not quite comfortable at being left alone with Sir Philip.

"Please sit down, Lady Rosalind," he smiled. "I won't eat you, you know."

Lady Rosalind blushed, feeling gauche and unsure of herself, but acceded to his request.

"I would like to offer my belated thanks to you for rescuing my friend. You are, I believe, in safe hands, but if at any time you find yourself in need of a friend, I would be honoured if you would consider me at your service," he said seriously, bowing before seating himself comfortably opposite her.

Determined to deflect attention from herself, she

gave Sir Philip one of her direct looks. "You think, perhaps, we may still be in danger? You know who was behind it, don't you?"

It was more statement than question. Sir Philip looked across at the intriguing young lady, a look of mild surprise and indecision in his gaze. One moment she was an unsure child, without the usual flow of meaningless chit-chat that characterised her sex. She was, as George had pointed out, an innocent, and uncomfortable with any hint of flirtation yet when she found herself in a dangerous situation, she reacted with a quickness of thought and decision that was as rash as it was intrepid. Yes, by God, no fainting or tiresome fit of the vapours for her, and when she fixed those intense golden eyes on you, it was difficult to consider denying her anything.

"Although I have no wish to pry into Lord Atherton's affairs, you do not perhaps consider that as I have been so closely concerned in them, I might merit some sort of explanation?" she pressed quietly.

Although well aware it was not really his tale to tell, he nonetheless found himself filling her in on Lord Atherton's dealings with Lord Rutley. A large part of his success as a leader of soldiers had been dependent on reading the mood of his men. So although she remained silent throughout, he noted the flash of disgust that crossed her face at the mention of gambling, interestingly followed by one of guilt and chagrin when he mentioned the loss of the Rutley emeralds and the possibility that he had hoped to partially restore his failing fortunes by the acquisition of Lady Atherton's jewels.

Rosalind was relieved that the arrival of Mrs

Simmons to show her to her room put an end to any more confidences. This neat, efficient lady showed her an alarming amount of deference, informing her that Lady Atherton would see her in her private sitting room when she had had time to dress for dinner.

She had very little opportunity to reflect on Sir Philip's revelations as Lucy was waiting for her and in a very short time had her attired in a simple round gown of olive green, tied with a bronze ribbon under the square-cut bosom. She took extra care with Lady Rosalind's hair, piling it artfully on top of her head in a riot of curls, allowing a few to frame her face. She completed it by weaving some gold and green flowers into the arrangement and then stood back to view her handiwork.

Her eyes brightened with something suspiciously like tears. "Behold, thou are fair, my love," she sighed. "It makes my old heart glad to see you here in this setting, looking every inch the lady that you are."

Rosalind stared at the vision before her as if at a stranger; she had not had much occasion to wear any of the gowns they had altered and although she felt she looked well, she felt strange and unlike herself. Although she knew herself to be a lady, somehow she felt more like an imposter than ever. It was with some trepidation that she followed Lady Atherton's abigail to her private sitting room. She stood uncertainly on the threshold of the cosy and surprisingly, slightly shabby-looking room as she was announced.

Lady Atherton took in at a glance the coltish awkwardness of the very young lady before her, and one look at the wide, anxious, liquid gold eyes melted any reserve she might have felt. Quickly, she came forward both hands outstretched. "Welcome to Atherton, my dear child," she smiled. "I am delighted to make your acquaintance and have to thank you for rescuing my poor boy from his latest scrape."

Rosalind, looking into those kind, smiling eyes, felt more of a fraud than ever. "Oh no, please don't thank me," she begged, "I fear I am partly to blame. I-I don't deserve that you should welcome me so. When you know the circumstance of my meeting Lord Atherton..." Her voice wobbled as she faltered.

To her surprise, Lady Atherton put her arms around her and led her to a comfortable-looking sofa, drawing her down beside her. "You absurd child, you have been having a horrible time of it. I know all about it, but you will go on very much better now you are here, and how delightful it will be for me to have someone so charming to bear me company."

Rosalind returned the clasp of her hands, but incurably honest, was determined to make a clean breast of everything. "But you cannot have understood, Lady Atherton. I broke into your house, would have stolen from you. I don't deserve..."

"Hush," Lady Atherton interrupted. "You don't deserve all the horrid things that have happened to you. Poor old Barney was always a sad case before he met your mother, you know."

Rosalind's eyes widened in amazement. "You knew my mother?"

"Not well," Lady Atherton smiled, patting her hand. "But my husband and your father were bosom bows in their youth, you know, and we were present at their wedding. She seemed such a gentle, sweet creature and Barney settled down to a quiet life afterwards, didn't he?"

Rosalind nodded, tears misting her eyes. "She was a good, kind, creature and they were both very happy, we were all very happy. But Papa was never the same after... after she died."

Those silver eyes, so like her son's, darkened seriously. "No, no, but we mustn't judge too harshly, my dear. Men will often bury themselves in ridiculous distractions rather than face feelings they don't know what to do with." She looked into the troubled face before her and added, "I'm sure he loved you very much, and that in his mind he was trying to restore his fortunes so he could look after you."

Rosalind nodded, feeling the hard knot of tension that had held a stranglehold around her heart for so long, loosen. Just to have someone know her story and not judge too harshly brought tears to her eyes. Blinking them away, she straightened her shoulders, steeling herself to say, "You are very kind, ma'am, but I know you did not wish for a companion, and I will understand if you would prefer I seek another situation."

"My dear child, do I seem such a dragon that you want to run away already?" Lady Atherton laughed.

"No, no," Rosalind stammered, flushing as she remembered she had made just such a supposition to Lord Atherton. She had certainly not expected an elegant, beautiful lady with a quick understanding and a ready sympathy.

Lady Atherton got to her feet. "I am only teasing you, ridiculous child, come, or we shall be late for dinner. For now, you are a guest in my house, and when we have had time to get better acquainted, we will talk of the future."

It soon became clear that Sir Philip was a frequent guest and firm favourite with Lady Atherton and that she took no small delight in teasing him.

"Although it is always a pleasure to see you, Philip," she smiled warmly at him, "I am surprised you can spare the time away from town. There is not much more of the season left, after all, and I had quite thought you would have made your choice by now."

"Mother!" protested Lord Atherton. "I will not have Philip harassed over this matter. The more pressure that is brought to bear on a man to get leg-shackled, the more he is likely to make a run for it!"

"Oh, is that what you are doing, Philip? Running? Who is the unfortunate young lady you are running from?" she asked mischievously.

"You could pick any one of a dozen!" her son said drily.

"Really?" she said, interested. "And has not one of these fair maidens captured your heart, Philip?"

Rosalind sneaked a peek at him, half expecting him to be frowning, but he was his usual urbane self, and his eyes reflected the imp of mischief dancing in Lady Atherton's.

"Not a one, ma'am, although a couple are indeed beautiful, I might as well address myself to the roses they like to be compared to."

"Indeed!" replied Lady Atherton, laughing. "And do you often find yourself addressing flowers, Philip?"

He grinned. "No ma'am, but I might as well for all the sense I can get out of any of the debutantes. I have only to say the sky is green and they hastily agree with me, and then if I change my mind and decide it is purple, they would agree with that too!"

Lord Atherton gave a bark of laughter. "He speaks the truth, Mother, it is a truly insipid bunch this season."

Rosalind had said very little up to now but suddenly felt the need to speak up for her sex.

"I wonder what they truly think of you both?" she mused.

"They don't think, that is the point," said Lord Atherton. "They are only interested in how soon they can rob us of our freedom and how comfortable we can make them for the rest of their lives."

Rosalind tilted her head to one side and let her considering gaze roam unhurriedly from one gentleman to the other before voicing her thoughts. "You speak of them as commodities in a shop that you have the luxury of picking or not. As usual, the choice is yours. How much choice do they have? What other choice do they have? They must marry or live a life of dependency on their family, which in the end would be no life. They would dwindle into old maids and end up being little better than servants. You speak of them agreeing with everything you say, my experience is admittedly limited, but I had not noticed that gentlemen generally like being argued with. You speak of losing your freedom; I suppose you mean the freedom to come and go as you please, to indulge in whatever excesses you please, the freedom to shirk burdensome responsibilities. They have never known such freedom and whatever little freedoms society will allow them, can only be gained through marriage unless they are fortunate enough to have a considerable independence of their own. You speak of the pressure being brought to bear on you, what about the pressure each and every one of them is under? From their mothers, who have filled their head so full of what to do and what not to do that they hardly know which way is up, from their peers, who are naturally in competition with them and from a society that is looking on, ready to see if they will sink or swim. You talk of them having nothing to say, how much would you have to say if you had such a limited experience of the world? But you do have such experience, and as I can hardly believe that either of you has so little address that you could not draw them out and find a character beneath their society manners if you chose to, I must assume that you have chosen not to do so. That is again, your choice. It seems you think you can choose who and when, they have no such certainty and so can hardly be blamed for using what little stratagems they can to try and attract you and ensure their future security."

A stunned silence greeted this soliloquy, and then Lady Atherton smiled in genuine amusement. "You are very right, Lady Rosalind."

Lord Atherton had a small frown between his brows, but Sir Philip grinned ruefully at her. "Indeed you are, and you have shown us up for being the arrogant, selfish creatures we undoubtedly are!"

Finally, even Lord Atherton's lips twitched. He turned to his mother. "How is it all these limitations that hedge young ladies about never seem to apply to Belle? I am pretty sure she chose Hayward, not the other way around, and she has always seemed to feel free to live life exactly how she chooses."

His mother's lips stretched into a fond smile as she thought of her youngest daughter. "Ah, but there are always exceptions to every rule, George, and Belle has always been a one-off!"

"Indeed she has," said Sir Philip fondly. "If only she hadn't decided to marry when I was out of the country, who knows, maybe I might have been tempted!"

Lord Atherton laughed. "Ah, it's safe to say that now isn't it? At the risk of denting that arrogance further, my dear fellow, I must add that I fear you would never have been in the running. You would have been up to every move on the board and cut her off at every pass, something she is well aware of. Fond as she is of you, she has not forgotten the time you put her over your knee and gave her a good spanking!"

Rosalind's eyebrows shot up, and her fork paused on its way from the plate to her mouth.

Sir Philip gave her a wry smile. "You can now add brutality to all my other faults, ma'am!"

"No, she can't," said his friend. "She had deserved every single smack."

Rosalind turned her gaze towards Lady Atherton, who might have been expected to look shocked but was quietly laughing. "It is quite true, my dear," she agreed. "She must have been about ten at the time, and she decided to take Philip's horse for a ride. It was a very resty stallion and his pride and joy. She was lucky not to either break her neck or its legs. Our hearts were in our mouths when it returned without her, but thankfully, she had suffered nothing more than a tumble and bruised pride."

"Followed swiftly by a bruised bottom," Lady Rosalind smiled, getting into the spirit.

The rest of the meal passed without contention as many more examples of Belle's mad escapades were dragged up with a great deal of fondness, and it had to be said, a certain amount of pride.

CHAPTER 6

Within a very few days, Rosalind had begun to blossom under the kind attentions of her hostess. Sir Philip and Lord Atherton amused themselves with gentlemanly pursuits during the day, fishing, shooting or riding about the estate. Lady Atherton found a keen pupil in Rosalind, who enjoyed herself hugely rummaging about in the kitchen garden and exploring the park. Satisfied that her charge was safely and happily ensconced, Lucy departed Atherton, not trusting Ned's sister to look after things any longer than need be. Mary, one of the housemaids, found herself promoted to wait on Lady Rosalind which she did with eagerness and devotion. Rosalind awoke one morning to find a package waiting for her; a set of paints, paper and pencils were inside. Delighted, she didn't wait for her adoring attendant but hurried to get dressed so she could thank her kind benefactress.

When she entered the sunny breakfast parlour, only

Lord Atherton was present. He looked up from his paper as she entered and got politely to his feet.

"You look happy about something this morning," he commented, pulling out a chair for her.

Rosalind returned his smile and told him of her find.

He bowed again, and his smile widened. "I thought it might keep you out of mischief," he murmured.

Her brows shot up in surprise, and she looked adorably confused. "I have no intention of getting into mischief," she protested. "I thought they were from your mother."

"I hope the small gift is no less welcome for having come from me," he queried with awful politeness.

She was still blushing furiously at her rudeness and thanking him as Lady Atherton entered the room, laughing up at something Sir Philip was saying to her.

"Now what have you done to put Lady Rosalind to the blush?" she asked perceptively. "I hope you have been behaving yourself, George?"

When she learned about the gift she was delighted. "It is the very thing," she said approvingly. "If I had known you enjoyed painting, I would have seen to it myself. We are leading such quiet lives at present, you will be glad of the diversion."

Whilst she hastily denied any need of diversion, Rosalind admitted that when her services were not required, there were many beautiful vistas at Atherton that she would like to sketch or paint.

Lady Atherton tutted as she seated herself at the table. "How many times must I tell you, my dear, that you are at present a guest and not here to wait on me! I have taken great delight in your company." She had broken the seal on a letter as she spoke and became absorbed in its contents. As she read a low chuckle escaped her. "Our quiet is about to be broken," she announced, glancing up at her son. "It seems your sister has got wind of at least some part of your adventures and is about to descend upon us with Hayward in tow." She raised an eyebrow at his low groan and continued, "Not only that, but it seems your other sister, Harriet, has been paying her a brief visit and is also going to honour us with her presence, along with Sir Thomas and the two children!"

She had barely finished relating this startling information when Sedgewick entered the parlour and announced Lord Preeve. He entered the room, immaculately turned out as usual but somewhat ruined the effect by his sheepish manner. He offered a formal bow in the general direction of everyone before turning a half apologetic, half harassed gaze upon Lady Atherton.

"Good morning, John," she murmured, "what an unexpected surprise!"

"So s-sorry to intrude, m-ma'am, at such a time and w-with n-no notice. S-something o-of the f-first importance to d-discuss w-with G-George, you s-see."

She smiled kindly at him, tactfully overlooking the irregularity of receiving visitors at such an early hour and begged him to sit down and join them if he had not already breakfasted.

This seemed to throw him into even more confusion, and his stuttering became even more pronounced than usual as he tried to explain that he had only come to see George and wouldn't dream of intruding.

"Well, as you already have intruded, sit down and cut line," interrupted his friend rather peremptorily. "If it is to tell me my sister is about to descend upon me, you are behind the times; my mother has just received a letter informing us of this, er, delightful, if unexpected event. Anything to do with you, John?" he enquired gently enough, but he did not deceive his friend.

"There's n-no need to get on your h-high ropes, George," he protested. "I h-had n-no intention of opening my b-budget about w-what happened, b-but th-that dashed s-sister of yours would g-get blood out of a stone!" He paused to take a deep draught of ale from the mug that had been placed unobtrusively before him. "And t-to think I've h-hurried h-here as fast as p-possible to w-warn you, th-though why it m-matters is beyond me! B-but you s-seemed very set on it s-staying m-mum s-so I thought I had better come."

It was apparent that Lord Preeve was quite upset. Not only was his colour considerably heightened, but any of those intimately acquainted with him could have vouchsafed that it was very rare thing for him to breach the bounds of propriety by turning up uninvited and at such an hour, or to make such a long speech all in one go.

Lord Atherton softened. "Never mind, John, Belle wheedle it out of you, did she? I had hoped you might have avoided her as she is not going to formal parties just at present."

"Hyde Park," he explained. "And if y-you think I'm such a… a r-rudesby to c-cut one of m-my closest friends' s-sisters, y-you're all about in y-your head."

"No, no my dear fellow, not cut, but perhaps pretend you had not seen her?"

"W-well, there was no chance of that, not w-with her all but jumping up and down to g-get my attention. H-had s-some dashed odd-looking f-female with her, h-had a squint, v-very awkward, d-didn't know if she was l-looking at me or my h-horse."

Any residual tension in the room fled before the laughter that swiftly followed this tangled speech.

The earl racked his brains for a moment. "Probably a Miss Mowbray, she seems to be the latest oddball taken up by Belle."

"Y-yes, that r-rings a bell, b-but the thing is, I w-was unaware th-that Lady Hayward didn't know you were b-bringing L-lady Rosalind d-down, and w-when I mentioned th-that I h-had m-met her, there w-was no satisfying her until she h-had the whole t-tale out of me."

The earl could only be grateful that Lord Preeve was unaware of the whole tale.

"Poor, John. And was Miss Mowbray present to hear it?" asked the earl with some foreboding for if so there was no doubt it would be all over town by now.

"Now r-really George, I m-may not be as needle-witted as some, b-but I'm not such a knock in the c-cradle as that," he assured him. "I-I drew her aside and m-made sure she realised you didn't want it b-bandied about."

Lord Atherton dropped his head in his hands. "It wanted only that!"

It was left to Lady Atherton to settle Lord Preeve's ruffled feathers, telling him he could not be held to blame, that it was no very great matter after all, and that he was very welcome. She also extended an invitation for him to stay. "It seems we are to be a house party so you may as well." She then invited Rosalind to help her gather some flowers for the house, noticing how quiet and uncomfortable she had begun to look. She snipped, and Rosalind carried the basket, her thoughts clearly elsewhere.

"Do not be in a worry, my dear," she said gently. "It is a shame we are to be quite so inundated before you have had time to properly find your feet, but you would have had to meet them all sooner or later."

"But, ma'am, they are all coming to look at me," she said anxiously.

Lady Atherton nodded her understanding. "It is true, of course, but they know no more than you are come to visit me after all. I will tell them I invited you, for you know I might well have if I had fully understood your circumstances, and you may be sure they are not so rag mannered that they will pry too closely into them."

"Not even Belle?" Rosalind said, smiling despite herself. She had by now formed an image of a bouncing, lively and very inquisitive girl.

"Not even Belle, for I will inform her that you too are in mourning and so she mustn't inquire too closely. That puts me in mind of something, although I own it is refreshing to see someone not garbed in this hideous colour, we must provide you with some mourning clothes."

Rosalind coloured. "Yes, ma'am. I have only the one mourning dress, and it is a trifle shabby, I'm afraid, although I have been trying to wear darker colours than usual."

"Don't give it a thought, my dear, whilst it was only us it mattered not a jot, but we don't want to give rise to any more talk than necessary. I ordered far too much material for my own mourning, so we will put it to good use. Farrow, my abigail, is a very talented seamstress and between us, we will have it sorted in a trice." She paused, shaking her head. "It is a shame we have to bow so much to convention. My poor Frederick would turn in his grave to see us all decked out like a flock of crows."

"You must miss him terribly," Rosalind murmured shyly.

Lady Atherton smiled mistily. "Yes, it is so very strange not to have his large, gruff presence around the place. He was not always an easy man. Like most, he liked to have his own way and always thought he was right, but he was a caring husband and proud father, although he didn't always show it. He and George, in particular, were always coming to cuffs." She shook her head as if in doing so, she would dislodge unpleasant thoughts. "It had been sadly flat here until your arrival, and it will be nice to have the house full again."

Rosalind privately thought it quite selfish that Lady Atherton's children had left her alone at such a time, and although she felt apprehensive about their arrival, she felt pleased that she was in some way instrumental in bringing the family back together again. It was the least she could do for Lady Atherton who had been so very kind to her.

Most of the rest of the day was taken up with Farrow taking measurements and discussing the styles appropriate to such a young lady as herself. She might have expected to find Farrow resentful at having to wait on her, but she was pleasantly surprised to find this lady not only accommodating but also quite maternal towards her. She did not know how much of her story Lady Atherton had revealed to her, but she certainly did not turn her nose up at her lack of stylish mourning clothes. Little did it occur to her, that her strange mix of shy reserve together with a lack of condescension, portrayed her very much as the lady, not to mention the fact that she had such a good willowy figure and arresting face that it could not but add to Farrow's consequence to turn her out in fine style. Farrow had been with her mistress for many years, and if Lady Rosalind had been seen to be adding to her burdens, she would have had a very different reception. But it was plain to everyone that Lady Atherton had perked up considerably since her arrival and so she was deserving of respect.

The day the rest of the family were expected, Lady Atherton caught Rosalind gazing wistfully out of the window.

"Is anything amiss, my dear?" she enquired.

"Oh no, of course not, indeed I cannot remember when I have been so comfortable," Rosalind hastily assured her. "It is only..." She hesitated, uncertain how to convey how the open parkland and countryside beyond made her realise how very confined her life had recently been.

"Only?" encouraged Lady Atherton.

Rosalind smiled. "Lucy, Mrs Prowett, called me a hoyden because I was used to have the freedom to wander all over our estate. But I have always loved to be outside and although I have enjoyed wandering the gardens..." She trailed off, naturally reticent to give any suggestion of unhappiness with her situation.

Lady Atherton smiled her understanding. "You are feeling a trifle hedged in? You are so young and have so much natural energy, I am not surprised. Do you perhaps ride?"

Rosalind's expressive eyes suddenly burned with desire, causing Lady Atherton to laugh. "Of course you do! Have you a riding habit with you?"

Holding her breath, Rosalind nodded.

"Then you shall take my own mare out. She will be a trifle fresh, but I am sure you won't regard that in the least."

"Oh, you are so very, very good," Rosalind burst out.

Lady Atherton pinched her cheek. "Don't be so nonsensical, child, now hurry up and change whilst I send a message to the stables. My groom Henchcombe will accompany you."

Rosalind hastily summoned Mary to help her into her habit. It was of a severe masculine cut in black but with an amber braid around the collar, front and hem. It suited her long slender form to perfection, not that she ever considered that, to her, it was comfortable and serviceable.

She found a beautiful grey mare waiting for her, sidling a little as the stable boy held her. She stroked her head and offered her a sugar lump, murmuring softly to her all the time. "There, my beauty, we both need a run, don't we?"

Henchcombe came forward to help her up into the saddle and offered her some advice whilst he lengthened the girth for her. "She's as fresh as a daisy, miss, so just take it easy until you get acquainted, like," he advised gruffly.

She followed his advice until they were out of sight of the house, but then the long tree-lined avenue that led through the park beckoned, and she broke into a canter, then a gallop, a laugh of sheer joy escaping her as she felt the smooth power of the mare flying beneath her. By the time she drew rein, a firm understanding had been reached between her and her mount, and her wide smile went some way to taking the sting out of Henchcombe's protestations.

"You've a fine seat, miss, and no mistake, but if it's all the same to you, I'd be a mite happier if now that you have galloped her fidgets out, you'd let me lead, being as you don't know this country yet and my lady wouldn't thank me if I was to bring you home on a stretcher!"

She laughed at such a suggestion but beyond asking him to take her on a good run across country was content to follow his lead. The mare jumped well off her hocks, and it was just as she neatly cleared a hedge into a pleasant meadow that something caught her eye. It was not unusual to see a plume of smoke in the country, but this one rose into the sky like an accusing black finger. Henchcombe had noticed it too, and there was a gathering frown on his brow.

"That looks nasty, miss, and if I'm not much mistaken, one of His Lordship's tenants has a cottage in that direction. We better put 'em to but be wary o' rabbit holes."

The smoke was about a quarter of a mile away. They had to skirt around the edge of a hayfield but after that made quick progress. The back of the cottage was ablaze, but fortunately, the roof was slate, not thatch, so it had not become an inferno. The small back garden ran down to a brook, and there were six farmhands forming a line to pass up water in buckets. Jumping quickly off his gelding, Henchcombe gave the reins into the hands of one of two frightened-looking small boys and bade miss wait where she was. However, Rosalind was close behind him. How could he think she would stand by when clearly every hand available was needed? Apart from muttering something under his breath about shades of Miss Belle, he raised no more fuss. It was hard work; the buckets were as full as they could hold and consequently heavy, but it soon became clear they were winning. Before too long, only ugly black smoke belched through the kitchen windows. A clatter of hooves was heard on the lane, and in a few moments, Lord Atherton came striding around the side of the house.

He sent her a swift, keen glance as she stood stretching out her aching back but then turned back to the small group that had gathered around him.

"Was anyone hurt, Jenkins?" he asked a middle-aged man in a smock.

He shook his blackened face. "No, thank the lord, the missus had taken the boys down to milk the cows." He nodded in the direction of a barn in a field on the other side of the stream. "And the rest of us were working two fields over."

He nodded briefly before heading over to Rosalind. "I should have expected to find you here, I suppose," he said curtly. "I can't decide if trouble finds you or you find trouble!"

She gasped at the harshness of his words and

found her indignation rising. He cast a jaundiced eye in the direction of Henchcombe who was hovering in the vicinity. "I'll have words with you later," he snapped. "For now see Lady Rosalind safely home whilst I see what can be done here."

Jenkins had come slowly towards them as he vented his spleen. "Excuse me, sir, but I haven't had time to thank miss and Henchcombe yet. It was hard going with only a few us milord, and it was them arrivin' in the nick of time that turned the tide."

Rosalind, turning her back on Lord Atherton, gave him a friendly smile and said that she was glad to have been able to help and only very much hoped, not too much damage had been done.

"Well, miss, it's mainly the kitchin, but how it could o' started has me in confusion."

Lord Atherton looked thoughtful and then asked Rosalind to wait a moment. He headed back to the house and disappeared through the charred remains of the kitchen door. He picked up a small jar that was laid on its side, gave it a sniff and glanced at a thin snake-like trail that still showed on the blackened floor. He stood inside the still smoking blackened kitchen only for a few moments, but it was enough. Stepping back outside, he called to Jenkins, a frown between his eyes. "Do you use whale oil?" he asked him.

Despite the seriousness of the situation, he started to laugh, which induced him to start coughing. The wheezy chuckles caused tears to leave a whitened trail through the soot on his weathered face. "Lord bless you, gov'ner, as if I would waste the readies on such a luxury even if I could. Tallow does us, sir, or a rush-light or two."

"And had you any gunpowder about the place?"

As Jenkins replied in the negative, his frown deepened. "I'll send some men over to start sorting this mess immediately," he said. "Have you somewhere you and your family can stay for a few days until we make it habitable again?"

Jenkins assured him they had and thanked him for his consideration.

"Henchcombe, ride on ahead and let my mother know what has occurred, she will wish to send some provisions for the family. I will escort Lady Rosalind."

"To make sure I don't find any more trouble?" she challenged him, her eyes burning with resentment.

Henchcombe walked off, his face wooden.

Lord Atherton didn't choose to respond until he had thrown her up into the saddle and mounted himself.

"I suppose it never occurred to you that you were putting yourself in danger?" he said, speaking through his teeth. "But no, you thrive on it, don't you? What Henchcombe was thinking to allow you to involve yourself in the business is beyond me!"

Feeling this was grossly unjust, she hastily defended herself and the poor groom. "I was never in any danger! I never went anywhere near the blaze, and as for Henchcombe, he asked me to wait," she began but was rudely interrupted.

"And of course you didn't listen..." He broke off abruptly as he realised he was talking to thin air, for the lady he had impetuously taken under his protection had given her mare her head, and as he watched with reluctant admiration, she took the hedge that would lead her most directly back to Atherton without pause.

"Hell and the devil confound her," he muttered even as he gave chase.

She was as fearless and as reckless in the saddle as she was when confronted with danger, and it was not until they reached the park that he drew abreast of her. He reached over and grabbed her reins in an iron fist, bringing her to a not very dignified halt.

"Let me go," she hissed at him, her eyes blazing with anger.

"In a moment," he bit out, "you will take a hold of that temper, you little cat, and remember that you are a guest in my and my mother's house. If you have so little conduct that you wish to give rise to all sorts of gossip by riding in as if the devil and all his minions were after you, I do not."

Although she knew she was behaving badly, she could not back down. "Why is it that you take every opportunity offered to put me in the wrong when all I was trying to do was help?"

At that moment, the unmistakable sound of an approaching carriage saved him answering a question that he would have found awkward to answer. He barely had time to direct them both onto the grass before not one, but two carriages swept around the bend in the drive. One carried on towards the house, but the other drew up a little ahead of them, and even before it had come to a halt, its window was thrust down, and a head topped with a fetching bonnet poked through.

"Hello, big brother," said Lady Hayward, grinning engagingly at them.

He rode forward immediately, Rosalind trailing a little in his wake as he greeted his youngest sister.

Rosalind saw that she shared his eyes, but where his too often had a steely glint to them, hers shone with an engaging liveliness.

"Oh, I am so glad you ride," she said to Lady Rosalind, smiling saucily. "I can show you all my old haunts."

Rosalind noticed the way Lord Atherton cast his eyes up to the skies and instantly said she would be delighted to discover them.

Belle's smile widened as she drew her head back into the carriage. She had not failed to note Lady Rosalind's heightened colour or the tension that seemed to exist between her and George. Interesting, very interesting. She had a feeling this visit was going to be fun.

As they made their more sedate way towards the stables, Lord Atherton looked distracted.

"Belle is a sad romp," he finally said. "She is not much older than you and has a habit of falling into all manner of scrapes, as you know. She will naturally seek out your company as you are the nearest to her in age and as she is incurably inquisitive and also I might add, shockingly indiscreet." He paused as if trying to pick his words carefully for a change.

Rosalind decided to fill in the blanks for him, saying in a tight voice, "And you are afraid that I, who seem to always be in trouble, will lead her into some?"

He surprised her by laughing. "Even I would not be so unreasonable," he smiled ruefully. "I am afraid the boot is on the other foot. I fear she will undoubtedly lead you into some!"

Rosalind felt herself mellow, unable to withstand the smile that transformed his countenance.

"I will endeavour to keep us both out of trouble," she assured him.

He quirked an ironical brow. "Whilst I appreciate the sentiment, you must forgive me if an intimate knowledge of my sister leads me to place little dependence on it. But if you do find yourself in the briars, even though you feel I am always ready to place you in the wrong, please do not be afraid of turning to me."

They had by this time reached the yard that gave onto the stables. Barely had Lord Atherton reined in his horse before two sturdy-looking boys ran towards him.

"Uncle George, Uncle George," they cried simultaneously. Clearly, he was a prime favourite with them. They tried to shout over each other as they both begged him to take them up before him. He quickly dismounted and grabbed one in each arm, lifting them off their feet before they came to cuffs.

"Not now, you rapscallions," he laughed, giving them a brief hug before setting them on their feet again. "Escaped your mother already have you? Well Harry, George, make your bows to Lady Rosalind Marlowe, who is staying with us at present."

A mere female could not hope to engage their interest when their favourite uncle was present, so after bowing briefly in tandem, they turned their attention back to him. "Uncle George, Harry says he will get a ride first 'cos he is the oldest and so more important, but I have the same name as you, so it's not true is it?"

He was saved answering this thorny question by the appearance of his elder sister who came smiling up to them. "Ah, found you already, George? I told you both not to plague your uncle, so both of you go and find Nurse at once. What will Lady Rosalind make of your manners?"

Looking a little shamefaced, they made her another brief bow before racing each other back to the house.

"Lady Harriet Denby, Lady Rosalind Marlowe." Lord Atherton made the formal introductions.

Whereas Lady Hayward and Lord Atherton clearly favoured their mother, Lady Denby was built along more queenly lines and reminded Rosalind of the portrait of the late Lord Atherton she had seen hanging in the gallery. She was far more at home in the stables than the ballroom and her bluffness was only equalled by her good nature.

"Pair of rag-mannered brats aren't they?" she stated, her hazel eyes smiling. "It's George's fault, of course, he indulges them too much. There will be no peace until he has taken them for a gallop around the park! Should set up his own stable of course," she added. "Pleased to meet you, my dear," she said blithely, ignoring the long-suffering look from her brother. "My mother is full of your praises."

Rosalind coloured slightly at the compliment, said all that was proper and then hurried into the house to change her raiment.

Lady Denby gave her brother a frank stare. "Glad to see you've remembered your responsibilities at last," she said bluntly. "By the way, I like that young gal, knows how to hold herself together in the saddle and if I'm not much mistaken, not quite in the common style."

Deciding to ignore the second part of this speech,

he informed his sister he needed to see his mother on estate business and made his escape.

She was just coming from the kitchens when he came in and looked a little harassed. "Such shocking news! The poor dears, however could such a thing happen?" She looked like she was about to say something else when she thought better of it and asked George to come to her sitting room in five minutes.

He found her pacing the floor, but she came swiftly to him and took his hands.

"There is something more to this than meets the eye, George. What do you make of it?"

Her troubled eyes reminded him of a cloudy sky, and he longed to put her mind at rest. He decided to proceed with caution, after all, he hadn't had time to sift his own thoughts on the matter as yet.

"It could have been many things, a stray spark from the fire, a candle left burning, what has you in such a twitter, my dear?"

"George, I am more than seven, you know. Henchcombe told me it was quite a blaze and if you can explain to me how it took hold so quickly, I should be glad to know it."

"Damn Henchcombe," he muttered, "he had no business worrying you so."

"Don't blame poor Henchcombe," she scolded him, crossing the room and sitting herself down. "How you think he can pull the wool over my eyes when you can't, is beyond me. Where do you think Belle gets it from?"

Despite his annoyance, he smiled. "Indeed, the Spanish Inquisition would have been a far less barbaric affair if they had had the benefit of you two!"

She smiled, slightly mollified. "Yes, well just you remember it, and don't go blaming Henchcombe for not being able to prevent Rosalind lending a hand either. I admire her for it. She has a kind heart and a strong spirit, and it is just what I would have done in such a situation."

"I know it," he acknowledged, "but I feel responsible for her."

Lady Atherton patted the seat beside her. The haunted look that had been in his eyes since his father's death had been bothering her for some time, and she decided it was time to speak.

"George, I want you to listen to me very carefully," she instructed as he sat down and turned towards her. "You must stop taking the weight of the world on your shoulders. Every ill that happens to those nearest to you is not your fault. You had nothing to do with Rosalind's misfortune. You are not expected to worry yourself sick over what Belle will or will not do next, that is now Hayward's job, thank heavens. You must stop fretting about me, for I am much stronger than you think, and if you imagine I want my children permanently clustered about me, you are mistaken. And perhaps most importantly of all, you must stop blaming yourself for your father's death."

She heard his deep inhalation of breath and witnessed the colour drain from his face as a flash of pain changed his eyes to the dull pewter they always turned when he locked his feelings away. "Who else should I blame, ma'am?" he said with unprecedented formality. "If I had helped him bear the weight of running the estate, if I had not argued with him when last we met..."

Lady Atherton changed tactics. Rising swiftly to her feet, she said, "Enough, George, if you wish to wear a hair shirt that is your privilege, but it is quite unnecessary. If you think that your father was anything but proud of you, you are very wide of the mark. If his gout made him cantankerous when you last met that was quite his own fault, for he could not bring himself to forgo his wine with, and port after, dinner. As to your argument having caused him to have a heart attack, it is a great deal of folly for he had already had two minor ones when you were not here and not in his black books."

Her son looked shocked. "But you never mentioned this!"

"No, so now you can blame me if you will. He did not wish you to know, and although I may be a managing female, if you think I would go against his wishes..." She broke off for a moment, shielding her eyes with her handkerchief.

"Mama," he cried, getting to his feet and taking her in his arms. "Of course I wouldn't expect you to go against his wishes."

Lady Atherton gave something suspiciously like a sniff before continuing into his shoulder, "Whatever he may have said, the last thing your father wanted was to have you here for any other reason than that you wished to be and he was not at all ready to have you taking the reins out of his hands, so don't think it! He was very much ashamed of himself after you had gone away, but his health was unimpaired. The doctor assured me that it had only been a matter of time before it had happened, so now you know and can stop torturing yourself!"

Very much shaken, he sat back down again, drawing his mother with him. "I'm sorry, Mama," he said chastened. "I didn't mean to add to your troubles."

She smiled shakily at him, her heart feeling considerably lightened as she realised she had finally gotten through his defences. "From now on we will share our troubles, my darling. It is far more worrying to be left in the dark. Speaking of which," she muttered, crossing the room to fetch something from a side table. "Recognise this?" she asked, turning towards him.

In her hands, she held the package which had been stolen from him in Fenny Stratford. It had clearly been opened and roughly wrapped up again.

"Arriving as it does on the same day as this fire, I would say it is a clear message as to who is behind it, wouldn't you?" she said, a martial light in her eyes.

"Well, I'll be damned," Lord Atherton said slowly.

"You can be as damned as you like, dearest," his redoubtable mother concurred, "but all I can say is that in taking on the Athertons so, so blatantly, that pathetic excuse for a man has taken on far more than he has bargained for."

Lord Atherton's lips quirked as for a moment the picture of Rutley being confronted by his mother, Belle and Rosalind entered his mind's eye. His shoulders started to shake, and in another moment, both he and Lady Atherton were for some reason not entirely clear to either of them, laughing themselves into stitches.

## CHAPTER 7

To Rosalind, who was wholly unused to big dinner parties, never mind large family gatherings, once she got over her nerves, the evening was vastly entertaining. Nobody seemed to confine themselves to speaking to their neighbour but on the contrary, frequently interrupted conversations taking place across or even down the table, feeling free to contradict or challenge any comments made. Once she realised that although she may have been the lure that had drawn them, she was unlikely to become the centre of attention unless she brazenly put herself forward, Rosalind relaxed and found that she could quite naturally respond to any comment directed her way.

Lord Preeve was seated next to her, and she found him to be both amusing and sweet. Although he clearly enjoyed making her the object of his gallantry, she sensed that this was more because he felt it the natural thing to do rather than from any serious intent on his part, and so was able to relax and enjoy her dinner.

Little did she realise that her lack of predatory flirtatiousness (something which Lord Preeve's radar could pick up in the wink of an eye), had stirred a hitherto unsuspected hunting instinct in him. His cherub-like countenance, his good taste in all matters of dress and conduct, together with his vast fortune, made him a firm target with all ladies wishing to make a good marriage. It was not generally felt that his admittedly only moderate intelligence was in any way a hindrance to his eligibility, as it encouraged these ladies to think that they might (if they caught him), mould him to suit themselves. After racking his brains to hit upon some way he could attract the attention of a young lady, who not only was not afraid to brandish a pistol but thought nothing of aiding to put out a fire, he was finally hit by a sudden flash of inspiration.

"I s-say, L-lady Rosalind, I have heard what a c-cracking rider you are, b-but I wonder, are you a f-fine whip also?"

His ploy worked. She turned to him, a suddenly arrested look in her eyes.

"No, the opportunity to learn has never come my way." She smiled encouragingly.

"Well, I would be honoured to teach you if you would like it," he assured her. "Atherton has put his curricle and phaeton at my disposal, you know."

Rosalind offered him a blinding smile. "I would like it above all things."

"Oh, that is capital," interrupted Lady Hayward from across the table, not at all embarrassed to reveal that she had been shamelessly eavesdropping. "When you have had time to gather the basics, we can have a race!"

Her fond but wary husband, cast an uneasy eye in her direction. "Do you really think that is fair, my love, when you have been driving for so much longer than Lady Rosalind?"

"Oh, don't be such an old fusspot, Nat," she pouted. "Rosalind won't care a fig for that, will you?"

Lord Hayward took this in good part but cast a beseeching glance in Rosalind's direction.

"Well, we will wait and see," she said, aiming for the middle ground. "I may turn out to be shockingly cow-handed after all."

"In which case, you will be well-matched," interrupted Lord Atherton, "and will certainly not race any of my vehicles."

"I-I say, George, n-no need to be such a s-spoil sport. I'm sure L-lady Rosalind must add d-distinction to anything she t-turns her hand to."

Rosalind sent a smouldering glance in Lord Atherton's direction, the middle ground forgotten, before returning her attention to her stalwart supporter.

"I have always had a hankering to drive a phaeton," she revealed, smiling sweetly. "Preferably a high-perch phaeton," she dimpled. Then turning back to Lord Atherton, she added haughtily, "Do you have one, my lord?"

Realising he was being baited, his firm lips twitched, but he regarded her coolly. "Indeed I do," he admitted. "And I would certainly not wish to deny you any reasonable pleasure so you must certainly learn to drive."

"That's the d-dandy, George," approved Lord Preeve.

Lord Atherton began to smile. "Have you ever

tried to impart your skill to another before, John?" he asked gently.

"W-well no, b-but how h-hard can it be?" he replied cautiously. In his experience, his friend was always at his most dangerous when he spoke in those soft tones.

"That remains to be seen," he replied. "I look forward to observing your progress. But as Lady Rosalind is a complete novice, you will start in the gig."

Everyone around the table had to stifle their smiles as they tried to imagine Lord Preeve being seen in such an unfashionable vehicle. He was clearly having some difficulty in visualising it himself and looked comically crestfallen. However, he couldn't argue with his host's logic and so was forced to put on a brave face.

"Y-yes, w-well of course," he conceded. But seeing the disappointed look on his pupil's face, quickly added, "Don't w-worry my dear, as s-soon as you have shown m-me you can c-control the horse, we w-will move on to the curricle."

Lady Atherton decided it was time the ladies withdrew and left the gentlemen to their port. Lady Hayward linked her arm through Rosalind's as they mounted the stairs to the drawing room.

"I can see you are going to tease my brother nearly as much as I do!"

She laughed as Rosalind coloured. "Oh, don't be embarrassed, it will do him a world of good. He has been a trifle out of sorts recently, and it is just what he needs to have someone to spar with."

"I don't mean to spar with him, Lady Hayward, but he does manage to put my back up quite frequently," she admitted with characteristic honesty.

"Oh, please call me Belle. Lady Hayward sounds so stuffy, and that, I assure you, I am not!" she twinkled. "Besides, we are going to be the greatest of friends. How wonderful that you have such dark hair, we make quite an arresting couple, don't you think?"

Rosalind laughed. "Now how can I answer you?" she protested. "Either I will sound intolerably conceited or worse, insulting!"

"Did I sound conceited?" Belle grinned. "I didn't mean to but never mind that. I hear you were held up on the way here and shot the highwayman. It sounds vastly exciting. Tell me all about it!"

\* \* \*

As Lord Hayward and Sir Thomas teased Lord Preeve on his latest undertaking, Lord Atherton took the opportunity to discuss the day's rather startling events with Sir Philip.

"I rode over there myself, this afternoon," Sir Philip admitted, "and you were right; the fire was definitely set on purpose, and designed to cause the maximum damage in the minimum time."

"Yes," agreed Lord Atherton, "but I don't immediately perceive what the point of it was, or why he would alert us to his presence by sending Mother her package back."

Sir Philip flicked open his snuff box and took a thoughtful pinch. "It's all of a piece, George," he said slowly. "He's just the sort of spiteful type who probably pulled the wings off helpless insects or drowned kittens when he was a child. He's playing with you, dear chap. Wants you feeling uncomfortable wondering what he will do next. As for his ultimate aim, I'm not sure. He has nothing left to lose, and he hates you for some reason. He is probably jealous that you have everything he has not and wants to cause you some mischief before he is forced to leave the country. One thing you can be sure of, is that in this mood, he is undoubtedly dangerous."

"Well, I don't intend to wait to find out. This is my country, and first thing tomorrow I will set some enquiries afoot. If he is near, I will flush him out."

Sir Philip gave him a lopsided smile. "No, no George, as you say it is your country, and you are too well known; you will only set tongues wagging, something I am sure you wish to avoid. Leave it to me, dear chap. I have been itching for something useful to do, and I'd rather be hunting Rutley than watching John's efforts to teach Lady Rosalind to be a whip, or be cajoled into some hare-brained scheme by Belle!"

"Not interested in trying your luck, Philip? You could take the shine out of John any day of the week, and I might feel my cattle were in safer hands!"

Sir Philip grinned engagingly. "I am not so unfeeling. I have never seen John dangle after any respectable female before. I would not spoil his fun. It will also, I admit, be quite amusing to see if he can pull the thing off."

"By God, I hope you're wrong," Lord Atherton said, frowning. "She'd run rings around him!"

"No, no, I was referring to his teaching her to drive. I do not think he is serious in his intentions, merely enjoying a light flirtation, you know. I think he is a trifle piqued that she shows no interest in him. I have experienced that sensation myself. Have you not noticed that any attempt at engaging her in playful flirtation leads to her withdrawing into her shell?"

Lord Atherton looked rather haughty. "As I have not attempted to flirt with her, I wouldn't know. We are more likely to come to cuffs, you know."

His friend grinned. "Yes, I had noticed. Let's just say I'm not ready to be caught by any of the fairer sex yet, even if they are as alluring as Lady Rosalind. I feel there are one or two adventures left in me yet."

"Feeling restless, Philip?" Lord Atherton smiled. "Always, my dear fellow, always."

## CHAPTER 8

Rosalind proved to be an apt pupil. She was quick to pick up the gist of Lord Preeve's sometimes somewhat disjointed instructions. Her affinity with horses and her natural co-ordination stood her in good stead, as did her determination to prove to Lord Atherton that she was safe to drive his curricle.

It was barely three days before she had convinced her tutor that she was ready. Lord Preeve very quickly found himself at home with Lady Rosalind, he enjoyed her company, especially as he soon realised he wasn't expected to do the pretty. In fact, he discovered she was quite as likely to laugh at his compliments as to be thrown into maidenly confusion.

He was relieved to have his dignity restored when they graduated to the curricle. After half an hour or so tooling around the countryside, he allowed her to take the reins. As they passed no other vehicles and only one solitary person on foot on the way back, this excursion proved not too alarming, although he did feel obliged to curb her pace as they swung through the gates into the park.

He was just silently congratulating himself on avoiding any potentially embarrassing situations when Lady Rosalind came to a sudden halt by the home wood.

"Is aught amiss?" he asked, surprised.

"I'm not sure," she replied quietly. "Listen, can you hear anything?"

Lord Preeve dutifully listened. "I th-think I c-can hear a cat," he finally deduced.

"No, that's not a cat, not unless they can whimper! It's a child!" she said, throwing the reins at him and jumping down from the curricle immediately.

Lord Preeve was not used to the young ladies of his acquaintance being able to step down from a carriage unaided, never mind leaping from a curricle (thank heavens it wasn't the high perch phaeton), and so was thrown off balance.

"L-lady Rosalind whatever c-can you mean to d-do?" he said uneasily, suddenly remembering the highwayman.

"Find him, of course," she threw back over her shoulder somewhat impatiently. All feelings of self-congratulation fled as he observed her climbing onto the fence that separated the park from the home wood. He had a horrible vision of her falling, but as there was no-one to hold the horses and Atherton wouldn't thank him if they bolted back to the stables, he found himself helpless. He closed his eyes in a silent prayer as she balanced precariously on top of the fence before grasping the nearest tree. Slowly, he let out a sigh of relief. It was premature.

"Harry, is that you?" she called, craning her neck so she could look up into the tree.

"I'm up here," came a very small voice, and a tear-stained, grubby face peeped out from between the branches about halfway up.

"Uncle G-George made me promise not to talk to any strangers I saw, and there was this man with a face like a scrunched up muffin, so I climbed up but, Lady Rosalind, it's so very high, and I can't get back down again."

"Don't worry, Harry, I'm coming to get you," she said calmly, swinging herself up onto the nearest branch.

"L-lady Rosalind, c-come down I b-beg of you," groaned Lord Preeve, seriously alarmed. "We can get someone from the house to h-help!"

But even as he spoke, she had almost reached Harry. She stopped on the branch below him. "I won't let anything happen to you, Harry, but I want you to give me your hand and slide down next to me," she coaxed gently. "You don't want George to think you were a scaredy cat, now do you?"

That did the trick, and in a very few moments, he was on the branch beside her.

"That's my brave boy," she said encouragingly. "I'm going to go ahead to the next branch, and then we will do the same again. Do you think you can manage that?"

Harry nodded, wiping away his tears with his sleeve.

They had just reached the bottom branch when hoof beats were heard coming down the avenue, and Lord Atherton came into sight. He pulled up beside the curricle and followed Lord Preeve's rather stunned gaze.

"I tried to s-stop her, G-George..." he began.

"I don't doubt you, John," he said in a resigned voice.

"Uncle George," cried Harry thankfully. "I was hiding from the stranger like you told me to, and I got stuck in this stupid tree. But I have been brave, haven't I, Lady Rosalind?"

"Very brave," she smiled.

"Lady Rosalind is a really good climber, even though she's only a girl," he informed him.

Lord Atherton dismounted swiftly and tied his horse to the fence. "So I see. Lady Rosalind, you will pass him down to me and then wait for me to help you," he said tersely.

She obeyed the first request but had already dropped down onto the fence by the time he had put Harry safely down. Turning back to her, he grabbed her firmly around the waist and swung her around, holding her for a moment before letting her go.

It was a strange feeling to have his hands span her waist, and she felt the colour rise to her face, and her heart beat rather faster at the intimacy. Expecting a rake down, she was surprised when he merely bowed and thanked her before handing her back up into the curricle.

He took Harry up before him much to that little boy's delight.

"Thank you, Lady Rosalind," he called cheerfully as they set off towards the house.

"I hope I haven't shocked you," Rosalind said to an

unusually quiet Lord Preeve as they followed in the curricle.

"N-no, just w-worried me a little. Not at all the th-thing for you to b-be climbing t-trees though you know," he advised her kindly.

"Well no, of course not, but the thing is," she confided, "I climbed a lot when I was a child, and Harry looked so scared I had to help him."

Lord Preeve patted her hand almost paternally. "I'll t-tell you what it is, you've got a dashed k-kind heart."

Whilst this episode did not lessen his admiration for Lady Rosalind or his appreciation of her aptitude as a pupil, it did make him a trifle uneasy as to what adventures their future drives might include if her compassion was stirred.

Rosalind went straight to her room and after changing out of her carriage dress, sat down on her bed with her sketchpad. Harry's description of the stranger as having a face like a scrunched up muffin had not escaped her, nor did it seem incomprehensible to her. In fact, it had struck a chord, for the only person they had passed on their drive was a solitary man on foot. She had glanced at him and had been struck by his face. She had no trouble sketching it; he had a round face, rough and wrinkled with small button eyes. His nose had been wide and rather squashed, as if he had been unfortunate enough to be punched there on more than one occasion. He had been wearing a rather worn felt hat with a flat brim, a short black coat and a red neckerchief.

She found Harry enjoying a hearty luncheon in the nursery and happily investing his adventure with sinister overtones as he described it to his little brother, more often than not with his mouth full.

"He doesn't sound very scary," George said thoughtfully. "You said he had a face like a muffin; muffins aren't scary."

"They are when someone's face looks like one. You would have run home as fast as you could if you had seen him!"

George nodded in agreement. "That would have been more sensible than getting stuck up a tree and having to be rescued by a lady!"

Rosalind, who had entered the room quietly behind the boys, shared an amused glance with their long-suffering nurse before intervening, as judging by the way Harry was rolling his bread and butter into a ball, the argument was about to descend into a food fight.

"No, George, I am not a boy, although I often used to pretend I was when I was younger, and that is why I am quite good at doing the things boys usually do."

They had both turned round a trifle sheepishly, but this comment interested them deeply.

"Why didn't you want to be a girl?" they asked in unison.

She found herself being regarded by two pairs of almost identical, questioning hazel eyes, and for a moment was at a loss how best to answer them, then she offered them a grin. "Would you rather be fishing, climbing, riding or sewing samplers?"

Harry accepted this, but George was harder to satisfy. "But you're s'posed to like sewing and stuff," he persisted. "Besides, you're too pretty to act like a boy, isn't she, Uncle George?"

"Yes," he said, smiling disturbingly at Rosalind as she whirled around in surprise, "far too pretty."

Colour suffused her face at the compliment whilst the boys watched with interest.

"I came to ask Harry about the man he saw," she said, changing the subject firmly.

"So did I as a matter of fact," replied Lord Atherton, turning to his nephew. "Now you have had time to recover from your adventure, Harry, perhaps you can tell me what he was doing or where he was coming from before you climbed the tree?"

Harry thought about it for a moment. "I was chasing a rabbit," he said slowly, "so I wasn't on the path. I was kneeling by the hole it had disappeared into when I heard someone whistling, so I stayed quiet until he had passed and then climbed the tree in case he came back."

"And did he?"

"Yes, a few minutes later, but I don't know what he was doing."

"Did he see you?" asked Lord Atherton.

Harry shook his head. "I don't think so."

Rosalind opened her sketchbook and showed Harry the sketch. "Was this him?"

Harry nodded, looking astounded.

"You're right, Harry," said his brother fairly, "he has got a face like a squashed muffin!"

"I told you he had!" said his brother, flicking a small bread and butter ball at him.

"But I still don't think the muffin man looks scary," challenged George, casually wiping away the smear of butter on his cheek.

Lord Atherton had the presence of mind to withdraw with the re-opening of hostilities, taking Rosalind with him. He took her to his study to take a closer look at her sketch.

"Where did you see him?" he asked quietly.

Rosalind looked frustrated. "I don't know the area well enough to describe where, but I could show you."

She had promised Belle she would ride with her that afternoon, and she looked a little put out when she discovered her brother was to accompany them, suspecting him of wanting to keep an eye on her. But when she discovered Sir Philip was also to be of the party, she came out of the sulks.

They made the small market town of Shadbury their destination and had not gone far down the country lanes when Rosalind slowed down, looking carefully about her.

"Yes, it was about here I saw him," she said in a low voice to Lord Atherton. "But I don't think the information is going to be of much use to you," she added in a dismayed voice.

Just ahead of them was a crossroads, to the left the signpost indicated the narrow road ran towards Astley village, the one to the right leading to a hamlet named Lade. "He could have been going in any one of three directions," she mused.

Lord Atherton nodded. "Yes, but at least it gives us a starting point."

"What do you think he was up to?" Rosalind asked.

Lord Atherton shrugged. "Perhaps nothing. But I admit I would rather be sure of that and would ask you to keep your wits about you any time you leave the estate."

Shadbury was a very pleasant market town, and it soon became clear that both Lord Atherton and Belle were well known and respected there. After exchanging greetings with several acquaintances, the party left their horses at the George and took a stroll through the main street. As Belle decided she would like to go in search of some new gloves, the party split up, agreeing to meet back at the George in an hour.

Belle enjoyed herself hugely, purchasing two pairs of gloves, a new reticule and a silk scarf. Belle's assertion that they made a striking couple was surely borne out as the two young ladies attracted a lot of attention. But whereas Belle was happy to return a smile or flirt light-heartedly with any chance met acquaintance, Rosalind tried to melt into the background. She found herself looking over her shoulder more than once as an irrational feeling they were being followed refused to be shaken.

As they approached the George, they perceived Lord Atherton in close conversation with a beautiful young lady in a very smart barouche. Rosalind found herself being nudged in the ribs before Belle leaned in towards her.

"That is Miss Letitia Grey, she's the daughter of Sir Peter Grey, a local baronet, and she has wanted to sink her claws into dear George, forever! Fortunately, she has had no luck in attracting more than polite interest so far, for she is a spiteful little cat who thinks far too much of herself."

As they came up to the barouche, Rosalind found herself being closely scrutinised by a pair of hard blue eyes, and the small smile that curved the little prim bow mouth certainly didn't reach them.

"How delightful to see you, Belle," she said unconvincingly. "If I had known you were back I would have paid you a visit. However, it sounds as if you have quite the houseful at the moment." She gave a little titter, turning her eyes back towards Rosalind. "I must own that I am surprised your mother would be receiving visitors at such a time."

Belle gave her a sparkling smile, but there was a dangerous glitter in her eyes. "Oh, but only very close family and friends. We are not receiving in the normal way, you know. We feel ourselves very fortunate that Lady Rosalind could come to keep Mama company, for she has been like a ray of sunshine on a gloomy day, hasn't she George?"

Seemingly getting into the spirit of things, George surprised Rosalind by bowing low over her hand and kissing it. "Indeed, she has. She has brightened all our days at this sad time," he confirmed, bestowing an intimate and disturbing smile on her.

Even as Rosalind flushed up to the roots of her hair, Miss Grey suddenly remembered she must hurry back, or her mama would wonder what had become of her. She had barely pulled away before Belle went into peals of laughter. "Well done, George, that gave her her own again!"

Lord Atherton smiled crookedly at Belle. "It wasn't well done of me, you heartless baggage, but I have enough to do at the moment without having to fend off Miss Grey's less than subtle advances!"

Although Rosalind was not quite happy to be part of this game, she was forced to swallow any impolite retort as at that moment, Sir Philip strode out of the inn to enquire if they were coming in before the tea had gone quite cold.

"Some friend you are leaving me to the mercies of that man-eater!" complained Lord Atherton.

Sir Philip gave him an unrepentant grin. "You are unjust, my dear George, I merely considered myself de trop, her interests clearly lay elsewhere, and I simply beat a graceful retreat!"

"More like hasty retreat!" growled Lord Atherton.

Whilst Belle happily regaled Rosalind with tales of the lengths some of the local ladies had over the years gone to, to attract her brother's attentions, he drew Sir Philip to one side.

"Any news, Philip?"

"No-one saw anyone near Jenkin's cottage but there is some talk of strangers being seen near the old lodge on the east side of the old Hadley estate."

"But that place is going to rack and ruin, old Lord Hadley hates the country and barely steps out of his London house these days. In fact, my father considered offering to buy it from him at one point as it marches next to our own land, but when he saw the state of the place, decided it wasn't worth the effort to bring it about again."

"Worth taking a look?" asked Sir Philip.

"Yes, but it will have to wait until tomorrow. I have promised to look over the home farm this afternoon, and I want to see how the repairs on Jenkin's cottage are going."

Rosalind had enjoyed her excursion but still unused to always being surrounded by company, grabbed her paints and easel, quietly let herself out of a side door and made for the lake for some much needed solitude.

After choosing her vantage point, she sat for a few moments, just drinking in the peace. Closing her eyes, she let the gentle breeze wash over her face. She always tried to empty her mind before she began to draw or paint, it enabled her to gain the objectivity and creativity required to produce a work that would both represent the view but also imprint something of herself into it. Annoyingly, a dark, handsome face with eyes not unlike the sheen on the lake, kept intruding into the darkness. One moment it was all arrogance and annoyance, the next smiling and uncomfortably handsome. Although she knew he had only flirted to annoy Letitia Grey and probably embarrass her, it hadn't stopped her heart missing a beat. Opening her eyes, she pushed herself to her feet and walked briskly to the edge of the lake. Picking up a small handful of stones, she started throwing them in one at a time, punctuating each plop into the lake with a softly muttered utterance.

"He is a gambler. He is arrogant. He criticizes when he should say thank you. He thinks he can have anyone for the click of his fingers. He thinks he always knows best. I will not think of him!"

She watched until the ripples from the last stone dissipated, and then nodded to herself, turned on her heel and marched back to her easel. Soon she became lost in concentration and hours flew by without her realising it. Finally, she was satisfied, putting down her brush she planted her hands on her hips and leaned backwards to stretch out the back that still ached from heaving pitchers of water.

"Oh, how clever you are!"

Rosalind jumped; she had not heard Belle

approach. "You have caught the beauty of the lake and park beyond, but it is more than that. I can almost feel the air. You have caught the breeze skipping over the lake and rustling the trees. I can almost hear birdsong when I look at it!"

Rosalind smiled at her enthusiasm. "It's not bad, I suppose. It relaxes me."

"Not bad? I could not paint anything half so well, Rosalind."

"Well, thank you. It is my only real accomplishment, however, as I am sure climbing trees doesn't count. I am sure you have many."

Belle laughed. "You would think so with all the teachers I have had, but I am afraid I was a sad romp growing up. I could never be still long enough to learn anything of any great importance! I have been sent to find you as it is nearly time to get ready for dinner."

Rosalind blinked. "Already?"

"Yes, so come on, give me something to carry."

"Do you think your mother would like the painting?" she asked as they strolled up to the house. "I would like to repay her in some way for all her kindness."

"She'll adore it," confirmed Belle. She looked as if she would like to say more, but then they saw Lady Atherton waving from the terrace.

"Come on, girls, or you will be late!" she called.

She was as delighted as Belle had predicted with her painting, and Rosalind felt a little spring in her step as she went up to change for dinner.

CHAPTER 9

When Lord Atherton and Sir Philip rode out the next day, they found no evidence of habitation at the old lodge. The windows were shuttered and the knocker was off a door whose paint was peeling sadly. The whole place looked damp and neglected with ivy obscuring much of the house, so they were forced to conclude that the gossip had been incorrect. He was not really surprised; strangers were not that common in these rural parts and were often viewed with unwarranted suspicion as a matter of course. They had more luck with the elusive stranger who had been seen in the home wood, however. Astley village boasted only one inn, The Green Man. The landlord, a very respectable gentleman who ran a basic but tidy little business, was well known to Lord Atherton and recognised Rosalind's sketch straight away.

"Aye, he was staying here alright, a Mr Timms, but if you wanted to see him, milord, you're out of luck.

He left yesterday. My Tom took him to Shrewsbury in the cart, so he could take the stage back to Lunnon."

"And do you know what his business was, Scorton?"

"He was a friendly enough cove. He did ask a few questions about who was up at the big house, but only in a general way, like. Said he'd been looking for a nice quiet spot to recuperate after an illness and had heard the country around here was good for walking. He did seem to spend most of his time tramping about, but that's all I know, milord." He sucked his teeth thoughtfully for a moment, a slightly worried frown furrowing his brow. "Is there any reason particular like, as you are interested? He seemed a respectable enough cove."

"No, no, I'm sure he was," Lord Atherton reassured him, "but he was seen in the home wood, so I wondered if perhaps he had business hereabouts."

Scorton nodded. "He probably wandered in on one of his walks, sir, that 'ud explain it."

They rode slowly back up the lane towards the crossroads.

"Are you satisfied with that explanation, George?" asked Sir Philip casually.

Lord Atherton frowned. "It seems too much of a coincidence that a stranger should choose to stay in such an out-of-the-way place and at the same time the Jenkins' place was set alight. And something about that face seems somehow familiar, but you were right, Philip, I am looking over my shoulder all the time and perhaps overly suspicious. But if Rutley is behind everything, I wish he'd make his next move."

He was to get his wish sooner than he expected. As they turned into the lane that led towards Atherton house, he saw what was unmistakeably his curricle leaning at a drunken angle across the ditch that ran alongside the road.

"What the devil has happened now?" he growled, spurring his horse into a gallop. Vaulting swiftly out of his saddle, he saw the vehicle was empty, and his horses were sweating as they fretted in the traces. His eyes scanned the ditch, and a low moan directed his gaze some way further along. Lord Preeve was sprawled at an awkward angle, one leg twisted beneath him. In a moment they were both beside him.

"Overturned you, did she, John?" Sir Philip said softly, casting an experienced eye over the leg and gently easing it out from under him. This caused Lord Preeve to let out an anguished cry.

"I'm sorry, old fellow," he murmured, "it's almost certainly broken."

"S-so is my h-head," groaned that unfortunate gentleman.

"Yes, you must have hit it when you were thrown, nothing too serious, I think," Sir Philip soothed.

"N-nothing t-too serious! It's th-thumping l-like a d-drum, and I c-can see t-two of you," he moaned, closing his eyes again.

Lord Atherton looked at his friend, a sharp, worried look in his eyes. "Where is Lady Rosalind?"

"Probably gone to get help, George," suggested Sir Philip.

"Then why didn't she take one of the horses?" he mused. "It would have been much faster. Besides, I can't see her leaving John in that state or not calming the horses. Go and get help, Philip. I'll stay with John and free the horses."

"Do you remember what happened, John?" he asked but was not surprised when he was answered only with a negative grunt.

As his eyes ran over the curricle, he saw that the pole was broken, whether it had happened during or before the accident was not clear. However, when he returned to the house, there was a note waiting for him.

"It was found by one of the stable hands," explained Sedgewick, "most irregular."

Quickly, he strode into his study and unfolded it, his mouth thinning into an angry grimace as he read. It was short and to the point; Lord Rutley had Lady Rosalind, and if he wanted to ensure her continued wellbeing, he would come to the lodge on the Hadley estate alone and prepared to play for high stakes.

Sir Philip found him there a few moments later. He had seen his friend in many moods but never had he witnessed him looking quite as bleak as he did now. His eyes were quick to notice the scrunched up paper that protruded from one of his balled up fists.

"Vaughen, my groom, has had a look at the curricle, George, he is almost certain that pole was tampered with. Rutley?"

Lord Atherton nodded, and the bleak look disappeared as one of pure rage replaced it. He reached for the riding crop he had thrown onto the desk. "He has gone too far this time, and he is going to be made to regret it. Out of my way, Philip," he growled, crossing the room in two long strides.

Sir Philip did not move out of his path but put a firm hand on his friend's shoulder. "Gently now, my buck," he said quietly. "Never go into action without a cool head; that way lies disaster. A clear plan of action is required if we are to bring this thing off neatly. I don't think there will be any difficulty, from what I have seen, Rutley chooses his tools poorly. Sit down and open your budget."

\* \* \*

Rosalind had been bowling along quite happily and was just about to slow down for the approaching bend, when a horse and cart had swept around it on her side of the road. The high stepping, well-bred pair attached to the curricle had shown their objection by rearing, the pole had snapped, and the curricle tipped onto its side, flinging Lord Preeve out. Rosalind had been thrown onto his side of the seat, banging her head on the side of the curricle and had been momentarily stunned. Before she knew what was toward, she found herself being roughly manhandled out of the vehicle, a rough sack was thrown over her head and her hands tightly bound behind her. She then found herself deposited none too gently onto what she assumed was the floor of the offending cart, and a rough voice warned her to keep her mummer shut, or she would be knocked senseless. As her head was already swimming and she felt quite sick, she had no difficulty in obeying these instructions. She only hoped that Lord Preeve had not been too seriously injured and would set up the call for help before they had gone very far.

That the men who had abducted her shared this same fear soon became apparent, as judging by the way she was thrown about, they were pushing the horse as hard as they dared. When they finally slowed down, it was small comfort as they seemed to have turned onto a very rough track so that she was jolted about as if she were a sack of potatoes.

She was 'helped' somewhat unceremoniously out of the cart and led up a small flight of mossy steps. A smell of damp pervaded whatever abode they had taken her to. At last, they removed the rough sack from her head, and she found herself in a dark shuttered room. A small fire flickered fitfully in the grate but barely took the deep chill out of the air. A candelabra set out on a small side table gave out a little light, illuminating a threadbare rug and two chairs whose covers had seen far better days, the rest of the room was cast into shadow.

"Here you are, guv'nor, the booty has been delivered as requested."

"So I see," came a soft voice and a man stepped out of the shadows. "Any problems?"

Although he addressed the rough-looking man who had brought her in, Rosalind felt herself stiffen as his cold eyes leisurely surveyed her from head to toe. She felt a shiver of fear snake down her spine as his repellent gaze stripped her naked.

"Not to speak of, sir, the flash cove as was drivin' with her took a tumble and was knocked unconscious, but he was breathin' when we left him."

Lord Rutley showed no interest in this news but carelessly threw a handful of coins at the man's feet.

"You have done very well. There will be more of that later when this business is finished. Now get outside and make sure that Atherton is alone when he arrives. If there is anyone with him, shoot 'em!"

The huge sense of relief she had felt at hearing

Lord Atherton's name mentioned, fled at these last words.

Determined not to show her captor fear, a display of which she had no doubt he would enjoy, she put on her most haughty expression. "So now you are prepared to add murder to your other crimes, Lord Rutley?"

He shrugged negligently. "I may as well be hung for a sheep as a lamb."

"I hope very much that you will be!" she spat at him, her eyes blazing.

The slender figure smiled, and his green eyes glowed with sudden interest. He stepped forward and ran one long white finger down the side of her face, from her temple to the corner of her lips. "Oh so fiery, so passionate, perhaps I should have kept you to myself for at least one night before letting Atherton know where to find me."

His sibilant words made her tremble with revulsion and her hands, still tied behind her back, curled into fists. How she wished they were free so she could strike him across his smirking face.

"Yes, now that I have seen you for myself, I think that would have been the ultimate punishment for the arrogant pup."

He turned away from her, and she found she could breathe again. He wandered over to a table ranged in front of the shuttered window. She saw that it was laid with a bottle of wine, two glasses and a pack of cards. He poured himself a glass of wine.

"Could you at least untie my hands? The rope is bound very tightly and is most uncomfortable, or do you only threaten females when they are completely defenceless?" she asked, her voice scathing. If he would only untie her hands, she might be able to escape.

He raised his glass to her, and insolently took a deep slug of wine. "Still so spirited. Therein lies the problem, my dear. Loath though I am to disappoint you, it has come to my attention that you are a young lady of great resource, and I wouldn't want to encourage you to do anything rash."

He sat down in one of the chairs at the table and nodded in the direction of the fire. "Please sit down. I don't wish you to be any more uncomfortable than necessary."

She gave a rather wild laugh. "And I suppose it was my comfort you were thinking of when you had me roughly manhandled, covered in a filthy sack and thrown into an even filthier cart?"

"Crude, I admit," he acknowledged, "but I had to think of a plan even those idiots couldn't fumble. Now sit down."

He waited for her to comply before carrying on conversationally, "You're not at all like your father, you know. He didn't show any of your spirit, quite the broken man the last time I saw him."

Rosalind felt a cold rage fill her veins. "No, I am not much like him. Though I believe you find yourself in a very similar position, but unlike him, I doubt very much you will take the honourable way out."

Lord Rutley shrugged, but a dull colour had crept into his cheeks. "I have never thought killing oneself is anything but foolhardy, where there is still life there is still a chance the luck may turn."

At that moment, the sound of a door being

pounded on was heard. Rosalind offered Lord Rutley a sour smile. "I think yours is about to, for the worse."

A hurried footstep in the hall sounded, and then the door was flung open. Lord Atherton stood on the threshold for an instant, his hard stormy eyes scanning the room. Ignoring Lord Rutley completely, he strode swiftly over to Rosalind and dropped to one knee before her. He looked even grimmer as he took in the darkening bruise on her forehead and her bound hands.

"I am so sorry, my child. Do not worry, he will pay dearly for this!"

She smiled shakily at him. "I think he is mad, my lord."

"No, just desperate," he said softly.

Rising, he turned swiftly towards Lord Rutley. "I take it you want your chance to redeem some of your losses to me in play?"

"Just so, Atherton," he agreed smoothly. "Although this time I thought we would see how lucky you are at cards."

"Did you really think it necessary to go to such extreme lengths?" he bit out, walking over to the table and giving the deck a cursory inspection.

"But you are always so busy," complained Lord Rutley softly. "I really did feel that I must get your attention."

"You have it, but I will not play you for any stakes until you agree to release Lady Rosalind from her bonds."

Lord Rutley nodded at the man who had followed Lord Atherton into the room. "Release her and then keep her covered."

"No!" Lord Atherton barked out. "You will not touch her! I will do it myself." He made quite a show of having difficulty untying her bonds and used the time to quietly warn her to move quickly if anyone else came through the door or at a signal from him.

Lord Rutley's henchman retreated and withdrew a pistol which he kept trained on Rosalind.

"One foolish move, Atherton, and I'm afraid Lady Rosalind will suffer."

He nodded briskly. "Let us get this over with; name your stakes."

Rosalind's attention was distracted for a few moments as the blood rushed back into her hands, creating an excruciating pain. She closed her eyes and bit her lower lip, determined not to distract Lord Atherton with her distress.

An intense silence descended on the room, only broken by the hissing of a log or the turn of a card. Rutley won the first few games and then leant back in his chair and gave his opponent a long look.

"Careless, very careless, Atherton. This is no sport; you are throwing the games intentionally, and I am not such a flat to be taken in, so let us raise the stakes. Lady Rosalind will also suffer if I consider you are not playing your best."

"What do you hope to gain, Rutley?" queried Lord Atherton. "It is highly unlikely that you will win enough from me to reinstate your fortunes, and you know that if you harm anyone close to me, I will hunt you down, however long it takes and whatever it costs me."

"Ah, you don't understand after all," his opponent murmured. "It is all a game, my dear fellow, just a game. What is there to gain from this life but the pursuit of amusement to relieve the unutterable boredom the rules of society impose upon us? But I admit I hate you. You are an arrogant young pup. You have everything on your side; wealth, looks, infinite opportunities, but I doubt very much you know what to do with them. I was you once, but the thought of getting leg-shackled to some broodmare to propagate the line and settle down to run my estates never appealed to me," he drawled, his eyes flickering towards Rosalind.

"If you didn't wish to run your estates, why didn't you employ someone with an eye for business to do it for you? You talk of opportunities, and it is true there are many beyond even your estates, investments you could have made, ships or the canals for instance. But you have been too short-sighted and selfish. Do you care for anyone other than yourself?"

Lord Rutley gave out a grating laugh. "Why should I? I will have to flee the country after tonight anyway, but at least I will go knowing that I have had some sport. Your father was just like you, you know. Always looking down his long nose at those he considered inferior."

"We will leave my father out of this," Lord Atherton snapped. "Do you want to play or talk?"

The game continued. As far as Rosalind could tell, neither player had the upper hand for long; fortunes fluctuated fairly evenly between them for some time, but then Lord Atherton started winning. The pile of coins and notes in front of him began to mount steadily. Lord Rutley was beginning to fidget, at one moment twitching his cravat, the next twisting his emerald ring around his thin finger. For a moment, her vision blurred, and it was another scene which swam before her.

She was back outside the library window at Roehaven, her father reached into his pocket and withdrew a handkerchief which he used to mop his sweating brow. Even though she was outside, she could feel his desperation. She could almost smell it. She could smell it now. It was coming from Lord Rutley, pouring off him in waves, like the ripples the stones she had cast into the lake had spread ever outwards until all became still and peaceful again. Grimacing, she realised it was extremely unlikely that there would be just such a peaceful ending to this encounter. Glancing up, she saw that the man who was supposed to be keeping her covered was watching the game, the gun hanging loosely in his hand. Straightening her spine, she sat up and refocussed her attention. Whatever Lord Atherton had planned, she would be ready.

Lord Atherton was watching Rutley closely, and Rosalind kept her eyes trained just as closely on Lord Atherton, her eyes straining as the fire burned low. Time seemed to slow, the world outside seemed far away, then she heard a muffled sound coming from beyond the room and saw Lord Atherton's eyes swivel towards her. He gave her a brief nod. She dived to the ground as he pushed the table forcefully into Lord Rutley, sending him tumbling backwards in his chair. His henchman hesitated for an instant, and it proved his undoing. In that moment, Lord Atherton had retrieved the knife from his boot and threw it unerringly across the room. It hit him in the thigh, and he dropped the gun as he clutched at the knife. Lord

Atherton sprang across the room just as the candelabra went out.

The room was plunged into darkness as the door was thrown open, and someone barrelled into the room. In the ensuing confusion, Rosalind felt about for a candle and held it to the embers of the fire. She held it up just as the shutters were thrown open, letting a little of the fading daylight through the ivy-covered window. Sir Philip stood in his stockinged feet, taking in the scene before him. Lord Atherton had overpowered his man, who now lay unconscious at his feet, but of Lord Rutley, there was no sign.

"After him, Philip," he grunted, as he retrieved the rope that had bound Rosalind earlier and tied up the unconscious man.

An extensive search of the house and grounds revealed nothing; the bird had flown. The other hired thug ordered to watch the approach to the house had stood no chance against a hardened campaigner used to guerrilla warfare, like Sir Philip. He had left his horse tied to a tree some distance from the house and approached it in ever decreasing circles until he had spotted his prey. The snap of a twig had alerted him but too late, as he had turned he had received a thundering right hook from a hand that felt like a sledgehammer and had been knocked out cold.

When they eventually came round the men were questioned, but it came as no surprise that as hired thugs, they knew nothing more about Lord Rutley's future plans. Lord Atherton deemed that there was nothing much to be gained from informing the local magistrate, particularly as he was Sir Peter Grey. He didn't want to have any more to do with the family than absolutely necessary for if Letitia got wind of the story, it would be all over the county before long.

It was decided that they would be given a taste of their own medicine. Sir Philip would drive them in the cart to some isolated spot and then release them. The threat of incarceration or worse if they returned would be enough to ensure their compliance.

"I don't like the idea that Rutley is still on the loose," grumbled Sir Philip.

"I think his game is played out," countered Lord Atherton. "I will be very surprised if we hear from him again. He has nothing left to do but get himself out of the country."

Lady Rosalind rode Sir Philip's mount home. Dusk was falling, the silence only broken by the birdsong that filled the air as they said goodbye to the day. A day that filled the thoughts of both riders.

"Thank you for coming to my rescue," murmured Rosalind. "Again."

Lord Atherton offered her a wry smile. "We seem to make a habit of rescuing each other."

Rosalind returned a rather wan smile. "I am sorry I overturned your curricle. I hope Lord Preeve has sustained no lasting injury."

"He'll be laid up for a few weeks with that leg, but that's all. As for the curricle, it would have taken a very experienced driver to avert that disaster even if it had not been tampered with. I am only thankful that you have met with no serious injury."

Rosalind looked thoughtful. "I know you think it over," she said slowly. "But I truly think he is mad. He told his thug to shoot anyone that followed you and the way he spoke to me," she shuddered, "was not gentlemanly."

"If he laid a finger on you, I will hunt him down and make him wish he was never born," Lord Atherton growled through gritted teeth.

"No, no," Rosalind hastily assured him, surprised by the vehemence of his response. "He just taunted me in a horribly insulting way. I don't think he has a soul."

Lord Atherton's lips quirked in humour. "I don't think he took your last message to heart, that's for certain. What was it I read in the paper now? 'For what shall it profit a man, if he shall gain the whole world, and lose his own soul?' Mrs Prowett certainly chose an apt quote."

Rosalind laughed at the thought of her old friend. "So you guessed then."

"Yes, a redoubtable woman, Mrs Prowett. I seem to be surrounded by them!"

Rosalind was glad when the house finally hove into view. She ached all over, and her head had begun to thump again. She gladly allowed Lord Atherton to lift her down from her horse and raised no demur when his mother bustled out of the house, hugged them both fiercely and insisted she was put immediately to bed.

"No, no, I am quite able to walk," she protested blushingly, when Lord Atherton lifted her into his arms as if she were light as a feather and strode towards the house. But she was overruled by Lady Atherton.

"That's the way, George," she said approvingly. "Just you lie still, my dear, and we'll soon have you more comfortable."

Lady Atherton tucked her in herself, drawing the curtains and ordering a fire to be lit. "I know it's not cold, my dear," she said, "but everything always seems so much more cheerful and cosy with a fire, doesn't it?"

Rosalind was glad to sink back against her feather-soft pillows, idly watch the flickering flames and letting her thoughts meander over the day's events. If they wandered back rather frequently to the part Lord Atherton had played in them, it was hardly surprising after all.

The relief which their safe return was met with, was only matched by the rampant curiosity of the family. Lady Atherton convinced her reluctant son that things had reached such a pass they should be shared with everyone. Whilst she agreed that it was doubtful Lord Rutley still posed any danger, she felt everyone should be put on their guard, just in case he was deranged enough to still want to damage the family in some way.

The story was met with varying responses at the dinner table. Belle, whilst admiring Rosalind hugely, was desperately disappointed to have had no part in such an exciting adventure. Lord Hayward could only be thankful that she hadn't known of it as he could not place any reliance on her not having ridden off hot-foot to help in the rescue.

"I would not wish you to place yourself in such a perilous and uncomfortable situation, my love," he protested gently. "I am convinced you would not have enjoyed it nearly as much as you think."

"Perilous, pooh," she laughed. "Anyway, I am sure you would have come to my rescue, dear Nat."

Although Lord Hayward could not help but feel gratified by the innocent trust she placed in him, Lord

Atherton frowned at his sister. "Do not underestimate the danger Lady Rosalind was placed in today, Belle. I cannot think you would have found it any great fun to be overturned in a curricle, thrown in the back of a filthy cart with your hands bound and to find yourself, still bound, alone in the company of an unscrupulous gentleman."

"I hardly think we can any longer attribute the term 'gentleman' to Rutley," interjected Lady Denby scathingly.

"No, indeed not," agreed Sir Thomas sternly. "And I must question your wisdom, George, in deciding not to deliver those two rascals into the hands of the local magistrate and report Rutley's doings. Sir Peter Grey, isn't it? A sensible enough man, I believe."

As Sir Thomas was magistrate of his own parish, these sentiments were understandable and not easy to counter.

"Yes, I have nothing against Sir Peter, a sensible man as you say," agreed Lord Atherton politely, although the slight thinning of his lips signalled he was not quite happy to have his decisions questioned. "However, the same cannot be said of either his wife or his daughter. I stand now in my father's shoes and he, I know, would not have wished his family's name bandied around the neighbourhood as an object of conjecture and gossip, and although we disagreed on many things, I am as one with him on this."

Hearing her son, finally accepting the mantle of head of the house brought tears to Lady Atherton's eyes. She smiled mistily at him. "Quite right, my dear, quite right."

"However," he continued, "if any of you feel

uncomfortable with the situation, particularly you, Harriet, with the boys to consider, I will understand if you wish to bring your visit to an end."

This brought a chorus of disapproval. In one respect the family were united; such a thing was not to be thought of. The Atherton clan closed ranks; no one was prepared to leave until they were convinced any danger had passed.

"However," added Lord Hayward in an unusually grave tone, "there has been a lack of openness in you, George, that I do not pretend to understand. If anything else does occur, you might consider that Sir Thomas and I are also here and quite able and willing to offer our assistance. In fact, I insist you keep us informed at all points."

Belle looked at her husband with surprise and admiration. "Well said, Nat. I had not thought of it before, but I agree it was quite selfish of George to keep the adventure all to himself."

Her brother merely rolled his eyes and addressed himself to his dinner.

Deeming it best to stay within the grounds for the next few days, new amusements were looked for. On visiting Rosalind's bedchamber the following morning to see how she went on, Belle was surprised to find her already up, the resilience of youth having rapidly overcome the discomforts of the previous day.

She gave her new friend a swift hug. "You poor thing, tell me all about it!"

Rosalind shook her head and gave her an apologetic smile. "If you don't mind, I'd rather not. I'd rather keep busy and not think about it."

Belle accepted this without any obvious signs of

disappointment. "Well, busy you shall be then," she smiled. "We can work on those accomplishments you would like to acquire as we are to be housebound for a few days. I know you can ride, but can you dance?"

Rosalind shook her head. "Not really," she admitted. "I have never even been to an assembly."

Belle clapped her hands. "We will start there then. It will be such fun! It is a fortunate circumstance that Sir Philip is here, you know, for he is regarded as one of the most accomplished dancers and is a most amusing partner. He will be happy to lead, and I can accompany you on the pianoforte," she said, confidently disposing of that gentleman's time.

"You sat still long enough to learn to play then," Rosalind smiled, buoyed up by Belle's high spirits.

Belle laughed. "Well, I had to do something during the winter. We get torrential downpours here you know!"

Her words proved prophetic as the next afternoon it came on to rain. Belle wasted no time but let Sir Philip know what a treat he had in store. Even a hardened campaigner like himself, armed with an intimate knowledge of the young lady concerned, was not proof against her cajoling ways. He was obliging enough to agree to the scheme, and although Rosalind felt awkward at first to have a man in such close proximity, Sir Philip's good humour as she stepped on his feet more than once, soon put her at her ease. Her natural aptitude for all things physical and love of a challenge presently took over, and it was not long before she had mastered the rudimentaries of the dance.

"Very good, Lady Rosalind," he praised her as they

got through a whole dance without her bruising his toes further. "Now it is customary to converse whilst performing the dance, so although I realise the way I tie my cravat is quite mesmerising, if you could endeavour to raise your gaze, we shall try it."

Rosalind raised a laughing countenance to his. "I was concentrating on my steps!"

"Even so," he murmured, nodding to Belle to begin again. "How are you enjoying your stay in the country, ma'am?" he enquired, all formality as he led her into a graceful turn.

"Oh, vastly diverting, sir," she replied, joining in the game and putting on what she imagined would pass for society manners. "One never knows what might happen next."

His lips quirked in amusement. "How refreshing. You are not perhaps missing the amusements of Town?"

"Oh no, a select party of friends is such a relief after all the sad crushes of recent weeks," she assured him blandly, blithely ignoring the fact that she had never been to any society crushes, sad or otherwise.

"How true," he concurred. "Although I am sure your many admirers would not readily agree."

Rosalind, by now thoroughly enjoying herself, dimpled roguishly at him. "Ah, but it becomes so tiresome trying to keep them all accommodated, for if I agree to dance with one, I leave another downcast and disappointed."

"A circumstance you must find very gratifying," her partner stated, his shoulders beginning to shake.

"I am not so heartless, sir," Rosalind protested.

"Unlike you, for I believe you are a shocking flirt and have left a string of broken hearts behind you."

At this point, he gave up trying to contain his amusement and let out a bark of laughter. It was thus, Lord Atherton found them.

"I am glad to see you are all enjoying yourselves. The lesson went well, I presume?" he stated dryly, sounding slightly prosy even to his own ears.

"Oh Lord, yes," agreed Sir Philip, wiping his streaming eyes. "Lady Rosalind will be an accomplished dancer and flirt in no time at all! Keep her here, George, for if she is ever let loose on the town, she will be a match and more for any of the incomparables!"

"I was only playing at flirting," Rosalind protested, not quite comfortable with this description.

Lord Atherton had a suddenly arrested look on his face. "You have no need to play at it, my dear, it comes quite naturally to your sex, I believe."

Rosalind was quick to hear the slight sneer in his words and flushed up to the roots of her hair. "I will go and see if Lady Atherton requires me to do anything for her," she said, hastily marching towards the door.

"A good idea," agreed Lord Atherton, holding it open for her. "That is what I brought you here for, after all."

Rosalind dropped him a curtsy subservient enough to have come from the lowliest maid whilst sending him a searingly hot glance of resentment.

Sir Philip and Belle exchanged a knowing look.

"Feeling a trifle out of sorts, George?" enquired Sir Philip, gently.

"Not at all, dear fellow," Lord Atherton replied blandly. "Come and play a game of billiards with me."

Belle raised no objection to being so summarily deserted, but let her fingers play idly over the keys, a distracted but not unsatisfied smile on her face.

## CHAPTER 10

Lord Atherton had remained closeted with his steward, Mr Kingston, for most of the morning. By the end of their interview, his head was buzzing with the alien ideas of crop rotation, high yielding crops, the importance of nitrogen in the soil and role of legumes and clover in achieving this, and much more. He was just considering a ride to shake his crotchets out when Sedgewick announced he had a visitor; Lord Gifford, Marquis of Stafford, had come to call. A tall, rather spare man, with a restless energy and a pair of astute, twinkling blue eyes entered the room. Lord Atherton rose hastily from behind his desk to greet him.

"Lord Gifford, this is an honour," he said, bowing.

"Nonsense, my dear boy," smiled the older man, taking the chair on the other side of the desk and accepting a glass of claret. "I have had no opportunity to pay a visit since your poor father's death. He was a good friend and will be missed, but I am glad to see you at home, taking an interest in your affairs."

Lord Atherton grimaced slightly. "I have a lot to learn, sir," he admitted ruefully.

"Of course you do," he laughed, "but Kingston is a good man and will show you the way all right and tight."

"How are your mines and quarries running, sir?" he enquired politely.

They were Lord Gifford's favourite topic, and he did not hesitate to expound upon them.

"We have increased our small canal network to carry the loads from the mines to the quarries and wharves, and it has increased productivity greatly. Unfortunately, one of the underground subsidiary passages in Wormbridge wood has recently collapsed, only a minor inconvenience and I will soon put it right. You have no interest in investing, I suppose?"

Lord Atherton smiled. "Not at the moment, sir. We have some interest in the Grand Junction, and it has begun to pay good dividends, but I must admit I am more than a little interested in the steam engine. I remember going to see the Catch Me Who Can in Bloomsbury, created by Richard Trevithick when I was a lad. And although it came to nothing, it was the fault of the rails not the locomotive. I am sure it is the future. Have you any steam engines at the mines, sir? I would be very interested in seeing them if you have."

Lord Gifford smiled at his enthusiasm. "We use them on our inclined plane and to pump water out of the mine. You are welcome to a guided tour anytime, my lad. It is refreshing to meet a young man with more in his head than whoring and gambling. You are your father's son, after all."

"I am beginning to understand the balls he juggled

more every day," Lord Atherton admitted wryly. "I hope to take you up on that offer very soon, sir, if I may?"

"I will look forward to it, come in the afternoon and then dine. You will stay the night, of course."

A knock on the door interrupted them, and then a fair head in a very fetching lace cap peeped around the edge. "Oh, it is you, Miles." Lady Atherton smiled, coming into the room. "I am sorry to interrupt, but I did not want you to run away without saying hello."

Lord Gifford rose to his feet and came forward to take both her hands in his. "My dear Sophia, I don't know how it is but you look younger every time I see you, damned if you don't!"

"Oh, don't you flummery me, you old rascal," she laughed. "I know I look quite haggard in this miserable black, but please come up to my sitting room and take tea with me and let me know what is going on in the world. I feel sadly out of touch."

"Of course I will, and I must say, Sophia, you must be very proud of young George here. He has more sense in his cockloft than many a young man."

"I am very proud of my son," she agreed, smiling at him fondly. "Could you arrange for poor John to be carried down, George? He must be sadly bored. I have asked Rosalind to try and do what she can to entertain him."

"I brought her here to help you, Mama, not entertain my friends," he grumbled.

Lady Atherton's finely curved eyebrows lifted in surprise. "Entertaining my guests is a great help I assure you, dear. Why don't you go for a ride? You have been cooped up too long, and it is clearly irritating your nerves. Now Miles, how is dear Dorothea? It is an age since I have seen her, although her last letter was a great comfort."

"I expect to see you soon, my boy, been a pleasure talking to you," Lord Gifford flung over his shoulder as he was led out of the room.

Knowing John as well as he did, Lord Atherton was fairly certain he would refuse to come downstairs undressed, so he instructed his valet, Townsend, to offer whatever assistance Wrencham might require in achieving this. They walked into Lord Preeve's chamber to find this fastidious person in an unusually agitated state, wringing his hands and looking extremely harassed.

"Please sir, do not get up today, I am persuaded it will cause you a great deal of pain."

"N-nonsense, Wrencham. I c-cannot spend the next few w-weeks lying in bed," blustered his employer.

"Lord Atherton, sir, could you please persuade his lordship to stay where he is?" he pleaded.

"My good man," he replied somewhat haughtily, "I have come to offer our assistance in dressing him so he can come downstairs, and I cannot think it of so serious a matter as to cause all this heart-burning anxiety!"

Lord Preeve let out a crack of laughter. "That's given y-you your own, y-you old fusspot!"

The real cause of Wrencham's distress soon became apparent.

"But please, sir, not the Petersham trousers! I cannot think it will add to your or my consequence to wear such outrageous garments!" he complained almost tearfully, casting Townsend a fleeting glance.

"D-don't be such a s-sapskull, what other g-garment h-have I that will f-fit so easily over this d-damned splint?"

As this was unanswerable, the offending Cossack style trousers were retrieved from the wardrobe. If Townsend was startled by the lurid yellow and blue stripes of the voluminous garment, he gave no sign and proved his worth by helping Wrencham ease them on with the minimum of fuss and discomfort to their owner.

"Might I suggest that you will be more comfortable in your dressing gown than a coat?" he suggested politely, casting a not unsympathetic glance in the direction of his fellow valet.

Feeling a small measure of relief, Wrencham hurried to produce a splendid double-breasted gown of quilted blue satin which largely covered the offending trousers.

Fortunately, Lord Preeve had suffered a straightforward break in his lower leg. However, it was still of the first importance to keep it as still as possible whilst the bone knitted back together. Therefore, he was carried down by two footmen on a board, protected on both sides by the assiduous valets.

Once settled comfortably on a sofa in the yellow salon with his leg elevated by cushions, he pronounced himself to be perfectly comfortable.

"S-so th-thank you but you c-can t-take yourselves and your d-damned f-fussing off now!"

Lady Rosalind entered shortly after, her face wreathed in an apologetic smile as she dropped to her knees and took his hand in hers. "I am so very sorry to have, in some part, been the cause of your injury, my dear Lord Preeve."

He returned the smile and patted her hand in an avuncular way. "Ah, d-don't talk n-nonsense my ch-child, I have already h-heard enough of that to l-last me a l-lifetime. It w-was not your f-fault anyway, I d-doubt even Atherton h-here could have p-prevented it and he c-considers himself a top-sawyer, d-don't you know."

Getting to her feet, she acknowledged Lord Atherton with a frosty inclination of her head. "I am sure he does. Lady Atherton requested me to see if I might find a way to entertain Lord Preeve, sir," she informed him with icy civility.

"I am aware," he replied with equal coolness. "What a shame he can't help you indulge your newfound talent at dancing. What other amusements do you have in store for him?"

Turning her back pointedly, she gave the invalid one of her rare, wide smiles.

"H-how about a g-game of cards, my d-dear?" Lord Preeve suggested, hopefully.

"No, I have something better than cards," she said decidedly, flourishing the book she held in her hands. "It is Pride and Prejudice by Jane Austen. I found it in the library and have always wanted to read it."

Lord Atherton raised surprised brows at his friend, reluctant amusement creeping into his eyes. "I didn't know you enjoyed novels, John. You are in for a high treat!"

"I – er, d-don't as a r-rule, are you sure y-you wouldn't r-rather play c-cards, my dear?" he asked a trifle desperately.

"Quite sure, if you are thinking this is one of those fanciful novels full of improbable happenings, where the heroine is forever fainting, and the villain lives in some horrid gothic castle, let me reassure you. I believe it to be a most improving work and quite believable."

"Improving d-did you s-say?" Lord Preeve answered faintly, his startled eyes darting back to his friend. "It is m-most kind of you, Lady R-Rosalind, but you m-must have m-much better things to do than read to an invalid. P-perhaps George w-would l-like to p-play cards?"

Lord Atherton smiled sweetly. "I'm sorry to be disobliging, dear fellow, but I was just about to go for a ride, must keep up the practice if I am to remain a top-sawyer!"

He returned an hour later, feeling much refreshed and couldn't resist a peek into the yellow salon. He expected to find Lord Preeve with his eyes glassed over, if not snoring quietly. Instead, he found a very cosy scene; ranged around the room sat not only Lady Rosalind but Belle, Lord Hayward, Harriet and Sir Thomas. None of them appeared to be in the least bored, but on the contrary, were hanging on Rosalind's every word. Not only was her well-modulated voice easy on the ears, it seemed she also had a hitherto unsuspected talent for play-acting, and each character came alive as she spoke their words.

He quietly took up a position by the door and watched her read. Most of the words washed over his head as he watched her mouth move and her animated face take on various expressions from comical to deadly serious.

Presently Lord Preeve looked up and spotted him still leaning against the wall, his arms folded.

"I s-say, G-George, you h-have missed out m-my boy, it is almost as g-good as being at the p-play. Although this D-Darcy chap sounds like a dam-dashed r-rum un, my m-money's on Wickham to b-bring the thing off."

It was like a painting become animated; everyone started moving and chatting, so Rosalind closed the book. It took her a moment to come to herself for she had really got lost in it. When she did, she realised she had become the centre of attention with everyone singing her praises. Blushing, she got to her feet.

"It was nothing," she smiled. "I was really indulging myself. I must go and see if Lady Atherton requires anything."

She was not allowed to leave before she promised to let everyone know when the next instalment would occur.

She visibly stiffened as she neared Lord Atherton. He held the door open for her and followed her out into the hall.

"Wait!" he called as she carried on walking towards the staircase.

She turned and lifted her chin. "Is there something I can do for you, sir?"

He looked uncharacteristically uncertain for a moment. "No, no. It is just that… what I mean to say is… that was very well done. You have entertained practically the whole household, I am grateful and…" He paused, looking awkward. "And I apologise if I have been somewhat tetchy. I have had a lot on my mind."

Rosalind curtsied before turning and mounting the staircase. Lord Atherton followed her slowly, on the way to change his buckskins, a small frown puckering his forehead. His excuse had sounded weak even to himself, but it was no less true for that. He realised just what a cushioned life he had been leading, but now he felt hedged about by responsibilities. Although his mother might try and convince him otherwise, he knew he, and he alone was responsible for the well-being of his tenants, his family and guests. He straightened his shoulders. They were broad enough, after all. He could and would carry the weight with pride and dignity.

Sir Philip had been absent most of the day, he arrived back an hour before dinner and hurried up to his room to change. Lord Atherton found him there just putting the finishing touches to his cravat. He remained silent and watched in amusement as Sir Philip lowered his chin, inch by inch until he had achieved the desired result.

"Anyone watching you, Philip," he smiled, "would not believe you have carried honours on the field of battle."

"Ah," his friend smiled, "therein lies my advantage. Always fool the enemy into thinking you are weaker than you appear."

Lord Atherton waited for his valet to shrug him into his well-fitting coat, which anyone with any fashion sense would have known was designed by Schultz; its neat lines and military cut were unmistakeable.

"Where have you been all day, my dandy?" he enquired as soon as Farrow had softly closed the door.

Sir Philip offered him a wry smile. "I have never been one for the indoor life. I have been tooling your phaeton about the countryside with skill and finesse if you must have it."

"Ah, cutting a dash I perceive. But if you think I am to be taken in by such a Banbury tale, you are mistaken. Cut line. What have you really been up to?"

"It is not a Banbury tale, oh suspicious one. I have been driving your phaeton, just seeing how the land lies, you know. I may have partaken in refreshment at one or two hostelries, keeping my ear to the ground, so to speak."

Lord Atherton laughed. "Now who is the suspicious one? Did you hear anything interesting?"

Sir Philip offered him an unrepentant grin. "No, nothing at all, but I discovered there's a damned fine serving wench at the Angel in Shrewsbury."

"Ah, indulging your taste for low company!"

"I am not so high in the instep as you, dear fellow. Besides, there was nothing low about Molly's charms!"

They were still laughing as they made their way down to dinner. Rosalind, who had just come out of her room, stepped back into the shadows before they caught sight of her. Seeing Lord Atherton laughing in such an unrestrained fashion caused a strange, fluttering feeling inside her. He looked much younger and carefree than she had seen him before. She hardened her heart; she had felt they had reached some sort of understanding, almost friendship on their ride back from the lodge, but she had clearly been mistaken, for he had very soon reverted to type, taking every opportunity presented since to criticise her and make her remember her place. And although he had apologised earlier, it had been delivered in so stilted and awkward a fashion as to lack any warmth or conviction.

The following day brought fine sunshine, and it was decided they would picnic by the lake. It boasted a very pleasing aspect, looking down over the park and had a small island in the middle which sloped up towards a cluster of trees. Hampers and blankets were carried down, and they made camp near the small boathouse. It housed not only a punt but also two rowing boats. Sir Philip and Lord Hayward commandeered one of the rowing boats and scooped up George and Harry to go fishing.

Lady Harriet settled back on a blanket, content to be a spectator. "I'll lay any of you odds that one or other of the rascals will fall in before long," she said, quite unconcerned.

"I certainly went in enough times!" laughed Belle. "Oh, here comes John."

They all looked up to see two intrepid footmen carrying him down, in what appeared to be a pair of curtains which they had turned into a sort of hammock.

"C-careful," protested Lord Preeve tetchily as they lowered him down beside the blankets, nearly tipping him out. "I-I'm not a s-sack of d-dashed turnips!"

With humble apologies they fussed about for a few moments, propping him up on a bank of cushions and arranging a parasol to cover him before beating a hasty retreat.

Something had caught Belle's attention, and she shaded her eyes from the glare of the sun as she continued to look towards the house. She gave a low groan. "Quick, George, take us out in the punt. If I'm not much mistaken, that is Letitia coming towards us!"

They followed her eyes and saw that a very elegant figure holding a parasol was being escorted towards them by Lady Atherton.

"Quick," Belle repeated, grabbing Rosalind's hand and dragging her towards the punt.

"Not a word about what caused your accident, John, or anything else if you can help it," Lord Atherton sent over his shoulder as he swiftly followed them.

"I-I s-say, L-lady Rosalind, I thought you were g-going to r-read me some m-more of that b-book!" he called after them.

"I will later, I promise," she called back as Lord Atherton pushed the punt away from the bank.

"Oh, let them go, John. I will bear you company and shield you if you think you need it," Harriet said drily, getting to her feet.

Rosalind was not best pleased at having herself dragged aboard by Belle but could hardly say so. Leaning back, she watched as Lord Atherton skilfully poled the boat away from the bank. He was grinning down at his sister with such a look of genuine affection that for some reason, she felt her heart tighten in her chest.

"You rag-mannered brat!" he laughed.

She twinkled back up at him. "But dear George, it is not me she has come to see. I was protecting you!"

"Lord help me, if the day that I need your protection, ever comes!"

She pouted slightly at that. "I can do more than you give me credit for! I could pole this boat as well as you, for instance. Give me a go, and I'll show you!" she cried, jumping to her feet with all her usual impetuosity.

Rosalind grabbed hold of the side of the boat as it started to rock quite alarmingly.

Any chagrin Miss Grey might have felt at witnessing such a scrambling departure was well hidden, and she was all smiles as she greeted Lady Harriet and Lord Preeve.

"What on earth have you done to your leg, Lord Preeve?" she asked with great concern.

"Oh, it is n-nothing, d-don't give it a th-thought, a s-silly c-curricle accident, n-nothing more," he assured her, then winced as he belatedly remembered George's instructions not to say anything about it.

"May I?" she asked, all politeness as she gestured at the blanket next to him.

"Of c-course," he stammered, reddening slightly. "F-forgive me n-not standing up."

"Oh, don't be silly," she tittered, settling herself comfortably. "Now, tell me all about how such a thing could have occurred, for I am sure such a nonpareil as yourself, could not have been the cause."

"Talk about tipping the butter boat over someone," whispered Harriet to her mother.

Lady Atherton merely smiled, her gaze taking in the scene on the lake. "How lovely it is to see everyone here together, oh, watch out Harry," she murmured as she saw him suddenly get to his feet and lean over the side of the boat.

Harriet's eyes crinkled in amusement as she saw a hand grab him by the collar and casually pull him back again. "Well done, Nathaniel," she murmured approvingly. "He will make a good father. It would be good for Belle too," she stated, her eyes swinging over to where her younger sister now stood poling the boat. "Calm her down a bit," she added as she saw her nearly lose her balance.

"Hmm, who do you think will go in first, Harry or Belle?" Lady Atherton smiled.

"I'd say the odds are even," said Harriet resignedly. "But I know who has the least excuse!"

Harriet grimaced as another irritating titter floated her way, but she was a good-hearted woman and on glancing down, could not mistake or ignore the desperate plea in Lord Preeve's panicked gaze. She was glad, however, when the others, at last, joined them for some luncheon, the fresh air having given them all appetites. Kind-hearted she might be, but she was not known for suffering fools gladly, and it took all her patience to parry the little questions Letitia would slip into her conversation of nothings, clearly designed to find out more about Rosalind or any of the eligible gentlemen at present residing at the house.

As Lady Atherton laid out a cold collation consisting of cold meats, fruits and sweet biscuits, Letitia turned her attention to Rosalind.

"You are so brave, Lady Rosalind, to sit out without a parasol. Are you not afraid of ruining your lovely complexion?"

Her tone clearly suggested that she considered this disastrous event already to have occurred, but if she had hoped to discompose her quarry, she was disappointed. Rosalind merely shrugged her shoulders carelessly. "If my worth is to be judged by whether or not I have a freckle or two then so be it. I would rather by far enjoy the fresh air and sunshine than either closet myself away, or forever be worrying about taking out a parasol, or if the brim of my hat was wide enough."

Letitia's eyes turned a shade colder even as her smile widened. "Yes, I have heard how intrepid you are. Perhaps it was the sun in your eyes which led to you overturning Lord Atherton's curricle and breaking poor Lord Preeve's leg? I am sure that would account for it."

Lady Rosalind coloured even as Lord Preeve jumped to her defence. "No, n-no, y-you are quite out, Miss Grey. It was the f-fault of the c-cart coming the other w-way, n-no blame attaches to Lady R-Rosalind!"

"How chivalrous of you to say so," she simpered to him, "always so much the gentleman."

Rosalind caught Belle rolling her eyes and had to bite her lip not to burst out laughing.

Intercepting a stern look from Lord Atherton, Lord Preeve cast about wildly for something to change the subject. His eyes alighted on Harry and George, who were very interested in something they had in a small bucket.

"I s-say, lads, what h-have you got there?" he asked jovially.

Harry didn't immediately respond, he was too busy poking something in the bucket with his finger, but George raised his head and considered Lord Preeve seriously. "It is our catch, sir," he explained. "It is p'raps not a very big fish, but it is our first catch, and we shall eat it for supper."

"C-caught something did y-you? W-well done, b-bring it over h-here and let me see," he encouraged them.

They both grabbed the bucket at the same time and came towards Lord Preeve, each tugging it this way and that as they argued over who should carry it.

"But I caught it on my hook," insisted Harry.

"Yes," agreed George, "but I held the net that landed him!"

By the time they reached Lord Preeve, most of the water had spilled, and the inevitable accident happened. As Harry gave the bucket one last huge tug in his direction, George let it go. Harry went toppling backwards and whilst the bucket remained firmly gripped in his rather grimy little hands, the remnants of the water and one quite small fish sailed in a graceful arc through the air before landing in Letitia's lap, where it wriggled about quite frantically.

After looking down at it for one horrified moment, she gave out an undignified scream and leapt to her feet with more haste than grace.

"Ughh! That is disgusting!" she complained shrilly. "And just look at my dress! It is damp, slimy, and no doubt smells of fish!"

Both boys froze for a moment, before George said in a small voice, "We are very sorry, miss, but it is only a very small fish."

Letitia had gone red in the face and now turned a very unforgiving gaze upon them.

"Your turn to apologise, Harry," quickly intervened Harriet. "Apologise, and then both of you go back to the nursery. I will come and see you presently."

Harry duly apologised politely enough, but the

effect was ruined by the giggles that drifted back on the breeze as they raced up to the house.

"Now now, my dear, it is a very distressing accident, I'm sure, but boys will be boys you know," said Lady Atherton soothingly as Letitia continued to rant and rave.

"I'm glad to say, I don't," replied Letitia through gritted teeth.

Sir Philip choked back a bark of laughter, rather unconvincingly turning it into a cough, drawing Lady Atherton's attention in his direction. She raised her brows at him for a moment before smiling kindly at him. "Ah, Philip, my dear, you are just the person. I know how much you enjoy driving around the countryside so I won't hesitate to request you drive Letitia back home. I am sure she has had enough sun and won't want to delay in changing out of her present attire."

Sir Philip swallowed his punishment, bowing gracefully in both their directions.

"It would be an honour," he avowed, offering his arm to the offended lady. "Miss Grey?"

The transformation was immediate. Gone was the petulant, disgruntled young person of a few moments before, now she smiled coyly up at her escort.

"Oh, thank you, Sir Philip, it is most kind of you." Looking over her shoulder, she smiled sweetly at the rest of the party. "Thank you for a very pleasant luncheon, for I won't allow such a trifling incident to spoil my day."

The various members of the party either bowed or curtsied and watched the couple's slow progress towards the house, nobody daring to look at anyone else. However, when they were judged to be out of hearing distance, Lord Atherton took his mother's hand and kissed it. "A masterful move, Mama."

Then the dammed up laughter broke forth in a gushing torrent until more than one person was clutching their sides and had tears running down their faces.

Lady Atherton was the first to pull herself together. "This is most unseemly, a well-bred person should never show an excess of emotion!"

"Not even when a wriggly fish lands in their lap?" gasped Belle, and they were all overcome once more.

CHAPTER 11

The following day also dawned fair, and the boys were so much in charity with Belle, she offered to play a game of hide and seek with them in the gardens. Rosalind did not take much persuading to join them. Steering them clear of the lake, Belle took them to the Italian gardens which lay to the east of the house.

In the main part, all was balance and symmetry. A mermaid fountain set in an oval pond was the focal point from which gravelled walkways radiated. Small hedges lined the walks and four square flowerbeds filled with geraniums offered a small splash of colour amongst the predominant green supplied by cypress, myrtle and bay trees as well as a variety of topiary. Here and there a heroic statue or carved urn set upon a stone plinth added to the classical feel, and at the far end, two shallow flights of steps leading in opposite directions both converged at an impressive balustraded terrace. The whole was surrounded by taller, well-clipped hedges with archways cut into them to provide access to a wilder arrangement.

Here, the influence of Lady Atherton could be detected; narrow paths led between higher growing shrubs and flowering plants. Oleander, honeysuckle and roses vied with rosemary and lavender for space until you came to a jasmine-covered pergola leading to a small classical-style temple. It was the perfect choice for the game as its design created many opportunities for concealment.

Rosalind volunteered to be the first to be blindfolded by the fountain whilst they all hid. After a good twenty minutes of ignoring the giggling and rustling that came from various bushes, she finally caught Harry. His turn lasted a much shorter time, for knowing George's dislike of being alone, he very quickly found him under a bench not very far from the bush he had previously hidden behind. George had a much more difficult time of it, and finally, Rosalind took pity on him and began to cough or sneeze to aid his cause. She was eventually caught, but Harry was not satisfied.

"Have you a cold, Lady Rosalind?" he enquired suspiciously.

"No," she answered, "but I admit the leaves of the bush were tickling my nose!"

Harry thought about this for a few moments. "Well, that would explain it, I suppose," he conceded.

"Where is Aunt Belle?" asked an impatient George.

Rosalind knelt down beside him and smiled. "Do you think she is playing a trick upon us?" she asked him.

George thought about this and then nodded, a slow smile spreading across his face. "P'robly. Aunt Belle likes playing games."

"Well, let's go and find her," Rosalind suggested.

But after a good half an hour of searching, even Rosalind grew weary and anxious. She knew Belle to be one for a joke but not for a moment did she really believe she would tease her little nephews in this manner. Finally, she turned to the two boys and suggested they went back to the house.

She sent the two boys to the nursery and went in search of Lord Atherton. She ran him to ground in his mother's sitting room, where they were both involved in a game of chess. She wasted no time with preamble.

"Belle is missing," she blurted out breathlessly.

Two pairs of startled grey eyes sharpened their focus on her.

"What do you mean, missing?" Lady Atherton asked intently.

Rosalind explained quickly, adding, "I cannot think she would have abandoned the game in so precipitous a manner."

"Did you see anyone else in the vicinity?" Lord Atherton enquired.

Rosalind shook her head. "Only a gardener; he was collecting clippings from the hedges he had been trimming."

Lady Atherton nodded decisively. "You round up some of the others and organise a search, George. I will talk to Jackson and discover if he had set anyone to work in that part of the gardens today."

Remembering the criticism he had previously received from Lord Hayward, he included all the available guests apart from Lord Preeve, but there was no sign of Belle.

Lady Atherton hurried to join them once she had interviewed her head gardener.

"All of the under-gardeners are accounted for, and no-one was working in this part of the grounds today," she informed them all seriously.

"Where exactly did you see him, Lady Rosalind?" Lord Hayward asked tersely, worry overriding his normal placidity.

"It was when we first arrived," she said, thinking rapidly. "Yes, over there." She pointed to where a neat row of clipped box hedges marked the east side of the garden. "He was putting clippings into a wheelbarrow."

Sir Philip immediately strode over to the area indicated and gave the ground a close scrutiny. "Yes, the ground is quite marked. The wheelbarrow must have been quite heavy to have left such an imprint, but there are tracks only going one way, and as hedge clippings are not heavy, I can only presume that Belle was carried off in it towards the east gate."

All eyes turned again to Rosalind.

"You didn't hear or see anything?" asked Sir Philip.

Rosalind thought hard. "It was George's turn, and we were all hiding; he was finding it hard to find anyone, so I began to sneeze and cough to help him. Perhaps that covered any other sound. I'm sorry, but I don't recall anything that could help. Maybe one of the boys saw something?" she added, looking quite distressed.

"I will go and talk to them," said Harriet, marching off towards the house.

"It's not your fault," Sir Philip said briskly to Rosalind. "Hiding in plain sight is a very clever trick; even if you did see the gardener, your mind might not register it particularly as it is what you might expect to see, whereas if someone was acting furtively, you would notice immediately. Nat and George, come with me, we will follow the trail to the east gate. Sir Thomas, go inside with Lady Atherton and Lady Rosalind, in case Belle turns up. It will only give food for gossip if we all hare off like a herd of cattle stampeding."

The boys could throw no more light on the situation, and so they gathered in the drawing room and gave way to useless conjecture. They were all agreed, at last, that Lord Rutley must be behind it.

"Both George and I were convinced Lord Rutley would flee the country after his last failed endeavour," fretted Lady Atherton, pacing up and down. "What can he hope to achieve?"

Rosalind shivered. "Lord Atherton was convinced he was merely desperate, but I wondered if he had not run mad."

"If it is madness," Sir Thomas interjected solemnly, "it is a very calculated sort. Desperate, he is of a certainty. If we do not presently receive a ransom note, I will own myself very surprised."

"He is a despicable creature, and if he harms a hair on Belle's head, I will see him in Newgate, scandal or no scandal," Lady Atherton declared passionately.

"I very much think that if he is caught this time, it is highly likely that either George or Nat will run him through!" suggested Harriet, the thought clearly giving her some satisfaction.

"A very understandable sentiment, my dear," her

esteemed spouse allowed, "but great as the provocation is, as none of us would benefit from either of them being tried for murder, let us hope that it doesn't come to that."

There was nothing else to say, so they all relapsed back into pensive silence.

It was some time before the others returned, looking tired and somewhat dishevelled. Lady Atherton flew out of her chair the moment they came in.

"What have you discovered?" she demanded urgently.

Lord Hayward walked over to the unlit fire, leant on the mantelpiece and gazed down at a slightly besmirched boot but said nothing.

"We found the wheelbarrow and this," said Lord Atherton, drawing a bright blue ribbon out of his coat pocket.

"Belle was wearing that this morning," confirmed Rosalind quietly.

"Oh, how roughly must he have treated her for it to have come loose," cried Lady Atherton tearfully.

A sudden noise drew all eyes to Lord Hayward, he had been fiddling absent-mindedly with a small, delicate figurine that had been on the mantle, it now lay smashed on the hearth.

"Knowing Belle, I would not consider it unlikely that she had dropped it intentionally, to give us a clue," Lord Philip suggested calmly. "Which at least points to her not being too badly hurt."

Whilst such a suggestion may have given relief to some people in the room, a grinding sound was heard as Lord Hayward, not satisfied with merely breaking the figurine, now crushed it almost to dust beneath his boot.

"When I find Rutley," he said in a deep, quiet voice that was filled with resolution, "I shall give him the same treatment."

For a moment, his audience were stunned into silence; never before had any of them seen this side of their relative or friend.

"Shouldn't we be out looking for her, George?" asked Lady Atherton at last.

"We found no sign in the immediate vicinity. Until we receive some communication from Rutley, we can do nothing."

A timid knocking on the door was followed by the entrance of Belle's abigail looking tearful and pale.

"Excuse me, ma'am," she said to Lady Atherton as she curtsied, "but is it true Lady Hayward is missing?"

On hearing the affirmative, she turned paler still. "If you please, ma'am, could I have a private word?"

That drew the attention of all but especially Lord Hayward.

"There will be no secrets between any of us here, Sheldon," he said tersely. "If you have any information pertinent to the situation, out with it!"

"I don't know where she is, sir, I only wish I did. It's her condition as is worrying me," she said tearfully, wringing her hands.

His eyebrows shot up. "Her condition? What can you mean?"

Her eyes turned to the dowager countess. "I told her she should at least tell Lady Atherton, but she would have it that it was too early and that she couldn't bear any fuss or botheration," she blurted out.

Comprehension dawned on this lady, shock swiftly superseded by incredulity were written clear. "Do you mean to tell me, Sheldon, that my daughter is in the family way?"

"That's it, ma'am," she affirmed guiltily and then burst into tears. "And I wish I had gone against her and told you for then she might have stayed in and rested like I told her more than once she should."

"I doubt it," she said drily but seeing that the maid was genuinely in distress, Lady Atherton shepherded her out of the room and handed her over to the calming ministrations of Mrs Simmons.

This latest titbit of information could not but increase the anxiety of all and not having heard anything more, it was a dismal party that made up dinner that evening. No one had any appetite for any of the splendid dishes set before them and conversation was desultory.

Everyone was at breakfast when the missive finally arrived. Sedgewick presented it with a suitably solemn countenance to Lord Atherton, to whom it was addressed. It was brief and to the point.

*Dear Atherton,*

*As you have no doubt guessed, I have your esteemed sister. Lively, isn't she? She is at present unharmed. If you come to The Blue Bell Inn near Donnington this evening, you will find her still in this much to be desired condition. You will come alone this time, for although I am loath to question your honesty, I have taken the precaution of hiding her elsewhere. If this condition is not met, I will not reveal her location, which I admit, is not an entirely safe or comfortable one. Although it pains me to be vulgar, you will also bring with you jewellery to at least the worth of 5,000 pounds and 200 of the new gold sovereigns (I really cannot be expected to flee this dismal country without some means of supporting myself).*

*Rutley*

A few moments' silence greeted the reading of the letter, emotions ranging from relief that the means of recovering Belle had been revealed, to anger, amazement and incredulity. Then they all started speaking at once.

"But that is nearly twenty miles away," Lady Atherton said. "Why so far?"

"Why does he not just ask for money?" asked Rosalind in a small voice. "Why the jewels?"

Lord Atherton met her clear gaze and read the worry that she might still be responsible in some way for planting the idea in his head.

"They are portable," he said briefly, "small, light and easily sold; perfect for a man wishing to travel swiftly." He transferred his gaze to his mother. "He would not be so foolish as to come too close again. I have taken steps to be informed if anyone answering his description comes into the neighbourhood, something I am sure he has thought of. He may be desperate, but he is not stupid."

"I always thought h-he w-was a d-dashed loose s-screw," avowed Lord Preeve (who determined not to be absent when such stirring events were afoot, had managed to master the crutches which were to be his constant companions for some weeks to come), "b-but George, you d-don't really m-mean to reward h-him for his d-damned infamy, d-do you?"

"There can be no question of trifling with him when Belle's safety is at stake," protested Lady Atherton. "I will willingly give my jewels to ensure her safe return!"

"It will certainly be best to proceed with caution," concurred Sir Thomas. "A man who will resort to kidnap, blackmail and extortion is not to be underestimated."

"You will not go alone, however," stated Lord Hayward in a steely voice.

"No," agreed Sir Philip firmly. "His mind is so twisted that we cannot rely on his honouring his side of the agreement, after all."

"Well, do not think that I will sit here and meekly await your return whilst you all go off in hot pursuit," Lady Atherton informed them. "Who knows what state she will be in? She will need me."

Her son looked exasperated. "We cannot all go, he will not be so easy to deceive this time."

"No," agreed Lady Atherton, "you are going to have to come up with a very clever plan, George. Lady Rosalind and I will go and pack whilst you are about it, for Donnington is very near to Uffington Hall. Miles and Dorothea will be delighted to have us."

Her son looked startled. "You cannot mean to acquaint Lord and Lady Gifford with all the details?"

Lady Atherton's glance strayed to her son-in-law. "How very right you were, Nathaniel, when you commented on his lack of openness. George, Miles and your father were very close friends, and Dorothea and I have always shared a close understanding. Not only that, but Miles is also a magistrate, not to mention knowing that area like the back of his hand; you may have need of him. Besides, I doubt very much Belle will be in any fit state to be driven far when you find her."

Despite feeling his consequence to have been somewhat diminished by this masterful speech, a glimmer of admiration shone in his eyes as he watched his parent transform from panicked mother to purposeful avenger.

As Rosalind held the door open for her, she looked back over her shoulder. "Oh, and no one will stir from this house until I have heard all the details of Belle's rescue and approved of them."

Within half an hour, the plan was set. Lord Atherton was to go first, alone, in case Rutley had set any spies along the main roads. Lady Atherton and Rosalind were to go a little later in the family carriage, which thankfully did not bear the family coat of arms.

Sir Philip insisted that they take his groom, Vaughen, with them as an out-rider. "He was with me in France and Spain," he explained, "and if you have any trouble, he will know how to deal with it."

Sir Philip, Lord Hayward and Sir Thomas were to make their own way cross country to the vicinity, keeping well away from the main roads. Once there, they would scout the roads that Lord Rutley was likely to take in his escape, splitting up to keep them covered. Each would take a groom (Sir Philip borrowing Lord Atherton's) so that whoever found him, could send word to the others.

Rosalind could not help but feel anxious at the thought of Lord Atherton facing Rutley on his own; she felt certain he did not take as seriously as he should the danger he represented. Feeling she could not reconcile it to her conscience to let him go without mentioning her concerns, she overcame her diffidence and made her way out to the stables just as he had climbed into his phaeton.

"Please take care, my lord," she said seriously. "I feel sure he will cross you still if he can."

Lord Atherton stared down at her for a moment, an unreadable look in his quicksilver eyes. "I am honoured by your concern, Lady Rosalind. I assure you I shall take every care for I am well aware that my sister's fate depends upon it. I wish you a good journey and know you will take good care of my mother," he said, glancing over her head.

With that, she had to be content as he swept out of the yard at a spanking pace. Turning, she found Lady Atherton had come up close behind her. She felt a blush stain her cheeks as she realised she must have heard her warning and only hoped she would not suspect her of having feelings towards her son that would be inappropriate to her present situation.

Lady Atherton merely took her arm and led her back towards the house. "Wise words, my child, it was what I had come out to say myself. Now, we must make haste for I do not intend to be far behind him. It may be that he will need Lord Gifford's assistance, and I must acquaint him with the situation before that need arises."

It was early evening when they arrived at Uffington Hall, a fine example of a Tudor manor house, all mellow brick and towering chimneys. Lady Atherton had sent a stable boy ahead with a letter informing Lord and Lady Gifford of their imminent arrival. She had been in such haste that she had merely mentioned her need for her good friends' help in a matter most urgent and of the utmost delicacy, so it was hardly surprising that before the coach had come to a stop outside the front door, Lord Gifford himself rushed out to greet them.

"My dear Sophia," he exclaimed, helping her down from the carriage, "you know without my mentioning it that you are always a most welcome guest, but what can have occurred to occasion such a hasty arrival?"

Lady Gifford, a small, smart lady with a rather brown complexion and quick, restless movements which had earned her the nickname sparrow from her fond lord, was not far behind him.

"Welcome, my dear," she greeted Lady Atherton.

"Come in out of this cold wind and then when you are quite comfortable you can tell us all about it."

After the introductions had been made, Rosalind retired to her room ostensibly to freshen up, but mostly because she could not help feeling that her absence would allow Lady Atherton greater freedom to share her worries and Rosalind's own part in the story. The others retired to the panelled drawing room, where over a glass of wine Lady Atherton related the family's recent history with Lord Rutley. To say her audience was amazed would not do their reaction justice; for a full two minutes, they were silenced, until finally, Lady Gifford found her voice.

"But this is incredible!" she exclaimed, shocked. "I would not expect to find such a story even between the leaves of one of Mrs Radcliffe's novels!"

"You are very right, Dorothea, but unfortunately, it is just such a nightmare that we are cast into," replied Lady Atherton.

"I have heard the rumours that he was so badly dipped he had fled the country, of course," acknowledged Lord Gifford. "But that he was such a villain, I had no idea! He must be brought to justice, Sophia!" he insisted.

"I am not unsympathetic to your argument," Lady Atherton replied. "It does seem the outside of enough that he should get away with behaviour so unbefitting to a gentleman and so potentially dangerous to all involved. But consider, Miles, would you want your name bandied about in connection with such incredible events? If you had a daughter, would you want it known that she had been taken in such a manner and held alone, with such a one, overnight? Although we can only pray that nothing untoward has occurred, would you place any money on the chance that those who live for scandal will not whisper about the possibilities?"

This gave Lord Gifford pause for thought, and he found himself in reluctant agreement.

* * *

Lord Atherton had made good time, which was just as well for the Blue Bell was not a well-known establishment. Every respectable inn he enquired at disclaimed all knowledge of it, whether that was because they hoped to gain his custom he could not be sure, but eventually, he found a farmer driving a cart of turnips who had some pertinent information.

"Aye, I know of it, milord," he confirmed. "But it's not the place for a fine gentleman like you. It's a flash house, full of those on the prigging lay, yer more likely to leave with yer pockets empty than yer stomach full."

"I have no intention of dining there, and I believe I am an ill pigeon for plucking," Lord Atherton assured him. "Besides, it is just such a one as you describe that I am looking for."

"And you looking so respectable and all," the bucolic gentleman said mournfully, shaking his head. He nevertheless gave him a convoluted set of instructions which took him down a series of ever narrowing lanes until he came upon a rough-looking building on whose creaking sign he could just make out the outline of a bell through the peeling paint. It might have been a pretty inn in its day but now had several panes of glass missing from the small windows, which had been boarded up rather than replaced. The roof looked more moss than straw and driving his phaeton around the back, he found a small neglected yard where weeds had been given free rein for some time. There was, however, a serviceable barn, at present housing two horses; one a glossy chestnut, presumably belonging to Rutley, and the other a sturdy cart horse.

Within a few moments, a thickset, rather vacuous-looking young man appeared.

"Cor blimey guv'ner, that's a bang up set-up!" he said, very much impressed.

"Exactly so," agreed Lord Atherton, dropping a coin into a rather grimy hand. "See to the horses and make sure it is ready in half an hour. I don't expect to be much longer."

"Yes, sir," he breathed, gazing down at the shiny silver coin in his hand.

"There will be another of those for you when I

return, if all is in order," he called over his shoulder, feeling sure that would provide enough of an incentive for him to guard his means of escape well.

Entering the door at the back of the inn, he found himself in a narrow corridor. Before he had gone many steps, a small man with a sharp face appeared and nodded to the staircase.

"The other flash cove is up there, first room on the right," he said shortly before disappearing back into the tap room.

Lord Rutley sat in a rickety chair opposite the doorway, a pistol in his hand. He was not looking at his best. His normally pristine appearance was marred by a wilted cravat and slightly grubby shirt. His face was pale and his eyes bloodshot, as if he had been dipping too deeply into whatever limited spirits the hostelry had to offer.

"Blue ruin?" Lord Atherton said laconically, stripping off his gloves.

"As you say," replied Lord Rutley, "it's the only palatable drink this godforsaken tavern has."

"Was it really necessary to meet in such a place?"

"Beneath your touch, Atherton?" Lord Rutley sneered.

"Indeed, but I'd say you have found your level."

"Be careful, my buck," said Lord Rutley softly. "What is there to stop me shooting you and taking what I am sure you have in your pockets? And what would happen to dear Lady Hayward then?"

Clenching his fists, he fought down the almost overpowering desire to take Rutley by the throat and throttle the life out of him. "Are you really so lost to all sense of honour that you would harm a blameless young lady of quality in such a way? Where is she?" he demanded.

Rutley touched a livid red scratch that ran down one cheek, and Lord Atherton's emotions veered from pride that Belle had not taken her situation without showing fight, to fear that his subsequent treatment of her might have been less than gentle.

"A blameless young lady with claws! Besides, honour is overrated," he snapped back. "First let me see the ransom."

Disgusted, Lord Atherton reached into the voluminous pockets of his greatcoat and withdrew a jewellery case containing a set of very fine sapphires. He threw it on the floor at Rutley's feet along with two bulging bags of coins.

"There, you have it. Now for God's sake, man, where is Belle?"

"All in good time," Rutley murmured. "Sit on the bed over there. I cannot promise the blanket is entirely free from fleas, but I am sure you will endure it."

He waited until his instructions had been followed before retrieving the items before him. After a brief inspection, he nodded, satisfied.

"My own jewels were returned, you know. The irony of it was they were only paste copies! Something tells me these are not, however."

"They are genuine," snapped Lord Atherton. "Now it is time for you to keep your side of the bargain."

"Indeed. I am afraid I am going to borrow your phaeton, my dear chap, as your finely matched bays, will get me out of this damned country all the quicker.

You may have my horse in return. You see, I am not entirely unreasonable."

"And Belle?" demanded Lord Atherton impatiently.

"Ah, yes. If you ride to the village of Donnington, you will find a much more respectable hostelry named The Swan. You will find a letter awaiting you which holds the information you so ardently desire."

A red mist descended upon Lord Atherton, and he launched himself off the bed.

"I wouldn't if I were you," Lord Rutley said icily. "Although I am sure you display to fine advantage, you really do not have time for fisticuffs, a barbaric sport if you ask me. If you do not collect the letter within the half-hour, you will find it has been destroyed."

That halted him in his tracks. "How did you know when I would arrive?"

Lord Rutley smiled thinly. "You young are all so impetuous. It really was not very hard to conclude that you would leave Atherton immediately and driving like the devil, I imagine. Now time is ticking, shall we?" he said politely, nodding towards the door. "After you, dear chap."

Rapidly calculating in his head, Lord Atherton estimated that he would just make it. He only hoped that the others had been able to locate the place and cut off Rutley's means of escape.

"Were you so sure I would come alone?" he asked as he mounted his horse.

"Your affection for your sister and dislike of scandal, combined with your undoubted arrogance, assured me that you would not fail to heed my warning. Your sister, was, after all, gone for a night, albeit untouched. I cannot think you would like it known. You may perhaps have had to pacify Lord Hayward. He must, after all, have been very concerned. However, as he is not known for acts of derring-do, I felt tolerably safe from his interference."

A wry smile twisted Lord Atherton's firm lips as he remembered the crushing of the figurine beneath his boot.

"Be careful not to underestimate your opponents, Rutley. If he ever catches up with you, I would be very concerned."

Wasting no more time on him, he galloped off. Like its owner, his steed presented a fine appearance, but there was little substance beneath. He had decided to go cross country to save time, but he found he had to force the sluggish steed below him over hedges and ditches and felt quite exasperated by the time he reached the outskirts of Donnington. No wonder Rutley had wished to exchange their modes of transportation! He was not known for his sporting proclivities and had probably been taken for a flat by a quick-talking horse dealer.

The Swan was a respectable coaching inn, situated just off the village green, which boasted a pond where some of the creatures it had most likely been named after, glided peacefully. He handed the reins of the horse over to an ostler and strode into the inn. The letter was waiting for him, and he impatiently scanned its contents.

*Dear Atherton,*

*You mentioned investing in the canals, I believe, at our last unproductive meeting. I have taken your advice to heart, and so that is where you will find what you seek. I am afraid Lady*

*Hayward might not share your enthusiasm, however; rather dark, damp and cold for her taste, and who can blame her? If you search in the vicinity of Wormbridge Woods, I am sure you shall find her, eventually. Good hunting!*

*Yours Rutley.*

Cursing long and fluently under his breath so that even the ostler looked impressed, he retrieved his mount and was gone in moments. He made hell for leather for Uffington Hall, or at least as close to it as his horse would allow. His mother was right, he would need Lord Gifford's knowledge of the locality and the canals if he were to find Belle.

His arrival was eagerly awaited and barely had the butler shut the door of the drawing room before his mother flew across the room and took his hands.

"You are safe," she cried thankfully. "But where is Belle?"

"He has played the scoundrel until the last, I am afraid," Lord Atherton said bitterly, withdrawing the crumpled note from his pocket and reading it to his audience.

"He is a detestable man," Lady Rosalind said in a low voice.

"Indeed," Lord Atherton concurred. "Whether this last throw of the dice was to enrage me or to give him time to escape unheeded I am unsure," he said scathingly. "Either way, I don't much care, if only you might be able to throw some light on it, sir?"

Lord Gifford nodded quickly. "If it is dark, I must assume that he is talking about one of the underground passages, and if that is so, the only one that is not being worked on at the moment is the subsidiary passage at Wormbridge Wood that has partially collapsed. He would not be able to hide her without being seen or her being discovered, anywhere else, I am sure."

"Let us go at once," Lady Atherton said impatiently, her voice trembling with emotion. "There is no time to lose! If part of the passage has collapsed already what is to stop the rest of it coming down? What my poor girl must be suffering in the dark all alone!"

"I agree with your sentiments exactly, Mother, but we will make much faster work of it if it is just Lord Gifford and I."

Lord Gifford had already had enough forethought to change into his riding gear, and so they were away in the time it took two fresh horses to be readied.

Lord Gifford led them along a winding path through the wood and down to the canal. A long, narrow boat with a prow at each end was tied up there, and Lord Atherton could see a tunnel cut into a rock face ahead of them.

Quickly tying their horses to a nearby tree, they stepped into the boat and paddled towards the tunnel. There were two doors at the entrance which swung inwards as the prow of the boat came into contact with them. As they closed behind them, it was as if they had stepped into another world; gone were the bright sunlight and cheerful birdsong, and they were cast into an intense, inky darkness.

In a few moments, Lord Gifford had retrieved the tinderbox he had brought and lit the candle lantern that had been in the bottom of the boat. This served only to make the darkness ahead more profound and cast eerie shadows on the damp, dripping walls near them.

"Belle!" Lord Atherton shouted. The dismal gloom was made even more unsettling as his anxious voice returned to him in a series of ever fading, solemn echoes.

Visibility was only a few feet ahead, and so they almost passed the small rocky outcrop, but Lord Gifford swiftly turned the boat as an incongruent flash of green caught his eye.

They found Belle in a half swoon, gagged and bound upon the cold, unyielding stone. She opened eyes that looked blindly around her as her brother removed her bonds and lifted her in his arms. It seemed to take her a few minutes to focus but slowly sense returned to them.

"Georgie," she murmured, using the name she had used to call him when a young child. "I am so cold." Her teeth were chattering in her head, and she was shivering uncontrollably.

"I will have his liver for this," Lord Atherton growled as he wrapped his coat around her and stepped into the boat, cradling her on his knees. "It is all right, Belle, I have you, you are safe now."

A small, sweet smile curved her lips. "You have always rescued me, thank you. Dear Nat will be so cross. I am going to sleep now."

Sensing this was not a good idea and unable to bear seeing one who was so usually full of life, energy and mischief, lying so still, he gave her a firm shake. "No, you must stay with me, Belle, you can sleep later."

Her eyes fluttered open again. "But I am so weary."

"Even so. I need your help, Belle. I will have to carry you before me on my horse which will be a much harder task with you asleep. Besides, Rosalind managed to ride herself back home after her ordeal, you surely do not want to show less spirit than she?"

His appeal to her competitive nature worked. She frowned up at him. "I do not believe I am known for lacking spirit."

Her fond brother smiled down at her. "Then show it, my dear. You do not want Lord Gifford to think you one of those swooning females you are usually so contemptuous of."

Lord Gifford paused in his paddling to reach into the pocket of his coat. "Give her some of this," he said, passing a small hip flask to Lord Atherton.

"Here, just a small sip," he said, gently tipping some brandy into her mouth. It made her cough but seemed to revive her.

Lord Atherton took a swig himself before passing it back. Darkness had fallen by the time they pushed through the doors again, but the moon was up, and it felt almost like daylight compared with the dense black of the tunnel.

Lady Gifford had ordered water to be readied, and after warming Belle by the fire, wrapped in blankets, Lady Atherton and Rosalind bathed her and put her to bed. She was soon in a deep sleep, her breathing regular, and had regained some colour. Feeling there was nothing more to be done, the ladies returned downstairs to await events.

## CHAPTER 12

They had not long to wait. Soon footsteps were heard in the hall, and the entire party got to their feet as Lord Hayward, Sir Philip and Sir Thomas were announced. They looked tired and rather careworn. Lord Hayward had a handkerchief tied around his forearm, and it was noticeable that the knuckles of his right hand were red and swollen.

"Belle?" he demanded imperatively as soon as the door had shut behind him.

"She's safe upstairs, asleep. But I am afraid she had a tough time of it," Lord Atherton replied.

When he had given his brief recital of his part in the evening's work, Lord Hayward shook his hand.

"If ever you are in the briars, George, I am your man," he said gruffly. "Now, I am going to see my wife."

It was understandable that etiquette should have been overlooked under such circumstances, but now the men exchanged greetings with their hosts.

"I hope that scoundrel came by his just deserts,"

said Lord Gifford sternly. "If you have him incarcerated somewhere, all the better. I will know how to deal with him."

Lord Atherton had his eyes fixed on Sir Philip. It had not escaped his notice that his friend looked exceedingly grim.

"That won't be necessary, sir," he said softly. "As to his fate, I suppose that depends on your definition of justice, but I have seen too many dead men to take it so lightly."

"Dead!" exclaimed Lady Atherton, shocked. "Not that he didn't deserve it, but I would rather he lived than any of you should be had up for murder! Do not tell me Nathaniel was responsible! It would be more than Belle could bear!"

"Only indirectly, ma'am, do not disturb yourself. He did not murder him," he assured her. Turning back to Lord Gifford, he added, "Though we will need your help in tidying up, sir."

Overcoming her amazement, Lady Gifford remembered her duties as hostess and insisted that her guests should sit down and be fortified with a glass of wine before sharing their tale.

It seemed that they had had just such a difficult time locating the inn as Rutley had hoped when he had chosen it, but eventually, they had discovered its whereabouts by asking at a local farm. They had discovered that he had not many options if he stuck to the roads, and as he was not known for hunting, they felt it was fairly certain he would. He could head only for Shrewsbury, Telford or Stafford initially.

It was Lord Hayward to whom the luck, if you could call it that, fell. He was covering the smaller roads that led indirectly to Shrewsbury. He had been startled at first to see George's phaeton coming towards him but had soon realised who was driving, and sticking to the agreed plan, had sent his groom off to alert the others. However, he found when confronted with the man who had had the audacity to steal his wife, he could not stick to the rest of it, and instead of waiting for the others' arrival before he began his pursuit, he had drawn his horse across the road.

Rutley must have been mad, for he whipped his horses harder, driving them at him. His blood was up, however, and there was no way on earth he was going to let him go by. At the last possible moment, Rutley had pulled them up. He had managed to control them, just, but in doing so he had lost his advantage and found himself plucked from the phaeton in an undignified manner.

Lord Hayward had never before experienced the blood-thumping anger that had taken him over at that moment, and he found he was holding Rutley down and repeatedly punching him in the face before he knew it. That he was very likely to murder him if he carried on did vaguely cross his mind, but it was not enough to stop him.

It was a sudden sharp pain to his arm that temporarily disabled him (Rutley had had a knife concealed about his person). It was just enough of a distraction for him to try to make his escape. Ignoring the pulsating burn in his arm, Lord Hayward had hastily mounted his agitated steed and given pursuit.

Unlike Rutley, Lord Hayward was a hunting man and having acquired an intimate knowledge of the road earlier, he did not hesitate to take a high hedge into the field beyond. He knew that he would cut off at least a half a mile this way, and when he again jumped a hedge to land on the road below, he landed only a few feet ahead of a sharp bend in the road.

Rutley swept around it moments later at an insane pace. Lord Hayward could have been killed but Rutley panicked, as did his horses, and as they swerved sharply to avoid him, the phaeton slewed dramatically before coming to an abrupt halt, half in and half out of the ditch that lined the road. Rutley was thrown over the ditch and into the field beyond.

Stopping only to calm the horses, Lord Hayward had swiftly followed. His rage was still up, and he would have liked to have continued where he had left off, but what he saw had sobered him in an instant. Rutley lay unmoving, his pallor ghastly, and it had suddenly hit Lord Hayward that his neck was broken.

"We arrived soon afterwards," explained Sir Philip. "We managed to rescue the phaeton, so I drove it back, carrying Rutley with me."

"He is here?" Lady Gifford said, alarmed, looking about her as if she expected to see his lifeless body stretched out in her drawing room.

Sir Philip nodded. "I am sorry for the inconvenience, but we could hardly leave him there for the crows to peck at."

"No, no, you did the right thing," said Lord Gifford. "I will have him carried up to a room and send for the doctor, keep everything above board."

"But what will you tell him?" asked his good lady.

"Why just that these good fellows are my guests and they came across the accident whilst out for a ride.

Nothing more will be needed for the doctor, a bit of a rum fellow; looks like he lost his sense of humour and never found it again! However, I will also send for the coroner tonight, Squire Fellows. As the death was sudden, he needs bringing in. He will need to record the death formally. We will have to tell him the truth, but he is a reasonable man, and once we have the inquisition we can send Rutley home."

"I will have a cold supper laid out in the dining room, no doubt we are in for a long evening," said Lady Gifford faintly before bustling out of the room.

The doctor and the squire arrived within the hour and were in stark contrast to each other. Doctor Swallow was spare, with a long, thin face and a serious demeanour, whereas the squire was of a more portly nature, with a jovial round face dominated by a pair of bushy sandy eyebrows.

They became quite animated as he nodded at the doctor in a friendly manner. "Well met, Swallow. I see you're still looking as sour as if you'd swallowed a lemon!"

The joke was obviously an old one as the good doctor all but rolled his small, close-set eyes.

"I believe I have been sent for on quite a serious matter, sir," he said punctiliously.

"Indeed, indeed," rumbled the squire, "but let's get over heavy ground as light as we can, eh?"

The good doctor merely bowed his acquiescence.

"Well, lead on, Miles. We had better see the body first, although I had a damned good venison pie for dinner tonight and no doubt it will curdle in my stomach! Still, I'll have a good snifter of your fine brandy afterwards, which will no doubt set me to rights!"

It was not a pretty sight. Lord Rutley had always been pale but now the chalky pallor of his face jarred against the dried blood and livid bruising around his nose and eyes.

The doctor looked dourer than ever. "You did say he was thrown from a vehicle and not in a skirmish?" he asked at first sight of the body.

Lord Gifford merely nodded, exchanging a serious look with the squire as the doctor bent to examine the body. After a few moments, he straightened again. He confirmed that although Rutley's face was quite bruised, the cause of death was undoubtedly a broken neck, consistent with his having been thrown out of a vehicle, which may or may not have also accounted for his other injuries.

Having been told that Belle had got lost and come home very chilled and was in a delicate condition, he took a look at her but thankfully pronounced her to be in need of no more than some rest.

Lord Gifford was closeted with Squire Fellows for some time. On hearing the unvarnished tale, the squire, much amazed, had asked to see Belle, to verify her part in the events. Afterwards, he felt he was in need of more than one glass of sustaining brandy.

"I felt it best to tell him everything as I know it," Lord Gifford explained to the others. "He has seen Belle and is very much shocked that she should have been used in such a manner. Fortunately, it has made him very sympathetic to our situation," he said, his glance encompassing everyone but especially Lord Hayward, who had finally torn himself away from Belle's bedside with the attendance of the doctor.

"He will need to interview everyone who attended

his death. It is just a formality really. He has already seen the grooms who all confirmed what I had told him. He will see you next, Lord Hayward."

Nodding, he rose and silently left the room.

"Poor Nat is very quiet," said Lady Atherton into the ensuing silence.

Rosalind had kept very much in the background throughout the evening. The relief and happiness she had felt at the safe return of Belle and Lord Atherton had been overshadowed by the disturbing knowledge that Lord Rutley was lying dead upstairs. It had unsettled her and tapped into some of the emotions she had generally kept under a tight guard since the death of her father.

"It is a sobering thing to see a dead man who has died violently. Especially if you feel you are in some way responsible," she said softly, almost before she had realised it.

"Indeed it is," agreed Sir Philip. "As usual you say little, Lady Rosalind, but what you say is to the point and worth listening to. If we don't feel some ember of sympathy or regret when we see another's death, what is to separate us from animals?"

Rosalind blushed as she realised she had spoken her inner thoughts aloud and that all eyes were upon her. "I think I will go and check on Belle," she said, hurrying from the room.

She expected to find her new friend either fast asleep or chomping at the bit to get up. Neither possibility was, in fact, the case. Instead, she found Belle awake but pensive and unusually subdued. She was sat up against her pillows, her golden hair falling about her shoulders, looking more like the young girl she was than the society Belle she liked to play. Her quicksilver eyes, so usually full of mischief, had dimmed to the dull pewter Rosalind was more used to seeing in her elder brother.

"Rosalind." She smiled tremulously, patting the bed beside her. "Come, join me. I bet it is all horridness downstairs. Nat told me everything, is it not awful?"

Unable to resist such an affectionate appeal, Rosalind overcame her normal reserve, clambered up beside her friend and took her hand.

"Yes, it is not very pleasant, but at least it is over," she said gently.

Belle's eyes suddenly glimmered with unshed tears. "I have been such an idiot," she declared with her usual frankness. "I remember that I was so cross that I hadn't been part of your adventure with Lord Rutley, and George took me to task for wishing any such thing, assuring me that I would not have enjoyed it at all. And he was right. Rosalind, dear Rosalind, it was horrible!"

Turning to her friend, she sobbed unreservedly into her shoulder for a good five minutes before she finally hiccupped and gave a shaky laugh. "Look at me, I believe I am having the vapours. What a lowering thought when I have always scorned those ladies who are so easily overcome by the merest mischance!"

Rosalind smoothed her hair, suddenly feeling older than her years. "But you were not easily overcome, and you did not suffer the merest mischance, so on this occasion, you are allowed to cry," she replied. Then lowering her voice to a whisper, she added, "Don't worry, your secret is safe with me."

Although Belle smiled warmly at her, Rosalind could still see the trouble in her face.

"What else is worrying you?" she said calmly. "Come on, you might as well get it all off your chest."

Belle's face puckered up again but she took a resolute gulp and scrubbed quite roughly at her eyes with her handkerchief. "I have not just been an idiot," she admitted quite vehemently. "I have been a selfish, unthinking idiot!"

"Indeed!" exclaimed Rosalind with mock severity. "Welcome to the club, but you will have to get behind me in the line for that particular award!"

That did the trick; Belle's inquisitive nature was never far beneath the surface, and this brought it right back to the fore.

"I knew it!" she breathed. "I knew there was something more to your sudden arrival in our lives than my close-lipped brother would admit, but Mama warned me off from enquiring too closely because she said it would upset you greatly. Do tell me, Rosalind."

Feeling that anything was better than seeing the wounded look in Belle's eyes, she finally told her all her story. Surprisingly, she found it was less painful with each telling. But this time it gave her pause for thought. She had found Lord Rutley contemptible in all her dealings with him, but she now found herself questioning what was ever more appearing to her as her own prejudices and hypocrisy.

"You see, I am not so different from Lord Rutley after all, am I? Finding himself in a corner he tried everything in his power to gain back some sense of justice, some control of his life, as did I," she said thoughtfully.

Belle considered this for a moment, then squeezed Rosalind's hand. "No, it is not at all the same thing. You were not responsible for the position you found yourself in, and you were trying to avenge the wrongs done to a loved one. I would not have hesitated to do the same. Lord Rutley was alone responsible for his downfall and was only trying to put the blame for it on dear George's shoulders. People like him never like to accept the blame for their own actions," she pointed out with unusual perspicacity. Then she looked solemn again.

"Thank you for sharing your secret with me, Rosalind. It was a secret worth keeping. But I, I kept mine to myself from purely selfish motives," she said quietly, her hand unconsciously moving over her only slightly rounded stomach. "It is my duty and my pleasure to give my brave, darling Nat an heir, but I kept it to myself, frightened that all my pleasure, my gallivanting, would be at an end."

"It is understandable..." Lady Rosalind began, but Belle fiercely cut her off.

"No, no, it is not!" she cried. "When I was tied up in that cold, dark place, wondering if I would ever be found, I realised for the first time that it wasn't only me! I had another life inside me, one that I had ignored, one that I had placed in jeopardy for my own selfish ends. At that moment, I realised that I loved it, that more than anything in the world I wanted it to be safe and ashamed though I am to admit it, it is the first time I realised that it was more important than me!"

"No, Belle," Rosalind disagreed, "but as important as you. Without you, Lord Hayward's life would be a desert. He loves you to distraction."

A little imp of mischief once again danced into Belle's eyes. "He does, doesn't he?" She smiled. "When I saw his poor hand, I almost felt sorry for Lord Rutley. I never thought Nat was the sort to beat anyone!"

Happy to see her friend restored to some semblance of her former sense, Rosalind got up to take her leave. "You need to sleep now, and so do I!" she said.

"Wait," Belle insisted. "There is something else you should know as we are being so honest tonight."

Turning obediently back towards the bed, Rosalind raised her brows. "Such as?"

Belle began a little awkwardly, "It is something I overheard. I had not meant to listen, but that's me, incurably nosy and forever listening at keyholes!"

Rosalind waited calmly, her amber eyes fixed with the unnerving focus she had whenever she was interested in something.

"It's about my father," blurted Belle. "He didn't win any money from yours, although I understand why you thought he did. My father hated gambling. He thought it a fool's game."

"Whilst I understand that you wouldn't want to think so, Belle, his name was on the list," Rosalind said with certainty. "Not that it really seems to matter anymore."

Belle shook her head. "Well, it matters to me. I heard raised voices coming from his study the last time George was down before Papa died, and wondering what trouble he was in now, I listened outside the door. Papa was suffering with his gout, which made him out of reason cross, and when George asked him to advance him some of his allowance to purchase a new horse, Papa kicked up all sorts of dust! He ended up calling poor George all sorts of things, but when George protested that he was not as bad as a certain person my father was known to have lent a large sum of money to, he went apoplectic! He was very harsh with George, and that was the last time he saw my father before he died. I am afraid he feels he is in some way responsible as if that last argument brought on his heart attack. It is all nonsense, of course, it was just a coincidence."

Rosalind had gone very still. "Are you trying to tell me that my father was the person to whom he lent that large sum of money?" she asked quietly.

Belle nodded. "I discussed it all with Mama. Your father and mine were bosom bows when they were young, despite being quite opposite in character. Yours was the more flamboyant, mine was always quite conservative. Apparently, yours settled down quite happily when he met your mama, but when she died, he was all to pieces. My father thought that if he could but lend him enough to pay off his immediate embarrassments, he might come about."

There was an uncomfortable buzzing in Rosalind's ears. "But of course, that was just a drop in the ocean. How kind of your father. Thank you for telling me." Rosalind forced a smile. "Now, I am tired. I will see you tomorrow, sleep well."

She wasn't sure how she exited the room, having no recollection of having opened the door, but once inside her own, she sank wearily onto the end of her bed, her mind reeling, her thoughts chasing themselves around her head until she felt dizzy. Oh, what a fool she had been! Why had Lord Atherton not corrected her misapprehension in the beginning? What must Lady Atherton think of her? How could she have been so kind? Perhaps it went some way to explaining why Lord Atherton swung from friendliness to disdain when around her? Her thoughts whirled around and around in such a fashion until she felt she was in danger of losing her senses.

"My lady? Are you alright? Shall I send for someone?"

The panicked voice broke through her disordered thoughts, and she came back to herself to find Mary looking at her with great concern.

"No, no, it has just been such a very long day," she murmured.

"And so it has, my lady," Mary agreed. "Let's get you into bed, you look completely done in!"

Rosalind allowed herself to be undressed and felt soothed somewhat as Mary brushed out her long raven locks until they shone. As she thankfully sank into her soft mattress, she allowed drowsiness to overcome her. She would think about it all tomorrow, perhaps it would all make more sense then.

Downstairs, Squire Fellows joined everyone in the drawing room.

"Well well, this is a rum business," he declared. "Rutley was undoubtedly a cad, but on reflection, I do not think it will be of benefit to anybody for the full truth to come out. He is dead, and I think that is punishment enough. As regards the inquisition, I only need record the injury that caused his death, as well as the time, place and circumstances. My verdict will be accidental death caused by a carriage accident. I agree that the body may be transported tomorrow to his family home along with this document."

A collective sigh of relief went around the room. "Now, I must take my leave of you whilst the moon is still out. I should think you're all wishing me at the devil anyhow, eh?" he said. "It has been a horrible business, but it is over now. I hope to see you all again under happier circumstances."

After his departure, the party broke up. It had been a trying day for everyone involved.

CHAPTER 13

After a restless night tossing and turning, Rosalind lay staring at the gold velvet curtains that surrounded her comfortable bed. It had seemed like fate when Lord Atherton had offered her the position of companion to his mother. He had led her to believe that he wanted to make reparations to her for any harm his father might have caused her, but that had been a lie. His motives, though praiseworthily altruistic, had now placed her in a very awkward position. She was being given charity by the family she already owed so much to. She would have to return to Lucy or ask Lady Atherton to recommend her for another position. She could not impose upon them any further. Feeling that it would be bad manners to bring the subject up whilst they were all guests in someone else's house, she decided to wait until they returned to Atherton Hall and she could have a quiet word with Lady Atherton.

Everyone was rather subdued at breakfast, so Rosalind's preoccupation went largely unnoticed.

"Miles and Dorothea, I cannot thank you enough for your help and hospitality," said Lady Atherton, smiling, "but I am afraid we must get back today. Harriet and Lord Preeve will be on tenterhooks until they know what has happened."

"You are all welcome to stay," Lord Gifford offered. "I will be happy to show you those steam engines, George."

"Thank you, sir, perhaps another time. We have imposed enough for one visit."

Their journey home was without incident and rather dull. The whole party seemed overtaken by the lethargy that sometimes follows the dissipation of adrenaline and stress after tense and stirring events.

Lord Hayward rode alongside the carriage, seemingly unwilling to let his wife out of his sight, and Rosalind was filled with a bittersweet melancholy at such an obvious display of devotion. How nice it must be to have someone's whole happiness and delight dependent on your wellbeing and presence in their lives. Belle would never want for admirers, but she had something of far more value; the undoubted love and protection of a good man.

Blinking away tears, she took herself roundly to task. She was not some romantic idiot who would hanker after a knight in shining armour, she would rescue herself and somehow forge a meaningful life for herself. She would have to, she thought wryly. What man in his right senses would take on a penniless girl from a discredited family?

The party began to break up the next day; Lady Harriet and Sir Thomas had upcoming social engagements at home, and Sir Philip felt it was time he paid his estates a visit.

"So my watchdog finally feels it is safe to leave me to manage my own affairs," Lord Atherton smiled as he took leave of his friend.

"That remains to be seen, dear fellow," he returned cryptically, putting his horses to.

Lord Atherton stood still for a moment, staring after him. "Now what the devil did he mean by that?"

He was not given much leisure to think it over, however, as his two nephews tumbled out of the house, followed by his eldest sister.

"Uncle George, we have been playing St George and the Dragon, but I am the eldest, so I have to slay the dragon, don't I?" cried Harry.

"But I am named George, so it has to be me, doesn't it?" insisted his youngest nephew.

"You wouldn't be strong enough!" insisted Harry.

George frowned. "But I would kill him by tricking him. That would be possible, wouldn't it, Uncle George?"

"Enough!" said Lord Atherton with just enough hauteur to reduce them both to silence. "You would need both your qualities to slay a dragon. Strength, skill and cunning would all be necessary."

"Have you ever killed a dragon?" they asked as one.

Lord Atherton knelt down until he was on their level. "No, not a dragon, but I have seen off an enemy or two."

They tried to hide it, but they not unnaturally felt a little disappointment.

"Did you ever rescue a princess?" Harry asked hopefully.

Lord Atherton laughed. "No, not a princess, but perhaps the odd damsel in distress!"

His young admirers looked a little relieved at this.

Lady Harriet decided now was the moment to take charge and shepherded her irrepressible sons into the family carriage before turning back to her brother.

"Well done, George. You have handled most things very well," she said, kissing his cheek. "Keep an eye on that fine gal though; something is bothering her."

Sir Thomas rode up at that moment and bent to shake his hand, grinning as he caught his brother-in-law rolling his eyes. "Don't know what advice she gave you, my lad, but if I was you, I'd heed it. Not much escapes her, you know," he said, not without pride.

Lord Preeve, Lord Hayward and Belle were to stay another couple of days; Lord Preeve's leg and Belle's health being deemed too delicate yet to travel.

Lord Atherton had little occasion to speak to Lady Rosalind alone though, between reading to Lord Preeve, who wished to know how the novel ended (without the trial of having to read it to himself), and trying to bolster Belle's unusually low spirits, she was kept fully occupied and he only saw her at mealtimes.

He found her polite but withdrawn, and he found himself driven to uttering the odd provoking comment in the hope she would rise to the bait, but apart from giving him a considering look, she refused to be drawn. He finally resorted to asking his mother if she thought Rosalind unusually subdued, but on considering the matter, she had merely suggested that the recent disturbing events were enough to have sobered anyone.

Rosalind had not wavered in her determination to leave Atherton but found the idea of it an increasingly lowering thought. Each day that had passed, she had felt more like part of the family – a large, warm family – and it would be very hard to return to the lonely life she had been leading. However, the morning that she said goodbye to Lord Preeve and Belle, offering hollow promises to keep in touch, she decided to broach the subject. After all, the longer she left it, the harder it would become.

She found Lady Atherton in her kitchen garden, sitting on a bench, with her face raised to the sky and her eyes closed. They reluctantly opened as Rosalind blocked out the sun. Rosalind realised that she looked tired but firmed her resolve and plunged in.

"Dear Lady Atherton, may I speak with you?"

"Of course, my love, come sit by me." She smiled. "I must admit that although it was lovely to see everyone, it is nice to have some peace at last!"

Rosalind smiled uncertainly, she had an inkling she was about to disturb Lady Atherton's peace.

"I am considering leaving," she opened.

Lady Atherton sat bolt upright. "This is very sudden!" she protested. "Has George upset you?"

Rosalind clasped her hands in her lap and kept her eyes firmly fixed on them. "No, not at all. You have all been so kind," she said hurriedly. "And please do not think me ungrateful. I count my stay here as amongst the happiest times of my life!" She stalled and covered her eyes with her hands, briskly blinking to head off the tears that threatened. This was not going to plan; she had meant to be cool, calm and collected.

Lady Atherton put her arm around Rosalind and

leant back, pulling her with her. "This has been an eventful and emotional time for us all," she said softly. "Do you really think this is the moment to be making such important decisions?"

"I having been your guest under false pretences." Rosalind groaned. "If I had known my family was already in your debt, I would never have come."

Lady Atherton sighed, long and slow. "Then I am glad you didn't know! Do I detect the indiscreet tongue of my beloved daughter?"

Rosalind pulled herself together and sat up, turning to face her kind hostess. "You must not blame Belle. We were pulled together after everything that happened and both of us shared some confidences. Understandably, she didn't want her father to appear in an unjust light."

Lady Atherton frowned. "No, of course not. But it was your father that was in debt, not you, and as good as my husband's intentions were, he only fed fuel to the fire when he gave your father the money. It may as well have been a gift, you know, for I don't think he ever expected to get it back."

"But that just makes it worse," Rosalind cried.

"How?" countered Lady Atherton. "My husband made a bad investment, but it was knowingly and willingly done. What this has to do with you is beyond me."

Rosalind was silenced, she did not know how to answer or explain the confused feelings inside her. Finally, Lady Atherton raised her chin and made her look at her.

"Rosalind, I value your company and presence in my house. I invited you to stay as my guest, not my paid companion. If you really wish to worship at the altar of pride, stay as my unpaid companion until such time as you feel you have paid off your debt, but please do not disappear into the ether as swiftly as you came. It would make all of us extremely unhappy, and I cannot think that we have deserved that."

"No, of course not, but perhaps you could recommend me to someone else who needs a companion?" she asked tentatively.

Lady Atherton raised her brows in the haughty manner that all her children would have recognised as extreme disapproval, and her eyes became steely. She spoke in a voice Rosalind had never heard before.

"Are you suggesting that you would be happier working for someone else?"

Rosalind was no match for someone who had successfully manipulated a headstrong family for many years and swiftly backed down.

"Oh no, you must know I don't mean that!" she protested but was quelled by the raised eyebrows just as surely as her children were.

"It is my pleasure to serve you," she assured her hastily, "but I do not wish to impose upon your good nature."

"Rosalind," Lady Atherton sighed, softening. "I admit I had not realised just how lonely I was until the descent of my lively family, and although you found me enjoying a morning of peace, I know it will begin to pall before much longer."

"But you have George," she pointed out.

"For the moment," Lady Atherton smiled. "He is, at present, throwing himself into learning the business of his estates, but I cannot expect a young man of his energy to bury himself here indefinitely. He is much sought after in society, you know. He is a man possessed of good looks and fortune, so it could not be otherwise."

Seeing that Rosalind was wavering, she finished with a clincher. "Besides, if you go, he will only replace you with someone else to salve his own conscience when he is off gallivanting. I enjoy your company, my dear. I have come to depend on you in many small ways, and I do not wish to replace you with someone else."

Rosalind felt a weight slide off her shoulders. "Thank you," she said softly. "I will stay if that is what you really want and if I can be of real use."

Lady Atherton rose to her feet. "It is and you can. Whilst sitting here sunning ourselves like hothouse flowers is very pleasant, that bed will not weed itself. I'll start at this end, you take the other."

When she returned to the house sometime later, she saw Lord Atherton on his way to the stables. He was dressed impeccably as usual and aware that her gloves were slightly muddied and her dress sadly crumpled from kneeling on the grass, she would have hurried on with no more than a nod had he not stepped into her path. Irrationally, she felt irritated. Whereas she could forgive Lady Atherton for keeping the truth from her, she felt that in some way her son had made a fool of her.

"Lady Rosalind, I see you have been helping Mother in the garden," he smiled.

His acknowledgement of her disarray annoyed her even more. "It is what you brought me here for, after all," she pointed out, throwing his own words back at him through gritted teeth.

His mobile brows rose in just the same style as his mother. "Oh, we are at dagger drawing, are we? Well, hold fire, I come in peace. The curricle is now mended, and if your last expedition has not given you a distaste for it, I would be happy to continue with your driving lessons."

"How very kind of you," she replied coldly. "Your charity knows no bounds, quite the philanthropist aren't you?" She knew she was being unreasonable and rude but couldn't help herself.

"My charity?" he said abruptly.

"Yes, for what else can I think it when you brought me here knowing that my family was already so much indebted to yours?"

It was his turn to look annoyed. "Would you rather I had left you to starve in the gutter?" he snapped.

Her eyes flashed fire. "I was hardly in the gutter!"

"Well you were not many steps from it, were you?"

"How ungentlemanly of you to remind me!" Lord Atherton, not trusting himself to speak, bowed and strode off to the stables.

Rosalind was left feeling churlish and ungrateful. Frustrated, she turned away from the house and decided to go for a brisk walk to shake out her crochets.

She was punctiliously polite at dinner, forcing herself to make conversation, partly in an attempt to make up for her earlier behaviour and partly to try to fill the gap the others leaving had left behind. Her efforts were met with icy politeness and indifference.

"I am thinking of going up to town for a few days, Mother," Lord Atherton said suddenly.

"As you wish, dear," she said calmly, sending Rosalind a meaningful look. "Will you be gone long?"

"I have no firm plans, but I will keep you informed."

Rosalind was conscious of a curious mix of relief and disappointment.

"Please give my love to Belle," she said quietly.

He offered a small nod in her direction by way of reply.

"Oh, and I have just written a letter to Mrs Prowett. Would you be so kind as to arrange for it to be delivered?" she asked, determined not to be daunted.

"Of course, only let me have it tonight for I intend to be off early in the morning."

He couldn't wait to be away, she thought wryly. Who could blame him with her acting like an angry hornet?

Lady Atherton was true to her word; she kept Rosalind very busy. She took her with her on visits to tenants, to Shrewsbury shopping, taught her the delights of her garden and consulted with her on various changes she thought she might make to her sitting room. She asked Rosalind to sketch and paint the ideas so she could envisage them more clearly.

Although happy enough to be useful, Rosalind was aware of a vague feeling of dissatisfaction for which she took herself roundly to task, her present situation was a far cry from Prowett's Coffee House, after all.

A few days after Lord Atherton's departure, Rosalind found a letter laid beside her breakfast plate.

She picked it up eagerly, assuming it would be from Belle, who had promised to write. Lady Atherton entered the room a few moments later, to find her looking as if her mind was far away. She had to speak her name twice before Rosalind came out of her reverie.

"Is everything all right, dear?" she asked, pouring herself a cup of coffee. "Not bad news, I hope?"

Rosalind blinked, clearing her head. "No, yes, no, at least, I don't know."

Lady Atherton smiled wryly. "I believe I am usually fairly good at reading between the lines, but I will need a little more to go on if I am to come to any satisfactory conclusion in this instance."

Rosalind smiled ruefully. "I'm sorry, I sound horribly missish, don't I?"

Lady Atherton looked at the usually self-possessed young lady before her and noted the bewildered look in her eyes. "Would it be easier if I was to read the letter?" she suggested gently.

Rosalind handed it over. "Read it aloud, if you will. Perhaps it will make more sense to me then."

It was brief and to the point.

*Dear Lady Rosalind,*

*I have expended much time and effort in locating your whereabouts. I have some news that will be of great interest to you and would appreciate your attendance at my offices as soon as may be convenient for you.*

*Your servant,*

*Mr S. J. Creevely.*

Lady Atherton frowned down at the missive. "I understand your confusion. He is not a man of many words, is he?"

Rosalind looked anxious. "It must be something to do with my father."

"Perhaps, perhaps not," murmured Lady Atherton. "Either way, there is only one way to find out," she said decisively. "We must go to London, and there is no time like the present."

Rosalind looked startled. "There is no need to accompany me, Lady Atherton. I would not cause you so much trouble!"

But the formidable lady had already pushed back her chair. "Trouble? No such thing, I am persuaded it will do me a lot of good, and whilst we are there we can visit some furniture warehouses and source some new material for chair coverings and curtains. Come on now, go and pack. We leave within the hour."

Rosalind was beginning to see where Belle got her impetuous nature from.

They were two nights and three days on the road, and Rosalind had plenty of time to speculate as to what the summons might mean, but it was useless, of course. Finally giving up, she tried very hard not to dwell on it or what Lord Atherton's reaction might be to their unexpected arrival.

It was late afternoon when they arrived. Radcliffe opened the door, and in a heartbeat, his face turned from shock to delight.

"My dear Lady Atherton, what an unexpected pleasure. Why did you not warn us of your arrival?"

She smiled graciously, an imp of mischief dancing in her eyes. "Why Radcliffe, I like to keep you all on your toes, you know!"

The smile was returned. "I think you will find that we are always ready to receive you, ma'am."

He took both of their arrivals in his stride as did Mrs Harvey, the housekeeper.

Lord Atherton had gone out and was not expected back for dinner. Rosalind was quite thankful; she was tired, had a nagging headache and certainly did not feel up to any sort of confrontation.

After partaking of a light supper, she took herself off to bed and dropped into a deep slumber. Waking some time later, she found that as usual, once disturbed, she could not drop back off to sleep. The house was silent, and after tossing and turning for a while, she decided she would creep down to the study to find a book to read.

She listened carefully at the top of the landing, but there was no light in evidence and no sound. She glided down the stairs silently, her white nightgown billowing around her and her long dark hair falling loosely down her back. She listened for a moment at the door of the study before quietly pushing it open.

How strange it felt to be standing in this room again. She felt a twinge of shame at the memory of her last visit. She no longer felt like the avenging housebreaker of a few weeks ago, so much had happened in such a short time. Everything had seemed so black and white then; men were the enemy. They were selfish, indolent, degenerate beings with no sense of loyalty or shame.

How ignorant she had been. Her exposure to the Atherton family and their friends had forced her to re-assess. Sir Philip was an honourable man who had proved to be a brave and loyal friend. Lord Preeve did not seem to do anything useful with his life, but he had also proved to be a loyal and kind friend to her. And then there was Lord Atherton.

Rosalind thought back to her accusations against his character at the lake. She had accused him of being a gambler, but apart from the forced game with Lord Rutley, he had shown no disposition to gamble whilst at Atherton, but on the contrary, thrown himself into the business of his estates. It was true that his gambling had fuelled Lord Rutley's hatred and led to all the more alarming events of recent weeks, but Lady Atherton's words had stayed with her. *'We mustn't judge too harshly, my dear, men will often bury themselves in ridiculous distractions rather than face feelings they don't know what to do with.'* She had been talking about her father, of course, but she now realised those words could also be applied to Lord Atherton and herself.

It was what she had been doing when Lord Atherton had caught her red-handed and made her face up to her situation. She had accused him of being arrogant, a charge he was not altogether innocent of, but on consideration, his high-handedness, she realised, often sprang from a sense of his responsibilities rather than an overinflated sense of his own worth. *He thinks he can have anyone for the click of his fingers.* Well, even that was hardly surprising if he was used to being hounded by predatory females like Letitia Grey.

All this didn't excuse his frequent rudeness to her, of course, he had more than once snapped her nose off. On the other hand, it was understandable that he should have mixed feeling towards the person whose father had added the fuel to the fire of his last argument with his own parent. He had tried to extend an olive branch to her when he offered to resume her driving lessons, but she had flung it in his face, her pride wounded by the realisation of just how much she was in his debt.

Sighing, she moved over to the bookshelves that lined one wall and raised her candle to scan the shelves. It seemed someone in the family had at one time had a scholarly frame of mind. She was confronted with lines of leather-bound books, beautifully tooled with gold leaf, ranging from religious tracts, philosophies, and atlases to histories about Greece and Rome. She finally found a less dry section and passing over works by Shakespeare, Scott, Swift and Dryden, finally settled on *The Corsair* by Byron. She had just pulled the book from the shelf when a soft voice spoke behind her.

"If it be thus to dream, still let me sleep."

She turned swiftly, dropping the book, her hair flying and her lips opening in a gasp as she saw Lord Atherton framed in the doorway. He slowly advanced with careless grace, and as he came to a stop before her, she saw a wild glitter in his silver eyes. Her throat was suddenly dry, and she found she could not move. He slowly reached out and gently traced the contours of her face.

"And ne'er did Grecian chisel trace, a Nymph, a Naiad, or a Grace, of finer form or lovelier face!" he murmured before lowering his head and pressing his firm lips against hers. Her shocked gasp allowed him entry to her soft mouth, and as his tongue slipped between her lips, she found herself momentarily overcome with a myriad of new sensations. Her breasts felt suddenly heavy, and an arrow of intense pleasure shot down to her core. Her instinct was to press herself closer against him, but the candle came to her rescue. Some of the hot wax dripped onto her fingertips, its sharp burn recalling her to her senses. She stepped back, and Lord Atherton opened eyes of molten liquid. Holding the candle between them in one slightly shaking hand, she burst into speech.

"My lord," she said quickly. "I have taken you by surprise, but I am no dream or Nymph, it is I, Rosalind. Your mother and I arrived this afternoon!"

Mention of his mother seemed to do the trick. He shook his head as if to clear it and ran his hand through his thick curls, his gaze recovering some of its usual lucidity.

"Lady Rosalind," he said slowly, taking a step back and offering her a small bow. "Forgive me. I am afraid I have been imbibing rather heavily this evening, and when I came upon you, I felt I must be dreaming. No offence was intended."

"I understand," she said with quiet dignity. "I will see you in the morning, sir."

With that, she fled back to her own room as quickly as her shaking legs would allow. Sinking onto her bed, she traced her full, swollen lips with her fingertips, a small, amazed smile curving them. It was going to be awkward tomorrow, but it would be useless to deceive herself into thinking she hadn't enjoyed it. She had seen enough inebriated young men in their cups from her bedroom window when she was staying with Lucy to set any store by the event. Although Lord Atherton had spoken beautiful words to her, she was sure he had not been in his rightful senses and fairly certain that he had not even recognised her.

The first part of her surmise may have been

correct, but the second was far wide of the mark. At that moment, Lord Atherton was in his own chamber, vigorously washing his face in a basin of cold water. Rubbing fiercely at his face with a towel, he cursed long and fluently under his breath. She had been a thorn lodged deep within his flesh ever since he had met her. Always fiercely attracted to her, the knowledge that she was under his family's protection and an innocent who had yet seen nothing of the world in which she was supposed to move, had held him in check.

Her evident resentment of his handling of the situation concerning her father, and the forced intimacy that remaining at Atherton would have engendered, had precipitated his bolt to town. It had been supposed to provide him with enough distraction to forget her but the blatant, simpering attentions he was on the receiving end of from the more experienced society damsels had left him cold.

Rosalind's strange mixture of self-possession and innocence was captivating. Embarrassed by situations other society damsels would have carried with aplomb, yet intrepid whenever danger threatened, where they would have had the vapours. What the hell was she doing here anyway? Why had his mother not informed him of their impending arrival? Tonight would never have happened if he had been expecting to see her. He prided himself on being a gentleman, and therefore, would never attempt to seduce a lady of quality, particularly one staying in his house. However, arriving on the threshold of his study, he had seen the ghostlike figure that had been haunting him for the last few days, all floating nightgown and ebony hair. And when she had turned, those luscious lips parting and her hair falling like a rippling black river around her shoulders, he had been drawn by an invisible thread that seemed to bind them together. He could no more have stopped himself kissing this vision than he could have stopped the sun from setting! Typically, she had accepted a situation where others would have tried to force a declaration out of him, with relative equanimity. He was experienced enough to realise she had also enjoyed it, which led him to believe she was not as indifferent to him as she liked to portray. For a moment, she had responded deliciously.

Groaning, he threw more cold water over his face. This was going to be a long night!

## CHAPTER 14

Lord Atherton rose unusually early and summoned a surprised Townsend.

"Is everything alright, sir?" his valet enquired solicitously, taking in the purple shadows beneath his eyes with a swift sideways glance.

"I believe it is not that unusual for me to be up at this hour," he snapped in reply.

"Well, not in the country, sir, but I admit I had not expected you up after a night on the town."

A stormy glance from beneath haughty brows had him scurrying to the wardrobe and pulling out the various garments necessary for a gentleman's morning attire.

"I do not believe I pay your very handsome wages to interrogate me first thing in the morning," he said in the deceptively soft voice all his dependents knew not to cross. "Although you generally do me great credit, I believe I could dispense with your services if you felt my demands unreasonable."

"No, no, my mistake. I apologise, my lord," he

said, bowing deeply, however with the air of one cut to the quick.

Disgusted with himself for taking his bad humour out on his servant, he offered a conciliatory grin. "Oh, stop humbugging me, Townsend. You know you were not mistaken, now see if your talents stretch to making me presentable at this ungodly hour. I wish to see my mother before she goes down to breakfast."

Half an hour later, he knocked on his mother's door. Farrow opened it, not looking best pleased.

"My lord, your mother is not yet up and should be allowed to rest after the tiring journey she had yesterday," she protested.

"Oh, stop being such a dragon," came an amused voice behind her. "I am not in my dotage yet, you know! Come in, George."

Farrow stepped aside, disapproval etched into every line of her stiff posture and then left the room without another word.

Far from looking in her dotage, he found her sitting up in bed with a very fetching lace cap atop her golden hair. She laid down her cup of chocolate as he approached and patted the bed in invitation. There was a sparkle in her eyes and a suppressed energy about her that brought a smile to her son's face.

"Well you don't look at all knocked up, Mama. In fact, you look like you are plotting and scheming."

His mother pulled a face. "No such thing, but I have a list of shopping as long as my arm. Rosalind and I are giving my sitting room a new touch."

"And this was so urgent you came hot-foot to town without a word?" he queried.

"Well no, but Rosalind has had a letter from a

solicitor in the city, claiming he has news that she will want to know."

He let this sink in for a moment, a frown of concentration creasing his brow. "Do you think it is concerning her father?"

Lady Atherton shrugged. "It seems likely, but it was so brief it is hard to tell."

"How do you think she will take it, if it is bad news?" he asked quietly.

"Not well," admitted his mother. "She has her own share of pride, and I have already had to exert some pressure for her to remain with me since she discovered the truth about the loan Frederick made to her father."

Lord Atherton looked startled. "She wanted to leave?"

"Indeed she did, I had to persuade her that it was not her fault and that I would not relish having her replaced," Lady Atherton verified, suddenly finding her hot chocolate of interest again.

The end of this brief interview had two very different effects on its subjects; Lady Atherton once again sank back into her pillows with a pleased smile, whereas her son went down to the breakfast parlour and started pacing up and down in such an agitated manner that the servants scattered before him. If Rosalind had thought of leaving before, any bad news now received was likely to tip her into precipitate flight. Lord Atherton suddenly realised he found the thought of this completely insupportable.

Rosalind found him staring out of the window onto the square, his hands clasped behind his back. She realised that her heart was suddenly beating uncomfortably fast and took a slow deep breath. She would not be missish.

"Good morning, Lord Atherton," she said, with admirable composure.

He whirled around and pinned her to the spot with a hard, intense look that stopped her breath.

"Rosalind," he said, taking two quick steps towards her. "I have wrestled with my better self, but it is useless! Although it goes against my judgement, I must ask you if will do me the honour of becoming my wife."

Rosalind's amber eyes widened in surprise at this unexpected and not very gallant proposal. She had played a variety of scenes in her head for this first awkward meeting since the events of last night, but this one had not figured in any of them. Then, as his words sank in, her surprise was overtaken by irritation.

"Why? Because you kissed me? Do you think I am one of those manipulative ladies who would try and turn that to my advantage when I know you were not in your right mind? That is hardly flattering, my lord!"

He took another step forward and tried to take her hands, but she whipped them behind her back. She couldn't let him touch her, or she would not be able to think clearly.

He gave a sudden harsh laugh. "I am making a sad mull of it, I know, but I am trying to tell you that I love you and would be honoured if you would spend your life at my side."

Rosalind suddenly realised that in other circumstances, she would have been more than happy to hear those words, but in the present case, she could not forget the ones that had come before.

"But you love me against your better judgement, remember?" she flung back at him. "We would be in a sad case if I accepted and you came to your senses. No, I cannot accept your generous offer."

Lord Atherton looked as if he would say more, but Rosalind gave a dry laugh and started pacing the room. It had occurred to her that they were in danger of re-enacting a scene in the book she had so recently read to Lord Preeve. Elizabeth Bennett had reacted in such a way and had later regretted it. Rosalind might have had her feelings wounded by the manner of Lord Atherton's proposal, but she was fully aware that he had acted always in her best interests. Turning back to him, she took a deep breath.

"I am sorry if I sound ungrateful," she said. "I understand your reluctance. I have witnessed first-hand the lengths you will go to, to shield your family from any breath of scandal, so I suppose I should be honoured you would even consider tying yourself to someone in my circumstances."

"Your circumstances?" he queried. "I am the son of an earl, you are the daughter of an earl, thus far we are equal."

"My father..." she began, but he cut her off angrily.

"Do you really still know me so little that you think I would hold your father's mistakes as a marker against you?"

Rosalind looked confused. "But, my lord, if not that, then what?"

Lord Atherton gritted his teeth. "For God's sake, stop calling me 'my lord'. I have a name and I wish you would use it," he said, not sounding at all lover like. He stepped forward and grasped her shoulders firmly, and as he looked down into those light eyes, he saw uncertainty, confusion and vulnerability.

"You have seen nothing of the world yet," he ground out. "And I am a selfish cad to claim you for myself before you have had the chance to take your rightful place in society and been given the opportunity to look about you, to be courted by other men."

Rosalind's lips parted. "Oh," she murmured.

His eyes fell to them, and his grip on her tightened. "But I find I am such a selfish cad and do not wish to give any others the opportunity," he growled and pulled her against him, kissing her fiercely.

Radcliffe, who had entered the room unheard behind them, swiftly stepped back into the hall just as Lady Atherton came into it.

"You might want to wait a moment, ma'am," he said quietly.

She offered him a knowing smile. "I don't think so, Radcliffe," she said, stepping into the room with a light step.

"George!" she squawked in accents of outrage that would not have been out of place on any theatre stage.

Rosalind tried to step away but found herself clamped firmly against Lord Atherton's side.

"What is the meaning of this?" Lady Atherton continued sternly.

Lord Atherton had a moment of blinding clarity and suddenly realised what a master hand she had played.

He gave a wry grin. "I imagine you must know what it means."

His mother let a wide smile spread over her face.

"Well, that's alright then. I wondered how long it would take you to get round to it. Congratulations, my children."

Looking relieved, Rosalind smiled shyly. "You are happy then?"

"My dear child," Lady Atherton said, coming forward and kissing her cheek, "if you are prepared to take him on, I will be very happy, but beware, he will try to ride roughshod over you if you let him!"

"He can try," she said with a grin.

"That's the spirit," approved Lady Atherton. "Now, let's get some breakfast. We have your solicitor to visit."

Rosalind's smile faded. She turned to Lord Atherton. "If it is some horrible news, I will not hold you to your offer."

He quirked a haughty eyebrow at her. "It is a chaste experience knowing you. I had not thought myself such a fickle fellow."

"Not fickle, no," she protested quickly.

"Oh ho! What then? Do enlighten me. Arrogant? Shallow?"

"None of them," Rosalind admitted. "Proud, perhaps," she said gently.

"Madam," he said menacingly, taking her chin and turning her face up to his and dropping a light kiss on her lips, "what is sauce for the goose is sauce for the gander. Now listen carefully for I mean every word. I am not interested in the news, good or bad, and I will hold by my offer."

"Very proper, George, now if you will let the poor girl alone for a few moments, perhaps she can be allowed to eat something," said Lady Atherton with asperity, to cover how touched she really was.

He obediently held a chair out for his betrothed. "I am happy to escort you myself to see this solicitor, Rosalind," he said gently.

She shook her head. If it was some shameful news, she would rather not have him looking on. "Your mother has kindly offered to accompany me, and I think that will be best."

"As you wish," he conceded.

Rosalind felt extremely nervous as they were admitted into the offices of Mr Creevely. He was a slight man with a long thin nose on which sat a pair of small rimmed round glasses. Through them, a pair of unnaturally enlarged eyes viewed her keenly.

"Please be seated," he said, his lips quirking up slightly in an approximation of a smile.

They perched on the two upright chairs that faced his immaculately tidy desk.

"You are an extremely hard lady to find," he said, looking at her over the rims of his glasses.

"I was not aware that anyone was looking for me," Rosalind said quietly, her hands clasped firmly in her lap. "You are not, I think, the solicitor who came after my father's death?"

"No," he confirmed. "I do not act for your father."

"Who do you act for, and how did you find me?" she asked, curiosity overcoming her nerves.

He smiled. "Your father was a very late, only child. The title will die with him as he comes from a family who were either childless or only bore females. He had a cousin, Lady Brentwood, who I approached, but she made it clear that she had no interest in either your father or you. I am sorry if that is upsetting for you."

Rosalind shrugged. "It makes little difference to me. I don't know her."

"Yes, well, my general enquiries having failed, I left word with my contacts in Bow Street that if any rumour of your whereabouts be heard, I should like to be informed. It appears that you have been having an adventurous time, Lady Rosalind."

Enlightenment dawned. "Oh, the hold-up."

He nodded. "I hired one of the runners to go down to the area of Atherton House and discover if you were there."

Lady Atherton frowned. "But we received no such visitor."

Again the dry smile dawned. "No, I am a cautious man, and I did not encourage a direct approach," he admitted. "I did not want to cause any disturbance, excitement or potential embarrassment by the visit of a runner. I was not sure, after all, of Lady Marlowe's situation, and as I was not prepared to reveal the reason for the enquiry to the runner, it did not seem necessary to disturb you."

"The muffin man!" Rosalind suddenly exclaimed.

"Muffin man?" said Mr Creevely, understandably confused.

"A stocky man with narrow set eyes and a rather squashed nose," Rosalind clarified.

The solicitor looked amused at the description. "Ah, I see Mr Timms was not quite as discreet as I had hoped."

"Well, he was seen in the home wood, but we never found out what he was doing there," she explained.

Lady Atherton gave a delicate cough. "Perhaps we could get back to the main point of the interview?" she suggested.

"Ah yes, now we come back to the first part of your question, Lady Rosalind. For many years I looked after the affairs of your maternal grandfather. You have his eyes by the way."

"My grandfather?" said Rosalind, surprised. "I think I saw him when I was a small child, but I do not remember him very well."

"Well, he did not forget you. As you may be aware, he disapproved of your mother's marriage to your father. He thought him very likely to come to ruin and so set up a trust for you to be managed by me. You were to be made aware of it on either your marriage or if at any time I felt you to be in dire need of it."

Rosalind went very still, her wide, surprised eyes never leaving Mr Creevely. "He left me some money?" she asked, hardly daring to believe her ears.

He nodded his assent. "Do not think you are an heiress, however, Lady Rosalind. You have something in the region of five thousand pounds, not a fortune but enough for a nice dowry or to command some level of comfort."

"Why that is wonderful news," said Lady Atherton, "and you shall keep every penny of it, my dear. You will be so much more comfortable with a little money of your own by you."

Mr Creevely steepled his fingers. "Well, let us not be too hasty. Remember, there were two conditions attached to my releasing the trust to Lady Rosalind."

Lady Atherton gave him one of her no-nonsense stares. "So there were. I think you will find that Lady

Rosalind qualifies on both counts; she has been staying with me as my guest but is quite penniless, something I am sure you are quite aware of. As for the other matter, she has just become betrothed to my son, the Earl of Atherton. It has not been announced yet, so I am sure I can rely on your discretion, Mr Creevely."

The solicitor sat back in his chair and allowed a full, genuine smile to transform his features. It was not his habitual look; any of his staff would have been quite taken aback to see it.

"Of course. That is indeed wonderful news, please accept my heartfelt congratulations. I must admit, I am pleased the mystery of your whereabouts is cleared up, Lady Rosalind. I do not like mysteries, and to find you in such happy circumstances is more than I dared to hope."

Rosalind felt like she was floating in a pleasant dream as they left the premises. The knowledge that she wouldn't come entirely penniless to the marriage was a much needed balm to her pride.

"Well, we have much to do, my dear," said Lady Atherton, when they were in the carriage. "George must send a notice to the papers, and although we are both still in mourning, I see no reason why you should prolong the engagement, as long as you have a small, private ceremony."

"Everything is happening so fast," said Rosalind.

"Well, judging by what I saw in the breakfast parlour, I'd say that is for the best, wouldn't you? George isn't known for his patience, you know."

Rosalind blushed up to the roots of her hair, which made Lady Atherton laugh.

"Don't be embarrassed, love. I stand in place of

your own mother, and if there is anything you would like to know, you only have to ask."

Rosalind could only be thankful that they drew up in front of the house at that moment. She loved this family, but she came from much more naturally reserved stock, and it would take some getting used to.

She realised her change in status the moment the door opened. Radcliffe bowed deferentially to her.

"I hope you don't think me too forward if I offer you my congratulations, my lady," he said. "And if you wish to see my lord, you will find him in the study." He smiled and added so softly she couldn't be sure she was meant to hear it, "wearing out the carpet."

Far from seeming offended, Lady Atherton laughed and turned to Rosalind. "Go to him, my dear, he will be worried for you."

As she started walking down the hall, she heard her say, "Come with me into the drawing room, Radcliffe, we have a small dinner party to organise."

She smiled to herself; life would never be dull in this household. As soon as she opened the door, Lord Atherton came striding towards her and took her hands in his.

"Well, my love, what news?" he asked gently.

"I hardly know where to begin," she said on a sigh. "It all seems so unreal."

Misreading her sigh, he pulled her tight against him. "Never mind, my dear, you are safe, and I will deal with anything unpleasant. You don't need to worry about anything."

For a brief moment, she gave herself up to the feeling of being enveloped and protected by his strong arms, but then stepped away and smiled up into his searching gaze.

"I am not penniless, after all," she almost whispered. "I have five thousand pounds."

His reaction was not quite what she envisioned. Instead of the smile she had been expecting, he took a step back, his brow furrowing.

"Five thousand pounds?"

"Left to me by my mother's father," she explained.

He now turned from her and resumed pacing the carpet.

"George?" she said hesitantly. "Are you not pleased?"

"No, yes, no," he contradicted himself, running his hand through his hair. "Do you not realise that now that you have a respectable dowry, coupled with your beauty, your field of possible suitors has widened considerably?"

Rosalind turned away from him for a moment to hide the small grin that curved her lips. Although she now knew his words sprang from chivalry, he deserved a little punishing, just a little, for doubting her.

"Oh, I see," she murmured softly. "Perhaps you are right, it has all happened so quickly. And I never gave you an answer after all."

"No, dammit," he suddenly exploded, pulling her around quite roughly. "You are mine, do you hear? Mine!"

He crushed her lips quite brutally with his own and only gentled his assault when he felt the unmistakeable quiver of response that ran through her. Finally, he drew breath and pulled a little away. "Lady Rosalind

Marlowe, will you or will you not consent to becoming my wife?"

Reaching up, she captured his face in her hands. "Yes, dear George, I will, for if I did not, I would be the most abandoned creature alive after kissing you again!"

Breathing heavily, he grinned wickedly. "We will be married as soon as possible, my love, and then you may be as abandoned as you wish!"

Lady Atherton chose that moment to breeze through the door. She looked at them both steadily for a few moments.

"Rosalind, it is not at all the thing for you to be alone with any gentleman for so long," she said, blithely ignoring the fact that she had sent Rosalind to him. "And, George, you need to send a notice to the Gazette, I believe. Also, you need to see about purchasing a special license."

"A special license?" he echoed.

"Yes, a special license. Although I am not generally in favour of young people rushing into marriage, I believe if the proprieties are to be observed, and I insist that they are, it had better happen sooner than later!"

Lord Atherton let out a crack of laughter and kissed his mother's hand. "You are quite as outrageous as Belle, you know!"

She smiled primly at him. "I don't know what you mean, I am sure. Come, Rosalind, we have much to do."

As they reached the door, she looked over her shoulder. "Oh, and George, make sure you are home tomorrow evening, we have a few guests coming for dinner."

Lady Atherton made sure they had no more time alone, becoming the most assiduous chaperone, finding a multitude of small tasks for Rosalind to do. Her previously easy-going employer had turned into the most demanding of future mothers-in-law. She found she needed advice on planning the menu for tomorrow's dinner, that she had letters to write, but her eyes were tired and so needed Rosalind to scribe them for her, and then discovered that she had not a decent pair of gloves in the house and so they must go shopping. Rosalind was glad when she could finally fall into her bed and for the first time since her father's death, slept the whole night through in a deep, dreamless sleep.

Neither did she see Lord Atherton for most of the next day.

"Do not be offended, my dear," Lady Atherton advised her, "I have given him a few things to do."

Rosalind smiled to herself, if he was anywhere nearly as busy as she was, her primary feeling was pity, not offence.

Lady Atherton had sent out the invitations to dinner herself and was strangely reticent as to who was coming.

"Oh, just a few close friends," she said offhandedly when applied to.

Mid-way through the afternoon, she suddenly looked up from her copy of *La Belle Assemblée* and caught Rosalind smothering a yawn.

"You are tired, my dear, you must go and rest, and I will arrange a nice relaxing bath to be drawn for you," she said kindly. "But before you go, tell me, do you not think this gown hideous?"

Rosalind dutifully took the magazine and gazed down at the page opened. Two gowns were depicted, and she judged that it must be the long-sleeved pink gown with a blue satin ribbon around its waist, the front decorated with a fussy double line of pleats.

"Yes," she confirmed, "the colour would certainly not suit me, pink has never been a favourite of mine."

Lady Atherton gave a tinkling laugh. "No, not that one. I find that one quite delightful. Take a closer look at the other one."

Hiding her surprise that someone of Lady Atherton's undoubted good taste could like such a dress, she dutifully paid attention to the other one and felt her confusion deepen. Of exquisite simplicity, of soft and flowing fine white cotton with gold embroidered scrollwork down the centre, around the waist and across the low bodice, it was the sort of dress she would have loved to own.

"But this is beautiful, so understated yet so feminine. I would certainly wear such a gown as this."

Lady Atherton merely shook her head and said with an amused look, "Well, each generation has their own preferences, I suppose, now upstairs with you and rest before dinner. I will need you to be ready earlier than usual to help with the final seating arrangements."

Rosalind smiled. "I would have done so already if you had told me who was coming!"

"Ah, but I like surprises," Lady Atherton laughed.

Rosalind was not as a general rule, so keen on them. She had suffered too many unpleasant ones in her relatively short life. She was to receive another one. Just as she was about to leave the room, Radcliffe entered.

"Lady Rosalind, a Lady Brentwood has come to call. I said I would see if you were at home."

Rosalind just stared blankly, her mouth suddenly dry. Why had her father's cousin who had up until this moment shown no interest in her, come to call?

"She has probably read the notice of your engagement in this morning's paper," said Lady Atherton dryly. "Would you like me to leave you to receive her alone, my dear?"

"No!" Rosalind cried, sounding slightly hysterical even to her own ears. She took a calming breath. "No," she repeated more gently. "Please stay."

Lady Atherton gave her a reassuring smile and turned to the butler. "You may show her in now and bring us some tea, if you please."

Rosalind stood as a lady of huge proportions, dressed in vivid purple entered the room.

"Lady Brentwood," she murmured, sinking into a brief curtsey. "I am Rosalind Marlowe, and this is Lady Atherton."

Their visitor was breathing rather heavily, and her neck disappeared behind a series of double chins as she gave Lady Atherton a regal nod before turning her attention back to her distant relation.

"Please, sit down," Rosalind said, moving over to a chair near Lady Atherton.

After she had lowered her bulk onto the small sofa indicated, Lady Brentwood gave Rosalind a long, considering look from a pair of close-set, cold eyes.

"So, you are Bernard's child."

It did not sound like a compliment, so Rosalind merely nodded by way of reply.

"Well, you are at least a well-looking girl, which is how, I suppose, you have had the good fortune to contract such an eligible connection."

As she did not know how to answer that either, she was glad when Lady Atherton stepped in.

"We are very fond of Rosalind and are extremely happy to welcome her into our family," she said graciously.

"You do know, I take it, of her circumstances? That her father came to the bad end we all had predicted and disgraced the name of Marlowe before taking his own life?" she snapped. "It is just as well he had no heir, there was bad blood in his family. It is at least a name you won't have to bear with much longer," she said to Rosalind.

Rosalind felt a slow, burning anger seep through her veins. This was meant to be her relation, who should have been pleased for her, and yet was prepared to perhaps put her position in jeopardy if she could by dragging up the sordid past.

"I was very fond of my father," she said quietly.

"As was my late husband," interjected Lady Atherton. "I presume you have come to wish Rosalind well in her upcoming nuptials?"

"Yes, well, I happened to be on a rare visit to Town when I saw the notice. Thought you might like to know you had some relatives. I have two girls about your age, one of which will be making her come out next season."

"Oh, really?" said Lady Atherton, raising her

eyebrows haughtily. "And do you have a house in Town?"

Lady Brentwood coloured slightly. "No, we don't often come to Town. The hectic life doesn't really suit me or my lord. But as we seem to be Rosalind's closest relations, she might perhaps consider getting acquainted with her cousin, Cecily."

Those eyebrows rose even higher. "No doubt you think she might be able to take her about a little, introduce her to the right people and so on?" she suggested.

"Well, and why not?" Lady Brentwood blustered.

"Perhaps because," said Rosalind softly, "there is bad blood in us Marlowes. We wouldn't want to taint Cecily now, would we? In addition, you speak of family, but you have until now shown no interest in my existence or well-being. This is now my family, and I find I have no need or desire to further my acquaintance with you or yours."

She watched with some satisfaction as Lady Brentwood turned an interesting shade of puce. Getting decisively to her feet, she rang the bell. "Now, if you will excuse us, we are really very busy today. We have a wedding to plan after all."

"Why you impertinent little baggage. I should have known better than to expect anything better from a Marlowe, but I thought I'd give you a chance. If I had thought for one moment, I would be treated in such a scandalously rude fashion, I would never have come."

With perfect timing, Radcliffe entered the room.

"Good day to you, ma'am," said Rosalind with quiet dignity and swept out of the door, closely followed by Lady Atherton. By the time she had reached her own chamber, her shoulders had begun to shake.

Following her in, Lady Atherton said in a soothing voice, "There now, don't be upset by that old dragon."

But when she turned around, she was laughing. Collapsing onto her bed, she gasped out, "She was such a fright! Can you imagine a more vulgar creature?"

Lady Atherton too began to laugh. "No, a country squire's wife with no taste or delicacy if I am not much mistaken. She probably cannot afford a season in Town and thought you might do the thing for her."

Rosalind's smile wavered for an instant; it wasn't Cecily's fault that she had such a mother after all. "You don't think..."

"No!" said Lady Atherton firmly. "Now, hurry up and take that bath before it goes cold."

As she lay back in the water's warm embrace, she floated off into a half-sleep, letting her mind wander over the turn of recent events. Lucy would be amazed! She suddenly opened her eyes wide. Lucy! She should have already sent her a note, no, gone to see her, to share the wonderful news. Tomorrow, she would do it tomorrow, she decided, drifting off into a pleasant daydream once more. This time the one where she replayed the experience of being held in a very passionate embrace by her future husband.

"My lady, wake up!"

Rosalind reluctantly opened her eyes to find Mary waiting with a large towel.

"The mistress is waiting for you in the drawing room, miss," she explained.

Realising her bathwater was now tepid, she did not demur but took the towel and wound it around herself.

"What is the hurry?" she said. "The guests aren't expected for a couple of hours yet."

"I don't know nothing about that, my lady, I'm just doing as I'm told," she said, not quite meeting her eyes.

Mary helped her into her undergarments before removing the screen that had shielded her modesty. Turning, Rosalind's eyes widened in surprise. There, laid out on her bed, was an almost exact replica of the dress Lady Atherton had claimed to despise. Walking slowly forward, she couldn't take her eyes from it. Reaching out a slightly unsteady hand, she gently touched its soft folds.

"It's beautiful, isn't it miss?" chirped Mary merrily. "It was one of Lady Belle's, but she didn't think it flattered her. It came back from the dressmaker's this morning. Lady Atherton had them make a few alterations and add all that gold embroidery to it."

"But we are in mourning," Rosalind murmured regretfully.

"You're all having an evening off from mourning on account of your engagement," Mary explained.

At that moment, Farrow entered, bringing her a pair of long gold gloves; the very expensive gloves Lady Atherton had purchased on their shopping trip yesterday.

"I have been sent to help you get ready, Lady Rosalind," she explained, smiling, "and may I offer you my congratulations on your engagement."

Half an hour later, she was ready. In addition to her other gifts, Lady Atherton had sent her a present of a simple pearl necklace. Farrow stood back and surveyed her handiwork. The gold tambour work in the dress brought out the golden tones in Rosalind's arresting eyes. Her hair had been swept up onto her head except for a long strand of curls that fell over one shoulder, a single white rose placed above one ear, creating a striking contrast to her ebony locks. The dress fitted her tall, slender form to perfection and as well as the elegant gloves, one satin-tipped slipper, also in gold peeped out from beneath its hem.

Farrow sighed and gave something suspiciously like a sniff. "Never have I achieved such results with so little effort," she said, her eyes shining. "You could almost be a Grecian Goddess come to life."

Rosalind laughed, feeling quite giddy all of a sudden. "Be careful, Farrow, all these compliments will go to my head."

Farrow became brisk to cover her emotions. "Now don't talk nonsense, I've never met such a modest young lady, nor one who deserved a bit of luck more than you."

"And I've never seen one as looks as beautiful as you do!" breathed her faithful Mary. "Just wait 'til His Lordships sets his eyes on you, he'll bust a gut!"

"Mary!" Farrow admonished all business again.

"You'd be better tidying up here than using language which no lady of quality can wish to hear!"

Rosalind hid a smile, she wondered if Farrow had realised that Mary's status would rise considerably once she was married.

Just then, there was a knock on the door, and she found Radcliffe on the other side.

"I've come to escort you to the drawing room," he said formally.

"Escort me?" said Rosalind, surprised. "I believe I know the way."

"Even so," he said. "And if I may be so bold as to speak, being an old retainer of this family you know, you look charmingly, my lady."

Somewhat bewildered, she accepted his escort. The surprises that had gone before were nothing compared to what awaited her there. Lucy, attired in what Rosalind recognised as her best gown and cap, was sat awkwardly on the edge of a chair. She stood as if to address her but was beaten to it by Lord Atherton. He looked extremely elegant, wearing white pantaloons and a black swallow-tailed coat. His black waistcoat had no ornament, but a white rose to match the one in her hair.

Grasping her hands, he raised them one after the other to his lips, murmuring, "If I could write the beauty of your eyes, And in fresh numbers number all your graces, The age to come would say, This poet lies; Such heavenly touches ne'er touched earthly faces."

Touched as she was by his words, a slow, wide grin crossed her face on hearing the small sob that came from behind him. Never taking her eyes off Lord Atherton's face, she said, "Lucy, I believe you have been outdone in the quotation stakes!"

As she had hoped, he shared her amusement, and they both turned to her.

"Your turn, I believe, Mrs Prowett," Lord Atherton gently challenged.

Blinking back the tears his beautiful words had brought to her eyes, she rose to the challenge. "She is more than just a pretty face, my lord," she said. "She is more precious than rubies: and all the things thou canst desire are not to be compared unto her. Length of days is in her right hand; and in her left hand riches and honour. Her ways are the ways of pleasantness, and all her paths are peace. She is a tree of life to them that lay hold upon her: and happy is every one that can retaineth her."

A slow clapping from the fireplace followed this short speech, and for the first time since entering the room, Rosalind saw the small, rather rotund vicar who was standing by the fire.

"Excellent, Mrs Prowett, most excellent. From proverbs, I believe."

"Indeed it is," she confirmed, "verses fifteen to eighteen."

Lord Atherton bowed low in her direction. "She is all the things that I desire, Mrs Prowett," he said boldly, "although I am not sure about the 'all her paths are peace' bit."

Lady Atherton chose that moment to come forward. "Darling Rosalind, you look divine. Let me introduce you to the Reverend James Philips, he is an old friend of mine."

Rosalind duly curtsied.

"He has come to marry you."

And so she found herself the Countess of Atherton before the dinner guests arrived.

Lord and Lady Hayward were the first to put in an appearance. Belle was glowing, pregnancy obviously suited her. She hugged Rosalind fiercely. "I am so glad to have you as my sister!"

Lord Preeve and Sir Philip arrived shortly afterwards, the former walking with the aid of a very elegant walking stick. He shook Lord Atherton's hand warmly and turned a beaming smile upon the new Lady Atherton. "By j-jove you are a s-sight for sore eyes, n-never saw you l-looking lovelier! C-can't s-say I'm that s-surprised," he declared. "M-might not b-be up to every r-rig in town but it s-suddenly s-struck me when you were r-reading me that b-book, y-you two were c-carrying o-on just l-like that Miss Bennett and that W-Wickham fellow."

Rosalind laughed. "I think you mean Mr Darcy."

"I-if y-you s-say so, anyway G-George was t-turning into j-just such a r-rum f-fellow before you came on the scene. B-best thing that c-could have h-happened to him!" he declared, then cast a wary eye at his friend. "N-no offence m-meant, George."

"None taken," he grinned.

Sir Philip smiled at him. "I find you are able to manage your affairs very well, after all, George."

Turning to Rosalind, he bowed low over her hand.

"My congratulations."

"We will all dance at your wedding, next," teased Belle.

Slowly releasing Rosalind's hand, he gave a lopsided grin. "Don't wager any money on the chance," he said. "I fear the prizes most worth winning have already been claimed."

# VOLUME TWO

SOPHIE

# SOPHIE

## BACHELOR BRIDES BOOK 2

CHAPTER 1

The air in the drawing room at Danesbury Manor was so thick with tension it could have been cut as neatly as the slices of seed cake that lay untouched on the small table, next to the rather austere lady who was presently busy pouring out a cup of tea.

"So, your year of mourning is finally over, Sophie," she said, her voice as brittle as the delicate china cup she held.

Sophie winced at the wealth of insincerity and irony couched in that one word; mourning.

"Come, come, child," she continued impatiently. "You can hardly pretend that it was a love match! Your husband was old enough to have been your grandfather!"

"Great-grandfather more like!" sneered Alfred, seventh Earl of Lewisham, forgoing the tea and taking a deep gulp of claret instead. A thin, red rivulet snaked down his chin as he continued almost before he had swallowed. "Thought he'd keep me out of the succession by mounting a girl just out of the schoolroom! The miserable old goat! Cost him a pretty penny too. Would have been laughable if they hadn't been pennies that should rightfully have been mine!"

"Alfred!" his wife protested.

"Sorry, m'dear," he mumbled unconvincingly, taking another swig from his glass.

Sophie felt a bright red flush steal over her cheeks but clasped her hands tightly around her reticule, determined not to give him the pleasure of a response. They had taken an early dinner at only four o'clock, but the lack of any other company had unfortunately encouraged Lord Lewisham to join them almost immediately.

Rowena, Lady Lewisham, turned her pale, wintry gaze back towards her guest. "As I was saying, your year of mourning is now up. I cannot fault you for the quiet way you have spent it, although I own, I was surprised that you chose to stay at the Dower House rather than return home to your family. However, I should not think that you will bury yourself there for the foreseeable future? I cannot imagine what you can have been doing to amuse yourself."

Sophie took a delicate sip of tea whilst she formulated her response. 'You would know if you had ever condescended to pay me a visit,' did not seem wise. Edward had warned her to expect a cool reception from his heir and his wife. Even so, he had suggested she stay at the Dower House after his death and had provided her with an indigent distant relative, Agnes Trew, as a companion. *You must continue to develop your character and independence,* he had advised. *Go back to your family too soon, and you will be drowned in their endless needs and demands*. He would be turning in his grave at the behaviour of his nephew and his wife. Both the topic of their conversation and the style in which it was delivered, showed a lack of breeding and good manners he would have deplored.

Putting down her cup, Sophie gently stroked her reticule as if for reassurance. "Reading mostly." Ignoring the rude exclamatory noise that issued from Alfred, she continued. "But you are right. I think a change of scene would do me some good."

For the first time, Rowena's mouth approximated a smile, (if a somewhat sour one). "Ah, your mother will be pleased to have you home again."

Although she clearly could not wait to be rid of her, Sophie found it hard to take any real offence. Edward had been very keen to keep Alfred, (whom he described as a weak, snivelling, maw-worm with few morals and even less sense), out of his shoes. As two previous wives had failed miserably to furnish him with an heir before throwing off this mortal coil, he had decided on one last throw of the dice. Not wishing for the inconvenience, expense, or effort of going to Town, Edward had looked about him. Sophie had been local, young, beautiful, and came from a large, impoverished family, (the last asset being of prime importance as it had made him eminently acceptable and he had taken it to be a promising indicator of her likely fertility). To close the deal, not only had he very generously provided for her family, but he had also agreed to leave Sophie the bulk of his unentailed fortune in the event of his death – if she had not conceived at that time. Only the knowledge that her deceased spouse would have thoroughly approved of her actions, gave her the courage to drop her next words into the conversation.

"I do not intend, at present, to go to my old home."

"Oh?" said Rowena, raising an enquiring eyebrow.

"No, I am thinking of going to Town," Sophie said quietly.

The quality of the silence was now rather like the unnatural calm before a storm hits. Whilst Sophie had been living a quiet, frugal existence, Alfred had been able to keep his simmering resentment towards her under control. Now that she was free to do as she pleased, it was close to breaking point. His usually somewhat bovine gaze now resembled more that of an enraged bull.

"Town? Town?" he spluttered. "Can't wait to waste your blunt on fripperies, I dare say! Barely a year up and you are going off gallivanting, probably ready to catch some other poor unsuspecting fool in your toils, eh?"

"Alfred!" His good lady did not so much as glance in his direction, but her tone silenced him in an instant. "It is understandable that you should crave some amusement," she conceded. "Is your mother going to accompany you?"

Sophie could not fail to notice the exaggerated intonation Rowena placed on the word 'mother' or the frequency with which she used it. On the surface, her enquiries were innocuous enough, but anyone of any intelligence would have picked up the sneering condescension behind the words and the implication that she was not quite a respectable person.

"No, my husband's cousin, Lady Renfrew, has invited me up for a visit."

This time the stilted silence had a slightly stunned quality.

"Aunt Lavinia has invited you for a visit?" Alfred finally repeated slowly. "Ha! She'll eat you for breakfast!"

"Or treat you like an unpaid servant!" chimed in his wife. "I have to admit I am surprised, a high stickler, Lady Renfrew."

"Indeed, she is," Alfred agreed with some feeling. "I don't like you girl, won't pretend I do, but I wouldn't wish Aunt Lavinia on you." He had straightened his posture at her very mention. "Wouldn't stay with her if I were you. If you must go, take your mother and stay in a hotel."

Rowena gave Sophie a hard, shrewd look. "Of course," she said slowly, "everything hinges on your ambitions. If you are on the catch for another husband, Lady Renfrew will certainly be able to introduce you to the most exclusive circles."

"I do not wish for the most exclusive circles or another husband." Out of the corner of her eye, she saw Alfred slump back in his chair at her words. "However, Edward encouraged me to continue with my studies of the classical world, and I can think of no better way to do it than by travelling."

"Continue your studies?" repeated Alfred, clearly flabbergasted. "Uncle Edward married a bluestocking?"

"Well, you can view those broken bits of stone Lord Elgin dragged back from Greece," Rowena said doubtfully. "Although why anyone would want to, is beyond me. I believe they are on show at The British Museum."

Sophie knew that it would probably be better to keep the reach of her plans to herself for now. She and Miss Trew had kept themselves occupied over the last year by planning a fantastical trip, a sort of grand tour. However, neither of them had ever really expected to put that plan into action. It was only when she had received the most unexpected invitation to visit with her husband's cousin in Town, the notion that she could use her time there to acquire the various permissions and letters of introduction she would need to travel across Europe, had begun to take hold.

"Yes, I will visit The British Museum, of course, but I was thinking of travelling on the continent to see such wonders in their natural context. I have a desire to stand in the places where momentous events have happened," she asserted boldly, feeling that somehow saying the words aloud would make her plan feel real.

Alfred had begun to turn an interesting shade of purple. "Have a desire to... momentous things..." he spluttered. "A girl as green as you and a widow, travelling alone? The only momentous event likely to happen is that you will drag this name even further into the mire than you did when your grasping little hands persuaded you to bed a man who was on the verge of senility. You will end up a whore to some dispossessed poet or foreign gentleman..."

"Enough!" Rowena snapped.

Sophie was on her feet, ready to flee. She had never enjoyed brangling.

"Wait." Rowena rose and looked imperiously at her visitor. "Although I cannot condone the extreme frankness with which my husband has spoken, I must agree with his sentiments, however inelegantly expressed. You have very little experience of the world at large, and so are hardly equipped to look after yourself on such a journey. Go to London, but postpone the rest of your plans, at least until you have formed some acquaintance with whom you could travel."

Sophie had an inkling that there was more than a grain of common sense in this advice, but she was too inflamed by Alfred's grubby insinuations to back down.

"Thank you for your advice," she said stiffly. "But I will not be alone; Miss Trew will accompany me."

Sophie marched back towards the dower house with a vigorous energy not usually associated with young ladies of quality, alternately grumbling under her breath and re-reading the letter from Lady Renfrew that had been a secret source of hidden support throughout the visit. How glad she was to be leaving this place! The only thing she would miss was the library, a room in which she and Edward had spent many happy hours. She suspected it would now be largely left to gather dust. She slowed as she neared her destination and briefly closed her eyes, her mother's strident tones ringing out across the small garden in front of the house, announcing her presence.

Sending a swift prayer of thanks that she had already accepted the invitation, and so could not easily be persuaded to change her mind, she stuffed it back into her reticule. Letting herself quietly in, she cast a wistful glance at the staircase, but before she could set foot on it, her mother's piercing voice carried clearly to her ears.

"It seems to me, Miss Trew, that you cannot be a fit

person to look after my poor, widowed child. When I think of the heartache and worry I have suffered, that she should be alone at such a time with only a stranger to bear her company. My dear, sweet girl."

*Dear, sweet girl?* This, from the woman who had never missed an opportunity to criticise her, and had accused her of being a changeling on more than one occasion? Feeling it would be unfair to leave Agnes alone with her any longer, she squared her slender shoulders and reminded herself that she was no longer a schoolroom miss to be bullied or used as the repository for all her mother's countless disappointments. She was that rare thing: an independent widow of means.

Pasting on a smile that was as false as her mother's sentiment, she pushed open the door.

"Mama, what a surprise. I am sorry I wasn't here to welcome you."

That lady's already ample bosom, swelled with indignation, putting the seams of the wide-striped calico dress she wore under severe pressure. Narrow, close-set eyes swept Sophie from head to foot, making her conscious of her muddied boots and wind-swept russet hair.

"So, this is what happens when you are left to your own devices! You look quite wild! Am I a visitor of so little importance, then, that you do not feel it necessary to run upstairs and change your boots, remove your bonnet, or drag a brush through your hair?"

Sophie eyed her mother's heightened colour warily. She was clearly agitated, and experience warned her that only careful handling would prevent one of her spasms coming on.

"Mama, I didn't want to keep you waiting any longer than necessary," she explained, calmly removing the offending bonnet. "But, of course, I will run upstairs and tidy myself up."

As she reached the door, Sophie cast an apologetic glance at Miss Trew, who was sitting ramrod straight on the edge of her chair. At least her mother could find nothing to fault in her appearance – she was as neat as wax, her mousy-coloured hair pinned in a rigid bun from which not a single tendril dared escape.

"Wait!"

Used to her mother's capricious ways, she came back into the room and sat down, folding her hands neatly in her lap.

"How you did *not* expect a visit from me after that letter you sent me, I do not know! What is this about you going to stay with Lady Renfrew? If she is that condescending woman whom I met after the funeral, I cannot think what you mean by it. She looked at me as if I was something that had crawled out from under a stone!"

"If that is true, I am sorry to hear it," Sophie said. "She was very formal when I met her, but polite. The invitation came out of the blue, and I think it very kind of her to think of me."

"Kind? If that woman proves to have a kind bone in her body, I will own myself amazed!"

Feeling that anything she might say would only inflame her temper further, Sophie remained silent.

"What about your family, Sophie? Alcasta and I would be only too happy to accompany you to Town. Whilst you were in mourning, you could be of no use to us, but now you are in a position to hire a house for us all. Perhaps this Lady Renfrew could introduce us to some people? Just in a quiet way, you know. Alcasta must make her come-out next season, or she will be quite on the shelf. Some experience first would be most helpful."

*Go back to your family too soon, and you will be drowned in their endless needs and demands.*

Sophie knew a cowardly impulse to withhold her full intentions until she was far away, but conquered it. Raising her large, green eyes from the floor, she plunged in. "Before I can help any of my sisters, I need some experience of the world myself, Mama. It was Edward's wish. I intend to visit London only for a short while and then travel on the continent as far as Italy. I want to see for myself the remains of antiquity. I would love to go as far as Greece, but it is too dangerous at present as the Ottomans and Greeks are fighting over Athens..."

"You always were a selfish, unnatural girl," her mother interrupted. "Perpetually having your head in a book rather than trying to attract a potential husband or help in any useful way! Have you any idea how difficult it is to bring up – never mind out – five girls on a shoestring? No, of course you have not, and why would you care? You have not changed; you are still obstinate and ungrateful. What useful experience will you get to help your sisters, by looking at a lot of old stones or paintings that I'll lay odds are indecent, is beyond my comprehension!"

Suddenly clutching at her heart, she sank back onto the sofa. Miss Trew was on her feet in an instant with the smelling salts she seemed to think necessary that every lady should keep close to hand. Kneeling in front of the afflicted lady, she waved them under her nose.

Sophie, more used to her mother's theatrics, stood her ground. Emotional blackmail, she knew, was an open book to her. She did not miss the moment her mother surreptitiously half-opened one eye to monitor the effects of her half-swoon.

"I did my duty when I married," she stated calmly. "Edward and I did not keep secrets; I know to the last sovereign how much you benefited from my marriage, and I am happy that it was so."

She meant it. Even though her family had been willing to sell her to a man who, as Alfred had so scathingly pointed out, had been old enough to be her grandfather, she harboured no resentment. She was not of a romantic disposition and had understood it was a business transaction that benefited all parties, securing her future and removing her from an uncomfortable position in her own family's household. Her mother's only words of wisdom at the time had been to assure her that her husband was unlikely to live for many more years, especially if she did her duty by him. Sophie had failed to appreciate this advice either then, or now.

Unexpectedly, she and Edward had developed a companionable affection for each other. He was surprised and pleased to discover that behind the beautiful façade, lay a brain and an insatiable thirst for knowledge; she to realise she was to be not only allowed unlimited access to his impressive library, but that he was happy to guide and teach her.

"Oh, get off me, woman!" her mother suddenly snapped, pushing Miss Trew away and making a miraculous recovery. "Your father would rather spend his blunt on his pack of dogs or his fine horses than his family, as well you know!" she complained bitterly. "But as it is useless to argue with you, I will only say this – don't come running to us when you have committed every folly going and find yourself shunned and without a character!"

She carried on raining criticism on her daughter's head all the way to her carriage. When Sophie returned to the drawing room, she found Miss Trew still perched on the edge of her chair, pale and silent. Kneeling in front of her, she took both of her hands in her own.

"Don't set any store by it, Aggie," she said. "It is all drama, mother lives for it."

"Did you mean it?" Miss Trew asked, raising her slightly myopic gentle, grey eyes. "Are you really intending to put our plans into action?"

Sophie squeezed her motionless hands. "I know, Aggie. It is a daunting thought, is it not? However, we are two intelligent, reasonable women. Is the continent such a wild place that two modestly behaved ladies cannot quietly make their way across it without being kidnapped by a wicked count or falling into a swoon at the sight of a naked statue? Did we both not thoroughly enjoy Marianna Starke's book, *Travels on the Continent*? We planned to use it as our guide, remember?"

Miss Trew nodded her assent. "It is true that remarkable lady has made the journey more than once," she conceded. "But Sophie, I am a vicar's daughter, until I came here to live with you, I had hardly been more than a few miles from my village.

London will be a great adventure for both of us, and I am looking forward to it. Do you not think you might perhaps meet some like-minded acquaintances there with whom you could travel onwards?"

Although Sophie had found it easy to ignore Rowena, Miss Trew's echoing of her sentiments was harder to dismiss.

She laid her cheek in her friend and companion's lap. "I suppose I might be getting a little ahead of myself," she conceded, striving to hide her disappointment. "How about we give London a try and then see how we feel?"

As Agnes gently stroked the disordered locks in her lap, a stray beam of sunshine suddenly set their red and gold tints alight.

"When you get to London, I predict you will be gay to dissipation and quite happy to bask in the glory of all the admiration you will attract," she said softly. "Now, upstairs with you. It will take your maid a good half an hour to brush the tangles out of your hair!"

## CHAPTER 2

Sir Philip Bray, ex-captain of the 15th Hussars, pulled up his smart curricle outside his townhouse in Brook Street, jumped down with a liveliness that belied the fact that he had been on the road for two days and nodded for his groom, Vaughen, to carry on to the stables in the mews behind. Having spent a very pleasant few days with his friends, the Athertons, celebrating their son's christening, it might have been expected that he would be happy and relaxed. However, he took the steps up to his front door two at a time, with a restless energy that suggested otherwise.

"Pleased to have you back, sir," said his butler, accepting the impressive many-caped greatcoat and hat offered to him.

"Thank you, Stanton," he replied with his usual charming smile.

"You will find quite a pile of correspondence on your desk, sir," he said apologetically and then paused as if uncertain of quite how, or if, he should continue.

Sir Philip was surprised; it was not like Stanton to be cagey or indecisive.

"Was there something else?" he asked quietly.

"Nothing important, sir, just something a trifle irregular," he admitted.

"Go on," Sir Philip encouraged him gently.

Stanton cleared his throat. "Ah, one of the letters awaiting you was hand delivered, sir."

Sir Philip merely quirked an eyebrow.

"By a lady," Stanton finished.

"Ah, I see. Thank you, Stanton," he murmured before striding off towards the library.

Throwing himself rather carelessly into the chair behind his desk, he swung one booted leg over the arm and frowned at the large pile of missives before him. When that didn't make them disappear, he thrust out his large, but perfectly manicured hand, and scooped them up. Most of them were clearly invitations to the latest round of dinners, balls, card or garden parties or heaven forbid, musical recitals, on offer.

He hastily discarded all of them without compunction. It only raised false hopes in the breasts of all the matchmaking mamas who were, he knew, speculating on when he would finally settle down and set up his nursery. Why turning thirty was seen to be such a watershed event was beyond him, but everyone seemed to think that he would now settle down and do what they saw as the responsible or respectable thing. Even though he had just witnessed a splendid example of married bliss, he believed George and Rosalind Atherton were the exception rather than the rule, and he felt no great desire to emulate them.

That left him with three items. The first was tied

with a pink ribbon and smelled of his latest widow's perfume. He tapped it against the desk twice and then threw it on the discard pile too. He was very much afraid the lady in question was about to suffer the same fate. He had always made it clear that he was not on offer for the long-game and favoured discretion in all their dealings. It seemed she was trying to redraw the lines of engagement, but calling in person at his house was a step too far.

The next letter had his instant attention. Swinging his leg down to the floor, he leaned forwards and leant both arms on the desk, looking down at it for a long moment. The paper was crumpled and dog-eared, but he immediately recognised the rather loopy scrawl. Harry Treleven. A crooked smile twisted his lips, and he slowly relaxed back in his chair as the image of his old friend and lieutenant swam before him. Tall, with broad shoulders tapering to a narrow waist, golden hair, sapphire-blue eyes flashing with mischief and excitement, his nose aristocratic, his bearing proud — Harry had owned a dash and gallantry that were irresistible. He had not known what fear was. A superb and reckless horseman, he had risked his neck on the most dangerous brutes. He had also excelled in swordsmanship and had proved to be a first-rate shot.

He had never been the same after Waterloo. The light had gone out of those eyes, he had taken to drink, and the mischief he had gotten into had been of the more serious kind, culminating in a duel. It had been unfortunate and avoidable as the lady in question had enjoyed a string of affaires, but Harry had broken the unspoken gentlemanly code: whilst in his cups, he had been indiscreet. The much put-upon husband, Lord

Worthington, had only two choices; call him out or become a laughing stock.

As one of his oldest friends, Sir Philip had, of course, been his second. Although exasperated that his friend was behaving so recklessly, he had not been unduly concerned. Everyone had known Harry was the better shot by far, including his opponent, but they also knew he didn't have a mean bone in his body. It was expected he would delope and indeed, that had been his intention.

It was not until he had begun raising his arm that Sir Philip had noticed how much his friend's hand was shaking; he had been dipping deep again – in itself not an unusual occurrence – however, the night before a duel it was ridiculously careless, even for him. The pistol had gone off early, severely injuring his opponent. It was extremely doubtful he would last the night, and it had been up to Sir Philip to get Harry safely out of the country.

"Don't worry, old chap," he had laughed, embracing his friend before stepping onto the smuggler's vessel destined to take him across the channel. "As there is no peace to be found on the land, I will become a pirate and live by the sea!"

That had been five long years ago, and he had not heard from him since. Nor had anyone else. The irony was, the cuckold had survived his ordeal, after all.

Sir Philip blinked, and a small glass filled with a deep red liquid swam into view. Stanton must have placed it there whilst he had been wool-gathering. One of the side-benefits of ending the war with France was having access to a good wine from Bordeaux. He fortified himself with a sip before opening Harry's letter.

*Hello, old chap,*

*I hope you are thriving in the land of our birth. I expect you have a wife and a bevy of children by now.*

*After spending the last few years at sea, I have put my privateering days, and many questionable deeds behind me and have landed in Pisa. My eyes have been opened! Tower, dome, arch, and spire are my new horizon. Everywhere is colour and light, and even the voices that speak a language I don't understand, are music to my ears.*

*It is ironic that I find that damned poet, Byron, here. I, who have lived the life of a Corsair, end up in the same city as the charlatan who writes about one! His latest mistress, the Countess Teresa Guiccioli has recently arrived, so perhaps the many fair ladies of this city, who are generous and friendly to a fault, will be safe from his philandering ways.*

*I have been fortunate enough to be befriended by one of these good ladies, as I am plagued by a recurring fever which has left me low. Maria Trecoli is an angel beyond compare; without her unremitting care, I would probably have departed this life.*

*I would dearly love to shake your hand again, my friend, there is something that I need to share with you. I would risk all and travel to you if I could, but in my current state of health, it is impossible. If you are passing this way, you can find me near the quay, in lodgings at Parte di Mezzogiorno. Just ask for Maria, and you will find me.*

*Your friend, Harry Treleven*

*P.S. Perhaps you could let my mother know I am alive.*

Sir Philip sat ruminating over this missive for some time before turning to his last communication.

In sharp contrast to Harry's well-travelled document, this one was pristine, folded with precision, and had just one, neatly printed word adorning the cover. Philip. The crisp, neat strokes commandeered his attention as effectively as its author's voice always had. As usual, it was short and to the point.

*Philip,*

*I expect you are back by now and trust you will call on me at your earliest convenience.*

*LR*

Would he? He frowned down at the summons. It was certainly not convenient; the urge to make all haste to Italy was strong upon him. However, his lips curled into an affectionate smile. He would, of course. He owed his godmother too much to deny her anything. After his mother had died attempting to provide him with a sibling, who had been stillborn, he had frequently divided his summers as a child between his godmother, the Athertons and the Trelevens.

It was the usual custom to receive guests in the drawing room, but he was not at all surprised when he was shown to the library. Lady Renfrew thrived on being unusual. The more masculine surroundings of this room exactly suited her no-nonsense demeanour, as well as being the cosiest in her large townhouse.

She sat by the fire, a small glass of claret on a table beside her, along with a book, and a rather splendid gold and blue enamelled snuffbox. She wore a long-sleeved high gown of dark ruby levantine and a quite exotic gold turban upon her steel grey locks. She was still a very handsome woman with a pair of piercing silver eyes. Even though he towered over her, she nevertheless managed somehow to look at him down her long, straight nose.

"So, you finally managed to fit me into your hectic schedule," she drawled, her voice unexpectedly low for a female. "I suppose I should be grateful."

A smile of genuine amusement lit his deep, blue eyes as he crossed the room in three quick strides. He took her surprisingly delicate hand in his, swiftly dropping a kiss on it before glancing surreptitiously around the room.

"Ah, don't tell me. You have finally run out of suitors and so pine for the company of a mere godson! Or is that fat, old cockerel I found strutting around you last time, hiding behind the curtain?"

Lady Renfrew gave a low, deep chuckle. "You leave poor Percy alone. He has been my friend since before you were born!"

"He has been deeply in love with you since before I was born," he grinned. "I can't decide if he has nerves of steel or none at all!"

"Hrmph! Enough of your insolence, you are a good for nothing here-and-therian with more money than sense! It is time and more you settled down. But no, you are one of those who prefers to chase women rather than catch 'em! As for your latest, a prime article if ever I saw one!"

A slightly pained look crossed Sir Philip's face. "I suppose it is too much to hope that you will develop some subtlety in your dotage," he parried.

Lady Renfrew gave another rich, throaty laugh. "Beyond praying for! I give the word with no bark on it, as you well know. But you're right, it is none of my business and not what I asked you to visit me for."

"Asked?" he said gently.

"Oh, sit, you're giving me a crick in the neck!"

Taking the chair on the other side of the fire, he accepted the glass of claret his godmother's butler unobtrusively offered him, crossed one leg over the other and unconsciously started drumming his fingers against the armrest. None of his barely suppressed impatience passed by the eagle-eyed lady opposite.

"Open your budget!" she said. "What tom-foolery are you about to embark upon?"

As she had invited Harry to stay many times during his childhood, he had no compunction in revealing his latest news.

When he had finished, she gave him a long, considering stare. "There is, of course, no question, you must go to him and bring him home if you can. His poor mother has never been the same since he left."

"I know. I will visit her before I leave. It is the least I can do."

"Still blaming yourself, then?" his godmother sighed. "I won't waste my breath trying to persuade you otherwise, but you will have to wait a couple of days to visit Lady Treleven, she is out of town but is due back by the end of the week."

Sir Philip nodded, not at all surprised that she seemed aware of Lady Treleven's movements; little went on in Town without her somehow knowing of it.

"I have a couple of things I need to tidy up first, anyway," he said briskly, getting to his feet and bowing politely. "Oh, what was it you wanted of me, Aunt Lavinia?"

"Oh, only to give you your birthday present," she said nonchalantly, reaching for the beautiful snuffbox beside her.

"Thank you, it is..." he suddenly stopped. He had thought how lovely it was when he had given it a cursory glance earlier. It was gold, inlaid with beautiful blue panels, but as he flicked it open with a practised flick of his left hand, he discovered that instead of snuff inside, there was a small, miniature portrait. He carefully took it out and raised his quizzing glass to his eye. It was perfectly executed. Raven black hair curled attractively around the face of a young woman, and it seemed her blue eyes stared rather wistfully up at him. He could almost have been looking at a female version of himself.

"Mother," he said softly, his lips curling into a small smile. Finally, he raised his eyes and looked across at the woman who had stood in her place throughout his formative years.

"Thank you, I only have one portrait of her alone."

"Don't get all sentimental on me," Lady Renfrew said briskly, clearing her throat. "There is one, small thing you can do for me, Philip."

"Name it," he smiled.

"Amelia Feversham is giving a ball on Thursday night, I would like you to escort me to it."

The smile slipped. Lady Feversham had two unmarried daughters: Lucinda, who was painfully shy in his presence – making it nearly impossible to hold a conversation – and Harriet, who was quite the opposite, making it almost impossible for him to edge a word in. However, in this instance, he could hardly accuse his godmother of matchmaking as it was no secret that there was no love lost between them.

"There's no need for you to look blue-devilled! Amelia Feversham has hardly two sensible thoughts to rub together, and those that she does have are inane or gossip-filled. Her mother was just the same! She also has an inflated sense of her own importance, always has had! To be truthful, it pains me to gratify her by making an appearance at her ball, but I have a guest coming to stay for a few days who will need entertaining. She is my cousin's widow, and as Percy is off to Newmarket for the racing, I thought you might escort us. However, if it is too much trouble..."

Bending over her hand again, he kissed it and then her cheek. "It will be my pleasure, Aunt Lavinia, but if your cousin is anything like you, God help me!"

Not more than half-an-hour later, Lady Lewisham and Miss Trew were shown into the library.

Sophie had felt a growing amazement and excitement within her as they had made their steady progress through Town and she had experienced a snippet of the constant life and noise that filled the metropolis through the window of her carriage.

However, she had also felt increasingly nervous as they approached Berkeley Square. If she had been shown into a formal drawing room and been received with due pomp and ceremony, she would have felt out of her depth. Instead, she felt the tension at the back of her neck ease and her shoulders relax as she took in all the cosy informality of the library. Her memory of Lady Renfrew had been somewhat fuzzy, but the animadversions on her character made by Alfred, Rowena, and her mother had left her expecting the worst sort of tyrant. Only the thought that Edward had been outwardly crusty but quite likeable underneath, had given her the courage to proceed with her plans. However, she had the advantage of catching that redoubtable lady off-guard, and one glance at the slightly rumpled, sleepy figure by the fire with a book open on her lap, melted her fears.

"Lady Renfrew," she said, stepping quickly into the room and offering a quick, graceful curtsey. "Please, do not get up, you look so comfortable there. The library has always been my favourite room in the house too. How wonderful that we share a love of books."

In other circumstances, Lady Renfrew, who was indeed known as a high stickler, might have given such informality and familiarity of address a deserved set-down. But in this case, she did indeed find herself at a disadvantage. The joint effects of the claret and the warm fire had lulled her to sleep, and so she was not at her most needle-witted. Besides, it was a hard heart indeed that could remain unmoved by the warmth and vitality encapsulated in Sophie's genuine, wide smile. It transformed her already pretty face into an animatedly beautiful one. Her colouring; rich auburn hair, jade green eyes, and creamy skin were not quite in the usual style either.

"You'll do," she murmured obliquely.

CHAPTER 3

Sophie and Lady Renfrew developed an almost immediate affection for each other, perhaps more deeply felt because it was such a rare occurrence for both of them. The former because her experience had been largely confined to her own household and Lady Renfrew because she did not suffer fools gladly and found the world unfortunately populated with a great many of them. Like her deceased cousin, she found it refreshing to be in the company of a young, unaffected lady with a lively, enquiring mind. Even so, after one stimulating discussion ranging from the merits of poets as diverse as Blake and Byron, she gave Sophie a word of warning.

"Although I enjoy our talks, my dear, it would not be wise to show yourself too clever in general conversation. Tonight will be your first real introduction to society, and it would be fatal to your reception if you are seen as a bluestocking."

Sophie felt herself bristling. "As I have no great

wish to figure in society, the thought does not worry me over-much," she shrugged.

She immediately realised her mistake as she found herself on the receiving end of what some disgruntled unfortunates who had experienced it before her, had named Lady Renfrew's basilisk stare (although never to her face).

"Don't be a fool, girl!" she snapped. "What is the use of all the intelligence in the world if you have no common sense or think that book-learning can replace experience or sound advice? You know nothing of the society of which you speak! Think of Byron, whatever your personal opinion of him, the fact remains that he was courted by everyone a handful of years ago when he first published 'Childe Harold's Pilgrimage'. Foolish women even carried his miniature around to swoon over if they could not get an introduction! A few years later, he had to flee abroad or be ostracised from the very society who had put him on a pedestal. Do you really wish to follow his example? If you must go abroad, go because you want to, not because there is no better alternative."

Until that moment, Sophie had not realised how much she had enjoyed the easy affection which had developed between them. An awkward, antisocial child, she had found it difficult to develop close relationships with her mother or her sisters, with whom she had little in common.

On the outside, she had had all the advantages; her appearance and figure were pleasing, her aptitude for learning, drawing and the pianoforte were exceptional, but she had always preferred to lose herself in a book than join in with the constant quarrels and arguments of her sisters. She had often slunk away to hide in a quiet corner of the library. Her father had not minded and had even gone as far as inviting her to hide in his study once or twice – perhaps not wisely telling her that he could not blame her for seeking a retreat from all the infernal squawking that always seemed to be going on as he often did so himself.

Mistaking her quietness for meekness, her mother had thrust her into social situations she had no desire to be in and discovered the underlying streak of stubbornness that lay within. From the start, she had refused to play the game of flirtation with her would-be admirers, not because she was contrary, but because she genuinely did not enjoy it. She found she had little in common with any of them and did not find their flow of empty nothings interesting or flattering. Her husband had been the first person, apart from her governess and perhaps her father, to find no fault with her character, and his cousin, Lady Renfrew – an original herself – had also seemed to accept her for who she was. Casting herself on her knees at Lady Renfrew's feet, she took her hand in both of her own.

"I am sorry," she said, blinking rapidly to hold back the sudden, unexpected tears that threatened. "You are right, of course. I would be foolish to ignore your advice. It is just that I have never felt quite comfortable at balls and dinners where I am expected to converse without actually saying anything."

Despite her annoyance, Lady Renfrew's lips quirked into a sympathetic smile. "Well, it is a skill you must learn, my dear. Unless you are royalty or an eccentric old lady like myself, you have very little choice!"

\*\*\*

"Are you not finished yet?" said Sophie rather plaintively to her maid, Burrows.

That lady gave a heartfelt sigh and said in a no-nonsense tone, "If you would stop fidgeting as if you were sitting on hot coals, my lady, I might be able to tame these unruly tresses of yours! His late lordship, God bless his soul, hired me to make sure you always looked your best and he would turn in his grave if I let you go out looking anything less than perfect!"

Knowing this to be true, Sophie submitted but her eyes watered as yet another section of her locks was pulled and pinned quite ruthlessly.

"You'll do," Burrows finally said.

"You look beautiful," breathed Miss Trew.

Sophie had never really given too much thought to her appearance, but perhaps surprisingly, her bookish husband had. He liked beautiful things and had taken an unexpected delight in seeing her becomingly turned out. He had even sent for a seamstress to take her measurements and provided her with a quite extensive wardrobe. She had always happily donned whatever Burrows had laid out without ever really paying any great notice to her attire. However, a year of mourning had given her a new appreciation for her raiment, and as she gazed at her reflection, she smiled as she took in the details of her dress. Both striking and elegant without being ostentatious in any way, it was, at heart, a simple white round dress composed of tulle over a white satin slip. It was the trimming of tulle, chenille, and pearls at the bottom of the skirt, arranged in wreaths of corn, flowers, and roses that set it above the ordinary.

Her hair was dressed artlessly, falling in ringlets to either side of her face and adorned only by a simple spray of pearls, the motif repeated in the pearl necklace that graced her long, slender neck.

"I wish you were coming, Aggie," she said, turning towards her as Burrows briskly rolled on her white kid gloves.

"I would not know how to go on at such a grand affair," she replied, handing Sophie her wrap and delicate ivory fan. "And anyway, you have no need of me with Lady Renfrew to chaperone you. I shall be quite happy at home with a book. Now, down with you, quickly. If I am not much mistaken, I heard a carriage arrive a few moments ago."

Sir Philip had excused himself from attending dinner, feeling that he was doing more than his duty in escorting his godmother and her relation to the ball. When Sophie entered the room, he had his back to the door.

"Ah, there you are, at last, child," Lady Renfrew said, pushing herself to her feet.

Sir Philip executed a neat turn at this form of address.

"Sophie, Lady Lewisham, my cousin's widow, let me present Sir Philip Bray, my godson."

It was not often words failed Sir Philip or that his famed charm and address deserted him, but the vision standing in front of him was so far removed from the image he had formed in his mind of an older lady, not unlike his godmother, that he was left speechless for a few moments. His eyes were not so incapacitated. They swept comprehensively over the young lady before him, taking in the elegance of her figure and dress, the way the simplicity of the white brought out the rich red tones in her hair and the arresting green of her eyes.

He belatedly offered a rather stiff bow, only his innate good manners preventing him from displaying the annoyance he felt that his godmother should have played him so. If she thought for one moment, that a beautiful widow would distract him from his present purpose, she was much mistaken.

Sophie's curtsy was also rather mechanical. She had not given their escort much consideration at all, but her first impression was that his eyes almost precisely matched the blue of his elegant, swallow-tailed coat. An inane thought that irritated her and that irritation only grew when she felt his assessing glance rake her from head to toe. Sophie did not have a very high opinion of extremely handsome men. She had met a few at the local assemblies and been forced to conclude that they were often brainless and almost wholly concerned with their appearance and consequence. They were free enough with their compliments, but she felt sure it was only because it reflected well on themselves both to say them and to be seen with someone who deserved them. Unfortunately, and to the despair of her mother, she had not developed the habit of being irresistibly pleased with a young man merely because he possessed the happy art of making her pleased with herself.

It was not a promising start to their evening, but despite his annoyance at being so clearly manipulated by Lady Renfrew, it did not take the astute Sir Philip long to realise that Lady Lewisham had had nothing to do with it. He did not think vanity was one of his failings, but it was, he had to admit, an unusual occurrence for the young, beautiful ladies of his acquaintance to observe him with an expression of some disdain, rather than throwing him an arch look or one of maidenly confusion. Either way, as he did not intend to devote his evening to any beautiful young ladies, it was neither here nor there.

Once he had seen his godmother comfortably situated, he disappeared in the direction of the card room, a show of uncharacteristic rudeness which did nothing to improve Sophie's initial impression of him. If Lady Renfrew was disappointed that Sir Philip had disappeared, she did not show it and, pausing only to introduce Sophie to an eligible partner, quickly settled down with her cronies.

Sophie had thought she knew what to expect from a ball, but she very quickly realised that what passed for a ball at a local assembly in the country, was a far cry from a London affair. Lady Feversham's ballroom was of a far grander scale, and she had certainly not spared any expense.

Once she felt confident with the steps of the first country dance, Sophie marvelled at the number of beeswax candles that glittered everywhere. She estimated there must be at least three hundred of them. They were reflected in the many gilt-edged mirrors that adorned the walls, as were the many coloured satins and silks of the ladies and the shimmering jewels that graced their arms, necks, and hair. The hum of voices greeting one another, the tinkle of laughter, added to the strong scent of the many flowers that festooned the room, made Sophie's senses swim for a moment. She was quite glad when the dance came to an end, and she could partake of a refreshing draught of lemonade.

She had hardly recovered when Lady Feversham descended on her. A very attentive hostess, she insisted on introducing Sophie to a succession of eligible dance partners.

Sophie found herself thankful, for the first time, that her mother had insisted on arranging impromptu dancing sessions for both her daughters and their friends, and ensured that Sophie had attended the local assemblies. Both the country dances and the quadrille proved to be lively and surprisingly enjoyable. The novelty of dancing with strangers, the snatches of new conversation and the exertion were exhilarating. So, when Sir Philip made an impromptu check on his godmother, he found Sophie all sparkling eyes, heaving bosom, and rosy-cheeked and impulsively solicited her hand for the next dance, just as the waltz struck up.

Sophie found herself in a dilemma – she could hardly decline without appearing unacceptably rude after having danced all evening – nor did she wish to upset Lady Renfrew, yet she felt strangely reluctant to experience her first public waltz with this man. It was not just his rude appraisal when he had first met her, or the fact that he was their supposed escort and had not been near them all evening that made her hesitate. She found something undefinable about him, unsettling. As it was, Lady Renfrew decided for her.

"That's the ticket," she boomed. "You won't find a better dancer, Sophie, so off you go."

As soon as Sir Philip's arm encircled her waist,

Sophie's mouth went dry. As the music started and he swept her across the floor, their eyes locked and Sophie gave herself up to the rhythm of the dance. For quite some time, neither said a word. The other dancers became a blur to her as he led her effortlessly around the room with only the lightest of touches.

"You dance very well, Lady Lewisham," he finally said with a rueful smile.

It transformed his countenance from forbidding to charming in an instant.

"You must have been married very young," he said softly.

His words broke the spell that had bound her, which was a relief for she had been feeling strangely breathless and unlike herself.

"I was just turned nineteen when I was married, not a particularly young age at all. If you mean that I was young to be married to my husband, Lady Renfrew's cousin, I cannot disagree."

"And were you happy?" he murmured into her ear. Somehow the question felt like a caress.

Sophie nearly missed her step, surprised at such a personal enquiry. "I find your question an impertinence on such a slight acquaintance," she protested. "My happiness then or now, is none of your concern."

Fortunately, at that moment, the dance came to an end. Sir Philip bowed and returned her to Lady Renfrew. Feeling a little out of sorts, Sophie swallowed a groan as Lady Feversham appeared in front of them. This time, however, her attention was directed at Sir Philip. She had a young lady in tow. The likeness between them was remarkable, each had a long nose and a receding chin, and bright, darting eyes.

"Ah, Sir Philip, there you are. So naughty of you to wait so long to dance when there are so many young ladies desirous of a partner," she smiled indulgently, tapping him on the arm with her fan. "How fortunate for you that Harriet has a dance still free."

Sir Philip said all that was polite and dutifully rejoined the throng of dancers.

Sophie found herself unaccountably warm and light-headed, and so made her way towards the end of the room that was less crowded. Her eye was caught by a very young lady, who stood on the edge of a group of giggling girls who were surrounded by a crowd of attentive young gentlemen. She was very pretty, with bright blonde hair and limpid blue eyes, but looked uncomfortable, her face a little pale and her eyes searching the crowd as if looking for someone. They met her own briefly before moving past her. Sophie was just considering introducing herself when a very modish lady in a beautiful rose satin gown glided past her with a light step, her hands held out towards the shy wallflower. Sophie saw a small smile of relief curve the young lady's rosebud mouth, and satisfied that she had been rescued from whatever awkward situation she had found herself in, sat on a sofa that was mostly hidden by an impressive fern, displayed in a large urn.

"They say he was quite *ancient* and has left her a *fortune*."

Sophie had relaxed back into her chair and had been cooling herself with her fan, but this overheard snippet had her full attention. Snapping it abruptly shut, she peeped between the fronds of the plant. She could just make out the rather buxom form of a lady in a rather low-cut ruby coloured dress. She half-turned to her companion, revealing a countenance that would have been pretty if not for the rather petulant droop about her full lips. A gold ornament glittered in dark hair that was piled unusually high. "It is fitting is it not, that such a blatant gold-digger, should be courted by all the fortune-hunters. The tables are turned, and if she is not very careful, she will find herself caught in her own trap!" the unknown lady tittered.

The titter was returned, and Sophie saw the gloved hand of her companion wave the pretty fan she had been languidly wafting herself with, at her friend.

"It is true that at least three of her partners are known to need a rich wife, but you surely cannot include Sir Philip. He is very well-off and seemed very taken with his partner, I thought."

They carried on their slow progress around the room, and Sophie lost sight of them. Feeling somewhat deflated and even more overheated than before, she stood up quickly and stepped back around the plant and into a room that suddenly swam before her eyes. She felt her arm taken in a cool grip.

"You are not well, Lady Lewisham, here, come this way," said a gentle female voice. "You are quite safe. I am Lady Isabella Hayward. I know just what will make you feel better."

A few moments later, Sophie found herself on a cool terrace, and her vision cleared. She looked into a pair of understanding, intelligent grey eyes. It was the same good lady who had gone to the rescue of the wallflower.

"Thank you, I feared for a moment that I was going to faint."

"Yes, it is insufferably hot inside and such a sad crush, it is hardly surprising."

"I saw you earlier," said Sophie. "Approaching a young, pretty girl who looked a little distressed."

Lady Hayward nodded. "Yes, that was Miss Treleven. A lovely, young widgeon and hopelessly shy. She has been living quite secluded and to be thrown into a situation such as this is torture to her. I merely returned her to her mama but not before I had noticed you dive behind the fern! I am incurably nosy, you see, and had already determined that I would make your acquaintance!"

Sophie smiled, finding her honesty refreshing. "I am glad of it," she said. "I know so few people and have also been living quite retired from society."

"Of course, as a widow, that is to be expected. But I think you had been enjoying your evening until perhaps you overheard Lady Skeffington gossiping, as I think you were meant to."

"Like I was meant to?" Sophie echoed, bewildered.

Her new friend nodded. "You are a beautiful, young widow who is rumoured to be very well provided for. You are bound to be an object of gossip and conjecture at first, you know."

Sophie let that sink in for a moment. "But why would Lady Skeffington want me to overhear?" she asked.

"Well, do not misunderstand me. Sir Philip is a very good, very old friend of mine, and I love him dearly, but he is quite determined to remain single. I had hoped that he might follow my brother's example now that he has finally settled down, but sadly this does not seem to be his intention."

Sophie blinked, she had not thought herself in the least stupid, but she was finding this conversation quite challenging to follow.

"Are you saying that Lady Skeffington wants to marry him?"

The fair-haired lady before her laughed, revealing two very appealing dimples. "Oh, I am sure she does! She is also a widow, Lady Lewisham, who is not getting any younger, and I do not believe her jointure is overly generous." She paused for a moment as if weighing her words. "Oh, you have been married, and though it is not good-natured or quite the thing to gossip, she started it, so I will tell you. She has made the stupid mistake of thinking a taste of her very obvious charms might do the trick, where all the hordes of innocent debutantes that have thrown themselves at him, have failed!"

Sophie's mouth dropped open at such frank talk. "She is his mistress?"

Lady Hayward shook her head, her golden curls bouncing around her animated face. Leaning a little closer, she murmured, "*Was* his mistress. He has been nowhere near her tonight."

"But what has all this got to do with me? I have never set eyes on him before today."

Lady Hayward's head tilted to one side as she considered Sophie seriously for a moment. "Lady Lewisham, you appear out of the blue, just after he has terminated their arrangement. You are younger than she is, prettier than she is, and he chose to ignore all the ladies in the room until he singled you out for the waltz."

"Ah, I see," she sighed. "And were all my other partners fortune-hunters?"

Lady Hayward linked her arm again with Sophie's and smiled. "No serious fortune-hunters have been invited. However, it is true that one or two of your partners need to marry money if they are prudent. But if they were charming and agreeable, what is it to you? If a woman has beauty, she may marry money; if she has money, she does not need beauty. You appear to have both, and so you have the world at your feet! Enjoy it! Only do not be surprised if you become the target of enmity from some who are not so fortunate and of a jealous disposition."

Sophie found herself smiling back. Lady Hayward possessed a joie de vivre, that was infectious. "Well, as I am not looking for a husband and will not be in town much longer," she said, her mind made up, "you are quite right, it matters not a jot. It does not reflect well on Lady Feversham, however, for she introduced them to me as desirable partners!"

Lady Hayward nodded in agreement. "But she has two daughters of marriageable age and Sir Philip, although not a marquis or an earl, comes from an old, respectable family and is very wealthy, as well as being extremely charming and well-looking."

"Surely, money cannot be of paramount importance to her? When I think of what the candles alone must have cost tonight, never mind the refreshments!"

"I can see you have a lot still to learn about the ways of the *ton*, Lady Lewisham. It is a shame you are leaving Town so soon because I think we are destined to be great friends and I would be happy to teach you. Suffice it to say, all is often not what it seems. I have a feeling you might be a case in point, now come, tell me all about your plans, for I can sniff out an adventure a mile off."

They returned to the ballroom together and slowly made their way towards Lady Renfrew, their heads close in conversation. Lady Hayward had just extracted a promise that Sophie would write to her about her adventures when they reached her.

"Ah, I wondered where you had got to," she grumbled. "Been making friends, I see. Well, Belle used to be a sad romp, but I am glad to say she has improved greatly since she married Hayward."

Instead of taking umbrage, Lady Hayward gave a tinkling laugh and leant down to kiss Lady Renfrew's cheek.

As she straightened, Sophie saw Lady Feversham wending her way towards them with another dashing young man in tow. She glanced over at Lady Hayward with a raised eyebrow. "Is he one?" she enquired with a slight smile.

"Yes," Lady Hayward confirmed seriously. "But very charming!" she added, sending them both into peals of laughter.

\* \* \*

Sir Philip duly presented himself at the establishment of Lady Treleven. It was the second interview he had undertaken this week, and he expected it to be as unpleasant as the first. Lady Skeffington had, at first, shed despairing crocodile tears all over him, and when he remained unmoved, taken to casting hysterical aspersions on his character, manhood, and mankind in general. None of which he had felt he particularly deserved, but he had cared too little to put forward any arguments to the contrary.

Lady Treleven had had some harsh words for him in the aftermath of Harry's duel. *'So, this is how you repay a friendship of longstanding and all the hospitality you have received in my household. I have treated you almost as a second son. I survived the fight against Napoleon, only because I knew you would look after Harry as well as anyone could in such a situation. No words could describe my joy when he arrived home, alive and with all his limbs intact. Yet not only did you not manage to keep him safe, but you also helped him in his foolhardy duel and then sent him packing abroad for no good reason as it turns out! If you want to be welcome here again, find him!'*

Each word had been a dart to his heart, for every one had only echoed those he had, for the most part, already said to himself. Lady Treleven had been reclusive for some years after Harry's disappearance. It was only for her daughter's sake that she had now made a return to society, and as he avoided most social functions these days, it was years since their paths had crossed.

Acting on impulse, Sir Philip had not informed her of his intended arrival or the reason for it, and so half expected her to refuse him entrance. However, to his surprise, he was given immediate admittance, the butler not even pretending to see if she was 'at home'. He was shown not into the drawing room but escorted directly to Lady Treleven's private sitting room, where she joined him not many moments later.

She had always been a beautiful woman – Harry's extraordinary good looks had come from her – and she was still very handsome. Her bone structure would always ensure this was so, but her looks had faded, almost as if someone had gone lightly over her edges with an eraser. He was grieved to see the lines of worry and sadness that had etched themselves into her face. All this registered in barely a moment, and then, to his great surprise, he found himself caught up in a fierce hug that nearly un-manned him.

"Philip, you have come at last!" she said as she released him, only to take both his hands in her own. "Let me look at you!"

The astute blue eyes looked at him closely. "Still so handsome," she murmured, "but not as carefree as you used to be."

"Lady Treleven," he began but was immediately cut off.

"Oh, shhh, I was for too many years, Aunt Dorothea, to you, to become Lady Treleven when we are private."

He would have spoken again, but she stopped his words, putting her gloved finger to his lips. "Philip, dear Philip. I must speak before I can allow you to. Come, sit with me."

She led him to a sofa by the fire and sat next to him, still holding his hands, hers lost within his. Her eyes filled with unshed tears, giving them the shimmering brilliance he remembered and reminding him painfully of her son.

"I saw you at Lady Feversham's ball, but poor Henrietta had the headache, and I had to take her home before I could speak with you. I was hoping you would come and informed Stanley to admit you if ever you did. Philip, I am so dreadfully sorry," she paused to dash away the drops that had now spilled over onto her cheeks.

He pulled her to him, enveloping her in a bear hug from which she emerged presently with a watery chuckle. "Enough, for I fear I have ruined your beautiful coat!"

Sir Philip returned her smile with complete unconcern. "I believe I have another."

Again, she took his hands. "Philip, I am finding it hard to put into words the feelings that are in my heart, so I will simply say this. I did not mean what I said to you in the deep agonies of worry I was suffering at losing my only son in such a way. You were not to blame, no one was, and I have missed you, my second son. At first, I thought that if I could not have Harry, I wanted no one, but that was all grief and foolishness. Please, tell me you forgive me."

Sir Philip kissed first one hand and then the other of the lovely woman in front of him, feeling the deep darkness that had long dwelled within him, lighten a shade.

"There is nothing to forgive. I too am sorry," he said. "I should not have stayed away. I took your words quite literally, you see."

Lady Treleven raised her hands to cup his face. "Poor, foolish, Philip."

She watched, as a slow, wide grin transformed the sombre countenance before her. "I have found Harry," he said softly. "Or rather, he has found me!"

Lady Treleven closed her eyes. Silent tears trickled again from beneath her lashes. Sir Philip wiped them away with his own handkerchief.

"He is alive, then," she finally breathed.

He silently pressed Harry's letter into her hands, and when she had read it through several times, the narrow shoulders beneath her shawl began to shake, this time with laughter.

Sir Philip could not recall any amusing anecdotes in the missive and for a moment, was worried hysteria was setting in. The upset of seeing him and the shock of his news must have been too much.

He was considering ringing for a servant when she raised eyes brim-full of amusement. "Do not look so worried, Pip, I do not need hartshorn! It is just so like Harry, to add as an afterthought the *'P.S. Perhaps you could let my mother know I am alive,'* bit. Now I know he cannot be at death's door!"

Her first instinct was, of course, to fly to him, but she was too sensible a woman not to realise that she would only slow Sir Philip down and ruin her daughter's chance of a successful season.

She smiled confidently at him. "You will bring him home, I know."

She also insisted on giving him a large purse of money for the woman who had nursed him. "I do not know what manner of woman this Maria Trecoli may be," she said, "and I care even less. Make sure she wants for nothing!"

CHAPTER 4

When Miss Trew saw how set Sophie was on carrying out the trip they had planned, she buried her doubts and agreed to accompany her. Their visit to The British Museum to see Elgin's marbles had made quite an impression on them. The spectacle of headless and sometimes limbless statues – which nevertheless still held an echo of the grace and beauty of their original execution, and in their natural setting within the Parthenon would have served the atmosphere of decaying grandeur well – in their present situation seemed only to highlight the fact that they had been ripped from their true home. They found they had some sympathy with Byron's view that 'Dull is the eye that will not weep to see, Thy walls defac'd...By British hands'.

The visit helped define the final itinerary for their journey. At first, daunted by the vast array of sights recorded in Marianna Starke's book and how long it would take to do even a quarter of them justice, they now agreed that they would make haste through France, before enjoying the experience of the Alps and then focus their experience on Pisa, Florence, and Rome. Miss Starke assured them that Pisa had not only been founded by Romans but still held some excellent examples of classical antiquity, as well as being the place where the revival of the style in the twelfth and thirteenth centuries could be seen. She maintained that 'Those persons…who contemplate the productions of the Greco-Pisano school as the earliest efforts of the reviving arts, cannot fail to be highly gratified…'

\* \* \*

There was one other important visit that Sophie chose to make, but this time alone. It was to the offices of a Mr Pickett. He was the attorney Edward had entrusted with his business. She was conscious of the vague feeling of anxiety that always assailed her when she expected an extremely formal encounter. She was shown into a meticulously ordered office and greeted by a white-haired old gentleman in a black suit, his wrinkled face a testimony to his age. But his hazel eyes were astute, alive with intelligence, and held a lurking twinkle.

"Lady Lewisham, I am honoured to meet you," he said, bowing as far as his back would allow.

Sophie smiled. Somehow, he had put her immediately at her ease.

"I must offer my sincere condolences on the loss of your esteemed husband. Lord Lewisham was a remarkable man."

"Indeed, he was," she concurred.

"I must also congratulate you on attaining your age of majority," he said. "You are a fortunate young lady. The private fortune Lord Lewisham's uncle bequeathed to him is now yours to do with as you will. I am more than happy to continue to manage it for you, but if you feel you would prefer a younger man to take on the office, I can proffer some recommendations that might suit."

"Oh no," Sophie said. "That is not the purpose of my visit, I assure you."

She proceeded to explain her current plans. When she had finished, the twinkle was even more pronounced.

"I see," he said. "You are an intrepid young lady, and I am happy to help in any way. I will acquire the passports you need, sufficient funds for your adventure and arrange for the purchase of a carriage in France. You will be much more comfortable with your own carriage."

"Yes, I think so too," she agreed.

"However," he added. "As you do not take a relative as your escort, would you mind if I offered you a few words of advice?"

"Not at all," she replied, pleased to hear an objective voice of reason. "I would be most grateful to hear them."

"Take a male servant as well as your coachman, and make sure you impose your presence on any foreign innkeepers or officials. If you do not, you will find yourself a target for impertinence or fraud, at the very least."

Sophie thought about that for a moment and then nodded decisively. "I find your advice sensible, sir."

Mr Pickett looked pleased. He hesitated over his next words, however. "Please do not take offence, Lady Lewisham, but would you object if I offered you some advice of a more personal nature?"

She looked intrigued. "Not at all, although I cannot imagine what it might be."

He gave her a rather old-fashioned look and said in a tone more fatherly than official, "You are very young and very beautiful. I say that as an impassive observer, you understand. However, it would not be surprising if you came to the attention of some, shall we say, more worldly gentlemen?"

Sophie nodded, raising an enquiring brow.

"Well, I do not wish to cast doubt upon your judgement, my lady, but if you feel inclined towards such a one to the extent that you might consider the sacrament of marriage again, might I suggest that you consult me first, on the matter of settlements. You have a very healthy fortune, and I would like to see you well protected in such a circumstance."

"I do not intend to marry again," Sophie smiled. "But if such a thing were to occur, you may be certain that I will follow your advice."

Expecting Lady Renfrew to try to delay her departure, Sophie was both relieved and surprised when, on the contrary, she proved most helpful, giving her letters of introduction to families she knew to be in Pisa and Rome, and assisting her in acquiring a male servant, a Mr James Squires, to help and protect them on their journey.

She had found him through a charity she patronised that helped find employment for impoverished ex-soldiers. Tall and skinny, with a jaunty grin and a slightly devil-may-care attitude, Sophie was not convinced about him. However, Miss Trew reminded her gently that often all someone who had been down on their luck needed was a chance to prove themselves.

"You'll have to train him up," Lady Renfrew warned her. "I am ashamed to say that whilst we were happy enough to pack off raw recruits to throw in Napoleon's path, we were not so good at ensuring their continued well-being if they were among the lucky ones who made it home alive. Remember, not all scars are visible. Treat him with a firm but fair hand, and I am sure he will be of service to you."

Sophie took her by surprise by hugging her fiercely as she departed. "I wish you could come with us, dear Lady Renfrew. I can never thank you enough for your hospitality and kindness," she said tearfully.

Unused to, and usually disapproving of such open displays of affection, that redoubtable lady nevertheless briefly returned the embrace.

"Ten years ago, I might have come," she said briskly. "But these old bones will no longer stand the nonsense. You can thank me by returning safely and coming for a proper stay. When you have got the travelling bug out of your bonnet, we will see about getting you properly established!"

Sophie had been looking forward to her first sea-crossing, but unfortunately, it did not meet her expectations. The weather had been inclement, and within an hour of leaving port, the ship had been rolling in a most alarming manner, which had given her vertigo, followed by horrendous sea-sickness. It was a fortunate circumstance that Miss Trew had been unaffected and able to look after her with the assistance of her maid.

She had been extremely grateful when she had stepped again onto dry land, and even then, the rolling sensation and feeling of nausea had taken some time to pass.

Their way through France proved largely unproblematic; travel was again a popular past-time and everywhere was set up well to accommodate the traveller. They found the roads were largely good, and if the signs of the revolution marred the beauty and edifices of several towns, the countryside as they approached ever nearer the Alps was clothed in vineyards and had a most pleasing aspect.

It was nearing dusk as they approached Dijon and they were fascinated to see a large party of women, colourfully dressed, down by the river, chatting and laughing as they washed an assortment of garments. As suggested in their guide, they found the Hotel de Parc a comfortable establishment with a good table and excellent wine. After a satisfying night's repose, they awoke early, keen to begin their approach to the Jura Mountains. They were thwarted, however, by Squires. The availability of cheap spirits at some of the establishments they had visited, had encouraged him to over-indulge and he had subsequently delayed them on more than one occasion.

Their coachman sat quietly, his face wooden – he did not approve of Squires and tried to have as little as possible to do with him.

"You leave him to me," said Burrows grimly. "I will fetch the useless good-for-nothing wastrel myself. I promise you he will soon regret the necessity!"

As she marched off purposefully towards the stables, Sophie and Miss Trew exchanged an exasperated glance, which turned to one of sternly repressed amusement as Burrows re-appeared, pulling Squires along by his ear, his posture stooped and water dripping from his hair and face.

"A bucket of water soon put him to rights," she said with some satisfaction. "That'll teach him to go on the cut!"

Miss Trew, although not conversant with that particular term, got the general gist and decided to offer a little further encouragement in her own style, giving him a gentle but stern sermon on the evils of strong drink.

"I am sure you wish to be useful, Squires, but you would do well to observe what it says in Corinthians: 'Nor thieves, nor covetous, nor drunkards, nor revilers, nor extortioners, shall inherit the kingdom of God'. Peter also advised: 'Be sober, be vigilant; because your adversary the devil, as a roaring lion, walketh about, seeking whom he may devour.' You must mend your ways, or you will be lost."

Squires's head had begun to droop – although whether from shame or a thunderous headache was not clear.

"You will most certainly be lost," confirmed Sophie, her tone acerbic. "For unless you can give me your word that you will mend your ways and tread a more sober path, I will leave you where you stand!"

That got his attention. His head snapped upwards, his eyes widening with sudden fear. "Please, no mi'lady, do not leave me in this godforsaken land, miles from home and with nothing but the shirt on my back! I will leave off the strong stuff, I give you my word!"

"See that you do," Sophie said sternly before turning to her carriage.

Nothing that had gone before prepared them for the breathtaking, natural beauty of the Jura. As wild and sublime as promised, at times towering perpendicular cliffs hemmed them in, the claustrophobic feeling exacerbated as they passed under deep archways hewn out of the granite rock-face. This was often followed by the sudden, unexpected appearance of lush pastures or proud glades of beech or fir trees, climbing the valleys like silent sentinels to the passes beyond. Their first view of Lake Geneva and the impressive glaciers which enclosed it took their breath away, the natural magnificence and beauty that surrounded them more than compensating for any fatigue felt in achieving the prospect.

"You cannot now wish that you had not set out on this expedition!" Sophie cried, turning to her companion. "One cannot help but reflect on the insignificance of mankind when confronted with such a truly ancient and immovable landscape."

Miss Trew answered with a smile and her usual placid common sense. "The world God has created is indeed a marvel, and I must feel privileged to see firsthand some of his most sublime work. But even though we may seem insignificant, like ants crawling over a huge mound, it is the mind and labour of man that has carved these pathways through seemingly impossible terrain. God instructed us to 'be fruitful and multiply, and replenish the earth, and subdue it,' but I can quite see that it would be a feat not to be desired or contemplated, that man would or could subdue such a place as this!"

The further they went into the Alps, the more the landscape defied their imaginations. Napoleon's excellent military road allowed for good progress, and the often winding terrain, bound by rock on one side and steep precipices on the other, frequently left them unprepared for the hidden treasures just around the corner.

The pass over the Simplon was rich with imagery. A lush natural valley of rolling orchards and meadows emblazoned with flowers would be swiftly superseded by swollen waterfalls that if caught by the sun, could be turned into shifting rainbows of colour and light. At other times, peaks would be obscured by shifting cloud and mist that would lift just long enough to give a tantalising glimpse of isolated monasteries or ruined castles perched on remote outcrops, recalling to mind The Mysteries of Udolpho.

At these moments, Sophie admitted to herself that although she had always disagreed with her siblings and berated Ann Radcliffe's novel as not worthy of any consideration, she could now appreciate how such a landscape could inspire such a fertile inner imagination.

Slowly, as they climbed ever higher, the temperate weather changed. Trees no longer flourished, and those that survived were bent like old men against the bitter blasts of cold wind that blew down from the icy peaks of the mountains. Some had been uprooted and thrown one upon the other, stopping just short of a yawning abyss, reminding them that their safe passage relied upon the mercy of natural elements outside of their control. The temperature continued to plummet as they approached an impressive glacier grotto carved from the ice. As they emerged on the other side, icy sleet started to fall, and they occasionally had to stop for the coachman and Squires to clear away drifting piles of snow.

Sophie shivered and thrust her hands deeper into her muff. She was glad when they began their descent. Beneath them, a huge reservoir of water stared blindly upwards with its milky eye at the snow-filled clouds gathering above. She was heartily relieved when they reached the inn, ironically called Le Soleil, in the small hamlet of Simplon. The threatening weather had encouraged many other travellers to break their journey here, and they were lucky to engage the last remaining room. Sophie and Miss Trew would have to share the bed, with Sophie's maid on a truckle bed, jammed in one corner. However, it was clean and comfortable enough.

Unfortunately, there were no private parlours to be had, and the dining room was full to bursting with guests eager for their meal when they came down for dinner. Two long trestle tables ran almost the length of the establishment, but there was not enough space, even for two slender ladies, to squeeze themselves in. The noise, heat, and smell, from so many crammed together like cattle in a stall, was for a moment overwhelming, but the growl of Sophie's stomach outweighed such trivial disadvantages.

The proprietor, a small man with a fat stomach and an avaricious gleam in his eyes, obviously felt that no extraordinary civility was necessary when his coffers were so full. He eventually waddled his way towards them, waving one impatient hand before him as if to swat away flies. "Later, you will have to come back later."

Miss Trew immediately stepped back as if to withdraw, but Sophie grasped her arm in a tight hold. Although she did not like wrangling, neither did she like to be dismissed in such an off-hand manner. If the innkeeper had apologised and shown some regret for their inconvenience, she would have been happy to comply, as it was, his attitude, coupled with another timely reminder from her stomach that it was many hours since she had eaten, put paid to any such compliant behaviour.

Her time with Lady Renfrew had not been wasted, with a fair imitation of her basilisk stare, she looked the offending gentleman up and down as if he was something nasty that she had found on the bottom of her slipper. "It does not suit me to come back later," she said icily. "You will find us a place now."

"But Madame..." he began to protest.

"Lady Lewisham," she corrected haughtily.

Sophie was pleased to see the look of uncertainty that crossed his face. If he had thought that two ladies travelling alone would be easy to fob off, he was fast learning his mistake.

He stretched out his arms in entreaty, his tone slightly more placatory as he pleaded, "But what would Madame have me do?"

Sophie nodded to a dim corner; now the serving girl had moved, she could see a small, empty table.

"That will do."

The man before her looked even more uncomfortable. "But that is already reserved..."

"Perhaps, I could be of some assistance," came a calm, cool voice from behind her left shoulder.

A voice she had only heard during the course of one evening but which she recognised immediately. Whirling around, she gazed at the gentleman in some astonishment.

"Sir Philip, whatever are you doing here?" she burst out.

His correct bow reminded her of her manners and colouring, she dropped a swift curtsy.

Ignoring her question for the moment, he turned back to the innkeeper. "I believe I reserved a small table?"

Sophie grimaced, why had she not thought of that?

The innkeeper was all obsequious smiles now and bowed so low he almost wiped his nose on his knee.

"As you say, sir. Please, come this way."

"One moment, I believe there will be room enough for these two ladies to join me."

"But of course, it is the perfect solution," he smiled relieved, weaving his way across the crowded room with surprising agility for one so large.

Sophie turned to Miss Trew, who was looking at her in some amazement. "Oh, do not look at me like that, Agnes. It is the outside of enough that we are treated with such insufferable rudeness, merely because a man does not accompany us."

"And that is an excuse for you also to be rude?" she chided gently. "Now, I suggest we accept Sir Philip's very generous offer or retire to our chamber."

Feeling like a gauche schoolroom miss, Sophie nodded and joined him where he stood politely waiting for them.

"Sir Philip Bray, this is my companion, Miss Trew," she said, aiming for a polite but business-like manner.

His bow was deeper than was strictly necessary for a companion, and the smile that accompanied it was friendly and open.

"It is a pleasure to make your acquaintance, ma'am," he said.

It was perhaps not surprising that Miss Trew was a little flustered at such attention and consideration from such a handsome and commanding person, but Sophie was surprised to see something suspiciously like a blush creep over her cheeks.

"And it is a pleasure to meet you again, Lady Lewisham, although quite unexpected. My godmother did not mention your intended journey to me."

"Nor yours to me," Sophie countered.

"And you are travelling alone?" he prompted.

"As you see," she replied, a slight challenge in her direct gaze.

"How very..." he paused as if searching for the right word, "intrepid."

It was perhaps fortunate that the soup arrived at that moment, for Sophie thought he might as well have said foolish and felt her hackles rise. She declined the offer of cutlery from the waiter as they had followed the advice in their guide and brought their own.

Sir Philip looked amused but said nothing, turning his attention to Miss Trew. When it was discovered that her father's parish was known to Sir Philip, they enjoyed quite a comfortable cose, and it was not long before he had, with considerable adroitness, drawn out of her all the information Sophie would have been reluctant to give about their plans.

Initially annoyed, Sophie found herself relaxing as he showed no inclination to criticise them, but on the contrary, was all politeness and interest.

"So, how have you found your first experience of the mountain passes, Lady Lewisham?" he suddenly asked her, drawing her back into the conversation.

Happy to converse on such a general topic, she replied with real enthusiasm. "Words cannot fully express how the magnificent scenes I have witnessed have impressed themselves upon my imagination! I had looked forward to expanding my mind and understanding upon this journey, but I had not before realised how such a varied and sublime natural landscape could speak to something within me that goes beyond the life of the mind, that touches something almost spiritual." She suddenly laughed. "I fear I am expressing myself poorly."

Sir Philip's lips twisted into a crooked smile. "On the contrary, your eyes express your feelings as clearly as your words." For a moment, they had locked with his, burning like a green flame with an intensity that had scorched him.

"It is all God's creation, after all," Miss Trew commented quietly. "But I must say it has been a delight and an education not to know what might be waiting on the other side of every hill."

Sir Philip was silent for a moment as if lost in thought. "Wellington would not agree with you, ma'am," he said eventually. "The secret of his success throughout the wars was knowing exactly what lay on the other side of the hill!"

"Ah, a soldier. I thought as much," Miss Trew said. "You were in the Peninsula?"

The trout they were served was delicious, and they spent an enjoyable meal discussing the differences between the mountains in Portugal and The Alps. Sir Philip was happy to draw a general picture for them of conditions there but seemed reluctant to offer any personal anecdotes or expand on the reason for his journey, other than to say he had urgent business with an old friend.

He insisted on escorting them both to their chamber after dinner and even went as far as offering to act as escort for them as they made their descent into Italy. An offer which took all parties by surprise.

"You are all kindness," replied Sophie, all frigid formality again at the implied suggestion that they needed the mantle of a man to protect them. "But you are in a hurry, and we have managed very well so far. As I believe we will continue to do so, I will politely decline your very generous offer."

There was nothing for Sir Philip to do but bow and wish them goodnight.

"You do not think that it might have been a good idea to accept Sir Philip's offer, my dear?" Miss Trew asked when they were cosily tucked up in bed. "He would easily iron out any difficulties we might encounter, as he did tonight, and he is a charming companion."

Sophie turned to her, a mischievous smile lighting her countenance. "Oh, Aggie, I do believe you might be just a little bit in love with him!"

Miss Trew did not take offence, but admitted, "I should think every lady must fall a little bit in love with him. His countenance is so handsome, and he is so, so big! One cannot help but feel safe with him."

Sophie could hardly deny him his appearance, however, could not agree with the final sentiment. He had occasionally looked at her in a way that made her insides flutter, and it was not a sensation which she had enjoyed. If anything, he made her uneasy. It was then she remembered the bitter tones of Lady Skeffington at the ball.

"Tell that to his latest mistress, a widow he has discarded as he would an old coat!"

Miss Trew looked shocked, and Sophie felt a stab of remorse at destroying her rose-tinted image of him. "I am sorry, Aggie, but it is true. In accepting his offer of protection, I would perhaps save myself from the frying pan only to jump into the fire!"

If he were honest, Sir Philip was a little relieved that his offer had been declined. He was a man who generally kept firm control of his actions, with a clear head and an objective eye. These traits had saved his life and those of others, on more than one occasion. It was also true of his dealings with women. A very energetic man, it could not be expected that he would live like a monk, although his inherent honour (as well as his desire to avoid marriage), had ensured he had steered clear of innocents, and his fastidious tastes, that he gave ladies who were too loose with their favours, a wide berth.

A widow – who was used to male company and missed it – was his compromise. It was meant to be a mutually beneficial experience that harmed neither party. If he felt the lady was becoming too attached, he would end things, hopefully amicably. He was not in the business of breaking hearts.

But where had his clear head and firm control of

his actions been when he had, first, invited Lady Lewisham to waltz with him at a ball where he had had no intention of dancing, and then offered to be her escort on a journey that he really should not dally on? He found himself faintly amused when she put on her prim and proper face or when she attempted his godmother's trick of cowing someone into obedience with a haughty manner, almost as if she were trying on different roles for a play. However, his objectivity and control were unimpeded. But when her feelings were engaged and she started to talk passionately about a subject she was interested in, or when she was simply enjoying herself as she had been at the ball, her eyes lit up like emerald beacons that beckoned a man hither and halted all rational thought for a moment. He knew from bitter experience that it only took a moment of rash behaviour to create a landslide of unforeseen consequences.

Closing his eyes, he sighed deeply and tried not to think about the fact that, at that moment, she was lying in a bed just across the corridor from his own.

CHAPTER 5

The snow clouds that had looked so threatening the evening before, had obligingly moved off elsewhere to drop their load, and so Sophie and Miss Trew, not wishing to run the gauntlet of the other guests, set out early the next morning, taking some freshly baked hot rolls to eat on the journey.

The day had a grey, sombre feel to it, not helped by the towering cliffs that, at first, marked either side of the road, hemming them in – the feeling further exacerbated when they, every now and then, passed into the gaping mouth of another grotto cut through the rock. After leaving a particularly fine example, they turned an extremely sharp bend and were suddenly deafened and much startled by a violent torrent of water hurtling down into the yawning precipice that now marked one side of the road.

It was with some relief that they entered the small hamlet of Isella, a poor place, mainly consisting of a few cottages, a customs house, and a posting inn. The feeling was to be short-lived, as barely had they pulled up outside the inn when they were approached by two indolent-looking customs officers. For some reason, they did not seem pleased with their papers. Sophie tried to argue her case, but the two men before her did not seem to comprehend a word she said. Before she quite understood what was happening, one let out a low whistle and two rough-looking men in home-spun tunics with rough clogs on their feet came running up and started to throw their baggage unceremoniously into the road.

"Lawks, my lady! Whatever are they up to?" squealed Burrows, before jumping down and giving them a piece of her mind, using language that under other circumstances would have earned her a sharp telling off, but in the present case, Sophie felt far too grateful to cavil at. Squires soon joined her, but they might as well as have been addressing one of the many large boulders they had passed on their journey, for all the effect they had.

"This is ridiculous," Sophie muttered, alighting herself.

"Stop this at once!" she ordered furiously. "I am sure our papers are quite in order and insist that you put everything back immediately!"

To her consternation she found herself completely ignored, the customs men having the temerity to turn away from her, apparently admiring the view of the mountains with rapt attention as if seeing them for the first time.

Even as she spoke, their two lackeys opened her trunk and began rifling through it.

"Here, leave my Lady's things alone, you ruffians!"

screeched Burrows grabbing one of them by the arm, outraged that her careful packing was to be so disturbed. He shook her off as if she were an irritating insect, causing her to fall onto the rough road.

"You foreign, good-for-nothing bully," she cried from her prone position before bursting into tears. Squires tried to comfort her, but she rounded on him fiercely. "What use are you, you good for nothing clodpole? Leave me alone and do something for my lady!"

Goaded into action, he stepped purposefully forward but found himself floored by a giant fist, anchored to an arm that bulged with sinew and muscle.

The sound of hoof beats cantering towards them could just be heard above the din. Sophie turned her head to see three horses approaching at an impressive rate. Two had riders, and the other seemed to be carrying their baggage. A magnificent black stallion led the way.

The words she had uttered the evening before were forgotten in the rush of relief she felt as she recognised the dark hair and fine form of Sir Philip. He and the horse moved as one. She had just time to register the firm muscles that guided the great beast, (and which his serviceable leather breeches did little to hide), and that his expression was unusually forbidding before he reached them, dismounting in one fluid, graceful movement.

"Stay, Alcides," he said in a commanding tone before striding purposefully towards the two men still intent on their task.

He grabbed them roughly and banged their heads together. Grunting, they both fell swiftly to the floor.

"Sophie, get back in the carriage," Miss Trew pleaded quietly as she pointed with one shaking, outstretched finger, towards the customs men. Their attention was now entirely on the scene before them, and one had a gun pointed directly at Sir Philip, the other had a supercilious grin etched across his smug face.

Sophie gasped and felt herself begin to tremble, her treacherous limbs turning to jelly. Her instinct was to help Sir Philip, but she could not see how it could be done or bring her wayward legs under enough control to move an inch.

He looked as calm as ever, however, merely nodding towards a point beyond their shoulders. "I wouldn't if I were you," he said coolly, with quiet authority.

They had all forgotten his companion, but now turned their heads to see him still sat astride his bay gelding, a pistol held in each steady hand and a reckless grin spread across his face.

It was all the time Sir Philip required. He moved as swiftly and silently as a panther. The smug one did not see the hammer-blow coming that knocked him instantly unconscious, and the other had barely time to register the occurrence before he found himself relieved of his pistol, his arm twisted painfully behind his back, and his feet almost leaving the ground as he was marched back towards the customs house.

As they disappeared inside, Sir Philip's companion approached, still mounted, guiding his horse by his knees alone, just as the two ruffians got to their feet, rubbing their heads and muttering curses under their breath.

He briefly nodded respectfully towards Sophie. "Vaughen, Sir Philip's batman, I mean groom, at your service, my lady," he said shortly before turning back towards the men.

"Put everything back as you found it!" he said menacingly, both pistols now firmly trained on them.

His character was hard to read from his weathered face – for although his countenance was not unpleasing, with lines radiating from his eyes, suggesting he was not a stranger to laughter – the deep scar that ran from just below one ear to the edge of his mouth, suggested that he was someone who was not to be trifled with.

Sophie finally found her voice, concerned that Sir Philip had not, as yet, re-appeared. "Thank you, Vaughen. Perhaps if you would lend me one of your pistols, I could oversee things here whilst you check on Sir Philip."

He did not withdraw his keen eyes from the two men busily re-packing her bags, but they crinkled with amusement. "Bless you, lass," he began, then hastily corrected himself, "I mean, my lady. Don't fret yourself. The day I have to help him sort out one fat, lazy official, is the day – god forbid – he has been given notice to quit!"

When she still did not look convinced, he added, "Believe me, Lady Lewisham, when I tell you that he would not thank me for interfering."

As at that moment, Sir Philip and the customs officer re-appeared, the question became a moot point.

They both approached her and seeing their advance, Miss Trew bravely stepped down from the carriage and stood beside her charge, all quivering indignation.

They came to a stop before them, the customs officer's face a mixture of resentment and shame. It seemed that he had suddenly rediscovered his command of English. "I am sorry for the trouble, Lady Lewisham. Having re-inspected your documents, I find them in order, and would ask you to forgive any inconvenience and feel free to be on your way."

About to answer herself, she was startled and surprised when her retiring companion took a step forward and answered for her.

"You are a disgrace to your office, sir," Miss Trew exclaimed earnestly. "How proud your mother must have been when you attained your current position, but how do you think she would feel now if she had witnessed your recent behaviour towards two defenceless women?"

His amazed glance swivelled in her direction, taking in the pristine, if rather drab, figure before him.

"She died last year," he eventually admitted.

"How fortunate for her that she is now experiencing the joy of meeting her maker rather than witnessing the perfidy of the child of her loins!"

Sophie gasped in shock and admiration as his face twisted in embarrassment, and he shifted awkwardly from foot to foot like a schoolboy caught out in some misdemeanour. "I am sorry..." he began but was mercilessly cut off, for Miss Trew had been overcome by the zeal of a believer who has the chance to spread the word of God in all his righteousness and perhaps redeem a lost soul.

"Do not try to exonerate yourself from your outrageous behaviour," Miss Trew continued like a stern governess, much to Sophie's continued amazement. "Our good Lord said, 'joy shall be in heaven over one sinner that repenteth, more than over ninety and nine just persons, which need no repentance.' Learn that lesson well and make sure you do not disgrace your name – whatever that is – or your calling further!"

To the astonishment of all and the embarrassment of Miss Trew, suddenly there were tears in his eyes, and he dropped to his knees, taking her hand in his own and weeping unashamedly all over it. She had not taken into consideration the less guarded emotions of the foreigner before she had begun her sermon.

"Control yourself, man," said Sir Philip disgusted, helping him to his feet. Then offering a brief bow in the direction of the ladies, continued, "I suggest we partake of whatever light refreshment this hostelry has to offer whilst your baggage is stowed. Go ahead, I will join you in a moment."

"An excellent suggestion," agreed the customs man, recovering his poise and eager to make amends, moving with unaccustomed alacrity towards the inn to ensure that a private parlour and free refreshments were made available to them.

Sir Philip found both ladies still a little shocked, huddled together as if for comfort on the settle beneath the window. He was immediately followed into the chamber by a serving girl who served them a glass of wine each. Sophie took a grateful sip and tried to gather her scattered thoughts together.

"I cannot thank you enough, sir, although I admit I am at a loss to understand why we were treated so."

"Indeed, I shudder to think what may have

happened if you hadn't arrived so fortuitously," added Miss Trew.

Sir Philip stood looking seriously down at them. "Oh, nothing too grave. After an exhaustive search of your baggage, you would have been allowed to continue. At some point on your journey, however, you would have discovered that various items of value were missing."

Miss Trew gasped. "The scoundrels!"

Sir Philip smiled gently at her. "I am afraid this is one of those occasions when book-learning is an inadequate chaperone. If you had greased him in the fist, in the first place, I believe you might have avoided any unpleasantness."

Sophie, recovering some of her natural energy, pushed herself to her feet and began pacing up and down in a decidedly unladylike manner, her indignation clear.

"Oh, a bribe! How foolish of me! I should, of course, have invested in a book that informed me of when and how much I would need to bribe corrupt public officials! Oh, and let us not forget, greedy innkeepers! I suppose if I had greased the fist of that bumptious little man last evening, a free table would have miraculously become available."

She had come to a stop directly in front of Sir Philip, her eyes ablaze and her bosom heaving at the exertion. He looked distinctly unimpressed with her outburst.

"Undoubtedly. But is all this heart-burning necessary?" he said, quite harshly. "Did you not wish, how did you put it – to expand your mind and understanding? If you insist on travelling without the protection of a male relative who would already understand these things and take care of them for you, then you will have to expand your understanding in ways that you have not imagined!"

Sophie heard the censure in his tone both at her loss of composure and her ignorance and felt heat rush into her cheeks. She was relieved when she became aware of the comforting presence of Miss Trew beside her and the tension that seemed drawn between herself and Sir Philip, eased a fraction.

"Perhaps you will let us re-pay you whatever sum you were required to expend on our behalf," Miss Trew said gently.

Sir Philip's face softened as he looked down at the diminutive, little lady before him. "I believe I can stand the nonsense. You were quite remarkable, Miss Trew," he said, making her blush. "You gave him something far more valuable than mere money, you gave him the chance to redeem his behaviour and become a better man!"

"It is true, Agnes. I never knew you could be so stern. You were wonderful!" agreed Sophie.

Miss Trew smiled mistily up at Sir Philip. "You were very impressive yourself, and I am quite sure your mother would have been very proud of you!"

His smile faded, and they both felt his withdrawal. "She is also dead," he said flatly, his suddenly inscrutable countenance not inviting platitudes.

"I have already offered to act as escort to you both, and although I am not a relative as such, I feel our mutual connection to Lady Renfrew impresses some obligation on me to ensure your continuing safety. I am afraid I am not on a sight-seeing tour but have some business that I must attend to in Pisa without delay, so you must resign yourself to travelling hard for a week or so. I will be ready to leave in five minutes."

With that, he bowed and left the room. Sophie looked rebellious, but Miss Trew merely said in a matter-of-fact way, "Well, we already seemed to have jumped into the fire, my dear, so come, let us go. I do not like to disappoint you, but I confess I will feel far more comfortable with Sir Philip's escort than without it."

The scenery was at first as dramatic as that which had gone before, with bridges thrown over wild gorges, where torrents plummeted downwards into the bowels of the earth. But gradually, softer hues gentled the prospect until at last, they had a glimpse of the vast plains of Italy. Imperceptibly, the vegetation became more exuberant until they were surrounded by acres of vines, groves of olives, and generously laden fruit trees.

When they came to Lago Maggiore, whose shores were a hive of activity, dotted with towns, villas, churches and castles, Sophie fretted that they were not to be given time to explore them as Miss Starke had detailed several places of interest. The same thing happened at Milan, with Sir Philip pressing on to the smaller town of Lodi.

"I particularly wished to see the Cathedral at Milan," Sophie said wistfully. "It is one of the largest in Italy."

"We had already agreed that we could not see everything," soothed Miss Trew. "Console yourself with the reflection that Miss Starke herself suggested that the buildings there, in point of architecture, are in no way remarkable. When we reach Pisa, we will be able to dispense with Sir Philip's escort and take our time to look about us, and at least we will get there without being swindled or robbed!"

The day had been persistently gloomy with some fierce downpours, and after travelling for several hours, the sight of the city gates was a welcome relief, until Sophie realised it was past dusk and they had already been closed.

"Wonderful!" she exclaimed. "He has made our teeth rattle in our heads, travelling at a quite ridiculous pace to reach this insignificant place, for no good purpose!"

Miss Trew decided to let this pass. Sophie had always studied, but she had also balanced this with vigorous exercise as she always said it allowed her thoughts and ideas to percolate somewhere in the back of the mind until they were ready to form into coherent theories. It was indeed hard on her to spend all day in the close confinement of the carriage.

"Ah, look, my dear," she said suddenly. "Sir Philip has done the trick, they are opening!"

"Of course, he has," Sophie muttered darkly. "I expect he has greased the fist of another public official! I wonder what budget he sets aside for the purpose?"

CHAPTER 6

The following day dawned fair, and Sophie, keen to be up and exploring, stood at the window watching the sky as it gradually lightened, drawing on a rose-pink cloak shot through with orange threads. Unable any longer to still the increasing desire to be out in the beautiful morning, she silently left the inn and the town; the tall walls, which had offered such a welcome embrace to tired travellers last evening, now felt like an encumbrance to be shed.

She walked out as far as the bridge that spanned the River Adda, the wide waterway that stood beside the town and leaned against the parapet, looking down at the gently murmuring waters below. She watched as they meandered around some obstacles and over others, quietly determined to continue on their way.

"It is a beautiful spot, is it not?"

Sophie jumped, and Sir Philip put out a hand to lightly steady her.

"Sir Philip! Are you following me?"

He quirked an eyebrow and immediately she felt foolish, conceited even.

"Not at all, it is mere coincidence. You must share my love of early mornings, Lady Lewisham."

"I felt the need for some exercise," she explained, annoyed that she sounded slightly defensive. "We have spent so much time shut up in a carriage, you see."

Sir Philip nodded but looked a little stern. "Your need for exercise is understandable, Lady Lewisham, but it was not wise to wander out here alone."

Sophie's eyes narrowed. "I thank you for your concern, sir, but I hardly think I stand in any danger at such an hour and in such a peaceful setting."

Unconsciously, she had begun tapping one little foot, and she winced as it came into contact with a sharp stone on the downward beat. Bending swiftly, she picked it up and threw it into the clear waters below.

They both watched as it briefly agitated the smooth surface before disappearing from sight.

"Even in a small, unassuming place such as this, a single event can occur which sends out world-changing ripples," Sir Philip said quietly.

Sophie looked interested. "Oh? Did something of that nature happen here?"

"Indeed – it is where Napoleon faced the Austrians in his first Italian campaign. The Austrians were in a strong position on one side of this bridge, yet he inspired his men to charge across it in the face of awful gun and artillery fire. It is the battle that earned him the confidence and loyalty of his men and persuaded him he was a superior general, destined for great things."

Sophie looked intrigued and surprised. "You speak almost as if you admired him!"

Sir Philip regarded her seriously. "And why not?"

For a moment, Sophie was lost for words. "But you were a soldier!"

He nodded once.

"You fought against him?" she prompted.

He nodded again.

Feeling a little exasperated, she said, "Then he was your enemy, he killed people you knew and would have killed you without a thought, so how could you possibly admire someone like that?"

Sir Philip looked pensive for a moment and then smiled wryly. "The French would no doubt say the same of Wellington. Both Napoleon and Wellington were great leaders in their own ways. Both could inspire and motivate their men in the face of overwhelming odds, both were usually the master of sound strategy, and both did not hesitate to put themselves in danger. The real difference between them was motivation. One was driven by the need for glory, the other by duty. I intend to be driven by neither!"

"What are you driven by?" Sophie bit her lip, drawing his gaze, as she belatedly realised how personal and potentially provocative her words were.

His smile grew wider, and a predatory gleam entered his eyes. Sophie felt powerless to move, even as she realised his head was moving closer to hers. Her eyes fell to his finely moulded lips, a moment before they whispered against her own. He laid no hand upon her person, and it was the lightest of touches, yet when he pulled away, she found she was trembling.

"Your problem is that you see everything still in

black and white," he murmured. "But as a widow, I think you will find there is a whole world of greys in-between!" He began to lower his head again, but she took a step back, snapped shut her parasol, and prodded him sharply with it.

"Oh, you – you, rogue! I had just thought you might be worth getting to know after all!"

Sir Philip winced and held one hand over his heart. "Ouch! Your words are far deadlier weapons than your parasol, ma'am! If you find my boring on about military history more fascinating than my kisses, I really am losing my touch!"

"I know nothing of your touch! Nor do I wish to!" she added hastily seeing that predatory look return. "It seems you do not hold a very flattering opinion of widows, but let me make it plain to you, sir, I am not now, nor will I be, at any time in the future, interested in a, a ..."

Sir Philip leant his back upon the wooden parapet, folded his arms, and waited with apparent interest. After he had watched her flounder for a few moments, he took pity and filled in the gaps for her. "A slip on the shoulder? Carte blanche? Affaire? Dishonourable Proposal?"

Colour flared into her cheeks, and she found both her tongue and her parasol, which she used to great effect to punctuate each utterance that followed, forcing Sir Phillip to retreat before her or risk being turned into a pin-cushion. "I am an independent woman of means! It is my firm intention to stay that way! I am not interested, now, or at any time in the future, in relations with any man and with you in particular. I do not want you, I do not need you, and neither do I wish to see you again after your disgraceful behaviour! Napoleon may have won his battle at Lodi – you will not!"

On that delightful utterance, she turned smartly around and marched back in the direction of the town, her nose tilted towards the sky and her parasol back where it belonged.

Sir Philip shook with silent laughter as he watched her progress. The little termagant! He had indeed served under Wellington, and one of that man's strengths had been to know when to retreat. It was something he ought to do now, of course. But he had felt her tremble, and if he were honest, he wanted to feel it again.

It was strange that a widow responded like an innocent. If it were a ploy to keep him interested, it was working – if it was not, then she was deceiving herself – the red tones in her hair, the way her emerald eyes flashed with anger, all spoke of a passionate disposition. That all that passion should be focussed on events and objects that were ancient history was a tragedy. Clearly, her experience of marriage had not been satisfactory. The age gap between his own parents had not resulted in a happy union either. A wry smile curled his lips as he acknowledged that he was some years older than her himself, but then he was not proposing marriage. *He was not proposing anything!* he reminded himself ruefully. The kiss had been rash. Ungallant even. He had promised her his protection. Sir Philip groaned. He was going to have to apologise.

Sophie's heart was beating at an alarming rate of knots as she climbed the stairs of their Hotel, not only due to the impressive rate she had maintained all the way back. Her cheeks were flushed and her eyes bright as she burst into her room.

"My dear, whatever has occurred to occasion this wild appearance?" exclaimed Miss Trew, alarmed.

"It would appear I have jumped out of the frying pan, into the fire and now into the furnace!" she said vehemently, yanking at the ribbons of her bonnet, and casting it carelessly aside. "Your Galahad is no more than a – a rake!"

Miss Trew paled at these words. "Oh, my dear, no! Do not say he has forced himself on you for I could hardly bear it!"

That gave Sophie pause for thought. She could not in all good conscience accuse him of forcing himself on her, she had seen the kiss coming after all and to her shame had made no move to avert it. Bursting into sudden tears, she shook her head. "No, he did not do that."

A little colour returned to her companion's cheeks and taking Sophie's arm, she led her to the bed. "Sit down and calm yourself, my dear. If not that, then what has happened for you to defame his character so?"

As she told the story of their meeting, Miss Trew's expression became thoughtful, her myopic gaze staring into the middle distance.

"It seems to me, my love, that you got off quite lightly. Another gentleman, finding an attractive young lady unattended, might not have found the fortitude to stop at one light kiss, parasol or no parasol!"

Sophie's jaw dropped. "Got off lightly? Aggie, you cannot deny that his behaviour was ungentlemanly, surely?"

"Perhaps not," she admitted. "But was it the behaviour of a young lady of quality to venture out alone to such a public spot?" she queried gently. "It hardly seems fair that you expect Sir Philip to follow the conventions when you so blatantly break them yourself. What is he to think? You had only needed to remain in my company, and it would not have happened, after all."

As Sophie found this unanswerable, she changed tack. "Be that as it may, I am tired of travelling everywhere without seeing anything. Miss Starke mentions a church that has some remarkable works by Callisto, who was a pupil of Titian, you know. I suggest we go and view them before we are closeted up for the day once more."

Miss Trew was happy to comply with this suggestion. They had just donned their bonnets when following a brief knock on the door, Burrows entered carrying a letter.

*Dear Lady Lewisham,*

*I offer my most sincere apologies for behaving in such an ungentlemanly manner. I am fully aware that I have offered your party my protection and can assure you that such a lapse of judgement will not happen again.*

*I would have suggested you visit the church of L'Incoronata this morning, as it boasts several impressive frescos and paintings by Callisto, but unfortunately, I have discovered it is temporarily closed for renovations due to water ingress.*

*As you have already visited the only other place of note, I suggest we set forward as soon as you have taken some refreshment.*

*Your humble servant,*
*Sir Philip Bray*

CHAPTER 7

Forced to satisfy her curiosity by what she could glimpse from the windows of her carriage, Sophie took to studying the peasantry. She found it intriguing that those nearer the Simplon were often of fair complexion with blue eyes, and of quite a slight stature, but even as the vegetation had grown more exuberant the further south they travelled, so the people had also flourished.

Sophie found the men tall, robust, and finely proportioned, but it was the women who most excited her admiration. Their dark hair and expressive black eyes were exotic, their movements earthy, yet graceful. They seemed to embody an inner life and vibrancy that shimmered in the very air around them.

However, even this occupation grew wearisome after a few more days of travelling and the rolling olive groves and rows of vines, that had, at first, delighted the eye, even acquired a sameness that she would not have believed possible not so long before.

"Thank heavens we will be in Pisa tomorrow," she

said wearily as the road curved down into a dip, surrounded on both sides by the seemingly ever-present trees in this part of the country. Sophie saw a small group of sun-kissed boys by the side of the road waving grapes and other fruits at them. One of them began to run along beside the carriage shouting, "Uva! Uva!"

Sophie and Miss Trew exchanged a smiling glance and then on a sudden impulse, she demanded the coach be stopped, climbed down, and enjoyed a lively exchange with them, laughing when they bowed deeply and shouted, "Bella, Bella!"

Smiling widely, she curtsied to them as if they were dukes.

"Get in the carriage, NOW!" Sir Philip suddenly shouted.

Something in his tone made her comply with unusual meekness. He had been a little way ahead but now galloped back towards them with some urgency. He drew to a halt beside the carriage, throwing a pistol at Squires. "If anyone comes near, use it!" he ordered, before disappearing off into the olive groves that lined the road, Vaughen following close behind.

Alarmed, Sophie leaned out of the window to suggest the children get in the carriage with them, but they had melted away, a few bunches of dropped grapes the only sign they had ever been there. The sudden crack of a shot in the distance had both occupants of the carriage on the edge of their seats, craning their necks to try to see where it had come from, but the trees obstructed their view. Neither spoke, but clasped hands as they waited for events to unfold, their eyes never leaving the spot where Sir

Philip and Vaughen had disappeared in a cloud of dust.

They returned at a more moderate pace. Vaughen retrieved their packhorse and sent them a pitying glance before taking up a position behind the vehicle. Sir Philip approached the window of the coach and sat frowning at them for a moment, a muscle ticking in his firmly clenched jaw.

"What just happened?" Sophie asked urgently.

Eyes that were chips of ice, raked her face, sending a quiver of apprehension through her.

"What just happened, ma'am, is that you disobeyed my orders," he said harshly.

"What orders?" Sophie asked, bemused.

"I made it clear when I offered my escort, that we would only stop to break our journey at places of my choosing."

Sophie felt confused and a little hurt. Although she had not appreciated the liberties of a few days ago, she could not deny that the admiration and latent passion that had turned his eyes into endless pools that had beckoned her into their depths, had haunted her dreams. To see them look at her so scathingly now, made her feel somehow bereft, as if in losing his good opinion, she had lost something important.

"Yes, you have urgent business in Pisa," she said haltingly, "and so we have accommodated your wish to travel incessantly all day, every day! I cannot see how my stopping for a few moments..."

He cut her off. "Your stopping for a few moments, at such a secluded and largely hidden spot, gave a few banditti the perfect chance they had been waiting for!"

"But my book says rumours of them are much exaggerated..."

"Damn your book!" he said, his slip of composure shocking her into silence. "We have run them off for now, but we will not stop again unless I order it!"

He made to move off. "Wait!" begged Sophie. "What about those lovely children? They may also be in danger!"

"Indeed," said Miss Trew, finally finding the courage to speak. "We cannot leave the poor lambs in the middle of nowhere when there are such rogues about."

Sir Philip let out a long, low sigh. "Why do you think those 'poor lambs' were here, in this particular spot, in the first place?"

Miss Trew looked non-plussed, but a look of chagrin crossed Sophie's face, and Sir Philip's glance gentled a fraction.

"You mean, of course, that it was their job to lure us to stop, that they were hand-in-glove with the banditti," she said slowly. "And I fell straight into their trap! I apologise."

Miss Trew's hand flew to her mouth, her eyes glinting with tears.

"I am sorry for your distress, ma'am," Sir Philip said more quietly, "but they are hardly to be blamed, after all, for they are poor and were probably offered enough reward to keep their families in comfort for some time to come."

As they travelled onwards, clouds that had been but a speck on the horizon earlier in the day, steadily closed in. Grey but with a tinge of red, they smothered the sun, casting the day into gloom. The wind also picked up, swirling dust into the air, causing the ladies to firmly shut the carriage window and Sir Philip to loosen his neckcloth enough to pull it half over his face.

When they finally broke their journey, he did not join Sophie or Miss Trew in the private parlour he acquired for their use. It was a desultory meal, with Miss Trew's thoughts on the infamy of men who would corrupt poor innocent children, and Sophie trying to fathom why such an obvious withdrawal of his approval, should disturb her quite so much.

* * *

The closer they had drawn to Pisa, the more Harry had filled Sir Philip's thoughts, driving him to maintain a pace of travel that he knew must be trying for the ladies. He had been lost in them when some instinct had caused him to pause – perhaps it had been the cessation of the steady rhythm of the carriage behind or his soldier's intuition kicking in – but something had made him glance back over his shoulder.

His initial feeling had been one of irritation at the delay, followed swiftly by one of amusement as he saw Lady Lewisham cavorting happily with the ragamuffins at the side of the road. He had thoroughly agreed with their shouts of 'Bella!', for she had indeed looked beautiful and absurdly young as she laughed with them in an unrestrained moment of happiness. A sudden twinge of something uncomfortable in the region of his heart had been quickly usurped by a feeling of tension, making him glance away into the olive groves – just at the moment when the sun had glinted brightly off something in the distance. It was a sight he had witnessed before, and his reaction was swifter than thought.

They had seen off the banditti with no great difficulty; they were after easy pickings. A warning shot that had cleanly removed the hat from one of them had settled matters. He was, however, furious with himself for the lapse in concentration that had allowed the ladies to fall behind and the subsequent unpleasantness he had subjected them to – but realised that it would be easier and quicker to deliver them safely to their destination if they were a little in awe of him. If he had dined with them and faced the inevitable look of reproach in their eyes, he would, undoubtedly, have been tempted to apologise.

He found sleep an elusive bed partner that night. The storm that had been threatening the best part of the afternoon, finally burst into life with an impressive rumble of thunder, followed soon after by a flash of lightning that seemed to rend the sky in two. The wind moaned fretfully around the corner of the building and arrows of rain bounced off the many small-paned glass windows of his room.

*I hate rain!* he thought, crossing his arms behind his head and staring up at the ceiling. Without warning, he was hit with a series of flashbacks that came to him unheralded and unwanted.

He and his regiment were bivouacked in a field near Waterloo. Rain lashed down, turning the field into a muddy quagmire. The struggle to stay dry was largely futile; the ground was sodden – rivulets of water poured down collars and off cuffs making any chance of sleep, negligible – particularly for him.

Whenever he closed his eyes, incongruent, vibrant, shameful images of the Duchess of Richmond's ridiculous ball intruded.

The Gordon Highlanders danced gracefully to the sound of bagpipes, candlelight glinting off the swords at their feet. The ladies clapped along, the liveliness of the dance dispelling much of the formal frigidity that often marked such affairs. Spirits were high, everyone determined not to face up to the ever-present danger of imminent battle.

Sir Philip was dancing with Miss Frances Bowles, the daughter of a very wealthy merchant. His acquaintance with her was slight, but he recognised two things about her immediately; she had a pretty face and the soul of a courtesan.

When a dispatch arrived, and the word for the soldiers to slowly start withdrawing went round, she grabbed his hand and all but dragged him into a small, courtyard garden. They were in quite a compromising position when they were discovered by his good friend, Lieutenant William Hunt. He grinned sheepishly at William, assuming he had come to drag him off to the front but then saw the stunned expression on his face and the guilty one displayed by Miss Bowles.

Without saying a word, William turned on his heel and left. Miss Bowles stamped one angry little foot and descended into an energetic bout of weeping. It seemed that an announcement of her betrothal to his friend had been imminent.

"Don't you understand?" she all but screamed at him. "You were the forbidden fruit I wanted to taste before a lifetime with one man!"

"Whereas you, ma'am, were just forbidden," he

snapped coldly before hurrying to catch up with William.

Now he walked tiredly among a field of corpses. Sightless eyes stared upwards, wounds gaped open as if crying out in silent distress and furtive scavengers moved silently among them, not averse to taking the clothes off their backs, the coins out of their pockets, or even the teeth out of their heads. They filled him with a rage that was both useless and futile. He began to move more quickly through the motley throng. Please God, they hadn't found Harry or William!

A blur of movement by a stand of trees to his left caught his eye. As he turned, Harry sat up among the countless dead, his blond hair streaked red and a dazed expression dimming his usually expressive eyes.

"Harry!" he called, a flood of such intense relief rushing through him that his own exhaustion was forgotten, and he managed to close the distance between them at a loping run.

Harry did not seem to hear him but just sat, staring blindly ahead. Sir Philip dropped to one knee beside him and took his dirt-streaked face in his hands. "Harry?" he said gently.

The blue eyes slowly focussed on him. "Hello, sorry, old chap, I can't hear a thing! Do I know you?"

With that, he passed out again.

"Don't worry, sir, I'll help you get him back. Thought you might need a hand."

So intent had he been on searching for his friends, he had not been aware that his loyal batman had been following in his wake.

Sir Philip nodded. "We'll just move this unfortunate fellow out of the way," he said, for the first-time glancing at the poor departed soul who was draped face down across Harry's legs.

He began to reach out his hand and then stopped short – for beneath the dirt, blood, and grime, he could see the torn coat was a Hussar uniform. With a deepening sense of foreboding, he gently turned the lifeless body and drew in a deep, painful breath, feeling a fist close around his heart as he recognised the blank countenance.

"William," he whispered softly, cradling his friend in his arms. "I'm so sorry, William!"

Even though he was bone-weary and bloodied himself, he somehow managed to stand, with William still held in his arms. Vaughen hoisted Harry over his shoulder, and together they made their slow, silent progress back across the field.

Another clap of thunder seemed to burst right over the inn, wrenching Sir Philip back to the present. He sat up with a start, covered in a light sweat. Giving up on sleep, he drew up a chair before his window to watch the storm play itself out. He had failed William in so many ways, but he was damned if he was going to fail Harry!

He suddenly tensed as he heard a floorboard creak just outside his room. Grabbing the pistol he always kept beside his bed, he sat astride the chair and listened as the handle of his door slowly began to turn. The door inched open, and a dark furtive shadow moved silently into the room, holding a cudgel of some sort in front of him.

"Drop it!" growled Sir Philip.

Just then a flash of sheet lightning briefly lit up the chamber, revealing Vaughen carrying a bottle of something. "If it's all the same to you, sir, I'd rather not. I was reconnoitring this establishment when I stumbled upon a very fine cellar. This is a bottle of what they call grappa hereabouts. I thought you might like to try it."

"You fool!" Sir Philip said. "You could have been shot!"

Vaughen offered him an unrepentant grin. "You are many things, Captain, but trigger-happy ain't one of them. I have never known you to shoot the wrong man, yet! Now get a bit of this fire-water down you, it'll do you more good than being sat there looking at that gloomy scene! It's a good storm, to be sure, but I reckon we've seen more impressive ones!"

Sir Philip's lips twisted. "So we have, Vaughen, so we have. Now stop cradling that bottle as if it were your sweetheart and pass it over!"

\* \* \*

Despite having an air of fallen splendour, Sophie thought that on first acquaintance, Pisa looked like an ancient and beautiful town. Divided by the Arno river which had a broad quay on each side, the many faded yet noble buildings that lined it, had a decaying grandeur that suggested a rich and interesting past.

The main streets were wide and excellently paved, and the bridges over the Arno were elegant and graceful. They stopped near one such structure, at the hotel L'Ussero.

"Aggie, we are finally here!" she said, alighting without delay – her pent-up excitement barely contained. She turned full circle, trying to take in everything at once, a wide smile slowly dawning. "It is as if the very buildings breathe their history!"

"It is probably the damp!" came the dry voice of Sir Philip.

Sophie turned to him her smile undimmed, any awkwardness between them forgotten in the joy of their arrival. "Oh, even if that were true, what matter? How can I thank you for your care? We have been a sad trial to you, I know. How glad you must be that having seen us safely to our destination, you can carry out your business without delay."

Her openness of manner, vibrant demeanour, and glowing eyes were bewitching. She had stated nothing but the truth, yet now the moment had come, he felt reluctant to leave her. Widow or not, she had all the naivety of a newly emerged schoolroom miss but none of the protection.

"It has been my honour to serve you," he smiled, bowing to them both. "You have your letter of introduction?"

"Indeed, it is safely tucked in my journal," she said.

He nodded. "When I have confirmed my plans, I will send you word where you can contact me if I can serve you further," he said. "But as I have some enquiries to make for my friend within, I will ensure you are comfortable before I leave."

He struck lucky first time and was directed to an old Palazzo that had been divided up into private apartments a little further along the river. It bore the signs of some neglect, but a slovenly porter soon directed him to the correct door with an uninterested nod of his greasy-haired head.

It was opened by a weary-looking lady with black

eyes, bruised by purple shadows underneath and a full mouth that drooped at the corners, as if borne down by life's burdens. In ordinary circumstances, she must have been beautiful, but in her present ravaged and dishevelled state she looked what she was; desperate. He had no more than bowed and introduced himself when she burst into loud, unrestrained sobs.

"Lui è gravemente malato!" she cried, over and over.

It seemed that his sudden appearance had broken the final thread of her forbearance, so putting her gently aside he strode through the high-ceilinged, sparsely furnished, marble-floored reception room to the tall wooden door at the end. It gave directly onto the bedchamber, and there lay his friend.

The bedcovers were tangled as if he had been thrashing in his sleep, his blond hair was dark with sweat, his face alabaster. The shutters were closed and the darkened room stank of rank sweat. After one comprehensive glance, he turned on his heel and returned to the greatly afflicted lady who had thrown herself down onto a day bed, still sobbing noisily. When his words had no effect, he dealt her one sound slap and called her name imperatively, "Maria!"

The noise ceased, and she stared mutely up at him.

"Dell'acqua calda!"

Nodding she hurried over to a small wood-burning stove that crouched in one corner of the room. Returning swiftly to the bedroom, he wrenched open the shutters and threw open the doors that led onto a small balcony, letting some much needed fresh air in, and the rank smell, out.

In a matter of moments, he had stripped the sheets

from the bed and the soiled nightshirt from his friend. Just as Maria Trecoli entered with the hot water, a knock sounded at the door.

Taking the bowl and cloth she carried, he nodded for her to answer it, breathing a sigh of relief that Vaughen had been so prompt. Between them, they soon had Harry washed and in fresh laundry.

"You want me to find a doctor, sir?" asked Vaughen once they had finished.

"Immediately," confirmed Sir Philip. "One competent in dealing with malaria!"

CHAPTER 8

In Pisa, social visits were paid in the evening, and Sophie and Miss Trew wasted no time in visiting Lady Bletherington. The cameriere who admitted them conducted them through a long, narrow suite of rooms, their appearance somewhat dingy owing to each only being dimly lit by a single lamp. However, the sitting room into which they were announced, was both elegant and light, and the lady herself could not have been more welcoming.

Somewhere in her forties, she was still a handsome woman. Her light brown hair was topped with a lace cap, the only nod to her age, for her dress was fashionable, cut quite low and perhaps not quite the most flattering to a figure that was rather full. Having risen to greet her guests, she invited them to sit and sank gratefully back in her chair, hastily reading Lady Renfrew's letter. Disconcertingly, she read it under her breath, occasionally uttering a much louder exclamation, such as "Ah! Oh! or Indeed!"

"How pleased I am," she eventually declared, "that dear Lady Renfrew has guided you to me. It is a pity my daughter has gone back to England with my husband for the season, for I am sure they would have liked to have met you. Her aunt is kindly bringing her out as I have been advised to stay here for my health."

Sophie murmured a polite response. Lady Bletherington did not attend to it but resumed the thread of her discourse as though it had not been interrupted.

"We have quite a community of English here, you know, but it is always a delight when we get some new blood to liven us all up! And you are interested in antiquity, delightful! You will, of course, visit the Campo Santo and the Cathedral with its extraordinary bell tower, and then you must tell me what you think of them! Then there is the opera, I am myself going tomorrow and beg you and Miss Trew will join me! I have a box, you know."

Before Sophie could get a word of thanks out, she rushed on – hardly pausing to draw breath. "And then, every so often I hold an evening salon, you will enjoy that, I know. I will hold one in honour of your arrival. It will be the perfect opportunity for you to meet other congenial persons who are interested in literature, classical antiquity, and the fine arts! Byron is here in Pisa, did you know? Although he has not yet graced us with his company at any of my select little gatherings."

By the time a somewhat stunned Sophie had thanked her kind hostess for her generous invitations, the proper length of a first visit was up, and so they took their leave.

"I wonder what Lady Renfrew wrote in that

letter?" she mused. "For once Lady Bletherington had read about me, it appeared that there was no need to hear anything from me! Not that she was not good-natured and all kindness."

Miss Trew smiled, amused. "She is probably lonely, my dear, garrulous people often are. She has perhaps not quite got used to the absence of her husband and daughter. Your lending her your company will in some way recompense her for her kindness in taking you under her wing a little."

In respect of architectural splendours, the guide books assured her that Pisa could not be compared with Florence, but as Sophie had no experience yet of the latter, she could not help being more than pleased with the former. The Cathedral, its famous leaning bell tower, the Baptistery, and the Campo Santo would individually have been impressive, but together they were breathtaking. The sunlight reflecting off acres of white marble was blinding, however, and once the overall impression of magnificence had been appreciated, they discovered it was best to only look at a small segment of these glorious edifices at a time.

The bell tower, an elegant building, leaned at an angle that defied gravity and could not fail to please. The Cathedral also did not disappoint. It was built on a scale that was both magnificent and awe-inspiring, home to over seventy lofty columns and adorned by many alters, some designed by Michelangelo. The Baptistry, however, was on a more manageable scale; its interior resembling an ancient temple. Sophie was drawn to the pulpit, whose marble columns and impressively carved reliefs were the work of Niccolo Pisano.

In particular, her eyes were repeatedly drawn to the statue that represented the Christian virtue of fortitude. It was a beautiful example of the classical revival. The naked statue designed on classical lines, held a lion cub on his left shoulder, clearly referencing Hercules.

"He is beautiful, isn't he?" Sophie breathed, her eyes wide with admiration.

"Indeed," agreed Miss Trew and then stifled an unexpected giggle. Sophie looked enquiringly at her as she struggled to retrieve her usually calm demeanour. "I'm s-sorry," she whispered shakily, "but I was just thinking that your mother may have been right when she suggested I was not a fit companion for you, as I was just imagining her reaction if she were here looking at these 'indecent bits of old stone'!"

That set them both off and they had to hastily leave lest their laughter be taken for a lack of appreciation of this place of reverence or worse, a ridiculously missish reaction to seeing a naked statue!

It was the Campo Santo which affected them most, however. Gothic marble cloisters with delicate traceried windows, housed fine examples of Roman sarcophagi, and in the galleries, many frescoes dating from the fourteenth and fifteenth centuries impressed them with their scale and execution.

They found themselves both fascinated and repelled by those that illustrated *The Triumph of Death*. Their subject matter was not easy to look upon – it was to be expected that they would be instructional in character – but the details of death and desolation were unlike anything they had seen before. Depicted as an old woman with long white hair, bat wings and claws in the place of hands and feet, the terrifying figure of death hovered over a scene where various corpses were amassed, their souls being drawn from their mouths by devils or angels depending on their ultimate destination. It effectively dampened any desire to laugh, and it was in a thoughtful frame of mind that they returned to their hotel.

\* \* \*

Vaughen did not fail in his objective but returned with a Doctor Johnson, who was enjoying a sabbatical from his profession in order to enjoy the rumoured delights of the continent. He had run him to ground at the hotel L'Ussero.

"I thought it might be better to have someone who understood the constitution of the Englishman," he said to Sir Philip.

Doctor Johnson was a distinguished looking gentleman somewhere in his fifties. He had intelligent light-grey eyes, a shock of thick white hair, formidable side-whiskers, and a pair of bushy eyebrows that were at present drawn together in a rather peevish expression. He did not appear to appreciate being the object of Vaughen's careful selection, especially as he had been interrupted at his dinner. He was quite red in the face due to the pace at which he had been unceremoniously marched by someone he considered to look quite disreputable, and the state of the building he entered did not encourage him to think he would be well imbursed for his troubles.

However, one glance at the formidable countenance of Sir Philip, silenced the many and varied objections he had been about to make on the manner and haste of his procurement. After listening to a halting description in broken English of Harry's recent symptoms by Maria and inspecting Harry for himself, he agreed that Malaria was the likely cause.

"Fortunately for you, I provided myself with a plentiful supply of sulphate of quinine before setting out. It should reduce the fever and sweating within a week. He is likely to have a sore head so keep up cold applications to his temples. I am here for another week or so, so if there is no improvement, you may send a note to the hotel."

He left in a more cheerful frame of mind, having been more than amply rewarded for his efforts.

\* \* \*

Sophie was looking forward to her first opera and insisted that Miss Trew overcome her natural reticence to put herself forward and accompany her.

"For I do not know anyone and rely on your presence and support to bolster my confidence," she explained. Although this was true, she was also quietly determined that her dear Aggie, would enjoy all the opportunities Pisa had to offer.

Lady Bletherington duly collected them, accompanied by a young relative. Her nephew Mr Maddock, having completed his university education, was enjoying a little grand tour before applying to one of the Inns of Court to become a barrister. He wore his wavy hair slightly long and had a rather careless way with a cravat. His demeanour was aloof, his brow often frowning, and his conversation erratic, largely consisting of what he thought were witty or satirical interjections, which were made with a strange curl of his lip. Sophie was just wondering if he was suffering from some sort of tic when Lady Bletherington leaned towards her.

"He is a big admirer of Byron," she confided in a whisper. "Writes reams of awful poetry!"

The truth of this statement was made apparent when his fitful attention suddenly became fixed on a box on the other side of the theatre. Leaving Miss Trew to enjoy the meandering flow of Lady Bletherington's conversation, she followed the line of his gaze and observed a dark-haired man with a high forehead and pallid countenance. His full lips had a sneering look about them. This, she assumed, was the man himself. She had heard him called handsome but could not agree, although even from this distance she could sense something of his impressive aura. Although he seemed to hold himself aloof from the others in his box, preferring to scan the theatre below, he somehow drew the eye, making his guests fade into the background.

"And on that cheek, and o'er that brow, So soft, so calm, yet eloquent, The smiles that win, the tints that glow, but tell of days in goodness spent," Mr Maddock suddenly sighed, tragically.

"Ha!" exclaimed Lady Bletherington, nodding at the lady in Byron's box, whose red-gold hair and blue eyes were strikingly pretty, and whose extremely low-cut silk gown revealed fine rounded arms and a generous bosom. "How any of her days can be said to be spent in goodness when she left her husband to be Byron's mistress, is beyond me! That's what happens when girls barely out of the schoolroom are married to men old enough to be their father! She is pretty enough, I suppose, but unfortunately suffers from being rather short in the leg, everybody says so."

Colouring, Sophie said, "*She Walks in Beauty* is not typical of his work, but I must admit I enjoyed the sentiment that beauty comes from within as well as without."

But Mr Maddock was not attending, and Sophie realised that his gaze was now fixed on the stage. There was a sense of barely repressed excitement and impatience about him as he waited for the performance to begin.

"So, what do you think of the great man?" asked Lady Bletherington. "It is true he looks a trifle gloomy just now, but then he has just lost his daughter, poor soul!"

It was just as well the curtain went up at that moment, for Sophie found she could not sympathise with a man who deserted the poor mother when she was increasing, denied her access to her own daughter, and then left the child to die alone in a nunnery at the tender age of five.

It was Rossini's opera of Otello. Sophie found herself entranced from the first. The energy of the performances and the quality of the acting outshone her expectations. In particular, the soulful singing and heartfelt rendition of the voluptuously beautiful leading lady playing Desdemona was spellbinding.

With hair and eyes as dark as midnight, smooth pale skin and ruby lips, she brought her character to life with a passionate interpretation of the role that was filled with drama and expression.

As the spectacle reached its tragic conclusion, she found herself rapidly blinking to dispel the tears that had suddenly filled her eyes.

"Did you enjoy it, Agnes?" she said quietly.

"I found the singing most superior and the performance moving."

A finely dressed gentleman had entered their box and was bowing elegantly over Lady Bletherington's hand, enquiring politely about her health and her family.

His entrance had a startling effect on Mr Maddock, who jerked suddenly to his feet, offered only the slightest of bows, mumbled something unintelligible under his breath and left the box.

"Oh, oh dear," said Lady Bletherington a little flustered. "He is probably overcome, poor lamb, although it is the second time he has come so one would have thought he would know what to expect. Never mind. Lady Lewisham, Miss Trew, let me introduce my good friend, Count Maldolo."

Tall with dark eyes, he greeted them both with a dignified reserve that was pleasing.

"And how have you enjoyed your experience of the opera?" he asked in perfect English.

Sophie expressed her enthusiasm fully and unreservedly, earning her a wide smile, which showed to advantage his even teeth that flashed white against his tanned skin.

"It is refreshing to hear an opinion expressed with

such intelligent vivacity," he said. "I also enjoyed it. Giselda Sirena is a rare talent who captivates all who see her. Although I fear your fellow countryman, Lord Byron, did not share our view as he disappeared after the first act!"

Sophie thought she heard a slight sneer in his voice and was glad when he continued, for she did not know how to answer.

"I think only someone native to the country where opera was born can fully express the range of emotions necessary for such a performance."

"You were going to tell me what you thought of the Campo Santo, Lady Lewisham," Lady Bletherington interrupted, eager to edge her way back into the conversation. "I always think..."

What she always thought was to remain a mystery as Count Maldolo, perhaps used to her ways, interrupted.

"Yes, please, Lady Lewisham, I would be most interested in your observations."

Miss Trew unobtrusively moved her chair a little closer to Lady Bletherington and leant towards her.

Sophie mentioned the frescoes to him. "They were very well executed," she said. "And I suppose the preoccupation of death in what is, after all, a cemetery is understandable. Yet they held a disturbing quality that spoke to something within me that I cannot quite explain..." she trailed off, not quite able to effectively voice the unsettled feeling that had remained with her since their visit. "Do you know the paintings?" she asked.

He nodded. "Of course. You must not feel disturbed because you feel something you do not fully understand. All good art should have such an effect on a person with sensibility and an enquiring mind. A guide book will speak to you of the pre-occupation with death at a time when plague was rife. It will try to tell you what to think by placing it firmly in its own historical and religious context. But for me, this is missing the point. You could just as well glean those facts from a dry history book. Surely the role of all good writing or art is to speak to something within us, even it is only a half-formed thought or feeling. Something beyond the obvious. What I see or feel when I look at those paintings, will differ widely from your view, because we differ widely in our experience of the world – neither of our feelings will, however, be correct or incorrect."

"It is interesting that death is personified as half-demon, half-woman," she said, realising that this had been bothering her.

The count merely laughed. "Ah – but Eve tempted Adam astray and so introduced sin into the world! A woman opened the door to the devil, therefore is it so surprising that one might also represent him?"

Sophie wrinkled her brow in consideration of his opinion for a moment. "Did not Adam also have free will? Is it not a weakness to put the blame for our failings on another because we are tempted, rather than accept that we chose to succumb to temptation?" she countered, blinking away the sudden vision of a certain kiss she had tried very hard to forget.

"Indeed," agreed Miss Trew. "It is infinitely easier to decry and expose the sins of others than to correct our own."

The count bowed. "I cannot deny your wisdom, Miss Trew."

Sophie found herself approving of him, both the elevation of his mind and the gentleness of his manner were very agreeable. He soon took his leave, and Lady Bletherington could talk of nothing else but him all the way back to their hotel.

"He showed you a considerable compliment in his attentions, Lady Lewisham, for he is a considerable Patron of the Arts and is an important person hereabouts. He has a villa somewhere in the countryside. I have never been, you understand, but I have heard that he has some impressive works by the Florentine artists…"

*** 

Sir Philip was not enjoying such a convivial evening. Harry's fever had mounted, and he was raving, uttering various inchoate phrases. However, two names were decipherable and were repeatedly and sometimes desperately uttered; William and Philip. Whatever troubled him clearly harked back to that fateful day in June 1815.

Sir Philip added another cold compress to his fevered brow, murmuring, "Peace, Harry, I am here."

His voice seemed to reach him, and for a moment he opened his eyes, gazing wildly about. "No fault!" he cried before closing them again and sinking into a more settled rest.

"Seems he's sorely troubled by something," said Vaughen, coming quietly into the room, carrying a one-pot stew he had created over the wood-burning stove.

He laid it down on the small table that lay against one wall of the chamber. "It's been a while since I've cooked your supper, sir, but I don't think you'll find I've lost my touch being as I had access to a much wider range of fresh local produce than has, at times, been the case!"

"Still no sign of Maria?" he asked.

After the doctor had visited, he had taken her to one side and thanked her for her unremitting care of his friend. When he had handed her the generous purse sent by Lady Treleven, she had broken down into noisy sobs once again. Indeed, she was so overwrought she seemed to have an inexhaustible flow of them, and so he had sent her home with instructions to rest and not return until she felt more the thing.

Vaughen gave him a wry smile. "I took it upon myself to make a few enquiries," he admitted. "It seems that the Trecolis were in a spot of bother, sir, pockets quite to let. They seem to have left town in a hurry rather than put the dibs back in tune!"

Sir Philip's lips twisted dryly. "Ah, I see."

"I don't suppose as she had much choice, sir, if it was the will of her father," Vaughen said generously.

"Perhaps not," Sir Philip acknowledged. "But as we have received no word or letter for Harry, I must assume she did not care enough to write one."

Vaughen knew better than to continue the subject; his master was fiercely loyal to those he considered his friends.

"And the ladies?" he enquired after a moment, in an off-hand manner, as if it were a passing thought.

"Gone to the opera, sir, though why anyone would want to listen to that infernal warbling is a mystery to me."

Sir Philip nodded absently. "Keep your ear to the ground, Vaughen. If she gets into any trouble, she will in all probability be too stubborn to ask for help."

Vaughen grinned and began to clear away the pots. "You can rely on me, sir."

CHAPTER 9

Lady Bletherington's assertion that Sophie would enjoy her salon proved to be far from accurate. She found a small group of English ladies who were none of them distinguished by any remarkable understanding. Mr Maddock was the only gentleman present but made no effort to converse, preferring to strike an interesting pose against the fireplace and gaze off into the middle distance as if lost in deep thought.

Their hostess, having just received a copy of The Literary Gazette, tried to open a discussion on the merits of L.E.L's latest poem, 'Sappho'. However, it appeared that she could not render what her imagination compelled her to say with any clarity, leaving the unfortunate but accurate impression that she did not entirely understand what she endeavoured to make intelligible to others. After a tangled speech which referred to the pain of loving not one, but two men, who did not return the lady's passion and most probably did not deserve it either – (though how you could fall in love at the sound of a voice, she did not know) – and the compassion one must feel for someone driven to suicide, whilst at the same time condemning such an act as selfish, cowardly and ungodly, she trailed off into an uncharacteristic silence.

Sophie had not as yet acquainted herself with Miss Landon's poem and so could not come to her rescue. She noticed the satirical glances and smiles that passed amongst Lady Bletherington's guests and felt annoyed that Mr Maddock, who might, if he had any real literary pretensions have stepped into the breach, had now positioned himself as far away from the guests as possible but very near to a bottle of wine, from which he was replenishing his glass with remarkable and increasing frequency.

Rather than consider the pain of unrequited love or compare her verse to other representations of Sappho, they preferred to discuss the recent revelation that the poet was a woman and the likelihood of the poem being autobiographical, and if so, to whom the poet might be referring as rumour had it she was increasing.

She was forced to conclude that they had come merely to listen to – or spread themselves – malicious gossip. At least she was on her guard when she suddenly found herself the object of their barely veiled interest and speculation and was forced to parry impertinent enquiries into her age, deceased husband and income.

"I hear you and Miss Trew are travelling without a male companion," said one of the ladies. Lady Montrose wore a rich dress of purple with a matching dyed feather in her hair. She was a handsome woman, and her eyes shone with a sort of malignant intelligence. "How very... brave you are!"

"Is Italy such a dangerous place?" countered Sophie with icy politeness, refusing to give fuel to the fire that would blaze if she shared the experiences that Sir Philip had rescued her from.

"Not generally, no," the lady said, "but one widowed so tragically young and in the possession of a fortune, cannot be too careful! If you feel you need it, you may come to me for advice."

Sophie cast a quick glance at Lady Bletherington whose tongue had clearly been wagging and saw that she had at least the grace to look a little shame-faced.

"Indeed?" parried Sophie. "And what is it, exactly, that I must be careful of? Is it perhaps something unfortunate that you have experienced?"

Lady Montrose, on the shady side of thirty, looked a little haughty. "Experienced, of course not! However, if you think that all the young gentleman currently on the grand tour are here merely for the history, you are sadly mistaken!"

"I am not sure exactly to what you are referring, Lady Montrose, but as the only gentlemen I have met here are Mr Maddock and Count Maldolo, who seemed a very elegant, restrained gentleman, I hope I have nothing to fear."

"Ah, yes," she said with a small smile that did not quite reach her bird-keen eyes. "Lady Bletherington mentioned that the count had seemed very pleased with you. His manners are indeed very becoming, and he has a handsome countenance, does he not?"

"I cannot say that I formed an opinion on the matter, he must be above forty, after all," Sophie replied. "But it seemed to me that he had a pleasing intellect."

When she proved such a disappointing source of information, they inevitably turned their attention to Byron.

"It is no wonder he is looking so pale. I hear he is at present living solely on a diet of vegetables!" one lady began.

From there it was a small step to tearing apart the character of Byron's mistress, Countess Teresa Guiccioli, whilst all the time pretending to admire her fortitude in putting up with the whims and moods of her capricious lover.

Feigning a headache, Sophie made an early departure much to the relief of Miss Trew.

"I declare, I have rarely been more disappointed," Sophie said as soon as they were in the carriage. "I had expected an evening of rational conversation."

"It is a shame, my dear," concurred Miss Trew. "And I must own myself astonished that Lady Renfrew, who has such a fine intellect herself, should have recommended to you a lady who may have a kind heart, but has remarkably little sense or reason."

"Perhaps she had no other acquaintance presently residing here and thought that Lady Bletherington would be better than no acquaintance at all," she said, unwilling to hear any criticism of the lady to whom she had taken to so readily.

"Indeed, it can be the only explanation," agreed Miss Trew faintly.

By the following morning, they had begun to see the more amusing aspects of their evening but had tacitly agreed that Lady Bletherington could be of very little practical use to them. As they lingered over breakfast, a card was delivered to their private sitting room. Count Maldolo had come to call.

His appearance was immaculate; his buff coloured coat fitting his broad shoulders perfectly and his linen, crisp and white. Showing an elegant leg to the ladies, he bowed and apologised profusely for intruding on them so early.

"But it occurred to me after our interesting conversation at the opera, Lady Lewisham, that although you have witnessed some of the architectural splendours Pisa has to offer, you may not have experienced some of the beautiful scenery we have, that perhaps only a local could show you. I have come to see if you and Miss Trew would like to drive out with me before the day becomes too warm."

"That sounds delightful, but we are not quite ready..." Sophie began.

"It is of no moment," said the count. "I will await you downstairs, take your time."

By the time Burrows had attired her mistress in a simple Pomona green carriage dress of cambric muslin and chip hat with matching ribbons and parasol, twenty minutes had passed.

"Very becoming," approved Miss Trew, herself plainly attired in a light beige pelisse and straw bonnet.

"I am sorry to have been so long," Sophie said ruffled, "but Burrows will never be satisfied until I am as neat as a pin."

"Quite right," Miss Trew approved.

Count Maldolo showed no signs of impatience, however, merely giving her an approving glance. "I am impressed that you could be ready in less than half an hour," he admitted.

"It is a minor improvement," Sophie said with a wry smile.

"I am afraid it may be a bit of a squeeze," he apologised, handing Sophie first into the gig. "But this way we can easily explore some of the smaller tracks that would be impossible to navigate with a larger carriage."

It proved a very pleasant morning. The count led them a winding way through a country of enchanting scenery where the fecund plains, dominated by the vines and olives, were at times interrupted by sun-baked fields of golden wheat. Every cottage they passed had a small garden filled with an abundance of vegetables. He took them through gentle glades of shade and past small meadows filled with a profusion of wildflowers, pointing out pomegranates and junipers, rosehips and the sweet-smelling sambuca.

"What is that lady doing?" Miss Trew asked interested, when she saw an old lady dressed in black making her way around the bases of the trees and a small stone wall that separated them from the road, every now and then bending low to pull something from the earth and place it in her roughly woven basket.

"She will be picking wild asparagus or fennel, mushrooms or nepitella, a sort of wild mint," he explained seriously. "There are many poor people here, but for those with wisdom the land provides plenty."

As they made their way back into Pisa, they passed quite near the residence of Lady Bletherington.

Perhaps it was this circumstance that made Count Maldolo enquire if they had attended her salon last evening.

"Yes," Sophie said carefully, unwilling to denigrate Lady Bletherington in any way. "But it was not as interesting as I had hoped. I was surprised to find no local ladies present."

"Ah," said the count with a small amused smile. "But the adventurous English like to travel all this way and then gather together like homesick children. They have already experienced Italy in their minds through literature, paintings, and travel guides and so find confirmation of their opinions or disappointment everywhere."

"You are cynical, sir!" Sophie said, surprised.

"Perhaps. I have too often witnessed discussions at these salons that merely regurgitate whole passages that have been read in books with no reflection or recourse to their own imaginations. They freely give of their opinions without feeling the merits they praise or the defects they censure. But you, Lady Lewisham, impressed me when you strove to understand the feelings your imagination could not quite grasp after having seen the frescoes in the Campo Santo."

Sophie felt a desire to defend her countrymen and women, but her experiences of the evening before and the flattery to her intellect, made her struggle to find an adequate defence.

"And do Italian ladies hold salons?" asked Miss Trew quietly.

"Not any that I would grace with the name of lady," he said. "My daughter is very knowledgeable," he admitted. "But she would not choose to use in company knowledge which she has acquired in private. A lady may read much, but it is sometimes wiser to conceal all."

"I thought Italy would be more enlightened," Sophie said, surprised. "But it is not so very different from home in this respect."

"Is knowledge any less valuable to an individual if it is not brought out into a public discussion where it is often misunderstood, argued over endlessly and then dismissed?"

Even as he spoke, they pulled up outside the hotel, just as Doctor Johnson rushed out of the door, his black bag in hand, followed swiftly by Vaughen. They had several times exchanged greetings with the doctor, and Sophie felt a sudden twinge of alarm.

"Vaughen," she called as the count politely helped her descend from the gig. "Is anything amiss? Is Sir Philip ill?"

"No, my lady," he said hastily. "But the friend he came to see is and he is concerned for him. It hasn't helped that the lady who was caring for him has disappeared, and Sir Philip insists on looking after him single-handed. I daresay lack of sleep is making him fret, so excuse me, but we must be on our way."

"Wait!" Sophie said as he turned away. "Is it far?"

"No, ma'am."

"We will also come then. It may be that we can help in some way."

"I'm not sure..." he began, but Sophie impatiently cut him short.

"Nonsense, it is the least we can do when he has taken such good care of us."

Sophie turned to take her leave of Count Maldolo.

He took her hand and looked at her intently for a moment. "This Sir Philip," he said. "He is a friend of yours?"

"Yes, he escorted us part of the way here," she confirmed.

The count bowed. "Then I will send you the directions of my own doctor also."

"Perhaps my services will not be required, after all," grumbled Doctor Johnson, clearly offended.

Miss Trew smiled gently at him. "Oh, Count Maldolo is just being polite. I am sure you are very accomplished, sir. Come," she said, taking his arm, "we must not keep Sir Philip waiting, for I am sure he must be very anxious to have disturbed you."

Sophie hid a smile at Miss Trew's masterful handling of the situation. She was finding herself respecting her companion's judgement more every day. She supposed as a vicar's daughter she had been used to dealing with her father's parishioners.

The count watched them go, a small frown creasing his brow. He suddenly cracked his whip driving off at a spanking pace, causing an unwary gentleman to hastily jump out of his way.

Sir Philip was indeed anxious. Harry's fever had continued unabated even with the quinine, and although he had occasionally opened his eyes and been persuaded to drink, he had not shown even a flicker of recognition when he had gazed straight at his old friend.

He had left the door ajar and so did not immediately perceive that he had extra visitors. As Doctor Johnson entered the room, he briefly shook his hand before turning back towards the bed as Harry cried out something unintelligible.

"His head seems to be causing him much discomfort, he keeps clutching it and thrashing from side to side. He must not die!" he said imperatively. "I do not care what it costs or how it is to be done, but you must bring him back to me!"

Sophie and Miss Trew, who had hung back in the main reception room, exchanged a speaking glance, for it was impossible to miss the depth of affection in which he held his friend or the agony of worry he was in. Sophie could not help wondering what it would be like to have someone feel such a deep affection for her that they would do anything to keep her close.

Sir Philip strode into the room a moment later, running a hand through his dark locks. Judging by their disarranged appearance, it was an act he had repeated many times before. He wore no coat or cravat, and his shirt was open at the neck, revealing the strong column of his throat. He looked tired, dishevelled, and vulnerable, yet incredibly virile at the same time. He stopped short when he saw his guests.

"Ladies," he said surprised and then bowed, swiftly recovering his poise. "How may I be of service to you?"

Ignoring the fact that her heart had begun to beat a trifle faster, Sophie stepped forward. "We require no service from you, Sir Philip, but on the contrary, are here to offer our own. And by the look of you, not a moment too soon."

He coloured slightly. "I am sorry you find me so disarranged. I am unprepared for visitors."

"It is of no moment," she said. "It is we who

should apologise for having burst in upon you unannounced, but having heard of your friend's indisposition, we came with all haste to see what we could do."

He rested his hooded gaze on her for a long moment, taking in the clean crispness of her gown. The colour emphasised her emerald eyes – she looked like a fresh spring flower. The idea of her spending tedious hours mopping his friend's fevered brow did not sit well. "I thank you for your kind consideration," he finally said, "but the sickroom is no place for such a fresh daisy as yourself, Lady Lewisham."

"Is that so?" she challenged, tilting up her chin slightly. "Perhaps you have forgotten that I was married to a man who was much older than me and sick for some time before he died? Or did you think that I would leave all his care to his attendants whilst I occupied myself shopping for fripperies?"

Perhaps fortunately, Doctor Johnson, having finished his inspection of the invalid, joined them at that moment, saving Sir Philip from the necessity of making a reply, for he did not have the energy or appetite for an argument.

He looked solemn. "Things are indeed at the critical point. The disease has gone too long unchecked, and so the symptoms are strong. We must up his dose of quinine in the short term for if he falls into a coma, there is nothing else to be done."

Sir Philip looked grim. "We must not allow that to happen!"

"I could bleed him..."

"No!" Sir Philip snapped. "I have witnessed too many soldiers die after such a procedure. I believe it drains the spirit and he needs all the energy he can muster if he is to fight this, his hardest battle."

"Daisies!" said Miss Trew suddenly.

All eyes swivelled in her direction at the unexpected utterance.

"Doctor Johnson, when Count Maldolo was driving us through the countryside this morning, I am sure I saw some feverfew. If I could make an infusion of the plant, surely it would help with the fever and the headaches, in particular?"

"Indeed, it could," he agreed. "At least it will do no harm, and it may do some good."

Having not been brought up to an idle life, Miss Trew warmed to a useful role. Turning to Sir Philip decisively, she said, "Your care and concern for your friend whilst admirable, cannot be maintained if you take so little care of yourself, sir. You not only look dishevelled but half-deranged into the bargain! We will indeed collect some feverfew and make it up, but we will share the care of ... your friend."

"Harry," he said. "Viscount Treleven."

Although naturally shy and retiring when taken out of her natural milieu, Miss Trew had indeed been used to offering succour to the needy in her father's parish, and found her competence for managing difficult situations overtaking her usual reticence when dealing with the gentry. Glancing at the bundle of blankets folded neatly on the day bed, she continued undaunted. "And I see no good reason for you to be sleeping rough in this lodging, it is far from ideal and in the present circumstances, quite unserviceable. I shall book rooms for you and Lord Treleven at the hotel, where you will find it easier to access both the esteemed Doctor and the basic comforts necessary to your wellbeing, as well as making it less difficult for us to offer our assistance."

Doctor Johnson observed Miss Trew with some respect. "You speak a great deal of sense, ma'am," he said approvingly. "I will happily administer the required dose myself and judge when it is time to lessen it again, for too much for too long will also be injurious to Lord Treleven's health."

His natural inclination towards privacy together with his anxiety over his friend had prevented Sir Philip thinking with a clear head, but now he saw all the advantages of this proposal. A slow smile eased some of the worry that etched his brow, and Sir Philip took Miss Trew's hand and kissed it lightly. "Did I not say you were a remarkable woman?" he said. "But as for sharing the care, I would not presume to intrude on your time..."

"Our time is ours to do with as we choose," interjected Sophie, decisively. "I will send my carriage so you can transport Lord Treleven easily to the hotel. And we will help you care for him, for I think you will find that even a daisy, whilst preferring the sun, is hardy enough to cope with inclement conditions when necessary."

Sir Philip bowed low over her hand, his eyes never leaving hers. "You are all consideration, Lady Lewisham. I fear I did not do justice to you when I compared you to a common daisy; you are more like an orchid, rare and beautiful."

"And hard to cultivate," she added dryly, her antipathy to flattery automatically kicking in. "One kind act does not an orchid make! I prefer to be a daisy."

## CHAPTER 10

Lord Treleven was moved in remarkably little time and now finding himself surrounded by an unexpected network of support, Sir Philip allowed Vaughen to persuade him that he should take a truckle bed in Harry's room.

"For if you are going to tell me that I am incapable of caring for him, all I can say is your memory must be failing you. If you have forgotten the times I have tended to you..."

"Enough!" said Sir Philip with a lopsided smile, clasping him on the shoulder. "It is not my lack of faith in you that has driven me, and well you know it! Now, I will leave Harry to your tender ministrations whilst I bathe, for I have agreed to dine with the ladies."

Doctor Johnson also joined them for dinner. Between them, they came up with a schedule which would not be too demanding on the ladies but would allow Sir Philip time to rest and exercise.

"I will agree to this arrangement but only when Harry has shown significant improvement," he said.

"And on the understanding that if he becomes lucid and wishes to speak to me, I will be fetched immediately."

After dinner, both gentlemen excused themselves. Sophie and Miss Trew settled by the fire; Sophie with a book, Miss Trew with some embroidery. Sophie was aware of a strange sensation of comfort at knowing Sir Philip was under the same roof. As this feeling ran contrary to her desire for independence, she tried to analyse it and come up with some rational explanation for it.

She had not got very far with this endeavour when they were interrupted. Two Italian ladies were admitted to the parlour – one young and pretty with thick, glossy dark hair and a shy demeanour – the other much older and quite stern-looking. The hair that peeped beneath her hat was pure white, and she had small hard current-like eyes. The Marchesa Rossanna D'Orza introduced herself and her niece.

"I believe you have already met Contessina Isotta's father, Count Maldolo?"

Sophie smiled widely. "Oh, how wonderful to meet you both! Contessina Isotta, your father spoke very fondly of you. I am delighted you have come to visit!"

The young lady offered a small smile in return and said in a low musical voice, "My brother also speaks of you with respect, Lady Lewisham."

"We cannot stay," said the marchesa briskly, refusing to be seated, "but would like to invite you to a small breakfast at our villa outside town tomorrow. It is the Villa Maldolo, ask anyone, and they will direct you. Come at ten, before the day gets too warm to enjoy the gardens."

Hardly waiting for a reply, she then swept regally out of the room again. Contessina Isotta again smiled but said nothing, following in her wake with a quiet grace.

Sophie stood looking after them for a long moment. She felt undecided as to her own desires in the matter, feeling that they had rather been ordered than invited. However, she could not deny that she had a strong inclination to visit the villa and see the impressive collection of art Lady Bletherington had mentioned, as well as to get to know Contessina Isotta a little better.

"Do you think we should go?" Sophie finally said to Miss Trew. "We have promised to help with Lord Treleven, after all."

Miss Trew looked unruffled and re-applied her needle to her work. "Well, my dear, as Sir Philip made it quite plain that he would not accept our assistance until the viscount is much improved, I do not see the harm. That is, of course, if you wish to go. If you do not, you could always develop the headache," she said with a small smile.

Sophie laughed aloud at her friend. "Then we shall go. I own that I am a little intrigued to see if the elegance of his villa will match the elegance of his person."

Burrows dressed Sophie with her usual care in a round robe of jaconet muslin under an open pelisse of pale grey sarsnet. Her satin straw hat boasted three rows of matching grey ribbon around the crown. A few rich ringlets peeped from beneath it.

"There," Burrows said satisfied. "You're pretty as a picture, my lady."

"Thank you, Burrows," she smiled. "As usual, your taste is impeccable."

"It wouldn't matter how impeccable my taste was if I didn't have such good material to work with," she grinned. "I once worked for a lady who always looked like a pudding no matter what I did!"

Sophie was still laughing when she stepped onto the landing just as Sir Philip came out of his room further along the corridor, dressed for riding. Her laughter drew a smile from him, and he bowed briefly before crossing the distance between them in a few long strides. He already looked less care-worn, and his appearance was immaculate.

"You look charming, Lady Lewisham," he said lightly.

Sophie dropped a brief curtsey and dimpled prettily. "Why, thank you, kind sir. I have it on the best authority, my maid's, that I do not, at least, look like a pudding!"

His smile widened, and his eyes crinkled in amusement. For the first time, she noticed the fine laughter lines that radiated from them and thought how much they suited him.

"As you are going out, can I hope that Lord Treleven is perhaps a little improved?"

"His fever is not quite as virulent, and he spent a more restful night, so I am cautiously optimistic that the increased dose of quinine has begun to work. I am loath to leave him for long. However, I need some exercise and fresh air. You are going out yourself, ma'am?"

Sophie told him of the kind invitation they had received. "It will be interesting to get an insight into the manners and customs of some local people rather than just sight-seeing."

"Yes, a place is not defined solely by its art or the stones with which it was built," he agreed. "I will enquire the way and escort you as I am going for a ride anyway. Perhaps Miss Trew might show me the feverfew she prescribed for Viscount Treleven, for his head is still bothering him."

As he led them past the gentle murmur of a limpid stream, a wild meadow spread before them covered with the daisy-like feverfew, the white and yellow of the flowers occasionally broken by a splash of red as wild poppies sprang up amongst them.

Sir Philip left Alcides to drink from the stream and found himself drawn by a sweet, fragrant scent to the fringe of the meadow. It reminded him of something that nudged the edge of his memory. He came to a stop in front of a wild myrtle shrub. Its deep green leaves contrasted pleasingly with the many pure white flowers that decorated it, a plethora of golden-tipped stamen erupting from their centres like delicate starbursts.

Sophie left her parasol in the carriage and at the last moment, also stripped off her kid gloves lest they get covered in green stains. Curious as to what had caught Sir Philip's attention, she wandered over to him.

"Oh, they are beautiful," she said, bending low to breathe deeply of their heady scent.

It was her scent, he realised, only magnified by the huge array of blooms. From this moment on, he would always associate her with the myrtle. Acting on impulse, he broke off a spray and handed it to her. In doing so, he disturbed a butterfly the colour of lapis lazuli. It fluttered agitatedly into the air, alighted on the flowers she held for a moment, and then darted away on the breeze.

Smiling widely at him, she slipped it through a button hole on her pelisse.

"The Greeks knew the plant as Myrtos and associated it with Aphrodite," he said softly. "The Romans, as Myrtus and associated it with Venus. Ovid describes her rising from the sea, holding a sprig."

"Of course," said Sophie. "I have read of it somewhere. Thank you. You have brought the myth alive for me!"

Sir Philip smiled wryly. It was typical of her to be more interested in the classical overtones of the plant, whereas the usual innocent society maiden would have blushed and fluttered her lashes – aware of the romantic ones – and the less innocent would have been more interested in the aphrodisiac properties associated with it!

"We had better help Miss Trew gather some specimens," he murmured dryly. "Or she will read us a lecture on the iniquities of idleness!"

"And she would be quite right to do so!" Sophie said, turning and making her way into the meadow.

The feel of the warm sun on her back and the gentle breeze rippling through her hair was delicious, bringing a soft smile to her lips. She began to hum an old nursery tune as she moved amongst the feverfew. Leaving the tiny white flowers, she bent low to pick the feathery leaves that gave off a strong citrus-like aroma. The sweet sound of birdsong filled the air, and she thought that it felt like a long time since she had so thoroughly enjoyed the calming effects of nature.

Realising that despite her wide-brimmed bonnet the sun was now full on her face, she swivelled, still low to the ground and reached for the next nearest plant. Her pale, smooth hand brushed against another, much larger and stronger than her own.

Feeling a fizz of energy shoot like lightning up her arm and through her body, she gasped and raised two wide luminous eyes. She felt as if time itself had stalled. The scent of the meadow and the sound of birdsong faded away until only they remained, and she found herself drawn towards and lost within Sir Philip's ocean-deep gaze.

"I think we have enough leaves to last us for quite some time," came the gentle but clear voice of Miss Trew.

Sir Philip sprang upright immediately and offered his hand to help Sophie to her feet. She did not take it but slowly straightened as if in a half-dream and turned towards the calm voice that slowly filtered through her stunned senses, grounding her and enabling her to breathe once more.

Miss Trew took her arm and led her back towards their carriage, at the same time, filling the silence with her gentle chatter.

It was not long before they turned a bend in the road and were confronted by two large gates that had been thrown open in anticipation of their arrival. A long avenue lined with cypress trees led towards the villa, a loggia ran along the front of the upper floor supported by a series of classical looking columns. Spread out in front of them were impressive gardens.

As they made their way towards the villa, they admired the well-kept ornamental parterres which were occasionally interrupted by invitingly shaded paths, some lined with classical statuary. Nearer the villa, the soft breeze carried a fragrant smell. They saw that here, the neatly clipped box-hedges framed beds filled with herbs. In the centre, a three-tiered fountain was displayed, topped by a graceful nymph and, to either side, were two fierce lions from whose mouths water also spouted.

They pulled up beside an elaborate balustraded front, which was reached by two opposing sets of steps and gave entrance to the villa. Count Maldolo was waiting for them there. Sir Philip did not dismount but gave the count an appraising stare before briefly nodding. The count also took his time surveying his unexpected visitor before running lightly down the steps and returning the acknowledgement by the briefest inclination of his head.

Sophie felt the strange tension between the two men and hastily introduced them.

"Sir Philip was kind enough to show us the way," she explained, glancing from one to the other.

Neither broke their stare.

"Thank you for seeing the ladies safely here, please stay and refresh yourself," the count eventually said – politely enough – but his countenance remained grave and offered little encouragement.

"Thank you for your kind offer, but I cannot stay," Sir Philip replied, somewhat tersely.

"Ah, your friend is still sick?"

"Yes, so if you will excuse me," he said, offering a brief bow in the general direction of all before abruptly wheeling his horse about and cantering back down the avenue.

"I would have escorted you myself if I had thought you would have had any difficulty finding the way," the count said a trifle stiffly, unable to keep a hint of disapproval from his tone. "But come, the ladies are ready for you."

Sophie was surprised when instead of mounting the steps to the villa, he led them to a side garden. It was delightful. Bordered by pots of lemon and orange trees, its central focus was a large shaded pergola draped with vines, with tubs of rosemary and lavender at its base. Underneath a long table was filled with a great variety of cakes, bread, fruits, ham, and figs.

The marchesa and Contessina Isotta both stood and offered them a small bow. Dropping a light curtsey, Sophie smiled. "It is nice to see you both again, and how wonderful that we can partake of our meal in such a beautiful and fragrant setting."

"Ladies, I have a little business to attend to but will join you later," said the count, bowing briefly before disappearing back around the side of the villa.

An awkward silence followed, and Sophie found that she did not know quite how to break it. The contessina was dressed rather plainly in a cotton print dress with a warn shawl draped around her shoulders although the day was already warm. She kept her hands demurely folded in her lap, her smooth face expressionless, and her eyes downcast.

An old servant dressed in faded livery, who looked like he should have been retired years ago, served coffee and then withdrew. Then and only then, did the marchesa speak, proceeding to a diligent cross-examination of Sophie's birth, marriage, and the reasons which had brought her so far from her own country.

"You were fortunate that your family managed such an advantageous marriage for you," she said.

"But I am surprised that they would approve of you travelling such a distance with only one female chaperone at such a young age."

"But then I am a widow and not dependent on their approval," Sophie said quietly.

"But surely you would not go against your families' wishes?" she probed.

"I would certainly never wish to behave in a way of which they would disapprove," Sophie hedged, sending Miss Trew a rather desperate glance.

Miss Trew knew her duty and began to address a series of questions on the medicinal qualities of the various herbs she had seen, drawing the marchesa's attention away from her employer.

"You must forgive my aunt," Contessina Isotta said, her voice barely more than a whisper. "Things are different here, and she is somewhat old-fashioned in her views."

Sophie felt sorry for the girl, who barely seemed to dare utter a word in her aunt's presence. By gentle questioning, she managed to discover that she had not long returned from the nunnery where she had been educated, and it was hoped that a marriage for her would soon be arranged.

Sophie smiled. "And who is the lucky man?"

The contessina merely shrugged, but her soft mouth drooped sadly. "I hardly know, some marchese from an ancient family, like your husband he is much older than me. I will not get to meet him until the contract has been signed."

Sophie was a little shocked, although a similar arrangement had been made for her, she could have refused, and she had certainly met her future husband on more than one occasion before she had accepted his offer.

She had no opportunity to probe further as at that moment, the count returned.

"If you have finished, might I suggest a turn about the gardens?" he suggested.

The marchesa declined, so Sophie and the count went ahead down the narrow walkways, with Miss Trew and Contessina Isotta following behind. They came to a shady walkway where a series of classical statues were placed at even intervals. All were toga-clad ladies who were looking over their shoulders towards them.

"They are beautiful," said Sophie, pausing to run her hand over one.

The count regarded her thoughtfully for a moment. "In their way, but you are more so."

Sophie felt something in herself recoil at the cool delivery of his words. "Please," she said, putting out a hand as if to ward them off.

But the count took her gloved hand in his own and bent to brush his lips against it. "How is it that you can admire and comment on the beauty that surrounds you, yet you would disparage those who find within themselves a similar sentiment when they look upon your form? You dismiss it immediately as artifice and empty of all true sentiment, and where this is true, you do no harm and maybe even some good. But where the feeling is truly felt, you wound the bearer of it and in doing so diminish your own worth!"

Sophie had felt no depth of sentiment in his words, and neither did she wish to. She had the feeling that he viewed her as another object he would like to add to his collection. She had, at first, been drawn to the elegance of his person and the gentleness of his manners. He had always displayed a dignified reserve that in no way threatened her and that he had not uttered meaningless nothings to her had been to his advantage. Now, she realised that behind that reserve lay a lack of any human warmth that was chilling.

"I have no wish to wound you or any man," she said. "If beauty I have, it is through none of my doing. I admire these statues for their form, yes, but I would rather be admired for a virtue that I have cultivated, for some act or achievement that is worthy of merit, than for merely possessing the face and form that God gave me."

The count released her hand and offered her a small bow. "Forgive me if I spoke out of turn. I meant no disrespect."

Miss Trew and Contessina Isotta had at last caught up with them. Sophie noticed that the young girl sent an anxious glance from beneath her lashes in the direction of her father. Sophie took her arm and turned back towards the house but found it difficult to draw any conversation out of the contessina. Each enquiry had her sending a nervous glance over her shoulder, reminding Sophie of the row of statues so recently observed. The formal gardens, where every tree and border were clipped, suddenly felt oppressive, and she realised that she had preferred the more natural, wild beauty of the meadow.

As they approached the villa, Sophie thanked Count Maldolo for his hospitality and asked for her coach to be summoned. Any feelings of disappointment she might have felt at not having seen the rumoured treasures within the villa were superseded by the desire to avoid any opportunity for another tête-à-tête with him.

She pondered on what she had observed as they made their way back to town.

"That poor girl hardly dares to breathe without her father or aunt's permission," said Sophie.

"She has indeed been brought up very strictly," agreed Miss Trew. "I believe it is the custom to keep the girls close until they are married so that no whisper of scandal can attach to their name."

"It is more than that," Sophie said. "I could not help but feel that there was a well of sadness within her, and I did not hear one kind word addressed to her. I hope her marchese proves to be as kind and generous as Edward proved to be."

\* \* \*

As soon as Sir Philip was through the gates, he let Alcides stretch into a gallop. He had not liked leaving Lady Lewisham and Miss Trew, just as he had not liked leaving Harry. He generally trusted his judgement, and he had not liked Count Maldolo. There had been no warmth in his offer of hospitality, and he had felt the underlying resentment at his presence that had bristled through the man.

That he had some interest in Lady Lewisham, he had no doubt – that she was unaware of it – he also had no doubt. The feeling that he had left a lamb to the slaughter niggled at him and only the knowledge that Miss Trew would watch over her had enabled him to take his leave. He had done so with alacrity as the desire to ruffle the count's feathers had been very tempting. In all truth, he would have liked to have pushed him up against the wall and threatened him with all manner of unpleasant things if he dared to so much as breathe too close to Lady Lewisham.

He groaned. He was in trouble. When she had been happily moving through the flowers in the meadow, humming a sweet melody, utterly unconscious of her grace and beauty, he had felt himself drawn to her like a moth to a flame. When she had turned so suddenly and their hands had met, skin on skin, that flame had burned in her eyes, sending a dry heat through him, igniting a desire that whispered to him to lay her down among the daisies and sip her nectar.

Thank heaven for Miss Trew! One calmly uttered, commonplace phrase had been more effective than a douche of cold water. Much more worrying, though, was the wave of fierce protectiveness that had possessed him as he had watched her return slowly to herself. The urge to sweep her up into his arms and carry her somewhere, anywhere he knew she would be safe from anyone who might try to corrupt the innocence that he had felt within her, even as he had felt her desire burst into life at that brief touch. Widow or not, she was that rare thing, an innocent temptress. Only a snake would try to take advantage of that.

Only marriage would do for Sophie, Lady Lewisham, but marriage was something neither of them wished for.

Harry, he must concentrate on Harry. He would make sure that Lady Treleven would know the happiness of being reunited with a son whom she loved unconditionally, even as his own mother had loved him.

CHAPTER 11

That evening Lady Bletherington came to call with the reluctant Mr Maddock in tow. Dressed as carelessly as usual, he bowed politely enough and then went and sat on the window seat and stared down into the street below – as if whatever was going on there, was bound to be more interesting than anything the ladies might have to say.

"My dears," Lady Bletherington said as soon as she was through the door, "how cosy this room is. No wonder you are tempted to stay in by the fire. These old grand palazzos are all very well but not always very comfortable. Now tell me everything. How have you been spending your time in this delightful city?"

When told of their invitation to visit the Marchesa D'Orza and Contessina Isotta, she looked amazed, but perhaps more surprising was Mr Maddock's reaction. Rising from his perch in the window, he came and sat next to his relative, his eyes fixed rather unnervingly on Sophie.

"You were honoured indeed to be invited to their estate for it is not as it is at home, my dear. Italians prefer to visit at the opera or theatre rather than entertain at their homes. The count must be very impressed with you. Yes, indeed, very impressed," she trailed off, already writing in her mind the letter that she would send to Lady Renfrew, as she was sure to be interested in such a promising event.

Sophie felt a twinge of irritation. She had purposefully not mentioned Count Maldolo, unwilling to give Lady Bletherington food for the gossip that she knew would be spread around her circle without delay – not because she was malicious – but because she could not help herself.

"Tell me, what did you make of the marchesa? She is very proud, is she not? It is said she was very much in love in her youth with some count or other, and there was an arrangement between the families that they would wed, but he all but left her at the altar. Apparently, he fled afterwards for fear of terrible reprisals! She was then married to an ancient marchese who made her miserable, and when the present count's wife died, she came to live with him."

"I know nothing of this," said Sophie, wondering why, if it were true, she was complicit in forcing Isotta into such a similar situation. "She was certainly very reserved. Contessina Isotta seemed a very gentle creature."

Mr Maddock sighed deeply at the words.

"Her beauty is divine, her bearing gentle, her brow pure, her gaze soft..." he trailed off.

"You know her?" Sophie said surprised. "It seemed

to me that she was kept very close." She certainly could not imagine someone of Mr Maddock's stamp being let anywhere near her.

"I saw her at the opera the other night," he said dreamily. "The Maldolo box is next to Byron's. But you are right," he said bitterly, "there is no way of getting near her. She is guarded as if she is a prisoner, and he her jailor!"

"Surely, you exaggerate, sir," said Miss Trew gently. "Would a jailor take his daughter to the opera? Perhaps she is more like a precious jewel, that may be occasionally displayed but must be kept safe at all times."

Mr Maddock ran a hand through his long, limp locks and got swiftly to his feet. "Pah! She is displayed only as her beauty reflects well on the owner of it! Like all his other treasures! He thinks as highly of himself as if he were a Medici. Come, aunt," he said with uncharacteristic firmness. "We must not take any more of these good ladies' time, we have other visits to make, remember?"

Sophie was amazed that Lady Bletherington responded with such alacrity to his unusual display of decisiveness, laying her hand on his arm and smiling warmly up at him. "How right you are, dear. Where would I be without you?"

Sophie, though relieved at their departure, was conscious of a nagging worry. "Aggie," she said slowly, "do I imagine it, or did you think that Mr Maddock knew more about the family than he should have?"

"Well, my dear," said Miss Trew thoughtfully, "if the poor boy is forced to escort his aunt everywhere and retreats into the background regularly, I should think he hears all sorts of odd bits of gossip that could lead him to draw a quite false picture of the situation."

Sophie smiled warmly at her friend. Just because he had echoed some of her own feelings after her visit, (feelings that on reflection seemed out of proportion and exaggerated), did not mean he had formed them at first hand. "You are right, of course, but he spoke of Isotta with such reverence that I find it hard to imagine he has not somehow met her."

"Ah, but unlike you, my dear, he is of a romantic disposition, or thinks he is which amounts to the same thing! The beauty that is witnessed from afar will never be tainted by the realisation that she has a shrill voice, freckles or bad teeth..."

Sophie started to giggle. "Oh, stop it, Aggie, for you know the contessina suffers from none of these terrible afflictions!"

A timid knock at the door brought them to their senses. Recognising the knock, Miss Trew bent over the fire, removed the kettle she had placed there, and filled a cup with its steaming water. A pungent, bitter smell filled the room as Sophie opened the door.

Doctor Johnson came in, smiling warmly at the ladies. He seemed to enjoy sitting with them for half an hour in the evening, almost as if for that short time, he could imagine he was enjoying the comforts of his own home.

"How is our patient?" enquired Miss Trew.

The Doctor's smile widened. "His fever becomes less virulent by the hour, and his head does seem to be improving."

"How kind of you to administer to him so carefully and patiently," she said, real admiration in her warm tones. "I have prepared another infusion. I will just pop it up to him."

"Let me," said Sophie, taking the steaming cup from her hands. "You entertain our visitor. I will not be above a moment."

A gentle smile curved her lips. She was reasonably sure that Doctor Johnson's admiration for Miss Trew was also at the heart of the visits. He was far too proper a gentleman to take advantage of her good nature, however, and so she felt no qualms in leaving her with him. They usually fell into a discussion of various herbal remedies versus more traditional ones, and although they often disagreed, it was in such a gentle manner that you would have had to be listening very carefully to have noticed.

Sophie did not knock; she did not wish to either disturb the patient or his watcher if they were asleep. As she peeped around the door, she saw Sir Philip was in his shirtsleeves, a book in his hand and his eyes firmly fixed on his friend. The viscount was still and pale, but his breathing was quiet and regular.

"How is Lord Treleven?" Sophie said in a whisper, coming fully into the room. "I have brought another one of Miss Trew's infusions."

Sir Philip moved as if to stand, but Sophie waved him back. "Please, don't. The sickroom is no place for such formality."

Sir Philip's lips twisted into a smile. "He is sleeping so peacefully, I am not sure I should wake him."

As Sophie glanced towards the patient, he opened his eyes and looked straight at her, his gaze clear.

"If that potion tastes as disgusting as it smells, you can take it away again!" he said with a weak grin.

"Harry, do you know who I am?" Sir Philip said, surging to his feet.

A twinkle came into his eyes. "Hello, old chap. Had to wake up – couldn't stand any more of that twaddle you were reading to me. I would have thought my letter made it clear that I didn't think much of that Byron fellow. Happy to see you of course, but just at this moment I'm more interested in the vision of loveliness hovering at the end of my bed as if she had seen a ghost."

Sophie's dimples peeped out as she offered him a small curtsey. "Do not be mistaken by outward appearances, my lord," she said, "for I am determined you will partake of this potion, however disgusting it may smell."

"You are clearly a witch, and I have not the strength to argue," said Lord Treleven, holding out a recalcitrant hand that refused to do the dictates of his will, but shook alarmingly.

"Here, let me," said Sophie, gently lifting the cup to his lips and offering him a small sip. When he wrinkled his nose, she murmured, "Just a little bit more, my lord."

As he drank, her eyes lifted and locked with Sir Philip's. There was a wealth of relief and something else she could not quite identify in his glance.

"Give me a hand, will you, Philip?" said the viscount, trying to push himself up into a more upright sitting position. "I'm weak as a kitten!"

Between them, they raised him without difficulty, and Sophie adjusted the pillows behind him with a proficiency that suggested it was not the first time she had taken part in such a manoeuvre.

"That is hardly surprising, sir, when you have hardly swallowed a mouthful of food for the better part of a week. I will ask the kitchens to send up a chicken broth," Sophie said firmly.

The viscount closed his eyes wearily, but a small grin still played around his mouth. "I can hardly wait! Where is Maria?"

Sophie withdrew discreetly as Sir Philip perched on the edge of his friend's bed.

"She's flown the coop," he said gently, before explaining the situation.

Harry closed his eyes as he listened. They sprang open at the mention of his mother, and a small laugh shook him.

"Thank heaven she did not accompany you. Maria had a dramatic flair that would not have sat well with her."

"If you mean she was fond of hysterics, I know!"

"Poor Maria! She deserved the reward, you know. She looked after me even after my own funds ran out. Her father ran a café, but unfortunately took part in the more serious gambling sessions that went on in private upstairs, unsuccessfully as it seems!" Harry's head sank back against his pillows as if the very act of speaking had drained what little energy he possessed.

"And my father?" he asked softly.

"He was thrown from his horse and broke his neck not long after you left," Sir Philip said gently.

Harry's jaw clenched, and his hands curled into fists. "My poor mother," he finally said.

"Yes, she did not take it well and has only recently

come out of seclusion. The sooner I get you home, the better," said Sir Philip.

Harry's eyes shot open again. "Home?"

"We have much to discuss, Harry, but it can all wait until you are much stronger. The only significant things you need to know are – Worthington did not die, and I intend to return you to your mother as soon as possible."

Harry closed his eyes again and the sigh that he slowly exhaled, seemed dragged up from the depths of his soul. "Worthington did not die!" he whispered. "Yes, take me home, old chap. Take me home!"

Sir Philip watched his friend fall back into a deep sleep and realised that his jaw was rigid with tension. Slowly massaging it with his hand, he came to a sudden decision. He withdrew a leather pouch from his discarded coat's pocket, strode over to the window that looked out onto the courtyard below, threw it open, and let out a low whistle.

Within moments, Vaughen appeared. Sir Philip threw the pouch down to him, not at all surprised when he caught it without a fumble. "Get yourself to Leghorn and in the morning book us passage on the first sea-worthy vessel that will take us home."

Vaughen grinned up at him. "Will do, sir. Good English air is just what his lordship needs!"

They were in luck, an English merchant vessel, The Minerva, was due to leave for London in two days.

"But do you think Lord Treleven is in any fit state to be moved by sea?" Miss Trew said in her gentle way when Sir Philip broke the news to them.

"He will cope with it far better than a land journey,

which would jolt his emaciated form and aching head quite horribly. He is used to sailing and the voyage will give me time to feed him up a bit, for I dare not hand him over to his mother in his present condition!"

"But what if he suffers another relapse?" said Sophie, aware of a sinking sensation in the pit of her stomach.

Sir Philip turned to Doctor Johnson with a wry smile. "This is where I hope I can persuade you to accompany us, sir. I will, of course, pay your passage and you may name your price for your time, services and the early end to your tour."

Doctor Johnson looked torn. Although he had been able to afford to come on this trip, he was by no means so well off that he could easily dismiss both the payment and privilege of serving the gentry. Also, he had come to a slow realisation recently that he was indeed missing the comforts of his home. He suspected that he might be a little too old and set in his ways to be experiencing his first grand tour. Involuntarily, his eyes turned towards Miss Trew.

She smiled gently at him. "It would be a prudent move indeed, for I am quite certain the Doctor's presence must make all the difference to the continued improvement and management of Lord Treleven's condition."

Finding he could not bear to see himself diminished in this good lady's eyes, he had agreed to it before he had quite realised what he had done.

Sir Philip bowed first to Miss Trew and then Sophie. "Your willingness to offer support to myself and Lord Treleven will not be quickly forgotten. Do you head to Florence soon?"

Sophie forced words past the strange lump that had formed in her throat and said with a small smile, "We were becoming quite a cosy party. Count Maldolo would condemn us as a party of home-sick English, so perhaps it is for the best!"

Sir Philip's brow puckered slightly. "Is his opinion of such importance to you?"

Sophie laughed and shook her head. "Only in that, I would not wish to prove him right!"

Sir Philip took her hand for a moment. "I have spent a large portion of my life avoiding my own home and country, but now that I have found Harry, I wish for nothing more than to be back there. I will admit to both a feeling of homesickness and uneasiness at leaving you behind. If you do wish to return, you only need say..."

Sophie withdrew her hand from his gentle grasp and clasped it firmly behind her back because for a mad instant, she had been tempted to curl her fingers closer around his and concede that there was nothing she would like more than to return with him. Not because she had tired of Italy, but because she felt that she would be less disappointed with the loss of the sights Florence and Rome had to offer than with the prospect of his absence.

This thought frightened her more than a little. *You must continue to develop your character and independence.* These had almost been Edward's last words of advice to her, and she had faced the disapproval of her family and the discomforts and dangers of her journey in an effort to follow them. Was she really ready to give up that independence and entrust her character to a gentleman who though a loyal friend to Lord Treleven and a charming and capable companion to her and Miss Trew, was still a confirmed bachelor and known womaniser? She could not see that becoming any man's mistress could help her develop either her character or independence, and as Sir Philip had assured her that he did not intend to be driven by duty, she could not imagine that he had any other motivation in mind.

"If you had seen how I fared on the relatively short crossing to France, you would be grateful that I will not be accompanying you. At least this way, Doctor Johnson will be able to concentrate all his efforts on Lord Treleven! If you would like to borrow my carriage to take him to the port, consider it at your disposal."

Sir Philip looked stern for a moment before bowing and offering a crooked smile. "That won't be necessary. I will be taking Harry down to the port by canal tomorrow. I hope you enjoy the rest of your visit. If you run into any trouble, send word to the British Consulate in Florence."

Sophie raised her chin slightly at this. "So, you still think that we are incapable of looking after ourselves?"

Sir Philip's grin widened. "I may have been mistaken when I compared you to an orchid, after all, you are as prickly as a cactus! Lay your prickles, Lady Lewisham, for I shall allow that you are more than capable of adapting to the conditions in which you find yourself."

Deciding that the hotel would be a little flat after the departure of Sir Philip and Doctor Johnson, the ladies were also packed and ready to leave the following morning.

Harry was carried down in a chair, too weak and dizzy yet to walk that far but too proud to allow Sir Philip to carry him.

"Ah, there you are, my sorceress!" he said, spying Sophie stood amongst her luggage. "You can be no less for you silenced the army of tiny hammers that were attacking my poor skull! For such a service, I will be eternally grateful!"

Sophie smiled as she saw his eyes were glowing with a sort of feverish anticipation. He was obviously pleased and excited to be going home. She shuddered as she briefly contemplated the weeks at sea he would have to endure first.

"It is rather my companion, Miss Trew, whom you should thank, sir, for both the inspiration and the recipe for the potion came from her."

Sophie's opinion of him grew as he immediately turned his attention to Miss Trew, his gallantry undiminished.

"Miss Trew, you are an angel. I would ask you to come closer, please."

Smiling at Lord Treleven as if he were an amusing child, she approached him and offered him a small curtsy. He beckoned her closer as if he wanted to impart something of a private nature to her, but when she bent forward, he kissed her soft cheek as if she had been his old nurse.

"Thank you."

To Sophie's surprise, rather than becoming flustered, she merely smiled indulgently down at him. "Well, by rights, it is Doctor Johnson you should be thanking, for I think your recovery is largely down to him."

"Well, if we have all finished praising everybody else, it is time we were going." Sir Philip was brisk and business-like.

Sophie handed him the letter she had stayed up late composing. Knowing how sharp Lady Renfrew's observation skills were, she had found it surprisingly difficult to write. She had been very careful not to refer to Sir Philip too regularly or too warmly, and she had struggled to mention Lady Bletherington at all without making her appear the foolish creature she undoubtedly was.

To relieve her feelings somewhat, she had sacrificed Mr Maddock, and sketched for Lady Renfrew an image of his outward appearance and erratic behaviour that would, she hoped, amuse her. And then she had come to her visit to the Maldolo estate. She could not omit it as she was very sure that Lady Bletherington would also be writing to Lady Renfrew and would be sure to mention it and invest it with a significance that it did not merit. She saw no reason to keep from her the awkward scene he had initiated or her unequivocal response to it. Her finished letter was no masterpiece of the epistolary art, but she hoped conveyed a coherent, lively account of their experiences so far.

Their boat was waiting on the canal just outside the hotel. Lord Treleven made as if to stand, but his legs buckled.

"Damn your pride," muttered Sir Philip, picking him up as if weighed no more than a small child and striding off with a final nod to the ladies.

"When you return to England, please feel free to

call on me at any time," Doctor Johnson said, colouring slightly as he pressed his card into Miss Trew's hand, before hurrying off after them.

Both ladies were unaware of the other's long sigh as they watched the barge slowly disappear around a bend in the river. Their carriage swept out onto the road at that point, snapping them out of it. They had agreed they must pay a call on Lady Bletherington on their way out of town, and Sophie unexpectedly found herself looking forward to the empty stream of her chatter, hoping that it would fill the emotional void which she had felt suddenly close around her.

They knew something was amiss as soon as Lady Bletherington's cameriere admitted them. He had always been silent and distant before, so Sophie was unprepared when he suddenly clutched her arm, pulling her along, excitedly saying, 'The Inglese mi'lady has turned into a donna Italiana!"

At first bemused by this odd comment, all became clear as they were shown into her sitting room and found Lady Bletherington half reclining on a sofa, her lace cap wildly askew, weeping and wailing in quite an abandoned manner. She was attended only by her maid, who stood by uselessly wringing her hands.

Miss Trew was immediately before her, waving her small vinaigrette beneath her nose. When this failed to make her more coherent, Sophie retrieved a small vase from a nearby table, unceremoniously threw the wilting flowers on the floor, and dashed the remaining discoloured water over the poor, afflicted lady.

Her maid gasped audibly, but the effect was immediate. The smell and the slime from the liquid caused

Lady Bletherington to cease her shrieking as she found it necessary to hold her breath whilst she frantically scrubbed at her face with her sodden handkerchief.

Sophie turned to the maid. "Stop standing there gawking and go and fetch her ladyship a glass of wine!"

As she scurried from the room, Sophie perched precariously on the small amount of sofa remaining and took her hands.

"I am sorry, ma'am, but if we are to help you with whatever has caused this distress, you must calm yourself."

Lady Bletherington shuddered and took a great gulp of air but gradually contained her emotions until only the odd, small sob escaped her. The wine seemed to restore her further, and she managed to sit up a little.

"It is my poor Bertie," she finally said. "You must help, Lady Lewisham, he has gone!"

"Bertie?" Sophie asked bemused, trying to recall if Lady Bletherington owned a dog by that name. It seemed the sort of name one might give to a dog.

"Mr Maddock," she said a trifle impatiently. "He has become quite infatuated with the daughter of Count Maldolo! He imagines her persecuted and himself in the role of her noble rescuer!"

Sophie felt quite stunned. "But where would he get such an idea?"

Lady Bletherington looked a little uncomfortable. "Oh, I don't know. Where do romantic young men get any of their ideas? Some ridiculous poem? Some hypothetical discussion?"

Miss Trew looked askance as the latter suggestion. "And has he been witness to such a discussion?"

A pink tinge infused Lady Bletherington's pale cheeks. "Lady Montrose has quite a wit," she admitted. "She likes to weave amusing tales around some of the Italian characters who hold themselves aloof from us, no one seems to know quite what happened to his first wife after all," she broke off at Miss Trew's amazed stare. "But it is all nonsense, everybody knows it is all nonsense!"

"Clearly not everybody!" Sophie said drily.

This brought Lady Bletherington back to the matter-in-hand.

"Oh, my dear girl! You are the very person! I fear he has gone to abduct her! With only honourable intentions, of course! You must go after him... explain to the count... do something, anything! When I think of what he might do to my poor nephew!"

"Lady Bletherington, you cannot consider it an honourable act to attempt to remove a gently reared girl from her home!" Miss Trew protested. "It is wicked, quite wicked!"

"And most unlikely," interjected Sophie. "How would he achieve it? He can hardly drive up to the villa unnoticed! Even if he could, I can hardly imagine Contessina Isotta would agree to such a thing! She has been strictly reared in a convent after all!"

"So was Byron's mistress," Lady Bletherington said tearfully, "and look where that has ended! Please, help me. I am sure poor Lady Renfrew would wish it."

That had Sophie's full attention for she would never have ascribed such an adjective to that particular lady. "Poor Lady Renfrew?"

Lady Bletherington suddenly covered her mouth with her hand as if to cram the words just spoken, back in.

"I am sworn to secrecy," she whispered. "Forget I said anything!"

For such a loquacious lady, she suddenly became remarkably clam-like, a sly look in her watery eyes. Nothing Sophie said had any effect.

"Oh all right," she finally muttered, exasperated. "I will go to the Maldolo villa but only on the condition that you will immediately tell me what it is you wish to keep from me concerning Lady Renfrew."

Clearly, that had been what Lady Bletherington had been waiting to hear for her lips sprang open on the utterance.

"Thank you, Lady Lewisham. I am sorry to report that I have indeed heard from Lady Renfrew and she is mortally sick. Influenza! You know how it is with these persons with unusually strong constitutions. They are hardly ever ill, but when they are... and of course, she is not as young as she used to be. Her letter was very affecting, but she insisted I say nothing to you or her godson, who I believe is also in Pisa. Although as he has not seen fit to visit me, it is hardly likely that I could say anything to him."

Her suddenly peevish tone was quite lost on Sophie, who had gone very still and pale. She had a sudden image of Lady Renfrew, alone and unattended apart from her servants. She knew this was unlikely as although she was a childless widow, she had plenty of friends and acquaintances. She had been the only one of Edward's relations he had seemed to have any fondness for, and she was not surprised for they shared the same irreverent sense of humour and acute understanding.

Sophie's troubled eyes turned towards Miss Trew. "I think we should go to her," she finally said.

"I agree, my dear," Miss Trew said calmly. "We must also send word to Sir Philip, for he will want to know, I am sure."

"We will do better than that," Sophie said decisively. "We shall join him on his journey!"

Miss Trew looked a little worried at this proclamation. "But, my dear, you suffer horribly with sea-sickness."

"Oh, what matter?" she said impatiently. "Lady Renfrew was so kind to us. Indeed, I felt more at home in her house than I ever did in my own!"

"Don't forget my poor Bertie," interjected Lady Bletherington.

"The villa is not far out of our way to Leghorn," Sophie assured her. "But we will not be returning, so send a servant with us who can return to you with any news."

"My dear, how will we explain our uninvited visit?" asked Miss Trew, once they were shut up in their carriage once more.

"We are merely taking our leave," said Sophie firmly, "for if we find any sign of 'poor Bertie', I will own myself amazed!"

She was mistaken. As the carriage approached the house, they heard a piercing scream. Glancing up towards the source, they saw Contessina Isotta leaning precariously over the parapet that framed the loggia on the first floor.

Mr Maddock and Count Maldolo were struggling

together in front of the steps. The count, the taller of the two, pushed Mr Maddock roughly away, causing his unbound hair to fall in front of his face. As he impatiently pushed it out of his eyes, he received a punishing right hook to his jaw that sent him sprawling in the gravel. Count Maldolo then picked up his whip which had fallen to the ground in their struggle, and with a practised flick of his wrist cracked it ominously above the prostrate Mr Maddock, who began to scramble backwards as fast as he could on his elbows.

Sophie had seen enough. Jumping down from the carriage, she perhaps unwisely placed herself between the two gentlemen.

"Stop this at once, sir. I cannot believe you would attack a man who is already down!"

The count raised eyes that boiled like black oil. "He is still breathing," he said between clenched teeth. "A man who would try to sully the name of my daughter with his grubby English ways does not deserve to be still breathing. He is not at home now. In Italy, we know how to look after our own!"

"Papa!" Isotta's voice was low and urgent.

Miss Trew gasped, and all eyes swivelled upwards. Isotta was now standing precariously on the parapet of the loggia, one arm wrapped loosely around a pillar.

The count froze as if turned to stone. Sophie witnessed an expression of such bleak torment twist his features that she half-raised one hand towards him in a futile gesture of support. She had thought he was bereft of all feeling, but now she sensed the deep well of anguish he carried within himself, the lid of which had been blown clean off by his daughter's reckless action.

"Isotta, cara mia," he gasped, his unsteady hand reaching up towards her. "You are so like your beautiful mother! Please, get down. Does this imbecile Inglese mean so much to you?"

The sadness Sophie had sensed in the young lady now overflowed, and great tears rolled over the smooth skin of her face unchecked.

"He is nothing to me," she cried, "as I am nothing to you! As my mother was nothing to you! I may as well follow her example and throw myself from here to the hard ground below, which will be as unyielding as your will! I will lay as cold and broken as the marble statues that you love so much! Perhaps then I will fill a very small corner of your shrivelled heart!"

"Noooo!" he cried, the words torn from him as Isotta swayed forwards.

But even as they watched, horrified, two arms came from behind her and pulled her back away from danger. Squires had her safe. Turning, he relinquished her to the silver-haired servant in the faded livery, who held her sobbing body until the marchesa appeared by his side, and between them they bundled her back inside the villa.

"Oh, well done, Squires!" Sophie murmured.

The count fell to his knees and dropped his head into his hands.

Sophie turned to instruct Mr Maddock to make himself scarce, but he seemed to have already seen the wisdom of this course of action for both he and Lady Bletherington's servant, were nowhere to be seen. Sophie and Miss Trew positioned themselves on either side of the count, gently encouraged him to his feet and helped him the few steps to a bench that looked out over the gardens.

He sat staring straight ahead, but Sophie felt certain it was not the garden he saw.

"I loved her mother," he finally said, his voice hoarse and low. "She was grace. She was beauty. She was life."

"Count Maldolo, you do not need to explain..."

"I do. There have been too many secrets," he insisted. "I had been conducting some business in Pisa and was late returning, Livia was waiting on the balcony. As I neared the villa, she was waving and calling to me. She was with child again and could not wait to tell me her news. The doctor explained that she might have felt dizzy, whatever the cause, she leaned out too far. She fell. I loved her more than life itself and yet I killed her," he said bitterly. "If I had not appeared at that moment, she might still be alive."

"You were not to blame," Sophie said softly. "It was a tragic accident."

"I told myself that a thousand times, but it did not help; it always felt that way." He closed his eyes on the words. "Isotta was the living image of her mother, but every time I looked upon her, I felt guilt and grief burrow ever deeper within me, becoming a canker in my heart. As soon as she was old enough, I sent her away to the nuns. When I saw Isotta standing there, it seemed as if history was about to repeat itself, but this time the blame would have been all mine. I have continued to push her away, even arranging her marriage to an old friend of the family who lives far away. I thought I could then start again, perhaps even marry."

He turned his head and looked at Sophie. "I could not bring myself to replace Livia with another Italian woman. You have something of her grace and vitality, but your colouring is so different, I even considered you, but when I touched you, I felt you shrink..."

"I knew there was no genuine feeling there," she explained.

"You were right," he said harshly. "Until I allow myself to love Isotta and through her, her mother again, I am only a – a spettro – a wraith. All this," his hand gestured towards the gardens, "is as nothing."

"Papa?"

They stood and turned as one. Isotta stood a few feet away, a fragile hope shone in her huge dark eyes.

"Is it true? Can you love me?"

The count could find no words, but it mattered not, he opened his arms wide, and she walked straight into them. As they clung tightly to each other, Miss Trew and Sophie discreetly made their way back to the coach.

The marchesa was waiting for them. Her small black eyes gleamed with joy, and she took Sophie's hand in both her own.

"Thank you, child," she smiled. "You are not the one for him, but it is sometimes easier to talk to a stranger, is it not? Now my brother will find himself again, and my Isotta will not be sent away to marry an old foolish man who should know better."

Sophie smiled at her and suddenly on impulse kissed her cheek. "I hope you will all find the happiness I am sure you deserve."

"And you, my child. Go home, for whatever it is you are searching for, you will not find it in a pile of old stones or a gallery of paintings. Most people are running away from something, but you can never run away from yourself."

CHAPTER 12

The Minerva was a large merchant vessel carrying a cargo of valuable white Carrera marble back to England. Its cabins were functional rather than comfortable. They were just large enough to house two sets of opposing bunks, set one above the other, with barely room to stand between them. Sir Philip lay on the bottom of one, Harry on the other. Both had their hands folded behind their heads and their legs crossed at the ankles. They stared at the empty bunk above, each lost in his thoughts.

The vessel had left at dusk to catch the tide, and the gentle rolling of the ship indicated a fair wind.

"It is many years since we shared a room," Sir Philip said quietly.

Harry smiled. "Do you remember the summer we built the tree house by the river and camped out in it?"

Sir Philip laughed. "Yes, of course. We insisted we were going to be self-sufficient and catch and cook our own food, but after one inedible rabbit stew we decided that we were pirates and so free to raid the kitchens under cover of darkness!"

After a short silence, Harry murmured, "As you would expect, the reality did not match the fantasy. I did not make a very good pirate."

Sir Philip sat up, swivelled, and planted his feet on the floor. Leaning his forearms on his thighs, he looked searchingly at his friend. Harry continued to stare at the bunk above.

"You did not make your fortune then?" he finally asked.

A small frown puckered Harry's brow. "There were fortunes to be made," he acknowledged, "especially in the West Indies, but I found there was no honour amongst thieves and that I had seen enough bloodshed to last me a lifetime."

"Ah," smiled Sir Philip. "You wished to be an honourable pirate!"

Harry let out a harsh laugh. "They named me Honest Harry! I became an honest smuggler instead and took to smuggling European goods into America. But I have been homesick of late and met an English merchant in Leghorn who suggested I might be of use to him running goods into England. I was sorely tempted, but whilst visiting Pisa, this damn fever struck!"

"Thank God it did! If I had not received your letter, you might never have discovered that you were safe to come home!"

"About my letter," Harry mumbled, still not meeting his friend's eyes.

Sir Philip stilled, not sure of what Harry was about to say or if he would want to hear it, but somehow aware in every fibre of his being that it would be important.

Finally, Harry turned his head. "You know that I lost my memory of the latter events of that day," he began.

There could be no question of which day he referred to. "I had hoped that might prove to be a blessing," Sir Philip said gently.

Harry's eyes darkened with remembered pain. "It was no blessing, for although I could not remember how I came to be where you found me, I was haunted by a feeling that I may have done something dishonourable, something cowardly!"

"Not you, my friend. You were always 'Madcap Harry', or 'Brave Harry', but never 'Cowardly Harry'!"

The viscount's lips twisted in a grimace. "I did not feel as if I had been brave," he said quietly. "For although I had forgotten much, one thing I could remember was a feeling..." he paused to lick his lips as if they were suddenly dry, and Sir Philip bent to retrieve something from the worn leather saddlebag which lay under his bunk. He passed a small silver hip flask to Harry.

"Gently," he said as Harry took a large swig and began to cough. "That is no way to treat a particularly fine brandy, nor will Doctor Johnson thank me if he finds his patient drunk as a wheelbarrow!"

A brief smile flitted over the viscount's face but quickly faded. "That feeling was terror, pure unadulterated terror!"

"Harry," Sir Philip sighed softly. "Only an insensate fool would not have felt terror at some point during that day. You had more excuse than most, for I saw three horses shot beneath you and each time you quickly found another riderless mount and re-joined the fray!"

Harry nodded briefly and took a deep, slow breath. "Be that as it may, I could not rid myself of the notion that in my terror, I may have fled the scene. When you told me you had found poor William's lifeless corpse laying across me, the idea that perhaps he had died trying to stop me deserting would not leave me. That would make me not only a cowardly deserter but also the murderer of one of my best friends! At first, it was just a vague, nagging worry that I tried to dismiss as ridiculous, but as time went on it claimed more and more of my thoughts until I tried to drown them out with whatever drink I could lay my hands on!"

Sir Philip grimaced, retrieved his flask from Harry, and ignoring his own advice, drank deeply.

"I wish you had shared these fears with me," he said so softly, his words could hardly be heard above the creaking of the ship and the low roar of the waves beyond. "I would wager my life against the chance of events unfolding as you have described. If anybody killed William, I fear it was more likely to have been me."

In a low voice full of self-loathing, he shared his encounter with Miss Bowles and William at Lady Richmond's ball. "I did not get to talk things out with him before the battle, and I have wondered ever since, if perhaps, the shock of his betrayal at the hands of not only his love but also myself, may have led him to conduct himself in battle with a rash recklessness that may have gotten him killed! I had meant to keep an eye on him, but I lost him in the chaos."

Harry now sat up and faced his friend, their knees only inches apart.

"What a pair we are," Harry said with a small smile. "I have not been much of a friend to you in recent years, Philip, but I can at least put your mind at rest now. I have remembered, you see. It is why I sent for you."

"Go on," Sir Philip said softly.

"William was indeed angry," Harry confirmed. "But not with you! More than one of his friends had warned him about Miss Bowles, including me. She was an outrageous flirt, but when they hinted as much to him, he would not believe them. You gave him all the confirmation he needed!"

"I did not know," Sir Philip said, pushing an agitated hand through his dark locks. "I had been busy drilling some of our greener recruits and only returned to Brussels for the ball. God knows why Wellington always insisted his best dancers attended such events!"

"William knew you were ignorant of his relations with Miss Bowles," Harry said gently. "After we retreated from Quatre Bras, he told me as much. He was embarrassed he had been such a fool and was glad he had discovered it before any announcement had been made. Philip, he was not suicidal, he even managed to laugh about it in the end, saying how relieved his mother would be that he would not be marrying anyone whose parents were engaged in trade."

Sir Philip felt a subtle shift within himself. The burden of guilt, which had lightened a shade with

Lady Treleven's forgiveness, now eased further with the ray of hope Harry had shone into that dark place.

"I had a fourth horse shot from under me," Harry continued after a moment. "All was confusion. I will never forget the infernal noise of Boney's drums or the explosions that stung my ears. The ground beneath my feet rumbled as if a sleeping giant had awoken as the cannon balls tore into the earth all around me. My eyes were watering with the smoke that filled the air, and I saw another horse go down, trapping one of ours beneath it. I ran half-blind towards him." Harry gulped and reached for the flask again.

"William?" Sir Philip said softly, handing it over.

Harry nodded. "Yes, it was William. He was alive but grievously injured. I managed to pull him free and began to drag him towards a stand of trees where he might hope to have some cover. I had just reached them when I felt a sharp pain in the side of my head and blood began to run into my eyes. I fell. William had blood seeping from the corner of his mouth and knew he was done for. 'I'm finished!' he said to me. 'Tell Philip, no fault!'. They were his last words, even dying he knew you would blame yourself, and he did not want that. I am only sorry it has taken me so long to remember."

For a long moment, they held each other's gaze and then moved together into a brief, fierce embrace. When they broke apart, they were smiling.

"So, you are not a coward," murmured Sir Philip.

"And neither of us killed poor William," said Harry.

"We must begin again," said Sir Philip firmly. "We will do better this time."

"I'll drink to that," smiled Harry reaching for the flask.

Sir Philip whisked it out of his hands. "No, we will shake on it! The last thing I need is for you to succumb to fever again!"

A shrill scream rent the air and acting on instinct, both gentlemen leapt to their feet at the same time, effectively blocking the other in. Sir Philip pushed Harry back down. "Rest, I will see what is afoot."

It took only one stride to reach the door and as he pulled it open, a second scream directed him to a cabin, a little further along the dim corridor. Without pause, he threw it open, and a large rat ran over his boot. Kicking it viciously away, he glanced into the small cabin that mirrored his own. Two ladies were perched precariously on one top bunk, another on the opposite one. He rapidly blinked his eyes to clear his vision as the pale, horrified faces had for a moment resembled Lady Lewisham, her maid, and Miss Trew. However, their faces did not transform into those of strangers, and Sophie's lips widened into a rueful smile.

"Sir Philip, you come to our rescue yet again! I am sorry to have disturbed your rest, but although I feel I have learned enough to deal with rats of the human variety, I fear I am no match for the furry kind!"

"I am surprised you did not snip off its tail for use in one of your potions, my green-eyed witch," grinned Harry, peeping over Sir Philip's shoulder.

Sir Philip felt a heaviness in his legs as the ship pitched suddenly. He braced them just in time to catch Sophie as she toppled forward off the bunk and straight into his arms.

"What in heaven's name are you doing here?" he said, bemused as he stared down into startled eyes that had deepened to the colour of fresh moss.

"You do not deserve to cradle such a treasure," complained his friend. "Stand aside. I will show you how to treat such a lady."

Putting Sophie down, he looked over his shoulder and grinned. "Calm yourself, Casanova, for you would, without a doubt, have dropped her!"

Embarrassed, Sophie hastily told him about Lady Renfrew's condition.

"She did not want us to know of it," she assured him. "But Lady Bletherington let it slip..."

Sophie looked on astounded as Sir Philip threw back his head – causing Harry to take a hasty step backwards – and began to laugh.

"Sir?" she said uncertainly, grabbing hold of the bunk from which she had so ignominiously just tumbled, as the ship pitched again.

"Lady Lewisham," he replied. "Believe me when I say you still have a lot to learn! Do you not know, that for a moment, Lady Bletherington would have relished that she had a snippet of knowledge that no one else was aware of, but that feeling would have been swiftly superseded by the desperate desire to share it with whomever next crossed her path? I only have a vague recollection of the lady in question, but of this, I am in no doubt. You may be just as sure that Lady Renfrew was fully aware of this fact!"

Sophie's mouth dropped open. "Are you suggesting that Lady Renfrew is not ill? That she would worry us so for no good reason?"

"I have never known my godmother to suffer a

day's illness. She has the constitution of an ox! As for whether her reason is good or not, we will find out soon enough."

Sophie had turned even paler than when he had first set eyes on her and now covered her mouth with her hand, her eyes suddenly huge in her face.

"There is no need for this distress..." he began, but Sophie cut him short with a shake of her head.

"Please, leave, now!" she said from between her fingers.

"There is no need..."

"There is every need," she gasped as the ship rolled again. "For if I am not much mistaken, I am about to be violently sick!"

The gentlemen retreated with all the alacrity she could wish for.

Harry improved day on day, until before long he was making himself a nuisance above decks, offering the captain unwanted advice on the trimming of the sails, and only Sir Philip's close watch prevented him on one occasion, from climbing aloft in a sudden violent squall to help reef them in.

Sophie did not fare so well. Doctor Johnson's cheerful proclamation that she would grow accustomed to the rolling and pitching of the ship within a few days, at first resigned her to her situation. As she experienced vertigo each time she attempted to stand, she spent the time laying patiently in her bunk, waiting for the nausea and sickness to pass. It refused to do so, however. Sherry laced with quinine did not help, and as the days passed, she fell into a deep, misery-filled lethargy. She survived mainly on a diet of tea and dry biscuits and welcomed the carefully administered doses of laudanum that Doctor Johnson eventually resorted to, to ensure at least some temporary relief from the worst of her symptoms.

It was fortunate that the wind was with them for most of the journey and so they made outstanding time, arriving at the docks in Wapping, London, in just under three weeks. However, she arrived in a much weakened state and Miss Trew, growing increasingly concerned, confided tearfully to Doctor Johnson that she was not sure how much longer her dear Sophie could have survived such an ordeal.

"It has been distressing indeed to witness her suffering," the good doctor confirmed. "Your tireless, tender ministrations have been invaluable. However, I think you will find that a few days in a bed that does not move, and a few good meals will largely restore Lady Lewisham to her usual robust health."

"It better had!" Sir Philip said grimly. "And if I do not find my darling godmother at death's door, she will have some explaining to do!"

"Oh ho!" laughed Harry. "If I weren't in such a hurry to see my dear mother, I would be tempted to come along to witness you put that esteemed lady in her place! If you manage it, you will be the first!"

As the only hardened sailor amongst them, the viscount had been the only one not to take too dismal a view of Sophie's situation. "Trust me," he had reassured his brooding friend. "As soon as she is ashore, this will all become a distant memory!"

As soon as the ship docked, Sir Philip sent Vaughen ahead to warn Lady Renfrew of their imminent arrival and Lady Lewisham's ill health, and Squires to organise a hackney cab as the Captain had refused to accept Lady Lewisham's carriage on board, claiming the ship was already heavily enough laden.

As before, Sophie did not find that the world stopped moving as soon as she stepped ashore, and when she discovered her sheets warmed and a fire lit in her chamber, she immediately retired, too poorly yet to feel any relief at her change in circumstance. Doctor Johnson administered another dose of laudanum to help her sleep and promised he would call in a couple of days to see how she went on.

Sir Philip ran Lady Renfrew to ground in her library. She sat in her usual place by the fire, but she was not alone. Sir Percy Broadhurst had somehow wedged his ample figure into the opposing chair. He sported an impressive neckcloth tied in the style known as the waterfall, a smart coat of claret superfine and a satin waistcoat daintily embroidered with flowers and vines. He had curly, greying hair and a pleasing if rather florid countenance. A twinkle lurked in his warm, brown eyes. His stays creaked as he leaned forward, preparing to get up.

"Don't trouble yourself, Sir Percy," said Sir Philip, a trifle shortly. "You don't need to stand on ceremony with me. I am pleased to see you here as I take it as an indication that Lady Renfrew is on the mend."

He turned and bowed in her direction as he spoke, sending her a keen glance as he did so. Expecting to see she was in her usual robust good health, he was shocked to see that her countenance did indeed show the ravages of a recent illness. Her complexion was much paler than usual, and there was a lacklustre air about her. Her sharp, silver eyes remained undimmed, however – even if the wrinkles around them seemed carved a little deeper than before – and they returned and held his close scrutiny.

"It is good to see you, my boy," said Sir Percy, struggling to his feet, after all. "It will do Lavinia good to have some young people around her. I won't pretend that she hasn't been a trifle down pin of late, never seen her so fagged to tell the truth! Had me worried for a while but as you say, she is on the mend now."

"Do stop prattling on like an old windbag, Percy!" Lady Renfrew snapped. "Anyone would think I had been at death's door!"

"Lady Bletherington certainly had that impression," Sir Philip murmured.

"Hrmpf!" she snorted. "She would turn a touch of influenza into a huge drama!"

"Was that not your intention, ma'am?" Sir Philip asked rather sharply.

"Now, just a minute, you young jackanapes," Sir Percy protested. "I don't know what Lady Bletherington has to say to anything, but there is no need for you to talk to Lavinia in that tone!"

"Oh, go home, Percy, do! The day I need you or anyone else to fight my battles, I'll lay back and cock up my toes there and then!"

Her words bounced off him harmlessly, and he chortled deep in his chest. "That's the ticket," he smiled. "Well, I'll be off then, leave you two to catch up."

Sir Philip opened the door for him and found himself the recipient of a sly wink. "Go easy on her, my lad," he said softly. "She's not quite up to full sail yet!"

Taking the vacated seat, he said a little more gently.

"I am sorry that you have been ill, Aunt Lavinia, but you are not alone. Lady Bletherington did indeed give Lady Lewisham the impression that you were in a desperate way, and it has caused her to suffer almost three weeks of unremitting sea-sickness!"

That formidable lady coloured slightly at his words. "I did not expect that you would both jump on the first ship home," she said with a touch of humility.

"Then why write to Lady Bletherington? Come to think of it, why on earth would you recommend her as a suitable acquaintance for Lady Lewisham?"

"Oh, climb down off your high-horse," she said, recovering her momentary lapse of composure. "How else was I to get news of you both? If there were any gossip to be had, she would be the possessor of it!"

Despite his best intentions, Sir Philip's lips twitched with amusement. "You are an incorrigible, shameless..."

"That is enough, Philip," she said warningly.

Sir Philip reached into his pocket and withdrew Sophie's slightly crumpled letter. "Lady Lewisham asked me to give you this before she decided to come home," he said thoughtfully, holding it by one corner, so it dangled invitingly in the space between them. "I had until this moment, forgotten that I still possessed it. But as she is now here herself, perhaps it would be better to return it to her."

Moving surprisingly swiftly, Lady Renfrew plucked it from his grasp.

"There, you have successfully carried out your commission. Now, tell me about Harry. Have you got him safely home?"

CHAPTER 13

A few days' rest did indeed restore Sophie's spirits and appetite although she still looked rather frail. She and Miss Trew were sitting in Lady Renfrew's comfortable morning room whilst that good lady took her customary afternoon nap, the sun pouring in through the windows when they received a morning call.

Sophie laid aside the journal she had been idly doodling in and stood to greet her visitor. Lady Hayward tripped into the room, her golden curls gleaming beneath a dashing bonnet of primrose satin, ornamented with a bunch of Provence roses.

"Lady Hayward," she smiled.

Her visitor came forward, both hands outstretched. "Please, call me Belle when we are private, for didn't I tell you we were destined to be great friends?"

Miss Trew dropped a brief curtsey and received a friendly nod in return.

"It is a pleasure to make your acquaintance, Miss

Trew," smiled Lady Hayward, "for I have heard some very good things about you!"

Miss Trew coloured slightly and bent to retrieve her sewing. "It is very kind of you to say so," she murmured. "I will leave you to be private."

Lady Hayward pulled Sophie down onto the sofa and looked her over carefully, noticing the slight violet shadows under her eyes. "You poor thing," she said softly. "I heard how very ill you have been, and I see it is quite true."

Sophie laughed. "I look positively haggard, don't I?"

Lady Hayward gave a tinkle of laughter and shook her head. "That was clumsy of me," she said. "I have never quite broken the habit of saying aloud whatever pops into my head. And it is not true, my dear, not at all, just a trifle below par. It is a beautiful day, please say you will come for a drive around the park with me. I am convinced it will do you the world of good."

Sophie smiled – her glance had strayed to the sunlit windows on more than one occasion this afternoon. "It would be just the thing! A breath of fresh air would be most welcome. I will have to change, but it will be the matter of a moment," she declared, determined that for once Burrows would get her ready in less than twenty minutes.

Left alone, Lady Hayward began to fidget. She soon stood and started wandering aimlessly around the room. Eventually, her eyes alighted on the discarded journal. She looked at it and then away again, but as the minutes ticked by her eyes were repeatedly drawn to it. She knew she should not, but finally, the temptation became too strong. Suddenly she snatched it up and carried on her progress around the room as she began idly flicking through the pages.

It was not quite what she had expected. Instead of the usual diary-type entries, she found a cleverly executed series of cartoons wittily drawn with snippets of speech or comments below. Seating herself again on the sofa, she perused them intently. She smiled as she saw a person who looked like a groom, dripping with water, an exasperated lady standing over him, hands on hips, a bucket discarded at her feet. The comment, *'Wherein Squires meets his nemesis!'* was written in a neat hand beneath.

She had heard of Miss Trew's encounter with the customs officer only the evening before when Sir Philip had come to dine and entertained them with a few choice snippets of their adventure. The spectacle of him kneeling before the modest Miss Trew, her hand clasped in his, great tears spurting from his small eyes in all directions – her face aflame and alarmed – brought forth a chuckle. The comment read: *'Miss Agnes Trew reveals her backbone and redeems a lost soul!'*

She laughed aloud at the representations of Mr Maddock. The sketches presented him as a distant Byronic figure, but the deft strokes of her pencil had somehow rendered him ridiculous, capturing his foolishness and a certain vacuity in his expression. Various snippets of hackneyed poetry were also scattered around his image. However, the sketch where he lay on the ground, his eyes popping out of his face in terror, a menacing figure who was the epitome of every gothic villain ever written looming over him with a whip, made her curious. What had happened here? The brief comment, *'Where the Pretender experiences a rude awakening!'*, shed little light on the situation.

Flicking back a few pages to see if she could glean some more of this story, she stumbled upon a page that made her take a slow, deep, inhalation of breath. Two figures bent low over a field of wild daisies, their hands just touching, their faces only inches apart, their gazes locked.

Lady Hayward felt a blush creep over her face, for the first time feeling the enormity of her intrusion. The intimacy of the scene was palpable, and there could be no doubt as to the identity of the man for Sophie had also drawn his face in the sky above. The likeness she had captured of Sir Philip was remarkable, but it was not the Sir Philip Lady Hayward knew. The eyes were gentle, yet intent, capturing a yearning and desire that made her heart skip a beat. Every line had been drawn with care, almost reverence, revealing much about the sketcher's feelings.

Lady Hayward shut the book firmly, feeling slightly ashamed and returned it to its original position on the small table by the sofa only moments before Sophie entered.

She was immaculately dressed in a half-dress of white poplin finished with a single flounce of deep blonde lace. Her pelisse was slightly shorter than her dress, of a pale blue Levantine and on her head was a simple straw bonnet, lined and trimmed with a similar blue silk and decorated with matching ribbons.

"I am so sorry to have kept you waiting," she said, rolling her eyes. "But my maid, Burrows, is a high-stickler when it comes to my appearance."

Lady Hayward smiled. "I can see that. You look delightful."

At that moment, a slightly rumpled Lady Renfrew strolled into the room, her turban slightly askew.

"Ha! Belle! I thought we would see you before too long! Taking Sophie out for an airing, are you? Well good, good, it will do her no harm, but don't keep her out too long, she has barely risen from her bed, you know. And don't wear her out with your constant tittle-tattle!"

Belle dimpled, not at all offended. "Of course not, Lady Renfrew. We are just going for a quick turn about the park."

"Hrmpf! There will be nothing quick about it. Between all the mincing fops, ridiculous dandies, and would-be corinthians, keen to show what tremendous whips they are, all the while keeping an eye out for the ladies, you will be lucky to maintain more than a snail's pace! Spare me a few minutes when you return, will you, Belle?"

Not waiting for an answer, she turned about and walked back out of the room.

Sophie and Belle exchanged a laughing look. "She is an original," said Belle, "but I wouldn't have her any other way!"

"I may be an original, but I am not deaf!" came a deep, booming voice from the hall.

Sophie and Belle clapped their hands to their mouths to stifle their giggles.

Lady Renfrew's words proved to be no less than the truth. The park was crammed full of a wide array of gigs, phaetons, barouches, and curricles – scores of riders weaved their way amongst them showing off their mounts and hailing acquaintances – and the walkways were packed with afternoon strollers. Sophie, having never experienced Hyde Park at the fashionable hour, felt a little conscious as Belle seemed to know everyone and so every few yards, she was returning nods and bows or stopping to have a brief word with a group of ladies who were ambling along the path that ran beside the carriageway.

"Belle," Sophie said, her voice hushed, "who is that man over there?" She nodded at a group strolling just ahead. "I have never seen such an extraordinary outfit!"

Belle could not doubt who she meant, for one amongst the group wore a pair of hugely voluminous trousers with wide blue and white stripes. They were cinched in at the ankle and waist, exaggerating the effect. He wore a matching waistcoat, and his shirt-points rose halfway up his face.

"Oh, it is John!" she exclaimed. "He is a friend of my brother's and a dear, although in recent years has become increasingly eccentric in his dress. If he weren't as rich as Golden Ball, his poor valet would have left him years ago!"

She signalled for the barouche to stop as they pulled alongside the walkers. The gentleman concerned kept looking straight ahead, however, and did not immediately perceive them. Sophie suspected that the height of his shirt points probably rendered the simple act of turning his head a little awkward. Not put out at all, Belle simply called out his name.

Sophie's suspicions were confirmed when he swivelled his whole body around to see who was trying to attract his attention. He had a pleasing countenance, dominated by a pair of slightly startled wide-blue eyes. As he saw Belle, his expression relaxed and he smiled, sweeping off his beaver hat and offering them a bow, revealing gleaming golden locks that were perfectly coiffed in the style known as the Brutus.

"B-Belle," he said, coming up to their carriage. "A-Always a d-delight to s-see you!"

She laughed down at him. "What a plumper! I can recall more than one occasion when you have wished me elsewhere!"

"N-nonsense," he protested, refusing to admit to such an ungentlemanly inclination. "Y-you m-must have been m-mistaken."

Deciding this was not the time to draw several examples for him, she let it pass.

"Lady Lewisham, please let me introduce Lord Preeve. Lady Lewisham is at present staying with Lady Renfrew," she informed him.

"P-pleased to m-meet y-you," he said. "S-Staying w-with Lady R-Renfrew, are you?" His eyes became more protuberant as they always did when he was alarmed, and even though he was famed for his good manners, he could not prevent himself from saying, "R-Rather y-you than m-me! I h-hope you h-have nerves of s-steel, Lady Lewisham, f-for y-you will n-need them." On that note, he bowed and re-joined his friends.

Sophie raised one neat brow at her friend.

"Poor, John," said Belle, a gleam of mischief in her quicksilver eyes. "Although the rest of us have got used to his love of the Petersham trousers and his garish waistcoats, Lady Renfrew has not and never fails to tell him so!"

Sophie laughed. She could just imagine it!

Even in such a throng, she found her eyes drawn towards a distant figure on horseback. Although his features were not yet clear and the horse was not Alcides, she had no doubt as to his identity. The set of his broad shoulders, his erect carriage, and the accomplished way he guided his horse, were achingly familiar to her. As he drew closer, she saw that he was not alone, Viscount Treleven was also enjoying an airing, it seemed.

As soon as he spotted them, the viscount broke into a trot, only his excellent horsemanship making it possible without causing mayhem.

"Ladies," he grinned as he came up beside them, bowing deeply from the waist and waving his hat in an extravagant manner. "As glorious as this day is, it is dimmed by your combined beauty!"

"I thought you had an aversion to trite poetry, Lord Treleven?" said Sophie saucily.

"Lady Lewisham, I am glad to see you somewhat restored," said Sir Philip, coming up at a more sedate pace.

Harry clapped a hand to his forehead. "Somewhat restored? Even my poor effort at a poetic greeting was better than that, would you not agree, Lady Lewisham?"

Her eyes met Sir Philip's as she answered Lord Treleven's quip. "No, I would not," she said with a small smile, 'for Sir Philip's greeting was by far the more accurate."

Belle had watched this exchange with interest and was slightly disappointed to feel the slight air of restraint between the pair.

"You are not riding Alcides today," observed Sophie, a trifle stiltedly.

"As you see," replied Sir Phillip, stroking the neck of the rather fine gray beneath him. "He is not particularly fond of crowds, and I felt he needed a rest, even as Harry and you do!"

"He is like an old mother hen," complained Lord Treleven. "Always clucking about taking things slowly! I am feeling quite the thing, now, I assure you."

"If you insist on gadding about town at a rate of knots, I think you will find that soon changes!" Sir Philip said dryly.

It was true that Lord Treleven's spirits were up, but on closer inspection, Sophie could see he was still quite pale and thin. However, neither of them were children to be scolded by Sir Philip.

"I hardly think that a short ride in this comfortable carriage is going to stretch my reserves too far," said Sophie bristling. She knew she was not yet looking her best, but he did not have to labour the point!

"It is but a few days since you could hardly put one foot in front of the other!" Sir Philip reminded her.

"Well, never mind, we were just about to return as it happens, so we will wish you gentlemen good day," said Belle, stepping neatly into the breach.

"He is quite insufferable," Sophie muttered under her breath as they drove away. "He must always think he is in the right!"

"You will find no argument from me on that score," smiled Belle. "But the most annoying thing of all is that he usually is!"

As they neared the gates of the park, a dashing high-perch phaeton, pulled by two beautifully matched bays swept through them at such a pace, they had pull smartly over to one side of the road to avoid it. It was driven by a gentleman who must have been in his late fifties, although he was still quite handsome in an old-fashioned sort of way. Lady Skeffington sat next to him, her eyes fixed firmly ahead, her chin held high.

"That is Lord Bexley," said Belle. "He is probably trying to impress as he has recently become engaged to Lady Skeffington. He had been interested in her for some time but..." she trailed off, aware that she had wandered into awkward territory.

"But she had hoped to catch another fish," Sophie finished for her.

"Indeed," said Belle briskly, "but that is all in the past. Come, tell me your impressions of Italy. I never did receive that letter you promised me."

Sophie's head had begun to ache by the time they reached Berkeley Square, and so after taking leave of her friend, she retired to her room. The butler showed Belle to the library.

"I knew you would be an age," snapped Lady Renfrew. "Sit down and cast your eyes over this." She picked up the letter that lay on the table beside her. "Sophie wrote it to me before she decided to return, and I want a second opinion on it. You may be a little bit flighty, but one thing I will say for you, Belle, you are not at all stupid!"

Intrigued, Belle took if from her. After she had read it through a couple of times, she looked up thoughtfully.

"Well?" Lady Renfrew said impatiently. "What do you make of it?"

"I think," said Belle slowly, "that she has been very careful about what she does and does not say."

"My thoughts exactly!" Lady Renfrew concurred.

The picture in the journal swam back into her mind. "But she is not, I think, impartial," she added.

"Ha! And neither is Philip if I know anything at all! But what are we going to do about it? They both have a stubborn streak a mile wide! Left to their own devices, they will slip into their old habits. Sophie will be off to see some other relics, and he will carry on in his old restless way! Why he is so set against marriage is beyond me. It is true that what he remembers of his own parents' misalliance is not ideal, but I had hoped that seeing your brother so happily married to that delightful girl, might do the trick."

Belle absently stroked her still slender midriff. A sudden vision of Sir Philip at the christening of young Frederick, the latest addition to the Atherton clan swam into her mind. Her brother had chosen Philip as the godfather and his wife, Rosalind, had insisted he hold him, laughing when he had taken a step back as if reluctant to do so.

"He is not made of china and will not break," she had assured him, handing him over. "Besides, you need the practice – you will have a son of your own one day!"

Sir Philip had stood still for a long moment gazing down at the little bundle tightly wrapped in his christening blanket. His face had twisted into an odd sort of grimace, and he had said, "I am not at all sure that I will."

"She is not up to a round of parties just yet," continued Lady Renfrew, "and neither am I for that matter. Even if she were, it wouldn't answer, for you cannot depend on Philip to put in an appearance at such events! Also, she is bound to attract a host of admirers once she finds her feet, and I am not interested in a horde of lovelorn swains traipsing across my threshold!"

"I quite understand," said Belle, a light frown marring her otherwise smooth brow. "Philip's mother died in childbirth, did she not?"

Lady Renfrew's gaze suddenly narrowed. "What has that got to say to anything?" she said abruptly. "It was a tragedy to lose poor Arabella so soon, but it was not unusual."

"Exactly," murmured Belle. "We can all name someone, in addition to Princess Charlotte, who has died in such a way. Philip was extremely close to his mother, was he not?"

"Worshipped the ground she walked on!" confirmed Lady Renfrew. "They were peas from the same pod. Her husband took little interest in either of them and was not of a social disposition, so she lavished all her affection upon him. The poor boy was sent up to Eton only weeks after her death. But what has all this got to do with our current problem?"

"He lost a woman he worshipped to childbirth. He was forced to bottle up his feelings and go to boarding school. He has buried them, not faced them! If he marries, he risks history repeating itself, only this time with his wife, not his mother."

Lady Renfrew was stunned into silence for once. "Of course," she said eventually. "How could I have been such a fool not to have seen it?"

Belle smiled at her. "You are no fool, Lady

Renfrew, but neither have you ever been a mother. It is natural that your mind might not dwell upon such things."

"That is true," she conceded. "But you have, my dear, and if I am not much mistaken, you are increasing again."

It was Belle's turn to look stunned and a little dismayed. "However did you know? I am sure I am not showing yet. Please, tell me I am not showing yet."

"No," Lady Renfrew smiled, pleased to have the upper hand again. "You are not yet showing, my vain little puss! You have sat there rubbing your stomach for the past several minutes, however, and as you do not appear to be ill, it was not hard to deduce!"

"We need a plan," sighed Belle, straightening in her chair and adroitly turning the subject. "And it must be subtle for they are neither of them slow-tops. Philip will certainly not tolerate any kind of interference."

"Don't I know it!" Lady Renfrew exclaimed. "Have you any sensible ideas to offer?"

Belle's lips began to curl up at the edges. "Do you know, I might have, at that. I will sleep on it and come to see you tomorrow when they have become a little more clear."

"See that you do! The last thing we need is for him to take another mistress. That would really set the cat amongst the pigeons!"

CHAPTER 14

Very early the next morning just after the sun had risen, casting its shimmering, slanting rays through the branches of the tree-lined avenue, a black stallion and its rider galloped flat out through the hazy dappled light as if the devil himself were after them. The few grooms who were exercising their masters' horses, cast a wary eye in their direction and kept firmly out of the way.

*'He is like a mother hen always clucking.'* To think that he would ever be described in such a fashion! There was, he acknowledged, a kernel of truth in the accusation. Both his charges were safely returned home and how they conducted themselves from now on was not his concern. At least, it should not be. So why was he still fussing over them, kicking his heels in town? The season would be over soon, and it was high time he paid a visit to Eastleigh. He had, as usual, neglected his estate in Wiltshire for too long.

That he was attracted to Lady Lewisham, he could not deny. That she was no longer under his protection, was also true. However, she was as far from his grasp as she ever was, for she was honourable and good and true. The way she had jumped on board a ship, knowing she suffered horribly at sea, to offer whatever succour and help his godmother might require, proved it. By God! When he had heard the moans issuing from her cabin and indeed witnessed her curled into a ball, all the vitality he associated with her drained from her frail form, he had known anxiety the like of which he never wished to experience again. Only the pleasure of becoming re-acquainted with Harry or the necessity of preventing him from committing some folly had kept him sane. Thank heavens he had persuaded Doctor Johnson to accompany them home for he was sure things would have been far worse without him.

*You could offer for her.* The traitorous whisper floated through his mind causing him to grimace and push Alcides even harder. He had not gone many yards further when he saw a lady in a smart, close-fitting bottle-green riding habit on a bay mare coming in the opposite direction. He recognised her immediately. Lady Skeffington. He slowed to a trot as he approached her.

"Elizabeth," he said, pasting on a grim smile. That he had even for a moment considered placing Lady Lewisham on a similar footing left a bad taste in his mouth. "How have I known you so... well, and not known that you enjoyed such early mornings?"

Signalling for her groom to fall back, she brought her mount closer. He saw that her hazel eyes were heavy as if she had had a late or a sleepless night.

"I do not as a rule," she confirmed. "But I am aware that you do."

He quirked an eyebrow in surprise, for he had heard of her recent engagement.

"I must felicitate you on your betrothal," he said. "I must admit, I had not been aware that you had a partiality for Bexley."

They turned their mounts and began to walk them back down the ride.

Sending him a sideward glance she said pointedly, "Bexley would not have been my first choice, but he is a decent enough man and can give me the security I find I need, after all."

Sir Philip reached across and placed his hand over hers. "Then, I am genuinely happy for you."

She turned her own to grasp his, but he had already withdrawn it. She blinked and looked away as if momentarily overcome with emotion. Within a few seconds, however, she straightened her spine and managed a small smile.

"We did not part on good terms," she said coolly. "I may have behaved badly. I wished to apologise. I am sure you know that I did not mean all that I said. I did not wish you to think ill of me, when or if, I ever came to your mind."

Sir Philip felt a twist of remorse slice through him. He had seen Elizabeth Skeffington sober, drunk, happy, angry and in the throes of ecstasy, but he had never seen her vulnerable. He had taken everything she had offered him at face value, and although he had set out the terms of their 'arrangement' at the start, it offered him little comfort now when he understood he had caused her genuine pain. The conditions had been laid down by him, for his own benefit and protection.

"I will always remember you with affection," he said gently. "And if you ever need a friend, you may call on me."

She smiled at him through suspiciously bright eyes. "Thank you, Philip."

They had reached the gates of the park and their ways parted. As she turned her horse in the opposite direction, she looked over her shoulder.

"I suspect it is a lady with a pair of fine emerald eyes and a captivating smile who had you riding hell for leather down the avenue this morning. Do not let her slip through your fingers, Philip," she said softly. "If you do not claim her, another eventually will. If she has not already discovered that her independence is a hollow prize, she will in time."

Tipping his hat to her, Sir Philip made his way home, brooding on her words.

\* \* \*

The hot, humid weather had left Sophie feeling quite lethargic. Her room faced south, and the sunshine poured in. If she had been in the country and could have found a shady tree to sit under, she would have been tempted to go out, but in town, it seemed impossible to find a quiet corner where one could enjoy the scene in solitary peace. She opened her sash window to let in some air, but not a breath of wind stirred the stuffy atmosphere. Having finished the latest sketch in her journal – (this time Lord Preeve had been the victim, his eyes bulging in alarm, his trousers gloriously depicted with the comment, *'At least the air can circulate!'*) – and not feeling like reading, she decided to slip into the drawing room and practise on the pianoforte, which was placed unobtrusively in a dark corner. She would be horribly rusty, but that was all the more reason to practise. Who would hear her, after all? Miss Trew had gone with Burrows to purchase various items they considered her in need of, and she did not think her playing would penetrate as far as the library.

When she was not being called on to display her skills to anyone who would listen, it was a pastime she had always enjoyed. Once she had haltingly made her way through a Haydn Sonata, she found her fingers moving with increasing rapidity over the keys. An old favourite of her father's came into her head – *'The Soldier's Adieu'* by Charles Dibdin – and having performed it for him many times, she found she could play it from memory. When she had gone through it once, she played it again, this time singing along with the music, her voice clear and sweet. As the last note faded, she jumped, startled as a chorus of applause broke out behind her. Turning swiftly, she saw five people had entered the room.

Miss Trew, Doctor Johnson, Lady Renfrew, Lady Hayward and a lady she had not been introduced to but realised almost at once must by Lady Treleven, (for the likeness between her and her son was marked), stood beaming encouragingly at her. She felt a blush steal into her cheeks. She had never enjoyed putting herself forward and had applied herself to her lessons for her own pleasure rather than to please others.

Standing hastily, she murmured, "Thank you, but I am afraid I am really terribly out of practise!"

"Nonsense, child," said Lady Renfrew in a bluff manner which failed to completely obscure the pride she felt in her guest. "You would put most of the young ladies who have assaulted my ears over the years to shame!"

"I agree," said Lady Treleven. "Your rendition of the piece was most proficient."

After the introductions had been made, Lady Treleven said, "I am fortunate to find you all present, for I cannot thank you enough for the care you have all taken of my son." Her glance rested on Sophie, Miss Trew, and Doctor Johnson in turn. She regarded the last seriously for a moment before adding, "I have been extremely impressed with all I have heard of your care of both Lord Treleven and poor Lady Lewisham. If you give me your card, I will certainly call upon you if we ever need a physician. I will also ensure that my friends and acquaintances are aware of your excellence."

Doctor Johnson bowed deeply and accepted her praise with a pleasing modesty.

"I will send for some tea," said Lady Renfrew suddenly. "I must confess I have become quite addicted to the beverage and cannot wait until after supper to refresh myself with it. I am sure it is good for your health. I have taken it every afternoon since I have been ill, and it seems to do me far more good than the glass of claret I used to take."

"I quite agree," Lady Treleven said, "but whilst we await the tea tray, do please play us something else, Lady Lewisham, for I will feel myself very privileged to listen."

Not trusting herself to play any longer from

memory, Sophie picked up the only pieces of sheet music she could see, which lay as if discarded long ago, on top of the instrument. She took a long, slow breath as she saw it was Beethoven's Sonata No. 14, 'Quasi una fantasia'. It was a wonderful piece but complex.

Her husband had also enjoyed her playing, and again she heard his words whisper to her; *'continue to develop your character and independence'*. She was beginning to understand that these few simple words could have a far wider interpretation than she had at first credited them with. 'Thank you, Edward.' The thought had barely formed before she plunged in.

As the minutes passed by, she forgot her audience and became lost in the piece, remembering each breve, crochet, and quaver as if they were old friends. She did not solely concentrate upon accuracy but allowed the music she created with her fingers to connect with something within herself, and so managed what few could: to bring out the emotional depth of the sonata. When the final note shimmered through the air, she did not move for a moment, feeling drained and elated at the same time.

This time the applause brought a wide smile to her mouth, as still looking down at the keyboard, she realised that giving pleasure to those around her was its own reward and that hoarding her music to herself was a selfish act.

"Bravo!"

That one, deeply spoken word caused a strange fluttering sensation in her stomach. Turning slowly, she nodded towards Sir Philip, who stood by the door as if only recently arrived. "Good Afternoon, sir."

Striding forward, he bent over her hand. "That was a heartfelt performance," he said softly.

She looked at him archly. "Are you suggesting it was technically lacking?"

"No, my cactus. It was all the better for it!"

How being compared to a spiny, unattractive plant could sound like an endearment, she did not know, but on Sir Philip's lips, it did. Glancing past him, she noticed that all eyes were interestedly watching their interaction and could only be pleased that at that moment, the tea tray arrived. It was closely followed by Sir Percy, whose eye immediately alighted on the plates of cakes and sweet wafers laid out.

"Hello," he said casually. "Looks like I arrived in the nick of time!"

"Hrmpf," snorted Lady Renfrew. "You can wait your turn, Percy, or our guests will get nothing but crumbs!"

Undaunted, he cast an eye around the room, politely nodding at everyone, but looked a little crestfallen when he saw quite how many visitors there were.

Once everyone was settled with a cup and their dainty morsel of choice, Lady Renfrew addressed Sophie. "Lady Treleven, Lady Hayward and I have been putting our heads together and have hit upon an idea we hope you will approve of, my dear," she said.

Sir Philip let out a crack of laughter, causing all three ladies to send a quelling glance in his direction. "Hold onto your resolution, Lady Lewisham! For whatever little scheme they have been plotting, approve it or not, you will be ridden rough-shod over until you give in!"

Sophie smiled sweetly at him. "It is a stratagem I

would expect you to admire, Sir Philip, for are you not an expert at using such tactics yourself?"

The ladies smiled approvingly, and Sir Percy let out a guffaw of laughter. "Well done, Lady Lewisham, that has given him his own again! Serves you right, Philip, had to remind you of your manners only the other day," he said, reaching for another wafer.

"What is this idea?" enquired Sophie.

"We are planning a bolt to the country," said Belle. "Town has become insufferably hot and as both Lady Renfrew and you are still a trifle under par, and I am in a delicate condition, we thought it would do us all good."

"Increasing again, Belle?" said Sir Philip, looking at her intently. "You don't look as if you are, and there is a very healthy bloom in your cheeks."

It was her turn to smile sweetly at him. "Why, thank you, Philip. I always am healthy when I am with child, but it is early days yet, and Hayward thinks I should take it easy."

"Good advice," confirmed Doctor Johnson, nodding sagely. "Nice to see a young lady taking care of herself instead of sacrificing her health and potentially that of the baby by gadding about!"

Sir Philip gave Belle a knowing look. She frowned.

"Do not bring up old history," she said tetchily. "I am much wiser than I used to be. I have already told Hayward this time, have I not? And he is the biggest, dearest, fuss-pot there is!"

"And then there is Harry," said Lady Treleven before they could drift too far from the matter-in-hand.

"Harry? He is not sick again?" said Sir Philip quickly.

"Well, not as yet," Lady Treleven replied. "But despite your best efforts at encouraging him to take things slowly, he was out last night very late and looked white as a sheet this morning!"

Sir Philip nodded briskly. "I agree that country pursuits would be of far more benefit to him, but how are you to persuade him? He seems set upon visiting all of his old haunts and friends."

"I am sure when he realises how fagged I am feeling after such a long stay in Town, and how much his sister, Henrietta, is suffering from her shyness and wishes to be anywhere other than at a dinner, ball, or any other squeeze, he will soon be persuaded to accompany us wherever we wish to go."

Philip knew this to be true and felt a little relieved that he hadn't been saddled with the task of persuading him. His 'mother hen' days were firmly behind him.

"The trouble will be in keeping him there," she added softly, looking at him with wide, beseeching eyes. "That is where I hope you will come in, dear Philip. If you come too, he will have someone to fish, ride, or play billiards with." She sighed a little wistfully. "It would be quite like old times."

Beginning to feel hedged in, he said, "Could not Hayward perform that office? I assume he will be of the party? I had intended to pay a visit to Eastleigh."

"He will, of course, join us, but not immediately," said Belle. "He has some business to finish in Town first, and he is not such a close friend as you, after all."

Sir Philip frowned, feeling himself being drawn further into their net despite his best intentions. "I really must show my face in Wiltshire," he said doggedly. "Perhaps I could persuade Harry to join me there?"

Lady Treleven's eyes filled suddenly with tears. "Surely you would not take him from me so soon?" she said, retrieving her handkerchief from her reticule and dabbing delicately at her eyes.

"Don't be so thoughtless, Philip," said Lady Renfrew sharply. "If Harry goes with you, so must we all!"

Lady Treleven looked much struck by this. "It would be the perfect solution! Eastleigh has been standing empty for too long! It is not good for your servants to have nothing to do, you know. A small house-party will liven the place up, and you can conduct whatever business you feel is so suddenly urgent. If I take Harry home, he will not rest, for he will feel the burden of running the estate suddenly fall upon his shoulders, and I do not think he is quite ready yet!"

Belle clapped her hands as if entranced by the idea. "Oh, do say yes, Philip. I cannot go home just at present because my poor little Edmund has the measles, and I have been advised to stay away."

"Sound advice, ma'am," said Doctor Johnson.

"You could all come to me, I suppose," said Lady Renfrew begrudgingly. "I am feeling a little stronger every day. I don't suppose that organising my household to accommodate so many visitors will be beyond my ability or upset my servants too much. It is not what they are used to but..."

"No, no, it is not to be thought of, Lavinia!" said Sir Percy. "Not when this young jackanapes has that barrack of a place and nothing better to do!"

"I suppose you wish to come too!" Sir Philip said, exasperated.

"By Gad! Wouldn't I just!" he exclaimed. "How very kind of you to invite me. It would be just the thing for my constitution – I have been feeling a touch out of sorts myself now I come to think of it."

"Too many sweetmeats!" Lady Renfrew said. "A few long tramps in the country will do you good, Percy!"

"That only leaves you, Doctor Johnson," Sir Philip said wryly. "Don't tell me you have a desire to retreat to the country as well?"

"Oh, but that would be ideal!" said Lady Treleven. "How clever of you to think of it, Philip. When so many of us are feeling so delicate, it would be a great comfort to know a physician was on hand, and Doctor Johnson has certainly earned such a treat!"

Casting his eyes up to heaven, Sir Philip finally conceded defeat.

## CHAPTER 15

Having not discussed his home with Sir Philip, Sophie had not been able to form any clear picture of what to expect of Eastleigh. She had vaguely imagined somewhere that would be Palladian in style, with formally landscaped gardens, reflecting some of the qualities of order and decisiveness of the man himself. The reality could not have been further from the truth. She had gleaned an inkling of her mistake when they had passed a castellated gothic gatehouse as they turned into the park.

The manor was approached from the west by a long, curving avenue lined with noble, ancient oaks, but the parkland had been left naturalistic in style with a scattering of mature trees dotted in small clumps without any discernible pattern or design. There was no lake, but a river snaked through it, spanned by a series of simply constructed bridges of wood or stone, enabling grazing animals or people to cross at various points. The parkland flowed all the way to the gravelled sweep in front of the entrance of the mansion, rising steeply as it approached. A deer park stretched from the east of the building, fringed by woodland which ran behind the house, up a steep hill and descended again on the west side, parallel to the drive.

The house itself was made of an attractive soft-golden stone but was a hotchpotch of styles. The central façade of the main building had undergone considerable alteration at the end of the last century and was fairly typical, with evenly spaced symmetrical sash windows. A lower, older wing was joined rather incongruously to the house by an ancient porch and huge doorway, leading to an immense hall that was still in the style of the fifteenth century, with high narrow windows, an uneven flagged stone floor, an immense fireplace and the requisite suits of armour guarding the entrance.

On the east side, a slender round tower abutted a square one with five floors, which loomed above the main building. The whole edifice was castellated, and the overall impression was one of confusion.

Inside followed a similar pattern. The main dining and drawing rooms were decorated in a light, if slightly old-fashioned style, as were the principal bedchambers, whilst other rooms were covered in old wood panelling and dominated by huge stone fire-places. The tower could be accessed from the main house at the end of a dark, narrow inner corridor. However, the only time Sophie had tried the ancient oak door, she had found it locked.

The somewhat eclectic edifice did not form a coherent whole. Sometimes a small corridor or even a staircase would be stumbled upon, which led to nowhere but a blank wall. Whilst offering every convenience and comfortable furnishings, it nevertheless felt unloved and impersonal. It did not feel lived in, as indeed it was not for large parts of the year. Sophie thought it was a shame as once she had accustomed herself to the odd arrangement, she discovered she rather liked the erratic nature of the building. She felt it only needed a few feminine touches here and there to transform it from awkward and functional to unconventional and charming.

Although she was not aware of it, she was not alone in this opinion. Sir Philip had arrived only a day before his guests and Mrs Lemon, his diminutive housekeeper, had blinked away tears at the unprecedented advent of a house party and said she hoped it meant that Sir Philip intended to make an extended stay this time, for it was about time the corridors at Eastleigh rang with laughter and chatter.

Jenkins, the rather austere butler, had remained unruffled and impassive by the prospect of the descent of a stream of guests, merely ensuring the two footmen knew what was expected of them, that the cellars were well-stocked, and the silver polished to his satisfaction. Lady Treleven may have been correct in her assertion that it was not good for his servants to have little to do, but Sir Philip's long absences, whilst lessening their workload, did not make them lax in their duties as they all knew he could arrive, without warning, at any time and would expect all to be in order.

Mr Charles Carstairs, his steward, also shared the hope, if not the expectation, of a long visit. He had been born on the estate, his father having been steward before him and it was in his blood, but he was a modest man and knew his limitations. He was efficient, capable, and fastidious in his duties and knew the community of people who made up Eastleigh as intimately as anyone raised as a gentleman could, but firmly believed that only the personal interaction between a landlord, his tenants, and servants, could create the harmonious whole which he longed to see.

Determined to make another push to bring Sir Philip to a realisation of how much he was needed before he disappeared again, he kept him fully occupied with estate matters for the first two days of his guests' arrival. He was pleasantly surprised that he proved so amenable and took such a rare interest, happily riding about the park, visiting tenants, or discussing mundane matters such as crop rotation or the acquisition of a new seed drill. Used to being fobbed off with an off-hand comment to do as he thought best, he began to harbour hopes that his employer and childhood friend had finally decided to take an interest in his affairs – little realising that Sir Philip was still a little annoyed at allowing himself to be hijacked by the guerrilla tactics so shamelessly deployed by his godmother, Lady Treleven, and Belle, and was punishing them just a little.

Whether they felt punished seemed unlikely, however. Harry (who had the advantage of having several times visited Philip there as a boy), was easygoing by nature and happily showed the younger ladies around the park and woodlands, frequently having them in tucks of laughter as he related some of his and Sir Philip's more absurd childish escapades. Miss Trew and Doctor Johnson accompanied them on these excursions, the former to lend a touch of respectability to the party and the latter to keep an eye on his charges. However, it was remarkable how often they found themselves adrift from the main party. Lady Renfrew and Lady Treleven made the sunny drawing room their own and settled down to less robust pursuits.

That afternoon, Sir Philip and Mr Carstairs visited a Mr Throckston, one of his oldest tenant farmers, who had suffered recently with an inflammation of the lung. He had vague memories of him slipping him the odd apple or piece of cheese when he had been a child. They found him sitting at the kitchen table of his farmhouse and received a warm if unceremonious welcome.

"Well, if it's not Sir Philip himself come to call!" he said unfazed, whilst his good wife curtsied low, and a trifle flustered, tried to usher him and Mr Carstairs into her good front room.

"You are just in time, for the missus has made some of her jam tartlets," Mr Throckston said, ignoring his wife's efforts and nodding towards the vacant chairs around the table.

"It's not fitting, Jeremiah!" she protested sharply.

"Nonsense, it won't be the first time he has sat around this table," the irreverent old gentleman said, winking at Sir Philip. "You used to love her jam tartlets when you were a nipperkin!"

"Well, he ain't a 'nipperkin' anymore, and if you don't show him the respect he is due, there will be no more tartlets for you, you old cadger!" she said, whipping the plate from the table.

Sir Philip's wide, charming smile dawned. "Please, do not worry about me. I have sat in many places far more uncomfortable than this cosy kitchen," he said, taking a seat and raising an eyebrow at the plate of tartlets which she still held half-raised above her head, a slightly dazed expression on her homely face.

She placed them quickly back on the table. "Of course, Sir Philip," she said, curtseying again and dabbing at her eyes with her apron. "It is just that for a moment, it could have been your poor, dear mother sitting there," she sniffled. "She had just that sweet smile. She used to insist on sitting there too when she came a-calling."

"Aye, he be the spit of her," concurred her husband.

"Sometimes she would bring you too and sit you on her lap." She smiled at the recollection. "Not that you ever stayed there for very long!"

"Too busy playing with the dogs or trying to sneak off to ride the cart!" Mr Throckston confirmed, shaking his head ruefully. "You were never one for staying put."

As they rode back through the park, it was as if a treasure trove of memories, locked away and largely forgotten long ago, were suddenly released.

"Do you remember the time we went fishing and thought we had caught a monster, Charles?" he said as they crossed a bridge over the river.

Mr Carstairs chuckled. "Of course! You were standing in the boat, pulling for all you were worth when suddenly your hook was released, your line went loose, and you toppled backwards into the water!"

Sir Philip grinned. "We never did find out what it was."

"It was the one that got away!" laughed Mr

Carstairs. "Ergo, it must have been the finest fish never to be caught in the county!"

When they arrived at the stables situated behind the east wing, Sir Philip saw an unfamiliar horse being walked up and down by one of the grooms. Handing his mount over to Vaughen, he said, "Visitors?"

"Aye, a Lord Russell has come to pay you a visit," he said. "Seemed a nice sort of gentleman. Nothing starched up about him."

Sir Philip frowned. He never usually stayed long enough on his infrequent visits to receive callers, and his servants knew better than to gossip. One of the girls Mrs Lemon had hired from the village to help with the extra visitors must have been talking.

Turning to Mr Carstairs, he grimaced. "Those accounts you wanted me to cast an eye over will have to wait, Charles."

"Understood," the steward replied. "I will see you at dinner."

Sir Philip took a few long strides towards the back of the house, paused for a moment, and then pivoted neatly and headed towards the south-west corner of the building. Lord Russell was an old friend of his father's, and he found himself reluctant to greet him at this moment when his head was so full of unexpectedly warm memories.

He soon came to the walled kitchen gardens. Noting absently that they looked very organised and productive, he strolled past the neatly planted beds and stopped for a moment before the far wall. It was covered in long tresses of violet flowers. Closing his eyes, he took a long, slow breath, inhaling deeply the faint, sweet scent he associated with his mother. He had ordered the wisteria to be planted in this particular spot only five years before. This was the first year it had bloomed.

Gently parting some of the flowers, he bent and slipped through an archway behind into a hidden garden. Here, borders were filled with flowers of various heights and colours. Towards the back was a profusion of orange and crimson oriental poppies and beautiful blue delphiniums, towards the front, zinnias in various shades of yellow and pink added further to the explosion of colours. But the main feature of the garden was the roses. They had been his mother's favourites. His head gardener, Jones, had been instructed to take extra care with them, and it was clear that he had been assiduous in his attentions to the beautiful plants. Ranging from white, pale pink to deep damask red, hundreds of blooms covered the bushes.

Seating himself on a bench placed against the wall, Sir Philip let his eyes wander slowly around this haven of peace and tranquillity. Eventually, he put his hand into his pocket and pulled out the snuffbox Lady Renfrew had given him. Its bright colours glinted in the sunlight. He turned it between his fingers for a moment before flicking it open and withdrawing his mother's miniature. Feeling slightly foolish, he nevertheless held it up between his finger and thumb, so that she could survey the garden in all its glory. Then smiling wryly, he placed it in his warm palm and looked down at her image.

"I think you would approve," he murmured before putting it gently back in its box and slipping it again into his pocket.

Lord Russell awaited him in the cosy library that occupied one of the rooms in the old wing.

"I thought it best to put him in there," explained Jenkins. "For I heard gentle snores coming from the drawing room."

Lord Russell was dressed neatly in the traditional country attire of buckskin breeches, a dark clawhammer coat, and riding boots. He still looked fit and trim as he fluidly rose to his feet and offered Sir Philip a small bow.

"It is good to see you, my boy," he smiled, "although you are a boy no longer but have grown into a fine figure of a man if you don't mind me saying so."

"Thank you, sir," Sir Philip said politely. "Please, sit."

"I cannot stay above a moment," Lord Russell said. "One of my finest mares is in foal, and I am keen to see the outcome."

"Of course," murmured Sir Philip.

It was many years since he had last seen Lord Russell, and he was not quite how he remembered him. His face was softer, his tone more congenial.

"Now, I hope you don't mind if I speak my mind, sir," he said. "But I was a good friend of your father's and if I don't open my budget now, who knows when I will see you again?"

Sir Philip felt himself stiffen but nodded for Lord Russell to go on.

"I never got to have a private conversation with you after his funeral, my lad, but I wanted to."

Sir Philip's raised brow was his only encouragement.

"If you think to dampen my pretensions with that

haughty look, think again. I remember having to rescue you from a tree when you not much higher than my knee! Gave your mother a horrible fright!"

A small smiled cracked Sir Philip's face. "I believe you gave me a ride home on your horse," he said, suddenly remembering.

"Aye, I did at that. Your mother asked me to. She spoilt you rotten."

"Indeed, I was very fortunate," he agreed.

"Well, that brings me to what I wanted to say to you. Your father was not an easy-tempered man, but he had your interests at heart, my boy. He allowed your mother to indulge you because he could see how happy you made her, but he was worried it would spoil your character. He sent you away a little too soon after she died, I think, but he was keen you learnt to be a man. There is nothing like boarding school to sort the chaff from the grain!"

"I made many friends there," Sir Philip acknowledged.

"I'm glad to hear it. Now, you may not want to hear this, but you are going to. Your father was heartbroken when you joined the army. He was terrified he would lose you."

"You mean lose his heir, I think."

"I do not need you to put words into my mouth, Philip," Lord Russell snapped. "I meant exactly what I said. He was always scanning the papers for news of you or going up to Town to see what he could discover of your progress."

Sir Philip looked surprised.

"Aye, that has taken the wind out of your sails. He could not have been more proud of you, as it turns out. That's all. I thought you should know, and as he was never any good at expressing his feelings, I had an inkling he would never have told you." Lord Russell got to his feet. "Now, I must be off. I hope you stay around this time, Philip. You are a grown man now, and it is time to put off childish resentments and get on with what you were born to do!"

It was some time before Sir Philip left the library to get ready for dinner. He paused outside Doctor Johnson's room for a moment and then wrapped his knuckles firmly against the door.

Doctor Johnson opened it in his shirtsleeves. "Come in, come in, Sir Philip. What is it I can do for you?" he smiled, firmly closing the door behind him.

\* \* \*

Dinner was a lively affair. A little country air and a pause from the many and varied diversions of the season had refreshed everyone. Even Henrietta, who had been causing Lady Treleven a great deal of worry, had relaxed a little, and although she did not initiate any topics of conversation, she listened with interest and replied sensibly enough when directly addressed.

Lady Treleven was aware that her season had been a great trial to her, for although she possessed the Treleven good looks – her hair golden, her eyes blue – she lacked the natural confidence of her brother. Lady Treleven, being a sensible woman at heart, realised that it was primarily her own fault. After Harry's self-imposed exile she had retreated both to her estate and within herself. The loss of her only son, followed closely by the death of her husband, had left her bereft and lost. Whilst she had not insisted Henrietta become a hermit like herself, neither had she made the least push to encourage her to overcome her natural shyness and socialise more with the local families. It had been a shock to realise that her daughter was close to reaching her seventeenth birthday, and only the unpalatable thought that Harry might never return, causing the estate to be passed on to a distant relative, had goaded her into reluctant action – her motherly instinct to ensure that her daughter was amply provided for – overcoming her inclination to remain removed from society.

Coming to Eastleigh had been a very good decision. To her shame, she realised it had been a long time since she had given Philip the thought he deserved. He had taken the opposite course to herself, his dislike of his father and his unhappiness, driving him away from his home and making him unwilling to wear his father's mantle or fulfil his rigid expectations in any way. Her own rejection of him had been both cruel and unworthy of her, and after meeting Sophie, she had been overcome by a crusading spirit to see him happily settled.

Having been wracking her brains for the past several minutes for a way to bring the two together, she suddenly smiled gently and said, "Do you ride, Lady Lewisham?"

Sophie had been quietly discussing something with Mr Carstairs but now glanced across the table at Lady Treleven.

"I do," she answered a little wistfully. "Although it seems like an age since I have enjoyed a good gallop. The present Lord Lewisham felt it unnecessary to keep another horse – eating its head off – in his stables, so I was obliged to sell it."

"The miserable skinflint!" said Harry.

"I did, of course, offer to pay for its keep but he felt it would not be fitting for me to be gadding about the estate whilst I was in mourning."

"I can almost hear him saying it," murmured Sir Philip.

"Oh, do you know him?" said Sophie, surprised.

"Not well, but our paths have crossed," he said.

"He is a vulgar, bacon-brained, elbow-crooker!" snapped Lady Renfrew. "Least said about him, the better!"

"It is a shame you have not enjoyed a pursuit that you clearly enjoy for so long," said Lady Treleven, adeptly bringing the conversation back to the point. "Philip, I am sure you have something suitable in your stables?"

"I am not sure I have," he said a little ruefully. "There are some fine mounts, but I doubt any are suitable for a lady."

Lady Treleven opened her mouth to reply, but Sophie was before her.

"Really?" she said, her eyes alight with challenge. "I will have you know, that when I was shut up in that carriage for hour upon hour on our way to Pisa, I often wished I could take your place and ride Alcides. What is more, I am certain it would not be a task beyond my ability!"

"Oh ho!" grinned Harry. "Now that is something I would like to see!"

"My father is horse mad," she added. "He threw me on a horse almost as soon as I could walk!"

Sir Philip gave her an enigmatic look, his frown deepening. "Nevertheless, much as I hate to disappoint either of you, it is not an event that is ever likely to occur. I allow no one to ride Alcides."

"He has never liked people riding his horses," chirped in Belle with a mischievous twinkle. "What was the name of that horse of yours I sneaked out of the stables when I was a girl?"

"Ignis," said Sir Philip drily.

"Oh, that refers to flame or fire does it not," Sophie said, interested.

Sir Philip nodded, smiling ruefully. "Indeed, he was of a fiery nature and if Belle had ever applied herself to her studies as assiduously as you, Lady Lewisham, she might have saved herself a winding and some nasty bruises!"

"Oh, were you thrown?" said Sophie, sympathetically.

"I was," she admitted with an unrepentant grin. "But the spanking Philip doled out to me afterwards was by far the more humiliating experience!"

"Eh!" Sir Percy spluttered, quickly swallowing the rather fine claret he was as that moment sampling. "I worry about you, Philip, really I do! Spanking a girl! I would never have thought it of you!"

"If Lady Atherton was not upset by the event," said Sir Philip a trifle exasperated with his guest, "I do not think you need concern yourself. Belle must have been all of ten years, and if she had taken him out again, she might well have suffered far worse!"

"Quite right, Philip," approved Lady Renfrew. "She always did need a firm hand. I am at a loss to understand how Hayward has managed her half so well. He doesn't seem the spanking type!"

"No," said Belle, a secretive smile on her lips. "He does not need to resort to such cave-man tactics. I would never go against dear Nat."

Sir Philip raised a slightly sceptical eyebrow but merely said, "I am glad to hear it, Belle, but your example highlights exactly why Lady Lewisham should not ride Alcides!"

"Well, let the gal choose another, then," said Lady Renfrew. "If Lady Lewisham says she can ride, I believe her."

"I'll tell you what it is, Philip," said Sir Percy helping himself to a third portion of roasted pheasant, "you are getting set in your ways. It happens to us all as we get older. But I will say this for you – you keep a damn fine table and a marvellous cellar!"

Deeming Sir Percy's remarks unworthy of comment, Sir Philip looked across at Sophie. "I usually ride early, before breakfast," he said.

"I will be ready," she assured him, her eyes gleaming with satisfaction.

"But if I decide you cannot handle your mount, we will turn back immediately with no argument," he added.

"Agreed," she said with a confident smile. "As long as I get to choose which one I ride."

A gleam of reluctant amusement crept into Sir Philip's eyes. "Apart from Alcides, you may have free rein."

"I think I will join you," said Harry grinning. "For you may find you need an independent witness in case of any dispute as to Lady Lewisham's competence."

"I wish I could join you," said Belle smiling gently, "but I am a trifle delicate in the mornings at the moment."

Sir Philip sent a look of sympathy in her direction. "Never mind, Belle, think of some other entertainment that will amuse you, and I will do my best to accommodate you."

CHAPTER 16

Sophie awoke early, leapt out of bed, and ran over to the window. The sun had just risen, and the sky was a blaze of gold. Impatient to be out in such a glorious morning, she turned swiftly, smiling widely as Burrows came in.

"Burrows, we must be quick this morning as I need time to have a good look at Sir Philip's horses!"

"Of course, ma'am," her stalwart maid said, holding up a tastefully designed if unremarkable habit of a soft, green hue. "I believe this one was always your preferred choice."

Sophie's eyes narrowed as she observed it thoughtfully for a few moments. "Have we the grey one with us?" she finally murmured.

Burrows regarded her mistress rather sternly. "You mean the one that is in the military style, more silver than grey, frogged and braided in gold, the one that I picked out for you and you have never yet worn because it is too form-fitting and of a severely masculine cut?"

Sophie's smile dimmed a little, and she looked wistful. "It would have been just the thing for this morning," she murmured, "but I quite see that it is unreasonable of me to expect you to have brought it. This one will have to do."

Burrows returned the green riding habit to the little dressing room that was attached to the chamber and re-appeared with the desired one, a small smile of satisfaction on her face.

"I brought it just in case you fancied something a bit different," she said.

Sophie, delighted, gave her a quick hug – an unusual display of affection that left the competent lady's maid a little flustered.

"Come along now, ma'am," she said brusquely, "we will have to bustle, or you will be late."

"I knew it," she said triumphantly when Sophie was ready in unusually quick time. A tall hat of silver satin with a fine gold plume that curled attractively towards her cheek finished the dashing outfit off nicely. "You look stunning!"

Turning to look in the glass, Sophie gasped in delight, turning this way and that to see it from all angles.

"It is perfect," she said, elated. "No one looking at a lady dressed like this would expect to see her on a sluggish mount!"

The feeling was quickly succeeded by a moment of self-doubt.

"You do not think it a trifle too flashy?" she said hesitantly.

"No, now get moving or you will find a horse saddled for you by the time you get to the stables!"

Sophie hurried down the dark inner corridor that led to a side-door she knew would take her almost directly to the stables. Pausing in front of the narrow, wooden door that was set into the archway of the tower, she wondered for a moment what was beyond it. If one were of a romantic turn of mind, it would be the perfect setting for a headless spectre to walk about groaning and clanking its chains. Laughing softly at such a fanciful thought, she picked up the train of her skirt and carried on swiftly.

"Morning, Lady Lewisham," said Vaughen, touching his cap as she entered his domain. Alcides was already saddled and pawed the straw with an impatient hoof, shaking his head and letting out a low snort through his flaring nostrils.

"He is magnificent," said Sophie softly.

"That he is, ma'am, but I'd give him a wide berth if I were you. He needs to run his fidgets out."

"I can see that," she replied softly. "But I have the choice of the rest!"

"So I hear," Vaughen said, shaking his head as if bemused. "I only hope you've got a fine seat, ma'am, for you will need it!"

Sophie merely smiled and walked slowly along the row of stalls, tapping her riding crop absently against the palm of her hand. There were some fine hunters to choose from, but she knew which horse she would choose the moment her eyes alighted on him.

"Oh, you are handsome," she breathed softly, her keen gaze roaming over the dapple-grey gelding who had a proud bearing and was at least sixteen hands.

"Be careful, Lady Lewisham," said Vaughen

quickly. "He is a fine choice but does not usually take to strangers."

"We will not be strangers for long," she murmured.

Letting herself quickly into his stall, she stilled as he backed away and shook his head, whinnying.

"Lady Lewisham…" Vaughen said warningly, keeping his voice low.

Ignoring him, she held her position, turning her head slightly away. "Come now," she said gently, "can you not see we are destined to be friends?"

After a few moments, the gelding tentatively approached her. Sophie turned her head towards him but kept it bowed, a small smile playing about her mouth, her hands behind her back until she felt his face only inches from her own. Then raising her head slightly, she rubbed her nose against him and held her hand open beneath his muzzle.

He accepted the carrot she had pilfered from the kitchen the night before, and then gently nudged her as she cooed sweet nothings into his ear.

"We are going to have a fine run," she murmured, gently running a hand from his beautifully arched neck to his well-muscled hindquarters. "There is nothing of the commoner about you."

"You have bewitched him already, my sorceress! I could almost wish I was a horse," came a laughing voice from behind her.

If any other man had uttered those words to her, she would have felt contemptuous, but there was something about Lord Treleven's light-hearted banter that made it impossible to take offence.

She straightened slowly and patted her mount firmly. "Whereas you are certainly a commoner, sir. If you were related to the horse," she said softly, "you would be an ass."

"Well said," a deeper voice murmured. "Ne'er did Eos speak a truer word!"

Casting a glance over her shoulder, she smiled at Sir Philip, gave her new friend one last pat and left the stall.

"Saddle him up," she said to Vaughen peremptorily.

He sent a quick look in Sir Philip's direction. Sophie was pleased to see him nod his prompt acquiescence, his eyes never leaving hers.

"What have you named him?" she asked.

"Apollo," he replied.

Her smile widened. "Perfect."

As they walked together out into the yard he said warningly, "Whilst it is clear that you know your way around horses, Lady Lewisham, if I am not happy in any way as to your safety, we will cut short our ride."

"Of course," she said demurely, placing her right arm on the saddle, her left hand on his shoulder, and her booted foot firmly in his cupped hands.

He tossed her up into the saddle with ease.

"Thank you," she smiled, settling her knee between the pommels, quickly arranging her skirts and taking the reins in her gloved hands. Although Apollo sidled a little, a quick touch of her crop against his side soon brought him under control. Nodding approvingly, Vaughen stepped back and ceded control to her.

Lord Treleven came up on a glossy chestnut, casting an appreciative glance at Lady Lewisham. "You have one of the finest seats I have seen in a long time, Lady Lewisham," he grinned.

"But then, unless you have seen a mermaid riding a hippocampus, I don't suppose you have had many opportunities in recent years to witness many ladies riding at all," she said dryly.

"Stubble it, Harry," laughed Sir Philip. "You will find that Lady Lewisham is quite impervious to flattery."

They maintained a decorous trot down the avenue until satisfied that Lady Lewisham could indeed handle Apollo. Sir Philip turned off the road and into the park. Once there, he allowed Alcides to lengthen his stride into a canter and then a gallop. All three horses matched each other stride for stride.

When they finally pulled up, Sophie was grinning from ear to ear.

"Flattery aside, you are a fine rider," smiled Sir Philip, turning Alcides and walking him back towards the house.

Sophie nodded, accepting her due. "Thank you, Sir Philip. Flattery also aside, I will admit that you are one of the finest horsemen I have had the privilege to ride with."

"We should not be surprised that Lady Lewisham is such a fine rider," said Lord Treleven seriously but with a warning twinkle in his eyes. "It is all that practice she has had on her broomstick!"

Sophie rolled her eyes in a distinctly unladylike manner. "If I were a witch, Lord Treleven, I would turn you into a toad!"

"No, no, you wouldn't do that surely?" he said grinning. "What would you tell my poor mother?"

"I would offer to turn you back again as long as she

removed you to your estate until you had learned how to behave in the company of ladies."

"You are cruel, ma'am," he protested.

"Not at all," she said, smiling sweetly at him. "I am sure your mother will wish you to marry one of these days, but if you carry on in your current manner, you will have no hope of attaching a female with any sense or reason."

Harry's face twisted into a comical grimace at her suggestion. "Marry a female for her sense and reason? You have slipped up there, Lady Lewisham," he said, "for that is just as good an argument for me to remain unreformed!"

As they reached the stable yard, Sir Philip quickly dismounted, handed his reins to Vaughen and turned to Sophie. Leaning down to place both her hands on his broad shoulders, she allowed herself to be lifted down. The contact was brief, but it was enough to send her heart racing. Stepping quickly back, she busied herself shaking out the creases in the skirt of her habit.

"I will see you at breakfast, Lady Lewisham," Sir Philip said, bowing briefly before disappearing into the stables.

Hurrying to her room, she found Burrows waiting for her and a simple gown of white muslin, embroidered delicately with green leaves at the scalloped hem – the motif repeated at the wrists of the long narrow sleeves – laid out neatly on the bed. Fortunately, both Sophie and Burrows shared a mutual dislike of the increasing use of frills and furbelows that seemed to adorn the latest fashions.

"Did you enjoy your ride, ma'am?" Burrows asked

as Sophie availed herself of the warm water she had ensured was ready for her return.

"Mmm," she mumbled as she dried her face. "It was very invigorating."

"And did your habit have the desired effect?" A small smile played about her lips as she opened a drawer and selected a new pair of fine kid gloves.

"Well, Lord Treleven was impressed," Sophie said, "but as he is full of nonsense, I do not think we should set any great store by that!"

Once Sophie was gowned and seated at her dressing table, she submitted herself with unusual meekness to her unruly hair being assaulted mercilessly by the brush Burrows wielded like a weapon of warfare.

"And did Sir Philip notice your attire?" her assiduous maid mumbled around the long pin which hung from the corner of her mouth.

Sophie's eyes fell to her hands which were clasped lightly in her lap. "Well," she said softly, "he did compare me to Eos."

"Now don't you go spouting that gibberish to me," Burrows complained. "I'm an honest woman and don't hold with all that Greek nonsense!"

Sophie raised admiring eyes. "Why, Burrows, how did you know it was Greek?"

"I didn't," her maid said a little sourly. "Do not tell me that a lady of your fine intellect does not know the term 'it is all Greek to me'!"

Sophie's eyes crinkled in amusement. "Of course, I do, but how was I expected to know that you were also aware of it?"

"I have served in I don't know how many fine

houses these past twenty years," she replied a little stiffly. "It is my job to keep my ears open and my lips closed. I would have to be very dim-witted not to have picked up a thing or two!"

"Of course," Sophie conceded gently. "Eos is the goddess of the dawn."

She winced, her eyes watering, as Burrows slipped the pin smoothly out of her mouth and into her burnished locks, scraping her scalp on the way. "That's all right then."

Sophie was the last guest to arrive in the breakfast parlour. She was famished. Her appetite had been increasing as each day passed, but this morning's splendid exercise had whetted it even more. Loading her plate with eggs and ham, she sat down and applied herself to it with unusual vigour.

Lady Treleven and Lady Renfrew usually kept to their rooms at this hour, partaking only of a roll and some chocolate, but this morning they had bestirred themselves enough to join the others. Only Belle was absent, finding that she could not stomach the sight of a breakfast buffet in her present condition.

"Did you enjoy your ride, Lady Lewisham?" asked Lady Treleven in a disinterested tone, taking a sip of her chocolate.

Sophie's smile was like a ray of sunshine. "How could I not?" she said. "The morning was glorious, my mount splendid, and the company congenial."

Sending a warning glance in the direction of her son, who had at that moment choked on his bacon, she said, "I am glad to hear it."

"What did you make of the park?" asked Sir Philip. "It is a far cry from Count Maldolo's estate."

Taking a sip of her hot, sweet tea, Sophie considered her answer. "Indeed it is," she said. "His gardens were perfectly proportioned, manicured, and graced by the finest statuary."

"And so superior in every way," said Sir Philip coolly.

"Not at all," she replied. "At first glance, I admit they were impressive. Yet they lacked something that I have discovered is of prime importance to me."

All eyes (apart from Sir Percy's), swivelled in her direction at this remark. Lady Renfrew was the first to crack.

"Out with it, girl, we are not mind readers! What is it that they lacked?" she snapped.

"Who is this Count Maldolo?" asked Sir Percy, bewildered.

"Not now, Percy," Lady Renfrew hissed.

By now used to their odd interactions, Sophie was not put off her stride, although her brow furrowed as she searched for the words to express the feelings that had been slowly blossoming within her.

At last, she spoke. "They lacked the music and melody that only divine nature provides. The poetry that is in every wildflower, the wise benevolence of every ancient tree, the lyrical babble of a naturally flowing brook, the freedom of a wide expanse of rolling green meadow..."

"So much for sense and reason," Lord Treleven murmured.

This time it was a hard look from Sir Philip which silenced him.

"Yes, the grounds here are very pleasing," said Lady Treleven. "But I think a little landscaping in front of the house would not go amiss. Nothing much, but perhaps a few borders, a terrace and some steps leading down into the park."

"Do you agree, Lady Lewisham?" Sir Philip looked at her intently.

"Perhaps," she murmured, still a little embarrassed by her romantical flight of fancy. "But only because I feel that the house would benefit from a natural source of flowers."

"How right you are, dear Lady Lewisham," said Lady Treleven. "I have been thinking the same thing myself. The rooms here are charming if a little dowdy, some fresh flowers would freshen them up in an instant."

Sir Philip seemed to come to a sudden decision. He stood abruptly, screwing up his napkin and dropping it carelessly upon the table. All eyes now turned in his direction.

"If it is flowers that you wish for, it is flowers you shall have. Follow me!"

Recognising the tone of command and hopelessly intrigued, they all found themselves rising to their feet, even Sir Percy, although he could not resist a wistful backward glance at the table as they left the room.

Doctor Johnson and Miss Trew brought up the rear. Although they had both been treated with the utmost politeness during their visit, neither of them harboured any desire to rise above their station and so they naturally retreated to the edges of every gathering.

"Whilst I have every respect for Sir Philip," said Doctor Johnson quietly, "I cannot imagine even he can conjure a garden of flowers out of thin air."

Miss Trew was less sceptical. "I think you will find him a gentleman of infinite resourcefulness."

More than one worried look passed amongst them as he stopped in front of the kitchen garden wall. The wisteria was pretty but would not make a satisfactory flower arrangement.

Sophie, however, did not seem in the least disappointed. Stepping forward, she bent over one of the bright purple clusters.

"What a lovely fragrance," she said.

"Indeed," said Lady Treleven, "this is a good start, Philip. If you would like some advice on what else to..."

Her words died on her lips as he reached out a hand and revealed the hidden archway.

They formed an orderly line as they trailed one after the other into his secret garden and then stood in stunned silence, for a moment overcome by the riot of colour and sweetly scented air.

Sophie walked into the centre of the garden and then turned slowly in a full circle, her wide smile dawning as she did so.

"It is glorious!" she said.

"Indeed, it is," murmured Lady Treleven, taking her arm and leading her from one beautiful rose bush to another.

Suddenly everyone was talking and moving about as if every bloom was a revelation, but Sir Philip remained by the archway, tense and unsmiling. Only Lady Renfrew remained by his side.

"The roses are beautiful, Philip," she said, her tone unusually gentle. "They were your mother's favourites."

He nodded, his features relaxing a little. "It is the garden I keep in remembrance of her."

Lady Renfrew brushed her hand against his for a moment. "I know. But you are right to share it."

"We shall see," he murmured.

CHAPTER 17

When the men joined the ladies after dinner that evening, it was plain for everybody to see that Sir Percy was limping.

"A touch of gout, Percy?" said Lady Renfrew.

"It is nothing," he said, easing himself into a chair and stretching his leg out in front of him.

Miss Trew hurried to get him a footstool.

"Keep it elevated, Sir Percy," she said. "It will encourage the swelling to go down."

"Ha!" said Lady Renfrew. "So will restricting your diet, Percy, and keeping off the port for a few days!"

Sir Percy blanched at the thought.

"Would you like me to take a look, sir?" asked Doctor Johnson. "It might be that a few leeches and a mustard poultice will help."

"Some juice of Pennywort might be the very thing," added Miss Trew.

"No, no, I tell you it is nothing," Sir Percy protested looking distinctly alarmed but lifting his foot onto the stool, clearly deciding that this was the least nefarious option.

"Well, what shall it be tonight?" he said, turning the subject. "A game of cards?"

"I thought we might play Blindman's buff," said Belle dimpling.

"I think not, Belle," smiled Sir Philip. "I thought you had outgrown such childish parlour games. We cannot risk someone stepping on Sir Percy's toes after all."

"By Gad, you're right!" Sir Percy said. "My big toe is already throbbing as if a horse had stamped upon it!"

"Hrmpf! I thought it was nothing, Percy," muttered Lady Renfrew.

"Well, let us change it to Buffy Gruffy then," Belle suggested. "That way, Sir Percy can remain seated. You did say that if I hit upon something which would amuse me, you would try to accommodate me."

"Come on, Philip, when did you become such a stick in the mud? I remember the time..." Lord Treleven began.

"We shall play," interrupted Sir Philip with a wary eye on his friend, fairly certain that the anecdote he had been about to relate would not be fit for the ladies' ears.

"I will play cards with you, Percy," said Lady Renfrew gruffly. "If you sit sideways to the table you can keep your foot up. You are the only one worth playing with after all."

The chairs were soon arranged in a circle.

"Who shall begin?" said Belle.

"As it was your idea, you can have the pleasure!" said Sir Philip dryly.

Once her eyes were covered, Belle was led to the centre of the circle, and the remaining guests chose a seat.

Lord Treleven clapped his hands and the game began. Belle moved tentatively forwards with small dainty steps until her knees brushed against someone.

"How old are you?" she asked.

"Older than I have ever been," came a heavily disguised muffled voice.

Belle wrinkled her brow in thought.

"What gives you a fluttery feeling in your stomach?"

"Eating caterpillars!" came the reply.

When the chuckles had died down, she asked her final question.

"What is your best feature?"

"My pretty blue eyes!" came a high-pitched reply.

Belle smiled. "Lord Treleven, I believe."

"How did you know?" he asked, laughing.

"No lady would display such vanity, and Sir Philip would never refer to himself as pretty!"

Once he stood blind-folded, the players silently changed positions. He too moved with care until he felt the brush of something solid. Sophie braced herself, ready for his nonsense.

"How much do you love me?" he asked saucily.

"Not as much as you love yourself," came her immediate reply.

A wry smile twisted Lord Treleven's lips.

"What is the first thing you do in the morning?"

"Open my eyes."

"What is to a young woman hope or ruin and to an old maid charity?"

There was a momentary pause before Sophie replied softly. "A kiss."

"Lady Lewisham, I believe," said Lord Treleven, removing the blindfold.

"How did you know?" she asked, smiling.

"Too quick and clever for your own good!" he grinned.

Sophie knew whom she had stumbled upon the moment her skirts brushed against his knee. It was only the lightest of touches, yet the slight tremor that always ran through her whenever she came into contact with Sir Philip gave the game away.

"What is your favourite flower?" she asked.

"The flower of the Myrtle," came his gentle reply.

A small smile curved her lips as she remembered the meadow outside of Pisa.

"What is one of your most pleasant memories?" she probed.

"Sunrise at Lodi," he murmured, his low voice sending a thrill through her as she remembered their brief kiss. The air between them seemed suddenly thick with longing, and a little alarmed, she asked the first thing that popped into her head.

"Why is the tower locked?"

Even with her eyes covered, she could feel his sudden tension.

"Because someone turned the key," he finally said, his voice flat.

"Sir Philip," Sophie said, removing the blindfold

and offering it to him, colouring a little as she realised her question had been unacceptably intrusive to him.

He took it but said, "There, Belle, you have had your wish, and now I think it is time to call a halt to this particular game."

Lady Hayward did not protest but on the contrary, stifled a yawn. "I agree," she said. "I do not know why it is, but I am suddenly very sleepy. If you do not mind, I think I shall retire."

"It is not unusual for someone in your condition," said Doctor Johnson.

Still feeling a little awkward, Sophie said that she too was tired and followed Belle out of the room.

Belle took her arm as they mounted the stairs.

"So, what happened at sunrise at Lodi?" she asked cheekily.

Sophie tried to look nonchalant. "Oh, we both went for an early walk to enjoy the morning and found ourselves on the bridge outside Lodi."

"It sounds terribly romantic," she prompted gently.

Remembering how infuriated and confused she had felt at the conclusion of that encounter, Sophie smiled and said quite truthfully, "No, not really."

Belle looked a little disappointed.

"Do you know why the tower is locked?" Sophie suddenly asked. "Sir Philip did not seem to like me asking him."

Belle's brow furrowed as she thought about it. They came to a stop in front of the large portrait that dominated the wall at the top of the stairway before the landing branched in opposing directions. It was the only family portrait they had discovered. A rather joyless looking man with a stern expression stood next to a pretty woman with anxious blue eyes and a timid smile. Her slender hand rested upon the shoulder of a little boy, who held himself rigidly upright, staring straight ahead with a challenging look and a proud air.

The likeness between mother and son was remarkable, but although he could not have been above seven years at most, he seemed the more determined of the two. Both his allegiance and his protectiveness towards his mother were only revealed to the astute observer. Although the arm nearest to her was held rigidly by his side, the fingers of his small hand curled almost possessively backwards around a fold of her skirts, in a gesture of discreet reassurance.

Both Sophie and Belle were astute observers. Sophie because she was used to studying the symbolism embedded in the poetry and art of classical antiquity, and Belle because she had lived and breathed the air of the *ton* where nuance was all important if one was to survive unscathed.

"I don't know for sure," Belle finally said, "but have you noticed how empty of all personal touches the main rooms are?"

"Indeed," said Sophie. "But then Sir Philip lives alone, so perhaps it is not surprising."

"He did not always live alone, however," said Belle softly. "And he was very fond of his mother."

Sophie's brow puckered in thought. "Oh, you are right. There is no sign that she was ever here!"

"No, yet I cannot imagine he would destroy any of her things."

"So perhaps he keeps the things that remind him of her safe in the tower," Sophie said slowly. "Oh, I wish I had never asked. I did not wish to cause him pain!"

Belle gave her a quick kiss on the cheek. "Do not fret, my dear," she said. "I do not think that you caused him pain, but he has been used to hiding his feelings and holding his secrets close. A brave man, especially a soldier, is taught to take physical pain in his stride, but the agitation and agony caused by a strike to the heart is not openly acknowledged or admitted, and so it is buried deep inside until it is forgotten or destroys him."

Sophie drew in a deep breath of surprise. Lady Hayward might be mischievous, manipulative, and light-hearted, but it was clear that she had acquired her fair share of wisdom.

Before they parted, Belle gave her an impulsive hug and whispered into her ear. "I do not think Philip has forgotten but nor is he yet destroyed. It may be that you can prevent that from happening."

Sophie had much to think on as Burrows helped her prepare for bed. She was indeed tired, but her brain refused to let her rest. Sir Philip's intentions towards her were as unclear as ever. The attraction between them was undeniable and that she felt more alive in his presence than she had ever felt, was also true.

She realised she wished him to be happy. The very thought that his own personal demons might destroy him was unpalatable to her. That she might be able to alleviate them was a heady and frightening thought. That she loved him was not a startling revelation. The realisation had crept upon her gradually in many small ways; the feeling that something important to her happiness was missing when he was absent, the worry and hurt she felt if his good opinion was withdrawn, or the pure joy she had felt when they had been galloping side by side, were all testament to her true feelings.

As she tossed and turned restlessly in a fruitless attempt to find a position so comfortable she would be able to sleep, the words that had been so repugnant to her that morning at Lodi, now whispered treacherously through her unquiet mind. *'Your problem is that you see everything still in black and white... but as a widow, I think you will find there is a whole world of greys in between!'*

They no longer felt quite so unpalatable as before. She did not need or particularly wish for the approval of the *ton*. She had no need to ever marry again for money or status. In denying herself the possibility of becoming Sir Philip's mistress, was she denying them both something they both wanted and perhaps even needed for no good reason? Was she really displaying her independence of thought and action by clinging to a morality that only really applied to unmarried young ladies or newlyweds who had not yet produced an heir?

*You would prefer he asked you to be his wife.* Sophie's eyes sprang wide open. It was true! She, who had always put sense and reason ahead of romantic notions, now found herself the victim of unrequited love! Unlike Saphho, however, she would not find relief from her unfulfilled desire by throwing herself from a great height. The real decision for her then, was whether it would be better to take action and become Sir Philip's mistress and risk her heart breaking into a thousand little pieces later, or put aside both Sir Philip and her desires and direct her energy into trying to establish first, Alcasta, and then her other sisters.

Eventually, Sophie gave up trying to sleep and rose, dressing as best she could and carelessly pinning up her hair. Throwing a cloak over her shoulders, she crept out onto the landing. A brisk walk might alleviate the worst of her agitation. Relieved to find the house in darkness, she moved like a shadow down the stairs, grateful for the moonlight that shone through some of the high, small windows of the hall. As her slippered feet touched the cold flagged floor, she stilled, cocking her head to one side and listening intently.

She could hear the faint strains of a pianoforte playing somewhere in the distance. Following the melody, she found herself outside the door to the tower. It was ajar. She realised she was listening to the same Beethoven Sonata she had played at Lady Renfrew's house, yet her rendition now felt like a pale imitation. The sonorous music spoke of loss and sorrow, the notes entwining in the air to create a soulful yearning that tore at her heartstrings. She moved without conscious volition up the curved stairway until she stood in the open doorway of the room on the first floor, her eyes drawn to the figure who sat at the instrument. Sir Philip's eyes were closed, his expression pained as his fingers moved increasingly rapidly over the keys until they flew through the final movement. The music gradually soared until it achieved a tempestuous tempo that rang with a passionate ferocity that left her breathless.

As the final notes died away, silent tears coursed down her face unchecked. Stifling a sob, she turned and raced with reckless speed down the dark stairwell and out through the side door.

"Sophie!"

The urgent call of her name only sent her running again, this time around the side of the house and down towards the river, the music still ringing in her ears. His playing had magnified the longing, indecision, and turmoil that lay within her. But all that yearning and sorrow had not been for her; he had been playing for his mother. She could not bear it. She must have been mad to even consider for a moment the idea of becoming his mistress! To know the depth of feeling he was capable of, but never capture it for herself would be an agony beyond compare.

She came to a halt on a small wooden bridge, her chest heaving, gasping for some much-needed air.

Curling both hands around the wooden rail, she focussed on the moonlight reflected on the water and strove to regain a small measure of composure.

Before many moments had passed, she felt the wooden floor give as a steady, firm stride sounded against its boards before two large hands appeared on the rail beside her own.

"It is a beautiful spot, is it not?"

Sophie nodded, not trusting herself yet to speak. Her heart still hammered in her chest, but no longer from lack of breath.

They both watched the shimmering flecks of moonlight dance across the water like silver sprites as it flowed gently towards them, softly murmuring sweet nothings to the night.

"I have loved and hated this place in equal measure," Sir Philip said quietly. "My mother made it a magical place, she touched the lives of everyone she came into contact with. She had a gentle spirit and a kind heart. After she had gone, it was nothing to me. I despised my father for not making her happy and went against all he stood for. I joined the army against his wishes. I refused to settle down and show an interest in my inheritance both before and after his death. I made the foolish mistake of burying many happy memories and dwelling only on those that had caused me pain. In all likelihood, he is not the ogre I have made him, but just another gentleman who was led by duty and did not know how to make a young, shy bride with whom he had nothing in common, happy."

Sophie's heart swelled with compassion for him. She yearned to cover the hand so close to hers with her own, but her fears and uncertainty prevented her. Out of the corner of her eye, she saw Sir Philip suddenly straighten and reach into his pocket. He withdrew a pebble and held it deliberately over the water for a moment before letting it fall.

"We have stood on another bridge far away, Lady Lewisham, and watched the ripples of a small stone spread out across the water."

"Yes," she replied in a small, wistful voice. "But they were world-changing ripples."

"Indeed, they were," Sir Philip murmured. "For my world changed on that day."

A small, sliver of hope lightened Sophie's heart as she straightened and turned cautiously towards him. "How so?" she said warily.

"It was the day I first knew how much I wanted you," he said quietly.

"Please," Sophie whispered, feeling pain knife through her. "Do not offer me a carte blanche, for I do not think I could bear it."

"Shhh," he said, placing his warm finger gently against her lips. "I have not finished."

She stood rooted to the spot as he pulled out the pins she had thrust haphazardly into her hair, watching it fall in a wild wavy mass almost to her waist, a predatorial gleam in his eyes. "Eos," he murmured, pulling her against him and dropping his head on top of her own. Her nostrils flared and filled with his musky, masculine scent. She drew a long, deep breath, drawing his essence deep within herself.

"It changed my world because it planted a seed of desire and need that has steadily and stealthily grown until it has twined its shoots around my heart, body, and mind."

Taking her face in his hands, he gently tilted it up and looked deeply into her eyes with such tenderness, she felt the world tilt. Her lips parted in a soft gasp.

Sir Philip's intense gaze dropped to them for a moment before he lowered his own, inch by slow inch until they met hers in a soft, achingly sweet caress.

"I want you, Sophie," he said in a low voice that throbbed with longing, moving his lips along her jawline.

She shivered as he found the sensitive spot beneath her ear.

"But not as my mistress, as my wife."

His hands moved back into her hair, and he pulled her fiercely to him, capturing her mouth in a deep passionate kiss. His tongue moved against hers with the same urgency and dexterity that his fingers had displayed as they had moved across the keys, this time, creating a silent symphony of desire that existed only within and between the two of them.

Sophie was lost. Sensation, perception, and emotion overwhelmed her with their combined power. Her lips felt swollen and bruised. She felt... happy was not an adequate term – she felt fiercely joyous – as though in embracing the flood of feelings that consumed her rather than running from them, she acknowledged and accepted something true and essential within herself. Her burgeoning desire was now an elemental force that spiralled like a whirlwind of flame, tearing through her, scouring her soul of any doubt or deceit until only the truth remained.

"I want you. I need you. I love you," she gasped, sagging against him.

Sir Philip lifted her into his arms and strode back to the tower, carrying her up to his private sanctuary. Seating himself in a deep, comfortable chair set before the fire, he held her close, gently stroking her silken locks until her trembling subsided.

Slowly she came to herself, for the first time taking in the details of the room. His mother's room. A huge portrait of her was mounted above the fireplace. Her expression was gentle, her azure eyes soft with love.

Colourful rugs covered the floor, rose-patterned cushions brightened the chairs, and various watercolours graced the walls. They were well-executed depictions of various pastoral scenes but nothing above the ordinary. One painting outshone all the others, however. She had painted her young son, her love shining through in every brushstroke. She had captured each wave and curl of his blue-black locks, his eyes were serious but with a lurking twinkle, his smile sweetly affectionate, his small hand curled around a toy horse.

"Why did you run?" he asked quietly.

Sophie's gaze was drawn back to the portrait above the fire. "I thought you played for your mother," she murmured.

"I usually do, it was her favourite sonata, but tonight I played for you." He smiled wryly. "I was not at all sure of your feelings for me, my cactus."

"And now?"

"Now, I will never let you go, even if I have to lock you in this room!" he growled.

Sophie grinned and eased her head back on his broad shoulder so she could look up into his face.

"Do you think she would approve?" she asked gently.

"Without a doubt," he smiled, dropping a light kiss on her nose.

"I shall have to write to my parents," she said, squirming a little uncomfortably in his lap.

"Sophie," he said warningly, "please sit still, or I will not be answerable for my actions!"

She looked surprised and then coloured deliciously.

"You are still an innocent," he said softly.

Sophie nodded shyly. "Edward lost his gamble. He was too old and ill as it turned out."

A slow smile of satisfaction spread across Sir Philip's face. "I suspected as much. However, he did not lose; his last years were filled with companionship and a desire to nurture another."

"Anyway," Sophie gulped, getting to her feet and walking to the other side of the fireplace. "The thing is..." she paused as if unable to find the right words. Both Contessina Isotta and Sir Philip had lost their mothers at an early age causing them both grief and pain. Whilst she might never feel any great affinity with her own mother, she was beginning to comprehend how lucky she had been to grow up in a lively, noisy family. How did she explain her mother and father without denigrating them?

"The thing is," Sir Philip smiled. "You are worried that your father will try to wheedle some settlement that he is not entitled to out of me and that your mother will try to foist your sister onto us as soon as we are wed."

Sophie's eyes widened in surprise.

"Harry was right," Sir Philip murmured, getting to his feet and moving purposefully towards her. "You are a green-eyed witch."

Sophie's heart leaped, however, she put her hand out. It barely grazed his chest, but he came to an abrupt halt.

"You are the one that can read minds," she said, bemused.

"Not at all. I paid them a visit before I came home," he admitted.

"Why?" Sophie said. "You do not need my father's permission, after all. Or was it to see if I was worthy of you?"

Sir Philip took the hand that lay against his chest and raised it to his lips. "You are enchanting," he said. "Curious and educated but not always wise, spirited and passionate yet innocent, sometimes a woman sometimes a child."

"Then, why?" she whispered, her hand curling around his.

"Because, my cactus, although I did not need his permission, I wished to show him the courtesy that he deserved. He is perhaps not always sensible, but he is your father, and wise enough to be very fond and proud of you."

Sophie smiled. "I am fond of him too. I think I was the son he never had."

"Perhaps," smiled Sir Philip. "It would at least explain how you are such an accomplished and intrepid horsewoman as well as a scholar."

Whereas a compliment on her beauty would have left her cold, the accolade bestowed on a genuine accomplishment sent a warmth flooding through veins. The wide smile that always enhanced her looks distracted Sir Philip, and he claimed her generous lips in a lingering kiss.

"Enough," he finally said, putting her from him. "I am determined to honour your innocence until we are wed, but you are testing my resolve."

Sophie smiled, for the first time understanding the primaeval power a woman had over a man.

"And what did you make of my mother?" she asked tentatively.

He smiled ruefully down at her. "She is not unlike many society mamas that I have met. Her whole world revolves around making marriages for her daughters. But she has good reason. Without a brother to protect them all, their only security lies in her finding partners who can provide for them. To wed five daughters suitably, is a hard task indeed for a family who is not wealthy and does not move in the first circles."

This time it was Sophie who stepped towards him, her head dropping in shame against his chest. "You are right, but I did not see it," she admitted. "I did not wish to thwart her, but neither did I feel able to please her. I could not be other than what I was."

Sensing her vulnerability, his strong arms closed around her, gathering her close.

"How could you?" he said gently. "Your father pulled you one way, your mother another, neither accounting for those independent qualities that are uniquely your own."

At last, Sophie raised her face to his, her eyes sparkling with unshed tears and amusement.

"And did he fleece you?"

Sir Philip quirked an eyebrow. "Not at all. I am an ill pigeon for plucking. However, I did suggest that I could send poor Charles down to run an eye over his estate and perhaps offer guidance to his steward."

Sophie smiled. "And how did you feel about bringing out Alcasta? If my mother did not at least hint at it, I will own myself amazed. And in all honesty, I do feel I should make a push to do something for her."

"Of course," Sir Philip agreed. "But at a time of our choosing, and in our own way. We will take a long honeymoon, my dear, and only when we are both ready, will we engage ourselves on her behalf. Where would you like to go? If it is within my power to grant your wish, I will."

"Nowhere." Sophie took both his hands in her own. "Eastleigh holds all your strongest memories for good or ill. We will create new ones that reinforce the good and drive out the bad."

Sir Philip closed his eyes for a moment, but then a slow, rueful smile curved his firm lips. "How they will all crow tomorrow," he said. "Our engagement will be all of their doing and none of our own."

Sophie laughed. "They will have a point," she conceded.

"God save me from managing women!" Sir Philip murmured.

"I do not think you will need his intervention," she smiled. "It is poor Harry who will have to deal with their good intentions now!"

Sir Philip's shoulders began to shake. "By God, he will lead them a merry dance!"

Sophie gave him an arch look. "If they could manage you, sir, I would not be so sure. I will own myself surprised if he is not caught by the end of the next season!"

Sir Philip pulled her close and kissed her thoroughly.

"You are a delight, my love, and may well be right, but at this moment, I find I have more important matters to consider," he growled.

"Wait," she insisted breathlessly, turning her head so that his kiss landed haphazardly on her ear. "We do have more important matters to consider. What is to become of Agnes?"

For a moment he did not answer, apparently determined to search out every sensitive hollow and curve of her neck. "I think you will find that Doctor Johnson has plans for the remarkable Miss Trew."

"Of course," Sophie sighed blissfully, for a moment giving herself up to the delicious sensations that were coursing through her.

"And I have not yet heard you agree to be my wife, my cactus."

Sophie chuckled. "But then I have not yet heard you ask me!"

Sir Philip raised his head and looked steadily into her eyes, his feelings laid bare for her to see.

"Lady Lewisham, will you consent to be my wife, my love, and my companion in this life?"

"Yes," she said softly, reaching up to plant a soft kiss on his lips. "In this life and the next."

# VOLUME THREE

## KATHERINE

# KATHERINE

## BACHELOR BRIDES BOOK 3

CHAPTER 1

A travelling carriage and a lone rider turned through the gates of Elmdon Hall and made their unhurried progress along the well-kept drive that was lined with the trees it was named after. The rider made no attempt to communicate with the occupants of the carriage, his bright blue eyes too busy drinking in every detail of the achingly familiar vista before him, as a man dying of thirst might view the sudden appearance of an oasis.

It had been five long years since Harry Treleven had seen his home and as the sun made a sudden appearance from behind the sullen grey clouds, the many small-paned windows of the Elizabethan manor began to wink brightly as if in welcome.

"Elmdon," he whispered, a slow wide grin transforming his unusually sombre countenance. Suddenly impatient to be within the portals of his home again, he touched his heels to his horse's flanks and encouraged the weary beast into one last gallop.

Elmdon Hall had been the principal home to the

Trelevens for seven generations. It had first been gifted to Marcus Treleven, who had been a reckless but successful privateer and an annoying wasp to the Spanish, frequently intercepting their ships and filling Queen Elizabeth's coffers as well as lining his own pockets. She'd rewarded him with a knighthood and his son, a courtier to James I, was later awarded the title of viscount.

Perhaps it was this illustrious history that had tempted his descendent, the present viscount, to attempt such a lifestyle when he had been forced to flee the country after a duel over a lady that had left her husband, Lord Worthington, at death's door. That door had remained firmly closed however, and Lord Worthington had made a slow but steady recovery. It had only been when Harry had become dangerously ill with malaria and in serious danger of crossing that threshold himself, that he had discovered his mistake and returned to the shores of his birth. This could not have been achieved without the aid of his good friend, Sir Philip Bray, who had travelled to Italy to bring him home and entered the state of connubial bliss soon afterwards. Indeed, it had been his nuptials that had delayed his return further.

The house was generally acknowledged to be a gracious building of pleasing proportions, the Trelevens not succumbing to the temptation that so frequently gripped their acquaintances, to add to their consequence by adding on wings that they could have little use for and more often than not, detracted from the handsomeness of the original building. Containing only ten principal bedrooms, it was not so large that a visitor might easily lose their way nor yet so compact that its occupants could never find a quiet corner in which to relax and contemplate their good fortune.

It sat in rolling parklands that spread in all directions as far as the eye could see, and although the park was mostly naturalistic in style, it still boasted an authentic knot garden and well-tended maze that dated back to the house's Tudor origins.

It took a good twenty minutes at least to arrive at the house once any visitor had passed through the gates, and much longer on foot, although as it sat on a small rise towards the centre of the park, it could be seen long before this.

The clattering of hooves on cobbles brought Kenver, the head groom at Elmdon, out of the stables. He was a small, wiry man with a weather-beaten face and a naturally taciturn disposition. He was not best pleased at being interrupted, as he had been busy mending one of the stall doors, which a bad tempered mare had kicked half off its hinges. He strode into the yard, his mallet still clutched in one fist and his annoyance writ large upon his dour countenance.

He stopped short when he saw his long absent master, dropped the mallet, and blinked rapidly as if to clear his vision. As Harry swung down from the saddle and strode towards him, he put his hands on his hips and let out a low whistle. For a moment it looked like Harry might actually embrace him and he thrust out a work-roughened hand to discourage such an unthinkable occurrence. However, he shook his hand warmly and the lines around his small, dark eyes deepened as a rare wide smile crept across his face.

"Lord Treleven," he said. "Welcome home, sir. Welcome home!"

Harry grinned. "Hello, Kenver, glad to see you, even if you do still look like you've lost a sovereign and found a farthing!"

"Is that so, sir? Well you may be right, but if you don't mind me saying so, you've turned into a right spindleshanks and no mistake. Best get yourself in to see Mrs Kemp, she'll soon put some meat on your bones!"

"I will, for I am famished. You can show me what cattle we have later, Kenver."

He shook his head ruefully. "The stable's not what it once was, sir."

"Not to worry, Kenver, not to worry, we'll soon sort that out!" the viscount assured him breezily, already striding towards the back of the house.

Mrs Kemp had been the cook at Elmdon ever since Harry could remember and a firm ally. Always active and usually hungry, he had been forever haunting the kitchens as a child, knowing she would give him something tasty to keep him going until dinnertime. She was busy pummelling some dough, with an energy that belied her age, when he entered the kitchen, and did not so much as glance up. Shutting the door behind him, he leant against it nonchalantly.

"What has taken you so long?" she snapped, clearly mistaking him for one of the scullery maids.

"That is a long story, but I came as soon as I could, I assure you," he replied softly.

The pummelling stopped. Mrs Kemp's head whipped around, revealing a round rosy face and a satisfyingly startled expression.

"Master Harry! Master Harry!" she squealed, his

boyishly cheeky grin causing her to slip into the form of address she had used when he was but a child. "Is it really you?"

Pushing himself away from the wall, he strode forwards and caught her up in a hug. "Mrs Kemp, Mrs Kemp!" he laughed. "It is indeed, me. A very famished me! Please say you have something to stop the infernal rumbles that have been issuing from my unruly stomach for the past hour and more!"

She emerged from his warm clasp, slightly flustered, with her cap askew and her eyes suspiciously bright.

"Now, that's enough of that, sir. You are the viscount now and need to remember your station *and mine*. It is most improper that you manhandle me in such a fashion! Or that you should creep in through the back door like a servant."

Harry hung his head as if in shame. "I must apologise, Mrs Kemp, I did not mean to wound your dignity, but I really am very hungry you know."

She was not fooled for an instant by his humble display. "Oh, sit down, Lord Treleven, do. I don't know what you've been up to or where you've been but there is nothing to you, and that's the truth! But don't you worry none, we'll soon have you fattened up!" Disappearing for a moment into a small adjacent pantry, she re-emerged with a jug of ale and a plate of cakes.

"Here you are, sir, get this down you for starters!"

"Mrs Kemp, Mrs Kemp!" This time the refrain came from the inner corridor. "Lady Treleven's carriage is coming up the driveway. Why she didn't write to warn us, I don't know!"

The door opened on these words to reveal the harassed looking housekeeper. Harry's back was towards her, so all she saw was a strange man wolfing down cakes.

"Who is this?" she said sternly. "This is not the time to be feeding all and sundry, Mrs Kemp, not with her ladyship being almost at the door!"

Harry hastily swallowed, took a swig of ale, and turned to greet the newcomer. "Have you already forgotten me, Biddy?" he twinkled.

No one else would have dared address Mrs Bidulph, a very correct housekeeper, in such a fashion. She pressed her hands over her heart as she gasped, "Lord Treleven? Can it be you?"

Pushing himself to his feet, he took both her hands in his own and dropped a swift kiss on her pale cheek. "Indeed it can. Now bustle about, Biddy, you must go and greet mother, remember."

"Of course, sir," she said, pulling herself together. She paused at the door as if something had just occurred to her. Turning back she said, "Will you be changing rooms, my lord?"

A shadow seemed to flit across Harry's face. "No, my own room will do nicely for now."

Nodding briskly, she bustled out, all business again.

Word about Viscount Treleven's return soon got out in the mysterious way these things do in the country and it was not long before a stream of visitors made their way to Elmdon. Families who had long since given up trying to engage with Lady Treleven, who had become quite reclusive after the disappearance of her son followed shortly after by the death of her beloved husband in an unfortunate riding accident, now made a concerted effort to renew their acquaintance; especially if they had daughters of marriageable age.

They found Lady Treleven quite transformed and even her shy daughter Henrietta, slightly less awkward than before. Although this was generally viewed as a welcome development, more than one ambitious mother found herself disappointed, for Lord Treleven proved annoyingly elusive during these frequent visits.

This was only partly due to him throwing himself into learning the business of running his estate, something he did with great energy and application; he had never been one to do anything by halves, but also because he had made it crystal clear to Glasson, his butler, that he expected him to pronounce him 'not at home' if anyone arrived with their daughters in tow.

This instruction had not been issued because he held females in contempt, far from it, he had always had an eye for the ladies, but he preferred to further any acquaintance on his own terms and avoided matchmaking mamas like the plague. Although he was pleased that his friend Philip had finally found his life's partner, he had no intention of following his example any time soon. He was fairly certain he would be the devil of a husband! Not one to deny his own weaknesses, he knew he had a roving eye and had never yet met a woman he had not wearied of within a sennight.

At the present time, he preferred to re-acquaint himself with his country. His estate was on the north coast of Cornwall and it ran all the way to the wide expanse of sea that bordered the county.

It was here that he had ventured today, escaping both visitors and his steward. Mr Hewel was honest enough and had served the family, like most of their servants, for a long time, however he was not as young as he once was and Harry feared he had quite exhausted him as he had endeavoured to acquire as much information as possible in a relatively short time. His estate was huge and he had not yet surveyed above half of it, but it was already clear to him that much needed to be done. Mr Hewel had fallen behind the times and no new investments or innovations had been attempted for some years. He should perhaps pension him off, but he sensed that Mr Hewel was not yet ready for an idle life and he would not repay loyal service in such a way.

A warm wind buffeted him as he approached the cliff, and he took a long breath inhaling deep the fresh sea air, tasting the salty tang upon his tongue. The recent rains had encouraged a riot of growth and a luxuriant carpet spread before him, embroidered with splashes of blue, white, pink and yellow as sea campion, thrift, stonecrop and alexanders threaded their way through it. He picked his way carefully towards the cliff edge, wary lest the growth hid a rabbit hole or two.

Allowing his mount to drop his head and enjoy the small, yellow flowers of the alexanders, he let his eyes rove over the wide expanse before him. The choppy grey-green waters were flecked with angry flurries of white foam which scornfully burst over or rushed around the dark rocks which stood like silent giants, barring entry to the clean, empty stretch of golden sand beyond. Above gulls wheeled and gannets dived, their raucous calls striking a discordant note above the ever present rumble of the crashing surf.

By God, he had missed this country! It spoke to something deep within him, stripping from him all artifice and calling to his most primitive self. If the day had been calmer he would have been tempted to make his way down the narrow path that wound towards the beach below and dive into those cold, clear waters, and celebrate his homecoming with a baptismal swim. It would be foolhardy today however, as not only was the sea rough, but from his vantage point he could clearly see the white and brown rush as waves and sand were sucked under and dragged out again by a strong current.

Only a fool would underestimate the sea; beneath those waves lay the wrecks and bones of many ships and sailors who had come to grief on this treacherous stretch of coast. Shaking off this melancholy thought, he turned his horse and made his way back to the cliff path. He could see the tall granite chimney and engine house of Wheal Trewith in the distance. Although the mines offered much needed employment to the local people, he could not help but think they were a blight on this naturally wild and beautiful landscape.

He knew that Lord Trewith had at one time suggested his father invest and even that they explore the possibilities of tunnelling into his own land, but he could not say he was sorry that the idea had come to naught. He would much rather invest in farming the land, providing jobs and much needed sustenance rather than plunder it for its natural resources. He was however, going to have to expand his interests sooner or later; a combination of poor harvests and a drop in the price of crops had seriously undermined the productivity of the land, eating not only into his own profits but those of his tenant farmers.

Lord Trewith, like his own father, was no longer of this earth and his son, not sharing his head for business or love of the West Country, which he had been known to refer to as a social wasteland, had sold the estate whilst he had been away. He had not yet met Mr Caldwell, the current owner and his nearest neighbour of any note, but no doubt he would soon enough. He could only give him credit for giving him time to settle in before paying his visit and could wish that a few others had shown such forethought.

He turned away from the mine and headed towards the village of Langarne. The ride had given him a thirst and if his memory served him correctly, The Anchor served a decent brew. It had also used to boast a very cosy armful who went by the name of Mollie Penrose.

Langarne was reached down a long, winding, steep lane. Tall hedges and towering trees threw it almost constantly into shifting shadow and in winter it could be treacherous. At the bottom of the hill, the village spread out along the banks of a river, made up of mostly small thatched cottages, the inn, and a church and vicarage, which stood slightly apart across a small green. Other than a few women washing clothes down by the river, and an old man sunning himself outside his cottage, sucking on his pipe, it was largely deserted today. The man nodded at Harry as he passed.

"Glad to see you back, Lord Treleven, and not before time, if I may say so," he said, removing the pipe from his mouth. "Things go to ruin when those as knows the land and its people leave it be."

Harry gave him an intent stare, vaguely aware of currents flowing beneath his words that he could not quite navigate.

"Well, I am back now, my good man, and I will do my best to set it in order, you may be sure."

The wizened old man regarded him just as closely for a moment and then nodded, put his pipe back in his mouth, and spoke around the obstruction. "Happen you will, sir, happen you will."

A young lad came running as he turned into the yard of The Anchor. Harry dismounted, tossed a coin to the boy and strode into the inn. It was a warren of small rooms, with low beams and flagged floors, and he was surprised to see sullen men who should have been out earning a crust, occupied more than one.

"Lord Treleven!" beamed a tall, spare man with a thatch of dark hair, putting down the cloth he had been wiping the bar with. "I heard as you were back and was wondering how long it would be before you paid us a visit. I told Mollie as how you wouldn't think yourself too high and mighty just because you have a title now!"

Harry grinned and shook the huge hand offered to him. "I should think not, Joe. I have been looking forward to a tankard of your fine ale. Is old Jack about?"

Joe shook his head and began pouring his ale. "M'father died of pneumonia last winter, sir. I run the place now."

"Oh, do you now, Joe Phelps? We'll soon see about that!"

"Mollie!" Harry roared, his eyes lighting with laughter. Spinning around he lifted the curvaceous red-haired woman who stood before him, her hands on her nicely rounded hips, clean off of her feet, twirling her around before planting a brief kiss on her smiling lips.

"Put me down, Harry, do, afore you drop me. I don't know what mischief you've been up to but you're thin as a cord. There was obviously no decent food to be had on whatever godforsaken shore you washed up on!"

"Ahem." The noise was quietly made, but they both glanced over to see Joe observing them, a small frown furrowing his broad brow.

"No offence, Lord Treleven, sir, but I would rather you weren't quite so familiar with my wife," he said, his voice gentle but quite firm.

Harry took a step back as Mollie flushed slightly. "You're married, Mollie?"

"She is that," confirmed Joe seriously. "And I would remind you, Mollie, that what is past is past and best forgotten and as his lordship has come into his title, an all, you should address him as Lord Treleven from now on."

Mollie's rueful eyes might have held a smidgeon of regret but she curtsied briefly to Harry. "Joe's right enough, everything is different now, H-my lord, we was wed last year and I have never been happier."

Harry's smile was a little lopsided. "I am pleased for you both," he assured them glancing around the room, suddenly aware of more than one pair of resentful eyes upon him.

"Why aren't these men out working?" he asked quietly.

Joe lowered his voice and leant in a little closer. "You'd be better asking Mr Caldwell the answer to that, sir, he's a deep 'un and proud as Lucifer. A lot of things have changed, my lord, and not for the better neither."

"Go on," Harry murmured.

"Seems he wasn't satisfied with Cornish miners who were born and bred to the trade. Brought a load over from Wales along with his coal, and on the last setting day they bid so low, they were awarded the contracts. There's a lot of bad feeling round here and no mistake and I wouldn't be surprised if there was trouble afore long. A few have got work in the boatyards at Padstow, the rest sits in here, nursing their resentment over a drink they can't afford and will likely never pay for."

"I see," Harry said frowning. "I will indeed ask Mr Caldwell for his reasons, Joe, of that you can be sure. Meanwhile, I'll have a word with Mr Hewel and my mother, it may be that we could do with some extra help."

Joe nodded tersely. "I 'as always said you were a good 'un, honest as the day is long."

Leaving his horse at The Anchor, Harry strode across the village green towards the vicarage. A few women had just come from there, and passed him with their eyes downcast, the aroma of freshly baked bread wafting from their cloth covered baskets.

A squat housekeeper with a fierce beetle-black glare opened the door, her expression as sour as curdled milk.

"I've no more bread to—"

Harry grinned at her. "What about one of your biscuits, Mrs Creedley?"

Harry had been sent down from Oxford on more

than one occasion, and his father, though secretly admiring his pluck, had insisted he spent some of the time studying with the Reverend James Gulworthy, a widower, who had the reputation of being something of a scholar.

"Lord Treleven! The prodigal son returns, at last. You'd best come in," she sniffed, "as if I haven't got enough to do with looking after the vicar and the new doctor, as well as feeding half the village!"

Not at all put out by the lack of ceremony with which she greeted him, Harry followed her down the dark, panelled hallway into the large kitchen. She went to a covered plate that sat on the scrubbed wooden side and plonked it none too gently on the large pine table that ran almost the length of the kitchen, then stood glaring at him with folded arms.

Glancing out of the window, Harry saw the balding pate of Mr Gulworthy bent over a small rose bush. Mrs Creedley followed his gaze.

"He'd be better tending his flock than his precious roses! If he were one of those methody preachers he'd be turning them out of The Anchor and giving them a lecture on the evils of drinking. Instead he preaches about how the bountiful eye shall be blessed for giving his bread to the poor, and I'm the fool that has to make it!"

Harry glanced at the housekeeper, surprised. She might appear curmudgeonly but he knew that she had a good heart and he had never before heard her berate her absentminded master.

"And you needn't stand there looking down your nose, neither. You're no better!"

Harry felt himself stiffen, his eyes hardening. Mrs Creedley suddenly burst into tears.

"I'm sorry, my lord. I didn't mean it, but everything's topsy-turvy round here at the moment."

Flicking back the cloth that covered the plate, he took a biscuit and laid a hand briefly on her shaking shoulder.

"Calm yourself, Mrs Creedley, you may be sure I will look into matters here."

The afflicted lady rummaged for a handkerchief in her apron pocket and promptly wiped her eyes and blew her nose.

"I know you will, sir, you always were a good boy, really."

Mr Gulworthy glanced up as Harry approached, unhurriedly finished deadheading a few more roses, then smiled and held out his hand.

"Lord Treleven. Welcome home, sir, welcome home. Your return is the best news we have had in these parts for some time."

"That is not a view shared by all, I think," he replied a little grimly.

Mr Gulworthy shook his head. "Things are not as they once were, Lord Treleven. The villagers feel let down, abandoned, hopeless and bitter."

Harry sighed. "Mrs Creedley also seems deeply affected."

"Yes, well, her favourite nephew has just sailed from Padstow for America, hoping to find a better life, so we must forgive her if she is a little more crotchety than usual."

Harry frowned. "Have you had any dealings with Mr Caldwell?"

The vicar's gentle gaze hardened. He turned back to his flowers and firmly snipped the wilting head of another fading rose.

"I reminded him of proverbs 22:1," he assured him.

Harry raised a quizzical brow.

The vicar sighed. "You never were one to stick to your books. 'A good name is rather to be chosen than great riches, and loving favour rather than silver and gold'."

"And his response?"

"The heathen laughed in my face," he said gravely.

CHAPTER 2

Miss Katherine Lockhart stretched weary limbs and sighed. She had been on the road for almost a week but it felt like forever. Her brother, Sir Richard Lockhart, had informed her that the ways into Cornwall were much improved in recent years, but if this were so, she shuddered to think what they had been like before. If it remained dry they had to negotiate ruts and dips that jolted all occupants of the carriage mercilessly – and no matter how stuffy and hot it became they were forced to keep the windows shut to prevent the dust from choking them – but if it came on to rain the road became a treacherous quagmire in a matter of moments. It was perhaps these indisputable facts that had discouraged her brother from making the journey himself when a distant relation he had never met had unexpectedly bequeathed him his property, Helagon, more than a year ago. His solicitor had informed him that it was a modest house in quite an isolated spot and might benefit from some slight renovation. It was to this property that Katherine was now making her plodding way.

She had really been left with very little choice. She had only once met someone she had felt the slightest tendre for and he had turned out to be a sad disappointment. Having a natural inclination to manage, she had been happy enough running Sir Richard's elegant house for him, but it could not be contemplated that she could continue to do so as he had recently been married. His wife, Caroline, understandably wanted to put her own mark on Felsham Court, and this was not always easy when the servants were used to the way Miss Lockhart ordered things. When, exasperated, Caroline had suggested it might be time to replace some of them, Katherine had realised that her continued presence was quite untenable. Unwilling to see any loyal retainers turned off or to remain a drain on her brother's resources when she no longer held any useful role within his household – and having no considerable fortune of her own – she had suggested she look about her for a post as governess or companion.

Sir Richard had looked horrified, but fully aware that the continued presence of both women under his own roof would inevitably disturb his peace, had offered her a compromise; she would travel to Helagon and put it in order, and if she liked it there, she could have its use for as long as she wished. Despite her four and twenty years, he had insisted she take a companion. Mrs Abbott was some sort of distant cousin to their departed mother and lived in a small cottage on his estate. She had been more than happy to accompany Katherine, delighted to feel that she was needed and could finally be of some real use.

And so they had set out on this interminable journey. Their slow progress was not due to the poor state of the highways alone however; if her brother had been prepared to lend them his best carriage and horses, they might have been much more comfortable and made swifter progress, but as Caroline had assured him that she could not do without it, that had not been an option.

"I am sure Katherine cannot mind taking the other coach, dear, for she is not in a hurry after all," she had said winningly, serving up the smile she reserved only for him. "And I really cannot be expected to be jolted about by that horrid rickety old thing in my present delicate condition."

Sir Richard's strong sense of decorum had not allowed him to entertain, even for a moment, the idea that his sister should make use of any form of public transport, and his penny-pinching ways had encouraged him to take notice of his wife when she had pooh-poohed the notion that they should hire a private post-chaise and four to convey his sister to her destination.

"It is such a shocking expense!" she had exclaimed. "And you have already been so very generous in gifting dear Katherine the use of Helagon for as long as she wishes. Although I hope I value my sister-in-law as I should, I am sure that it would cause her much discomfort to think that she had been such a burden to you, Richard. Do not forget that she will have the benefit of an experienced coachman who has known her all his life and if it *is* a little slow, that cannot signify for she will have the benefit of Mrs Abbott to keep her company."

That part was at least true. Mrs Abbott was perhaps not the brightest penny in the purse, but she had a good heart and a sweet disposition and Katherine found this refreshing after fielding Caroline's barely veiled barbs for the past six months.

Katherine turned her gaze to the open landscape beyond the window of the carriage, it appeared to stretch endlessly before her and was quite alien in its character. It was a rough hardy terrain, strewn with large grey boulders and scrubby brush, but here and there bright bursts of yellow gorse or purple heather relieved the monotony. The huge sky cast an ominous feel over the whole, bruised lowering clouds stretched almost to the wide horizon and beneath them a fiery orb of molten gold threw its munificent soothing rays over strange outcrops of granite and stunted withered trees, which leaned towards it as if in silent supplication. It was a far cry indeed from the fertile, gently rolling hills near her own home, yet she felt herself somehow moved by the ancient unadorned scene before her.

Slowly the prospect gentled, the land showing signs of cultivation, and they descended into a deep wooded valley.

"It cannot be much further," Katherine murmured as they turned into a road so narrow that the twigs of untended bushes and trees scratched the sides of the lurching coach like skeletal fingers.

"I do hope not, dear," said Mrs Abbott a trifle anxiously, "for it is almost dark."

"It's an ungodly place if you ask me," muttered the

other occupant of the carriage. "It wouldn't surprise me if there were hobgoblins out there."

Mrs Abbott looked a little alarmed.

Katherine favoured her maid with a stony stare. Caroline had recommended her, and wishing to avoid any unnecessary unpleasantness, she had agreed to give her a trial. Her disposition was surly however, and Katherine would have been tempted to replace her if she had had the time. But although she had resigned herself to tolerating her sour disposition, she would not countenance her upsetting Mrs Abbott.

"I do not believe anyone did ask you, Ayles, and if you cannot keep your tongue between your teeth, you shall ride on the roof next to coachman John."

Ayles bowed her head as if in deference, but Katherine noticed the sulky pout that she could not quite hide.

Dusk came on quickly and the dense woodland that bordered the road on either side intensified the gloom. The ladies were aware of a feeling of relief as they heard the crunch of gravel beneath them and realised they had turned into a driveway. As they descended from the carriage a sliver of moon appeared between the shifting clouds, casting its silvery light over the granite house in front of them, bathing it in a ghostly glow. No welcoming flicker from a fire or candle could be discerned behind any of the dark blank windows that seemed to stare blindly down at them.

Signalling for coachman John to stay where he was, Katherine stepped forwards and pulled the large iron bell that hung by the front door. It had clearly not been oiled for some time and squealed its protest at being thus awoken. The flapping of wings could be heard above its low sonorous chimes as roosting birds were disturbed, adding their disgruntled cries to the cool night air, and somewhere in the distance the mournful hoot of an owl completed the eerie atmosphere. Katherine shivered and pulled her cloak closer around her, at the same time silently castigating herself as a witless widgeon. She had always prided herself on her calm good sense and reason and here she was behaving more like her namesake Catherine Morland in Northanger Abbey! A novel she had not managed to finish as, although she could admire the wit of its writer, she was less able to bear with the overactive imagination of the heroine.

Nevertheless, she was grateful when a few moments later, a stooped, elderly gentleman who looked as if he should have been retired a long time since, opened the door. He attempted an unsteady bow and almost toppled forwards. Katherine automatically put out her hand to steady him and offered him a small smile.

"Good evening, I am Miss Lockhart, I do hope you were expecting us?" She glanced past him uncertainly into the dark panelled hallway.

"Forster, ma'am," he said, standing aside to let them pass. "We knew you were coming, Miss Lockhart, but were not sure exactly when to expect you."

Katherine was relieved. For a moment she had wondered if they had come to the wrong house and the awful prospect of resuming their journey had loomed before her. "I can see that," she said drily as she looked about the hallway. Even in the light of his flickering candle she could see that the wooden floors were dull and the table that stood at the base of the staircase, covered in a film of dust. Her housewifely instincts were revolted but she refrained from comment.

A little more light was shed upon this rather dismal scene as a door at the end of the corridor burst open and a short, stout lady hurried forwards.

"Oh my, oh my," she said in a worried voice. "Miss Lockhart, I only had the letter two days ago and as there is only me and Forster left, everything is not yet as I would like, or at least as good as I could make it."

"There are only the two of you?" Katherine said, surprised.

The agitated lady before her nodded. "We had a maid or two and a gardener when Mr Jenkins was alive, but after he died they bailed. Said they weren't staying around in this gloomy place with no guarantee of getting paid anytime soon."

"Well, I must thank you, Mrs…?"

"Mrs Nance, ma'am."

"Mrs Nance and Forster for at least staying," she continued. "It is an unfortunate circumstance to be sure, but I am sure there will be no great difficulty in hiring a few more servants. But we can discuss what is to be done in the morning. Now, is there any chance of a fire and some supper?"

"I will go and lay the fire directly, ma'am," said Forster.

"Wait," said Katherine, thinking better of it. "Is there a fire in the kitchen, Mrs Nance?"

"There is indeed, ma'am."

"Good," Katherine said decisively. "We will take our supper there. We only require some tea and perhaps some cold meat and bread and butter before we retire."

"As you wish, ma'am, I have at least prepared the bedchambers and a room over the stables for your coachman."

She found things much more to her liking in the kitchen. A cheery fire burnt in the hearth, its flickering flames reflected in the gleaming copper pans that lined the walls and the table on which Mrs Nance laid their simple repast, was scrubbed spotlessly clean. Once they had eaten their fill, the housekeeper showed them to their rooms.

As they ascended to the first floor, many of the stairs creaking beneath them, Katherine shivered. A cold damp seemed to penetrate through the very stones of the house.

Her chamber was of a comfortable size, and apart from a bed hung with red velvet drapes that may have at one time been quite luxurious but were now sadly faded, it boasted a small threadbare armchair that was set before the empty fireplace, a washstand, a large armoire, a squat ugly dresser made of a dark wood and a toilet table upon which sat a slightly hazed mirror. Crossing to the window, Katherine firmly closed the worn curtains against the flickering shadows cast by the trees, which somehow rendered even the most ordinary items of furniture slightly menacing, blew out her candle, and climbed into bed. Her sheets were cool and unwelcoming but even this inconvenience could not keep her tired eyes from closing almost immediately. Her last cogent thought before she fell into a deep slumber was that she was sure everything would seem much better in the morning.

When she opened her eyes, the first thing she saw was a nasty crack running across the ceiling above her. Sighing, she sat up. Mrs Nance had thoughtfully placed a small silver bell by her bedside and she rang it. The sooner she was up, the sooner she could assess the magnitude of the task she had undertaken.

Ayles eventually answered the summons on the third ring. Her eyes bore witness to her restless night, purple shadows and swollen eyelids a testament to her fitful sleep and her downturned mouth a clear indication of her feelings.

"Is everything all right, Ayles?" Katherine asked gently.

Her maid pursed her thin lips. "Oh, I've nothing to complain about, Miss Lockhart. I daresay I will become quite used to mice running across my bed during the night, not to mention the branches of a tree scraping against my window, and I am not one to moan about the wind howling around the house as if a demented lost soul was trying to find its way in."

"I am sorry that your rest was disturbed, Ayles," she said, not unsympathetically. "But every house has its own foibles after all, and whilst I can do nothing about the wind, I am sure we can remedy the other annoyances."

Not wishing to put Mrs Nance to the blush, after breakfast she and Mrs Abbott made their own tour of the house. It was to be expected that after lying empty for some time it should bear an air of neglect, but judging by her growing list of problems, she could only imagine that their distant relative, Mr Jenkins, had been too tight-fisted to spend any money on its upkeep. He had certainly not been constrained by poverty for he had also left her brother quite a tidy sum, which he had begrudgingly put at her disposal to carry out whatever improvements were needed to make the house habitable.

"And if you don't like it, Katherine, once you have put it in order, you must come straight back," he had advised her, his sense of duty overcoming his dislike of being made uncomfortable. He was also fully aware that she had always managed his house extremely well on a modest budget, and had cast a wary eye over all the improvements that his new wife felt were necessary to her comfort. "I am certain it is Caroline's condition that is making her so crotchety, but once the child is born I am sure she will be only too grateful for some extra help with everything."

Katherine had repressed a shudder at this ingenuous speech, the implications of the word 'everything' conjuring up visions of herself dwindling into a maiden aunt who would be expected to fetch and carry for a never satisfied Caroline, or take care of her offspring when she inevitably discovered that the expense of a nursemaid was really not to be thought of when *dear* Katherine could have nothing better to do. She had determined there and then, that whatever she found awaiting her, she would make the best of it. However, she had certainly not expected Helagon to be quite so rundown.

"Might benefit from some slight renovation?" she muttered, not for the first time as they came upon yet another room with moth-eaten furnishings. She was, by now, expecting the patches of damp and windows that rattled in their frames rendering the simple act of keeping the draught out, quite impossible. Worse was to come, for two ceilings had partially collapsed in the servants' quarters and some of the floorboards were quite rotten.

Katherine was not one to make a drama out of a crisis, but felt her spirits sink at this scene of devastation. "It seems Richard's solicitor has quite a talent for understatement," she said grimly.

Mrs Abbott looked worried. "Perhaps it has deteriorated greatly over the last year?" she said, giving him the benefit of the doubt. "But, Katherine, dear, I do not see how we can expect to hire any more maids when we have nowhere for them to sleep."

"There can be no question of it," she agreed. "I presume the problem is with the roof, the tiles have probably slipped. Let us go into the garden and see."

They found the back of the house covered in climbing ivy, and the garden predictably dishevelled and neglected. A weed-choked path was just visible beneath the long, unkempt grass and they made their way along it as best they could in order to attain a better view of the house.

"Oh, Katherine, come over here, dear."

Turning her head, she saw that Mrs Abbott had wandered off the path into the jungle beyond. She found her struggling to hold back the grass in order to take a closer look at something.

"Let me help," Katherine said, pulling back another section of undergrowth.

"Be careful, dear," Mrs Abbott warned. "There are some nasty brambles hidden in there."

It was a small but perfectly formed fountain, with a cherub standing on a plinth in the centre. Its mouth was pursed and in the absence of any water issuing from it, the winged child had an air of being surprised at the disturbance.

"It is a sign, my dear," Mrs Abbott said gently. "Everything will work out for the best, you wait and see. I think this garden could be quite lovely underneath this riot of grass and weeds."

Despite herself, Katherine smiled. Mrs Abbott was a keen gardener and had lovingly tended her own small patch of garden at Felsham. Her optimistic words strengthened Katherine's resolve; if Mrs Abbott could see through this wilderness to the potential that lay beneath, then she must do the same with the house.

She could clearly see now where some tiles had slipped and others had been blown clean off the roof. Plants had already started to take their place, but taking Mrs Abbott's lead she tried to look at the house with new eyes. It was larger than she had expected and not unpleasing in its proportions. Once the ivy had been stripped away and some of the trees that grew too close to the building, chopped down, it would look quite attractive. She would have to throw an army of workmen both into the house and garden, but it could be done.

The small stables that were set a little back at the side of the house were sheltered from the prevailing wind by a stand of trees, and were not as dilapidated as she had feared. Apart from her own carriage, there was a rather forlorn gig covered in dust but apparently still in one piece.

"All's well, John?" she asked her coachman, who was busy sweeping the floor.

"I've seen worse, ma'am," he said gruffly, "but I'll

be needing some help if you want things set to rights anytime soon."

"I will set about getting some help immediately," she assured him. "But in the meantime you are only to do what is necessary to make your own living arrangements more comfortable."

Mrs Nance looked up a little anxiously as they entered the kitchen and she reassured her with a calm smile.

"Mrs Nance, I am all admiration. I cannot imagine how you and Forster have managed in such a ramshackle place."

"Well, miss, it wasn't always as bad as this. But if you don't mind me talking frankly about a relation of yours, Mr Jenkins was not one to spend a penny when a ha'penny would do. He became quite eccentric in his last years; lived and slept in his library and ignored the rest of the house. I expect as you'll be off now you've seen it for yourself." Her tone was resigned and she bowed her head. "I don't know what's to happen to old Forster and me."

"Well I can tell you, Mrs Nance," Katherine said firmly. "You are going to be very busy presently, for we are going to turn this place about. I think this house could be quite charming with a little restoration and Mrs Abbott and I have already agreed that the garden will be delightful."

When Mrs Nance raised her head, her face was wet with tears. "It's what I've always said, miss, it's wrung my heart to see such a fine residence turn to wrack and ruin so it has."

Mrs Abbott took her arm and led her to the table.

"There, dear, sit down and rest for a moment. I'll

make you a reviving cup of tea. You'll need all your strength presently for you'll have an army of hungry mouths to feed."

Mrs Nance revived at the very thought and stepped away from the table.

"That's as music to my ears, Mrs Abbott, but I'll not have you waiting on me, it's not fitting. We'll have a cup of tea but I shall make it."

"I am going to need a little advice on how best to proceed," Katherine said thoughtfully. "Where do you suggest I seek it?"

"There's only one place near here where I think you'll get any useful sort of advice, and that'll be at Elmdon Hall, ma'am. The Trelevens have farmed the country around here for generations."

Katherine nodded decisively. "Well, then it is to Elmdon Hall I shall go, and there is no time like the present."

CHAPTER 3

Katherine's suggestion that she drive herself in the gig did not go down well with coachman John, who had had the privilege of teaching Katherine to both ride and drive and so did not hesitate to speak his mind.

"Now don't be hasty, ma'am," he said in his unhurried way. "It's not that I question your ability to drive it, you're a fine whip and do me credit, but what I do doubt is its ability to be driven. That gig has not been used for years and will need a proper looking at before it can be deemed serviceable, like everything else around here. Besides, you can't take it before you get a groom, for I'll not try and squeeze these old bones into a seat that is only fit for a lad, and if you think Sir Richard would thank me if I was to let you go haring about this countryside on your own, you've got windmills in your head. It won't take me many minutes to get the carriage ready, she's a fine old gal for a short journey, after all."

Katherine had had no thought of asking him to

accompany her, only wishing to allow him a rest after their tiring journey, but she supposed she should have known better; coachman John took his duties very seriously.

Although there was still a strong breeze blowing, the day was fair, white puffs of cloud chased each other across an azure sky and the narrow lanes seemed far less daunting when bathed in glorious sunshine. Once out of the valley, the trees marched in ordered lines along the hedgerows and the warm air shimmered with birdsong. Relaxing back against the squabs of her seat, Katherine allowed her mind to wander as her eyes roamed over the tranquil rural scene.

As they approached the wide gateway of the Elmdon estate, a deer ran across the road in front of them. The carriage had already slowed to turn into the drive so neither the graceful creature or the horses were much alarmed by this event – but the short explosive crack that snapped through the air moments later had them jibbing in their bits.

Startled, Katherine pushed down her window and leaned out. "John?" she called.

"Don't you go fretting, ma'am," he said, with his usual calm. "It'll be some gentleman or other after a pheasant or two, I'll be bound."

They had not gone many yards into the park however, when they saw someone stagger to his feet clutching his arm and a riderless horse tearing down the avenue. Barely waiting for the carriage to come to a halt, Katherine jumped down into the road. Brushing down her skirts she turned to the stranger.

"Sir, you are hurt, can I be of some assistance?"

she asked, her cool tone at variance with her impetuous action.

Harry offered her a small bow and a rueful smile. "It is nothing, ma'am, a mere scratch. I have suffered much worse I assure you and have had some practise at being thrown from horses."

"Then you have either been most unfortunate or very careless, sir," Katherine said, her small smile taking any sting from her words. "But please, allow me to bind your arm and take you up to the house."

"It is quite unnecessary," he insisted.

Katherine's clear hazel eyes dropped pointedly to the glistening dark red stain that had ruined his coat.

"Come now, sir, if it is only a scratch then it will not hurt very much to get that coat off you, and if it is of a more serious nature, the sooner we remove it the better, for you do not wish any stray threads to get into the wound."

Her patient, reasonable tone was very much in the style of a nurse re-assuring a recalcitrant child.

"I thought any lady worth the name was meant to faint at the sight of blood," Harry murmured provocatively.

Katherine merely raised a haughty brow leaving him in no doubt at all that she was every inch a lady. Before he could argue further, John was behind him, helping ease the tight fitting coat over his shoulders.

"Best do as you're told, sir," he said encouragingly as Harry winced. "Miss Lockhart is in the right of it."

Once the coat was removed, Katherine took a step forwards. She had retrieved a small pair of scissors from her reticule and began to snip at the material around the wound in an efficient manner.

"I have been a keen supporter of the infirmary in Bath," she informed him conversationally. "I discovered I have quite an interest in medical matters, and have frequently observed the surgeons there treat a variety of wounds."

"Really? And that makes you an expert, I suppose," Harry said, eyeing her scissors warily.

"No," Katherine replied unruffled, "just an enthusiastic amateur."

In a matter of moments the wound was laid bare and Katherine bent closer to observe it more closely.

Straightening she smiled sweetly at him. "I would not call it a mere scratch, sir. It runs quite deep and is bleeding quite profusely at the moment but it is not, I think, too serious. Have you a flask of brandy about you?"

"No, Miss Lockhart, I do not." Annoyed at her interference, Harry was terse. "I am not in the habit of imbibing spirits every time I take a ride."

If he had thought to wrong-foot her, he was sadly mistaken.

"I am glad to hear it, sir, but as you seem so accident prone it occurred to me that you might have become accustomed to carrying one to fortify yourself whenever you were thrown."

A glimmer of appreciation shone in the bright eyes that were suddenly closely regarding her and an appealing dimple was revealed as his lips reluctantly twitched into a grin. For the first time Katherine realised how very handsome he was. She pushed that thought firmly away; she had fallen for a handsome face but once in her life and it had been a salutary experience.

"I am not thrown as a matter of course, my hornet, but was referring to my time at Waterloo. It usually takes more than one shot to dismount me, but thankfully I am out of practice at dodging bullets."

"Then you should not allow your friends to shoot across the road," she said a little tartly; the handsome gentleman who had disappointed her had also been a soldier.

"My friends?" Harry queried.

"Could you take off your cravat, sir? I need it to bind your wound. You are, I assume, Lord Treleven?"

Harry inclined his head.

"Well if the shot wasn't caused by one of your friends shooting pheasants, how do you account for it?"

"Probably a poacher," Harry said, wincing as he lifted his arm to loosen his cravat.

"Here, let me," Katherine said briskly. "You are making the wound bleed even more."

She dealt with the neckcloth in a businesslike manner, keeping her eyes firmly fixed on the job in hand but not quite managing to avoid them slipping for the briefest moment, to observe the strong column of his throat as it was revealed.

"Very efficient," he murmured softly, causing her to glance up. His eyes had darkened to a disturbing sapphire blue. "Anyone would think you had done this before."

Katherine yanked the now undone cravat none too gently, causing her patient to wince as the friction caused a momentary flash of heat to sear his neck. "It is hardly a difficult task," she snapped. Retrieving her scissors she cut it neatly in two.

Harry groaned. "First my shirt, now my cravat, you are quite ruthless, Miss Lockhart, whatever will my valet say?"

"Are you never serious?" she chided as she folded one half of the cravat into a neat pad and pressed it quite firmly against the wound.

Harry sucked in a deep breath.

"I am sorry but it must be done if we are to stop the bleeding," she informed him, wrapping the rest of the neckcloth around his arm and tying it as tightly as she could.

"There," she said, finally satisfied. "That should do until the doctor is fetched."

The sound of hooves galloping towards them caught their attention.

"Ah, Kenver," Harry smiled, as he pulled up beside them. "I thought you might arrive before too long."

"An' well you might, sir, what with that showy new stallion of yours arriving in a lather as if all the hounds of hell were after him!"

"We must not blame Hermes, Kenver, someone has been shooting in the woods and he has not been trained to ignore gunfire, after all. I hope he has taken no hurt?"

"No, sir, he's just spooked is all, but seeing as you're one of the best horsemen I've ever seen, I couldn't account for it unless something serious had happened."

"It is nothing," Harry assured him. "I was caught napping, Kenver, wool-gathering, so my reactions weren't quite up to the mark. I do hope you did not mention your concerns to my mother?"

"Didn't have to, sir. She saw the horse come flying back alone and came immediately to alert me."

Harry frowned. "I am afraid I am going to have to relieve you of your mount, Kenver, but Miss Lockhart has been most eager to help, so I am sure she will not mind if you ride with her coachman on the roof of her carriage."

Katherine followed this exchange with some interest; she always felt you could tell a lot about a person by how they dealt with their servants. It had been immediately apparent that Kenver had been concerned for his master; his deep-set dark eyes had held a world of worry as he had galloped up and his brow had been deeply furrowed. It was still furrowed, as if he were not quite happy about Lord Treleven's explanation although he said nothing more.

"You cannot be foolish enough to ride when you have lost so much blood!" she protested. "I am quite prepared to take you up in the carriage, Lord Treleven."

Harry mounted the horse with ease and grinned down at her. "I am not such a poor creature. I will go ahead and warn my mother of your arrival, Miss Lockhart. Thank you for your kind ministrations, but I will do now."

With that he took off down the avenue at quite a pace, his blond locks flying and his white shirt ruffling across his broad back in the breeze.

"Of all the stubborn, foolhardy—" Katherine broke off as she remembered Kenver.

"He may be both of those, ma'am, but he could ride a horse in his sleep," he said, picking up the ruined coat that still lay in the dust. He observed the torn, bloodied sleeve for a moment and shook his head. "Barring unusual circumstances," he added under his breath.

\* \* \*

What an extraordinary woman, Harry mused as he rode back to the house. There was nothing remarkable in her looks, apart from her hair, whose glossy brown sheen reminded him of a ripe conker, and perhaps her eyes. Yes, it was her eyes that gave her distinction, they were, he supposed, hazel but their predominant colour seemed to alter with her mood. At first they had reminded him of clear warm honey but when they had flashed at him, the bright emerald flecks that had darted across them had made them appear more green than gold.

He gave a dry laugh. Distinctive they might have been, but he was not at all sure he approved of the possessor of them. He liked his women feminine and skilled in the art of flirtation and Miss Lockhart was anything but; her pelisse had been of a dull grey that had leached all the colour from her complexion and her bonnet had been practical but unadorned with any frivolous ribbons or flowers. Managing and eccentric were far more appropriate epithets for her.

He unconsciously rubbed the back of his still warm neck. Most of the respectable females of his acquaintance would have blushed adorably and fluttered their eyelashes at him if they had had the audacity to remove his cravat in the first place, something he took leave to doubt, but not Miss Prim and Proper; instead her eyes had flashed disdain as she had torn it from him. Any delicate female could also have been expected to at least feel queasy at the sight of his wound, but Miss Lockhart's warm smile after she had been allowed to inspect it had been of the sort he usually received after delivering a well-chosen compliment. He wondered from where she had sprung.

More pressing however was the question of the poacher in his home wood. He had made light of it, but either things had become very lax in his absence or the locals were getting desperate for food. Either way, it was an unwelcome development he would have to deal with. He would go and see Mr Caldwell tomorrow. He could not imagine why he would bring in his own workforce when there were plenty of willing and able men and women in the vicinity.

He found his mother pacing up and down in the stable yard, wringing her hands. Almost as soon as he had dismounted she crossed quickly to him and clasped him to her as she choked back a sob.

"Come now, Mother," he soothed, returning her embrace and holding her to him for a moment. "There is no need for you to be so distressed, I met with a small accident but am not much hurt as you can see."

Putting her gently from him, he looked down into the blue eyes so like his own, which were at that moment brilliant with unshed tears.

"No need to feel distressed?" she gasped. "The last time a horse came home alone your father had been thrown and broken his neck!"

Taking her arm he led her back towards the house. "I am sorry to have caused you such worry and reminded you of so sad a time," he said softly. "But fortunately you will have no time to dwell on what might have happened for you have a visitor coming up the drive even as we speak."

"Oh no," Lady Treleven said reflexively. "I shall be away from home for I cannot face anyone just at the moment, you cannot expect it of me."

As they entered the house, they found Glasson, their butler, waiting for them.

"I am glad to see you safe, Lord Treleven," he said calmly, his impassive glance resting briefly upon Harry's arm. "I have already sent footman James to fetch Doctor Fisher in case he is required."

"It was quite unnecessary," Harry said, a trifle shortly.

"Thank you, Glasson." Lady Treleven managed a small smile. "Let me know as soon as he arrives. We are about to receive another visitor, you will tell them—"

"That Lady Treleven will receive them," interrupted her son, leading her firmly into the morning room.

"Really, Harry!" she protested. But once he had explained the circumstances of his accident and Miss Lockhart's unusual reaction to them, she changed her mind.

"What a remarkable young lady," she murmured. "I will of course receive her and thank her for her kind services to you, but I will have something to say to Mr Hewel presently, some measures will have to be put in place to keep future poachers out."

"You can safely leave all that to me, Mother," Harry said firmly. "Now, if I am not much mistaken your visitor has arrived and so I will leave you."

"No, Harry," Lady Treleven replied, just as firmly.

"You will remain with me for the duration of her visit or until the doctor arrives, at least."

As Miss Lockhart was just then announced, he was left with very little choice, but relief that his mother had regained her usual equanimity overrode any slight irritation he might feel.

He turned and made his bow as she entered the room. "Please let me introduce you to my mother. Lady Treleven, Miss Lockhart."

Lady Treleven's face was wreathed in smiles as she came forwards and took Katherine's hand. "I am very pleased to make your acquaintance, Miss Lockhart, and must thank you for coming to Lord Treleven's rescue."

"No thanks are necessary," she smiled. "He would, after all, have been rescued anyway, only moments later."

"Nevertheless, your prompt actions were admirable and so very resourceful. Please sit down and tell me what I can do for you, for I am fairly certain we have not met. You are not, I suppose, related to Amelia Lockhart who was Amelia Grantley before she wed?"

Katherine's brows rose in surprise. "Indeed, ma'am, she was my mother."

"Oh, she has passed then? I am sorry, child. I made my come out with your mother and we were friends for a few years, but we eventually lost touch when we married and moved to the country. My husband was not overly fond of town."

"Your brother wouldn't happen to be Richard Lockhart would he?" Harry asked.

"Why yes, are you a friend of his?" she asked, surprised.

"More acquaintances," acknowledged Harry. "I haven't seen him for many years but we were at school together." He looked a touch rueful. "If I remember correctly he was quiet and studious whereas I was always kicking up a lark so our paths did not cross very often."

"You surprise me, sir," Katherine said drily.

Lady Treleven hid a smile. "Your estate is near Bath is it not?"

"Yes, I have until recently been living with my brother at Felsham Court."

"You are a long way from home, Miss Lockhart."

They both listened with interest as she explained her present predicament. As she described the state of the house and gardens, Lady Treleven shuddered.

"It sounds quite uninhabitable, I am surprised you didn't turn around and head straight back home."

It was Katherine's turn to look a little rueful. "It was not an easy situation for either my new sister-in-law or myself," she admitted. "I have been used to managing everything, you see."

"You surprise, me," Harry murmured, throwing her own words back at her.

Ignoring him, Katherine addressed Lady Treleven.

"Apart from anything else, I think the property worth saving, only I need some advice on how to acquire so many persons almost immediately."

"Well, you could try Penzance, it is the largest town within easy reach," Lady Treleven suggested.

"No!" Harry interjected, rising to his feet. "Miss Lockhart, if you will be advised by me, I know where a number of local men and women who need work can be found instantly."

"Well, that's settled then," beamed Lady Treleven. "You may leave it all up to Harry, Miss Lockhart, one good turn deserves another, after all."

Harry noticed the slightly stubborn tilt to Katherine's chin and thought she would refuse his suggestion but after a moment's hesitation she nodded decisively.

"As long as they are hardworking and honest, I would be grateful for your assistance in this matter, Lord Treleven."

"And in the meantime, you and Mrs Abbott must come and stay with us. You cannot remain at Helagon until the work has been done, you will be most uncomfortable."

Katherine looked a little startled. "I would not impose on you so, Lady Treleven."

"Nonsense, child," her hostess said, getting to her feet. "It is the least I can do for the daughter of an old acquaintance and besides, you will be company for my daughter Henrietta, she is very shy and has few friends."

After a brief knock, Glasson entered the room. "Doctor Fisher has arrived, sir."

"I will take my leave," Katherine said rising to her feet.

"Not staying to observe the doctor's work, Miss Lockhart?" Harry quipped.

She smiled archly at him. "Not in this instance, Lord Treleven, your injury is not interesting enough to merit a second look."

Harry let out a bark of laughter and strode to the door. "On this point, at least, we are in agreement. I will come over in the morning with my steward, Mr

Hewel, to cast an eye over what needs to be done, Miss Lockhart."

Lady Treleven walked her to her carriage. "I will expect you by tomorrow afternoon at the latest," she smiled. "And I will not take no for answer; if you do not arrive by then, I will come and fetch you myself."

CHAPTER 4

Doctor Fisher appeared to be a serious young man, the impression reinforced by the small-rimmed glasses that he wore. He confirmed Miss Lockhart's diagnosis and praised her prompt action and the neat job she had made of binding his wound.

"For as you have been a soldier, sir, I am sure you are well aware that it is infection rather than the wound itself that often leads to the loss of a limb or a life."

"You really must meet Miss Lockhart," Harry murmured. "You both have so much in common."

The doctor's lips quirked in amusement. It had not taken him very long to get Lord Treleven's measure. Apart from the fact that he oozed restlessness and barely restrained impatience, he had heard a few stories about him from Doctor Peasbody on his retirement.

"It is a shame things turned out as they did," he had said. "He was a great gun as a lad, always up for some fun and gig and inevitably getting into some scrape or other, whether it was tumbling out of a tree or falling into the river!"

After cleaning the wound and dressing it in a lighter bandage, he gave him a shrewd look.

"I don't suppose there is any use in my suggesting you take things easy for a day or two, Lord Treleven?"

"None at all," Harry confirmed cheerfully. "I have sustained far worse injuries and not been unduly incapacitated."

Doctor Fisher merely nodded. "Then I won't waste my breath, but if you do feel at all feverish or any extraordinary discomfort, please send word sooner than later," he advised. "You will find me at the parsonage in Langarne."

"I know. It is a strange place for a young doctor to try and make his name," Harry commented.

"Ah, but I don't wish to make a name, but rather learn my trade and offer help to those that need it. I am fortunate that my uncle has offered to shelter me."

Harry's lips twitched. "Tell me, how do you find Mrs Creedely?"

The doctor chuckled. "Caustic!" He picked up his bag. "If I don't hear from you in the meantime, I will be back in a couple days to change the dressing."

He found Lady Treleven hovering on the landing as he gently closed the door to Harry's chamber.

"It is really not too serious," he assured her, noting her anxious look. She was a handsome woman, but he did not miss the fine lines that remained etched on her brow even as she smiled.

"No, of course not," she said calmly enough. "But he was extremely ill with malaria until very recently and I fear is not yet quite as robust as he was. I tried to delay his return as long as I was able, for I knew he would have much to do when he came home." She paused, looking slightly melancholy for a moment. "I have not kept as close an eye on things as I should have in recent years, you see."

"My uncle informed me of your circumstances," Doctor Fisher said solemnly. "You have had much to bear, ma'am. Your concern is understandable but if I may offer a little advice?"

"Please do," she invited.

"I speak now as a son as well as a doctor, you understand. It has been my experience that one cannot force someone to go against his or her nature and expect a happy result. Even if you could persuade Lord Treleven to take things easy, his spirits would be sadly affected and that in turn, would impede his recovery."

Lady Treleven sighed. "You are right, of course. Indeed, you are wise beyond your years, Doctor Fisher."

"I do not know about that, Lady Treleven, but I have always enjoyed studying the human mind as well as the body. I truly believe the health of both is intrinsically linked."

They had been slowly making their way along the landing and had come to the top of the stairs. Lady Treleven impulsively laid her hand on his arm.

"I think you are a young man of sound sense, sir. If you wouldn't object to me trespassing on your time a little further, would you very much mind taking a quick look at my daughter, Henrietta?"

"Not at all, ma'am," he said promptly. "What is it that ails her?"

A small frown deepened the lines on her forehead. "It is hard to say," she admitted. "You will probably think me a complete worrywart but she did not come down today pleading a headache. It is probably nothing, she is very shy you understand and found her season very trying, although she perked up considerably after her brother returned. But since we have come home, she seems very lethargic again."

They found her sitting in the window seat, her long blonde hair unbound and falling in soft undulations to her waist. Her legs were drawn up and encircled by her arms and she was staring blindly out at the rolling landscape before her. She did not even seem aware that she had company until her mother spoke a little sharply.

"Henrietta, you have a visitor."

Her head snapped round, her eyes huge in her pale face.

"It is only Doctor Fisher come to see you," Lady Treleven soothed. "Harry met with a slight accident today—"

"Oh no!" she cried.

"There is no need to be alarmed, my dear, it is nothing too serious, but as the doctor is here, I thought we might just check that you are not sickening for something,"

"Oh, Mama, it is not necessary I assure you. It was just a headache and it has gone now," she said in a rush, colouring slightly.

"Well, nevertheless, you will let him examine you."

"Examine me?" she said alarmed, swinging her slippered feet to the floor.

Doctor Fisher had stood immobile in the doorway, but at her evident distress he moved a few steps into the room and bowed. "Miss Treleven, please do not worry. I will not do anything intrusive, I assure you." His cool, impersonal tone seemed to reassure her.

Henrietta gulped and turned back to Lady Treleven. "Mama, you will stay won't you?"

"Of course," she replied.

Smiling gently, Doctor Fisher approached her slowly as he might a frightened animal. "Now, Miss Treleven, I am simply going to take your wrist in my hand so I can take your pulse, it will not hurt I assure you."

Henrietta obediently held out her arm and watched in wide-eyed fascination as the doctor gently gripped her wrist and closed his eyes as if to concentrate.

"Well, all seems well there," he murmured after a moment.

He then seated himself on the window seat beside her and took her head between his hands. He immediately felt her stiffen and released her.

"Do not be alarmed, Miss Treleven, I just wish to observe your eyes a little more closely and it helps if your head remains still. May I?"

Henrietta nodded and he repeated the gesture. "I am pleased to report, ma'am," he said gravely after a moment, "that they are not crossed at all."

Henrietta's face was transformed as she giggled.

Rising to his feet he smiled. "There, that was not so

bad was it? I hope next time I see you, you will not look at me as if I am an ogre."

Henrietta blushed slightly but shook her head.

"I will just see the doctor out, my dear," Lady Treleven smiled. "Then perhaps you will take a turn about the gardens with me. Some fresh air will do us both good, I am sure."

"Of course, Mama."

"That was well done of you," Lady Treleven said as they descended the stairs. "It is not easy to draw Henrietta out."

Doctor Fisher looked thoughtful. "Physically there is very little wrong with your daughter, ma'am. But I think you are right, her spirits are low. It would have been useless to enquire into the cause of her melancholy on such slight acquaintance, but perhaps if she sees me when I come to call on Lord Treleven, she may eventually be persuaded to confide in me."

"Yes, you may be right. When next you come to call on my son, come in the afternoon and stay for dinner."

\* \* \*

Harry was true to his word and called at Helagon the following morning. Miss Lockhart was busy writing a letter when he was shown into the library and looked up with a frown when he was announced. Clothed in a modest high-necked morning dress of jaconet muslin, her hair confined in a very severe style, she reminded him of a school ma'am who was planning her lessons and was not best pleased at being disturbed.

"Miss Lockhart," he said bowing. "I apologise if I

have interrupted you but you were, I hope, expecting me?"

She stood immediately and smiled distractedly. "Of course, forgive me, it is not your arrival that has caused my consternation, Lord Treleven. I am writing, or rather, attempting to write to my brother about the sorry state of this property. He wishes me to put it in order but neither of us expected it to be quite such an undertaking."

Harry glanced at the abandoned letter on the desk. As he had expected, she formed her letters in a neat, legible style, but many of the uniform lines had been crossed and re-crossed, suggesting an indecision he did not immediately associate with her on his admittedly short acquaintance.

"It must indeed be a difficult task," he acknowledged, suddenly recalling that the nickname, Lockpurse, had been attributed to her brother for his penny-pinching ways. "If you paint things in too good a light he will not understand why you need to draw on his funds quite so frequently, but if you state the case too baldly, he may baulk at the expense and order you home immediately."

Katherine looked surprised at his astuteness. "You have it in a nutshell, sir," she sighed. "You make me sound like such a scheming creature, and perhaps you are right, but I had hoped to make my home here and the idea that I might be forced to leave so soon, is a lowering one."

"Come now, Miss Lockhart, all is not yet lost. Mr Hewel is already casting his eyes over the house and it may be that we discover the case is not so desperate as you suppose – and even if it is – console yourself with the thought that once it is brought up to scratch, your brother can make back his money any time he wishes to sell it. A mouldering ruin is certainly of no use to him."

Katherine's expression lightened. "How very right you are, Lord Treleven, in fact he would be making a good investment. That is exactly how I shall put it to him." She smiled gratefully. "Thank you, sir."

"Rescuing damsels in distress is my speciality," he grinned, offering her his arm. "Come, show me around this palace."

"I knew it wouldn't last," she murmured, sweeping past him, leaving him to follow in her wake.

"What wouldn't last?" he asked.

"You being serious for more than a moment. I suppose it was too much to ask for."

"Far too much," he acknowledged as he caught up with her in the hall. The stairs groaned their protest as he mounted them. "Well, you are at least in no danger from burglars, ma'am, they would not be able to come up these stairs without being heard for certain."

"Even if they did manage such a difficult feat, they would be poorly rewarded for their ingenuity," Katherine said drily, "for I cannot imagine what they would find that was worth stealing."

Harry could only agree as more of the house was revealed to him. But he suspected he had been in the right of it, it certainly looked bad on the surface, but he thought that once the roof had been fixed the rest wouldn't be too difficult to rectify.

They found Mr Hewel in the gardens with Mrs Abbott, deep in conversation. Once the introductions had been made, Katherine braced herself for bad news.

"It was very kind of you to come, Mr Hewel, but please put me out of my misery. How bad is it?"

"Oh, it is not as dire as you think, ma'am. You've caught it just in time. If it had been left for another year now, it would be a different matter. Once the slates have been replaced on the roof and the ceilings in the attic sorted, you'll be watertight. A few of the window frames and floorboards are rotten and will need replacing, but we have plenty of skilled men hereabouts – more than one of them has built his own house."

"Mr Hewel is also very knowledgeable about gardens, my dear," Mrs Abbott said. "He could see the potential of this one immediately."

Katherine smiled at her companion. "I am sure he could not fail to be infected with your enthusiasm."

"Indeed, ma'am," Mr Hewel agreed. "Mrs Abbott knows a thing or two about horticulture and has an eye for design."

"How long will it take to have the house habitable, do you think?" Katherine asked him.

"Well, barring complications, a few weeks should do the trick. I can have some men down here this afternoon if that suits, ma'am."

"Excellent. Perhaps I should delay my visit to Lady Treleven until I have given them their orders."

"That will be quite unnecessary, Miss Lockhart," Harry assured her. "Unless you also have an unusual interest in repairing old buildings, I would leave Mr Hewel to oversee everything. He will appoint a trustworthy person to be in charge who will report to him."

For the second time Harry noticed the mulish set of her chin but her reason again overcame her desire to disagree with him.

"Of course. I freely admit that I would not know where to start, so I must thank you again, Mr Hewel, and can only hope the task will not be too burdensome for you."

The steward smiled. "I overlook repairs and maintenance to our properties all the time, ma'am, it will be nothing out of the way, I assure you."

"Then I can only thank you. You will, I hope, keep me informed of all progress and costs involved?"

"As you wish, ma'am."

"Oh, and Mrs Nance will need a hand in the house, do you know of some girls who live locally who could help her out in the short term?"

"Leave it to me, ma'am."

"I will no doubt see you at dinner, Miss Lockhart, Mrs Abbott," Harry said, bowing and turning to leave with his steward.

"You may leave some of your usual duties to me whilst you oversee the repairs at Helagon, Mr Hewel," he said as they rode up the hill.

"That won't be necessary, sir," his steward assured him earnestly.

"I will enjoy it," Harry assured him. "You have so much to do already, it has occurred to me that as the estate is so large it might be a thought for you to engage an assistant to help you."

"You are not happy with my work, sir?" his steward replied a little stiffly.

Harry discerned the anxiety that lurked beneath his gruff words.

"You have held the estate together in my absence, Mr Hewel, and I am very grateful to you. You have not had an easy time of it either, what with the fluctuating price of crops and some hard winters and wet springs and I do not see things becoming any easier in the near future. We must also lessen the rents to make life easier for our tenants for they face the same problems, but we will need to think of ways to make up the shortfall."

He saw the older man's shoulders droop slightly. "Come, man, I do not wish to replace you and neither do I blame you for things you can have no control over. However, I am beginning to realise just how much you have to do on a daily basis. You can hardly have had time to look into things like better drainage and so on, but if you employed an assistant you would have time to investigate the latest developments."

They had reached the brow of the hill and came to a crossroads.

"You go on to Langarne, Mr Hewel, I am going to see our new neighbour. What can you tell me about him?"

"I have only ever seen him from afar, sir, but he is not liked hereabouts. He's thrown up some houses near his mine for those he has brought in and they keep to themselves mostly. You can imagine the bad feeling that exists amongst those who have lost their jobs. But it is more than that."

"Go on."

"There was a wreck about a month back, sir, and there were rumours, only rumours mind, that things were not as they should have been."

"How so?" Harry asked.

"Well, you know how it has always been hereabouts, if a ship flounders, those as makes it ashore are given shelter and food, but the local people harvest any goods washed up along the beach. They have always seen it as a gift from the heavens to help them through the hard times. They only heard of the wreck the next morning but when they went down to the beach, there was nothing to harvest apart from a few wooden spars and not a soul to rescue. They reckon Caldwell's miners had taken it all and some say that they may have caused it in the first place."

Harry looked startled. "That is a serious accusation. Is there any proof to back it up?"

Mr Hewel shook his head. "Not that I know of."

"Then I would ask you not to repeat those rumours to anyone else, Mr Hewel, it could lead to someone hanging by the neck."

"You're right, sir, and I haven't done so. It is probably just the rivalry between the newcomers and the locals that caused the talk."

Harry thought that Mr Hewel was probably right. The tales of wrecking were greatly exaggerated and he had certainly not heard of such a nefarious act on this coast in his lifetime. There were many fishermen in these parts and they would try and aid a boat in distress if at all possible, believing that to do otherwise would draw bad luck down upon them. But the country people would greatly resent anyone other than themselves harvesting the goods of a wreck; a right they had always seen as their own. They normally shared the goods between them, and his own father had usually found some offering left for him.

Harry was aware of a feeling of unease. For all the

goods to have disappeared by morning, if indeed there had been anything washed ashore, there would have to have been an organised, coordinated effort to remove them. If there was another wreck any time soon, it could lead to a nasty confrontation between the country people and the interlopers. And whether it was intentional or not, Mr Caldwell was at the root of much of this discord.

As he turned into the gates of Thornbury House, the words of the old man in Langarne came back to him, *'Things go to ruin when those as knows the land and its people leave it be.'*

He was only just beginning to comprehend the murky depths beneath those words. It seemed he had come home not a moment too soon. One thing was becoming clearer to him, however, he could not burst upon his neighbour and start demanding explanations for his actions, not until he was sure of the lie of the land, at least. If he put his back up at their first meeting, he was unlikely to find out anything of use or be able to persuade him that it would be better to employ the native inhabitants hereabouts rather than bring in foreigners.

Thornbury House had not been the principal seat of Lord Trewith and the estate was much smaller than his own. It was a fine house however, built in the Palladian style, boasting an impressive portico and possessing a pleasing symmetry. It was some years since he had been within its portals and Mr Caldwell had certainly put his mark upon it. He seemed to remember that it had felt like a country home should, with comfortable furnishings and old portraits lining the walls. Now it was decorated in a lavish, opulent style, and anything that could be gilded, was, particularly the elaborate frames of the many pictures depicting images of ships and landscapes from the grand tour. Modern marble statues and busts based on ancient Greek design lined the hallway and the ceilings had been decorated with spectacular plasterwork surrounding mythological scenes, some of which bordered on the indecent.

It seemed that Mr Caldwell was a very wealthy man and was not at all shy of displaying it. But the most exotic and startling item of all was his butler, if he could be called that. The man who relieved Harry of his hat and coat was of Indian descent. He wore a rich red satin turban and a matching garment that fell to below his knees, tied at the hips with a white sash. Trousers that clung very cosily to the leg, peeped beneath the hem.

He was shown into the library, a huge room that was filled floor to ceiling with gleaming leather-tooled books, their sheen undisturbed by so much as a speck of dust. He wondered idly if Caldwell had read any of them. Chairs and sofas were scattered about the room, all of them elegant with delicately carved legs, but not a one of them promising any degree of comfort.

The only slightly ungainly item was a large desk set in front of doors that led onto the garden. The long ruby curtains were half drawn to block out the sunshine whilst Mr Caldwell pored over a huge ledger. He unhurriedly marked his place, closed the heavy tome and rose to his feet as Harry approached.

"Lord Treleven, welcome, welcome."

The two men exchanged bows.

"Please be seated," he invited, nodding to the

upright chair that faced the desk. "I must apologise for not having called upon you since your return, but I thought you would be inundated with old friends, at first."

"I appreciate your consideration, Mr Caldwell," Harry replied, noting that despite his jovial tone, his host's eyes were regarding him closely. He was, he judged in his late forties, his red face and rounded stomach suggesting he enjoyed an ample diet and a fine wine. Even as the thought flicked across his mind, Mr Caldwell reached for a fine cut glass decanter half filled with a rich red liquid.

"Claret?" he asked.

"I thank you, no," Harry smiled. "It is a little early for me and I have much to do today."

"I imagine you must," his host said, pouring out a generous glass. "It is never a good idea to take your hand off the tiller for too long."

"So I am discovering," Harry replied ruefully. "I have a lot to learn."

"Well, that is refreshing. I am afraid I have often witnessed young men who come into their inheritance arrogant and ignorant. Too determined to cling to the family traditions rather than branch out and ensure the continued fortunes of their families. But the world is always changing, young man, always changing, and if you don't move with it, I am afraid you will be left behind."

"I notice you used a nautical term, are you interested in ships?" Harry enquired politely.

Mr Caldwell chuckled. "I ought to be, I made my fortune through them, bringing goods back from India mostly, but it's a risky business and not as profitable as it once was. Besides, I'm not getting any younger and I've a fancy to settle down. When this place became available so close to the sea and with a mine attached, I snapped it up. I've never been one to let a profitable opportunity slip past me, you've got to keep your eye on the main chance, my boy."

Harry tactfully ignored such a term of address from one who was his social inferior. "I am beginning to think you are right, sir," he replied respectfully, "farming does not turn a profit as it once did. You must be doing something right for this house is quite splendid."

He had achieved his aim; the rather sharp narrow-set eyes of his host seemed to relax, as did the man himself. He leant back in his chair and steepled his chubby fingers, looking thoughtful.

"I do not think your reputation does you justice, sir," he finally said.

Harry was all wide-eyed innocence. "My reputation, sir?"

Mr Caldwell chuckled. "Well, you were very young when you fell into folly and I am sure it was the lady's fault, but I had not expected you to be such a serious, respectful young man."

Harry dropped his eyes as if in embarrassment. "A few hard years having to earn my own crust has changed me, I think."

Mr Caldwell poured him a glass of wine, despite his protests.

"Nonsense, my boy, nonsense. We have a lot to discuss."

CHAPTER 5

By the time Katherine had conferred closely with Mrs Nance about her most pressing needs and all of her and Mrs Abbott's things were packed again, it was late afternoon and Helagon was a noisy hive of activity. Mrs Nance was in her element, issuing orders to the girls Mr Hewel had duly procured and shouting at the men who traipsed into the house to inspect the most damaged rooms, to take off their boots before they stepped foot on the newly scrubbed floors.

They arrived at Elmdon Hall to find Lady Treleven on the point of changing for dinner and were bustled upstairs almost immediately. She was shown to a lovely bright room with views over the rolling parkland in front of the house.

As Ayles unpacked her trunk, Katherine sat in front of her mirror brushing out her long silken tresses, a soothing pleasure she always reserved for herself. She was aware of feeling both pleasure and relief to be in such welcoming surroundings. Although an old house,

Elmdon had been properly maintained and the furnishings were tasteful and comfortable without being at all ostentatious. She was, she acknowledged wryly, used to a certain level of comfort, and although she had been quite prepared to remain at Helagon during the renovations, she was glad for all concerned that this had not proved necessary.

Her family had never been fabulously wealthy but had always been able to command some of the elegancies of life. Their lands, whilst not overly extensive, were rich and fertile, bringing in healthy rents both from tenant farmers and a few modest properties they owned in Bath itself. Never having any inclination towards extravagance, they had always managed to live within their means and Katherine had learned well the arts of household economy from her mother.

She had always imagined that in the course of time she would meet some suitable gentleman whom she would wish to marry and impress with these much to be desired skills. She had had no firm picture in mind of what he would be like, only that he must be sensible and of a steady character. She had no illusions of attracting anyone of great wealth or good looks as she knew she was nothing out of the ordinary herself and had only a respectable dowry.

She had hoped that she would meet this rather nebulous ideal during her season in London, something she knew her mother had been setting aside money for every year since she had been born. But this much anticipated event had never materialised as both her parents had met with an unfortunate accident when she had barely attained her seventeenth birthday. None of their careful planning and sensible ways had been a match for cruel fate. On returning in her father's curricle from a dinner with friends to celebrate the victory at Waterloo, they had turned a bend in the road and crashed straight into a carriage that had lost its wheel only moments before.

Katherine had been fond of her parents and had felt their loss keenly. Her studious brother had retreated to his study and she had taken up the reins of the household. Her season had not been thought of again and they had gradually settled into a comfortable routine.

Bath had no longer been a resort of great fashion, but when Queen Charlotte graced the town with her presence in 1817 on the advice of her physicians, there had been much excitement. She had shown her approval of Lady Isabella King's latest scheme – The Ladies' Association – a charitable organisation whose aim was to offer a home at Bailbrook Lodge to single ladies of gentle birth but little fortune. Katherine, approving of an institution that might relieve the uncertainty and situation of members of her own sex, had subscribed in a small way herself to the cause, and she had been persuaded to attend some of the celebrations held in honour of Her Majesty.

She had met the Honourable Mr Sharpe at one of these gatherings. He served with the 15$^{th}$ Light Dragoons who had come to the town as part of Queen Charlotte's escort. He had been very dashing in his uniform and had always had a smile on his lips. He had shown great interest in the scheme for the relief of impoverished ladies and had singled her out at every gathering she had attended, to such an extent that her friends had begun to tease her about when he would formally declare his interest.

When Princess Charlotte had sadly died in childbirth, the queen had rushed back to London taking her dragoons with her. Soon afterwards, Katherine had received a letter from Mr Sharpe. She had held it for a few moments before opening it, savouring the anticipation, her hand a little unsteady and a tremulous smile on her lips. At first, she could not quite comprehend the words that danced before her eyes, and had had to start again from the beginning, her hand trembling more violently as comprehension slowly dawned. Each and every word was burned into her memory, as was the humiliation she had felt.

*Dear Miss Lockhart,*

*I am finding this letter a little harder to write than I had anticipated. I had not expected to genuinely enjoy your company, it almost made me wish to call a halt to the charade I was enacting. On reflection however, the discovery that you were a kind-hearted girl with an intelligent mind only further strengthened my resolve to bring you to a sense of your own folly.*

*You have fallen under the spell of the charismatic and influential Lady Isabella King and I am afraid are being led down a path that will not result in happiness for you or the females The Ladies' Association wishes to provide for.*

*Bailbrook Lodge will be a community of women – no more than a nunnery – but without the solemn vows that would bring the peace of an acknowledged vocation to God, or the security that such a calling might be expected to provide. Instead you will have an odd assortment of single ladies with no common cause to bind them apart from their indigence and desire to avoid the natural order that our society provides.*

*Some of these ladies, in their misguided quest for independence, will forgo and indeed reject the mantle of protection that their families can and should provide, thereby acting in a selfish and wilful manner. Others who are not so fortunate as to possess such a family, but having all the qualifications of a gentlewoman, and thus the means to provide for themselves through imparting their skills and knowledge to others – thereby becoming useful members of society – will instead band together like a disgruntled flock of crows. They will console each other over their perceived misfortunes until they can only be made happy by the misfortune of someone even more unfortunate or despondent than themselves.*

*The ideal of some sort of female utopia, in which females can live in harmony and somehow provide for themselves by pooling their limited resources is ridiculous in the extreme and can only end in failure.*

*My friends and I firmly believe this. We faced many dangers and hardships when we fought, and eventually conquered, Napoleon. Many of our friends lost their lives in the endeavour, but we willingly sacrificed much in the name of King and country. We wished to ensure and uphold the values of our own nation, a nation led by men for the benefit of all.*

*Do not waste your time on such a cause as this, Miss Lockhart, for you do no good for society by doing so and although I admire your desire to help those you perceive as less fortunate than yourself, I would suggest you turn your eyes in the direction of those that truly need your philanthropy; the poor, the hungry, the sick – in other words – those who cannot help themselves. The poor woman starving in the gutter would happily give up her 'freedom' to be able to look after another if it provided a roof over her head and put food in her stomach.*

*I am fully aware that you are not indifferent to me, Miss Lockhart, and I sincerely hope that I have not touched your heart too deeply. It was not my intention to cause you lasting unhappiness, but merely to show you that it can be engaged, and will be again if you but let it.*

*There, my lecture is over. I hope you will not dismiss my words out of hand because I have hurt you or let this lesson turn you into the very thing I wish you to avoid becoming, but fear you may if you continue to keep company with such ladies; a bitter spinster. Do not worry that your name will be bandied about in relation to this matter, it was not done to cause you harm.*

*Although I doubt you will believe it, I wish you well.*

*Your friend,*

*Mr Sharpe*

Hot tears had poured down her face on reading this missive, followed by a furious anger that she had been duped so. She had torn it into shreds and thrown it into the fire. She had never mentioned the letter to anyone and had laughed off any suggestions that she must be disappointed at losing her friend so soon, merely commenting that the light flirtation had been a pleasant distraction.

"Are you feeling quite the thing, ma'am?"

Ayles bustled into the room, her attitude as improved as her surroundings.

"Why, yes, of course," Katherine murmured.

"Only you looked as though you was carved from stone, ma'am, so still and bleak looking as you were."

"I was just daydreaming, Ayles. You may put up my hair now."

"How would you like it tonight, miss?"

"I really do not mind, do as you please," she said quietly.

A sudden gleam brightened her maid's eyes, although Katherine was too distracted to see it.

"That I will, ma'am, that I will."

All that abominable man had shown her was how easy it was to be misled by the tenderer emotions of the feminine heart, how vulnerable they made one to manipulation, and how infatuation or love clouded sound judgement. She had certainly not made hers available for such abuse again.

With hindsight, she could not deny that he had been correct on some points. The charity had indeed faced some financial hardships and their continued security was uncertain; the ladies had been forced to move to a house in Bristol when the owner of Bailbrook Lodge had decided to sell the property. Katherine had turned her attentions to the infirmary in Bath and so had ended up following some of Mr Sharpe's advice after all.

How he would laugh now when her own circumstances were as he described, she must live on her brother's charity, become her sister-in-law's slave, or turn her hand to some gainful employment.

She unconsciously let out a dry laugh causing Ayles to look at her in some concern. It had just occurred to her that the doubt Mr Sharpe had cast upon a group of women being able to live together in any degree of harmony now seemed quite prophetic when she had not even managed to rub along with Caroline. She was not, she accepted, of a meek disposition. It could hardly have been otherwise when she had taken on the running of a quite large household at such a tender age, and she would indeed find it difficult to bow to rules voted on by committee, whether it be made up of men or women.

That did not mean, of course, that she agreed with his wide sweeping generalisations on the selfishness of women living according to their own desires rather than within a patriarchal hierarchy that was hostile of any challenge to its authority, or that her admiration for Lady Isabella King had in any way diminished; the Ladies' Association had only been one of many charities she had supported.

She certainly did not think it inherently selfish for an impoverished but educated gentlewoman to wish to live outside of servitude, whether it was paid or not, and could only admire that a lady who was independently wealthy had spared the time to think of others less fortunate than herself. But she could now see that the world was not yet ready to accept the principle of a group of ladies living in a mutually exclusive beneficial environment as a general rule, and that it would not suit everyone, certainly not herself.

In setting Helagon in order, she was at least being useful to her brother in some small way. But the sad truth remained, once the work was finished, she must either agree to be dependent on his support or insult and upset him by applying for a genteel position that she had no wish to fill.

"There, Miss Lockhart," Ayles said, in an unusually softened tone.

Katherine raised her eyes to the mirror in front of her and blinked. Usually in a hurry and completely disinterested in impressing any of the males of her acquaintance, she generally asked for a simple, almost severe style that suited her no-nonsense personality.

But given the rare opportunity to display her own creativity, Ayles had created a gentler look.

Although her gleaming locks were pinned neatly, she had surrounded them with delicately woven plaits, and soft waving tendrils had been allowed to frame her face. The result was very feminine.

Katherine's eyes slowly rose to meet her maid's and a small smile curved her lips.

"It is very pleasing, Ayles. Thank you."

Her smile was tentatively returned. "You have such beautiful hair, ma'am, it is a shame not to show it to its best advantage."

She disappeared into the adjoining dressing room, in a moment returning with a simple dress of gold silk, rather short in the waist and sleeves. Katherine eyed it warily. It had been an impulse purchase that she had made when besotted with Mr Sharpe and she was yet to wear it. It hung a little off the shoulder and was cut lower around the bosom than she was used to.

"Come now, miss, it is really very elegant. Try it. It won't take a minute to change if you don't like it, after all."

Not having the heart to snuff out Ayles' rare good humour, she allowed her to have her way.

"There," she said satisfied, a few moments later. "You do me proud, ma'am."

Katherine looked uncertainly into the mirror. "You do not think it a little immodest?"

Ayles sighed. "No, miss, it suits your slender figure to perfection and adds length to your neck."

Katherine suddenly smiled, for the first time beginning to fathom the real source of her maid's dissatisfaction. "Poor, Ayles, I must have been a sad trial to you with my sober tastes and lack of flair."

"I have flair enough for us both, miss, if you would but let me show it."

Katherine laughed. "Be happy that I have let you show it tonight, Ayles. My wardrobe is not filled with dresses such as these."

The maid looked at her with an eager look in her eyes. "There's nothing wrong with your dresses, ma'am, that a needle and thread can't fix."

"Perhaps," acknowledged her mistress.

Katherine took another long look at herself in the glass as Ayles made to leave the room.

"Wait a moment," she said impulsively.

Ayles looked over her shoulder, her hand still on the door handle. When Katherine hesitated, she turned and waited patiently.

It had occurred to Katherine that only yesterday she had watched Kenver closely to see how loyal he was to his master, taking it as a measure of Lord Treleven himself if his servant showed concern. Yet she had not given her own maid much consideration at all. It was true that she had not been in her employ long, and that she had not seen much to impress her, but it now occurred to her that neither had she treated her with the kindness or the patience that perhaps she deserved.

"I think we may have got off on the wrong foot, Ayles. Not only have I not given you the scope to do the job you have trained for as you would wish, I may also have been a little prickly lately. I have had a lot on my mind."

Ayles nodded cautiously. "And so you have, ma'am.

I was not best pleased to be leaving Bath I must admit, but things are not as bleak as they first appeared." She suddenly grinned. "And it might have been for the best after all, for if I had had to put up with that trumped-up maid of Lady Lockhart's looking down her long nose at me much longer, I might have been tempted to tweak it!"

"She was not welcoming?" Katherine asked, surprised.

Ayles gave a harsh laugh. "About as welcoming as an upset stomach! She loved to brag about how fine her mistress looked and she had the effrontery to call you dowdy, ma'am. Not in front of the other servants mind, steadfastly loyal to you they were, wouldn't have stood for a word being said against you."

Katherine looked thoughtful. "Well, Ayles, you may take your needle and thread and do as you please with it. I will not have you suffer such an insult again."

Ayles curtsied briefly. "Indeed I will, ma'am, and there's no time like the present."

"Don't get too carried aw—" she began, but the reformed maid had already bustled out of the room with an air of purpose and a spring in her step that her mistress had never before witnessed.

When she entered the drawing room she found a young lady idly tinkling the keys of a pianoforte that stood in one corner. Any fear that she may have been overdressed for a dinner in the country was instantly dispelled for the young lady was very smart. Her attire was of the latest fashion – a round dress of delicately striped net over a white satin slip with pretty puffed sleeves decorated with small pink bows – the motif repeated above the trim of four rouleaux of pink ducape. It was charming and suited her fair colouring admirably.

"Hello, you must be Miss Treleven for you bear a striking resemblance to your brother," Katherine said conversationally.

The young woman stood and smiled shyly. "Yes, everybody says so, but I am not very much like him in character, I am afraid."

Katherine quirked an enquiring brow. "Why be afraid? I am nothing like my brother either, nor should I wish to be. I am sure you have a perfectly fine character of your own, Miss Treleven!"

"It is kind of you to say so, Miss Lockhart, but I am afraid I am a mouse and my brother a lion."

Katherine seemed to consider this seriously for a moment. "How splendid," she finally said. "I think lions are vastly overrated, don't you? It is easy to be brave when you are bigger and stronger than most of your prey but just consider for a moment, all the advantages of being a mouse."

Holding her hand up in front of her, she began to count them off on her long tapering fingers.

"One, they are curious quiet creatures and so may observe much to their advantage. Two, they are modest by nature and so must always please. And last but not least, they have very good hearing and so can easily avoid unwanted guests."

Henrietta's smile added a sparkle to her lacklustre eyes, transforming her appearance from insipid to quite beautiful.

"What is this about unwanted guests?" Harry strolled into the room with Mrs Abbott on his arm.

"You cannot mean this lady," he said, bowing over her hand, "for she is quite charming."

Mrs Abbott's face creased into a smile. "I think there are other ladies present who deserve your compliments more than I, Lord Treleven."

She looked at Katherine and Henrietta and sighed approvingly. "You both look beautiful, my dears."

"Please, come and sit down," Henrietta invited, taking her arm and leading her to a comfortable looking sofa by the fireplace.

Harry turned to Katherine, his eyes slowly drinking in her appearance. Katherine might have bristled at his leisurely appraisal if she had not been similarly occupied herself. He was dressed as exquisitely as his sister; his coat of dark blue superfine clung to his athletic figure and his neckcloth boasted a sapphire tiepin and an impossibly complicated knot.

"I am glad it was not tied so when we first met," Katherine said softly, almost to herself. "For I would never have undone it."

The blue eyes before her held a twinkle as their owner took her hand and murmured, "You are indeed…the prettiest Kate in Christendom."

It appeared for a moment that he might drop a kiss upon the hand he still held. Katherine withdrew it hastily for his words stung even as her fingers tingled. She recognised the play from which he had stolen the words – Shakespeare's *Taming of the Shrew*. Tilting her chin, she replied in kind.

"I see a woman may be made a fool, if she had not a spirit to resist."

Harry threw back his head and laughed. "I see I

must pick my words and plays more carefully, Miss Lockhart. Forgive me, I meant no offense."

"Of course, Lord Treleven," she replied stiffly, inclining her head graciously. "How is your arm?"

"There is no use expecting an honest answer, my dear," Lady Treleven said, coming just then into the room. "I do not pretend to understand why men must think it a show of weakness to admit to pain, but so it is. Doctor Fisher will be here tomorrow to ensure all is well, however. He is a very sensible young man, I warmed to him immediately and have invited him to stay to dine."

"Then we will be a small party, Mother, for I have also invited Mr Caldwell."

Lady Treleven looked surprised. "Oh, I see. Well, I suppose one must get to know ones neighbours, after all."

"Is there any reason you would not wish to receive him, ma'am?" Harry asked, picking up her doubtful tone.

"No, dear, we have never had much to do with him. He did not take up residence until just before we left for town, for he set an army of men from London to alter the house to his own personal taste before taking possession of it, although it was a perfectly presentable house when he purchased it."

"You would not recognise it, Mother. Mr Caldwell has everything of the finest."

"Indeed?" his mother said coolly. "Well, it does not surprise me. He did call on us once or twice before we left and was very affable, if a little overwhelming and a trifle vulgar." She turned to Katherine and smiled. "Perhaps it is for the best, my dear, for he is your neighbour too and you will be more comfortable meeting him in company. In fact it could not be better, for we will be a larger party than you suppose, Harry."

Katherine noted that Henrietta had begun to look a little anxious.

"I think you will be pleased, Henrietta, when you discover who it is," her mother reassured her. "I thought you and Lady Hayward had become firm friends whilst we were at Eastleigh?"

"Oh, yes, Mama," she smiled. "But I am surprised we are to see her so soon or that Lord Hayward will let her travel so far in her condition."

Lady Treleven laughed. "Oh, she is hardly showing yet and anyway, what Belle wants, Belle gets. But in this case he is the reason for the visit, my dear. It was unfortunate that some business or other prevented him joining us during our stay with Sir Philip, but it appears that he spent some happy times in this part of the country when he was a child and now that he has an expanding family of his own, is thinking of acquiring a property in Cornwall. In fact, they are bringing little Edmund with them, for Belle says that he has completely recovered from the measles and she cannot bear to be parted from him a moment longer."

"It seems you are to be inundated with guests, ma'am," Katherine smiled. "If the burden is too great we can easily remove either to Helagon or perhaps a hotel?"

"Nonsense, Miss Lockhart, it is far too long since this house was full of company. Oh, that puts me in mind of something, we will be an odd number for dinner. I shall also invite Mr Gulworthy. Doctor Fisher is his nephew, you know."

CHAPTER 6

After the ladies withdrew from the dining room, Harry retreated to his study to take his glass of port. Leaning back in his comfortable, leather, wingback chair, he stretched out his long limbs, crossed his ankles and sipped at the deep red liquid appreciatively. His father had always kept a fine cellar. He wondered how he would have dealt with Mr Caldwell. A sudden laugh shook him. He would have dampened his pretensions with a look. The old gentleman had been a high stickler. For a moment, Harry could almost feel his presence in the room and his voice sounded in his mind.

*"Don't have anything to do with him, my boy, he's a vulgar, encroaching mushroom. Worships at the alter of Mammon, doesn't care for anybody but himself."*

Harry sighed. He did not have the luxury of ignoring Mr Caldwell. He was fairly good at assessing his fellow man and had known he was not to be trusted the moment he had set eyes on him. Some instinct had warned him that he must play a deep game if he was to discover why he had really brought in his own men to the detriment of the country people. It had occurred to him that the cost of bringing them over and housing them must far outweigh any advantage that he might gain from them offering lower bids on their contracts. It also suggested he intended to keep them there for the foreseeable future.

He had not been best pleased to discover he was expecting houseguests and really did not have the time to entertain Hayward, someone he hardly knew. He could only hope that his hunt for a suitable property would keep him out from under his feet.

He was happy Henrietta would have the benefit of a friend, however, for he had been quite shocked at how timid she had become. She had only been a child when he had fled, and although quiet and sensitive, he could not recall her being as withdrawn as she was now.

He frowned and took another sip of his drink. He had a lot to answer for. His reckless behaviour had caused his family much anguish. It pained him that the last memories his father had of him were less than satisfactory. He had been so proud of him, at first, when he had returned from Waterloo and had not understood the gradual change in his son. Harry had hardly understood it himself. He had suffered a head injury and lost his memory of a significant part of the final day of the battle, but he had remembered feeling terrified and known that he had been found with one of his closest friends, Lieutenant William Hunt, dead atop of him. The nagging thought that he had done something cowardly had haunted him until he had all but convinced himself he had been trying to desert and William had died trying to stop him. Although he had told himself time and again that for him to act in such a way would be thoroughly out of character, he could neither bring himself to completely discount the theory or to share his fears with anyone. In the end he had attempted to drown them out with drink and wild living.

His mother's suffering at his antics and subsequent disappearance was carved into the lines that had etched themselves into her face. Poor Henrietta had lived in the long shadow cast by all the pain he had caused and it had all been so unnecessary as it turned out. The fever that had consumed him whilst he suffered with malaria had cast him into a nightmarish hell where he had relived every moment of that elusive day until he had finally remembered what had happened. He had not been cowardly at all, but had been trying to save his friend when a bullet had whistled past him, slicing the side of his head and sending him into oblivion.

Draining his glass, he reflected that he could not change the past, only shape the future. He was determined that Elmdon would become a place where they could all find peace and happiness again. Perhaps it was fortunate after all that they were to have visitors, for Lady Isabella Hayward was charming and had an infectious sense of fun, she could be relied upon to enliven even the dullest of parties.

He had been delighted when he had walked into the drawing room to see his sister's face lit by a smile.

His surprise that Miss Lockhart could make Henrietta laugh was only matched by the amazement he had felt at her altered appearance. It never ceased to amaze him how a change of hairstyle and apparel could transform a lady. The gold gown had suited her admirably, not only revealing a very slender figure that was rounded in all the right places, but an expanse of skin he would lay odds was as silky as the garment itself.

She had also been smiling when he entered the room and had looked warm and vibrant, it was a shame she had retreated behind the hauteur she donned like armour whenever she was made uncomfortable. That was his fault of course. For some reason he could not resist the compulsion to tease her. If he was completely honest, he had even for a moment wondered what it would be like to kiss those wide, plump lips. He gave a dry chuckle. Her gaze would probably have turned as deadly as Medusa's and transmuted him to stone in an instant.

\* \* \*

The following morning, Harry went out very early and made his way along the coast to Trenance, a small fishing hamlet that nestled between towering cliffs. As he had hoped, he found Joseph Craddock sat on a small upturned barrel by his boat on the narrow strip of beach, mending his nets.

He stood quietly behind him for a few moments, watching his nimble fingers deftly weave in and out of the fine mesh and then sat down beside him on the gritty sand. Joseph gave no sign he had noticed his presence but unhurriedly finished his task and then glanced at the long legs stretched out beside him.

"You've scratched those fine boots of yours, Lord Treleven," he finally said, turning his head slightly and giving him a sideways glance. "It's a shame after all the time your poor man must have spent polishing them until they be as good as a mirror."

He could not have been much more than forty and his tightly curling black hair was still unmarked by grey, but his tanned face was mapped with fine lines and broken veins from years of exposure to the wind and weather. His eyes were as deep blue as the seas he fished and of an unusual intensity. They were regarding him closely now.

"Did you get a good haul, Joseph?"

"Not bad, the pilchards are runnin'. You ought to come out one of these nights," he said with the ghost of a smile. "It always used to blow your troubles away."

Harry gave a wistful smile. "I'd love to but it's not fish I'm after today, Joseph, but information."

The small wiry man got to his feet and began stowing his net. "I'm listening."

"I hear there was a wreck not so long ago but there was nothing washed up on the shore."

"They still grumbling about the ghost ship, then?"

Harry nodded. "Were you out that night?"

Joseph shook his head. "No, 'twere blowing something fierce, only a fool would have gone out. Word got round the next day and me and some of the lads went to take a look, see if anything could be salvaged, but by then the ship had broken up on the rocks. We had the customs men prowling about soon after, asking questions that no one had the answers to. Apparently, it was taking on water out at sea and the passengers and most of the crew were picked up by another ship in their convoy, but a skeleton crew stayed on board, sure they could make Padstow. Seems they were mistaken, but neither them nor the goods has washed up anywhere that I know of. Probably at the bottom of the briny."

Harry looked thoughtful. "Some are saying Caldwell's men harvested it before anyone else got a look-in."

Joseph shook his head. "They would. Working underground too long has addled their brains. Who would have been out to see it? Caldwell's miners live over the headland and those sorry little cottages he has built 'em are set on the far side of the mine. And before you spout any nonsense to me about fire-setting to lure them in, there was no sign of any fires and how would they have known that the ship would have sprung a leak and be headed for land anyways?"

Harry couldn't argue with his reasoning. Indeed he had not said anything Harry had not already told himself.

"Why are you so interested, anyways?"

"I don't like the bad feeling that's brewing, Joseph. More than one good man has turned bad when he finds himself down on his luck."

"Well there's only one person round here who might wield some influence over Mr Caldwell, and that's you, sir."

"I'm working on it, Joseph," he assured him. His

countenance lightened with a grin. "I'll come fishing one of these nights, it will be like old times."

His eyes looked out across the deceptively calm water in front of him. Further out to sea he could see a dark heavy curtain of rain and knew that before long the water would have quite a different character as the wind beneath the approaching clouds whipped it up into a seething frenzy.

"Weather's changing, I'd best be getting back, Joseph."

The small, wiry man nodded. "Aye, but you've got a few moments yet. Before you go, sir, there's something I'd like to show you."

Harry followed him up the beach until it met the cliff. Here, a small recess in the rock housed a boat covered in a tarpaulin. Together they untied it and flipped it back to reveal a small boat in perfect condition.

"Betsy," Harry murmured softly, running a loving hand along the smooth wood. "You kept her for me."

Joseph's weather-beaten face broke into a broad grin. "I knew you'd be back some day, sir. You've got more lives than a cat and have always been able to look after yerself. I remember when I was first teaching you to sail, you'd had maybe two lessons but arrogant young cockerel that you were, you took her out on your own rather than wait for me to get back from the fish market. My heart was in my mouth when I sailed around the headland to find Betsy drifting and no sign of you to be had. How I would have explained it to your father when he had forbidden you to take up such a dangerous hobby, I don't know. I was never more thankful than when you swam in with no more than a graze on your head where the block attached to the clew of the sail had bashed you."

Harry laughed. "Knocked me clean overboard and the current swept me away from her. By the time I'd swum out of it the cold had sapped my energy and I only just made it to the rocks. I had to scramble around them until I could make the short swim back to the beach. I remember you tore a strip off me. It's the only time I've ever seen you angry."

"Aye, well you deserved it. Anyhow, I thought you'd be wanting her when you came home so I've kept her here, and made sure she's all's spic and span."

Harry shook his hand warmly. "You're a good friend, Joseph. I am most indebted to you."

"Ah, get away with you, sir. We know how to look after our own hereabouts."

\* \* \*

After breakfast, Henrietta offered to show Katherine and Mrs Abbott the knot garden. Small hedges wove an intricate pattern with gravelled paths winding between them. Fragrant scents drifted on the breeze as small beds filled with marjoram, thyme, lemon balm, hyssop, rosemary and lavender filled the delicate gaps between them.

"This is quite beautiful," exclaimed Mrs Abbott. "I do so enjoy it when design and practicality go hand in hand."

Henrietta smiled at the older lady. "It is one of my favourite places to walk and think."

"I should think it is," she replied. "Such a soothing,

sweet-smelling garden must be the perfect place for contemplation."

"And what is it you contemplate?" asked Katherine, privately finding the dainty walkways rather confining. She would rather take an invigorating walk through the parkland if she wished to chew something over.

"Oh, nothing really," Henrietta replied, colouring.

"Come, child," said Mrs Abbott gently, taking her arm. "Although we are only recently acquainted, you will find a sympathetic ear in both Miss Lockhart and myself."

"Oh, I know, you are both so kind," Henrietta acknowledged. "It is nothing really. You will say I dwell upon things too much and it is of no consequence, I am sure."

"Well, let us put it to the test," encouraged Katherine. "If you lock your troubles away they will worry at you until they make you ill or overcome you at the most inconvenient of times."

An image of her brother's face, shocked and immobile, as she had suddenly burst into tears at the dinner table floated into her mind. He had only asked her gently if she thought it had really been necessary to purchase quite such an expensive fabric for the new curtains in the drawing room.

"There's no need to take on so," he had said when he had finally found his voice. "I am sure you know best, after all. Whatever has come over you, Katherine?"

Pleading a headache, she had fled upstairs mortified by her loss of composure. She could never have confided in him – although they had a comfortable fondness for each other, they were not close above the ordinary, and emotional scenes were anathema to him.

"I did not enjoy my season," Henrietta began quietly. "I really did not wish to go, but Mama insisted that we must, for if Harry was away much longer he might be declared dead and then Elmdon would pass to some distant cousin."

"Where did he go?" asked Mrs Abbott.

Henrietta told them about her brother's duel, how he had fled the country and of his recent joyous return.

"Oh, how much your poor mother must have suffered," Mrs Abbott declared.

"Indeed she did," said Henrietta. "And then my father died soon afterwards. She shut herself up here and hardly ever ventured out for such a long time. So I agreed to go, to see if I could make her happy. I knew that if I found a husband it would be one less worry for her."

"But you did not find anyone who would suit?" Mrs Abbott encouraged her gently.

Henrietta shook her head. "I couldn't talk to all the fine London gentlemen. Not the way the other girls could."

"But surely all of that hardly matters now that your brother has returned?" Katherine said, putting aside the disgust she felt at his selfish and wanton behaviour.

Henrietta coloured. "No, no, of course not, I told you it was nothing."

But Katherine had not missed the flash of pain in her eyes and it struck a chord. "Are you sure you did not find anybody in whom you were interested?" she said gently.

Henrietta shook her head violently, but her eyes filled with tears that quickly overflowed and ran unchecked down her pale cheeks.

"Oh, my dear, whatever can have happened?" asked Mrs Abbott, rummaging in her reticule for a handkerchief and passing it to the afflicted girl.

It was some moments before she could contain her sobs, but slowly the tale came out in fits and starts. She had been at a ball when a Mr Carruthers had made her uncomfortable by being a little too free with his talk as they danced.

"T-told me I was a dashed fine filly and wouldn't he like to be the one who broke me in."

Mrs Abbott looked appalled. "Was he drunk? Or mad?" she exclaimed. "To talk to a young lady of refinement in such a way is despicable."

"Drunk, I think," Henrietta gulped. "For when he whispered it in my ear, his breath stank of strong drink."

"And what happened then?" asked Katherine softly.

"I wanted to run from the ballroom but knew I could not, it would cause such a scene and I would not cause Mama so much embarrassment. I tried to find her, but there was such a crush of people I couldn't immediately perceive her and I felt horribly faint. I went out onto the terrace for some cooler air; it was quite deserted and I tried to gather myself." Her shoulders started to shake and she returned the now sodden handkerchief to her face again.

"And did he follow you?" Katherine asked, beginning to guess the real cause of her distress.

Henrietta nodded, shuddering. "He pushed me

against the wall and kissed me with his foul smelling mouth, and his hands pressed me where they should not have. I fainted."

Mrs Abbott's eyes had also filled with tears. "You poor child," she cooed, wrapping her arms around her. "It was quite abominable. What did your mother say?"

Henrietta took a step backwards and mopped up the remainder of her tears.

"Apparently she found Mr Carruthers standing over me looking quite put out. He told her I had felt faint and come outside for some air and, concerned, he had followed me. I came around a few moments later and Mama took me home."

"You didn't tell her?" gasped Mrs Abbott.

"No, at first I was too ashamed," Henrietta admitted. "And then Harry came home and I could not destroy her happiness. If he had discovered what had happened he might have called him out and had to flee the country again. I could not have such a thing on my conscience, neither of us could have borne it if we had lost him again."

"No, of course not," Mrs Abbott soothed.

"Come, let us walk some more," Katherine suggested. "You cannot return to the house until your eyes are less red."

Henrietta offered a weak smile. "I will show you the maze."

Katherine had expected to find a series of small hedges and was surprised to discover they towered above her in neatly clipped lines.

"Oh, but how wonderful," exclaimed Mrs Abbott, delighted. "But what a lot of work it must be to keep them so well maintained!"

"Yes," agreed Henrietta, "our head gardener, Phillips, takes great pride in them."

Katherine suddenly grinned. "I like a challenge and shall try and find my way to the middle, but you must promise to rescue me if I get hopelessly lost."

Henrietta had recovered her poise and her smile this time was genuine. "Of course, I will go first and make my way to the centre. If you get lost, I will call out to you so you will know my general direction."

"We shall split up, Mrs Abbott," Katherine said. "The last one to arrive must accept a forfeit from the victor, to be given at a time of their choosing."

Mrs Abbott's face creased into a mischievous smile. "I accept your challenge, my dear."

They disappeared into the maze in different directions. Katherine strode out purposefully, laughing as she came upon a dead end, time after time. Eventually growing frustrated, she had to call out to Henrietta before she finally found her way to the middle. There she found a fountain, and Mrs Abbott and Henrietta awaiting her arrival on one of the benches that surrounded it.

"Congratulations, Mrs Abbott," she smiled. "I am bested. What is to be my forfeit?"

"Ah, you stipulated it was to be at a time of my choosing, my dear, and I believe I will hold you to that. I will choose a forfeit at a time that I feel will benefit you."

"You begin to make me nervous," Katherine smiled.

Mrs Abbott gave a tinkle of laughter. "Oh, you may be sure whatever I choose, it will be done with your own best interests at heart, I assure you."

"Did you also require Miss Treleven's assistance to find your way?" she asked.

"No, she did not," Henrietta smiled.

The mischievous twinkle re-appeared in Mrs Abbott's eyes. "I have often studied maze design," she admitted. "They are frequently built on a variation of a theme, and after a few false starts, I managed to work out the pattern of this one."

"Oh, then you had a hidden advantage!" exclaimed Katherine. "That is hardly playing fair, ma'am."

Mrs Abbott chuckled. "You should never issue a challenge without first considering the experience of your opponent, my dear."

Katherine looked at her with new respect. "I see I may have underestimated you, Mrs Abbott."

Glancing up she noticed a dark band of cloud had covered the sky.

"We must go or we will be caught in the rain," she said.

As they emerged from the maze, the wind that the tall hedges had sheltered them from whipped their dresses around their legs and tugged at their bonnets.

Katherine took Henrietta's arm. "You really must not blame yourself for that shocking incident, Miss Treleven. I will not say that it was of no consequence, it was horrid and it is understandable that you should have felt quite overset by the whole experience. But I do think that you have dwelt upon it perhaps a little too much. Your reputation remains intact as does your honour, thank heavens. If you can overcome the melancholy this incident seems to have caused you, there is no need perhaps to inform your family of it, but if it continues to haunt you, you must, for they will be worried for you."

She felt Henrietta tremble a little. "No, I cannot, and you must promise me, both of you, that you will say nothing without my permission."

"Calmly now, my dear," said Mrs Abbott, taking her other arm. "We will not betray a confidence easily, but Miss Lockhart is right, you must not allow one unfortunate incident to colour your view of the world. For every cad out there, there are many more honourable gentleman, I am sure."

Henrietta nodded. "I am sure you are right but I fear they will never be acceptable to me, for every time a single gentleman comes too near to me now, I feel quite sick."

"Give it time," Katherine advised. "I was once made a fool of by a gentleman and at first it felt as if the world as I knew it was turned on its head, but the feeling passed, eventually."

Henrietta looked a little more hopeful. "I am sorry you too had a bad experience, Miss Lockhart, and if you have recovered from it perhaps I will too. I must admit that I feel a little better for sharing my experience with you both."

The first heavy drops of cold rain began to fall just as they reached the house. As they smiled at each other in relief at having missed the downpour, they heard a bright trill of laughter coming from the morning room.

"Oh, that is Lady Hayward," smiled Henrietta hurrying forwards.

They found Lady Treleven and Lady Hayward seated together on a sofa, smiling indulgently at a very young child with a riot of blond curls, who, happy to be released from the confines of the carriage that had so recently imprisoned him, was running in circles around the room. A very large gentleman stood by the fireplace, one arm resting on the mantel, his lazy eyes also following his progress.

As the ladies entered the boy came to an abrupt halt by a small table holding a rather fine cut glass vase boasting a colourful array of flowers. His large grey eyes regarded them seriously for a moment before he placed one chubby little hand on the table to steady himself, and stood on tiptoes in an effort to reach one of the blooms. The delicate table wobbled ominously, threatening to spill both the vase and its contents onto the floor. Before that seemingly inevitable event could occur, the gentleman moved with surprising swiftness for one so large, and scooped his son up with one long arm even as he steadied the table with the other.

He looked down at the small boy he had cradled in his arm as if he were no more than a small babe.

"Whilst I appreciate your desire to greet the ladies with a floral offering, Edmund, you really must try for a little more finesse," he drawled softly, gently placing him back on his feet.

"A bow is all that is necessary on this occasion," he said, proffering them one himself.

They smiled as the little boy obediently followed suit. All three ladies nodded their heads regally in acknowledgement.

Once the introductions had been made, Katherine smiled but excused herself.

"I hope you won't think me rude if I run upstairs to tidy myself up a trifle? The wind has, I am sure, given me a rather wild appearance."

"Not at all," Lady Treleven smiled, glancing at the rain that now rattled against the small panes of the large windows. "You go and change too, Henrietta, for I can see a few spots of rain have caught you, I am only glad you did not get quite drenched. I do hope your brother has found somewhere to shelter for he went out very early and has not yet returned."

Once Katherine had changed her slippers and allowed Ayles to tidy her hair, she slowly made her way along the upper gallery, looking at the portraits of the Treleven ancestors. She lingered for a few moments in front of one. A tall, rather raffish looking gentleman stood by a harbour, a huge ship anchored behind him. Although his hair was both darker and longer, something about his confident stance and the lurking twinkle in his eyes reminded her of the present viscount.

"I see you have found my notorious relative, Sir Marcus."

Katherine turned, startled, her eyes widening. Lord Treleven stood before her as if her thoughts had conjured him up out of thin air. His hair was plastered to his head and his coat and breeches were soaked through, moulding them to him like a second skin.

"Notorious? I was just thinking that I could see a family resemblance."

He raised an amused brow. "Are you suggesting that I too am notorious, Miss Lockhart?"

She had simply uttered the first thoughts that had come into her head, not meaning to link the ideas, and was about to refute the suggestion when Henrietta's words came back to her.

"Well, you have, I believe, fought a duel," she said, raising her chin a little.

She regretted the words almost as soon as she had uttered them. The laughter died from his eyes and she recalled belatedly that it was not her place as a lady and a guest in his house, to remind him of his past indiscretions.

"Oh, Lord Treleven, just look at you dripping all over my clean floor, go and get changed do, before you catch your death!"

They both turned to Mrs Bidulph. The small, slender lady stood looking sternly at him but Katherine thought she could detect concern in her dark eyes.

Harry glanced down in surprise at the little puddle that was collecting at his feet and offered the housekeeper a rueful smile.

"I am sorry, Mrs Bidulph, I had not noticed."

He offered Katherine a brief bow and strode off.

Katherine descended the stairs feeling a little mortified. She could not explain her lapse in good manners. Whatever his past had been, he and his mother had been more than kind in welcoming her into their home whilst the repairs to Helagon were undertaken. And then there was the expeditious manner in which Lord Treleven had assembled a workforce, not to mention appointing his own steward to oversee the project.

If only she did not feel this absurd attraction to him; she did not trust or like it. She had not been surprised to discover his duel had been fought over a lady – flirtation seemed to come as naturally to him as breathing. It did not come naturally to her however, and made her uncomfortable. She paused at the bottom of the sweeping staircase as another unwelcome thought came to her. She had encouraged Miss Treleven in the belief that she had recovered from her own experience, hoping to offer her some comfort, but if she were so wary of being made a fool of again that she viewed any gentleman who paid her any attention with suspicion, then she really could not make such a claim. Was she turning into a bitter spinster, after all?

CHAPTER 7

Dinner that evening was enlivened by the vivacious presence of Lady Hayward. She was a very beautiful lady with gleaming golden hair and sparkling grey eyes. Her delicate condition seemed to suit her, for her smooth fair skin had a soft sheen that seemed almost to make it glow. She exuded happiness and Katherine could not help but reflect that it was a shame the condition had not resulted in a similar happy state for her sister-in-law.

She was clearly well acquainted with the Trelevens and was not afraid to interrupt conversations or address anyone, regardless of their position at the table, but she did so with a charm that made it impossible to mind her complete disregard for etiquette.

A very real affection seemed to exist between herself and her lord. Katherine noticed that when Lady Hayward made an amusing comment, a small smile would curve his lips and his eyes would flick briefly in her direction. Whilst never neglecting either herself or Lady Treleven who were seated on either side of him, he was, it seemed, aware of her at all times.

"I noticed a gig I do not recognise in the stables, could it be yours, Miss Lockhart?"

Katherine turned her gaze in the direction of Lord Treleven. He was immaculately turned out as usual, and his black swallow-tailed coat only served to heighten the gleaming lustre of his blond locks.

"Oh, it has arrived then," she said, surprised. "I found it in the stables at Helagon but my coachman would not allow me to use it until he had looked it over. It seems it must have passed muster. I thought it would be useful to have a light vehicle I could use to visit Helagon and check on the progress there. I had not realised it would be ready so soon or I would have asked your permission first. I hope it is not inconvenient for me to keep it and my horse in your stables, Lord Treleven?"

"It is not inconvenient at all, Miss Lockhart, although I would have been happy to drive you over myself anytime you wished."

"That is very kind of you, sir, but I am sure you have better things to do. Besides, I prefer to drive myself."

"Are you sure that is wise, my dear?" said Lady Treleven. "It may be better to let Lord Treleven drive you, for the roads around here can be very narrow and winding, I am sure they are not what you are used to."

Katherine smiled at her hostess. "You need not worry, ma'am, I am believed to be a competent whip, I assure you."

"Splendid," chimed in Belle. "Then you may take me up with you. I have a desire to see this crumbling ruin, it sounds terribly romantic."

Katherine laughed. "Well, it is not quite a crumbling ruin, Lady Hayward, and I must admit, I did not find it at all romantic. What say you, Mrs Abbott?"

Mrs Abbott shuddered dramatically. "Oh no, I remember us arriving in the dead of night, the house only lit by the moon and not a sign of life until you rang that creaky old bell, and then that owl started hooting and the bats started flying."

Katherine blinked. She had not seen any bats.

Belle was entranced. "Oh, but how exciting. What happened next?"

"We had supper and went to bed," Katherine said drily.

"Yes, my dear," agreed Mrs Abbott. "But do not tell me you did not hear the trees tapping on the windows as if trying to gain entry, or that dreadful wind wailing around the corners of the house like a lost soul screeching its agony?"

"It sounds deliciously frightening," Belle smiled.

"I would lay odds Miss Lockhart was not at all afraid," said Lord Treleven, smiling slightly.

"You would win your bet, sir," Katherine replied. "I slept the whole night through and never heard a thing."

Glancing at the slightly disappointed look on the face of the lady opposite, she smiled. "However, my maid did not sleep a wink and also complained of mice running across her bed in the night."

Lord Hayward grinned lazily. "Now do not say you

would have also have enjoyed that experience, my lady, for you dislike them above all things."

Belle gave a tinkle of laughter. "I know, it is quite ridiculous that such a small harmless creature can frighten one so much, isn't it?"

"I am not afraid of them, I once kept one as a pet," revealed Henrietta. "I kept it in a bird cage and fed it cheese. It really was very sweet."

Lady Treleven smiled. "Yes, one of the stable cats dropped it at your feet when you were just a girl and you scooped it up and insisted you keep it."

"What happened to it?" asked Mrs Abbott.

Henrietta shrugged. "It escaped. I found the door to the cage open and it had gone. Whether it managed to free itself or someone else released it, I do not know."

Katherine smiled across at her. "I would not be surprised if it had liberated itself, did I not tell you mice were observant creatures?"

Henrietta returned her smile. "I would also like to visit Helagon, I think."

"Then I will drive both you and Lady Hayward," said Harry. "For I believe Lord Hayward wishes to make some enquiries in Padstow tomorrow and you will certainly not both fit in Miss Lockhart's gig."

\* \* \*

By morning the dark clouds had drifted away leaving a clear sky. A brisk breeze still blew but it was not enough to make riding in an open carriage uncomfortable. Ayles dressed Katherine in a close-fitting carriage dress of mulberry-coloured velvet with a matching high-crowned bonnet. She had added a trim of white fur around the base of the dress and at the end of each tight fitting sleeve, and a plume of white ostrich feathers on the right-hand side of the bonnet, which fell in a graceful arc to one side.

Katherine smiled at her maid. "Thank you, Ayles. I don't know how you do it but you seem to transform things from plain to elegant with just a few light touches."

Ayles smiled, pleased with the compliment. "It was nothing, Miss Lockhart. Your figure made the dress elegant as it was and I know you like things kept simple, but there's no harm in a bit of prettifying."

At the last moment, Lady Treleven and Mrs Abbott also decided to join the party and so she called for her barouche to be fetched to accommodate the small party of ladies.

Katherine, still determined to drive, went to the stable yard to collect the gig. She found both it and Lord Treleven waiting for her. He was dressed for riding and was tapping his riding crop against his thigh as if impatient to be away. It stilled when he saw Katherine and he offered her a small bow.

"As my services are no longer required and I have some business to attend to, I will only accompany you as far as the gates, Miss Lockhart. Unless of course, you would like me to cast my eye over the work being done at Helagon?"

"No, they cannot have got very far with the renovations after all, and I would not wish to keep you from your business," she assured him.

He stepped forward and offered his hand to help

her into the waiting gig. She settled herself and took the reins in her hand before smiling her thanks.

"My stable lad, Jim, will accompany you in the seat behind," he informed her.

Katherine's brows arched upwards. "Thank you, sir, but I hardly think it necessary when Lady Treleven's party will also be with me."

"You will take him nonetheless," Harry said briskly. "If there were to be any sort of accident our coachman would be hard pressed to deal with both vehicles."

Katherine had not seen this side of Lord Treleven before and found herself bristling at his commanding tone, as well as his suggestion that there might be an accident.

Kenver walked Hermes into the yard and Harry mounted the chestnut stallion in one fluid motion. Katherine covertly admired his confident handling of the magnificent creature as he brought his skittish prancing under control with an iron fist on the reins. For the first time she caught a glimpse of the soldier he had been rather than the light-hearted flirt he had become.

Hermes was clearly longing for a good run but Lord Treleven kept pace with the gig as she tooled it down the long avenue, the barouche following sedately behind.

Katherine was aware that his eyes rested on her more than once, but she kept her gaze fixed firmly on the road ahead, not at all unnerved by the scrutiny; she knew her own ability.

"You have light hands," he finally said approvingly.

A small smile of satisfaction curved her lips and

she turned her head to observe him for a moment. "And you, sir, have a very fine seat."

Harry's eyebrows rose in surprise. "Was that a compliment, Miss Lockhart?"

"I am not such a hornet or shrew that I cannot give credit where it is merited," she said a little sharply, colouring slightly.

They had reached the gate and he doffed his hat to her. "Our ways part here. Be aware that the road down to Helagon may be slippery where the trees have prevented last night's downpour from drying."

Without waiting for a reply, he cantered off.

Katherine watched him for a few moments as she waited for the barouche to catch up. She was a little piqued that he had made no effort to apologise again for the shrew reference at least, but then he seemed unusually abrupt this morning as if his thoughts were elsewhere. She wondered idly what business could preoccupy him so.

Katherine had sent word of their visit ahead and they found Forster and Mrs Nance ready for them. The drawing room had been scrubbed and polished and it looked like they had scoured the house for the least faded chairs and sofas. They did not quite match and still looked a trifle shabby, but at least afforded a modicum of comfort to her visitors. The sun poured through the windows casting a cheerful light into the room.

"But this is quite civilised," said Belle, surprised.

"It is certainly much improved," smiled Katherine.

As she showed them around the house, they stumbled upon maids scrubbing and polishing in the bedrooms and workmen removing window frames or prising up rotten floorboards. The cracks and damp patches on the walls were still in evidence and where the ceilings were partially down in the attic rooms, buckets had been placed in various places to catch any leaks, some over half full of rainwater.

"Ah, now this is more hopeful," Lady Hayward declared. "If there are any spectres to be seen, it will be here that we shall find them."

Mrs Abbott looked much struck by this observation. "You are quite right, Lady Hayward, perhaps the wailing I heard was not the wind, after all."

Katherine smiled indulgently at her relative. Although she had called on her regularly at Felsham, her visits had often been brief and she had not suspected that beneath the gentle, meek appearance she presented to the world, lurked a mischievous humour. She rather enjoyed it and was thankful that her need for a companion had allowed her to get to know her more intimately.

The wind and rain of the previous day had prevented work on the roof, but a wooden scaffold tied together with rope had been constructed to allow access and a few men were removing the remnants of cracked and broken tiles.

The grass in the garden had been reduced to a much more respectable length and the paths were now accessible. The old beds had also been revealed and men worked to turn the long neglected soil.

Helagon was a hive of activity and Katherine received respectful nods or curtsies from the workers wherever they went.

"Lord Treleven chose well," she said to his mother

when they finally returned to the carriages. "Everyone seems very respectful and hard working."

Lady Treleven smiled at her. "They are very grateful to you, Miss Lockhart. They have lost their work at the mine and have been having a hard time of it. This may only be a temporary reprieve for them, but it is a welcome one."

She thought over the words as she made her way up the steep hill that led from Helagon. It was, of course, Lord Treleven to whom they really owed their gratitude. She remembered that he had overridden his mother's suggestions about where to find workers with alacrity and determination. He had been very keen to help these men and women; he clearly took his position seriously, at least.

When they reached the gates of Elmdon, she realised she was reluctant to turn into them. She had never seen the sea and realised that she wished to very much. She drew alongside the barouche.

"Is it far to the coast, Lady Treleven?"

"Not at all, my dear, but perhaps it would be better if you wait for another day as Henrietta has promised to take Lady Hayward and Edmund into the maze and Mrs Abbott has offered to help me with some flower arrangements for tonight's dinner."

"Oh, I think I will just go and take a quick look if you don't object, ma'am. I have Jim with me after all."

"I can see you are determined upon it," Lady Treleven said. "And I must say you handle that gig very well, Miss Lockhart. As it really is only a very short distance, I can see no reason why you should not. Jim will show you the way."

They turned into a smaller track further down the road that led through the home wood. It was a pleasant drive; the trees were mature and there was enough space between them to allow the sun to create dappled pools of light. Katherine was enjoying listening to the birdsong when she thought she glimpsed movement amongst the undergrowth. Her shoulders tensed and her hands tightened on the reins as she remembered the poacher who had lurked in the woods on her first visit to Elmdon. A few moments later she saw a squirrel dart up the trunk of a tree. She let out a small laugh of relief but nevertheless flicked her whip to encourage the horse to go a little faster.

Presently they turned onto another track that soon led them out of the woods. They bowled along between fields, the grass was rougher here, and grey boulders were scattered across them reminding her of her journey across the moors. The breeze picked up as the prospect opened, and she saw a stretch of blue topped with white-capped waves. She turned onto the track that ran along the cliff edge and slowed the horse to a sedate walk. The furze and ferns gradually became less dominant and wild flowers wound their way through the long grass that waved in the fresh breeze.

She came to a halt and climbed down from the gig, wanting to get a better look at the coastline.

"Hold the horse will you, Jim?"

The skinny stable lad jumped down from his seat and obediently went to the horse's head.

Katherine walked towards the cliff allowing her fingertips to brush against the long grass. She stopped a few feet from the edge and gazed at the wild untamed beauty before her. She suddenly felt invigorated and wished for a moment that she could soar above the wide blue expanse like the white gulls that drifted gracefully on the breeze. Her eyes dropped to the golden sand that lay at the base of the cliff and she wondered how it would feel beneath her feet.

As her eyes wandered to the cliff face she saw the winding narrow path that led down to the beach below. Taking a cautious step forwards, she followed it until she could see that it could be accessed a few hundred yards ahead. She turned decisively back to the road and walked briskly towards the gig.

"I am going down to the beach, Jim," she informed the boy. "Walk the horse for me, please, I shouldn't be too long."

The boy looked surprised but knew better than to question his orders and so merely nodded.

The path curved its way down, winding back on itself several times, only now and then steep enough to require extra care. Katherine picked her way along it, thankful that she had worn her jean half boots, for the small stones that littered it would have made it most uncomfortable in anything less sturdy.

It was further than she had first thought and her legs were aching a little by the time she took her first step on the golden sand. She felt herself sink slightly into the soft, fine grains and made her way nearer to the waterline where it was slightly firmer, occasionally glancing back at the single track of footprints she had left behind her.

She walked to the end of the small beach where a tall black rock towered above her and skirting around it realised she could walk into the next, larger crescent-shaped cove. She amused herself picking up a few delicately shaped shells, pretty patterned stones, and fragments of smooth coloured glass.

Laughing as a sudden gust of wind tugged at her bonnet, she tied her ribbons a little tighter. Surprised at how far she had come, she realised she had lost track of time and reluctantly turned and began to make her way back, pausing when she saw something glinting brightly in the sunlight. Stooping she picked it up, placing it in her palm with her other treasures. She turned it this way and that – it looked for all the world like a diamond. She smiled to herself, it was highly unlikely of course, it was merely another fine piece of glass that had been shaped and polished by the shifting sands.

As she raised her gaze, a movement at the top of the cliff caught her eye. She saw a very small figure that must be Jim, waving frantically at her. She thought she heard a faint voice carried by the breeze and realised he must calling to her but she could not make out any words above the sound of the surf. It was she realised, noisier than before and her eyes turned back to the sea. Alarmed, she jumped quickly back as it nearly rushed over her boots. She had wandered up the beach in her search for shells and the sea had, it appeared, followed her.

She glanced down the beach and her heart began to hammer in her chest. Her footprints had disappeared and the water now engulfed the tall lump of rock that marked the cove she had found at the bottom of the path. She rushed forwards and stumbled, falling to her knees. Scrambling hastily to her feet, she picked up her skirts in one hand and began to run. Before she had covered half the distance she realised it was futile, her way was blocked and waves spumed white foam as they crashed up the rock face. Telling herself not to panic, she scanned the towering cliff systematically, searching for another way up. Her mouth dried as she realised there was none.

CHAPTER 8

Harry hastily untied the tarpaulin covering Betsy and pulled it back impatiently, laying it on the ground next to the small craft. He shrugged off his coat and laid it on top of the discarded cover. He was aware of a niggling feeling of guilt that he was going to indulge himself in a sail when he had assured Mr Hewel that he would ride out to see one of his tenant farmers. Mr Treen had sent a note to Mr Hewel asking to see him, but as he hadn't mentioned anything in particular, Harry didn't think it could be too urgent. He would go tomorrow; the weather on this part of the coast was often unpredictable and he might not see such perfect conditions again for weeks.

It wasn't the only thing that was unpredictable, he mused, as he pushed Betsy along the greased wooden planks Joseph had thoughtfully prepared for him. Miss Lockhart had looked very elegant this morning. The rich colour of her gown and the artfully placed feather on her cap had been very striking and although he had not been surprised to see she handled her gig with competence, he had not expected her to have such a confident, light touch. She could leave some of the incomparables who fancied themselves whips and liked to drive their phaetons around the park in town, in the shade.

Her compliment on his riding had taken him by surprise. There had been approval in her softened tone. Yet again, the urge to spar with her had overcome him and she had soon reverted to type. He should, of course, have assured her she was neither a hornet nor a shrew, but if he were to be back in time to greet his guests for dinner, he must hurry.

He pushed the small boat into the surf and jumped in. He reached for the oars and began to row, annoyed when he became aware of a slight twinge in his arm. When he was beyond the breaking waves, he set his jib and mainsail and Betsy immediately responded, skimming over the gentle swell. He raised a hand to a figure that had appeared on the beach. Joseph had come to watch him, but after a few moments he turned and made his way back up to his small cottage.

As the wind ruffled his shirt and hair, a wide grin spread over Harry's face and his eyes sparkled with pleasure. He had sailed in many ships, but for him, nothing could match the simple delight of a small vessel. Its performance and his safety relied solely on his wits and skill alone.

He raced around the headland and into the bay that marked his own land. It was then he saw the small figure jumping up and down, waving both his arms at the top of the cliff. He sailed in as close as he dared, knowing of the hidden teeth that lurked just below the surface, and realised the person was now pointing to the next bay.

Harry could sense the urgency in his movements and hurriedly tacked back out beyond reach of the rocks and then resumed his original course. The tall chimney of Wheal Trewith rose above the clifftop reminding him that he had not yet tackled Caldwell about re-employing at least some of his tenants at Langarne.

This bay, he knew, was not littered with the rocks that marked his own, and he steered a course towards the shore. The chimney disappeared as he came closer and his eyes fell to the beach below. It was then he saw the small figure in crimson, backed against the cliff face as the sea raced up the beach with the incoming tide.

Miss Lockhart! Wasting no time on pointless speculation as to how she had got herself into such a precarious predicament, he quickly furled his sails and reached again for his oars. When he was within striking distance of the small strip of beach that remained, he dropped his anchor over the side and slid into the water. He strode thigh deep through the swell, the incoming waves breaking around him and spraying his white shirt until it was also soaked through and clinging to him.

He was surprised that Miss Lockhart did not make any move towards him, but when he got close enough to see her eyes, he saw that they were large in her white face, and glazed with terror.

"Miss Lockhart," he said in the gentle tone he would use on a panicked horse, "you are safe now."

Her eyes fixed on his and the sound of his words

seemed to slowly penetrate her senses. "You are real, then?" she whispered. "I have not conjured you up in my desperation to be rescued?"

"I assure you I am real." He smiled gently, stepping forwards and taking the hand nearest to him. It was cold and slightly damp from where it had been pressed against the slick cliff face. It curled tightly around his and he felt touched by her vulnerability. He quelled the urge to sweep her into his arms and reassure her further, sure she would resent him for it later and for once feeling no urge to tease her. Their eyes held for a long moment, the spell broken when something dripped on her face. They both automatically glanced upwards. Harry's brows drew together in a thoughtful frown as he realised they were stood beneath a dark opening in the rock.

"What is it?" Katherine suddenly asked, her voice a little stronger. "Is it a tunnel? I did wonder if I could escape that way only I could not find a way up there."

"It is a type of tunnel," Harry acknowledged, his urge to hurry tempered by his need to keep her calm. "It is called an adit, and its job is to allow the mine to drain so it does not flood. As it rained all yesterday afternoon and most of the night, I would expect it to be pouring with water today, spreading a red stain over the sea."

Imparting such a mundane snippet of information seemed to do the trick. She nodded her understanding and then glanced at the boat, which was swinging in the wind. Her gaze dropped to their still clasped hands and her brows rose as if in surprise. She quickly released his and took a small step away from the wall. A shaky smile curved her lips. "Whilst I am glad of your expertise in rescuing damsels in distress after all, sir, how is it to be achieved in the present case for I cannot swim?"

Aware that they had not long before the sea began to hurl itself against the unyielding cliffs, Harry scooped her up into his arms. "Like this."

He strode back into the water trying to protect her by turning his back on any waves that broke around them and hoisting her up as high as he could, but by the time he deposited her in Betsy, she was also rather damp.

He smiled as, regaining some of her usual dignity, she sat up ramrod straight, her clenched hands the only sign of her nervousness. He set his sails quickly before pulling up his anchor. A gust of wind immediately caught them and they shot forwards. Miss Lockhart looked startled and her hands opened as they sought to cling to the side of the boat. As they did so, the treasures she had collected went skittering across the wooden floor.

Harry let out a short laugh, aware of feeling a strange mixture of amusement and annoyance.

"So, you risked your life for a few shells and pretty pieces of glass?"

Katherine coloured. "I was not aware I was risking my life, sir. I did not realise that the water would come in as it did."

"No, but what were you thinking, exploring without someone to guide you?"

"Lady Treleven saw no harm in it," Katherine defended herself, "and I had Jim with me."

"Neither of these arguments detracts from the fact that you put yourself in significant danger. I don't suppose my mother thought you would descend the cliff to the beach and as for Jim, it probably didn't occur to him that anyone might not know about tides."

She coloured and Harry realised he was being a trifle hard on her. Now that she was safe, all the ramifications of what could have happened to her had rushed upon him. If he had been many minutes later she would undoubtedly have drowned and he would not have been entirely without blame, for if he had accompanied her this morning as had been his initial intention, this would never have happened.

"Forgive me." He smiled ruefully. "It was not your fault, just an unfortunate accident that does not bear dwelling on. Let us not quarrel but enjoy the sail back. There is nothing like it!"

The combined force of the wind and sun had largely dried them both by the time they reached the entrance of Trenance Bay, and Katherine had recovered from her ordeal enough to think that he might be right. Once she had become used to the strange movement of the boat and learned to move with it rather than brace herself against it, she had begun to enjoy the experience.

She watched, fascinated, as he constantly made small adjustments to the sails and the tiller and soon realised she was in safe hands. In truth, she had not doubted it from the moment he had taken her hand and she had realised he was flesh and blood, not a figment of her overwrought imagination.

Lord Treleven suddenly grinned at her. His eyes were glowing with pleasure and enjoyment. She found she could not look away.

"Give me your hand," he said softly.

It seemed to rise of its own volition. She looked on amazed as he stripped off her glove. He then placed her hand on the tiller where his own had rested only a moment before. It felt warm and smooth. As the small craft swung off course and the sails began to flap, he covered it with his own.

"Like this," he murmured, gently moving it this way and that. "You need to go where the wind can fill the sails. Close your eyes and feel it brush against your skin."

The moment she closed her eyes, she felt her senses heighten. The breeze whispered against her cheek, its cool kiss a counterpoint to the warmth of the hand that covered her own.

"Now, open them and lead us in to the shore."

She felt his hand lift away from her own and raised her gaze to the sails, gently altering their course to keep them filled. She felt exhilarated as the little boat responded to the lightest of touches.

"But this is wonderful," she said, a wide smile curving her lips.

"You are full of surprises, Miss Lockhart," he laughed.

When they reached the shore, a small wiry man with dark curling hair was waiting for them. He waded into the water and as the next incoming wave surged beneath them, pulled Betsy up onto the beach. He then held out a hand to help Katherine to alight.

"Seems as you caught a beautiful mermaid, Lord Treleven."

Katherine stepped out of the boat and smiled at him. "I could almost wish I were such a creature for then I would not have been foolish enough to have been stranded or needed rescuing from the incoming tide."

"Ah, so that was the way of it. Don't be too hard on yerself, ma'am, for you aren't the first to have been caught so and you won't be the last neither."

Lord Treleven vaulted over the side of the boat and shook the man's hand. Katherine's eyes followed his movements. She had never met a man with such vitality and natural grace, or, fortunately for her, one who had such a cool head in a crisis.

"This is Joseph Craddock," he informed her. "He taught me to sail."

Her smile widened. "Then I also find myself in your debt, Mr Craddock, for if you had not done so, Lord Treleven would not have been able to rescue me."

A slow smile spread across his weathered face. "Oh, he would have found a way, miss, of that you can be sure."

Harry nodded up the beach to where a white cottage stood. A small wooden bench crouched against the wall.

"If you'd like to sit for a moment, Miss Lockhart, I'll just stow the boat and then I'll take you back."

Joseph helped Harry haul Betsy back up the greased planks and then helped him into his coat.

"You leave the rest to me, sir, get that lovely young lady of yours back to Elmdon. She's holding herself together well but she's had a fright and no mistake. I'm surprised she's not in hysterics truth be told."

Harry grinned at him. "I don't think Miss Lockhart is the sort to have the vapours, Joseph, she's far too sensible and dignified."

"Aye, well, off with you, anyways."

Harry nodded briefly and turned on his heels but he had gone no more than a stride when he paused and swivelled neatly again. Leaning into the boat he began gathering the scattered shells and fragments of glass. As he strode towards Joseph's cottage, he glanced at the little collection that lay in his palm. He came to a sudden stop, picked up a couple of the pieces and slid them into his coat pocket.

He paused when he reached Katherine and offered her the remainder of her treasure.

She glanced at his outstretched palm for a moment and then shook her head.

"Thank you, Lord Treleven, but let them fall. Perhaps some things are better left where they are found."

"As you wish," he said, tilting his palm so they fell to the sand.

He retrieved Hermes from the small garden behind the cottage and rode around to where Katherine now stood waiting for him.

"I am afraid I cannot trust Hermes to carry you alone, Miss Lockhart, so I will need to take you before me."

He saw a look of uncertainty cross her face and reached down his hand. "Come. There is no time for argument, Jim will have carried the tale to Elmdon by now and everyone will be concerned, I do not wish my mother, in particular, to worry any longer than necessary. Place your foot on mine and I'll do the rest."

As he now expected, sense won out over pride and she clasped his hand, rested her boot on his and sprang up before him without much aid at all.

Hermes sidled a little in protest and he firmly clasped one arm around her slender waist, feeling her stiffen as he did so, grasped the reins firmly with the other and took them home.

As soon as they entered the house, the drawing room door flew open. Lady Treleven, Henrietta, Mrs Abbott and Lord and Lady Hayward poured into the hall. They were already changed for dinner.

"Oh, thank goodness!" Lady Treleven cried coming forwards and briefly embracing her son and then Katherine. Taking a step back she gave Harry a stern look. "You are very naughty going sailing without letting anyone know what you were about! Had you forgotten Doctor Fisher was to change your dressing today?"

Katherine had not immediately perceived him but on hearing his name he stepped out from behind Lord Hayward whose huge form had obscured him from view, and offered a small bow in their direction.

"It is no matter. I can look at it as you change for dinner." His kind but penetrating gaze rested on Katherine for a moment. "I would be happy to be of service to you also, Miss Lockhart, if you feel at all unwell."

Lady Treleven took both of her hands in her own.

"Yes, do let him, dear. How terrified you must have been! I have been berating myself all afternoon for allowing you to go off on your own, but I never dreamed you would go down that steep narrow path to the beach without anyone to aid you. You must let Doctor Fisher look you over and if you do not feel up to dinner, I will have a tray sent to your room."

Katherine returned her clasp and smiled gently

down at her. "It will not be necessary, as you see, I am none the worse for the experience. Please, do not blame yourself, ma'am, it was an impulsive decision, the sand looked so inviting." She glanced ruefully down at her dress. Swathes of white stained the velvet where the salt had dried against the fabric. "I cannot say the same for my gown, unfortunately, I fear it is beyond saving."

"Oh, a dress can easily be replaced, so what matter?" smiled Lady Hayward coming forwards. "And to be rescued in such a way must have been vastly exciting."

The sound of a bell ringing echoed through the large hallway. Glasson appeared as if from nowhere and glided by them with unhurried dignity.

"It appears Mr Caldwell has arrived," said Lady Treleven, beginning to usher her guests back into the drawing room.

"I must go and get changed." Katherine moved quickly towards the stairs. As she passed Lady Hayward, she found a light hand on her arm.

"I will come with you, Miss Lockhart, for I wish to hear all about it. I wonder if I would enjoy sailing?"

"You would be horribly seasick, my dear," Lord Hayward assured her as she set her foot on the first stair. "Remember our honeymoon trip? You turned green almost as soon as we left the harbour!"

His good lady looked a trifle disappointed but sent a not unhopeful glance over her shoulder in Harry's direction. "Yes, but that was on a large ship, surely it would not be as bad on a little boat?"

"It would be worse," he assured her, grinning.

Katherine noticed the look of approval Lord Hayward cast in his direction.

"Hold the fort for me will you, Hayward?" Harry said, slipping by them and mounting the stairs two at a time. Doctor Fisher followed him at a more dignified pace.

Ayles was pacing the room when they entered her chamber. "Oh, miss!" she cried. "You have given us all such a fright! And just look at your poor gown!"

Katherine was not quite sure which was the greater concern for her flustered maid. "Is it quite ruined?"

Ayles came forward and gently rubbed one of the stains. "Don't you worry your head over that, ma'am, there's nothing there that a good brush and a treatment of vinegar and water won't fix! Now, you wash quickly whilst I lay out a choice of gowns for you or you'll be late for dinner."

Lady Haywood smiled and sat herself on the damask covered chair that was set beneath the window. Katherine disappeared behind the screen that lay at an angle across one corner of her room and began to wash her face.

"Tell me, Miss Lockhart, is Lord Treleven as accomplished at sailing as he is at everything else?"

"As I know nothing about sailing I am hardly qualified to judge," Katherine said drily.

A tinkle of laughter greeted this. "I see you are a lady who is not easily impressed."

Feeling a twinge of guilt that she had not been more supportive of her rescuer, she added hastily, "But I certainly felt safe both in his boat and on his horse."

"He let you ride his stallion?" Lady Hayward sounded amazed.

Katherine briefly closed her eyes. She really must learn to consider her words before she uttered them.

"Well, no," she admitted. "He took me up before him."

There was a moment's pause. "I am glad to hear it, how dreadful it would have been if you had survived one horrid ordeal only to have been thrown by that fearsome creature."

She heard a rustling of silk as if Lady Hayward had got to her feet.

"Oh, definitely that one, I think."

It seemed Lady Hayward was to choose her raiment for her. Katherine did not feel too alarmed by this development as she knew she had nothing too daring in her wardrobe.

She stepped around the screen and stared at the dress laid out on her bed. Of course, she knew she had a silk evening gown in Pomona green but she saw that the previously square cut, high neckline had been lowered and shaped, a deeper green satin ribbon had been attached below it and scalloped rouleaux of a similar green satin and blonde lace had been added to the hem of the train. She glanced at Ayles who stood with an alternating expression of hope and worry in her eyes.

She smiled. "If ever you decide to change professions, Ayles, you will make an admirable seamstress."

When they entered the drawing room not quarter of an hour later, they found a rather awkward tableau before them. Lord Hayward sat next to Lady Treleven, whilst Henrietta and Mrs Abbott occupied the opposing sofa. Mr Gulworthy stood behind them, his hands clasped behind his back. All eyes apart from

Henrietta's, whose gaze was firmly riveted to the splendid Aubusson carpet at her feet, her cheeks echoing its red tones, were fixed with amazed fascination upon Mr Caldwell who stood leaning on the mantelpiece as if he were very much at home.

As the occupants of the room registered their arrival, the eyes swivelled towards them with no small measure of relief. Lord Hayward stood and bowed before coming forwards to take his lady's hand. He took it upon himself to make the introductions, placing a slight emphasis on the words, 'my wife' when he indicated Lady Hayward.

Mr Caldwell bowed politely to this lady before turning his attentions to Katherine. She was a little startled when the rather stout man in the garish waistcoat took her hand and bowed deeply over it. She thought she heard something creak.

"I am a fortunate fellow indeed to be surrounded by such perfection."

Katherine's brows winged upwards and she retrieved her hand from his clammy grasp glad of her long gloves, but still needing to resist the almost overpowering temptation to wipe it against her gown. She was saved the necessity of making a reply by the entrance of Lord Treleven and Doctor Fisher.

"At last," Lady Treleven gave a relieved smile. "I had begun to think something was amiss. I trust the wound is healing as it should, Doctor Fisher?"

"Wound?" echoed Mr Caldwell. "Have you met with an accident, Lord Treleven? I must say you look right as a trivet to me."

"I am," Lord Treleven assured him. "It is nothing, the veriest scratch."

Katherine flushed as she remembered the exertion which he had put himself to on her behalf. She was on the point of apologising to him when he caught her eye. There was a warning there and she held her peace.

Lady Treleven advanced towards Lord Hayward. "It is time and more that we went in to dinner."

He offered her his arm and Lord Treleven proffered his to Lady Hayward.

Mr Caldwell made a move towards Henrietta and she shrank backwards, sending her mother an alarmed glance.

"Doctor Fisher, you may take my daughter in, if you please," Lady Treleven said briskly.

That young lady visibly relaxed even as Mr Caldwell frowned. Mr Gulworthy offered his escort to Mrs Abbott, leaving Katherine to Mr Caldwell. She placed her hand lightly on his forearm but he drew it within his own, giving her hand a little squeeze as he did so. Keeping her gaze firmly fixed in front of her, she suppressed a grimace.

"And who are your people, Miss Lockhart?" he enquired almost as soon as they had been seated.

"My brother is Sir Richard Lockhart of Felsham Court," she replied in a colourless tone, hoping to discourage him.

"Baronet or knight?" he shot back.

She looked at him in astonishment. "Baronet."

"And what sort of place is this Felsham Court?" he continued between mouthfuls of soup.

"I do not believe I understand you, Mr Caldwell."

"How many acres?" he clarified, undeterred by her air of frigid dignity.

"I really could not say."

He laughed, wiping a smear of soup from his chin. "Of course you cannot, and why should you? A delicate flower does not question the soil that harbours it, after all."

Her glance collided with Lady Hayward's dancing eyes and a small smile tugged at her lips.

When the ladies left the gentlemen to their port, Lady Hayward took her arm.

"I don't know how I kept my countenance. He is an extraordinary man, isn't he?"

"You almost set me off, Lady Hayward," Katherine acknowledged. "I don't know what was worse – his impertinent questions or ridiculous compliments!"

"Oh, call me Belle, please, all my friends do."

"Very well, Belle. Let us put our heads together, for we must come up with a way to keep Mr Caldwell as far away from Henrietta as possible. He will terrify and disgust her."

"You are very right," she agreed. "I often rescued her from unwanted attention when we were in town. I am afraid her rare combination of beauty and shyness might have led one or two sprigs of fashion to behave a little too warmly towards her."

Katherine paused for a moment in the hall and said in a lowered voice. "Did she tell you about Mr Carruthers?"

Belle quirked an eyebrow and a dangerous sparkle came into her eyes. "So he *did* make her faint! I always suspected as much! Imagine Mr Caldwell but fifteen years younger."

Katherine shuddered. "I think even I would have fainted!"

"Precisely. To someone of Henrietta's disposition and innocence, to be mauled by such a man must have been beyond distasteful. It makes me very angry, one's first kiss should be a magical experience, not feel like a violation!"

* * *

"Was your business in Padstow successful?" Harry smiled across at Lord Hayward.

"Oh, I may have discovered a couple of interesting leads. Mr Boodle was most helpful."

"Boodle, eh?" interjected Mr Caldwell. "Bit of an old fusspot, if you ask me. Give me a London solicitor any day. More up to snuff on some of the more, er, intricate aspects of the law, shall we say?"

"I found him to be adequate," Lord Hayward smiled sleepily. "Seems to have a good local knowledge."

"Isn't he an investor in your mine?" Harry asked.

"*Was* an investor." Mr Caldwell gave a wolfish smile. "I bought him out. He was always nitpicking over things he did not fully understand. Besides, I prefer to choose my own partners. Speaking of which, have you considered my proposal that you should become one of them?"

"I may be interested," Harry said slowly, aware that all eyes were now firmly fixed upon him with expressions varying from disinterest, surprise, and in the vicar's case, horror.

Mr Caldwell beamed. "Capital!"

"Not so fast, sir," he added. "Various conditions would have to be met."

Mr Caldwell raised a surprised brow and then laughed. "There's more to you than meets the eye, my boy. I like the cut of your jib. Come tomorrow and we will discuss it further, but I warn you, I am an old hand at negotiation!"

Lord Hayward yawned. "I find all this talk of business quite tedious. Shall we join the ladies?"

Mr Caldwell gave him an indulgent look. "Well, we cannot all have a head for business after all. Just as well for me, eh?"

Lord Hayward gave no indication that he had heard him.

Colouring slightly, he stood up and clapped Harry on the shoulder.

"Well lead on, lead on. You have a damn fine sister, Lord Treleven, diamond of the first water. I cannot think of a pleasanter way to spend the evening than in her company! Miss Lockhart's not too shabby either, but so starched up, you'd think she was the sister of a duke rather than a mere baronet. No wonder she's been left on the shelf – who in their right mind would want to be leg-shackled to an icicle?"

It was perhaps fortunate that he turned away just at that moment or he would have witnessed the quite murderous expression that flashed in his host's eyes.

As the gentlemen entered the drawing room, Lady Treleven rang for the tea tray. Mr Caldwell drew his chair close to where Henrietta was seated, quietly conversing with Mrs Abbott. Before he could draw breath to speak, Belle turned towards him with a blinding smile.

"Mr Caldwell," she said, her eyes dropping for a moment from his florid face to his equally florid waistcoat. "You are clearly a man who knows his own taste. I feel sure you must enjoy the finer things in life."

"That I do," he concurred. "And nothing could be finer than the company in which I find myself this evening." His eyes rested hungrily on Henrietta.

"You are all kindness, sir," Belle said with a tinkle of laughter. "Such modest requirements for your entertainment are a credit to you, but you must, I think, enjoy music?"

Mr Caldwell returned her smile a little cautiously. "As much as the next man, I should think."

"I knew it," she said clapping her hands. "Then you are more fortunate than you are aware, for Miss Treleven is quite accomplished on the pianoforte, I believe."

That young lady's startled eyes shot up from the clearly fascinating pattern of the Aubusson carpet. "Oh, no, I have not prepared anything!"

Mr Caldwell looked a trifle relieved. "Please, do not trouble yourself, Miss Treleven. I am sure a little conversation is all that I require."

Henrietta blanched.

"It is an excellent idea," Lady Treleven concurred. "Come, Henrietta. There is no point developing accomplishments if you don't intend to display them."

Doctor Fisher came forwards and offered her his hand. "Don't be shy, Miss Treleven, you are amongst friends, after all. I will be happy to turn the pages for you."

She offered him a tremulous smile and got to her feet.

Mr Gulworthy took her seat and he and Mrs Abbott exchanged a friendly look. They had discovered their mutual interest in gardening during dinner and had soon established a comfortable rapport.

Despite her nerves, Henrietta managed a creditable rendition of a sonata by Haydn. She received a polite round of applause, extended by the heavy, slow clapping of Mr Caldwell, who had quickly recovered from his initial feeling of chagrin at having his quarry removed so soon from his orbit, when he had realised all the advantages of his situation. He had, in effect, been given license to sit at his ease and gaze upon her fair visage without occasioning remark or fearing interruption. If only Doctor Fisher had not leaned in quite so close as he turned the page for her, he would have been quite content. Determined that he should regain the advantage over the younger man, he rose even as he clapped and began to move towards them only to find Lady Hayward before him. She fluttered both arms in front of her, driving him back to his chair before he had taken more than a step.

"No, no, sir," she laughed. "This will not do. One piece does not an evening of entertainment make. I am sure you do not wish to deny any delicate flowers here, the opportunity to blossom."

Her eyes turned to Katherine on the words. "Perhaps you could sing for us, Miss Lockhart?"

"If you wish," she smiled, swiftly crossing to Henrietta who had begun to rise. "You play and I'll sing, if you please, Miss Treleven, for I am afraid I have not applied myself to the instrument for some years now."

Henrietta sank back on her stool.

Picking up a songbook, Katherine began to flick

through it. A loose sheet of music floated to the floor. She made to retrieve it but Lord Treleven was before her. He glanced at it for a moment and then smiled, a mischievous glint in his eye.

"Do you know 'From Night 'til Morn I take my Glass', Miss Lockhart? It was one of my father's favourites."

"I do, but—" Katherine glanced over to her hostess, unsure if she would approve of such a lively song about drowning one's sorrows to forget a past love.

Lady Treleven considered Mr Caldwell for a moment. "I am sure it will go down very well, Miss Lockhart. Harry, you must join in also for it is meant as a duet, after all."

Harry glanced at his sister and she gave him a small smile and a nod of her head. Their voices blended perfectly, Harry effortlessly finding a counter melody and Katherine matching his tempo, and, in the end, his enjoyment.

The room erupted into laughter and applause as they finished. Mr Caldwell beaming as broadly as any of them.

Harry took Katherine's hand and bowed over it, his twinkling gaze never leaving her own.

"You sing as sweetly as a nightingale," he murmured.

Even as she felt the heat rush up her arm and into her cheeks, she perceived over his shoulder Mr Caldwell again determined to approach. His eyes were only for Henrietta so when she moved very close to him, he did not immediately perceive that the train of her dress was in his path. Sending a silent apology to Ayles, she timed her moment to perfection, moving away at the very moment his heavy tread encountered her gown. The sound of tearing reached every ear.

Mr Caldwell reddened. "Miss Lockhart, forgive me. I do not know how such a thing could have happened!"

Katherine smiled graciously. "Do not disturb yourself, Mr Caldwell, I am sure it will take but a moment to pin it up." She turned to Henrietta. "Would you mind very much lending me a hand, Miss Treleven?"

"Of course, Miss Lockhart, please, come with me." She glided gracefully to the door, Katherine following in her wake, determinedly keeping her gaze far from Belle.

Barely had the door shut behind them before Henrietta covered her face in her hands. Katherine looked at her in surprise. She could not see any cause for her distress.

"Miss Treleven, Henrietta," she began, concerned, but came to an abrupt halt as Henrietta let her hands fall, to reveal two eyes that were shining with laughter, not tears.

"You guessed?" she gasped, surprised.

Henrietta nodded. "Did you not say that mice were observant creatures, Miss Lockhart?"

"Katherine," she smiled. "Indeed I did. But I may have failed to mention that they can at times be quite forgetful. It may take you some time to lay your hands on those pins!"

## CHAPTER 9

When Harry went down to the stables the next morning, he found Lord Hayward there.

"Morning, Hayward. Where are you off to this morning?"

"I thought I'd ride towards Hayle."

Harry looked surprised. "I would have thought Penzance would be a better bet. There are some fine houses in South Parade."

"I am sure you are right, but I fancied a coastal ride this morning."

Harry nodded briskly and mounted Hermes. "Then we'll ride together awhile. I'll take a closer look at Caldwell's set-up before I go and see him."

"Mr Gulworthy did not seem to approve of your interest in his mine," he mused.

Harry sighed. "He will when he understands that it may be the only way I can influence who is employed there. Many local hardworking men and women have lost out to the people Caldwell has brought in."

"I would not have thought it would have been worth his while," Lord Hayward murmured.

Harry gave him a close look, surprised that he was prepared to discuss a subject that had been so distasteful to him only the evening before.

"That thought has also crossed my mind," Harry admitted.

"And have you come up with any likely explanations?" Lord Hayward gently pressed.

Harry looked thoughtful. "Not likely ones, no, so if you don't mind, Hayward, I'll keep my thoughts to myself for now. I don't like to cast aspersions on a man's character before I have firm evidence to go on."

Lord Hayward smiled his sleepy smile. "Very admirable, Treleven. Miss Lockhart and my esteemed wife, seem already to have formed some firm conclusions on his character, however."

Harry's countenance lightened as he grinned. "I almost felt sorry for him. They thwarted him at every turn."

"Their performance was indeed masterful but their motives were, I think, to be applauded."

"That is why I said, 'almost'. It was not until he trod upon Miss Lockhart's gown that I saw their game. I really am very grateful to them for he would have overwhelmed Henrietta and in all likelihood, angered me."

"Quite so," Lord Hayward agreed. "Doctor Fisher handled himself well, I thought. Comes from a very good family, you know."

"Yes, he is related to Gulworthy, who is, if memory serves me correctly, a brother-in-law of the Earl of Gantray."

Hayward nodded. "Doctor Fisher is Gantray's son. I know his older brother, Gerald, quite well. It seems the earl withdrew any form of support from Fisher when he decided on a medical profession rather than going into the church."

"That seems rather harsh," Harry replied. "His profession is perhaps not quite as esteemed as the church or the law, but it is quite respectable, after all."

"Gantray does not like to have his will crossed."

They were approaching the mine and picked their way around heaps of spoil. The draughty sheds, which should have been occupied by busy bal maidens hammering the copper ore, were deserted. The reason soon became clear. A crowd had gathered further down the slope towards the cliff and faint moans and chatter drifted towards them on the breeze. Dismounting, they led their horses towards the commotion. Snippets of conversation reached their ears.

"Where is it all going to end?"

"He won't be happy 'til we've paid him twice over, in blood!"

"He'll lose that leg, you mark my words!"

As they drew closer, a keening moan soared above the rest. They found Doctor Fisher kneeling by an unconscious man, a woman stood by his side. She had torn the bonnet from her head and was kneading it in her hands. Tears poured unchecked down her face as she moaned her distress.

The man's trousers were muddied and torn revealing a mangled mess of blood and bone. A rough stretcher made of wood and sack lay next to him and at a nod from the doctor, two men stepped forwards and positioned it close to the injured man. Doctor

Fisher swiftly bound his legs together at thigh and ankle and then rolled the man onto his side. The stretcher was pushed beneath the body and the doctor gently rolled him back down. As he stood and turned, Harry stepped forwards.

"What has happened here?"

"Lord Treleven! Good morning. Poor chap fell down one of the ladders, bashed his leg on sharp outcrops of rock all the way down apparently. It is a mercy he has not yet regained consciousness."

Suddenly, a pinch-faced man erupted into the crowd, waving his hands at the women and children who had downed tools to take a closer look. "Get back to work! This is not a circus! Anyone still here in the next thirty seconds will have their wages docked!"

The crowd scattered like leaves blown in the wind.

The man turned to look enquiringly at Harry and Lord Hayward. "Mr Scorrier," he informed them. "Anything I can do for you gentlemen?"

"We were just passing," Harry said, frowning. "Does this sort of thing happen often here, Scorrier?"

"Mining's a dangerous business, sir. Accidents are bound to happen no matter how careful you are."

The men with the stretcher had begun moving towards a little row of cottages on the other side of the workings.

"Gentlemen." The doctor bowed and made to follow them.

Harry laid a restraining hand on his arm. He had seen enough wounds in his time to know when a leg could not be saved. "Anything I can do, Fisher?"

Harry thought he saw something like surprise in his eyes. "Thank you, but those two should suffice." He nodded to the two stretcher-bearers and offered a rather grim smile. "I came here to gain experience and offer my help to those who really need it. It seems both aims are to be achieved today. I cannot save the leg but let us hope I can save the man."

"Oi! You little rat, what have you there?"

Harry turned to see what had occasioned such outrage in Mr Scorrier. Lord Hayward was bent over a rather grimy little girl, her twig-thin arm grasped in his huge hand. She looked terrified and two large, silent tears traced their way through the dust that smeared her face.

"You thievin' varmint." Mr Scorrier raised a hand as if to strike the girl.

"Desist!"

Harry had never before heard that tone from Lord Hayward. It stopped the man in his tracks. In softer tones he added, "You are mistaken, fellow. This young lady is rather to be commended for returning the purse that I had carelessly dropped."

He held it up. "See, the string has broken." Opening it, he withdrew a few coins and taking the girls fist, opened it and dropped them there.

She looked at him for a moment as if he had lost his mind, eyes wide, and then turned and ran before he could change it.

He turned back to Mr Scorrier, a frown between his brows. "Is it really necessary to employ children at so tender an age?"

"We need them for the picking, sir."

"Picking?"

"Yes, sir. Separating the small bits of copper ore from the waste. Takes keen sight and nimble fingers."

Lord Hayward looked sceptical. "That one didn't look like she's had a good meal in a long time."

Mr Scorrier shrugged. "We pay 'em tokens so they can buy their food from us. Encourages them not to drink it away. There's not much more we can do."

"Tokens? You do not even give them coin for their back-breaking labour?"

Not waiting for the inevitable excuses, he mounted his horse. As they rode back up the slope, he turned to Harry.

"If the goods they are allowed to purchase for their 'tokens' are not inferior in quality and overinflated in price, you may call me a moonling! No wonder she tried to filch my purse."

He seethed with an indignation that was very much at odds with his usual air of placidity. They paused as a pack of mules carrying heavy sacks of ore plodded past them.

"I would not be at all surprised if you are right," Harry acknowledged. "One mystery, at least, becomes a little clearer, however. There is no way our men would have agreed to such a system!"

"*One* mystery?" Lord Hayward said softly. "May I enquire as to what the other might be?"

Harry shook his head. "It is all conjecture at the moment."

They had come to a small road. "Our ways part here," Harry said.

Lord Hayward nodded. "Be careful how you tread with Caldwell."

Harry raised a brow.

"You may or may not find yourself in a position to improve conditions here if you have a stake in the mine. Either way, I think you will find he will demand a higher price than you are prepared to pay. It might be worth your while to stall him if this occurs rather than turn him down outright."

Harry watched him ride off. He rarely underestimated his man but it suddenly dawned on him that he had been duped into believing Hayward a bit of a slow top. He had thought he and Belle were something of a mismatch but now a few things began to fall into place. The way he had steered her away from begging an invitation to go sailing came to mind, and the way a smiling look accompanied by a slightly raised eyebrow had silenced her once or twice at dinner. He undoubtedly held her on a light rein, but hold her he did.

This was not the only point on which his judgement had been at fault. Whilst it was natural that his sympathies should have been focused on his own people, he had hardly spared a thought for Caldwell's workers. He had condemned them out of hand. He was now inclined to think they were just as much victims of Caldwell's manipulation. The poor souls he had seen today had looked ragged and miserable. The likelihood was that they were hopelessly in his debt.

When he informed Caldwell of what he had seen that day, the man showed not a glimmer of concern.

"Come, come, sir," he said. "The accident was unfortunate but not unusual. There is no place for sentiment in business."

Even as he felt his ire rise, he remembered Hayward's words and damped it down.

"Perhaps so, sir. But I have been brought up to consider the wellbeing of my dependents."

Caldwell suddenly smiled. "Well, my boy, if you

decide to join with me, there may be some room for negotiation, after all."

"There would have to be," Harry said shortly. "I would require at a very minimum that some of those who lost their jobs would be re-employed and paid *in coin* a fair amount for their labour and ore. I would also like to call in an independent expert to assess the safety of the mine and would need assurances that any shortcomings would be swiftly and thoroughly addressed."

Mr Caldwell looked slightly taken aback and not best pleased by this list of requirements. His colour heightened even as his eyes narrowed.

"You are full of demands, Lord Treleven, but I think you will find negotiation is a two-way process."

"I am listening," Harry said.

Mr Caldwell relaxed back in his chair and steepled his fingers, a conciliatory smile curving his lips. "It is not outside the realms of probability that I might accede to some or even all of your requests," he admitted.

Harry let out a long, slow breath.

"And as you are so concerned with the wellbeing of your dependents, I hope my proposal will find favour with you."

Harry waited with barely restrained impatience as Caldwell stood and poured out two glasses of claret. He passed one to him before perching on the edge of his desk.

"Yes, on reflection, I think I might be amenable to all of your demands if you will but agree to support my claim to your lovely sister's hand in marriage. I told you, did I not, that I wished to settle down? Turn respectable if you will."

Harry's brows shot up. The very thought of his gentle, shy sister being aligned with Caldwell was anathema to him. Hayward's words of warning were forgotten as he surged to his feet. "Never!"

A slightly ugly look came over his host's face. "Never is a long time, Lord Treleven. Fortunes change, sometimes for the worse. Would it not be better to secure a comfortable and safe future for Miss Treleven, now, whilst you still have something to bargain with?"

Harry carefully put down the untouched glass of claret and surveyed his host coolly.

"I do not think you would suit, sir," he said with icy politeness. "Neither do I think we could ever do business together. It is not a fine house or a gently bred wife that makes a gentleman, Mr Caldwell. Good day."

Even though he had lost his opportunity to influence the mine owner, he could not regret his words. He was not prepared to even pretend to barter with his sister as collateral. If he had done so he would have had to ask Henrietta to play along, forcing her into the man's company. It would have caused her much distress and he doubted very much she would have been able to carry it off.

Although he did not much feel like it, he decided he must make the overdue call on Mr Treen on the way home. Knowing it was much quicker to cross the fields rather than navigate the maze of narrow, deep-set lanes, he unlatched a gate and left the road. He racked his brains to try and find another way to put pressure on Caldwell. There was none, of course. Then he recalled the conversation about Boodle. He had allowed Caldwell to buy him out and would know of any other investors, perhaps they could be persuaded to bring some pressure to bear on him.

Lost in his thoughts, he did not see the sudden dip in the ground that made Hermes stumble. Instinct came to his rescue. He raised the reins and leant back in the saddle, easing the weight on his horse's shoulders and allowing him to recover. His mount seemed unsettled by the incident, so he dismounted and went to his head. Stroking his muzzle gently, he calmed him with a string of softly uttered words. He was, he realised, standing in a large saucer shaped dip. The grass had been disrupted by wide cracks that ran through the soil.

"Lord Treleven, sir!"

He turned to see a ruddy-faced man striding purposefully towards him. Leading Hermes, he went to meet him.

"Good morning, Mr Treen. I had meant to come to you yesterday, but something else came up."

"I never expected you to come yourself, sir. Very good of you it is. And to think you nearly took a tumble for your troubles."

Harry grinned at him. "My own fault, I wasn't paying attention."

"To be honest, milord, I'm surprised as your horse stepped a foot in that dip. It appeared a few weeks ago and my sheep won't go anywhere near it." He shook his head. "Danged if I can explain it."

Having decided to take a trip to Padstow to visit Mr Boodle, he had little desire to discuss the vagaries of Mr Treen's sheep. "Well, never mind. Perhaps you *can* explain the matters which require attention?" Harry said gently.

"Oh, yes, well it's nothing too serious, sir. Some of the fencing needs redoing, some of my sheep got out and it was a right old job to round them up again. Come this way, sir."

* * *

Thoroughly enjoying having her son within her orbit again, Belle decided to take him to see the boats in the harbour at Padstow. Katherine and Henrietta accompanied her. Edmund clapped and wriggled in Belle's arms as they went down to the harbour. Several fishing boats were tied up together, and one larger, tall-masted ship towered regally above them.

They descended from the barouche and began to walk along the quay, the little boy held in a firm grip by Belle on one side and Henrietta on the other. They laughed as he tried to drag them forwards, clearly not comprehending why anyone would walk when it was possible to run. They passed a set of steps that led onto a narrow stretch of sand. A woman sat on each of the top three steps, each wrapped in warm woollen shawls. They were busy gutting fish. One turned a lined face and gave the boy a toothless grin. Edmund gave her a wide smile.

"Are they slipp'ry?" he asked.

The woman gave a throaty laugh. "Ain't you 'andsome? Come and feel for yourself."

She held out the fish but Belle shook her head. "Thank you, my good lady, another time perhaps."

"I want to feel the fish!" Edmund complained as she dragged him along the quay.

Henrietta squatted beside him, pointing down to the sand. "What do you think they are doing?"

Two men were wielding axes, slowly revealing a huge timber beam that lay hidden beneath several layers of barnacles.

The little boy strained to be free, clearly wanting to join in. "Let me go! Let me go!"

Katherine, who stood a little behind the others, felt a light hand on her arm. She turned her head and looked straight into the amused eyes of Lord Treleven. For some strange reason, she felt a blush steal over her cheeks. He winked and took a step forwards.

"Edmund, gentlemen do not whine!"

The boy's head snapped around at this authoritative utterance, his grey eyes huge and considering.

"Harry!" Henrietta smiled, rising to her feet.

He nodded and took her place beside Edmund. "It is probably from an old wreck," he explained.

"What's wreck?"

Harry pointed to the large boat. "See that ship?"

Edmund nodded enthusiastically.

"It's made from lots of pieces of wood, like that one. But sometimes the big ships fall to the bottom of the sea."

The little boys eyes widened. "They get covered in barnacles. That's what the men are removing with their axes."

Harry grinned at the little boy. "Would you like to go on that big ship?"

Edmund looked unsure. "Will it sink to the bottom of the sea?"

Harry laughed. "No, it will not, I assure you."

"Take me on the ship!"

Harry gave him a stern look.

"Please."

"I think you should apologise to the ladies first, don't you?"

Edmund turned solemnly and bowed. "I apol'gise."

Harry cast Belle an enquiring glance. As she smiled and nodded, he hoisted her son onto his shoulders. "I will meet you in The White Hart Inn, ladies."

They turned and made their way towards the town, past the tall three-storey customs house. They came to a small square, several narrow cobbled streets, crammed with houses leading off from it. It was market day and the space was filled with stalls selling everything from fish, fruit, and pies, to pots, pans, bonnets or fine examples of bone lace.

They paused at one that had an array of wooden toys.

"Oh, look at how skilfully made this is," Belle exclaimed, holding up a model of a three-masted ship. "I must have it for Edmund."

"It is indeed exquisite," agreed Katherine, considering the delicate masts. "But do you think it will withstand his enthusiastic attentions?"

Belle laughed. "You are right, it would probably not last the day."

Katherine picked up a more sturdy looking fishing boat and raised a brow.

"Not as pretty," Belle said a little regretfully, "but far more sensible."

"Miss Treleven! Miss Treleven!"

They turned to see two ladies approaching. One was young, tall and slender, with vibrant bright red locks peeping from beneath her bonnet, the other older, shorter, and quite stout. Her hair was also red, but had sadly faded.

"Lady Humphrey, Miss Humphrey," Henrietta nodded politely before introducing her friends.

"I was wondering why you had not returned our visit." Lady Humphrey's smile did not quite reach her eyes. "But as I now realise you have guests, I shall forgive the slight."

Henrietta coloured. "No slight was intended, ma'am, I assure you. We have many calls to make, but as yet we have had no time."

"Oh, what is it you have there?" said Miss Humphrey, eyeing the toy Lady Hayward held.

As it was quite clear what she had, Belle did not answer but held up the little boat.

"How quaint," Miss Humphrey continued, "and how *kind* of you to purchase something so crudely carved." She turned to Henrietta. "Is your brother with you today?"

"Yes," said Henrietta. "He is to meet us at The White Hart Inn."

Miss Humphrey's lips opened on a smile, revealing a set of very yellow teeth. It was a shame as, apart from that one imperfection, she really was quite beautiful.

"Oh, how splendid," she twittered, linking her arm with Henrietta's. "We will accompany you if you don't mind, for I, for one, am quite, quite parched."

Belle and Katherine exchanged knowing glances and fell in behind them as they threaded through the mass of people.

"It is strange, is it not," murmured Belle, "how

shopping can make one quite suddenly so very thirsty?"

Katherine bit her lip.

"So," Lady Humphrey said, almost as soon as they were seated. "How did you find your season, Miss Treleven? I would have asked when we called on you, but I am afraid with all the excitement of the return of your brother, it quite slipped my mind. I assume you did not catch an eligible bachelor? I am sure your mother must have mentioned it if you had indeed been so fortunate."

"No, ma'am," Henrietta confirmed quietly.

Miss Humphrey tittered. "Oh, but then you have never been very good at putting yourself forwards, have you?"

"I have never understood why some girls seem to think it so important to make a match when they are only just out," said Belle. 'It would be so dull to enjoy only one season before one settled down, don't you think?"

Lady Humphrey's suddenly narrowed eyes seemed to suggest that she did not agree.

"I often saw Miss Treleven positively engulfed by admirers," she continued. "I must say, I thought she displayed very good judgement not to make so important a choice so quickly, for I have seen some quite disastrous results when unions are made in such a scrambling way."

"A young lady should not be required to make any such judgement," Lady Humphrey said. "That is what her parents, or in this case, parent, is for. Do not tell me, Lady Hayward, that your own did not influence your choice."

Belle smiled, but her eyes glittered in a way that would have made any of her family, if they had been present, very wary.

"As it happens, Lady Humphrey, they did not. I had accepted an offer before they knew anything about it."

"Well!" Lady Humphrey said, her tone dripping with disapproval.

Belle smiled widely at her. "Do not look so shocked, ma'am. Their faith in my judgement was not misplaced. They thoroughly approve of my husband and I could not be happier. But, enough about me." She turned to Miss Humphrey, her eyes dwelling for a moment on her gown, which was not of the latest fashion. "I do not think I saw you in town, did you not come up for the season?"

Katherine felt it was time to step in. Although she understood Belle's desire to protect her friend, she could not help feeling some sympathy for Miss Humphrey, who had turned an interesting shade of pink, the colour unfortunately clashing with her lovely hair.

"I have not enjoyed a season myself," she smiled. "I expect you have some local assemblies that you attend?"

The young lady pouted. "Yes, of course, but they are sadly flat."

Her gaze suddenly shifted over Katherine's shoulder and her rather sour expression was suddenly transformed.

"Lord Treleven!" she exclaimed. "Who have you there? I declare, that sweet little boy could almost be your son!"

Katherine could not disagree. Apart from anything else he appeared quite at home handling a child so young. Edmund had been giggling as they entered the room and Lord Treleven's eyes were alight with laughter, but they lost some of their sparkle when he perceived the company.

Harry placed Edmund carefully on the floor and bowed politely. "I can assure you, ma'am, that he is not."

Edmund ran to his mama. Belle scooped him up and offered him the toy boat.

Miss Humphrey gave a trill of laughter. "Well, how could he be? But never mind that, we have just been saying how dull the local assemblies are, Lord Treleven, and seeing you has put me in mind of something."

"Indeed, Miss Humphrey?"

"I have often heard that your father used to hold the most splendid Michaelmas balls. Isn't that so, Mama?"

"Indeed it is. What a good idea, child. Miss Treleven was just saying how many visits she and her mama need to make – it would be the perfect solution."

Miss Humphrey clapped excitedly. "Oh, please say you will, sir. I vow I will expire with disappointment, if you don't!"

Katherine could see by the sudden stiffening of his posture that he was not overly enamoured with this idea.

"Although I would not wish to be the cause of so calamitous an event, Miss Humphrey, I am not at all sure my mother will be able to commit to such a vast undertaking at the present moment."

The pout appeared again.

"Nonsense," Belle said lightly. She considered Henrietta for a moment and then smiled. "I think it a splendid idea. You should at least put the suggestion forward, Lord Treleven. She has, after all, many hands more than willing and able to help her."

CHAPTER 10

Any hope that he might harbour that his mother would veto the proposal was quickly snuffed out at dinner that evening.

"Although I hesitate to satisfy such an impertinent request, coming as it does from a young lady I consider very coming and lacking altogether in modesty or manners, the idea does have some merit." She held up her hand before Harry could protest. "We do indeed owe several persons a visit, as do you I suspect. On top of this, we would not only provide entertainment for our guests, but Henrietta would, I feel sure, be more comfortable at a ball held in her own home than she did when surrounded by strangers in town. Besides all this, I feel some sort of celebration to mark your home-coming is in order."

Harry, driven to the last ditch, looked to his sister for support.

"You cannot wish for it, Henrietta."

His sister glanced at the other ladies seated around

the table, and received an encouraging look from them all.

"I think I might," she said slowly. "Could we invite Doctor Fisher? He makes me feel at ease, if I could dance with him first I would feel braver, I think."

"Bravo," Katherine said gently.

Harry's surprised gaze fell upon her. "Do not tell me that you wish to dance until dawn, Miss Lockhart?"

If timid Henrietta could overcome her fears, Katherine was determined she would match her. She would not only attend the ball, she would enjoy every moment of it!

"I love to dance," she informed him.

She looked over at Lady Treleven. "Please say you will let me help organise it. I would so enjoy it."

"Of course you would," Harry murmured.

Lady Treleven gave no sign she had heard her son. "I would be very grateful for the assistance." She glanced down the table. "You gentlemen may entertain yourselves this evening, we ladies have a lot of details to discuss, which you would find quite tedious."

Harry turned to Lord Hayward as soon as they left the room.

"Let us retire to my study, we will be both more private and more comfortable."

When they were both settled with a brandy, Harry gave his guest a very direct look.

"I think it is time we stopped fencing with each other, Hayward."

That gentleman turned his sleepy gaze upon Harry and raised an enquiring brow.

"Stop trying to play the slow-top," he said briskly.

"I have realised there is nothing much that passes you by. Furthermore, if you came down here to look for a property, then it is I who am the moonling!"

Lord Hayward dropped the act. His eyes sharpened. "I must be losing my touch. What is it that gave me away?"

"Your words of advice for a start. You were quite correct. Caldwell did demand too high a price."

Lord Hayward looked pensive. "And did you take my advice?"

Harry shrugged. "I tried at first, but I could not play with Henrietta as the bargaining chip."

"It is a pity," Lord Hayward sighed. "But I suspected as much."

"And then I visited Boodle today."

"Ah," Lord Hayward said with his customary calm. "Anything else?"

"Yes," confirmed Harry. "Whilst entertaining your son upon the Lady Lucy, which is at present docked in Padstow harbour, I met an old colleague of mine."

"Really?"

"Yes, a military gentleman. He was unfortunately quite vague about why his regiment were visiting."

"I commend his discretion," Lord Hayward murmured.

"Damn his discretion. What interest do you have in Caldwell?" he asked. "Be frank, man!"

"Ah, now we come to it," he said thoughtfully. "You must forgive my reticence to confide in you, Treleven."

"Must I?" Harry said tersely.

Lord Hayward smiled. "Yes, I really think you must. Although my wife spoke highly of you, and in general she is a good judge of character, I felt in this case, I could not trust her instinct alone. I'm afraid I was not convinced you were to be trusted in this *particular* matter."

"Why ever not?" Harry said, exasperated.

"Your reputation goes before you," Lord Hayward said briefly.

"My reputation? If you refer to my duel, I cannot think what bearing it might have on anything."

"No, no. Your duel was unfortunate, but it was what came afterwards that concerned me."

Harry's eyes narrowed. "What do you know about what came afterwards?"

"I believe you were involved in, shall we say, some illicit dealings?"

"How the devil would you know that?" Harry demanded.

"Lloyd's Coffee House," Lord Hayward said. "I do not know if you are aware of the fact, but most men interested in ships and their insurance gather there."

"And?" said Harry.

"And, Treleven, they base their speculation on the reputation of the ship owners and captains. Lloyd's have agents in ports around the world. They have been very useful to us in many ways. And sometimes they report things that might be of interest to certain of our agents. We were aware that you were operating between Europe and America."

"Were you, by God? And who, exactly, is we?"

"The government in times of war and certain members of it, who have invested heavily in shipping, at other times."

Harry began to see the light.

"Has this something to do with the wreck?"

"Indeed it does. It was an East Indiaman. It was carrying a very valuable cargo."

"But if it was insured, why this cloak and dagger investigation?"

"The usual channels were employed at first, of course. They turned up nothing. The insurers are not satisfied in this case. And then there is the king."

Harry looked startled.

"He also had an interest in this particular cargo. He had procured a number of jewels. In particular, a very rare and large sapphire, which cannot be easily replaced."

"He always has had a taste for the exotic," Harry acknowledged. "But why suspect Caldwell?"

"He had for many years a good reputation as a sound businessman. But he has himself lost two ships in the last year, both of which were heavily insured. There were suggestions that both ships veered from the usual route but he was given the benefit of the doubt on both occasions. However, the captain of the wrecked Indiaman used to work for him. It may be coincidence that the ship was lost so close to his new residence or it might not. But it has occurred to me that if something smoky is going on, and if he has something to hide, he has miles of underground tunnels which might come in very handy for the purpose."

"And you thought I might be a part of it?" Harry said, disgusted.

"Hardly," Lord Hayward said gently, "but perhaps sympathetic enough to turn a blind eye? Cornwall is renowned for smuggling and wrecking, after all. Very few of the salvaged goods from a wrecked ship are given over to the customs officer, after all, even though those who have them, may claim salvage."

"Intentionally wrecking a ship and harvesting goods washed up on the beach are two very different things. I know no wreckers. And you must be aware that it can take years for a salvage claim to be paid, if it is at all! The government cannot expect the poor and hungry to follow their system until they make it fair!"

"I sympathise," Lord Hayward said. "But if we all ignored the law when it did not suit, there would be anarchy. But you perhaps begin to see why I did not, at first, fully trust you in this matter?"

Harry was a fair man. He could see his point. "I suppose I do," he conceded.

"That has, however, ceased to be the case," Lord Hayward informed him, smiling. "As a matter of fact, I hope that we can work together. Our interests are now aligned, for I am sure you would like nothing better than for Caldwell to be removed from your vicinity."

"Wouldn't I just," Harry muttered.

Lord Hayward stood and held out his hand. "Let's shake on it."

Never one to bear a grudge for long, Harry shook his hand and smiled.

"You're a dark horse, Hayward. I think I may have something that will be of interest to you." He strolled across to his desk, opened a drawer and withdrew a small velvet pouch. He threw it over to Lord Hayward.

Catching it deftly in one hand, he tipped its contents into his huge palm. He glanced quickly up at Harry before reaching for his quizzing glass and examining them carefully.

"If I am not very much mistaken, Treleven, I have here a ruby and a rather fine diamond. Do you mind me asking where you acquired them?"

"Not at all. Miss Lockhart found them, on the beach below Caldwell's mine. She thought them bits of glass."

"And did you correct her misapprehension?" Lord Hayward enquired.

Harry shook his head. "No. I wanted time to work through my suspicions. They seemed outrageous, fantastical even. But I was uneasy about the wreck, there was wild talk of Caldwell's miners having harvested the goods and even of having caused it. Yet there was no evidence to implicate them, until those two little beauties turned up." He frowned. "I still don't think I believe it. He keeps his workers in abject poverty, treats them little better than slaves, I cannot think he would trust them with something that could ruin him. They can have no love for the man, after all."

"No" mused Lord Hayward. "I suppose it is not outside the realms of possibility that they were washed up on the shore. I certainly need more to go on if I am to apply to the local magistrate for the power of search and seizure."

"It may be within the realms of possibility, but not, I think, probability." Harry grinned at him.

"Go on."

"They were found very close to an adit that should have been pouring water after hours of heavy rain, yet was not."

A wide smile slowly spread across Lord Hayward's

face. "I think we have him, Treleven. I think we have him."

"There may be a conflict of interest there, I'm afraid," warned Harry. "The local magistrate is Lord Humphrey. He is also the only other investor in the mine."

"I am aware," Lord Hayward informed him. "But from what I have been able to discover, he leaves it all to Caldwell. I think you will find that he will very quickly distance himself from the man and help in any way he can in order to exonerate himself from any culpability in the matter."

## CHAPTER 11

The following day dawned overcast but dry. At breakfast, Katherine announced she was going to drive over to Helagon to see Mrs Nance.

"Would you like me to come with you, my dear?" enquired Mrs Abbott. "I am quite happy to although I was going to plan the flower arrangements for the ball."

"There is no need," Katherine said. "I wish to see if Mrs Nance would be willing to lend Mrs Kemp a hand with some of the preparations."

"That is a very good idea, Miss Lockhart," Lady Treleven said approvingly. "And it is very kind of you to think of it."

"I will aid you with the writing of the invitations," smiled Belle. "I don't suppose there will be time to send them to the printers."

"No," agreed Lady Treleven. "The moon will be full at the end of next week, so we cannot put it off."

"I will come with you," Harry said suddenly to

Katherine. "I wish to have a word with Mr Hewel and I think I will find him there."

"As you wish," Katherine said. She glanced a little wistfully out of the window at the rolling parkland beyond.

"Do you drive or ride?" she asked after a few moments.

"Ride. Hermes requires a considerable amount of exercise but stubbornly refuses to let anyone else mount him."

"I wonder," she began, and then hesitated.

Harry raised a brow. "What is it you wonder, Miss Lockhart?"

She looked a little bashful. "Would it be terribly rude of me, if I asked to borrow a horse? It seems an age since I have enjoyed a gallop."

He smiled at her. "Not at all. I'll meet you at the stables in half an hour, and you may take your pick of the few that we have."

He was amply rewarded by the wide, warm smile bestowed upon him.

Katherine hurried into her close-fitting pale blue riding habit; it was an old friend and severe in style. She had strictly forbidden Ayles to tamper with it in any way and raised a stern eyebrow when she regarded her habit shirt.

"Oh, it is only a bit of lace I've added to the collar," she said, as she finished tying the soft muslin cravat in a neat bow. "There's nothing wrong with a bit of—"

"Prettifying," Katherine finished for her. "I know, Ayles."

When she arrived at the stables, Lord Treleven was

speaking to Lord Hayward who was already mounted. He touched his hand to his hat and smiled, before trotting off.

"Where is he off to today?" asked Katherine.

"Oh, here and there," said Harry vaguely. "I am afraid our stable is not what it once was, Miss Lockhart."

Kenver nodded politely as they entered and touched his cap. "I was thinking you might like to take out Misty, ma'am," he said, indicating a placid looking mare. "She's Miss Treleven's horse and has a very nice temper."

"Perhaps," Katherine murmured, walking on until she came to the last stall. Here she found a bay mare of about sixteen hands. She looked powerful, her neck arched nicely and she had a proud bearing.

"This one, I think," Katherine smiled. "She has quality."

Kenver gave a short laugh. "She may have quality but she also has the devil's own temper, ma'am. We call her Countess, for she's very demanding and likes her own way!"

"That does not mean she has to have it." Katherine glanced at Lord Treleven. "You did say, sir, that I might choose?"

"By all means," he said and then suddenly grinned. "Perhaps I should fetch a flask of brandy in case you take a tumble, Miss Lockhart."

Katherine smiled at his sally, remembering their first meeting. "I doubt very much it will be necessary."

The mare behaved well enough as she mounted her, but as soon as she took the reins in her hands she snorted and reared. Katherine did not panic, but kept her weight well forwards and her hands soft. As soon as all four hooves were firmly on the floor again, she stroked her neck and murmured to her.

"There, Countess, you're eager for a run, as am I, but there is no need for these manners."

Kenver and Harry exchanged a look of approval.

"We will take a ride through the park," Harry said. "I usually do every morning, and we can cut cross country to Helagon."

"As you wish."

After a few minor skirmishes, Countess discovered that Katherine was ready for all her tricks and settled down recognising the skill and confidence of her rider.

"My compliments," Harry smiled. "I have only ever seen one other lady with such a fine seat."

"Oh? And who was that?" Katherine enquired.

"Lady Bray, who has just married my friend, Sir Philip Bray. You would like her, I think."

"Then I must hope to make her acquaintance," Katherine said.

"If you settle here, you no doubt will. They are bound to visit me some time or other. I would have invited them to our ball if they were not so newly wed."

"You have resigned yourself to it, then?"

He gave a short laugh. "I was outnumbered and outgunned! I did not object on principle but I would have preferred it to be nearer to Christmas, I must admit. I have a lot on my mind at the moment."

Katherine would have liked to know what was troubling him, but she did not ask as she was enjoying his company and did not wish to risk being rebuffed.

A long, flat expanse of grass stretched out before

them. Harry met her gaze and quirked a brow. "Shall we?"

Katherine answered by touching her heel lightly to Countess's side and moving smoothly into a canter. She felt a smile stretch across her face as they switched to a gallop her mount proving as swift as she had hoped. She exchanged a smiling glance with Lord Treleven who easily matched her pace and noted the sparkle in his eyes, realising he was enjoying this just as much as she. They gradually slowed as they neared a flock of sheep that were grazing nearby.

"It is good to see you enjoying yourself, Miss Lockhart. The exercise has put a bloom in your cheeks. It suits you."

"I used to ride out every day at home," she said a little wistfully.

"Do you miss it very much?" Harry enquired gently.

Katherine put on a brave smile. "Do not encourage me in melancholy reflections, sir," she said briskly. "I am sure I will grow very fond of Helagon once I become accustomed to it. It is just that it is a little strange to feel," she paused as if searching for the right words, "oh, I don't know, a little lost, I suppose."

"It is completely understandable, Miss Lockhart." His gaze drifted off into the middle distance for a moment as if his thoughts were far away. "No one understands that feeling more than I," he said softly. "You have lost your anchor and are drifting with the tide."

"Yes, that is exactly it," she said quietly.

Harry's gaze refocused, the lurking laughter that

was so often present, apparent again. "Tell me about this harpy who has driven you out."

Katherine laughed. "I would not call her a harpy!"

"No, I will not have it. She is a harpy, I am quite sure of it!"

"I will not say so," Katherine said. "She is just a little irritable, shall we say. But then she is in the family way so I am sure it is quite understandable."

"So is Belle in the family way," he pointed out. "And I would not describe her as irritable."

"No, she is delightful," Katherine smiled.

"I agree," Harry said. "As are you."

Their eyes met, Katherine's widening in surprise at the compliment, which somehow felt quite genuine. Her heart began to beat a little faster as he brought his horse closer to her own. He leaned towards her and the mad thought that he might kiss her flashed across her mind, and yet she did not move.

Her hands had gone slack on the reins so when Countess suddenly moved forwards and kicked out her back legs at Hermes, she was not prepared. She fell forwards and clasped her round the neck, only just saving herself from a fall. She thought she heard a high-pitched, faint whistling and looked around in surprise and then stilled, her eyes wide.

Hermes had reared at the attack, avoiding the intended blow, but Harry had him under control in a matter of moments.

"What is it?" he said quickly when he saw Katherine's expression.

She pointed to something behind him. He glanced over his shoulder and then swiftly dismounted, striding over to a sheep that had collapsed onto its side. It twitched quite violently for a few moments and then went unnaturally still.

She saw him pull something from it and examine it closely.

Dismounting herself, she walked over to him.

"I heard a strange whistling sound," she began, but her words dried up as she saw what held his attention.

It was some sort of dart. It was slender, made of a light coloured wood and had a white feather on one end and a very sharp, glistening point on the other. It occurred to Katherine that it was not long enough to have reached any vital organ.

"My God!" he breathed, his eyes flashing angrily. "This could have hit you!"

"Or you," Katherine said quietly, her brain working rapidly. "Are you going to tell me it is a poacher again?"

Their glances again met and held, this time her heart hammering for a quite different, but just as alarming reason.

Amazed at how calm her voice sounded, she said, "A poisoned dart seems a little exotic for a Cornish poacher, don't you think? Not to mention the fact that it is the second time you have come close to being killed, my lord."

Lord Treleven was suddenly full of urgency. "Get back on your horse," he snapped. "We must return to the house, quickly. Whoever did this, may have more of them!"

They both turned and ran. Harry threw her up into the saddle and then vaulted onto Hermes.

Without speaking they raced back the way they had come, not slowing until they neared the stables.

"I must request that you say nothing of this to anyone," he finally said.

"But, surely——" she began, but he cut her off.

"To anyone! I will explain more to you when I can, you have my word. No one else is in any danger I am sure, and informing them of this will only inspire terror in my mother."

"You cannot go out again!" she said, startled. "They may still be out there."

"Do not alarm yourself, Miss Lockhart. I will not be so predictable in my movements this time and I hardly think there is someone lurking behind every bush."

"Do you know who is responsible?" she asked.

"Yes. There can be no doubt. But I hope that he will be dealt with by the end of today."

With that she had to be satisfied for he suddenly veered off, heading towards the home wood.

When she entered the house, she felt suddenly drained.

"You are back so soon?" Lady Treleven said, surprised, just then coming into the hall with Belle.

"Why, you look quite pale," said Belle, concerned. "Are you ill?"

"Yes," Katherine murmured. "Yes, that is why I have returned. It is just a headache, I shall go and lie down for a while."

Belle came forward and took her arm. "Here, I will help you to your room."

When they were out of earshot of Lady Treleven,

Belle murmured softly, "I hope Lord Treleven has not upset you in some way? He is a card, always jesting and sometimes quite outrageous but he means nothing by it, I assure you."

They had reached the door to her chamber and Katherine found herself quite unequal to the task of fielding any more questions. "Please, Belle, I cannot talk just now."

She closed her door softly behind her and leaned back against it, closing her eyes. What could it all mean? He had nearly kissed her and then he had nearly been murdered. Her head really was beginning to ache, it was filled with a jumble of images and tangled thoughts.

The wall of protection she had built around herself had crumbled to dust in the moment he had leant towards her, his eyes full of a gentle tenderness that had stopped her breath. She had never allowed even Mr Sharpe, a man who she thought she had been in love with, the liberty of a kiss, yet she had made no move to deny Lord Treleven. The pain of Mr Sharpe's betrayal and loss had been nothing to the stab of agony she had felt when she realised just how close Lord Treleven had come to death.

She stumbled to her bed and sank face down into her pillows, clutching them fiercely. Even if he had been about to kiss her, it meant nothing. He had given no other sign that he felt any great affection for her, and as Belle had pointed out, he was known for being outrageous. She must not refine too much upon it, the shared exhilaration of their ride and his clear admiration of her skill as a horsewoman had probably caused the moment of madness. He did, after all, have a history of behaving rashly.

She rolled onto her back and sighed long and deep. If only he came back safe, she thought she would forgive him anything, even nearly making a fool of her.

\* \* \*

Harry's senses were heightened as he weaved an erratic course towards the Padstow road. But even though he remained watchful, part of his mind lingered on Miss Lockhart. What had he been thinking? He grimaced. He had not been thinking. When she had been flying along beside him, he had felt a kinship with her, the feeling deepening when she had shown her vulnerability by admitting to feeling lost. But the blush of pink in her cheeks and the green flecks dancing in her eyes had made him feel something else entirely. He had glimpsed the fire that lurked beneath her sobriety and self-possession. He wondered what had happened to her that she kept that side of herself locked away.

A wry grin curved his lips. Perhaps it was just as well for him that she did. The poise she had shown when presented with his bloodied arm had seemed to him unfeminine. He had not admired it then, but he was beginning to think he was a fool. She had displayed it again today, her cool head and clear thinking had understood the threat to them in an instant, but rather than falling into hysterics she had acted with alacrity, following his lead without a moment's hesitation.

He finally gained the road and saw a cloud of dust

in the distance. The familiar sound of a troop of horses galloping reached his ears, and then a host of blue and gold uniforms met his eyes. Lord Hayward led the way. Harry raised his hand in acknowledgement to the troop, many of whom he knew, and fell in beside him.

"You got your permission, I see," he said.

Lord Hayward grinned. "After much outrage and complaint."

Harry chuckled. "I can imagine, Lord Humphrey has pompous down to a fine art!"

"Doesn't he just," agreed Lord Hayward.

"There has been a development," Harry said.

Lord Hayward showed no great surprise at his news.

"I wondered about the first incident," he admitted. "But now it seems clear he wanted you out of the way. It seems he had a change of heart once he had met you. Probably thought he could get you on side. It would be far more to his advantage than to have an unknown neighbour replace you."

Harry frowned. "All this for the chance of getting Henrietta?"

"Without your protection his offer might have gained more favour. But now it is also personal, I think. Mr Caldwell does not strike me as someone who likes to be crossed."

"He must be mad!"

Lord Hayward chuckled. "More than one man has been made mad by love."

"You're a mighty cool fish," Harry said.

"Usually," Lord Hayward said softly. "But I nearly killed a man with my bare hands, once, for love."

"Who?" he asked, intrigued.

Lord Hayward gave him his sleepy smile. "Ask your friend, Sir Philip, he knows all about it."

"You may be sure I will."

"I would not, however, compare myself to Caldwell. It was not done in cold blood but in the heat of the moment, and the provocation was great."

As they came to the mine, the workers stopped what they were doing and stood, mouths agape, as the cavalcade passed them. Mr Scorrier was soon seen scurrying towards them.

"What is the meaning of this?" he exclaimed.

Lord Hayward retrieved a rolled piece of parchment from his pocket, unfurled it, and waved it under the man's nose. "This is a document giving me the right to search this mine and seize anything that I might find that I feel should be handed over to His Majesty's government."

Mr Scorrier grabbed it and rapidly scanned its contents. "I would ask, sir, that you wait until Mr Caldwell can be sent for."

"I think not," replied Lord Hayward. "I will send two men down to investigate the adit that leads to the beach below, you will provide me with someone to guide them."

Grumbling and cursing under his breath, Mr Scorrier walked over to two men who sat on a pile of sacks, chewing on some bread. One of them hurried off, the other approached.

"You're wasting your time," Mr Scorrier assured them.

"That remains to be seen," said Lord Hayward.

Two of the dragoons dismounted and followed the

man towards the mine entrance that was cut into the rock of the cliff.

"Get back to work, you layabouts!" Mr Scorrier shouted at the women and children who still stood, silently watching.

"He seemed very sure we would not find anything," Harry said. "Either he is a very convincing liar or he knows nothing about it."

"We can only act upon what we know," Lord Hayward said. "But I hope you are mistaken for we have truly shown our hand now. We will not get a second chance."

Mr Caldwell soon arrived, his colour high and his small eyes angry. He looked at Lord Hayward in some amazement. "You! What have you to do with this outrage?"

"Good day, Mr Caldwell. I am merely overseeing this investigation."

"What investigation?" he demanded.

"Calm yourself, sir," Lord Hayward said softly. "We are merely trying to discover what happened to the very valuable cargo that was aboard the East Indiaman that sank. If you have nothing to hide, you have nothing to fear."

A sly gleam brightened his eyes. "Oh, you will not find anything, of that you can be sure."

His eyes shifted to Harry. "And what right do you have to be here, sir?"

"Perhaps you should clarify that comment, Caldwell," he said softly. "Do you mean 'here' as in at the mine, or 'here' as in of this earth?"

Lord Hayward sent him a warning look.

"I wish you would not talk in riddles," Mr Caldwell

said tersely. "I have no idea what you are referring to."

There was a murmuring as the two men who had been sent into the mine reappeared, their uniforms damp and grubby.

"Well," said Mr Caldwell. "And did you find anything?"

The soldier addressed Lord Hayward. "Nothing there, sir."

Mr Caldwell gave him a cold stare. "If you have quite finished disrupting my day, you may leave. You may be sure I shall be writing to both Lord Humphrey and the home secretary to complain."

They moved off slowly, disappointment writ clear on their faces. This time Harry and Lord Hayward brought up the rear.

"I was so sure," said Harry.

One of the dragoons who had conducted the search, rode back towards them. He pulled a piece of sacking out of his pocket and a small silver key.

"I didn't want to say anything in front of the mine owner, sir," he said quietly, "but something was down there, only it's been moved. There was also a wooden plank and a pile of rubble and rock next to the adit, sir, almost as if it had been blocked and recently cleared."

"Thank you, Roberts," he said, taking both items from his grasp.

He turned to Harry. "He must have got wind that the dragoons were about and taken the precaution of moving his booty." He looked at the little key. "We missed our chance, this is very little to go on."

"Let me see it," Harry said.

Lord Hayward went to drop it in his palm, but Hermes sidled and it fell to the track. Harry quickly dismounted to retrieve it. He picked it up and glanced back towards the mine. A ragged little girl was running towards them.

"I do believe that is the little imp who you rewarded for trying to pick your pocket," he murmured.

"Sir, sir," she panted as she came up to them. "Ma said I should tell you, something happened last night. Everyone was told to finish their shift early 'n' that never happens. Likes his pound of flesh, she always says."

Lord Hayward smiled at her. "Thank your ma for me, will you."

"There's more," she said breathlessly, she was wheezing and suddenly she bent over, her emaciated body racked by a series of chesty coughs. "It's the dust," she explained. "Gets in the lungs, Ma says. Anyways, we were told to get home and stay there."

"And did you?" asked Lord Hayward.

She shook her head. "No, and I got a right clout for it."

"From Scorrier?" Harry asked, his face darkening.

"No," she grinned. "From Ma!"

"What did you see?" he asked gently.

Her eyes widened. "Ma told me I was making it up, but I weren't, honest."

"Making what up, child?" Lord Hayward said patiently.

"I saw old belly ache, that's Mr Scorrier, headed towards the mine, with four others. I think they were men, but they had a sort of dress on and a funny thing on their heads."

In a few swift moves Harry removed his cravat and

wound it round his head into something resembling a turban.

The little girl laughed. "Yes, like that."

Harry reached into his pocket and retrieved his purse. He took her dirt-smeared hand in his and dropped some coins into it. "Tell your Ma to take you and the rest of your family and go home."

The little girl was speechless for a few moments. Her small fist closed around the coins. "Thank you, sir."

They watched as she turned and fled back down the track.

Lord Hayward gave him a lopsided smile. "That was very generous of you, Treleven, considering the information only confirms most of what we already know."

Harry grinned. "Don't give up yet, Hayward. The cargo is still here. Somewhere. He will have to move it sometime, and we must make sure we are there when he does."

"I cannot keep the king's dragoons here indefinitely," he said. "And then there is the business of keeping you alive in the interim."

Harry grinned, the light of battle in his eyes. "I'm a hard man to kill. Besides, I don't think all my nine lives are used up just yet, Hayward."

They had come to a crossroads.

"I'm for Helagon," Harry said.

"Give me a moment and I'll be with you."

After a brief exchange with one of the regiment, he returned.

Harry gave him a quizzical look. "Fancy yourself in the role of bodyguard, do you?"

Lord Hayward gave a lazy grin. "I hardly think even Caldwell would have the audacity to try and murder you twice in one day. Especially now, when he knows you're on to him."

CHAPTER 12

Katherine could not rest but nor did she feel up to facing the concerned enquiries she was sure to receive if she returned downstairs. She was pacing up and down restlessly when a timid knock fell upon her door. It opened a fraction and Mrs Abbott's head peeped around it.

"Oh good, you are awake. I did not wish to disturb you if you were sleeping, my dear."

"No, I tried but could not."

"So I can see," Mrs Abbott said gently. "I always find that a breath of fresh air helps a headache. Would you like to take a turn about the gardens with me?"

Katherine looked into the kind face of her relation and knew she could not lie through her teeth to her. She needed to remove herself for a few hours until she had regained her usual composure.

"Actually, I am feeling much better already. I think I will take the gig and go and visit Mrs Nance after all."

"Are you sure, my dear?" she said concerned. "You do not seem yourself."

"Yes, yes, I am quite sure," Katherine assured her.

"Well give me a moment, my dear, I must just fetch my bonnet and pelisse and I will be with you."

"There is no need, Mrs Abbott," she said quickly. "You have your flowers to plan, remember?"

"Oh, that can wait. I am your companion first and foremost, and it has occurred to me that I have been very lax of late, yes, very lax. It will not do. I shudder to think what Sir Richard would say at you gallivanting all over unaccompanied, I really do."

She was gone on those words, but returned not many minutes later with Belle and Henrietta in tow.

"We bumped into Mrs Abbott on our way back from the nursery," Belle smiled. "Edmund is happily trying to sink his boat in a tub of water, quite determined to find a way to make it stay on the bottom. As my presence appears to be superfluous to his requirements and we are quite exhausted from writing reams of invitations, we shall accompany you also."

"But then there will be no one to help Lady Treleven," Katherine pointed out.

"She has gone to call on Lady Humphrey," Henrietta said. "She decided to deliver her invitation in person. She has taken the carriage but perhaps we could take yours?"

Having finally run out of obstacles to throw in their path, Katherine capitulated.

She sat back and listened with only half an ear to their chatter.

"Although writing invitations is always dreary,"

Belle said, "I find it quite amusing to try to conjure up an image of an unknown person merely from their name. Sir Miles Hawkmoore is a case in point. I imagine him as a tall, regal sort of gentleman with a large, slightly curved nose and keen, observant eyes."

Henrietta giggled. "I am afraid you will be sadly disappointed when you make his acquaintance," she said. "He is short, stout, and wears spectacles."

"Really? How very vexing. What about Mr Hogwood? He must surely be short, stocky and have little piggy eyes?"

Henrietta shook her head. "No, I am afraid you are again mistaken. He fits your first description much more accurately."

"How extraordinary. Are they of an age? Perhaps they somehow got mixed up when they were babes."

Katherine finally cracked a smile.

"I particularly enjoyed the appellation, Clutterbuck," chimed in Mrs Abbott. "It has quite a ring to it, don't you think? Although I think this person is harder to immediately envisage."

"Not at all," Belle disagreed. "He would be, I think, someone who dresses all by guess, nothing matching and his person would be decorated with an array of rings and fobs, but unfortunately none of his time pieces would be accurate, causing him always to be late."

She gave Henrietta an enquiring look.

"Mr Clutterbuck is nothing if not neat, I would go as far as to say he is austere in his appearance," Henrietta laughed.

"I wonder what you would have made of me, if

you had only heard my name," Katherine said with a wry smile.

"Oh, but I think we have just established that a name rarely defines the person, my dear," Mrs Abbott pointed out.

As they turned down the uneven lane to Helagon, the carriage lurched in its usual torturous fashion and Belle had to grab the strap to avoid being thrown against Mrs Abbott.

"Do not tell me you travelled all the way from Bath in this antiquated old thing?"

"Do not let my coachman hear you," Katherine smiled. "He assures me she's a fine old gal for a short journey!"

"He is mistaken," Belle said with some asperity.

As they neared Helagon they found their way blocked by a farmer's cart. He was drawn across the entrance to the drive. Katherine pushed down the window and peered out.

"Oh, his front wheel is damaged, we will have to walk the rest of the way."

"That will be no hardship," Belle said drily.

The unprecedented and quite alarming prospect of four very finely dressed ladies approaching him caused the farmer's eyes to widen and his ruddy cheeks began to glow as if lit from within.

"I'm mortified to have caused you such trouble, Miss Treleven, ladies," he said, touching his hat respectfully. "I knew it was loose, wouldn't have used the cart if it wasn't urgent."

"Whatever can have happened, Mr Treen?" said Henrietta gently.

"Oh, I'll not bother you with the details, miss, it's his lordship that I need to see."

"Well, my good man," Belle said, her eyes alight with curiosity, "you are about to have your wish granted."

Lord Treleven and Lord Hayward had just rounded the bend in the drive. When they saw the ladies clustered about the cart, they dismounted and walked to meet them. Harry threw Katherine an intent look and she shook her head slightly.

"In trouble, Treen?" Lord Treleven eyed the wheel that leant at a drunken angle.

"Never mind my cart, sir. You won't believe what 'as happened, it was like something out of the Bible."

Everyone stared at him in some amazement.

"Except o'course, my sheep aren't men and they never rebelled against anything in their short lives, apart from when they escaped the other day and I could hardly blame them for that."

"Are you feeling quite the thing, Mr Treen?" Henrietta said eventually.

"I knew you wouldn't believe it," Mr Treen declared.

"If you wish us to understand you, Treen, you must speak more plainly," Harry said brusquely.

"I think you will find," said Mrs Abbott, "that he is referring to the book of numbers, when the earth opened up and swallowed those who had rebelled against Moses."

"Didn't I just say so?" the farmer exclaimed.

"I have no idea," Harry admitted.

Lord Hayward exchanged a humorous look with

his lady. "Are you trying to tell us that your sheep have been swallowed up by the earth, my good fellow?"

That good fellow, feeling much exasperated, looked at him as if her were a simpleton. "What else could I mean? An' I thought the gentry was meant to have lots o' learnin'."

Harry's lips twitched. "You must forgive my ignorance," he said, "but am I to take it that you need some help rescuing your sheep?"

"That I do, sir. I've had to lay off the lads as helped me, times being a little hard. I thought you might send me a man or two. I've got a rope and trusty Ben here," he said, patting his horse. "But it'll take someone with a head for heights to help me out of this, that's for sure. It's a miracle any of 'em are still alive. But I heard 'em, they was still bleatin' when I left."

Harry looked startled. "How deep is this pit they have fallen into?"

Mr Treen gave a harsh laugh. "Pit? It's no pit, Lord Treleven. More what you'd call an abyss."

Harry and Lord Hayward exchanged a meaningful stare.

"We will help you, Treen," Harry said, turning to mount his horse.

"But, sir, it's not fit—"

"Treen, stop blubbering and climb up on that coach."

Harry's tone was commanding, harsh even. The farmer looked at him as if he were a stranger, but nevertheless climbed up onto the roof of the coach.

He turned to the ladies. "We will return for you later."

"I don't think so," said Belle, completely unimpressed by his display of authority. "Come, ladies, I for one, want to witness for myself this act of God!"

As they moved towards the carriage, Harry raised an eyebrow at Lord Hayward. He seemed unruffled by his lady's proclamation and merely grinned.

"I wouldn't waste your breath," he advised. "Once Belle sniffs out a mystery there is no stopping her."

They fell in behind the coach. "I thought you had better control over your wife, Hayward."

His companion chuckled. "When you have one of your own, Treleven, you may pass judgement."

Katherine sank back into her seat in the coach and breathed long and low. Her heart had jumped at first sight of Lord Treleven, drumming in her ears as relief had swept through her. She had stood back and covertly observed him as he had tried to untangle Mr Treen's explanation of events. She had not missed his arrested expression when the depth of the pit had been explained, or the flame of excitement that had suddenly lit his eyes. She had been just as determined as Belle to see what had caused it but was grateful that her friend had taken the initiative, not at all sure she could have disregarded his wishes with such equanimity.

"I must admit I am very curious to see this abyss," laughed Belle. "I only hope Mr Treen is not prone to exaggeration for I will be most disappointed if we do not find something of biblical proportions."

They had drawn up beside a gate. Belle craned her neck and saw that her husband was unlatching it.

"Brace yourselves ladies," she said, dismayed. "For I fear we are about to cross a field."

They all immediately reached for the strap that

hung by each door. They had not gone very far when Belle's usually rosy complexion, paled considerably.

"Belle?" said Katherine, "is something amiss?"

She received a frantic shake of the head by way of reply. They came to a stop not many moments later and Belle hastily opened the door, leaned out and was violently sick. Mrs Abbott searched in her reticule, retrieved her handkerchief and sprinkled it with the sal volatile she always kept there. As Belle straightened up, she offered it to her.

That grateful lady held it to her nose and breathed deeply. Almost immediately, her complexion improved.

"Thank you, Mrs Abbott," she said. "I will be quite alright now. That ghastly rocking made me feel just as I did when we were at sea. Say nothing to Hayward, I beg of you, he will only fuss."

Fortunately for her, he had not noticed. The reason for this lack of consideration on his part was soon made abundantly clear. It appeared that Mr Treen was not prone to exaggeration after all, for there was indeed a yawning abyss in the middle of the field.

"I told you my sheep wouldn't go anywhere near that dip," said the farmer to Harry. "But when I came to move them to another pasture today, some had wandered in there, must have got used to it, I suppose. I thought nothing of it at first, then I heard a low rumble and they just disappeared."

The ladies joined them on the edge of the precipice. It must have been ten feet wide at least and who knew how deep, for they certainly could not see the bottom.

"Oh, Mr Treen," said Henrietta. "I think I have just heard one of your sheep."

They all listened for a moment, none of them really believing that anything could have survived such a fall, but sure enough, a faint bleat floated up to them.

Katherine's eyes widened as Harry stripped off his coat.

"Get that rope, Treen," he ordered.

"Sir!" The words were out before she could stop them. "Surely you are not going to risk your life for a sheep?"

He grinned and strode over to her, his eyes alight with excitement. "Do not concern yourself, ma'am," he said softly. "I know how to tie a knot that does not slip."

He took her hand and dropped a light kiss upon it. "There is more at stake than you know. Wish me good luck, ma'am, I am sorely in need of it."

"Good luck," she whispered, "and… be careful."

The rope was fetched. He tied one end of it to the coach and the other around his waist. They watched him confidently descend into the darkness below.

"Harry," Henrietta cried as he disappeared from view.

Mrs Abbott wrapped an arm about her. "Hush, child. Have faith. He did not survive Napoleon and years at sea to meet his maker in a muddy hole."

Time seemed to slow to a crawl as they all stood unmoving, their gazes solemn, as if they stood at the edge of an open grave. It seemed an eternity later when the rope that lay taut against the side of the cavernous opening twitched.

Lord Hayward stepped forwards and began to haul it in, hand over hand. Mr Treen took up position behind him and aided him in his efforts. A bundle of white fluff slowly emerged, an outraged bleat preceding it.

Miraculously it had seemed to escape any serious hurt, for the moment they had untied it, it shook itself and gambolled off to join its fellows who were huddled in the far corner of the field.

Lord Hayward lowered the rope again. The next time it jerked Katherine and Henrietta exchanged a small smile both sure they would see Harry within a few moments. They searched the darkness for a sign of his shining blond locks. Instead two rough sacks appeared.

"What's all this?" said Mr Treen, bemused, moving to open one.

"Do not touch it." Lord Hayward's voice was stern and Mr Treen immediately ceased his investigation.

Again and again the rope was lowered. Each time it re-emerged with either a sack or box attached.

Belle was sorely tempted to take a peek into one and began to edge her way towards them. Without so much as turning his head Lord Hayward addressed her, but in much gentler terms than he had dissuaded Mr Treen.

"I think not, my dear."

With only the slightest hint of a pout, she re-joined the others. Eventually the blond locks that Henrietta and Katherine so earnestly wished to see, emerged from the dark. Harry was mud smeared but triumphant.

"We have him!" he grinned, shaking Lord Hayward's hand and laughing. "It seems there are no limits to that man's audacity after all, he has been mining under my own land! No wonder he either wanted me on side or out of the way! It seems however, that the workings were not well supported. They have collapsed and the tunnel is blocked. It is a shame your troop have gone on ahead, for we need to grab him before he realises."

Mr Treen looked bemused by this conversation. However he turned his mind to his most pressing concern.

"But my sheep, milord. Where are the rest of 'em?"

Harry sobered for an instant. "I am afraid they did not make it, Treen. The one I sent up had the good fortune to have a soft landing, it fell upon the others."

The farmer's face fell and Harry clapped him on the shoulder. "Do not fret, I will make sure you are compensated for every last one of them."

Mr Treen looked a little brighter.

"Help us get this lot onto the coach, will you? And not a word to a soul, you understand?"

"I can't say as I do, sir, but who would I tell anyways? The wife 'ud think I'd gone soft in the head if I told her this tale!"

"Good man!"

The ladies were bundled back into the carriage all their questions unanswered, whilst the sacks and boxes were tied to the roof.

Harry turned to the coachman who had remained stoically impassive throughout the proceedings, only offering advice on how best to secure the retrieved items on the roof.

"John, isn't it?" Harry said. "Take the ladies back to Elmdon and guard this carriage as if your life depends on it."

Coachman John nodded. "You may depend on me,

sir." He tapped his coat pocket and winked. "I always carry a pistol, not that I've ever had to use it."

Satisfied, Harry turned to Lord Hayward. "Come, I will take you cross country, we can cut them off before they reach Padstow."

CHAPTER 13

Lady Treleven had returned when they reached Elmdon. They found her in the drawing room, her colour rather heightened.

"There you are," she said, "wherever have you been? I am full of news and have had no one to share it with."

"So are we, Mama," Henrietta said, sitting next to her. "We have had a very interesting morning."

"Oh have you?" Lady Treleven said. "You are very fortunate. Mine has been hideous. I have had to bear with Lady Humphrey crowing it over me with the most extraordinary tale." She gave Belle a hard stare. "Something about Lord Hayward conducting a search of the mine for the lost cargo of some ship or other, which of course, didn't exist. He has caused Lord Humphrey and myself considerable embarrassment, and made himself and Harry, who was also present at this outrageous event, a laughing stock. A very odd thing for him to do considering I thought him to be interested in acquiring a property."

Belle coloured. "I am sorry, ma'am. He does not always take me into his confidence about his business affairs. But I think you will find your embarrassment somewhat alleviated when you hear our news."

With much questioning back and forth, and many interruptions, they found they had the final piece of each other's puzzle.

"Ha! It is I who shall crow now!" Lady Treleven said, her indignation forgotten. "Or at least, I would, if I were a vulgar, encroaching creature, which I am glad to say, I am not."

"But why would Mr Caldwell need to steal anything?" Henrietta asked. "He is already so rich."

"Oh, how should I know, child? Greed I suppose. There is a reason greed is one of the seven deadly sins."

Katherine, who had kept very much in the background during this exchange, did not mention that he was also guilty of attempting another of these sins, one that, in her eyes at least, was far, far worse.

The ladies attempted to occupy themselves with the preparations for the ball. But even though they had not so many hours before been fully occupied with this endeavour, now topics such as how many candles would have to be ordered in, or the order of the dances, could no longer hold their interest for very long.

It was late in the afternoon before the gentlemen finally returned by which time they were agog with curiosity. Lord Treleven went to change his raiment before showing his face and so it fell to Lord Hayward to satisfy it.

"Hayward," Belle said, her face lighting up as she

saw her husband. "Tell us everything, immediately."

Lord Hayward strode over to the fireplace, leant his arm on the mantelpiece and rested his booted foot on the fender. His face was a little grave.

"Is all well?" she enquired after a moment.

"We took Mr Caldwell unawares," he said after a moment. "He tried to deny all knowledge of course."

"Will you be able to prove his involvement?" asked Lady Treleven.

Lord Hayward glanced at her, his expression solemn.

"Without doubt, ma'am."

"To think of a neighbour of ours, having to stand trial."

"That will not be necessary," Lord Hayward said softly.

"Why ever not? Do not tell me that he can buy his way out of trouble?"

"It will not be necessary for Mr Caldwell to stand trial, ma'am, because he is no longer living."

The ladies gasped. After a moment Lord Hayward continued.

"He made the mistake of trying to throw the blame on Mr Scorrier who runs the mine for him. On perceiving the gravity of the crimes that were being laid at his door, that gentleman was easily persuaded to talk. Although this inevitably involved revealing his own part in the case, the crime of helping conceal the goods will carry a much lighter sentence than masterminding the whole."

"But how is Mr Caldwell dead?" Katherine asked. "Did he try to escape?"

"No, a couple of his servants made the attempt but

we had the house surrounded."

"Was that to do with the other matter, sir?" Katherine asked quietly.

Belle's brows rose and she gave Katherine an enquiring look. "What other matter?"

Katherine bit her lip, unsure if she should have said anything, but she could not see what harm it could do now.

"Sabotaging an East Indiaman and stealing the cargo were not his only crimes," Lord Hayward explained.

He looked at Lady Treleven. "Apart from being almost certainly involved in fraudulent insurance claims, he tried, on two occasions to murder your son. The first attempt was put down to a poacher in the woods. The second attempt was made this morning, the method a poisoned dart, which fortunately missed its target."

Her hand flew to her breast, her eyes widening. She remained very much in control of her emotions however. "Then I am glad he is dead," she said flatly.

Belle's eyes were again on Katherine. "No wonder you were ill! But you said nothing of it."

"No, you did not," said Lady Treleven, clearly much put out. "Perhaps you did not think I would be interested in such a trifling event?"

Katherine flushed. "Lord Treleven had told me I must not. He did not want you to worry, ma'am. He assured me he hoped to have the matter resolved by the end of today."

Katherine was relieved when she turned her attention back to Lord Hayward. "How did he die? Did Harry—?"

"No, ma'am. Lord Treleven had the presence of mind to keep the dart, and an extensive search of the house revealed others as well as the blowpipe used. Once Caldwell realised that he would also be facing a murder charge and the hangman's noose, and he took things into his own hands. He was seated at his desk in the library, and before we could stop him he had a drawer open and a pistol in his hand. He at first turned it upon Lord Treleven but then gave a queer sort of laugh and turned it upon himself. In short ma'am, he shot himself."

\* \* \*

It was perhaps only to be expected that dinner that evening was a rather subdued affair.

"I will have to go up to town to give my report of events here." Lord Hayward dropped the words into one of the many silences.

"Oh, will you, my dear?" Belle said. "Will you be back for the ball?"

"I should think so," he smiled.

"You are, of course, welcome to stay for the ball," Lady Treleven said a trifle stiffly. "But was it really necessary to be my guests under false pretences?"

Her gaze encompassed both Belle and Lord Hayward.

"I really did not know what he was up to," Belle said.

"But you knew he was not looking for property, I think."

"Do not blame Lady Hayward, ma'am," Lord Hayward said. "It was not her fault. I was not at all sure of my ground and the fewer people who were aware of my interest in this affair, the better."

"Very well," she conceded. "As you have rid me of that man, I will forgive you."

"Thank you, ma'am."

He glanced at Harry. "Your evidence will also need to be heard so I suggest you accompany me."

"Oh surely that is not necessary," Lady Treleven protested. "The ball is barely ten days away! We can hardly hold a ball in your honour, Harry, if you are not present!"

"I have covered further distances in less time, I assure you, ma'am. Do not fret."

With that she had to be satisfied.

When the ladies had retired, Harry reached into his pocket and brought out the small silver key.

"I had almost forgotten this. Shall we see which box it fits?"

"If you wish," smiled Lord Hayward.

Their haul had been stored in Harry's study for safety until it could be collected in the morning. Most of the boxes were too large, but they finally found a small one, hidden in one of the sacks. It was square, quite plain, and made from Indian rosewood. The key fitted perfectly. Harry grinned and opened the lid. Inside, on a bed of red velvet lay a huge blue sapphire. It twinkled in the candlelight, its glitter reflected in his eyes.

"This alone must be worth a king's ransom," he breathed.

"Indeed it is, it is rumoured to be the largest one ever discovered."

Harry carefully closed and locked the box,

returning it to where it was found.

"No wonder the king was so anxious it was found, he has ever been a collector."

"Have you considered what this might mean to you, Treleven?"

"To me?"

"Apart from the sapphire, it is a valuable cargo. There are other jewels, spices, tea, silk, and many other items. Items that you may claim salvage on as you recovered them."

"I had not thought of that," he said slowly.

"And I think you will find that I can ensure your claim does not take years to be settled."

They were away early, before breakfast. Katherine watched them for some time from her bedroom window, only turning away when they had finally faded from sight. She was glad, she told herself. She did not like her emotions to behave in the topsy-turvy fashion they had of late. By the time Lord Treleven returned the chances were she would have moved into Helagon and their friendship, if you could call it that, would become easier and more natural when they were not constantly thrown into each other's company.

The exciting events of the day before had precluded her visiting Mrs Nance and she mentioned her intention of rectifying this oversight at breakfast.

"I will come with you, if you like," said Henrietta.

That young lady seemed to be growing in confidence every day and although she did not much feel like company, Katherine did not have the heart to rebuff her.

"Yes, that is a very good idea, Henrietta," Lady Treleven approved. "I have asked Mrs Kemp to prepare some baskets of food and I would like you to take them to the vicarage, if you will. Harry mentioned that Mrs Creedley has been baking bread for the villagers and is quite at her wits' end but I am ashamed to say it had quite slipped my mind until he reminded me this morning."

At Helagon, they found the tiles had been replaced on the roof and work had started on the damaged ceilings. Fires had been lit in many of the rooms to dry them out and Katherine realised it would not be long before it was habitable again. She dashed a quick note off to her brother outlining the progress before heading for the kitchen.

Mrs Nance was more than happy to help with the preparations for the ball. She ran her eye over the list of items Mrs Kemp had suggested she help prepare. When she raised her head, it was Henrietta whom she addressed.

"If you don't mind, Miss Treleven, I used to be known for my lobster patties, might I add those to the list?"

Henrietta smiled at her. "Of course, Mrs Nance. We are very grateful for your help."

"You seem a little happier than before, Henrietta," Katherine said gently, as they approached Langarne.

"I am," Henrietta admitted. "I believe you were right, Miss—"

Katherine raised a brow.

"Katherine," she amended. "Both you and Belle have raised my spirits. What happened no longer seems quite so terrible. And I believe some of your confidence may be rubbing off on me!"

"I will remind you of that comment on the night

of the ball," she smiled.

"You may need to," Henrietta admitted ruefully. "As soon as a gentlemen starts to flatter me, I feel most uncomfortable and can find nothing to say."

"Do you know, I have been known to suffer from the same malady myself?"

"You are just trying to make me feel better," Henrietta said.

"Not at all, let us practise. We shall take it in turns to be the gentleman. Who shall go first?"

Henrietta laughed. "I shall."

She cleared her throat and then said in a gruff voice. "Your lips look sweeter than cherries, ma'am."

Katherine choked. "Do not tell me someone actually said that to you?"

Henrietta giggled and nodded. "But how would you reply?"

"Like all things tried out of season, they oftentimes prove sour, sir."

"Oh, I would never think of saying anything like that."

"Then you must practise," Katherine said. "If that is the flavour of your compliments, try this one: "Your complexion is as fresh as morning dew."

Henrietta's brow furrowed as she sought a reply. Then she grinned. "But will fade as quickly when too bright a light is shone upon it."

"Very good," Katherine smiled.

"Oh, I have one! You are as modest as a dove, my lady."

Katherine quirked a questioning brow.

"Oh yes," Henrietta assured her. "I have had that said to me also."

Katherine raised her chin in a haughty manner. "And can fly away from danger just as fast."

They had reached the vicarage. "Just treat it all as a game," she smiled. "And enjoy it, it is what I intend to do."

They found Mrs Creedley in a much improved humour.

"My mother has sent some baskets of food to hand out," Henrietta said.

"That's very kind of her." Mrs Creedley took them from her. "But let's hope there won't be any need for 'em much longer. Mr Gulworthy is just writing his sermon but I will fetch him directly."

They had not long to wait as the vicar soon came in, his faded blue eyes looking quite distracted.

"Ladies," he smiled.

"I apologise if we have interrupted your sermon," said Henrietta.

"Nonsense, nonsense, the distraction is welcome."

"I suppose you must have a funeral to prepare," said Katherine quietly.

Mr Gulworthy brushed his hand across his balding pate and shifted a little uneasily in his chair.

"Well that all depends, yes, it all depends."

"On what, sir?" asked Henrietta.

"Whether or not he is deemed to have been in his right mind."

The door opened on his words and Doctor Fisher came into the room.

"Jennings is much improved—" He paused when he saw they had visitors. "Miss Treleven, Miss Lockhart."

Katherine noted that a faint pink tinge had crept

into Henrietta's cheeks.

"Well that is capital news. Well done, my boy," the vicar said, stepping forwards to shake his hand. He turned to the ladies. "Jennings is the poor miner who lost his leg."

Katherine looked interested. "It is indeed a feather in your cap, sir, if he has not only survived the procedure but is recovering also."

"Well it was touch and go to begin with," the doctor admitted. His eyes rested for a moment on Henrietta. "But I am sure Miss Treleven cannot wish to hear of such things."

"You are mistaken, sir," she said raising her eyes to his. "I am happy to hear of your success."

"Of course you are," the vicar smiled. "We shall drink a toast to Mr Jennings. A small glass of wine will do us no harm."

They had all just lifted their glasses to their lips when Mrs Creedley bustled in with the tea tray. She put it down none too gently on a side table and put her hands on her hips.

"I'm surprised at you, Mr Gulworthy, serving the ladies wine and at such an hour. Does not the Bible say it bites like a snake and poisons like a viper?"

"Now, now, Mrs Creedley, did not Jesus himself turn water into wine?"

Ignoring this unanswerable conundrum, she poured out a cup of tea and passed it to Henrietta, firmly removing the glass from her fingers.

"Here you are miss, I think you will enjoy this far more than that muck."

\* \* \*

The work at Helagon was completed a few days before the ball but Lady Treleven persuaded Katherine to delay her departure until after it.

"I am sure we will find there are a thousand things that need to be done at the last moment," she assured her. "Besides, Henrietta is much improved since your arrival, Miss Lockhart, but it may well be that she becomes a little nervous on the evening of the ball. She will benefit from having her friends around her."

When her son had not yet arrived home the evening before the event, she grew very twittery.

"I knew it," she said irritably at dinner that evening. "He will not make it back in time. How I will explain his absence I do not know."

"Oh, do not be despondent, ma'am," Belle said confidently. "I am sure Hayward will have him back in time."

"Well, I hope he does. If he hadn't dragged Harry into this in the first place, we wouldn't be in this predicament."

"No, ma'am," Belle said meekly.

Lady Treleven threw her a suspicious look and then a reluctant grin twitched at the corners of her lips. "Belle Hayward, you are many things but meek isn't one of them. However, I apologise for being such a crosspatch. We are none of us able to control the actions of our menfolk after all."

They arrived soon after the tea tray had been brought into the drawing room. Belle flew out of her chair to greet her husband, who uncaring of his audience, caught her neatly about the waist and dropped a brief kiss on her upturned cheek.

"Forgive us for coming in in all our dirt," smiled

Harry.

Katherine noticed that he was looking tired but happy. She was aware her heart was beating a little faster and gave herself a little inward shake. She might not be able to help being a little in love with him but she would not add to the ranks of probably countless women, who had shown it before her.

"Never mind your dirt," said Lady Treleven. "I am just happy that you are home in time for the ball."

Harry kissed her hand. "Forgive me, Mother. I did not wish to worry you."

Lady Treleven sat a little straighter in her chair. "No, about a great many things it would appear." Her tone was astringent. "I wish to inform you, Harry, that I am not made of china, and will not break every time an ill wind blows. From now on, you—" she paused and her gaze swept over the other occupants of the room, "and everyone else will keep me fully informed of any and all events occurring that pertain to you, Henrietta or Elmdon. Do I make myself clear?"

His face remained grave but Katherine did not miss the twinkle that lurked in his eyes.

"Then I had better inform you, ma'am, that we will very soon own Thornbury House and be the major shareholder in the mine."

Lady Treleven blinked in astonishment. "But how can that be?"

"Although Mr Caldwell met his end here, it was felt that the inquest should be held in London as he was best known there and his crimes mostly affected various people who had interests there," Lord Hayward explained. "The king himself took an interest in the hearing."

"And what was the outcome of this inquest?" Lady Treleven asked.

"A verdict of felo-de-se was recorded, ma'am. It is more usual in these cases for a verdict of non compos mentis to be given but as Mr Caldwell does not seem to have any living relatives, and had severely depleted his resources with the acquisition and very expensive renovation of Thornbury House, it was deemed fair. His assets are now confiscated by the Crown and will be used to offset the cost of the ship that was lost among other things."

Lady Treleven was now receiving all the information she could wish for but seemed quite overwhelmed by it all.

"I am owed salvage on the items recovered," Harry explained. "As well as compensation for the unlawful intrusion into my land, not to mention mineral rights on the ore removed. The amount due will be offset against the property and the mine so, in effect, ma'am, we have acquired both for very little."

"I see," she said, a small frown between her eyes. "But, Harry, what do we want with them?"

Harry looked a little rueful. "A fair question, ma'am, and one I would have asked myself not so long ago. Whether we like it or not, however, mining is the blood of this county. I did not aspire to be a mine owner but it has been borne upon me that it is the only way we can ensure the continued wellbeing of our people, and ensure their working conditions are as safe as possible. As for the house, at least we can have some say in who becomes our neighbour."

"Very true," she said brightening. She cast a glance

at her daughter. "I have asked the vicar and Doctor Fisher to dine with us tomorrow."

She smiled as she saw the delicate flush that stole into Henrietta's cheeks.

"You must hope that he remains here," Katherine said. "For no matter how safe you make the mine, there are likely to be accidents. I was very impressed that he was able to save a miner's life even though he lost his leg."

"Managed it, did he?" Harry lips twisted into a lopsided grin. "How very disappointed you must have been not to have witnessed the procedure."

Katherine grimaced. "I do not think I would have had the fortitude to withstand such a sight."

"I think you underestimate yourself, ma'am," he said gently. "You have more fortitude than any other female of my acquaintance. A circumstance I have every reason to be thankful for."

Katherine saw admiration in his eyes and became quite tongue-tied. Fortunately Lady Treleven was not so incapacitated.

"Is there anyone in particular you would like to invite for dinner, Harry?" she enquired.

"We have enough geese to feed a small army," she added drily.

Harry raised an amused brow. "How so?"

"I have not been able to consult with Mrs Kemp any time in the last few days, without one or other of your tenants appearing at the kitchen door with a goose, hoping the offering would soften the blow that they need a little longer to pay their rent."

"Then it is fortunate that I am very partial to goose," he laughed.

CHAPTER 14

At last everything was ready. Torches and lanterns had been placed at intervals along the drive, the long unused ballroom gleamed by the light of hundreds of candles and the floor had been polished to a bright sheen.

Henrietta stood with her mother looking radiant and quite beautiful in her simple white gown, her golden locks crowned by a wreath of pomegranate blossoms. Her brother lounged beside her, his dark coat and silk breeches relieved by the white waistcoat and stockings he wore. Indeed, Katherine reflected, they made a startlingly beautiful picture.

As she passed Henrietta, she leaned forwards and whispered in her ear, "I do not think any compliment you receive tonight could be called exaggerated, but remember, view it is a game and enjoy it."

"I shall," she assured her.

As she dropped a light curtsey to Harry he caught her hand and raised it to his lips, causing it to tremble slightly in his grasp. His eyes surveyed her pale pink gown and then lingered on her cheek a moment.

"You look charming, Miss Lockhart," he smiled. "Like a delicate rose."

Determined to follow her own advice she ignored the fluttering of her heart and raised an arch brow. "Beware, sir, for there never was a rose without a thorn."

"Hornet," he murmured, grinning.

Mrs Abbott was behind her and he also bowed deeply over her hand.

"I do hope you will save me a dance, my good lady," he said.

Katherine smiled, it was quite clear from the long train of her gown that Mrs Abbott had no intention of dancing but she appreciated the kindness he had shown her companion. She had come to realise he was kind, in his own careless fashion. He had also shown great concern and care for both his family and his tenants. In short, whatever his past, he was a good man. One she had been too quick to judge.

Even though she had moved further into the room, she heard the high-pitched titter of Miss Humphrey. Looking over her shoulder she saw that young lady playfully rap her fan against Lord Treleven's arm. She sighed. It was a timely reminder that all the qualities she had just acknowledged in him did not alter the fact that he was a flirt, and not to be taken at all seriously as far as affairs of the heart were concerned.

"Oh, the orchestra is about to play, I think," Mrs Abbott said. "And I have not forgotten your forfeit, my dear."

Katherine smiled down into the suddenly mischievous eyes of her companion. "I had forgotten it," she admitted. "Come, I am ready, what is it to be?"

"You must dance every dance you are solicited for this evening, that is all."

"You have wasted your forfeit then," she said. "For that was already my intention."

At that very moment, a rather portly gentleman with twinkling brown eyes and a pair of small spectacles perched on his rather snub nose, bowed before her.

"Sir Miles Hawkmoore," he smiled. "Forgive me introducing myself but I think we can dispense with the usual formalities at a private ball. May I have the honour of this dance, ma'am?"

Katherine threw an amused glance at Mrs Abbott and smiled so widely at him that he flushed.

As she took up her place in the set forming she noticed Doctor Fisher, who looked quite splendid this evening, lead Henrietta onto the floor. Belle was not far behind. She was being remarkably unfashionable and dancing the first with her husband. She radiated happiness and love. They had been married for some years now but still only had eyes for each other. She sighed and was aware of a slight twinge of envy. How wonderful it must be to know you were truly loved and have the unshakeable faith in your partner that Belle frequently displayed.

She very nearly stumbled as her partner turned her, and shook off the thought. She would make some sort of useful life here and be content with her lot. And she would begin by thoroughly enjoying this evening.

It did not prove too difficult a task, for finding herself to have the merit of novelty amongst a set of people who had known each other all their lives, she found herself with a succession of partners, all eager to please. Witnessing Henrietta blossom enhanced her pleasure further. On more than one occasion she observed her cause her partner to laugh and could only assume she was enjoying the game of light flirtation.

During a lull between dances, Belle found her. "Is it not wonderful?" she smiled, pointing with her fan to where Henrietta stood surrounded by admirers, holding court. "I would not have thought it possible that the shy wallflower I knew would transform herself into the incomparable of the ball."

"It is as it should be," Katherine said. "For she outshines every other young lady present."

"Indeed," agreed Belle. "I can see one lady in particular who seems most put out."

Katherine followed her gaze and saw Miss Humphrey on the edge of Henrietta's group of admirers. Her shrill laugh rent the air causing them both to wince.

"If she bats her eyelashes or waves her fan any harder, the young man she is trying to engage will think she is having a fit," Belle said drily.

As they watched, Lord Treleven paused near the group and said something in Doctor Fisher's ear before sauntering in their direction. Miss Humphrey, catching sight of him, snapped shut her fan and hurried after him, leaving the young man she had so recently been attempting to beguile with her wiles, staring after her, his mouth agape.

Lord Treleven had nearly reached them when she caught up with him and snatched at his arm.

"There you are, Lord Treleven, where have you been hiding?" she tittered a trifle breathlessly, unfurling her trusty fan once more and waving it in front of her face. "It is dreadfully hot in here, is it not? I am sure you would know of a quiet spot where a lady could cool herself."

Belle's brow rose. "The little minx!"

The music struck up and the young lady glanced hopefully up at her quarry.

Harry bowed and she flushed with excitement. "Might I suggest you sit this one out, Miss Humphrey, as you are so warm? I believe I am promised to Miss Lockhart for this dance."

Turning neatly on his heel he took a step in her direction, bowing and offering her his arm. Following strictly the terms of her forfeit, she placed her hand on it lightly and allowed herself to be led onto the floor.

"That poor child," she murmured reprovingly.

His eyes laughed down at her causing her heart to miss a beat. "She will not be a child much longer if she carries on in her present fashion."

"Perhaps she was a little forward," she conceded.

"There is no perhaps about it," he said with some asperity. "If she tries that with the wrong man she will find herself in the suds. She is completely without the dignity and modesty that mark your manners, ma'am."

The dance was a cotillion and left them little opportunity for further private conversation. Katherine was grateful, for every time they came together and she was forced to look into his eyes, she found herself without a single sensible thought in her head. She certainly would not have been able to parry his compliments with the wit necessary to both keep him firmly in his place and conceal how deeply they affected her.

He bowed deeply before her as it came to an end. "You dance delightfully," he murmured. "I hope to claim another before the night is out."

She offered only a small smile by way of a reply.

She found Mrs Abbott enjoying a conversation with Mr Gulworthy.

"We are planning a rose garden for Helagon," she smiled. "Are you enjoying yourself, my dear?"

"Yes," she smiled. "I hope you are satisfied? I have followed the terms of our bargain to the letter and have danced every dance."

"Ah, but the evening is not yet over, my dear," she said softly. "And if I am not much mistaken you are about to be claimed again."

Katherine turned her head to see who might be approaching. And froze. The blood leached from her face and she had to fight the urge to flee the room.

A gentleman dressed in full regimentals stood before her. He had a handsome countenance and a fine figure.

"Miss Lockhart." He bowed, displaying an elegant leg. "Would you do me the honour of granting me the next dance?"

The denial that she longed to utter refused to push past the lump that had formed in her throat.

"Off you go, dear," Mrs Abbott gently encouraged her.

Unwilling to cause a scene, she capitulated. She had to stop a groan as the opening bars of what was unmistakeably a waltz drifted through the air. She could have sworn the next dance was meant to be a quadrille. She felt every fibre of her being stiffen as her partner placed an arm around her neat waist and took her hand in his.

They had danced many times before but she felt as if he were a stranger. The man she had thought she had known had been an imposter after all. She made no attempt to break the awkward silence that hung between them. She had nothing to say to him.

"I had not thought to find you here, ma'am," he finally said.

She merely raised an eyebrow.

"But I am glad," he continued. "I have often wondered what had become of you."

"I believe I am the spinster you had expected me to become, Mr Sharpe," she said through gritted teeth.

He had at least the grace to look uncomfortable. "You do not look like a spinster," he said softly, "but a beautiful young lady."

Her eyes flashed. "You cannot expect me to believe a word you say to me, surely?"

"I meant it, nonetheless," he said gently.

"What are you doing here?"

"My regiment has been stationed near here in support of an investigation into a missing ship. Most have returned to town but some of us remain whilst a few loose ends are tied up."

Everything fell into place. Lord Hayward had mentioned dragoons, but he had not said which regiment. It had not crossed her mind that it might be Mr Sharpe's.

"I hope they will be tied up soon, then," she said coolly.

He flinched a little at her words. "Come, Miss Lockhart. Cannot we at least part friends?"

She looked at him in some amazement. "An honest enemy is better than a false friend, sir."

She breathed a sigh of relief as the dance came to an end. Noticing Miss Humphrey hovering in the vicinity, clearly hopeful of an introduction, and overtaken by a sort of malicious humour quite foreign to her nature, she promptly obliged her.

Her enjoyment of the evening was at an end but she would not repay Lady Treleven's kindness or invite unwanted speculation or comment by retiring early, however much she might wish to do so. Feeling herself quite incapable of exchanging polite pleasantries with anyone just yet, she made her way to the retiring room hoping for a few quiet moments to collect her thoughts.

She was not to have them. Barely had she sunk into a chair before the door opened and Belle tripped into the room. To her great mortification it took just one sympathetic glance from her friend before she found her eyes suddenly swimming in tears.

"I thought something was amiss," Belle said gently, seating herself beside her and taking her hand, cradling it on her lap. "I know you are probably wishing me at Jericho but I think you will feel better if you share your troubles."

When Katherine remained silent, she rubbed her thumb gently over the back of her hand and said, "Shall I begin? I think you had met the gentleman you have just danced with somewhere before. Judging by your stiff posture and forbidding countenance throughout the encounter, he has perhaps injured you in some way."

Katherine gave a rather grim smile. "Lord Hayward is sadly mistaken not to take you into his confidence when he carries out his business, Belle. Your extraordinary prescience would prove to be invaluable, I am sure."

"I have often told him so," Belle said lightly. "But every man likes to think he is master of his own affairs after all."

Katherine gave a rather hard little laugh. "Some like to imagine themselves master of everyone else's affairs also."

"Well, you will have to tell me it all now, for I am quite intrigued. Come, unburden yourself, you will feel better for it, I am sure."

Belle allowed Katherine to tell her halting tale without interruption. When she had finished she said, "I think you will find that he is not alone in his opinions, my dear. But to treat you in such a way was quite unnecessary, callous even, and to practise such a deception on a young impressionable girl, unforgiveable. I am very pleased you introduced him to Miss Humphrey, I am sure they deserve each other."

Katherine gave a watery chuckle.

"There, that is much better," approved Belle.

"Thank you," Katherine said. "It is quite ridiculous that I was so overcome. I now realise I was not even in love with him, after all. But he took me by surprise and all the old feelings of humiliation and anger seemed very fresh again. But I am better now."

* * *

During his days away, Harry had found Miss Lockhart filling his thoughts with increasing frequency. Images of her smiling face as she steered his boat or rode Countess beside him had come unbidden as he had tried to sleep. He had found himself looking forward to coming home, knowing she would be there. Her quick tongue, swift intelligence and dignified demeanour had become increasingly appealing to him. She might have a managing disposition but she was also calm when other ladies he had known would have had hysterics. He would, he realised, like to know her better.

He strode purposefully over to the recess in the far corner of the room that housed the orchestra.

"Play a waltz next, will you?"

He turned and scanned the room. He saw his quarry in conversation with Mrs Abbott and a wolfish grin lightened his countenance.

"Ah, there you are, Treleven. I've been meaning to have a word with you. Like you to fill me in on the details of the inquest, if you would. Should have taken place down here by rights, but then everything about this business has been highly irregular."

Harry frowned down at Lord Humphrey. "Now is hardly the time, sir. I will call on you tomorrow."

He had taken no more than a couple of strides towards Miss Lockhart when he saw Hugh Sharpe was before him. Damn Humphrey, that pompous old windbag had made him miss his chance. Deciding if he could not dance with Miss Lockhart he would enjoy watching her instead, he retreated to the edge of the ballroom. Leaning his shoulder against the wall, he folded his arms and prepared to watch her glide gracefully around the room.

His brows rose in surprise and he straightened his posture before he had watched her for many moments. He had witnessed first hand her grace and elegance when she had danced with him earlier, but now, although her feet made all the correct steps, her posture was rigid where it should have been fluid and her face was like a mask, cold and pale.

He did not know Hugh Sharpe all that well, he had been part of what his friends had called the king's sect, a group of soldiers who were extremely patriotic but a little too serious and arrogant for his tastes. He could not imagine what he had said to disturb Miss Lockhart, but upset her he assuredly had.

Damping down the desire to march over there and wrench her out of his arms, thus causing a scandal he was sure she would deplore, he gritted his teeth and mustered what patience he could. He waited only for her to hurry off the dance floor in the direction of the retiring room before he made his move. Striding purposefully up to his guest and completely ignoring Miss Humphrey, with whom he was in conversation, he said peremptorily, "Sharpe, in my study, now."

Not waiting for a reply he turned on his heel and strode out of the ballroom. Mr Sharpe followed in his wake, a bemused look upon his face, leaving Miss Humphrey staring after them, her pout firmly in place.

Barely had he shut the door behind them before he said deceptively gently, "I did not invite you here, Sharpe, to upset my guests. You will explain to me precisely and without prevarication, what you said to cause Miss Lockhart distress."

"It was not my intention to—" he began.

"Did I not say precisely and without prevarication?"

This time the menace behind the words was unmistakeable. Mr Sharpe's colour heightened and resentment shone from his narrowed eyes.

"I do not believe I need to explain my actions to you, Treleven."

Harry reacted with lightning speed, his hands were around Sharpe's throat before he was fully aware of his own intentions. He pushed him up against the door and almost lifted the man off his feet. "If you wish to live very much longer, there is every need."

Mr Sharpe had gone very red in the face, his hands clawing ineffectually at Harry's arms.

"All right," he finally choked out.

Harry released him and he staggered to a chair, clutching his throat.

Harry strolled over to his desk and poured out a measure of brandy. He handed it to Mr Sharpe who swallowed it gratefully.

"I was unaware of your interest in that direction," he finally said, his voice hoarse. "Much can be forgiven a man who is in love."

Harry perched on the edge of his desk, his gaze hard.

"I am still waiting."

"Just remember, Treleven, that what I am about to relate to you happened years ago."

Harry listened with increasing disgust to his tale. No wonder Miss Lockhart had developed brittle armour to protect herself. Her confidence in her worth must have been decimated by this man's actions.

"What was wrong with you, man?" he snapped. "That you felt the need to humiliate a defenceless woman?"

Mr Sharpe sat a little straighter in his chair. "It is our job to uphold the values of our country, Treleven. We protect the natural order. There are many factions who could threaten it. Give a woman too much freedom and who knows where it will end? I have seen some who already try to rule their husbands, give them enough scope and they will think they can rule the country as well. You do not wait for a snake to strike but cut off its head before it gets the chance."

Harry saw the fanatical light in his eyes and did not waste his breath arguing with him.

"Get out of my house, Sharpe," he said walking to the door and holding it open. "You are the worst sort of fool."

"Oh, and what sort is that?" Mr Sharpe asked as he got to his feet.

"I saw you trying to engage Miss Lockhart, Sharpe. I cannot imagine that you have spent so much time in her company without realising what a fine creature she is. I think you held a torch for her. I think you may still. That makes you the sort of fool who cuts off his nose to spite his face."

Harry closed the door behind him and went again to the brandy decanter. He filled a glass and sat in his favourite wingback chair, swirling the liquid gently around the bulbous vessel, his gaze distracted. Although he wished to get to know Miss Lockhart better, Mr Sharpe's revelations had given him pause for thought. He could not in all good conscience trifle with Miss Lockhart's affections unless he was deadly serious in his intent. He had no desire to cause her pain. On the contrary, he was conscious of a desire to protect her, even if it was from himself.

* * *

It was perhaps not surprising that Katherine should have noted the absence of the two gentlemen who had affected her heart most deeply when she returned to the ballroom. But any measure of relief she might have felt was to be short lived.

Miss Humphrey, who had made it quite clear to all her friends and acquaintances, that it was she they had to thank for the much anticipated Michaelmas ball, (and may even have gone as far as hinting that Lord Treleven's acquiescence to the scheme was in no small part due to the flattering interest he showed in her happiness), found herself disappointed in her expectations of the evening.

That the two most dashing gentlemen present had both danced with Miss Lockhart, who was clearly on the shelf, in preference to herself was mortifying to one who had long considered herself to be the acknowledged beauty of the neighbourhood. That this was largely due to the absence of Henrietta at most social events had never worried her overmuch, for even when she did appear she was so shy and tongue-tied that most young gentlemen preferred her own more vivacious style. That she had been forced into the background by the quite startling change in Miss Treleven that had resulted in her stealing her usual crowd of admirers, completed her humiliation.

She had watched enviously as various ladies were

twirled around the room during the waltz, a dance that her mother thought scandalous and had strictly forbidden her to partake in. Her gaze had been inevitably drawn to the dashing Mr Sharpe. Although sensitivity to the feelings of others was not her forte, even she had noticed the constraint that had seemed to exist between that gentleman and Miss Lockhart, and she had quite correctly assumed that they had some sort of past connection that had not turned out well. As she saw Miss Lockhart return to the ballroom, she saw an opportunity to offer her low spirits some small measure of relief.

"There you are, Miss Lockhart," she said, hurrying up to her. "I have been so looking forward to furthering our acquaintance."

Katherine's mobile brows arched in surprise. "Have you?"

Undeterred by this rather dampening response, she rushed on. "Why of course, we so seldom have outsiders move to the neighbourhood."

She took Katherine's arm. "Come, walk with me a little."

Belle sent her a laughing look and went in search of her husband.

"I must thank you for introducing me to Mr Sharpe, a most interesting gentleman."

"I am glad you found him so," Katherine murmured.

"Oh yes, indeed I did. And I am glad that both he and Lord Treleven have shown you such a flattering amount of attention. It is always more comfortable is it not, to be made welcome when one is in new surroundings?"

"Indeed."

"And of course they are both firm friends, they served together at Waterloo, did you know? I thought it very kind of them to choose to distinguish a more, shall we say, mature lady, when there are so many others desirous of a partner. Although I wouldn't set too much store by it, if I were you."

"I set no store by it at all, I assure you," she said coolly.

"I am so relieved. You seem such a dignified lady but gentlemen can be so naughty sometimes, can't they? I think they cooked up some sort of joke between them, for I had only been talking to Mr Sharpe for a short while when Lord Treleven whisked him off to his study. They were laughing about something or other as they left, indeed they seemed most amused. I thought I heard them mention your name although I may well have been mistaken."

Miss Humphrey had been working her malice in the dark, not sure if anything she said would hit home. But it appeared she had struck lucky for her companion had turned quite pale.

"Oh, do not take it to heart, ma'am. I would not wish to cause you any distress and if they have been having a little joke, if not a wager, at your expense, I am sure they mean no harm. But I felt it only right that I put you a little on your guard."

Katherine gently disengaged her arm. "Thank you for your consideration, Miss Humphrey, but it was unnecessary I assure you. I really have very little interest in either gentleman."

Miss Humphrey smiled, baring her little yellow

teeth. "Well that is all right, then, now if you will excuse me I must just check on Mama."

Although it was clear to Katherine that Miss Humphrey's words were motivated by jealousy, their poison nevertheless seeped through her armour. Could it be that Lord Treleven knew of what had passed between her and Mr Sharpe? Had he invited him here knowing of their history? Had they both been laughing at her? Mr Sharpe had assured her that he had not expected to find her here. But then he had already proved himself a consummate liar. It was harder for her to believe that Lord Treleven would play so cruel a trick; indeed her heart assured her that he would not. But then her heart had been wrong before.

Katherine was glad that the ball was nearing its end and she could slip away to her room without occasioning any comment. It was a long time before she fell asleep however, her mind sifting through Miss Humphrey's words trying to separate the fact from the fiction.

## CHAPTER 15

Katherine awoke to a grey overcast sky, her eyes as heavy as the rainclouds outside her window. Her musings of the night before had not led her to any firm conclusions and she decided she would not give the matter any further thought. Even if Miss Humphrey's assumptions were correct they did not in any material way affect her future. She may have developed a foolish tendre for Lord Treleven, but she had never for a moment allowed herself to hope that the feeling might be returned and the gentleman in question had certainly never given her any cause to think so.

"Are we packed, Ayles?" she asked, lethargically dragging the brush through her hair.

"Yes, ma'am." She took the brush from Katherine's hand. "Here, let me, you'll be here all day at that rate."

She did not much feel like going down to breakfast but as she needed to take her leave of the Trelevens, it was unavoidable.

"Ah, there you are," smiled Lady Treleven, "we had almost given you up! Belle has not made it down, but I should think she needs to rest a little this morning."

"I'm afraid I slept in a little late," Katherine smiled.

"And no wonder, after all the excitement of the ball. It was a great success, I think."

"Yes, yes, it was," Katherine said, resisting the urge to look at Lord Treleven.

"There can be no doubt of it," agreed Mrs Abbott. "I have rarely enjoyed myself more."

"You left a little early, ma'am," Harry said. "I trust you did not feel unwell?"

Katherine's eyes lifted and she noticed he looked a little distant. "No, sir, not at all. But I am unused to dancing until dawn these days."

She turned to Henrietta and smiled. "You seemed to be enjoying yourself. You certainly proved to be a hit!"

Henrietta's eyes twinkled. "I did enjoy it. I played our little game and think I did you proud!"

"Game?" Lady Treleven said. "What game was this?"

"Miss Lockhart helped me learn how to reply to a gentleman's compliments. They had always embarrassed me before, but she taught me to turn it all into a game and how to answer the more silly ones."

Lady Treleven gave Katherine a look of approval. "Give me an example of this game, Henrietta."

"Mr Hogwood informed me that I was a bright shining star."

"Really?" said Lady Treleven. "He has always

struck me as very dignified, a little too puffed up in his own conceit even. I do hope you gave him a set-down for his impertinence?"

Henrietta assumed a haughty, bored look and said in a languid voice, "I do hope not, sir, for I do not intend to fade with the dawn."

Harry choked on his coffee.

Lady Treleven looked quite amazed. "Henrietta! Although I am glad you found a way to enjoy your evening, I do hope you will not put on those airs and graces as a matter of course!"

"No, Mama, it was just a game."

"Did Doctor Fisher pay you silly compliments?" she asked after a moment.

Henrietta laughed. "He is far too much a gentleman and has enough sensible conversation that he does not need to resort to such tactics, thank heavens."

"Oh, I see," her mother said. "And do you enjoy sensible conversation?"

"It is the only kind I enjoy," her daughter informed her.

"Miss Lockhart's influence again makes itself felt," Harry murmured.

The rattle of rain against the windows caught his attention.

"Are you packed, Miss Lockhart?" he said frowning slightly.

"Yes, everything is ready," she said stiffly. She had heard his comment and did not think it had been meant as a compliment.

"Then I suggest you do not delay your departure

as, if I am not much mistaken, we are in for a downpour and you do not want to get stuck in the mud."

Feeling as if she had been dismissed, Katherine stood. "I must thank you all for your hospitality. I only hope I can repay it in some way."

Lady Treleven rose and took her hand. "You already have, my dear. You have been a friend to Henrietta, I could not ask for more."

"I think you will find, ma'am, that she now has many more."

That young lady stepped forward and embraced Katherine. "Thank you," she said. "I am glad you are only going down the road, for I will come and see you often."

"Please do, I depend on it," Katherine said. "Please say goodbye to Lord and Lady Hayward for me, will you?"

"Of course," Henrietta said.

Lord Treleven stepped forward and bowed. "I will order your coach, Miss Lockhart."

That was all. No light-hearted compliments, no twinkle in his eyes, and no kiss of her hand. Katherine was beginning to think Miss Humphrey had been right, but perhaps the joke had started long before last night, perhaps both he and Mr Sharpe had thought it amusing to see if the bitter spinster could be brought to fall in love again. But even if that were the case, she would not fall into a decline. She was no longer an impressionable young girl, but a mature sensible woman, with far too much pride and strength to fall into the doldrums because of the pernicious behaviour of a man.

"Are you quite all right, dear?" Mrs Abbott said as the carriage drove down the main drive.

"Of course," she murmured. "I have a headache, that is all."

"It's probably the weather," Mrs Abbot said gently. "If we don't have a thunderstorm before the day is out, I will be surprised."

Mrs Abbott was not to be surprised, at least not by the thunderstorm, which did indeed break midway through the afternoon. The ladies retreated to the library as it was by far the most comfortable room in the house.

"Lord Treleven was quite right to encourage us to leave so soon," Mrs Abbott said gently as a flash of lightning brightened the room for an instant. She crossed to the window and drew the heavy curtains. "I would not have wished to be caught in this storm although I do quite enjoy sitting by the fire whilst it rages outside."

"Yes, it is very cosy," Katherine murmured absently.

The heat from the flames soon began to make her feel drowsy and her eyes had just fluttered closed, the book she had been attempting, but failing miserably to read, slipping from her fingers, when the sonorous chimes of the bell, followed swiftly by another clap of thunder made them jerk open again.

"Who on earth would come visiting in such weather?"

Mrs Abbott quickly stowed her knitting in her basket. "I cannot imagine, my dear."

They both looked up expectantly as Forster opened the door and stepped slowly into the room.

"Sir Richard Lockhart," he announced, shuffling to one side so the tall, slender gentleman behind him could gain entry. He was quite handsome in an austere, scholarly sort of fashion, with prominent cheekbones and a high sloping forehead that led to a slightly receding hairline, although he was only a few years older than his sister.

"Richard!" Katherine exclaimed, rising to her feet. "We were not expecting you!"

"I thought about sending you a letter," he said, strolling to the fire with a polite nod in Mrs Abbott's direction. He reached his hands out to the blaze. "But then I realised there was every likelihood that I would reach you before it did."

"But is aught amiss?" Katherine said.

He gave her a lopsided grin. "Does something need to be amiss for me to come and see my own sister?"

"Well, no," she conceded. "But I must admit I had not expected to see you so soon. Is Caroline with you?"

"No," he said. "She would have come but thought better of it when I described the tedious hours she would have to while away and the state of the roads she was likely to encounter."

"I see," Katherine smiled. "You put her off. You have made a bolt for freedom. She still has the crotchets then, I take it?"

He frowned a little and glanced at Mrs Abbott.

"Oh, don't mind me, Sir Richard," she said gently. "I am sure it is quite understandable if she has."

"Yes, well, she is finding her situation a little trying," he admitted. "But that is not why I came. I wished to see for myself all these renovations, they have cost me quite a tidy sum after all. I must say this room seems very comfortable."

"Yes," agreed Katherine. "But when we arrived it was the only one, apart from the kitchen, that was."

"That bad, eh?" he said. "Come, show me around, sister."

"I will ring for some tea," Mrs Abbott said. "For I am sure you must be in need of some after your journey, Sir Richard, and perhaps a slice of cake?"

"That would be most welcome, Mrs Abbott."

Although the building had been made watertight, and the rotten boards and windows replaced, Katherine had not been so extravagant as to order new furnishings or redecorate, apart from in the servants' quarters where two new maids had now taken up residence.

"I must say that when I got the bill I thought you had probably gone to town and expected to find a palace," Sir Richard said. "But I see that is not the case."

Katherine laughed. "When have you ever known me to be extravagant? Lord Treleven's steward Mr Hewel informed me that if the house had been left another year it would have been beyond saving! The money has gone on the fabric of the building not on luxuries I can well do without."

Her brother frowned. "I cannot say I was happy to hear we were so beholden to Treleven. I am not sure that he is a fit person for you to know."

"Oh, so now we come to it. You came because you feared I might fall in love with a wicked rake!"

"Katherine! I never thought to hear you talk in such a fashion."

"Oh, don't talk such fustian, Richard! I am hardly a green girl," she snapped, a sleepless night and the fact that his fears might prove to be quite warranted causing her loss of composure.

"If living away from my protection has caused you to talk in such a wild way, then perhaps it would be better if you returned home with me."

He looked as if would say more, but was prevented by the appearance of one of the new maids. She dropped them a curtsey and began to back out of the room.

"Rose, isn't it?" Katherine smiled at the girl.

"Yes, miss."

"There is no need for you to go, this is your room after all. We were just leaving."

Realising she had upset her very correct brother and having no wish to cause a rift between them, she took his hand as they reached the stairs.

"Forgive me, Richard, I am not quite myself, I admit. I have the headache. Mrs Abbott put it down to the thunderstorm."

He looked at her closely and appeared a little mollified. "I must say, you are looking a trifle peaky, my dear. And although you may still be green, I am well aware that you are no longer a girl and well past the age of falling in love."

"Yes, well, let us join Mrs Abbott for that cup of tea, shall we?"

His temper further improved when he inspected the shelves that spanned two walls of the library.

"I say, old Jenkins put together a fine library, I will easily be able to spend a few days in here perusing some of these books. Thank heavens he had the sense to keep this room dry at least."

Hiding a smile, his sister dutifully agreed with him.

It rained for three full days and Sir Richard soon made the library his own domain. He joined the ladies only for breakfast and dinner, but apart from that, was hardly to be seen. He had apparently stumbled upon three plays by Euripides that had not before come his way and was quite absorbed. It never once occurred to him that being smaller than the drawing room, it was far easier to heat or that the ladies might be much more comfortable there.

"I am sure I cannot blame Caroline for having the crotchets if he locks himself up all day with fusty old books," Katherine said. "He has only been here three days, and I am already nearly out of all patience with him. Whenever I try to discuss a few changes I would like to make, such as acquiring matching furniture for the drawing room, or replacing some of the sadly faded curtains, he smiles in that distracted way he has, his mind clearly upon something that happened eons ago, and murmurs whatever I think best. But I know full well that he has not heard a word I have said!"

Mrs Abbott smiled. "It is how he used to behave before he was married but he has not had so much opportunity to indulge himself since he wed. I think you will find that he looks upon his stay as a holiday and feels he can freely indulge himself without fear of reprisals."

The following day the heavens finally stopped weeping and the tedium was relieved by a visit from Lord Hayward, Belle, and Edmund.

"I could not return home without taking my leave of you," she said.

"I am so glad," Katherine smiled. "How is everyone at Elmdon?"

Belle laughed. "Busy. The weather has not deterred a stream of young gentlemen calling at the house, all delivering thank you letters from mamas I am quite sure had no idea they had such obliging sons! It is all a pretext to visit with Henrietta, of course."

"And does she seem taken with any of these gentlemen?" Mrs Abbott enquired.

"Not a one," said Belle. "I think her affections are engaged in quite another direction."

"Dr Fisher, perhaps?" Katherine said.

"Oh, undoubtedly."

"Do you think Lord Treleven would look favourably on such a match?" Mrs Abbott said gently.

Belle's forehead wrinkled in thought. "I am not sure. He seems a little out of sorts at the moment."

Edmund, who looked a little sleepy and had been quietly sitting on his mother's lap playing with the tassels on her shawl, suddenly piped up, "E's teasy as 'n' adder!"

"Edmund," Lord Hayward said a little sternly but with a laughing look at Belle. "Where on earth did you hear such language?"

The little boy was not fooled. He looked at his father and grinned. "Kenver said it."

Belle laughed. "You can hardly blame him, Hayward, when you have repeatedly taken him down to the stables over the past few days."

They did not stay long as they wanted to travel as far as they could whilst the good weather held. But as

Lord Hayward took his leave of Mrs Abbott, Belle pulled Katherine to one side and said in a low voice, "I am so sorry that we have had no chance to be private for I am sure something is troubling you. I do not know what it might be, but I think I may have an inkling who may be responsible. I will only say that since you left Elmdon, Lord Treleven has not been his usual cheerful self. Whatever he may have done, or not done, if he comes calling give him the benefit of the doubt for if you trust my judgement at all, believe me when I tell you that he is not like Mr Sharpe."

She kissed Katherine's cheek and pressed a card into her hand. "Write to me and let me know how you go on, won't you?"

Soon after they had left, Sir Richard wandered into the drawing room. Mrs Abbott had gone to give Mrs Nance her recipe for bramble jelly, so he found only Katherine there, embroidering some linen.

"Hello, my dear. Forster said we had visitors. Thought I'd better show my face."

"We did," Katherine said drily. "But they have gone. They were friends who had also been staying with the Trelevens, they only came to say goodbye."

"Well in that case I'll get back to my book, if you don't mind that is?"

Katherine who had been deep in thought pondering Belle's words, assured him she did not mind at all.

* * *

Harry had come to respect Lord Hayward and felt some affection for his lady, however he was glad when they left. Between entertaining his guests and vetting the constant stream of silly young puppies that had come calling on his sister, he had had very little time to himself. Although not much given to introspection, he was aware of a growing feeling of dissatisfaction. Not being able to blow off steam as he would if he were in town by visiting Gentleman Jackson's boxing saloon, he decided to take Hermes for a ride and pay his overdue call on Lord Humphrey.

He was relieved when he was shown into his study without having to run the gauntlet of Miss Humphrey's simpering nonsense.

"Ah, come at last have you, Treleven. Thought you'd forgotten me," Lord Humphrey complained.

"Not at all, sir," Harry said. "I came as soon as I was able, I assure you."

"Well, sit down and explain to me if you will what is to happen to the mine now I have no partner. I read in the paper that a verdict of felo-de-se had been given – most unusual."

Without preamble Harry launched into an explanation of the outcome of the inquest.

"So we are to be partners, eh," he finally said. "You have come out of this very well, I must say."

"Indeed, I have been most fortunate, sir. I should inform you that I am just waiting for official confirmation from the lawyers and then I intend to put some major changes into effect."

"Now don't be too hasty, Treleven. What do you know about mining after all?"

"I may not know much about mining just yet, sir, but I do know how to get the best out of the people in my charge. We must do away with this token system and pay the workers a fair wage for a start," he informed him.

"Sounds more expensive," Lord Humphrey said doubtfully. "Bound to eat into the profits."

Knowing that Lord Humphrey really didn't have a clue what he was talking about, Harry patiently explained his reasoning. "I think you will find that a workforce who are treated as the skilled human beings they undoubtedly are and not like slaves who find themselves constantly indebted to their masters for the tools they use and the expensive yet poor quality food they eat, will be far more productive and thus increase the profits."

"Perhaps," he conceded.

"And I am sure it is in your interests as a magistrate and an important figure in this community to show yourself to be a benevolent and fair shareholder in the mine. Although I am sure no lasting damage to your reputation has been done by your association with Caldwell, by showing your approval of various changes I intend to make you will win over any doubters."

Lord Humphrey coloured at the mention of Caldwell. "I knew nothing of what he was about," he blustered.

"Even so," Harry said.

"What are these other changes you intend to make?"

"For a start, I intend to take on the miners from Langarne who lost their jobs."

"Well you would wouldn't you?" Lord Humphrey snorted. "They can't pay you rent if they don't have work."

"A fact you must have been well aware of when

you agreed that the work should be offered to a group of foreigners," he said softly.

Lord Humphrey shifted uncomfortably in his chair. "Now, just hold on a minute. Remember I am a minority shareholder, I do not have the final say on these things."

"I have not forgotten. I intend to put my plans into action with or without your approval but thought I would do you the courtesy of informing you of them."

"What will you do with the miners Caldwell brought in? I believe most of them are in debt to us."

"Only because Caldwell ensured they were. They have more than worked off their debt, so they will be offered a choice to stay and work side by side with our own men under the new system, or I will send them home and their so-called debts will be written off. I think you will find that most will opt for the latter option. They were here under duress, not because they wished to be. I will also be offering Doctor Fisher a fee in return for him overseeing the health of the workers."

"I'm surprised you don't offer to provide them a good hot meal every day as well!" Lord Humphrey expostulated.

"That idea is not without merit."

"It is meant to be a business not a charity," Lord Humphrey said, banging his hand on his desk. "I have a good mind to sell my share."

Harry smiled and got to his feet. "Done. Tell Boodle your terms and I will buy you out."

Harry made his way to Langarne. He had a brief word with Joe Phelps at The Anchor and asked him to spread the word that any man who wished to return to the mine would soon be able to do so.

"I will hold a meeting here next week, Joe, and explain my plans more fully if you have no objection."

"Objection, sir?" he said. "I couldn't be more pleased. Molly's increasing 'an we're going to need help we could ill afford if things had carried on as they were. I'm that grateful to you Lord Treleven, have a drink on the house."

"Congratulations, Joe, but I won't stay. There's another visit I have to pay."

He strolled over to the church and quietly let himself in through a side door that led to a small private chapel. He sat on a bench and stared down at the polished granite ledger stone that marked his father's resting place.

"The Trelevens start a new chapter, sir," he said softly. "I hope you would approve."

He was about to rise when he felt a hand on his shoulder.

"He would be proud of you," Mr Gulworthy said gently. "He always was; he often came here and said a prayer for you."

CHAPTER 16

Much to Mrs Kemp's disapproval, Harry had still not rid himself of the habit of entering Elmdon by way of the kitchen. Not only could he often find some tasty morsel to filch on his way into the main house, but he could also escape detection and discover if they had any visitors before making his presence known.

He quietly opened the door. Of Mrs Kemp there was no sign but two maids stood with their backs to him, their heads together. A few of their softly murmured words reached his ears and he stiffened. As he shut the door behind him, they broke apart and offered him a respectful curtsey. He frowned.

"Emma, isn't it?" he said, looking at the elder of the two.

"Yes, sir," she said, curtseying again and looking a little flustered.

His glance strayed to the younger one. "I don't think I know you. What is your name?"

She flushed. "Mary, sir, Mrs Kemp only took me on last week."

"Do you like working here, Mary?" he asked gently.

She nodded her head enthusiastically. "Oh, yes, milord, Ma was pleased as punch that both me and me sister got hired at the mop fair."

"Your sister works here also?"

"No, sir, she got a place over at Helagon, down the way."

Harry looked interested. "Ah, things become a little clearer. Are you aware, both of you, that gossiping about your betters could get you dismissed?"

"Oh, we weren't—"

"Then why did I hear Miss Lockhart's name on your lips when I opened the door?"

He looked at them sternly and they dropped their heads in shame.

"Mary?" The word was softly spoken but brought the girl's head up. Her eyes were bright and tears threatened to spill over onto her flushed cheeks.

"Oh, don't turn me off, sir," she pleaded, twisting her hands in her apron. "We needs the money. I wasn't saying anything nasty, only that Rose – that's me sister – said as how Miss Lockhart's brother had come to stay, turned up in that nasty storm and she heard him being out of reason cross with her and sayin' as how he would take her back home. She only told me 'cos she were worried, sir. If miss goes away, Rose might lose her job."

Something in her master's face made her gasp and then the tears began to flow.

"Please, sir," she sobbed.

Harry's gaze gentled. "There's no need to cry," he said. "I have no intention of having you turned off. Now I suggest you get back to work. If Mrs Kemp sees you being idle she'll certainly have something to say."

He went straight to his study, paced up and down for a few moments, crossed to the brandy decanter, removed the stopper, held it for a moment and then replaced it. Turning on his heel he retraced his steps through the kitchen and went to the stables. The vague, nagging feeling of dissatisfaction that had plagued him the past few days had now crystallised into a feeling of loss, an emptiness he had not experienced before. If he had been in any doubt as to the cause of this malady, he was no longer. He strode up and down impatiently as he waited for Kenver to bring Hermes out to him.

The horse's nostrils flared and his tail twitched as he swung up into the saddle.

"I'm not sure you should take him out again, sir," Kenver said. "You're as twitchy as a toad on a hot shovel and he knows it."

"When I want your opinion, Kenver, I'll ask for it."

Kenver whistled and a slow grin crossed his face as he watched him race out of the yard. He might have his mother's colouring but the disdainful look he had thrown at him and his unusually sharp manner, were all his father.

\*\*\*

Katherine picked up her embroidery and then sat unmoving, staring into space for some time. Eventually she sighed and put it down again. She went up to her room and donned an old bonnet and a warm pelisse and went for a turn about the garden. It was now a blank canvas, a little like her life, she realised. She had been nowhere, done nothing of any import. Was she really content to dwindle into an old maid in this little backwater? Might it not be better to return with her brother and try to coax Caroline out of her sullens? That she made him uncomfortable she was sure. He certainly seemed in no hurry to return to her.

She came to the small cherub fountain. A gentle smile curved her lips as she thought of her companion. How disappointed Mrs Abbott would be if they left before she had the chance to see her plans for the garden come to fruition. No, she would stay until next summer at least. Richard had chosen his own bride after all. She did not wish to find herself in the middle of their dissatisfaction and they were far more likely to find a way to make each other comfortable without her interference.

She turned and began to meander back towards the house her eyes rising to survey the newly mended roof. It was easy to see where the repair had been made for the newly laid slate tiles gleamed brighter than all the rest. She came to a halt and a wide slow smile curved her generous lips, an inkling of an idea beginning to take hold. Perhaps there was something useful she could do here.

"Miss Lockhart."

Her eyes fell and her smile slipped. Lord Treleven strode around the corner of the house purposefully.

"John told me I would find you here."

Her heart started to beat a little faster as she registered the intensity of his gaze.

"I wish you would smile for me," he said softly.

"I cannot imagine why," she said coolly. "There is no one here to witness your success after all."

His brows snapped together. "What the devil do you mean by that?"

She suddenly felt uncertain of her ground. It was much easier to suspect him of enjoying himself at her expense in his absence. But when he stood before her, she was reminded that the vitality and energy which characterised him, his love of life and openness of manner, all spoke against his being capable of any sort of maliciousness towards her. She remembered Belle's advice and took a steadying breath. "I am not sure. Forget I said it. I am out of sorts."

"Walk with me," he said, still frowning.

A heavy silence hung between them and she sought in vain for a way to break it. They both started to speak at the same time and then broke off, this encounter attended by a constraint and awkwardness that had never before marked their dealings with each other. At least not on both sides.

After a moment he said, "I am glad to find you here, I had heard that your brother had come to visit and was afraid he might have whisked you away."

Katherine gave him a sideways glance, her brow furrowed. "You run too deep for me, sir," she finally said. "Your words imply that you would not wish for such an event yet only a few days ago you could not hurry me out of your house fast enough."

His smiled ruefully. "I did not wish for you to be caught in the storm, I—" he hesitated, "I needed some room to think."

"Does not Elmdon have enough rooms for you to think in?"

He took a few quick strides away from her, jerked to a stop, swivelled and returned. He took both her hands in a firm grip, his eyes burning bright. "It would not matter if it had a thousand rooms, for if I knew you to be in just one, it is to that room that I would be drawn."

He spoke with such tortured sincerity that she could not doubt the veracity of his words. Her heart trembled and her lips parted on a soft gasp. His eyes fell to them for a moment.

"Would that have been so terrible?" she whispered.

"I did not wish to hurt you," he said softly. "I had to be sure of my own heart before I could even attempt to find a place in yours."

"And you are sure now?" she murmured, her eyes searching his, hardly daring to believe that her own feelings might be returned.

He stepped closer until only a breath separated them. "I am not a romantic man," he murmured. "I had never met a woman who could hold my interest, I doubted such a one existed. But when I was away you filled my thoughts, I could not wait to return to you. I liked knowing you were under my roof. When you were there no longer, I felt your absence and could not be comfortable. There was an emptiness," he took her hand and pressed it against his heart, "here."

"I felt it too," she said, her voice catching.

"Kate," he groaned, "my Kate, my love."

The possessive way he uttered the words stopped her breath. He dipped his head and pressed his lips to hers and she was lost. Light and longing flooding her, she swayed and he caught her to him fiercely, parting her lips and deepening his kiss. The shock of his tongue sliding over hers sent pulses of tingling pleasure spiralling to all her hidden places. When his mouth finally lifted from her own, she whimpered, feeling the loss, then sighed as he trailed the lightest butterfly kisses along her jawline before gently sucking on her delicate lobe.

"Harry, Harry," she moaned.

"Treleven! Step away from my sister!"

She chuckled and said softly, "Now we are in the suds – my bookish brother thinks you a wicked rake."

"Is his opinion important to you?" Harry murmured.

"I would not wish him to be unhappy."

"Then I shall have to convince him that his beautiful sister has reformed me."

"And have I?" Katherine asked, a hint of vulnerability and uncertainty in her eyes.

Harry stepped back and bowed low over her hand, brushing his lips against it.

"Never doubt it, Kate."

"I knew you should never have stayed beneath his roof," Sir Richard said, closing the distance between them. "Just look what comes of it. Have you no honour, sir?"

"Lockhart," Harry offered him a small bow. "I hope I have my fair share of it."

"But you were kissing my sister, sir," he protested.

"Yes," he acknowledged, his eyes twinkling. "But I can assure you I did not when she was beneath my roof."

"That does not make it any better! You should not be kissing her at all!"

His eyes raked his sister. "I did not see you putting up much of a struggle, Katherine. What possessed you? I would never have believed you capable of displaying such loose morals and poor judgement."

She smiled gently at her brother. "It would appear I am not past the age of falling in love, after all."

"Climb down from your high horse, Lockhart," Harry said, unwilling to have his love the target of such disapproval for long. "Do not tell me you did not kiss your wife before you married her? Despite your sister's poor judgement and loose morals, I have every intention of making an honest woman of her."

He glanced down at her, his gaze warm. "As soon as possible."

"Oh, you have, eh? Is this what you want, Katherine?"

She took her brother's hands and squeezed them.

"Yes, there is nothing I want more." Her cheeks were flushed and her eyes shone with such radiant happiness that Sir Richard was left with very little to say.

He glanced at Harry. "Well, you'd better come into the house, Treleven, we need to discuss a few things."

Harry grinned. "Certainly, old chap. Give me a few moments first though, will you?"

"Oh, very well," Sir Richard said. "You'll find me in the library."

Harry led Katherine behind a nearby tree. He leant against it and pulled her hard against him claiming her mouth in another long, lingering kiss.

"Your brother is right," he murmured. "You are

quite abandoned, and to think I thought you old-cattish when we first met."

She opened her mouth to utter a scathing response but he covered it again with his.

"What were you smiling at when I came into the garden," he asked her as they slowly dawdled back towards the house.

"The slates," she murmured. "They had given me an idea I hope you will approve of."

"Go on."

"I think we should start a school for the miners' children."

He took her hand and raised it to his lips. "I do approve. I had already intended to improve conditions as much as possible but I had not, I admit, thought of that. It is an excellent idea."

She beamed at him. "I want to feel I have made a difference in some small way."

He looked at her with admiration. "You have already made a difference, to Henrietta and to me."

"Oh, I do not think I can take all the credit for Henrietta's transformation. You do know that she is well on the way to being in love with Doctor Fisher? Do you approve?"

Harry smiled down at her. "He is a good man from a good family. I think he will make his mark upon the world. If she is of the same mind six months from now, I will not object. Now, my dear, perhaps you will explain your earlier comment about my needing an audience."

She coloured and told him of her conversation with Miss Humphrey.

"I did not believe it in my heart," she assured him.

He drew her to him for an instant. "It is understandable that you should doubt. I know your history with Sharpe because I forced it out of him."

"Oh, how did you do that?" she said interested.

"I strangled him."

Katherine chuckled. "Your methods are a little crude, sir."

He grinned. "But effective. When we are married—"

"I know you are not romantic," she interrupted him gently. "But even though I may be old-cattish, I find that I am. Would you mind very much asking me?"

He laughed down at her and then framing her face with his hands, he gently stroked her soft cheek with his thumb and looked deeply into her eyes.

"Will you marry me as soon as it may be arranged, sweet Kate?"

"Yes, yes, dear love," she replied sighing. "I will."

## THE END

## ALSO BY JENNY HAMBLY

*Thank you for reading my Bachelor Brides Collection!*

Thank you for your support! I do hope you have enjoyed reading my Bachelor Brides series. If you would consider leaving a short review on Amazon, I would be very grateful. It really helps readers know what to expect, and helps raise my profile, which as a relatively new author is so very helpful.

### *Other books by Jenny Hambly*

**Belle – Bachelor Brides 0**

**Miss Wolfraston's Ladies Collection**

**Marianne - Miss Wolfraston's Ladies Book 1**

**Miss Hayes - Miss Wolfraston's Ladies Book2**

**Georgianna - Miss Wolfraston's Ladies Book 3**

**Allerdale - Confirmed Bachelors Book 1**

Belle is available, free, to anyone who joins my mailing list.

ABOUT THE AUTHOR

I love history and the Regency period in particular. I grew up on a diet of Jane Austen, Charlotte and Emily Bronte, and Georgette Heyer. Later I put my love of reading to good use and gained a 1st class honours degree in literature.

I now write traditional Regency romance novels. I like to think my characters, though flawed, are likeable, strong, and true to the period. I have thoroughly enjoyed writing my Bachelor Brides series. Writing has always been my dream and I am fortunate enough to have been able to realise that dream.

I live by the sea in Plymouth, England, with my partner, Dave. I like reading, sailing, wine, getting up early to watch the sunrise in summer, and long quiet evenings by the wood burner in our cabin on the cliffs in Cornwall in winter.

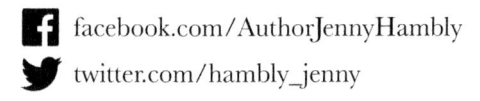

facebook.com/AuthorJennyHambly
twitter.com/hambly_jenny

Printed in Great Britain
by Amazon